Praise for *Mr. Darcy Takes a Wife*

"Wild, bawdy, and utterly enjoyable sequel.... Austenites who enjoy the many continuations of her novels will find much to love about this wild ride of a sequel."

—*Booklist*

"While there have been other *Pride and Prejudice* sequels, this one, with its rich character development, has been the most enjoyable."

—*Library Journal*

"A breezy, satisfying romance."

—*Chicago Tribune*

Darcy & Elizabeth

nights and days at Pemberley

Pride and Prejudice
continues

LINDA BERDOLL

Sourcebooks Landmark™
An Imprint of Sourcebooks, Inc.®
Naperville, Illinois

Published by Sourcebooks, Inc.
P.O. Box 4410, Naperville, Illinois 60567-4410
(630) 961-3900
Fax: (630) 961-2168
www.sourcebooks.com

Library of Congress Cataloging-in-Publication Data

Berdoll, Linda.
Darcy & Elizabeth : at home at Pemberley / Linda Berdoll.
p. cm.
ISBN-13: 978-1-4022-0563-7
ISBN-10: 1-4022-0563-5
1. Darcy, Fitzwilliam (Fictitious character)—Fiction. 2. Bennet, Elizabeth (Fictitious character)—Fiction. 3. Married people—Fiction. 4. England—Fiction. 5. Domestic fiction. I. Title: Darcy and Elizabeth. II. Title.

PS3552.E6945D37 2006
813'.54—dc22

2005033003

Printed and bound in the United States of America
DR 10 9 8 7 6 5 4 3 2 1

To Kathryn

Sister, Cohort, Friend

contents

Come live with me, and be my love,
And we will some new pleasures prove,
Of golden sands, and crystal brooks,
With silken lines, and silver hooks.

—John Donne

prologue

The inestimable Jane Austen had penned only six books when she died in 1817 at age forty-one. *Pride and Prejudice*, her third work, was published in 1813 and has been judged by many to be the finest novel in the English language. The story of the courtship of the beautiful and spirited Elizabeth Bennet and the handsome but haughty Mr. Darcy is as brilliant as it is brief.

As remarkable a writer as she was, Miss Austen wrote only of what a respectable unmarried woman in Regency society would be privy to. Therefore, *Pride and Prejudice* concludes with the nuptials. Regrettably, in ending her story upon the very cusp of what undoubtedly would be a marriage of unrivalled passion, she has gifted many of her readers with an unfortunate case of literary *coitus interruptus*.

This hunger has spawned a prolificacy of sequels—most attempting to replicate the original in restraint, if not wit. Readers of sequels seem to fall into two categories—those who are longing to learn what Darcy might have whispered into Lizzy's ear in their nuptial chamber, and those who fall into a swoon at the notion of such heresy.

If you, dear reader, happen to fall into the latter category, we offer this caution before you read further: *Hang onto your bonnet, you're in for a bumpy ride.*

As our story recommences, all should be bliss within the Darcy household. At long last, Lizzy has birthed an heir and Darcy is again by her side. Motherhood, however, has not only rendered her busy and distracted, childbirth itself has left her temporarily "indisposed." Although Darcy's heart aches for what his Lizzy has endured, it is not the throbbing of his heart that is most troubling to his serenity—it is the palpable pain in his loins…

Darcy & Elizabeth

New Pleasures Proved

To all the world the month of June in the year of our Lord, 1815 would come to be known as the season of Waterloo. To the members of the Darcy household, it would be called that, but not remembered as such. Far too many other events of greater personal importance to them had transpired to remember it so simply.

Although France was the conquered, England paid a harsh price for its victory. The county of Derbyshire was not immune to that heavy toll. So vast were the repercussions, they were felt even within the usually impenetrable walls of Pemberley. Lives were lost, marriages brought about, and babies born all in the space of a few months.

Having weathered these many woes within the bosom of her very own family, Elizabeth Darcy felt exquisitely compensated by the two babes nestled in her arms. Indeed, that her husband had survived war, quarantine, brigands, and pestilence and returned to her whole was all she desired. What wiles he employed and whose auspices he availed himself of as he trekked through the battlefields and drawing rooms of France to accomplish his mission of rescuing his sister was of no importance to her. Of even less concern was that the emissary he chose to send word to her of his progress was a woman with whom he had once shared uncommon intimacy. Indeed, when at last he had returned to his wife's waiting arms, all question of his connexion with that beautiful woman was forgot. At least at first, but not for long.

Of even less importance was whether George Wickham was actually dead and buried or was gallivanting about the Continent.

Whilst Wickham's fate remained unknown, there were other vexations. What with Mrs. Darcy labouring to withstand a growing curiosity (approaching to eclipse the Alps in dimension) as to just what went on between her husband and his fetching French emissary, and Mr. Darcy labouring with equal vigour to withstand a desire for his nursing wife aroused to a similar degree, a dance of uncommon peculiarity commenced.

It extended well into the next year.

Mr. Darcy's Dilemma

In the year '15, Fitzwilliam Darcy was five years more than thirty. Yet, save for a smattering of grey begging to invade his side-whiskers, neither his figure nor bearing had been influenced unfavourably by time or its toll.

The horrific ordeal he had undergone to retrieve his sister from the gaping maw of war had altered neither his stately carriage nor the composed hauteur of his countenance. He was still a tall, handsome-featured man of good leg. However, his impressive aspect had recently begun to be worried by a single fault.

To the detriment of his countenance, the imposing manner he had struggled with such resolve to vanquish in order to win Elizabeth Bennet's hand had resurfaced with a vengeance. Indeed, never was a chin more imperious, the turn of a countenance more proud. It was as if he once again stood, with all arrogance and disdain, at that country dance in Meryton absolutely refusing to dance. Granted, this supercilious turn was little noticed by those outside his immediate circle. He had always been reticent, but while he had once used a shield of arrogance to defend his social discomfort, this was an unease of a different sort.

On a fine day in autumn, decorum forced Darcy to engage in polite discourse with a gathering of neighbours. As was his habit, he stood transfixed as a fastidiously tailored statue with both hands in graceful repose behind an extraordinarily straight back. As Master of Pemberley Hall and a generous portion of Derbyshire County, that he was untitled grandson of an earl and not truly a member of the aristocracy was rendered entirely irrelevant to those who kept account of such matters. And, as a man who understood his position compleatly, his attitude rarely altered upon these public occasions. In a stance similar to one that might have been taken by a sovereign in audience with mere vassals, he presented himself by resting his weight on one foot, the other slightly foremost. Although in this posture his highly polished boots were seen to great advantage, it was not an air—it was a statement of eminence.

The statement of societal eminence *was* overt, but with this stance came an additional announcement—one quite explicit. (The level of design employed in this presentation, however, can only be conjectured.) For from those tall boot-tops up-welled a pair of legs bearing the unmistakable muscularity particular to one who devoted a good many hours to riding his horse. Moreover, his fashionable moleskin breeches bore an unambiguous bulge which did not originate (unlike those of many fashionable young bloods) from a carefully wadded shirt-tail. Given all that and the casual grace with which he moved, bearing testament to the hours he also spent with the foil, there could be absolutely no supposition that concurrent to holding the offices of wealth and leisure was he any part of a fop.

The only visible evidence of the horrors he had encountered upon his bold excursion the summer past were those silver threads infiltrating his side-whiskers. Behind the backs of hands, those few cynics who were unimpressed by such fortitude speculated upon whether Mr. Darcy had been fool-hardy or simply barking mad. It was of little importance to him that his actions were believed to be in any way heroic or himself thought valiant in undertaking them. Indeed, he would have cared little had he heard the twittering, but as it was, Mr. Darcy's ears heard little of the lowing of his company. They were recovering yet from a near-miss by a blunderbuss. As a man whose fortune was exceeded only by his pride, it had long been his study to avoid any weaknesses which might expose him to ridicule. Hence, this loss of hearing was a closely guarded confidence.

Herein, providence did bestow some fortune. This, because for the whole of his life Mr. Darcy had been understood to regard idle conversation with undue wariness. When forced to converse, he often did so in monosyllables. It was nothing to him to inhabit a conversation in which he spoke not a word for ten minutes together. It was said that he would but utter a word when he could not safely escape with a nod. A nod, offered with a soupçon of cunning, said volumes—particularly when one heard little of the conversation. Whether he would have had a comment had he been privy to just what was said, one can only hazard a guess. In all likelihood, however, he would not.

For Waterloo and its aftermath still hung heavily in the thoughts of the entire population of the land. In the months thereafter, little else occupied general discourse save when any member of the Darcy clan was within earshot. Indeed, although absolute facts were spare, gossip was rampant surrounding Mr. Darcy's pursuit particularly, and his family's activities in general, during those months. It was not that their neighbours despised rumour-mongering any less than most folk, it was simply a matter of possession. What else is one to do with gossip but pass it on? Indeed, what tale is so compleat without it takes a bend or two?

All of this prattle was not unbeknownst to Mr. and Mrs. Darcy. That was the true impetus for them to endure society's demands to see and be seen in the difficult months that followed Darcy's return. They knew it was mandatory not to surrender to the urge to close ranks. The death of Elizabeth's father granted them at least a year's reprieve, but they dared not take it. That would have been a capitulation. In their absence in society every rumour that abounded would have been repeated and exaggerated. The trip from scuttlebutt to outright scandal was but a short leap. With every fibre of their beings Mr. and Mrs. Darcy abhorred this pretence of normalcy, but defence of the Darcy name demanded it. With all that, upon the occasion of such a gathering as the one they hosted that day, it was not in any way regarded as a party.

Regardless of the occasion, it was Darcy's habit to claim a place upon his lawn overlooking a particularly pretty prospect. It was only one of the many in his rather estimable estate, but it served a specific duty. Darcy was only able to tolerate the toadying by looking beyond the genuflection of kith and kin and taking in the view. (It was an oft held defence, for Mr. Darcy excited a degree of deference in the county of

Derbyshire comparable to that of royalty.) The few neighbours, who competed for audience before him exhibiting an adequate level of sycophancy believed compulsory toward a man of his station, were primarily men-folk. Mrs. Darcy kept the ladies at bay with the proffering of ices and exhibiting the considerable charms of their younglings beneath the vine-covered loggia that adorned Pemberley's east wing. Therefore, amidst the masculine enclave came the predictable masculine talk—crops, politics, and the weather. Although there was an abundance of discord to explore upon all these topics, it was Sunday afternoon, and this assemblage dared not offend the Sabbath with less than geniality. And Darcy, with inherent magnanimity, endeavoured to bid consideration to all, but favour to none. He bowed with such grace and nodded with such sufficiently aloof benevolence—precisely as he would had he heard every word—not a soul suspected anything amiss.

Yet another sense beyond the auditory Darcy protected by claiming that view with proprietary vigour. He protected his sight as well. For thus engaged, he kept his gaze from alighting upon his beloved wife. At one time, when forced to suffer society it had been his habit for his eyes to seek her out as if she were some beacon in the night. The very sight of her soothed not only his manners, but his soul. Of late, that device had been little employed. He was quite unaware that this failure allowed his guests to note that his temper was far less amenable since his return from whatever covert mission had taken him to the Low Countries. And that fanned further speculation about the particulars. Although it would have been a great disappointment to the scandal-mongers, his appearance of being somewhat out of spirits was nothing as dramatic as having "been to the wars."

It was quite true; in company he was often out of temper since his return. However life-altering the throes of war had been, those memories alone did not ignite his pique. A large part of it sprung from a far less noble origin—the one ruled not by his heart, but a place a bit south and, for men at least, an often more influential region—his aching loins.

Hence, as the gentlemen of Derbyshire bobbed and weaved in deference to him as only free-born Englishmen could, little did they suppose that beneath that wall of hauteur, their dignified host struggled to kennel a most undignified hunger.

Intrusion into the Master's Bed-Chamber

In the year '15, life was forever altered in the Darcy household—and not just within the hallowed halls that traversed Pemberley's two hundred-odd rooms. Much to the master's qualified displeasure, an alteration also bechanced the master's bed-chamber.

From the beginning of their life together, Darcy and Elizabeth defied convention and took their sleep together. The master's bed-chamber and the mistress's bed-chamber had always been one and the same. Hence, when it came time to receive her newborns, Elizabeth believed it only fitting that she do so in the same bed in which they had been conceived. Although that decision was made in his absence, initially Darcy saw no reason for alarm. As time wore on and his sleep was disturbed and his nerves a bit frayed, he still held firm to that judgement. If it was a choice between Elizabeth and two little ones in his bed or no Elizabeth in his bed at all, he saw little to argue. Hence, it was without complaint (or at the very least, none audible) that he withstood the continued intrusion of two red-faced, interminably squalling infants as they took his rightful place in his adored wife's embrace.

There were other issues of propriety, however. Initially, Darcy thought it only proper to withdraw when the babies were brought to Elizabeth to nurse.

"I shall trespass no longer upon your privacy," he said stiffly.

But he had been away for so very long, she was loath to allow him leave her side at all.

"My privacy is yours as well, sir," she tartly reminded him, then more softly, "Please stay. We have been so very long apart, I long for your company. Furthermore, if you excuse yourself from me when I am in this attitude—I am so often thus—ere long I shall not know your face."

As ever, her sister Jane anticipated her and betook herself to find urgent occupation in another room. As for Darcy, every consolation to his wife was his ambition. Even so, he found it a bit unnerving to share the same room with his wife's undraped breast in the company of others—even if only her maid Hannah and the wet-nurse Mrs. Littlepage. He chastised himself for entertaining such squeamishness. To be disordered by one's lessers was insupportable—a failing to overcome. Time had gifted him with forbearance of Elizabeth's maid's bustling about over the years, thereby he lectured himself that a nurse was no different and set about ignoring her presence as well. Decorum was still a sizable consideration to him, but it had for some time been set aside in favour of his pleasing Elizabeth. Hence, however reluctantly, he did as she bid.

Although he confessed to no further disconcertion, his posture whilst Elizabeth nursed was quite formal. Indeed, it replicated the stance that he took upon more formal occasions—weight balanced on one foot, his hands carefully clasped behind him. Even after many days of witnessing of these feeding rituals, he stood with such rigidity that his wife grew impatient with such display of reserve—he had certainly had time to acclimate himself to the doings. She believed her motherly duties as no less than a communion—one that should be cherished by them both. Other husbands might eschew such an intimacy, but not hers. She knew better of his nature. He had no need of defending his manhood from what might be accused of being a purely womanly pursuit. What was important to her was important, in equal measure, to him. Their long separation could not have altered that. She would not allow it.

"Pray, come to me," she bid, holding out her hand.

He took a step in her direction but again reclaimed that oddly formal posture and stood there in that manner with all due diligence.

"Nearer, please," she insisted.

Although he shuffled his feet a bit, he moved not an inch nearer nor spoke a word until their son was at last sated.

"Ah," he said approvingly, clearly of mind that small exclamation was the extent of his duty as a doting father.

Indeed, he smiled with no small complacency.

From her place propped up amongst the pillows, Elizabeth looked not half so happy. She wiped Geoffrey Darcy's tiny chin and then handed him off to Mrs. Littlepage. Nurse carried him across the room and placed him in an ornately carved, over-sized cradle. It had been in disgraceful disrepair when Elizabeth had rescued it from the farthest reaches of Pemberley's attic rooms, but it had cleaned up nicely. There had been a different equally beautiful cradle crafted for her first confinement. It had disappeared after that stillbirth—she had never asked, but only supposed that her husband had it put away. When she began to feel movement with this pregnancy, she knew that preparations for a new arrival were imperative. She had inquired of Mrs. Reynolds of that cradle's whereabouts, but the old woman shook her head.

"Nay. It's done and gone, it is," she said. "Mr. Darcy himself took an axe to it—had it used as kindling, he did. He said he wanted nothing left of it."

It had been such a sorrowful time for her, Elizabeth had not fully realised the toll it must have taken on Darcy as well. The thought of what anguish must have driven him to split to pieces with his very own hands that tangible reminder of their loss grieved Elizabeth to the quick. When she saw her mistress's countenance troubled by her disclosure, Mrs. Reynolds did not regret that she spoke the truth, only the wound that the truth caused. She did, however, have within her means a salve. She snapped her fingers when the means of repair came to her.

"This way, m'lady," she said over her shoulder, for she was already scurrying up the corridor.

Elizabeth had to rest on the third set of stairs, propping her arms on her blossoming stomach. Mrs. Reynolds stopt as well, allowing Elizabeth to catch her breath and ascertain that what lay before them was, indeed, worth the bother.

"'Tis! 'Tis!" Mrs. Reynolds assured her.

At last they found the room that was a virtual treasure trove of infant paraphernalia. Mrs. Reynolds picked her way through the melange to where a cradle stood beneath a dusty muslin cloth. She pulled the cloth from the cradle with a flourish so grand that Elizabeth could not actually see the cradle until the dust had settled. When it had, she was unequivocally delighted. The cradle had once been white and only a trace of the gold leaf remained, but still quite evident on the headboard was the Darcy crest. Elizabeth couldn't imagine why Darcy had not offered this one for their own use before. But then, she supposed, if they had, it would now have been kindling. Mrs. Reynolds tsked at its condition, but Elizabeth saw its potential. Indeed, she oversaw its reconditioning herself—busy work she made for herself in the long, dark days of Darcy's away.

Now, the cradle sat in full view of Darcy upon a daily basis. Elizabeth knew that he must have recognised the crest, yet he had not inquired about it. Knowing her husband as she did, Elizabeth determined this was either because he knew its origin and therefore had no reason to ask or because it was a reminder of a past event of which he did not choose to speak. Either way, she let the subject alone and delighted in seeing their babies asleep in the very same cradle in which their father once lay. With the appetites they exhibited, however, she knew each baby would soon need its own.

Nurse sat herself down on the stool next to the illustrious cradle, crossed her plump arms, and commenced to rock it with one foot. Elizabeth had watched carefully as Nurse took the baby to the cradle, and kept her in her eye until certain her son was then settled into a nap. Thereupon, with precision that had come about by some innate instinct, Elizabeth expertly transferred the second baby to her opposite breast. Gently, she prodded the little chin with a forefinger, urging her to nurse. In due time, Janie did, but her eyes kept drooping. Elizabeth jiggled her several times to keep her awake long enough to take her nourishment. Darcy's ceremonious demeanour allowed him to go so far as to shift his weight to the other foot.

Without raising her eyes to her husband, Elizabeth inquired, "Pray, did you know that your lips are pursed of late to a vexatious degree?"

With some vehemence, he said, "They are in no such attitude."

He was quite certain he harboured no resentment of any kind, thank-you-very-much—and he most certainly did not begrudge such small bundles their mother's time. So emphatic was his non-perturbation, he felt compelled to alter the subject of such discourse. In preparation to do so, he moved nearer the edge of the bed and watched intently as Elizabeth idly drew her finger across their daughter's silken forelock. He cleared his throat. Thereupon, he frowned.

She ceased her caressing, but did not then turn her gaze in his direction.

Said he, "How long will they remain in their present state?"

"Pray, to what state might you refer, sir?"

"Misshapen," he said. "Their misshapen state."

"Misshapen?" she repeated, her lips now pursed, then added primly, "I have not the pleasure of understanding you."

"Yes. I must take leave to observe that they appear to have been pulled up from the garden—like some sort of squirming root vegetables."

She rose upon her elbow as far as she could without disturbing her nursling and looked directly and indignantly at him.

"That is an appalling thing to say! They appear to be no such thing!" said she. "Pray, how can you speak so ill of such adorable babies—your own babies?"

With this response, she settled back and busily set about straightening the rutabaga's gown before glancing up to gauge the impact of her retort upon the tuber's sire. She had to quash the inclination to remind him that said root vegetables were of his loins, but Hannah and Nurse were in easy listening distance. Hannah was compleatly trustworthy and inexplicably unflappable, but Elizabeth dared not speak so plainly in front of the newly employed nurse. Hence, rather than speak of his fruitful loins, she allowed her gaze to slowly take in the length of his frame. She did not see what this measure wrought upon his countenance for she looked away immediately, fearful that she had issued an invitation that she was, regrettably, in no condition to entertain. She substituted that overture for one of a less sensual nature by humming the familiar notes of a lullaby and patting the bed next to her in an invitation for him to join her.

He did not sit, but moved nearer and turned his head sideways in seeming rapt contemplation of his daughter's features.

He smiled and said, "I believe I see a distinct resemblance to your Uncle Phillips, Lizzy."

"I fancy not," Elizabeth retorted. "It could not be possible—he is but an uncle by marriage…"

She pondered the recollection of her Uncle Phillips's broad face—for the case could be made for his resemblance to a potato. Her eyes darted back to her husband whose countenance was entirely over-spread with mirth. Only then did she understand his tease. She narrowed her eyes at him, but could not keep from smiling in return. She even took a swat at the side of his leg. He threw his head back and laughed.

That was a fine sight for her to see. Almost every moment since Darcy's return had been so sombre that Elizabeth was overjoyed to recapture the gentle banter that had once been a daily treat. That above all else signalled a return to normalcy. Yet, she had no more than breathed that inward sigh than he undertook a most abnormal action. He reached out and grasped the straight-back nursing chair next to the bed and, in so swift a motion he might have done it every day of his life, turned it backwards against the bed and straddled it. He then rested his arms on the top of the chair-back and put his chin upon his folded forearms. From this attitude he watched the baby's doings quite intently. Elizabeth, however, was all astonishment at his manoeuvre and did not immediately realise their daughter had fallen asleep. He, of course, was one step ahead of her.

"The baby…" he said, pointing to the sleeping infant.

"Yes, yes, I see," she said with a small degree of irritation—somewhat discombobulated still not only by what he had done and that he had, with such undue haste, become her supervisor.

She daintily nudged Janie, but to no avail. Again she prodded her, this time more deliberately. The baby remained steadfastly asleep. Indeed, a slight snuffle came from the back of her throat.

"Perhaps if you tickled her feet," he suggested.

Stubbornly, she rejected such a notion. After a bit of jiggling and no tickling, Janie again began to nurse.

"One must not excite them unduly," Elizabeth lectured. "It disturbs the digestion."

"I see," said he with a smile (one she did not happen to observe).

Not one to harbour an injury, even one to her fledging mothering skills, Elizabeth loosed one hand from its hold on the baby and took his. He squeezed hers once, but did not let it go.

She rethought her pique. It was quite unreasonable to be both unhappy at his reserve and irked at his interference. Moreover, although her own life had been upended to a startling degree, she had near a half-year to adjust to the coming of a child (albeit that it was not one babe but two had been an enormous astonishment)—he had them quite unceremoniously thrust in his arms not a day after he returned to English shores.

Elizabeth looked down upon one-half of that surprise with uncommon tenderness and pride and was nearly over-whelmed by emotion. If her sensibilities were stunned, she could but guess her husband's disconcertion. Outwardly, he had been all graciousness. Still, she knew that his sensibilities had to have been abused abominably. These thoughts stirred her heart most profoundly. She tore her eyes from her daughter's contented face and looked upon her husband's. Behind doting eyes, his countenance bore an odd expression. If called to name it, had she not known better she might have concluded it was a bit forlorn. Although he prided himself upon his inscrutability, she recognised his moods and the tiny manifestations they took upon his aspect. Hence, when he exposed a disconsolation even to her, it was of no small significance.

"Nurse," she said abruptly. "Nurse!"

The nurse gave a start as if caught in her own nap, but quickly stood and curtsied.

"Leave us."

Although with this demand, Elizabeth's voice lost its initial stridency, it was still an order. Without looking in the direction of her mistress, Nurse hustled toward the door. Elizabeth nodded once to Hannah, who anticipated her own dismissal and was then on her way out the door as well. Elizabeth watched her cross the room and held them in her eye until the door had closed behind them both. Without looking to her husband (who looked almost as startled as had Nurse), she saw that Janie had once again fallen asleep. But this time Elizabeth did not rouse her. Rather, she gently shifted her tiny body to the side and adjusted her blanket.

"Shall I take her to her bed? Are you unwell?" Darcy queried, a little worry crease appearing between his brows.

"Neither," she whispered. "Leave her be. If you move her she might awaken."

Having her husband take his daughter in his arms and carry her to sleep beside her brother would have been a delightful sight to witness, but she dared not risk awakening her. For the first time she bethought her heretofore unwavering resolution about not allowing either baby out of her sight for a single moment. Fortunately, Janie continued to sleep and she did not have to make that decision.

"Come to me, my love," she said, arms extended.

He looked at her rather curiously before looking over to the peaceful, sleeping face of his daughter. A little bubble erupted from Janie's lips as she made sucking sounds in her sleep. With unparalleled precision, they turned to each other and silently shared their opinion of the unqualified adorability of such an act. Elizabeth had turned back to look upon her daughter's burbling when, as adeptly as he had brought it beneath him, he removed the chair and returned it to its place. Then, he carefully pulled himself next to Elizabeth upon the bed. Slipping his arm around her shoulders and stretching his long legs the length of the bed, he anchored one ankle over the other. He took a ferociously long time settling himself, perhaps in want of disallowing himself to notice that his wife had neglected to re-tie the opening of her gown. Happily unawares of the distraction she exacted, she nestled contentedly against his chest and let her fingers sneak between the buttons of his waistcoat.

To once again feel the indention of his frame and warmth of his body next to her upon the mattress was very nearly exhilarating. He had not engaged in such a posture since the day he had fallen fast asleep from sheer exhaustion after his furious ride across half of England to reach her. She looked lovingly upon him, for he was draped across the bed in incongruously formal attire. His impeccable grooming bid her recollect the disastrous state of his ensemble upon his arrival at that tumultuous homecoming. The summer heat had bid him to shed his coat and neckcloth somewhere along the road. Hence, he had lain across the counterpane in shirtsleeves and breeches, his face nearly as caked with dust as his boots. She had thought he had never looked more handsome.

Her reverie was disturbed by his inquiry, "How long shall the little one sleep?"

"It is not how long, but how deeply will she sleep," replied she.

"I see."

"I fear I am still…indisposed," she ventured, "from the rigors of childbirth. It will be some time before I am myself again."

"Do not trouble yourself, Lizzy. Such matters have not entered my mind," his voice was all assurance; his countenance, however, looked less certain.

For such matters had entered his mind. They had entered his mind on numerous occasions to the point of preoccupation. There was no one with whom he might inquire as to the length of her convalescence with any degree of decorum, hence he was quite happy that she had brought the issue to light herself. Yet, "some time" was not a comfort. It was, however, something to look forward to.

The Master of Pemberley Is Displeased

Mr. Darcy's lips were further pursed (was that humanly possible) by another undertaking required of him by his patriarchal duty. This one was not the astonishment of the one gifted to him by his wife, but it still took him quite unawares.

No sooner had he settled into his new role of fatherhood and begun to bask in its glow, he was informed that it was imperative that arrangements be set in place for a wedding for Georgiana and Fitzwilliam. As his glower suggested, the nature of this additional burden invited Mr. Darcy's most severe indignation. This abhorrence, however, did not fall to any inherent dislike for his sister's intended groom. Indeed, Col. Fitzwilliam was one of the few men he deemed worthy of Georgiana's hand. His displeasure was not because of the haste of the nuptials, but owing to the delicate condition in which Georgiana would be taking them.

Indeed, the same injured expression gifted to Darcy's countenance by reason of his newly apportioned bed was duplicated upon learning of his sister's indecorous condition. Such a pinched visage had only manifested itself lately in his wife's presence, thereupon influencing her conclusion that she was in some way responsible for it. Hence, it was with no small relief that she observed it again whilst he pondered this new outrage to his dignity. She came to understand that his unhappy mien was not one he employed strictly for her benefit. Frighteningly, however, so great was his distaste of this particular brotherly duty, his aspect was further aggrieved by the adornment of gritted teeth. This was not without due cause, for he believed himself additionally abused in that his sister had been compromised under his very nose.

Her deflowerment had undoubtedly come about during their summer's quarantine on the Continent. Their party had consisted solely of himself, Georgiana, and Col. Fitzwilliam. They were quite isolated by the threat of plague, abiding in a vacant cottage with borrowed servants. The colonel had been grievously wounded in a battle near Quatre Bas, Georgiana his dedicated caretaker. It had been inevitable that the foetid army hospital where Georgiana had nursed Fitzwilliam would beget disease. Regrettably, Darcy had been unsuccessful in expediting their return to England before a general quarantine had been mounted throughout the region. At the time he had thought the delay egregious—fraught as he was with anxiety to see his loved ones safely home.

He snorted contemptuously at the realisation that his beloved sister's deflowerment was a *fait accompli* whilst he strode about worrying for their very lives.

At the time, Darcy had believed his sister's solicitous attention to the colonel's convalescence to have been laudable. It may well have been admirable, but to Darcy nothing else about the entire nightmare of an ordeal was. It galled him still to realise that he had left his wife to chase halfway across Belgium to rescue his sister from the gates of hell when she had flitted off on a romantic adventure, thinking herself in love with Fitzwilliam. Her entire reason for absconding after his regiment had been to look after him were he wounded.

Darcy had been furiously worried for her safety when she left and furiously relieved when he found her amidst all the chaos. Her behaviour had been so indecorous that he had been beside himself with reproach, yet so unconditionally happy to find her safe that he had been unable to bring himself to chastise her with the proper vehemence. Seldom did he redress himself, but hindsight saw he should have extended a rebuke—for thereafter her conduct did not improve. He gave not a fig if she called herself a nurse—the familiarity with which she tended to Fitzwilliam was unseemly. He had disapproved of her engaging in her nursing activities even when exacted upon the ill inhabiting Pemberley's lands. But due to the seriousness of Fitzwilliam's condition, Darcy had always held greater concern for her sensibilities than her virtue.

He had been compleatly unaware of their intimacy throughout their stay on the Continent and journey's return to hearth and home. To be so compleatly insensible of what had clearly come to pass between them was a considerable blow to the ego of one who believed himself most wise in the ways of the world. Georgiana, clearly aware of the most advantageous method to advise her brother of her unfortunate situation, had confided in Elizabeth. It was Elizabeth who had the unhappy task of enlightening him of just how solicitous Georgiana's care of Fitzwilliam had been. Not only was Darcy incensed to have been so compleatly duped, he was of the opinion that having one's sister ruined was good reason to call the colonel out. That Fitzwilliam's blood was not spilt was due only to Elizabeth's earnest intervention—and undoubtedly, her insistent reminder that due to Fitzwilliam's situation as an invalid, Georgiana had hardly been coerced.

Uncertain whether or not that was a comfort, Darcy grudgingly gave his blessing to the union.

For preventing such a potentially volatile situation from escalating into a duel, Elizabeth was due the credit. But she would have disagreed. She believed that in allowing her to superintend the transferral of intelligence, Georgiana exhibited a degree of calculation that even her risky romp after Fitzwilliam would not have suggested.

There were far more sombre matters that attended Darcy's homecoming than scandalous liaisons. Equally disconcerting, but with other emotions, Darcy learnt of the death of Elizabeth's father. She had not told him of it; what he learnt, he learnt in a private moment with Jane. He consoled Jane perfunctorily, a lapse she ignored. It was apparent that his thoughts had already turned toward Elizabeth. Jane watched him as he stood silent for a moment before entering her bed-chamber.

Having experienced the loss of his own esteemed father and knowing full well how dearly Elizabeth held hers, he knew just how deeply she must be injured by his untimely death. His peek into the room saw her asleep but stirring. Although he crept quietly, she opened her eyes full and turned to him. He knelt beside her and took her hand. The smile that had begun to overspread her face, faded. He had not intended it, but his aspect betrayed such singular sympathy that it had not been necessary for him to wear a black armband for her to see that he knew of what sadness had come to pass.

"So," she said with finality.

To be spared the necessity of telling him was her only consolation. She had dreaded that. As the painful recollection revisited her, tears filled her eyes and she turned away.

"My heart is heavy for you, Lizzy," said he, smoothing her hair with tender care.

She wanted to respond, to offer *him* words of reassurance, but she had a catch in her throat that made it impossible to utter a sound. So choked was she, that she feared any attempt to speak would have her break into huge, gulping sobs. Indeed, she dared not look at her husband's face, fearing that too would send her into uncontrolled weeping. Her bereavement was not new. It was self-indulgent to suffer so deeply still. Her husband had not been home a day, she could better serve his ease by refusing to submit to maudlin thoughts...

With that, her chin began to quiver and she knew keeping her countenance was lost. Hence, she gave way to the weep that was so intent on having its way with her. She withdrew her hand from his and covered her face in vain attempt to hide her distress.

He would not have it and drew her into his embrace, pressing her tearstained face against his neck.

"Shush, dearest Lizzy, pray do not weep," he murmured. "I am here. I am here."

That reminder gave more consolation than any other she might have imagined. Therefore, in due time her tears ceased. She did not, however, give up her place against his chest and from thence she told the entire history of her father's death and those sorrowful days that followed. Common thought was to discourage the bereaved from lamenting a death in detail, but Darcy decided then to be of a different mind. Clearly, Elizabeth had pent her wretchedness for some time. He thought it best to allow her to have her say and did not endeavour to quiet her again. He petted her and soothed her until at last, spent of emotion, she slept. He was happy to be home and have the employment of chief consoler. He was happy too that office was aided by the two small nestlings whose constant care demanded she not surrender to melancholy. Although he believed the timing of their newborns a godsend, he knew better than to make any insipid platitudes upon the transference of life.

That truism was quite evident.

Thrust into this jumble of despair and beatitude was news of quite another sort. For word had arrived too of the supposed battlefield casualty of George Wickham, the scoundrel husband of Elizabeth's sister Lydia. This information, however, occasioned a feigned bereavement that was very nearly as oppressive as had it been real. All this equivocatory posing sent the Darcys' barely tethered sensibilities reeling to such a degree that they were eventually rendered again upright.

A reinstatement of his equilibrium was essential for Darcy to embark upon a reckoning of a peculiar type. This duty was less conspicuous than any other, even covert, but of no less importance. It was a surreptitious trip to Kent that he embarked upon one day not long after his return. He told no one of the nature of his visit or even his intended destination, for he had a matter of utmost confidentiality to attend. The reason behind all his subterfuge lay in the nature of his call. In that Darcy was a man who, above all else, held matters of family of considerable importance, what he meant to inflict was no small nub. It was his intention to levy an unequivocal threat upon his cursed aunt, Lady Catherine de Bourgh. Although his mother's sister, he granted her no quarter. Lady Catherine had been responsible for distress to his wife, an injury Darcy put higher than any other. Had the lady been a gentleman, no doubt a thrashing would have occurred.

Although this too was long in coming, it would not have come to pass in so timely a fashion had it not been for his aunt's unforgivable conduct toward his wife whilst he was abroad. She had threatened Elizabeth with eviction from Pemberley had he not returned. It was a risky ploy for even so cagey a lady as his aunt. Certainly she should have known that he would employ the Right of Dower on Elizabeth's behalf. He had seen to it not only would Elizabeth be free to live out her days in Pemberley, she would enjoy one-third of the estate's income. He seldom found himself suffering a misjudgement, but he believed keeping his own counsel on that matter had been a mistake. He should have seen to it that Elizabeth was privy to the provisions he had made for her.

This singular desire to protect his privacy had once again run afoul. Clearly, if he had not gone so far as to make Elizabeth aware of that which pertained to her well-being, it was unreasonable to expect his aunt to be. It was a lesson he learnt well. In face of the deaths their family had weathered of late, he observed how very quickly the pale horse of death could overtake anyone, regardless of the eminence of one's circumstance. It was imperative to bring his aunt to heel. He had to remind her that it was not she who stood at their family's helm.

"The long habit of living does not lend us indisposed for dying," he reminded himself on that singular trip to Rosings Park.

Darcy had been apprised beforehand of his trip that a retaliation of sorts had been issued at the time of offence. It was but a small one, granted, but one that was exacted at great injury to such a proud woman. Had Elizabeth not confided to him about the particulars of her confrontation with Lady Catherine, his actually doing her bodily harm might still have been a temptation. But, as it happened, Elizabeth, although alone and with child, was not without her own defences. Indeed, in protection of herself and her unborn, Mrs. Darcy discharged a cautionary pistol shot in Lady Catherine's direction. Although the primary victim was only the ostrich plume in her ladyship's bonnet, the intent of the shot was met. Either through the agency of an intimate look down the muzzle of Elizabeth's pistol or its deafening reverberation, her ladyship had added to the insult of unmitigated fright that of an unfortunate fit of incontinence.

As his aunt's chastening was compleat and the carpet long burnt, Darcy was in want of only one further commination. With the low voice that only considerable umbrage can engage, he advised his aunt that was she again to trouble his wife, he would see to it that she would find herself trussed and bound, and fast on her way to being the newest inmate in the Lyme Institute for the Indigent Insane.

She was most unamused at the notion, but of this, he was unaware. Before she thought to shut her gaping jaw, he was back on his horse and homeward bound.

5

Seduction of the Willing

It was pleasantly warm for so early in the day and the sun had by then worn away the morning dew. Therefore, lying in the grass beneath a small stand of trees, wearing no more than a knee-length, linen smock, Mrs. Darcy had no complaint of the air or the damp. Indeed, well above a month after the rigours of childbirth, she could not think of a single obstacle to mar the exquisiteness of the moment. She was quite happy to resituate the rolled up pair of breeches that comprised her makeshift pillow and bask in what was a supreme contentment. She looked lazily up through the swaying branches of a particularly handsome specimen of Spanish Chestnut. After a moment, she became aware of an intermittent glare caused by sunlight playing peek-a-boo through the leaves. It bid her use the back of her hand as a shield. She closed one eye and covered the other with her right hand, first widening and then narrowing her fingers to create a sort of simplistic kaleidoscope. Only then did she realise that she had been humming.

"Darcy," said she.

"Mmmm," he replied.

There was nothing that she was actually in want of inquiring of him. She simply sought reassurance that he had not fallen asleep. His response suggested that had he not been actually dozing off, it had been a contemplation.

It had been within the first few months of her marriage that she had come to understand that amorous congress begged sleep of her husband. As well-intentioned and considerate a lover as he was, she chose to believe that need to be a masculine inevitability quite beyond his regulation rather than to claim it as an insult against her company. Moreover, as his drowsiness came upon the heels of his rendering her unto the throes of exhilarating rapture, she thought it only fitting that she conceded him a rest. Occasionally, however, either playfulness or caprice would provoke her to rouse him.

This day she did not feel particularly impish, but she had just been the grateful recipient of those extraordinary attentions that turn up the corners of a woman's mouth and she was still feeling its after-glow. Her spirits in high flutter, she could not quite allow herself to leave him in peace. Perchance that was because their voluptuous connexion had been over almost before it began. She could not fault their ardour for being so inflamed, for their separation had been so lengthy that their anticipation was excited beyond all reason. Regardless, she could not quite surrender to that male proclivity for post-coital sleep with magnanimity when it countered her own predisposition so decidedly. Thus, she eyed him closely to determine if it might be necessary to call his name again.

They had come to this coppice by her design. She admitted freely that she had nothing less in mind than an outright seduction (if, indeed, a person quite willing to be taken advantage of could consider himself seduced). Although it was she who lured him, by the time they arrived, just who was the governor of whose libido was unclear.

The spot was idyllic for a tryst. It had been a favourite destination upon languid afternoons as she and Darcy rode stirrup to stirrup across the vast park that surrounded Pemberley. It was not unusual for them to dismount in this particularly secluded dale, for the surrounding trees with low-hanging limbs afforded ample privacy. Although the very act of turning in that direction made it a given that they would linger, the precise cue would be when she let go her reins and began to remove the pins that anchored her hat. He would throw one long leg over the pommel of his saddle and drop to the ground, then, with gentlemanly care, allow her to slide from her horse into his out-stretched arms. She could not be certain (and knew it to be unlikely, even chimerical to think it), but she hoped it was upon one of these rendezvous that she had been brought with child.

She had not ridden a horse since giving birth, but she thought it only fitting that she and Darcy revisit this bucolic (perhaps historical) setting to sate those passionate longings that had been forced by nature and happenstance into frustration. Darcy had been so adamant that she keep to her room if not her bed, to greet him on horseback was the most conspicuous announcement that she could devise to prove to him her nether-regions were quite willing and able for a turn of another kind as well.

It had been a long, arduous trek to return to some semblance of normalcy. The first step of that journey had begun when he had appeared at her bedside within hours of her giving birth. In the fog of pain and exhaustion that had overtaken her, when she had seen by her side the lover that she had longed for with such incalculable fervour, she feared it only a dream. When he spoke her name and she realised he was indeed home, the exhilaration of the moment caused a palpable shudder to overtake her being. The urge to both laugh and cry lent her very nearly speechless—but not quite. What she had said, she knew must have come out as a babble.

The single obstacle in that being the most rhapsodic moment of her life was the unhappy mischance that her husband returned from his extended journey at the very culmination of her lying-in. Of life's many travails, few left one's appearance more compromised than childbirth. It may have been an abominable conceit to be concerned for such a triviality, but she knew that her ordeal left her pallid, dishevelled, and altogether unappealing. She had dreamt and meditated on every possible aspect of their reunion, but no scenario included her looking a fright. It was, she supposed, to her great fortune she had the two most beautiful infants ever born to mankind to distract him from her lack of comeliness.

Despite her passionate response at the sight of him, she had been far too weak for thoughts of a libidinous nature to return with any haste. Indeed, in the next few weeks her emotions flew about quite without her regulation. One day it was all she could do not to leap upon her husband's virile figure and smother him with her wifely inclinations, the next she was full of nothing but motherly devotion. There was no greater indication of her changeability than her initial impetuous promise never to allow either child to leave her side. Ere long, sleep deprivation drove her to reconsider. The thought of time with her husband unattended by infant or nurse had not been the driving force behind this alteration, but it was an unintended windfall. Or at least should have been. For a shared bed, in cases such as these, did not promise connubial reward—particularly when one occupant not only slept intermittently but was so wretchedly sore that even the thought of physical congress was abhorrent. However, that second particular evil soon altered decisively.

Initially, so intense were her maternal inclinations, she feared they might compleatly usurp her womanly ones. In due time, as her body healed, so did her sensibilities. She began to take notice of her handsome husband lying beside her each night and watch with admiration as he arose from their bed each morn. He kissed her quite soundly, but made no other attempt at intimacy. To forgo more than affectionate nuzzling was becoming increasingly difficult. As was to be expected, time influenced maternal affection and marital ardour to find harmony within her increasingly lustful breast. Ever more frequently she had found herself gazing lovingly down at her infants only to have her thoughts invaded by recollection of those amorous acts from which they were created. She had begun to recall those deeds with unsettling regularity. But with the same unsettling regularity, her husband kissed her upon the forehead and bid her goodnight seemingly unaware of the hand that she shamelessly let linger upon his person. If he did not take a hint, she concluded that it was necessary that she make an overture that could not be misunderstood.

This was precisely the course that brought them to be lying side by side in the middle of a glen in the middle of the morning—in decided *déshabillé.*

For all her mooning and dreaming of how she might lure him, the specifics had all been done quite on impulse. Had she given it more thought, it was doubtful she would have kept her nerve long enough to come to him beneath the window wearing a riding habit that included of a pair of *his* breeches that she had pilfered. They were a pair of knee-pants, hence the length suited her but she had fashioned a belt about the waist to keep them up. She had little defence for choosing such attire (she did not admit to the desire to astonish him) beyond that it enabled her to sit not side-saddle, but astride Boots. If one were to race, a better seat was imperative. And it was a race that she sought both to engage in and to win. But to lure him, she had to catch him unawares. Hence, she came below the window of their bed-chamber not long after dawn. He was used to her arising at odd hours to tend to the babies whilst he still lay fast asleep. She had to call out several times to awaken him.

Answering her call, he came onto the balcony (she thought he looked quite fetching with mussed hair and sleep still in his eyes) but when he saw her there on Boots and leading Blackjack, he did not hesitate. Dressing was the work of but a moment. He leapt upon Blackjack and was after her in a flash. She knew that she took unfair advantage by not waiting for him to mount, but she cared little, for it had been her design all along to lead him to the bucolic shelter of trees that had played host to past pleasures. It was an ideal location to renew those ministrations that had been the glory of their marriage.

Under no other circumstances would she have capitulated a race. Upon this occasion, however, she allowed him to overtake her. If she had any misgivings having employed such a ruse, they were then compleatly soothed. It had been altogether divine—if far too abbreviated. They had shed their clothes and consummated their love with the same dispatch that he had dressed. Months of celibacy had been ended in a great hurry. She was only mildly disappointed. History suggested further loving rites were to be enjoyed.

He lay beside her, his bare back no more sensible of the damp grass than hers. He had not responded to her inquiry beyond his half-hearted murmur. Therefore she decided that to cajole him from what must be a satisfying rest she would have to offer more than conversation. Thereupon, she threw one arched leg over his and cupped her heel, closing the gap between their bodies with a small undulation of her hip. It was an infallible demarche for a woman who was in want of her husband's notice. Indeed, he opened one eye full and looked upon her, a notification that she indeed had his attention. Moreover, his hand found her bare thigh and began to stroke it. But he did so only for a moment.

He rose upon one elbow facing her and gazed into her eyes so deeply and with such intensity that she did not think that, was she so inclined, she had the fortitude to look away. He slid his hand beneath her leg and, without quitting her gaze, drew her knee purposely to his lips—a manoeuvre that suggested to her that her pleasure was of no less import than his own. It also pointed to the probability that he would have the strength for an encore. Only the thought of the bliss that was to follow allowed her at last to close her eyes. She lay back, transported to a place and time only known to infinity and could not keep a small sough from escaping the back of her throat. Her reverie, regrettably, was short-lived.

"Lizzy…"

Upon most occasions, it was with unadulterated joy that she heard him utter her name. This time however, differed. Although it was not in his nature to speak in an exclamatory fashion, it was implied. Such was her alarm that she thought someone might have happened upon them. She first shrank back and looked about. Seeing nothing, she endeavoured to sit up. To her further apprehension, he cautioned her otherwise.

"Pray, do not."

Although the timbre of his voice was in compleat disagreement, she was altogether relieved that they need not flee. She saw having to dress with all due haste in an unfamiliar garment to be no small challenge. If someone had trespassed upon them, it was likely she would have had to take leave with the tail of her shirt the only thing between herself and compleat exposure. The thought almost made her smile, but he interjected.

"You are…in distress," he said softly, but she detected a slight catch in his voice.

There was an intrusion upon them, but one of quite another nature than interlopers. She saw then that she had begun to bleed. She was truly horrified—but not from fear for her own well-being, but that *he* would fear for her well-being. She was also miffed. It had been a full ten days since she had last been vexed by such a bother and had believed herself essentially returned to her former robustness. She had given herself a week before she began to scheme. It had taken three full days to conjure just the right combination of seduction and playfulness with which to lure him. Hence, to have their idyll end so unromantically was an unmitigated abomination. She refused to admit that her health might be compromised even to herself. Until this moment, she saw all to be going quite splendidly. Even the fickleness of her spirits had waned. This was an unhappy setback.

"It is nothing," she assured him whilst abruptly drawing her knee from his grasp.

"Are you certain?" he asked, then thought better of it and altered his question, "How can you be certain?"

"I am quite sure it is nothing irregular."

She would not have it any other way. Regardless, it looked as if any possibility of a second voluptuous union had waned. He simultaneously stood and began donning his shirt, then hastily began to tuck it in. She sat immobile, transfixed—watching his hasty reclamation of his ensemble and thus the disintegration of what had been an idyllic reunion. With resignation over this unlucky perverseness, she looked to the rumpled pile that was the purloined trousers turned pillow and fretted about wearing them in her untidy condition. There seemed little choice, hence she picked them up and flicked them so as to get them into some sort of identifiable order. She had just begun to snake her foot down one leg opening and was silently bemoaning his overreaction to her little recuperative set-back when a cramp overcame her. Before she could stifle a slight groan, she felt herself expel an unseemly gush of blood. She had weathered enough days of womanly indisposition not to be altogether alarmed by this turn of events (although even by her account it was a ghastly amount), but the cramp was severe enough to give her pause. The pain, however, was not her primary concern. For while not unaware, she knew her husband was largely unschooled on the prolific nature of such flow. She would have been happy to spend all her days with him unknowing of just how indecorous feminine complaints could be.

"I can ride," she insisted, anticipating him contending otherwise.

She began pulling on the breeches, the legs of which were unspeakably uncooperative. He suggested himself of the opposite opinion of both her readiness to ride by herself and the necessity of her donning the breeches by pulling them from the feet that she was just beginning to fit down the narrow leg passages. The yank was far more abrupt than she liked and she almost said as much, but he had tossed the garment aside and then swept her up in his arms before she could utter a sound. In one motion he plopped her sideways upon Blackjack's saddle. He managed this with such economy of motion that she was still stuttering "but, but…" when he pulled himself behind her and gave Blackjack his heel.

"Boots…" she began, pointing behind them.

"Leave them," he demanded.

"No," said she, "my horse."

"She will follow," he assured her.

He dug his heels into Blackjack, demanding him into a canter, then bethought the situation and slowed him to a walk, clearly in a quandary whether speed or comfort held greater import.

As they got on fast to Pemberley House, she clung to his shirt. So tight was her grasp, she feared she might rend the fine linen. She was in no particular state of alarm, therefore she could not account for her own discomposure. Gradually, the realisation from whence it sprang occurred to her. He in his shirt and in great dismay, she across the saddle in front of him was the same attitude in which they took leave of the inn after her long-past and brief kidnapping at the hands of the villainous Tom Reed. It was disconcerting for that to be brought to her mind just then and she wondered if he recalled it as well.

They headed directly toward the courtyard, but public exposure of their little adventure was clearly something they most fervently did not wish to endure. Before she could bid him to find a more discreet entrance, he anticipated her, turning Blackjack toward the postern at the rear of the house (with Boots trailing loyally behind). When they gained the entrance archway shielding the steps, he leapt to the ground and held out his arms. Perhaps he had done just that at the end of that long-passed ride—she did not recall. But upon alighting from a horse on every mundane occasion, he had not drawn her down quite as tenderly as he did then.

Once upon the ground, she anticipated manoeuvring the steps under her own power. Again he thought otherwise. And again he swept her into her arms and with extraordinary purposefulness, took the steps two at a time. She was still a bit humiliated and would have preferred a less dramatic entrance.

"Pray, husband," she begged, "I am not so unwell as all this…"

Unthwarted, he did not alter from his hurried pace until they reached her bedchamber. Quite unceremoniously, he kicked back the door.

"Hannah!" he commanded.

Aware that her mistress was from her bed and the house, Hannah had kept a worried eye out for her return. She did not need to hear the commotion to be fast on their heels. Hence, when Darcy turned and called for her, they met—causing Hannah to come to a near skidding halt.

"Good. Good," he pronounced, then said, "Mrs. Darcy is unwell. See that the surgeon is called."

At last, Elizabeth's interjection was heard, "I am quite well. I do *not* need to be seen."

This too, was a repetition that recalled events that neither would have wanted to be brought to mind. Still, she insisted that all was well.

"'Tis merely a small regression," she insisted. "I need only to rest to repair fully."

She had finally made a statement with which he could at least partially agree.

"Yes, Lizzy. You do need your rest. Pray, is there anything than I can do to relieve your present suffering?"

She shook her head. However, he did not await an answer before he snapped his fingers at Hannah, who then hurried off to see that the doctor was, indeed, called. Once the maid had withdrawn, they could speak more plainly.

"It was unwise, I fear," he said.

As he had not specified "it," Elizabeth was left to wonder which of the various activities she had just undertaken was the one to which he referred. Any that he might have specified might not have found argument from her, for she had again begun to cramp. In fortune, she was by then beneath the bed-clothes and any unseemliness her body committed would remain between her and the maid.

She had been so caught up in denying her indisposition whilst simultaneously being thoroughly embarrassed by it, that the extent of Darcy's dismay had been lost to her. Only then did she become aware that his countenance betokened throes of uncommon anxiety. Clearly he was not acting, as he often did, as her overseer, but seemed, what was for him, highly alarmed. It was only to her veteran eyes that it was discernible as such. (Anyone else would have thought him only in a bit of ill-humour.) Hence, she repressed her ever-increasing pique at his officiousness and lent him all due allowance.

"I have been done no great harm. I shall be *fine*," she assured him, patting the top of his hand which rested proprietarily upon the bed next to her.

His gaze suggested that he was *not* particularly reassured. "May I safely leave it to yourself to determine…?"

"I *promise*," she did, in fact, promise him.

He smiled gamely, but did not leave her until the surgeon arrived some two hours later and offered similar sentiments. Mr. Upchurch stood over Elizabeth whilst Darcy looked on, hence the good doctor was unable to be more explicit with the couple than to inquire if Elizabeth had undertaken any unusual activities of late.

"She went out upon *horseback*," Darcy accused.

"Did she now?" the surgeon said mildly. "Now we mustn't do that for a while longer, shall we Mrs. Darcy?"

Having become quite familiar with Mr. Upchurch over the years, Elizabeth understood that the man suspected that her horse may not have been the only thing she had been astride. She blushed so profoundly that she felt it spread from her cheeks and down her throat and then invade her décolletage. His wife's reaction did not escape Darcy's notice. Her chagrin contaminated his composure, but to a far less discernible degree.

The expression of contrition upon his countenance very nearly made her laugh. He looked like a child caught with his hand in the sugar bowl. Wisely, she overcame that inclination. Her merriment, however, was not lost upon him and he managed to alter his aspect into her particular version of punctiliousness.

"I shall be much more circumspect," she solemnly promised Mr. Upchurch.

The surgeon left forthwith. Indeed, he left with such haste, it was unclear whether it was owing to Mr. Darcy's dour countenance or his own embarrassment over having to allude to Mr. and Mrs. Darcy's possible premature connubial connexion. Either way, he was out the door and down the hall so quickly that he almost tripped over their aging wolfhound Cressida upon his way.

Darcy and Elizabeth both heard Cressida whimper and Darcy walked to the door and looked out.

"She is uninjured?" Elizabeth inquired.

When he turned, he nodded his head and walked back to the side of her bed.

He said, "Cressida looks to be quite well. But, Lizzy, the question is, are you truly uninjured?"

As he said this, his countenance almost crumbled and he turned from her. Alarmed, she half-rose. He heard and turned about once more.

"Do not. Do not, please," he said, urging her to lie back.

In that brief moment, he had regained his composure. The happiness she had felt just that afternoon had now been usurped by self-reproach. She had selfishly pressed them to return to their previous intimacy. He was exposed not only to unseemly female emissions, but to profound apprehension.

The request was spoken with a level voice, but his eyes pled, "Promise me that you will see to your own well-being with greater resolve."

"I do promise," she said, then commenced to add a proviso, "But…"

"No," he said, "Please, no."

He looked away and began again, "Lizzy, my love, I have been far too deeply concerned for you to be soon at peace…"

She took his hand, but spoke no more. As much as she would have liked, there were no words to beguile him from his disquiet that day or for many days thence.

What Lengths Love Knows

From the very beginning, the throes of love in which Darcy found himself over Elizabeth had little to do with comeliness and everything to do with allure.

Although she was known as quite a country beauty, she had not the classic oval-faced, long-necked handsomeness of her sister Jane. Indeed, she was quick to assert Jane to be twice as handsome and thrice as good. Hence, she may have harboured some conceit of her own cleverness, but she believed her aspect quite unextraordinary. Her husband would not have disagreed that she was superior to most in wit and information. However, as he had been held in thrall of her physical charms for some time, he thought them nothing less than exceptional. These sentiments were largely unexpressed. His nature did not lend itself to expansivity. It had been only in their most private moments that he would speak rapturously of the fineness of her eyes and the turn of her countenance (not infrequently would his delineation of her charms wander into those phrases lauding attributes not normally employed in polite company). These flights of linguistics were infrequent even before his away to Belgium. Since his return to hearth and home and the arrival of new ones in their bed, he had little time to speak to Elizabeth in confidence at all, much less give her an accounting of how very much motherhood had improved her handsomeness. He was quite beside himself in admiration.

It was a muggy night, so damp Darcy's night-shirt stuck to his skin. He had thrown back the bed-clothes with disgust and had automatically reached out for Elizabeth. Her cool skin was always a comfort.

But she was not there.

It came to him then that she would be tending to one or the other of the infants. At that moment, even that usually sublime image was not a consolation to him. Restless, he turned upon his side and propped upon an elbow so as to gaze out upon the tree limbs that swayed beyond the railing of the balcony. The wide, double doors had been thrown open in a futile attempt to entice a cool breeze inside. Maddeningly, rather than come in, the wind stubbornly whirled about outside, enticing the drapes out through the doorway where they noisily flailed about. So blustery and oppressively humid was it, he wondered if a storm was brewing.

It was then that he saw Elizabeth.

She was leaning against the railing, her night-dress pirouetting about her ankles as if dancing with the wind. As it whipped about, the thin gauze of her gown alternately caressed her body and then capered away—revealing and then concealing her womanly curves. It was a voluptuous sight—one that beguiled him from the bed.

Bare-footed, he padded out the door and came quietly behind her. She did not give a start when he put his hands upon her hips. Rather, she reached behind and placed her hands upon his thighs. It would have been difficult to determine whether she rolled her head to the side to be kissed upon her neck, or whether he initiated it by drawing her hair to one side. Regardless, he kissed her there whilst allowing his hands to embark upon the familiar search of her body.

A sough was heard; whether it came from her, from him, or simply from the trees, he was uncertain. From whence it came proved irrelevant when she began a slow undulation against him. It pervaded his body with an unparalleled hunger for her. So hungry for her was he, that a moan escaped from the back of his throat. He turned her about, grasped her by the shoulders and drew her to him. His heart was beating so feverishly in his chest that he could hear it in his ears. She looked up and into his eyes, but her gaze turned impish and she slid her hand to his manhood and began to stroke it.

"Darcy?" Elizabeth said, shaking his shoulder.

She repeated, "Darcy? I beg you forgive me, but I cannot sleep whilst you make that noise."

Suddenly, he opened his eyes, blinking furiously in the dark, endeavouring to make sense of it. When he realised that he had been dreaming, he instinctively put his hand over his groin lest the specific nature of his dream be evident to her. That he was beneath the bed-clothes, in his night-shirt, and in the dark did not come immediately to mind.

"Yes," he said, rolling onto his stomach in embarrassment. "Yes, of course. I shall do my best."

"I do apologise," she said. "It is imperative that I sleep when I can." Then she asked with concern, "Are you unwell?"

Whether from the weather or his dream, perspiration had plastered his hair to his forehead.

"It is only these insufferable bed-clothes," said he, attempting to relieve himself of them without turning over.

"Return to your sleep, Lizzy," said he. "All is well."

There was a time when the discovery of his arousal would have delighted her. He no longer dared to expose her to such lustfulness. Even he had heard the tales old women told of what befell a nursing mother if frightened. It was said she might lose her milk. He could not risk that. He murmured his apologies for disturbing her and waited to hear the deep respirations of her sleep before closing his own eyes again.

In retrospect, he realised he had been inexcusably smug to think that he could share a bed with her and resist his husbandly urges, which was imperative, of course. She would be unwell for some time.

With the same meticulousness that he employed in all his endeavours, he had worked it out in detail so as to keep any inappropriate inclinations at a minimum. When they kissed, he allowed himself only close-lipped chasteness. (Under no circumstances was he to relax his guard against the soft warmth of her lips.) A far greater dilemma (one that would not be withstood whatsoever if the kissing business was not held at bay) was to lie next to her each night. After the initial exhilaration of his return had cooled, he had inquired as to the nursing duties necessitating separate sleeping arrangements. Never, in all of their marriage, had they been under the same roof and slept apart. After a brief exploration of the other's true wishes, it was determined that neither was disposed to forgo such intimate communion—even with such strong grounds against it.

There were hurdles to overcome. In order not to fall victim to his passion, his regimen was alternately to cling to the far edge of the mattress and to imagine at any moment the gnomish spectre of Mrs. Littlepage sitting between them with a baby in each arm. His sleep was negligible, but he managed to keep from disturbing Elizabeth's. Once came the dawn, there were fewer wrinkles to avoid, for if she were awake, she was nursing and if she was not, he would steal from their bed so as not to ruin her sleep.

Although he had thought out his every move with precision, sitting in his dressing-chamber waiting for Goodwin to ready him for his morning shave, it was of particular mortification to realise how tempted he was to resort to that activity particular to pubescent boys to relieve the palpable pain in his loins. Now it became clear that even in his sleep, his desire for her was ungovernable.

Regrettably, the rest of the day lay before him with unrelenting temptation.

To never again leave her side had been his initial compulsion and was honoured for weeks. It was only time and the aching in his vitals that bid him otherwise. He would have been quite happy to ride out each morning to engage solely in manly pursuits, eschewing such a female-dominated climate altogether. He could have made himself quite busy, not to return until supper was waiting. His temptation then would have been halved.

But he could not. Elizabeth had asked him to remain near her. He could never deny her anything—most certainly not himself. Therefore, he gathered his considerable dignity and reminded himself that he had endured war, pestilence, and a month on an ill-gaited horse—he certainly had the wherewithal to regulate his daily routine as he had the nights. But, alas.

The stark light of day did not diminish his yearnings. He found himself watching Elizabeth surreptitiously whilst she nursed. The loving gazes she bestowed upon their gurgling young ones as they took their nourishment from her, the babies' fingers tangling happily in errant strands of her hair—it was a display of pure angelic bliss, so beautiful it made his heart ache. If she saw him there, she encouraged him to come close. Thither went he to her side, but knew he was a clumsy outsider to such a gentle scene. Moreover, despite the sublimity he witnessed, the moment the children were taken from her arms and the room vacant of unwanted eyes, he felt the irresistable need to leap upon her fecund form, tear her gown from her luscious body and use every means within his power to impregnate her with another child.

Such a letch was an abomination unto the Lord, and of no help in his present situation, either.

The treasured miniature that had accompanied and comforted him upon his treacherous sojourn on the Continent was once again his constant companion. He drew a loving thumb across Elizabeth's likeness and pondered the conundrum he faced. For he would have paid any sum to exchange that tiny visage for her true aspect once again—

and he dared not. Her very countenance before him was a cruel taunt when he could not go to her—to brush the curls from her neck and press his lips to the warm indention just below her ravishing little ear—and from thence to the luscious treasures below. As it was, he spent half his time in miserable semi-arousal—and hiding it like some randy schoolboy behind whatever waist-high furniture was at hand.

The mercy she had shown him by enticing him to take her in so bucolic an assignation, and in so fetching a manner, was one of unparalleled generosity. Its ghastly ending was truly a disappointment. But he had certainly not been disgusted. Its single evil was to recall to him events that he had hoped were long-embedded in their past. The moment he saw her blood, his alarm, the panic, the sheer terror of that ancient event gripped him like a serpent's fang.

So firmly had he endeavoured to bury the memory, it was if it had occurred in another life.

It had been late one autumn, weeks before she had been expected to deliver their first child, when Elizabeth went into labour. It had begun in customary order, but as time wore on, hour after agonizing hour, no progress was made. The surgeon told them that the baby was not only quite large, but breech. With her usual pluck, she had endured a horrific labour. She had refused to cry out in her pain lest Darcy hear her—and he had pled for her to do just that. Servants covered their ears, Goodwin had been laid helpless, Fitzwilliam fled, and only Charles Bingley, Darcy's friend and Jane's husband, remained in the house to comfort Jane. And comfort her he did, for the outcome was grievous indeed. The baby was stillborn and Elizabeth was left clinging to life.

After the baby had been taken from her, Elizabeth had lain still as death. Darcy dismissed everyone from the room and had cleansed her himself knowing, even then, the unseemliness of his insisting on such duty. Jane was witting, but others in the household were unaware of it save Hannah. She had been the single other person who witnessed his tender ministrations (she undertook the conservatorship of that private hour as a sacred trust). Yet, it had been a fortnight before Elizabeth again opened her eyes. When she did, her husband was the first image she saw, for he had shepherded her care more devotedly than Jane. It fell to him to tell her that the baby was dead, and it was he who cried with her for hours after.

Upon that occasion long past, when Elizabeth's milk had come, it was despised, a heartless reminder of what was not to be. It was a trial for him not to recall that when he saw her now. Perhaps that is why the vision of her nursing now tugged so decidedly at his heart. Quite unreasonably, all of the heartbreak, all her pain, Darcy had concluded fell to him. His own imposing bearing (and his inordinate conceit of pride for it) bid him be wracked with guilt for fathering a child too large for her to deliver. She was not petite, but she was fine-boned. He, who prided himself upon being well-schooled in the nature of breeding—he, above all others—should have anticipated the dangers.

So great was his grief and his guilt, he truly thought that to run mad through the house would have been a relief. He vowed never to endanger her again. Looking upon her figure with desire had been unconscionable when he feared for her very life. He had shunned the notion of resuming connubial relations, fearing if she was brought to the straw again of another child, she would not survive. Were it necessary, he would bear celibacy. He even contemplated taking his sleep in another bed-chamber. She had been melancholy, even morose, hence temptation had not been keen. But her black spirits eventually diminished, and when at last the barrier was broken, it was Elizabeth who initiated love-making. In suggesting to Darcy that the time had come to reengage their marital rites, Elizabeth had to invoke all her powers of seduction. She told him unconditionally that she, and not he, was the governor of her life.

Her argument was so powerful that their recovery unto the boughs of amatory delight was consummated on one end of the fully set, mahogany dining table. Indeed, tiny bits of glass were discovered in the carpet by the maids for months. In the days that followed, Mr. and Mrs. Darcy might have been somewhat mortified over the obvious absence of the second-largest lead crystal decanter and what looked to be a half-dozen of the best goblets had they not had such a deliciously decadent love-fest whilst inadvertently destroying them. It was discovered that their dining-table was quite sturdy and had the silver settings not sported all six forks, neither of them would have recollected the occasion with anything but the utmost fondness.

They could laugh at their impetuosity later—but only much later.

Other husbands might have seen it as a mortification not to have been the one to assert matrimonial rights. But he was not. He saw it then as his wife's privilege, for it was her body, not his, which suffered for their newborns. Hence, it had fallen to her again to indicate when her body was sufficiently recovered from her lying-in. The morning she came beneath his window on Boots, she told him unequivocally that she was prepared once again to engage in those amorous acts that led to her confinement in the first place. Granted, when that time was nigh at hand, Mr. Darcy was in such a state of sexual deprivation, coaxing of mind or member was quite unnecessary. This time, however, theirs was a bed of wild flowers—but had it been rocks, that would have been no greater impediment than cutlery. It was maddeningly brief, but still a delight.

It was also clearly premature.

Elizabeth had been entirely mistaken in the supposition that his fastidiousness had been offended by her unexpected discharge. Had her mortification not clouded her judgement, she would have realised that. He had never been repulsed by the monthly evidence of her fecundity nor did he abhor the evidence of childbirth. She was, however, compleatly unaware that he alone had cleansed her body after the stillbirth. The blood was merely a reminder of how very close he once came to losing her. His reticent disposition always resurfaced in times of trial. Hence, he could in no way explain what terror took hold of him that day or why.

One of the many blessing their newborns bestowed upon him as a father had been to relieve him at last of his long-held fear for a safe delivery. Elizabeth had successfully birthed not one, but two babies. Granted, because there were two, neither was particularly large. In fact, he discerned that they were not as plump as Jane's newborns. However, both looked to be a bit long of leg—like their father. In truth, although they were fast plumping up, they both had been rather gangly. Their first-born had been exceptionally large—the physician had said so. If the twins had been but one, how large might they have been? That old bugaboo would occasionally seize him—that the children he sired were too large for his dearest Lizzy to bear. He endeavoured to remind himself of that with which they were blessed and fervently pray that if they were gifted with more children, all would be well.

When upon the heels of their abridged tryst he curtailed further advances toward marital fulfilment, she wholly misunderstood. He merely wanted to give her all the time she needed to recover. They must not rush her. All the planets would soon align, abolishing misapprehensions and misgivings. They would once again laugh together beneath the bed-clothes until frolicsome inclinations fell quiet, suffocated by a passion that had found no boundaries. He hoped.

Connubial Contemplation

Elizabeth Darcy was quite unaware of the many unprecedented dilemmas her husband carried with him as he engaged in his duties within and without Pemberley, as she was weathering internal disharmonies of her own. Having to nurse both hungry infants round the clock was no small bother either upon Elizabeth's time or vigour. But even so weary a difficulty as this had its merits, for it had relieved her of one potentially sticky dilemma.

Although Mrs. Bennet was still in deep mourning at Longbourn, she issued ultimatums to Elizabeth via the post. History should have suggested to Mrs. Bennet that issuing such demands to her second oldest daughter was unworthy of her time, but she had not heeded that lesson. Mrs. Bennet knew from Lizzy's previous pregnancy that she eschewed the notion of a wet-nurse. Mrs. Bennet, however, insisted (adamantly, even vociferously) that decorum demanded that her grandchildren have that service. It was no surprise that sweet, compliant Jane bowed to her mother's wishes, but Mrs. Bennet was most unhappy not to have that success with Elizabeth (Lydia needed no prodding to give up any duty which supplied her no diversion). If ever was the time, now Elizabeth must yield to her motherly advice, hence she wrote, "The very success of your marriage is at stake."

Medical advice, tales of abuse, or common sense could not sway Mrs. Bennet from her belief that a wet-nurse was mandatory. Were her grounds for this directive not well-founded? It was a proven fact that a woman could not possibly carry out her marital duty with a baby at her breast and if she could, excitement of a carnal nature spoilt a nursing mother's milk. Elizabeth may have birthed a Pemberley heir, but Mrs. Bennet knew having merely one was insufficient. Statistics were exceedingly unfavourable. It was far too likely that a baby would not live to see his first birthday. Some alarmists said only one in three would survive. (Although Mrs. Bennet had five who lived, they were all daughters and therefore unfit for numerical consideration.) An auxiliary son was imperative. Mr. Darcy had Mr. Bingley's money ten-fold. It was essential that the effervescence of Mr. Darcy's voluptuous fondness not be denied. Dear Lizzy must not waste a single fertile moment. No good came from nursing. It endangered the babe in her arms and denied further generation.

Indeed, Mrs. Bennet was unyielding on this point.

Elizabeth, unfortunately, was equally unyielding and as she was out from beneath her mother's eye, did what she pleased. She had initially refused on principle to turn either infant over to another woman to suckle. It was a proprietary issue. Little though she relished a contest of wills with her mother, Elizabeth's overabundance of mettle suggested that if it came to that, she would. However, after a perilous birth, she was slow to regain her strength and as a result her milk supply was a bit paltry—enough perchance for one hungry mouth, but not two. Necessity, regrettably, demanded the employment of a wet-nurse. In the end, the birth of twins rendered the disagreement moot. Elizabeth did not give up her nursing duties—she shared them with squat, bounteous-breasted Mrs. Littlepage. (Mrs. Bennet would have been unhappy she suckled them at all.) As in most disputes where both were sides are left equally unhappy, this incident could be viewed as a draw.

Mrs. Darcy may have settled that discord without undue privation, but upon other fronts, she was not so fortunate. Her mother was unconditionally oblivious to the passionate nature of the Darcys' marriage. Had she been witting, she would not have worried that Elizabeth would forsake her nuptial bed. Elizabeth Darcy was certainly not disinclined to disport amorously whether she was nursing or not. As determined a mother as Lizzy was and complicated as the manoeuvrings of twins were, she was determined nothing would interfere with the physical love she shared with her husband. She believed it a cruel evil to have to sacrifice one joy on behalf of the other.

However dedicated were her intentions, upon this vow she had been badly thwarted by practicality. Although Mr. Darcy had afforded her great affection atop the covers, from the very beginning, with babies and nurses about there had been little opportunity to creep beneath them. Indeed, what encounters they had managed had been somewhat furtive and not altogether rewarding. After the absolute fiasco she had subjected her dear husband to in the glen, she wondered if he would be permanently affrighted from attempting to scale those lofty summits their passion had reached in unions past. She prayed not.

Hence, it took all her concentration not to allow her mind to wander from those mothering arts, for if her thoughts drifted, their destination was not always to those many blessings she enjoyed, but to the single one she did not. In this instance, however, this preoccupation was not the usual penchant by the well-recompensed to long for that which they are denied. Intimate nuzzlings and erotic delights were most noteworthy omissions.

Mr. Darcy did continue to inquire after her health with all due determination, and with equal determination, Mrs. Darcy continued to deny that Mrs. Darcy's nether-regions had not been so anxious for marital rites as her libido. He, however, remained either unconvinced or uninterested. She had gone so far as to make certain that Mr. Darcy did not discover that the waddle she had not experienced since her honeymoon had once again afflicted her gait. (Upon that occasion she learned that time, and repetition, would heal all injury.) But, he made no request (by word or action) to engage in those acts that had once been an integral portion of their love. She should have been unconditionally miffed. As it was, her anticipation of renewing that very laudable part of their marriage was both barely containable and singly troubling.

For as much as her husband's adoration of her naked form knew no bounds in times past, he had yet to gaze upon her fully undraped shape now that she had carried and birthed twins. Indeed, her confinement had abused her figure so unmercifully that she had been loath to do more than take a quick peek at herself in the looking-glass. Not only was she more than a small part plump, there were horrid red claw marks striating upward on her belly. Those scars were quite evident because her stomach hung from her frame like an empty sack of salt. Elizabeth was far less vain than the average handsome woman, but she was appalled at the notion of her husband looking upon her figure in its present state. If she looked upon it with repugnance, she could not bear to imagine his reaction.

It was against her nature to admit to miscalculations, but hindsight suggested that it had been a misjudgement to have instigated marital relations so hastily *and* indulged the dual insult to her nether-regions by beguiling him to their tryst astride a horse. Ultimately, the only shrewdness involved had been that the method she had chosen for that seduction involved the open air and thus a minimum removal of garb. Indeed, although the outcome had distressed him to no end, her method did accomplish one important goal—physical congress was achieved without him catching sight of much skin.

The more that she thought of it, the more she considered their interrupted encore a blessing. If things proceeded in the same fashion as they began, it was likely nothing of her newly disfigured form would have been left to his imagination. The recollection sent Elizabeth into heart-palpitations of a sort that she had not felt since her wedding night—but now of an entirely different nature. Her current anxiety stemmed not from anticipating the mysteries of connubial pleasures, but from the enlightenment. She knew what immeasurable rapture they beheld. The rapture, however, was not what gave her pause. It was, indeed, the perfervid road thither.

From the very beginning, Darcy had been the most tender of lovers. He not only took his pleasure, but was generous in granting hers. His vigour was boundless (even indefatigable). He was impassioned, seductive, sensual, and romantic. (Just thinking of it gave her a voltaic frisson down her back that entered her innermost recesses.) So vivid was the recollection of his hand as it stroked the inside of her thigh, she was incited to reach for her fan. She did so reflexively, her hand absently searching the chair cushion until she found it by its tassel. She unfurled it, and began to flutter it demurely. But the recollection of his touch soon gave way to one that she had not seen for far too long—Darcy in all his naked glory. Hence, she began to flap her fan with greater and greater abandon—but to little avail. Once she began to visit her most intimate memories, they quite overran her thoughts.

One particular feature of their love-making, however, nagged her new-found inhibitions.

For, although their romantic idylls were many and their methods varied, a single aspect of her husband's love-making had never altered. Within the tenacious Mr. Darcy dwelled an unsparing meticulousness that demanded he do nothing in a cursory manner. That could be an unparalleled gift when it came to the art of sexual congress. However, much like his love-making, inspection of her would also be thorough.

No demure lifting of the hem of her night-dress would suit his leanings.

Even then, the memory of such investigations teased her thoughts.

Although of late, he had taken to wearing a night-shirt and she her night-dress, there was a time when they both were given to sleeping naked as the day they were born. That penchant had been established upon the first morning of their marriage. As it happened, the servants had slipped into the Darcys' bed-chamber early to light the fires and open the drapes. She had been mortified for it to be exposed to the household that their new mistress had taken her night so immodestly. Thenceforward, Darcy had gallantly undertaken the chore of opening the drapes each morning. That served the dual purpose not only of sparing her embarrassment, but also assuring the continuation of their eschewing night-wear. (Evidently, he had transgressed generations of morning ritual in telling the servants never to intrude into their bed-chamber unless the bell-cord was pulled.) Although they had not spoken a word of it between them, she had come to consider his assuming this duty as nothing less than a personal gift. Had he known of her feelings, he might have believed her gratitude was simply for his protecting her modesty before the servants. But it was not.

As it happened, when she would feel him leave their bed and walk to the windows each morning, she had not been above feigning sleep to peek at his naked figure. The sight of his broad back, sinewy limbs, and firm buttocks had been a voluptuous thrill that she never tired of viewing. Initially she had suffered a mild attack of panic when he turned about and sauntered back to the bed—torn whether to shut her eyes and continue the subterfuge of sleep or enjoy the pleasure of observing the more fascinating vision he presented as he walked towards her. (The first occasion upon which she had done so had been a small mortification in that it was probable that her gaze was not once cast upon his countenance.) Observing his appendages sway gracefully as he strode in her direction caused her heart to palpitate wildly. Initially, she had told herself that spying was merely investigative. Having only sisters and no brothers, she had absolutely no familiarity with the male of the species. As to why she continued to gaze upon him long after she was acquainted with every inch of his body, she unabashedly attributed to outright voyeurism.

When the weather was warm, he returned to their bed and drew the bed-clothes from her and awakened her from her pretended sleep by kissing her shoulders. Chilly days began much the same, but rather than remove the bed-clothes, he leapt beneath them to warm his cold feet against hers. With the same regularity that gifted her with his icy feet, she would protest—and he would pretend innocence. Playfulness often led to amatory embraces, but either way their mornings began, they commenced with some constancy.

At nightfall, a far different course was taken.

In the night, their pleasure was a sensual indulgence—lit by candles. Indeed, one candle was not enough. From their very first nights together, he insisted upon a twelve-pronged candelabrum—one that emitted more light than a blazing fireplace. But most unnerving to her, he had taken a single candle from its pricket, and with his soft palm guiding the path, drew it thither, illuminating the length of her reclining figure. It was an audaciously sensual act—an eroticism that did not diminish in repetition.

Not surprisingly, her modesty initially had forbid compleat surrender to his inspection. She smiled to herself when recalling that first intimate perusal for initially she was not altogether obliging—modesty bid her pull the counterpane across her bosom and up to her chin. But he was mindful of her misgivings and encouraged her with gentle insistence, beguiling her from beneath her cover whilst whispering words of adulation—words which encouraged her to believe herself to be nothing less than his heart's perfection. So often had he gazed upon her and extolled every inch of her form, her inhibitions had ceased to trouble her. Indeed, it was remarkable what abandon a woman could indulge when convinced of her own desirability.

Perhaps her husband understood that (it would be her guess that he did). What she did know was that when the candle was returned to its stand, pleasures of remarkable passion ensued—and hers very nearly eclipsed his. In due time, she was not merely the recipient, but a collaborator. When he drew himself to her, both were in such a state of quivering desire that she wrapped her limbs about him with a ferocity that matched his own. Their initial heat would find an urgent rhythm—purposeful and fierce. It was such sweet delirium that it was difficult to want to surrender to release.

The scent of his manliness—the sensation of him within her—was enrapturing. But for her, the apex of it was not her own ultimate pleasure. Rather, it was the Elysian moment of his. To feel the rush of his seed as it washed through was her ultimate bliss.

Contemplating their mingled effluences bid her fan flutter even more briskly, but only for a brief time. For her thoughts soon quit those past raptures and returned to her present apprehension. At times her innate mettle suppressed such dread as absurd. But then she would catch sight of herself in one of the many mirrors that she seemed unable to avoid, and be reminded of the one that lay beneath their bed. The very mirror that they had once employed for their own titillation had never been removed. It occurred to her that an amatory device such as that might not ever again be a temptation—her figure's alteration had been far too severe.

If she could only escape to take to the outdoors, she was certain the air and a brisk walk would lift her spirits—but she had not the opportunity or, truth be told, the strength. Her only comfort was knowing that this was her second pregnancy. Her body had weathered a stillbirth and Darcy had certainly not turned away from her then. Still, a double gestation was twice the ruin. That long-past ordeal was horrific to endure, but her figure had not noticeably suffered. At the time, she had thought it cruel to have absolutely no visible reminder that she had even carried a baby save for its tiny grave. Hence, she could not entirely despise swollen breasts and sagging belly when gifted with two such adorable reparations.

She remained conflicted as time allowed the gradual return to fitness of her insides but not the same kindness to her figure. Indeed, the belief that she might never regain any part of physical allure began to prick her pride. She felt ungainly and unattractive. Under such circumstances, most ladies would have diverted attention from an uninviting form through the adornment of lovely gowns. Alas, that avenue was lost to her. There were but two gowns with buttoned bodices in which she could squeeze her swollen bosom and still-shrinking belly—regrettably, both of them unflattering in cut. One was quite a pretty shade of lemon, the other forget-me-not blue, but mourning a father's death demanded that they both be dyed black.

Her night costumes fared no better. Both the size and employment of her bosom did not allow her to fit into her most fetching silk night-dresses. Hence, she was compelled to wear placket-fronted, muslin gowns. Jane had offered to send for the seamstress, but Elizabeth threw a shawl about her shoulders and refused. With more conviction than she felt, she told Jane that she would not remain in her present state long enough to merit new frocks. Her heart, however, told her that if she had new gowns fashioned to fit her newly bloated figure, it was a capitulation to the possibility she might not regain her old one. Had she not suffered enough humiliation, her husband made his displeasure abundantly clear in that for the first time in her recollection he intimated that her wardrobe was deficient, by echoing Jane's suggestion for new gowns. Undoubtedly she had reacted with excessive indignation at his possibly well-meaning interference. She did not truly take offence, she simply was unhappy to have tangible indication of his notice of her physical deficiencies.

Hence, she stole longing looks in her husband's direction, but loathed what visage he might observe in return. She pined not only for his touch, but yearned to stroke his manhood to arousal as well. (The single instance of intimacy had betided with such dispatch that they both had reached fulfilment before a caress was enjoyed.) Such ambitions were thwarted, however, by her own uncharacteristic reserve. Had the accusation of reticence been put to her, she would have categorically denied it. For her husband's virile figure inhabited all her dreams and most of her thoughts. She recalled the pleasures of marital rites past with imprudent constancy for a wife who meant not to engage in them. Indeed, so libidinously was she inclined, Lizzy could not sit two minutes in one place without leaping up on some pretext or another—not realising what a state she was in even when the insides of her knees began to ache from pressing them together.

The belief she once held that having enjoyed relations once, further pleasures would be anticipated, did not come to pass. But she was far too tenacious and had far too much to lose not to ponder every possibility. There was but one ultimate goal—she wanted to make love to her husband and have his in return. Her secondary concern was to keep the extent of her figure's ravagement unexposed.

If there was nothing she had learnt during marriage to a husband like Darcy, it was that there was more than one way to skin a cat. She knew that it was quite conceivable to have amorous connexion *and* hide her figure. The more she thought of the notion, the more sensible it became. The possibilities were endless—be it in the dark, lifting her skirts in the parlour, or standing on her head.

But of course, to exact any of these measures, she would have to have some part of cooperation from her partner. Regrettably, he remained present enough so as not to incite reproof, but entirely aloof.

The longer this deadlock persisted, the more earnestly she considered employing that blessed headstand.

Denial and Dedication

In the county of Derbyshire, the fortunes of several townships rose and fell with those of its largest land-owner. Hence, the tidings that were learnt to have occurred within the walls of Pemberley (or at least upon the road thereto) piqued furious interest not just in those who resided within its dominion. Not surprisingly, when it came to pass that an heir to Pemberley finally (if somewhat tardily in the opinion of some) was produced, it was heralded not just throughout the surrounding countryside, but parts beyond. Indubitably, however, the keenest interest was held by those whose very livelihood was contingent upon those of the Pemberley estate.

Owing to the very length of the wait, the all and sundry within this fraternity were delighted to the brink of giddiness to have their anticipation rewarded by not one child, but twins. (By virtue that the first of the two born to Mr. Darcy was the all-important son, everyone had found pleasure in near-equal measure for the happy surprise of the new young master's sister.) Therefore, it was of no particular astonishment that the celebration rejoicing this double blessing all but eclipsed that which was held to honour Mr. Darcy's wedding. To denote a milestone of such import, a repast of some extravagance had been furnished through the villages gratis by the Darcys. As the repast was complemented with an abundance of ale, there was no prompting needed for more than a few glasses to be raised to the health of the newest Darcys. So many glasses were indeed lifted that the health of those children was all but a foregone conclusion.

No one, however, felt more happiness upon their behalf than those in the Darcys' immediate employ.

Pemberley was an estate of illustrious repute. The previous Mr. Darcy was known to be a man of kindly intent and impeccable principles. Although young Mr. Darcy's aspect was a bit forbidding, he governed with the same firm but fair hand as had his father. An occasional tongue did pule that the son had not the amiability of the father, but that was the foulest complaint heard thereabouts. When the present Mr. Darcy married, his taciturnity was offset by the new mistress's easy manner. So unaffected were her ways, she seldom affronted anyone (save, it was said, Mr. Darcy's implacable aunt). Indeed, Mrs. Darcy's temperament redressed any deficiency of agreeability upon her husband's behalf. Despite Mr. Darcy's dour reputation, they were known to be very happily settled.

More telling of their true nature than what country gossips prattled was that those retainers nearest to the Darcys were their most loyal defenders. The couple inspired a fond admiration in their personal servants—a highly uncommon sentiment for one who carries a chamber pot. But this partiality held true to all who were in their service. Therefore, when the Darcys' marriage was at last blessed with children, joviality and elation competed for expression not only from housekeeper and steward, but from scullery maids to stable hands.

Chief amongst those well-wishers was Mrs. Darcy's lady-maid, Hannah Moorhouse.

She was not the most senior servant at Pemberley—that distinction was held by the housekeeper. In her few short years with Mrs. Darcy, Hannah was certain that no one surpassed her in devotion. Her office of lady-maid was held with the utmost diligence and utter dedication. Moreover, she had further distinction—although she was far too modest to remind other maids of the fact. She, Hannah Moorhouse, had been the only member of the Pemberley staff chosen by Mrs. Darcy herself. Still kept safely hidden amongst her personal effects was the sheet of vellum affixed with the Darcy seal that had summoned her to come for that initial interview. It was folded thrice and secured at the bottom of the bijouterie that Mrs. Darcy had given her the first Christmas after her employment. Had there been any question before, that beautiful gift secured the maid's undying esteem for her mistress. It was a regard that had only strengthened over time—seasons of joy and seasons filled with heartbreak. Had her lady not been so admirable, Hannah was of a sort who would still have been dedicated to do her bidding. She just would not have done so with such a full heart.

Hannah was prouder of nothing more than how closely she guarded Mrs. Darcy's privacy. Other maids could find no greater diversion than to titter amongst themselves whilst betraying their mistresses' confidences. There were certainly confidences enough for a lady-maid to betray. For she was privy to her lady's most intimate concerns, be it in what bed she slept or what she did or did not wear whilst there (with whom she slept was never a question). Hannah's office was simplified by her mistress's singular love-life, but what occasioned within the confines of her marriage would have been fodder enough to suit any busy-body. As an unmarried woman, Hannah was not so unschooled as to be unaware of the passionate nature of the Darcys' conjugal bed—or anywhere else they happened to engage in conjugal rites (and those places were legion).

It was Hannah who stood at her lady's door when Mr. Darcy made unexpected visits to her dressing-room. It was Hannah who saw to it that their soiled linens were not fodder for gossip. She knew almost before Mrs. Darcy when she might be with child and despaired with her when the monthly evidence arrived announcing that she was not. Hannah fancied she knew Mrs. Darcy well-nigh as well as Mr. Darcy did. Perhaps she did not love Mrs. Darcy as deeply as did he, but she cared for her just as truly. She did not suppose that Mrs. Darcy bestowed affection in the same fashion for her—that was not fitting. She was, after all, merely a maid. But she was certain that her lady harboured fondness for her. That was in Mrs. Darcy's nature. And as was in Hannah's nature, that small fondness was all she required.

Being Mrs. Darcy's lady-maid, Hannah's situation was unabashedly exalted so far as servants went, yet it was not without its tribulations. As tribulations went, however, they were very easily withstood. The merit of being in the household of so illustrious a family and personal maid to so fine a lady as Mrs. Darcy far outweighed the occasional trepidation she encountered when thrown into the company of maids of other genteel ladies. Mrs. Darcy had been so kind and unpretentious with her, Hannah had been quite unprepared to suffer the airs, not only of the high-toned lady-folk who sometimes came to call (women not fit to wipe Mrs. Darcy's shoes), but their hand-servants as well. Invariably, the worst offenders were those who claimed to be French—of course not all of them were truly members of that self-satisfied race. But as it was the height of fashion to have a French lady-maid, the back corridors of some of the grandest estates in England were thick with serving-wenches affecting some truly atrocious French accents.

It was a pleasure she was loath to admit, but Hannah did delight in seeing the alteration upon the countenances of those prissy maids from the time they laid eyes upon her broad, country face and simple manners and when they determined that she was lady-maid to *the* Mrs. Darcy. Sometimes it was all she could do not to laugh. Hence, what was once a trial now could be seen as a huge amusement. In that Mrs. Darcy was at last a mother and Mr. Darcy was by her side, all bothers were put to rest.

At least all bothers of any importance.

There were two other matters that worried her once her heart was spared the all-consuming apprehension for her mistress. Both involved persons of the opposite gender—one disturbance came about because of his being a man and the other despite it.

It was not truly a romantic entanglement. As a lady's maid, it was not in her province either to marry or to entertain the notion of a lover. Yet she had harboured tender feelings toward Mr. Darcy's man-servant for some time. Not initially—it was an attraction that had taken hold of her over several years. It was an altogether odd business for her to be attracted to such a man as Harold Goodwin. For although he was not physically repellent, neither was he particularly well-favoured by nature. His manners, however, were superb and his hair-tonic smelt like lavender—she could hardly be in his company without her heart skipping a beat. Moreover, the only thing that rivalled his devotion to his own toilette was his devotion to Mr. Darcy and Mr. Darcy's privacy.

Robust Hannah and the bird-breasted Goodwin would have made an unlikely pair with Goodwin's mincing walk and Hannah's earthy ways and cheerful demeanour. That incongruity might have occurred to Hannah as well had she allowed herself to think of them as a couple. But she had not. For it was understood that even if she was willing to leave Mrs. Darcy's service, a gentleman's gentleman could never marry. Both could not lose their positions. In some houses even a hint of romance between servants was reason to be let go. Hannah wanted to believe that Mrs. Darcy would not be so unyielding, but it seemed unlikely that several hundred years of custom might be rent on her account. Hannah was far too happy in her situation to risk losing it over what was only a distant possibility.

And a "distant possibility" was most probably an overstatement. For Goodwin had not given her any indication that he returned her esteem. In fact, his behaviour toward her was that of compleat indifference—at least when he was not carping over some offence against propriety that he perceived she had committed. It had always been a bone of contention between the two—Goodwin's family had been in service of the Darcys for generations and he considered Hannah an upstart. Despite that, Hannah knew they were quite of the same mind. Both served the Darcys second only to God. It was most likely the prominence of loyalty in his character that Hannah found most endearing—that and his seeming dismissal of her. (Although it was a truism that few things piqued womanly interest in a man with greater regularity than inaccessibility, Hannah was not worldly enough to have learnt it.) Harold Goodwin most certainly was not in want of inaccessibility. Her unrequited yearning was quite all Hannah desired from Goodwin. He had been the perfect gentleman in his aloofness. The single occasion on which she had dared breach his reserve, she had been rebuffed. It had been upon the occasion of Mrs. Darcy's stillbirth. He had stood upon the landing, clearly as wretched as was she. She had looked to him for sympathy, but he had turned away. She ran instead into the arms of old Mrs. Reynolds and never erred in that fashion again.

Nor did she once betray him to anyone when she learnt that he had repeatedly engaged in an unpardonable offence against his position.

There were others on the staff who would have delighted in disclosing his crime to his employer. But his employer had been abroad. That Mr. Darcy was abroad in peril without his loyal man-servant to aid him was why that selfsame man-servant committed the transgression in the first place. Goodwin hid it well, but it had not escaped Hannah's notice. Mr. Darcy's dressing-room and Mrs. Darcy's dressing-room were only steps apart. The paths of their respective servants crossed any number of times a day—even in Mr. Darcy's absence. When Mr. Darcy took his leave to the Continent, all notice was given to Mrs. Darcy's distress. Goodwin kept busy but his doings were all but ignored—his chief office was that of keeping himself out of Mrs. Darcy's eye. He knew instinctively that for her to see him would only remind her that her husband was in the very bosom of danger and quite alone.

Because Mrs. Darcy kept closely to her room during that time, Hannah was often at her leisure to see the surreptitious activity that Goodwin had undertaken. Hannah saw the flask that Goodwin thought was well-hidden beneath his waistcoat. Had he not been quite so thin or quite so meticulous with his person, a bulge of that size might have been overlooked. Because Hannah's gaze often caressed Goodwin's figure when he passed her, she had noticed that discrepancy in his form first. It was only later that she happened to uncover what it was. She had seen the object before. It was a handsome silver flask that had once belonged to Mr. Darcy's father. It was not an item that Mr. Darcy found useful, but Goodwin polished it with no less regularity than if he had. It did not occur to Hannah that Goodwin had done anything other than borrow it. She knew, however, a less forgiving eye might think it looked uncommonly like theft.

Hannah was uncertain just what liquid the flask contained—gin was her best guess. Regardless of its specificity, she knew the signs, for her father had been fond of the drink. Goodwin was quite adept at keeping his imbibing unnoticed. She rarely saw the flask come to his lips. Even less frequently did she see him tottering unsteadily down the hall. Everyone in the household was so out of sorts what with Miss Georgiana's disappearance, Col. Fitzwilliam's regiment in battle, Mr. Darcy scouring the battle-ravaged countryside in pursuit of his sister, and Mrs. Darcy, after all this time, finally with child, it was of no great surprise that the stalwart Harold Goodwin's need for liquid fortification went largely undiscovered.

When Lady Catherine de Bourgh came to Pemberley prophesying that Mr. Darcy would not survive his trip across the waters, Goodwin and Hannah shamelessly eavesdropped. Hannah had expressed her outrage by slinging silent curses behind that lady's back. Goodwin, however, guzzled the entire contents of a brandy decanter, thereby missing the exhilarating spectacle of Mrs. Darcy's having threatened her ladyship with gunfire.

Thereafter, a drunken stupor was all that stood between him and unfettered terror—first for Mr. Darcy and next for Mrs. Darcy and her unborn child when she accompanied her father's corpse to Hertfordshire for burial. People were falling dead right and left, he knew not which way to turn—hence, first he tippled then he swilled. It had been Hannah who saw to it that he was put to bed, a kindness he was in no condition to recall.

"It is all too much to bear," he whimpered.

"Shush. All will be well," she intoned—not compleatly certain of that herself, but had it been her place, those were the words of comfort she would have offered to Mrs. Darcy.

When Mr. Darcy did return upon the very heels of his wife's successful confinement, Hannah was so elated that she did not initially take notice that Goodwin stood upon the periphery of activity. In his extended arms was a silver tray bearing a dusting brush with a clean linen cloth draped over one forearm. He was pale and a little wobbly, but he was absolutely sober. The flask was returned to the drawer from which it had been taken. After his return, Mr. Darcy appeared, for all the world, to be compleatly unsuspecting that his own jeopardy had provoked poor Goodwin's falling afoul of the bottle.

But until then and within a fortnight, save for the newborns, one would have thought nothing extraordinary had befallen the denizens of Pemberley. Soon, Goodwin had reclaimed himself sufficiently to begin to cavil over her every step. Rather than being annoyed, she rejoiced. That was proof positive that their lives had regained a sense of normalcy. Moreover, once the blessed event became evident, the disagreeable country gossip that had abounded was effectively squelched.

It had been long in coming. The foundations of country life—church, tavern, and mansion house (up to and including, regrettably, a number of rooms in Pemberley House itself)—had been abuzz for months with talk both high and low of what had and would come to pass within the walls of Pemberley. Hannah was not so far removed from her roots not to have learnt of the gossip. But the bewildering range of case and canard that had been bandied about was astonishing even to her tolerant disposition. People gossiped—Hannah knew that was the way of the world. But some of what she had heard was outright calumny and to her, lies were lies. Knowing that prattle was ignited by ignorance and fuelled by fear did not make it any less objectionable. She could be a timid soul, but when her beloved mistress was slandered, she did not hesitate to defend her. Trouble was that most talk occurred behind her back and she had little opportunity to confront and thereby put an end to any particular rumour.

The single most troubling aspect of such low talk was that it would have troubled the Darcys had they been aware of it. Hannah fervently hoped that it remained unexposed to them.

Forthwith of Mr. Darcy's return and Mrs. Darcy's lying-in, the grumbling and sniggering citizens were finally and irrevocably hushed. The injurious accusation, which had been growing disturbingly urgent amongst its tenants and trades-people suggesting that the House of Pemberley had fallen fallow, was finally put to rest. The little matter of primogeniture was at last settled. With the simple act of giving birth to a male child, Mrs. Darcy terminated the winds which had shaken the georgic grapevine into a malicious frenzy. To one and all, mistress and maid, it was a time of contentment. All was as it should be. And because it was as it should be, that it was a long time in coming was hardly mentioned.

Still, there wasn't a rich man, poor man, beggar man, or thief in Derbyshire County who didn't know the particulars.

9

Mr. Darcy Loves Miss Bennet

As were many of the largest estates at the time, Pemberley was entailed to the male line. Therefore, the burden of producing an heir did not encumber the willowy figure of Georgiana Darcy—it fell squarely onto the exceedingly broad shoulders of older brother and only sibling, Fitzwilliam Darcy. (To those whose leanings embraced the tenets of good breeding, Mr. Darcy's exceedingly virile figure was seen as a great advantage.) Indeed, as Miss Darcy was, for all intents and purposes, exempt, successionally speaking, her single duty was to marry well. Her brother alone bore the responsibility of begetting an heir apparent. Of course, to do this properly, his foremost objective would have been to obtain a suitable wife. Providentially, the amplitude of Mr. Darcy's fortune was exceeded only by the liberality with which nature had blessed his propagational apparatus (a condition the unforgiving explicitness of masculine attire of the day displayed to great advantage). Whatever capital happened to incite their interest most keenly—that in his breeches or that with his banker—it was of no great astonishment that there had been no dearth of applicants for the office of Mr. Darcy's wife. Of the allurement of his wealth and position, he was well-aware. Just how cognizant he was of that of a more prurient nature must remain undiscovered.

In spite of the spate of ladies throwing themselves in his path, finding a potential wife who was not only of similar station, but met all the others of Mr. Darcy's notoriously stringent standards, was no easy quest. By the time he had reached the age of eight and twenty, no suitable prospect had excited his esteem. Accustomed as Darcy was to success in all quarters of his existence, it was with no small perturbation that he had come to understand that what reason demanded his matrimonial ideal to be was quite out of harmony with that of his heart.

When he first beheld Elizabeth Bennet, he thought her quite pretty but refused to risk further sentiment beyond that initial admiration. It took very little time before he determined that his well-guarded heart was in grave danger of being compleatly usurped. Indeed, with ferocity quite beyond his control, he found himself falling helplessly in love with a categorically unacceptable young lady. His struggle was substantial. For her countenance may have been lovely, but her less than illustrious connexions were not easily dismissed by a man whose filial pride, it could be said, was felt a little too keenly.

When at last he admitted to himself that Elizabeth Bennet, daughter of a simple country gentleman, was the only woman who could possibly make him happy, his arrogant presumption of her returning his esteem (or at very least holding exalted admiration for the estate that came with it) and the sheer impertinence with which he extended his hand very nearly derailed the entire engagement. In good time, they both overcame their battling prejudices and when he resubmitted his proposal, she happily accepted. However, the road whereupon happy wedlock travelled had not been without its occasional rut.

The first of these impediments was encountered before the engagement was in place.

Although Elizabeth Bennet was a gentleman's daughter, her mother's less than illustrious relations lent the Bennet family's circumstances little distinction. One uncle lived by trade and the other was a country attorney. Yet as undistinguished as these men were, it was Mr. Bennet's relation who ultimately endangered the family more directly—for his small estate was entailed to a nephew in consequence of Mr. Bennet's lack of a son to inherit. With no more than fifty pounds a year each to recommend themselves, it was imperative that his daughters be married—and if at all possible, married well. Mr. Bennet was a kind man, but as a father he could be accused of reserve. Hence, with five daughters in want of husbands, the duty of securing each a match fell to the conniving wiles of his wife. It was well-evident that Mrs. Bennet did not see gentlemen as possible suitors for her daughters, but rather as quarry carrying sacks of guineas on their backs. The size of the quarry mattered little, but the bigger the sack, the greater her esteem. Moreover, Mrs. Bennet gave not a fig for how these quarries were bagged.

Disreputably, the first to marry was not the oldest Miss Bennet, Jane, but the youngest, Lydia. She was barely sixteen when she ran off with that bounder Wickham, a major in the militia, but too smooth by half. Wickham hornswoggled more than a few creditors, hence it should have been of no surprise that the fatuous Lydia was duped by the artful swagger of a man in regimentals. Her chosen partner and the manner in which the marriage came about did not do her family credit. More than one opinion placed the blame for her wild actions upon her mother's over-indulgence rather than her father's indifference. The only good that came out of the entire debacle was Elizabeth's discovery that it had been through Darcy's auspices that Wickham went through with the wedding. (Only Lydia saw the devious Wickham as a good catch, for he lent no distinction to the family name.)

It soon came about that, also due to Darcy's influence, Jane Bennet became engaged to her beloved, Charles Bingley. Although Mrs. Bennet was much taken with Major Wickham's charms, she was pleased beyond words (this, merely a figure of speech) that Mr. Bingley's wealth reassured her that her last days would not be spent gumming mouldy bread in a poor-house. As if two daughters married was not bliss enough, simultaneous to that courtship was another conducted far more circuitously. When

Lizzy announced her engagement to ten-thousand a year, er, to Mr. Darcy, her mother's throes of passion were so rhapsodical, they were very nearly lethal.

All was not particularly well on the other side of the aristocratic fence in regard to this last engagement formed. For a man of Darcy's standing to disregard the inferiority of Miss Bennet's station and marry her for love and love alone not only flaunted convention, it very nearly kicked it in the knee. Mr. Darcy, however, answered to no one and the happiness of his alliance with Elizabeth was so absolute, he never once was plagued by regret. Indeed, Mr. Darcy, The Aristocrat, surrendered to the passion of Mr. Darcy, The Man, with all due haste. Although Elizabeth's virtue was pristine, this alteration in his demeanour (however gravely he endeavoured to conceal it) did not go entirely unnoticed. Indeed, upon this revelation (uncovered through a seriously compromising impetuosity at Netherfield), not only was she unruffled, she was unconditionally delighted. When at last their marriage bed was initiated, it was with equal parts tender desire and unrestrained lust. Thus, it was proven unequivocally that Mr. and Mrs. Darcy's union would be one of passionate heat, not cold indifference. And as befitting such a pair so well-matched in ardour but at odds in disposition and temperament, once the marriage was in place, Elizabeth and Darcy set about fulfilling their connubial obligations with considerable zeal.

Their dedication to begetting certainly could not be faulted, indeed, it was extraordinarily thorough. Yea, no couple could have executed their duty with greater frequency or more passion. Their happy existence, however, was trespassed twice by procreative failures—once through a miscarriage and once by a devastating stillbirth. Eventually, what should have been a pleasant and, insofar as this particular couple was concerned, an altogether delectable undertaking eventually assumed an unwelcome overtone. For these tragedies were followed thereafter, despite a renewal of the aforementioned dedication, by month after month of disappointment. Not only was it their plight to battle nature's impetuosity, but they were confronted with a more pitiless evil as well—their own singular torment for bringing to naught the Darcy ancestral duty. Although neither spoke a word of their own disquiet, guilt festered within the breast of each unreasonably.

Because she had been impregnated but unable to successfully deliver a baby, Elizabeth considered herself the culpable party. That his own virility was proven was of no particular comfort to Darcy, for he weathered guilt in equal measure. The child they lost was a hefty baby boy—and breech. Elizabeth's slight frame could not govern both trials. Darcy was quite tall, his frame not inconsiderable—it was not his most pronounced conceit, but he had always been well aware of his own impressive bearing. (Had he, by chance, been unaware of it, Elizabeth reminded him every time she stood upon her tiptoes to kiss his cheek.) Yet the very prominence of his own frame imbedded within him the fear that his attributes alone were accountable for the suffering she endured. That fear weighed so heavily on his heart, endowing Elizabeth with such a weighty encumbrance as the Darcy family legacy became the lesser evil. Yet, it was still a significant evil.

Understandably, it was with a joy bordering on the rapturous that upon his return from abroad Darcy was met with the happy news that he had finally (if unknowingly) saved the family name from oblivion. Granted, although it had been somewhat confounding for him not to be privy to this extreme turn of events prior to the newborn infants being thrust before him, it was quite agreeable in all other regards. Elizabeth had not disclosed to him she was with child before he left for the Continent because she did not want to further burden him, conflicted as she knew he already was over departing from his wife to pursue his errant sister.

He had only learnt of her condition upon his ship's docking in London. The trip from the Continent had been arduous, but he took little more time than to see that Fitzwilliam and Georgiana were situated before he made fast for Pemberley.

His horse was lathered to the point of exhaustion when he had finally arrived at the doors of his home. Although every fibre of his being told him he should be spent as well, he took the stair steps two at a time in order to make his way to Elizabeth's side with all due haste. He sprinted down the corridor and only stopt when he reached her bedside. When she grasped his hand and spoke his name, he at last allowed himself some relief. He had only been coaxed from her side by the opportunity to look upon his newborns. At the end of the bed stood Elizabeth's sister Jane Bingley and faithful Hannah, each holding a baby. Jane was so often with child that Darcy made the colossal error of supposing that one must be hers—a laugh that was to be enjoyed upon numerous retellings.

When he was at last convinced that, indeed, the two infants were both birthed by his wife, their swaddlings were turned back for him to take a peek. He then gazed upon his first-born son and second-born daughter with unadulterated admiration and no small astonishment. As one began to wail rousing the other to compete, he managed to marvel at the strength of their wails as well. But he had little to say beyond that. His relief had been so sweeping and profound for the health and well-being of all concerned that he had not even thought to inquire of their gender. It was not until someone offered up the small detail that one was a son, did the realisation descend upon him that he had, at long last, paid his patriarchal dues in full. (Indeed, as he looked down from one babe to the other, he thought from those dues, he may well have been owed some change.)

He was truly grateful that he had finally made his contribution to further generations carrying the Darcy name—but of far greater importance was that his beloved Elizabeth no longer bore that burden with him. Indeed, the gods were appeased, the populace elated, and Elizabeth excused from further service to that onus to which she had obligated herself.

When later he brought to mind all that had come to pass that day, he was overcome with a multitude of emotions. He recalled but vaguely how he had stood mid-most of the familiar carpet that covered the floor of their bed-chamber, yet he was keenly aware that his riding boots still bore a hundred miles' coating of dust. When the babies were quieted at last, he insisted that they be tucked into the crook of each of his arms. He wanted to gaze upon them together and appreciate their weight, be sensible of their immotility…kiss their foreheads. He was insensible of how malapropos such an inclination was from so new a father. Jane's alarm, however, reminded him of just how unpractised he was, for she held her arms extended, clearly in all readiness to catch whichever child he dropped first.

"Pray, should we not…can you not observe them better in another's arms?" she said.

It was not in his nature to do another's bidding, but as the babies began to simultaneously squirm and mewl, even he recognised the warning of another round of bawling. With all the same tenderness that he had taken them into his arms, he returned them to Jane's well-practiced ones. Jane quite adeptly handed them off to Hannah and they busied themselves with those matters mundane to infant care on the opposite side of the bed where Elizabeth still lay. Although his arms were empty then and hanging by his sides, he imagined he still felt their warm, writhing little bodies. It had seemed as if he had held them for a lifetime rather than for merely minutes—time had been temporarily suspended for him. Indeed, he could not draw his eyes away from the infants' tiny faces. It had been an immense struggle for his mind to absorb the vision his eyes insisted could not be denied.

There was then a specific moment that then and forever would be etched in his recollections. The babies' stirrings in his arms provoked an emotion in him that was only ignited when they were taken from him. It was only then that the realisation descended upon him that the red-faced, button-nosed bundles were the fruit of his love for Elizabeth. And it did so with the all the weight of a smithy's hammer. He recalled that sensation most particularly because upon the heels of that revelation, he had harboured the terrifying fear that he just might weep. He blinked his eyes madly and even bit the inside of his lip in defence of such a loss of composure. That he was successful in circumventing a loss of countenance, he could only attribute to a lifetime of practice. Had it been only Elizabeth there, losing himself so utterly might not have been admirable, but it would not be a compleat humiliation. Such an untoward display would have been insupportable with others looking on. His total reclamation of his emotions had come by looking down at his first-born son as he began to suck upon his tiny, pink fist with strikingly familiar single-mindedness.

Hence, rather than weep, he had laughed—which was nearly as unexpected from Mr. Darcy as tears.

Indeed, so startling was it, Jane turned to him and very nearly gaped. Hence, she did not observe her sister's countenance at that moment. But Darcy did—and the glow that then emanated from Elizabeth's eyes was not the same one of relief that had overspread her face when first she saw him (owing to the miraculously impeccable timing of his return). Her expression exuded pride, but to it was added more. It was a gaze they had not often shared before—one of absolute contentment.

It was only when he looked upon her then that he truly observed her. The trial she had endured was etched upon her through a complexion as pallid as death and the plum-coloured half-moons that lay imbedded beneath her eyes. Indeed, those dark circles looked to have been there for some time. But her eyes glistened and new to her aspect were two bright dots of red in the apples of her cheeks.

They were in company, still he said with uncommon resolve, "Never have my eyes beheld a sight quite so lovely."

Ironically, all who heard, except Elizabeth, thought he was speaking of his children. Without further comment he had then laid across the bed fully clothed and fallen fast asleep. Elizabeth had shooed all from the room to allow them to share the first peace either had had in months.

In the days and weeks that followed, Darcy allowed himself to imagine what their union might have eventually become had not the joyful event come about. He held no small fear that, in time, Elizabeth might have taken umbrage at being plagued by a debt not of her own making. If, indeed, she had been thusly disposed, there was little likelihood he could have faulted her for such a leaning—he was not so certain he would have behaved with such charity had their positions been reversed. He thought he would not like to have had the albatross of a family dynasty hanging solely up on the fruitfulness of his internal organs. Hence, beyond the boundless love and undying devotion he felt for her, he was exceedingly grateful that she bore him no lingering ill will.

Nonetheless, finding himself suddenly a father to not one, but two children was only the first of many stupefactions with which he had to contend upon his return. As was his nature, he confronted each odd twist life had presented him in his usual exacting fashion, one by one, as they arose.

And arise they did, certain as the sun.

Lady Catherine's Story

Descended from the same noble lineage as her nephew, Lady Catherine de Bourgh was also a woman of great fortune. She was sister to Darcy's mother and had made a very advantageous match in Sir Lewis de Bourgh. That union was not without its grief, but because the single occasion upon which that gentleman exhibited unerring good sense was to, quite expeditiously, drop dead, it was ultimately one of great success. Marrying, bearing a single offspring, and ridding oneself of the encumbrance of a husband all within one and ten years had been a comfort indeed for a woman such as Lady Catherine who prided herself upon efficiency in all matters. Therefore, Christian charity compels one to assume that it was this aspect of her nature, not a lack of affection for her husband, which directed her to oversee the digging of his grave and the setting of his stone whilst his deathbed vigil was still in progress.

'Tis always sadness for a soul to be wrested from the breast of his family and taken in wing'd flight. This was particularly true of Sir Lewis, who was still in the robustness of manhood (figuratively, for, in truth, only his pigment suggested him robust, and no one accused him of actual manliness) as he was but two and forty. One must concede, however, that owing to Sir Lewis's impressively…adipose neck, the suddenness of this tragedy was mitigated ever so slightly. So corpulent was his neck from the dutiful enjoyment of the feasts of life that it and several chins billowed over and about all sides of his neckcloth no matter how carefully it was arranged. Ergo, even the most optimistic of observers had to admit to no astonishment when he was struck by an inevitable attack of apoplexy.

Lady Catherine, good wife, never tired of telling each guest (both individually and in groups, so as not to miss an ear) who attended her in subsequent years that she saw the event coming and had counselled him most vehemently: Eat low on the hog and spare not the beans. (Those more speculative in nature whispered behind the backs of their hands that it was the gas, not the fit, that did Sir Lewis in.) Whether seized by wind or stroke was unimportant. Dead *was* dead. For regardless of the manner of his departure, his being church triumphant left Lady Catherine a dual office. She was from that day forward not only the heir to his estate of Rosings Park, which was much-admired by all, but sole parent to their daughter, Anne, who was not.

Used to obedience, Lady Catherine brooked disappointment no better from God above than man below. Hence, she was much put out about her own daughter's lack of comeliness. As it was, Lady Catherine's own strong features had lent her some handsomeness in her youth. But those same features when exhibited in Lady Anne's narrow face had not the same success. It might have been inferred that a bit of self-recrimination for her daughter's lack of pulchritude may have fuelled Lady Catherine's vexation in this matter, but no one was actually willing to make that observation. In truth, the blame did lie squarely at her feet (or, upon Anne's face, in this particular instance). Indeed, a strong, Roman nose, exceedingly long upper lip, and almost compleat absence of a chin grieved Anne's aspect most unkindly. This equine quality of her countenance might have been overlooked had not any small excitement effloresced the nasality of her voice into an outright whinny.

If her neighbours shared Lady Catherine's disappointment in her daughter's lack of comeliness, their commiseration also remained unspoken.

Anne's lacking may have been disadvantageous, but it was not disastrous. Anne's connexions were such that a good match was inevitable. What was potentially disastrous was that Anne had inherited (if those persistent little rumours about Lady Catherine's favoured footman were dismissed) a sickly constitution from her father. Yet unlike her father, Lady Anne did not harbour a prodigious appetite and, consequently, was thin rather than slim. With no padding with which to ward off the cold, she took chill easily and was often plagued by coughs and fevers. Her indifferent health was a great worry to her mother. Lady Catherine refused to entertain the possibility of losing her daughter, not entirely out of unconditional maternal attachment. If Lady Catherine looked meanly upon disobedience, interference fared no better. Her husband's untimely death was of little inconvenience, the forward progress of her life's design was not altered. Losing the trail of issue through a lack of grandchildren, however, was another kettle of fish entirely.

Although not a particularly contemplative girl, Anne was not compleatly dull-witted. Still, she might have passed blissfully unawares of the full extent of her own lacking had not her mother dutifully pinched her pallid cheekbones so fiercely, demanding them to rouge. Hence, Lady Anne passed her days in neither a dolorous funk nor effervescent bliss. She settled into a somewhat amiable melancholy. (Whether poor constitution induced this spiritlessness, or it fell to the consistent abuse of her sensibilities by an exceedingly dictatorial mother, can be but speculated upon.) The insult of a morose disposition, uninspired mind, pale complexion, and, if one were perfectly frank, a bit of a horse-face, was a heavy burden on such thin shoulders. Yet, in her favour, one must concede that Anne suffered the slings and arrows of Mother Nature's petulance altogether complacently. Those injuries notwithstanding, enduring Lady Catherine's unsympathetic eye in and of itself might have persuaded acquaintances to pity Anne. However, they did not.

Although the poor girl only had a single virtue, it was one valued above all others. For her father's immense estate was not entailed away from the female line. Lady Anne de Bourgh was to inherit it all.

A Horse of a Different Colour

All events, calamitous and merely annoying, Darcy not only withstood with dignity but bore with no small grace. Upon one issue, he was absolutely intolerant. Indeed, he was all but immoveable in his resistance. Surprisingly, the issue that caused such agitation and distress involved not a matter of the family—at least not their human family—but of one much loved all the same.

To understand compleatly one would have to know that of the many traits upon which Mr. Darcy prided himself, one he felt with particular keenness was his judgement of horseflesh.

He was put upon a horse's back for the first time when he was but three years old. This early introduction to the saddle set precedent for all time. The sheer magnificence of the seventy-odd horses that were kept in his stables reflected the priority he saw in their care and their lineage. His interest was not, however, merely administrational. Riding was his favoured entertainment. He partook of the hunt, but only because it was expected of him. He had hunters for that purpose, but Blackjack had been his favourite mount for a decade. As a stallion, Blackjack was a high-spirited and challenging mount, not a characteristic that Mr. Darcy avoided. (He never once considered having him gelded.) Indeed, for his own horse, he did not look upon docility as a particular asset. He had bought him as a colt and schooled him personally. In the days before he and Elizabeth married, there was no diversion he enjoyed more than sitting astride that horse as he took the trails beyond the park and woodlands to the surrounding leas across his vast estate. He was quite happy to take these excursions unaccompanied. If he was to be accompanied, he favoured the companionship of his cousin and friend Colonel Fitzwilliam.

Although Darcy had always understood it was his duty to take a wife, it had never occurred to him that he would eventually want to share this solitary pleasure with her. It was not a particularly feminine pass-time. The few young ladies who rode to hunt were in the mould of dear Lady Millhouse, whose robust visage was not the same image in which he had cast his future bride. Any young woman of his acquaintance who admitted an inclination to take fresh air was not much of mind to enjoy it upon horseback, but to be pulled in a carriage. He thought no more of it. Nor did he remind himself that he had inherited his love of horses from his own mother.

Once his marriage to Elizabeth was in place, however, he had a compleat alteration of opinion. It was then his wish that his wife join him whilst he inspected every lovely vista to which a day's ride would take them. That Elizabeth rode but little was of no impediment. He taught her to ride. (This tutorial was not the most favourite of those upon which he initiated her, but was the single one that he did not eschew speaking of in company.) The only thing lacking was an animal worthy to carry Mrs. Darcy. Indeed, it would be presumed that upon such rides the wife of Mr. Darcy be would carried by no other than a horse of the highest breeding. To assure this, Mr. Darcy and Fitzwilliam embarked upon a trip of such import that it incurred the first night Mr. and Mrs. Darcy spent apart after their wedding. All of this was done so as to locate and bring this horse to present it in time for, and in honour of, Elizabeth's twenty-first birthday.

It was an exceedingly handsome and thoroughly thoughtful gift, one with which Elizabeth was excessively pleased. Darcy's selection was a fine-looking, dusky-coloured mare. The horse was marked with a star on her forehead and white stockings up to her knees. Her name had been Dulcinea, but in what could only be called a fit of whimsy, Elizabeth renamed her "Boots." At the time, it had been supposed by the gentlemen that the mare had been named for her white feet. After the Darcys engaged in an extended thank-you session that, at her particular request, required his costume to entail nothing more than his tall riding boots, he bethought the matter. Regardless whence it sprang, the horse's name remained Boots and the affection Elizabeth held for the animal increased with time.

Due to both the vastness of his stables and the particular regard he held for the lineage of his horses, Mr. Darcy always deliberated with grave intensity upon their bloodlines. He plotted mare and sire with no less diligence than Wellington had for engaging Napoleon. He had long desired and planned for his Elizabeth's mare (for reasons of propriety, he refused to call her by her sobriquet, "Boots") to be bred by his own horse, Blackjack. It would have been a melding of the finest points and characteristics of two immaculate lines.

However, upon this intention, Mr. Darcy was thwarted.

After his return, when the onslaught of precipitating events had gradually waned, it soon came to his notice that his wife's mare was with foal. Although he had not dared to take Blackjack with him across the water, he had given no such order in his absence for her mare to be bred. Indeed, he had left no orders for any breeding, whatsoever. This, as in all things equine, he trusted no one to execute without his personal direction. Yet, before him stood poor, besmirched Boots bearing the unmistakable signs that she was to foal. With this single turn of events, Mr. Darcy erupted into a display of displeasure heretofore unseen in him—if one discounts the other single instance of a loss of temper by Mr. Darcy in front of his men.

That first of several unsettling events had occasioned upon the very evening that Darcy presented Elizabeth's horse. They had been still admiring the animal when all first heard, then caught sight of one of the footmen, the ignominious Tom Reed, whipping a horse. Mr. Darcy reacted before Fitzwilliam or Elizabeth had quite ascertained what was coming to pass. He raced to the scene (the first occasion Elizabeth had seen him move so swiftly), took the whip, and then laid it across Reed's back before banishing him from his service (the first act of violence she had witnessed as well). The story did not end then and there, but so rich in the memory of all who witnessed Mr. Darcy thrash the hulking Reed, it still provoked within them a distinct disinclination ever to incur Mr. Darcy's wrath. Hence, upon this occasion whilst he ranted, as only Mr. Darcy could (with a kind of peculiarly reserved fury), any grooms and stable boys about became unusually industrious lest they draw his unhappy attention.

Darcy's man at the stables was Edward Hardin. (He had been there to witness that event some years before.) He had been in the Darcys' service in some capacity all his life. Moreover, Edward Hardin personally discharged all of Mr. Darcy's instructions pertaining to his horses. Indeed, if any problems arose within the confines of the stables, Edward Hardin answered for them. Had not Mr. Darcy by chance seen Reed first that evening, Edward Hardin would have taken after Reed himself. He may not have laid a whip across Reed, for Reed was a brutish sort having near a foot in height and several stone in weight advantage over the wiry Hardin. But Hardin would not have hesitated in having Reed run compleatly out of the county.

Edward Hardin believed he knew Mr. Darcy as well as most anyone excepting Mrs. Darcy and although he respected his master implicitly, he did not truly fear him. Yet the sheer rarity of any overt display of temper by Mr. Darcy was, like the man himself, to be respected. He knew well what Mr. Darcy's design had been for Mrs. Darcy's favourite horse. He knew he intended to have that fine-configured saddle horse, Blackjack, as sire for Boots. Therefore, his horror had grown at the exact pace as Boots's belly swelled.

As neither Mr. nor Mrs. Darcy had been to the horses of late as they were much engaged with their own new little ones, it fell to poor Edward Hardin to share this odious state of affairs to his employer. Hardin did not exactly quake at the thought, but whilst he reported it, the hands in which he wrung his hat shook just a bit. Even decrepit old Cressida cupped her tail and made for a nearby waggon under which to cower until her master's displeasure abated.

This inadvertent breeding certainly should not have been an ordeal at all, much less one so disproportionately ill-taken. For although the care Mr. Darcy took with the lineage of all the horses in his stable was of legend, in the grand scheme of things, it did not seem the greatest of evils. Mr. Darcy's travails of late certainly should have reminded him of that, but this seemingly niggling matter inexplicably vexed the man to distraction. Initially, Mr. Darcy refused out of hand to accept that Boots was truly with foal. When that became conspicuously apparent, he still denied the only reasonable possibility. For despite great deliberation and careful watch, it was unmistakeable that the mare had fallen prey to an interloper, the identity of which was impalpable to him.

"I simply will not have it!" announced Mr. Darcy.

It was a demand as unyielding as it was unreasonable. Nonetheless, at this outburst Cressida whimpered and tucked her nose even further beneath her haunch.

His pique was too strongly felt to register his dog's disconcertion. He was far too caught in the throes of information that he abhorred. For Hardin said that in all probability (only couched in this manner because Edward Hardin was convinced that the lack of an absolute would be a brief comfort) that the sire had to be Col. Fitzwilliam's handsome mount, Scimitar. Edward Hardin recalled the night and the particulars well, for it foretold momentous events. Whilst doing his level best to avoid looking directly unto his master's unhappy countenance, he related that the event undoubtedly occurred the night Col. Fitzwilliam had visited Pemberley before he left with his regiment for France. Hardin particularly recalled the colonel remarking that, because of the impending war, it was apt to be a late night. As was the colonel's habit when his visit was to be lengthy, he removed his own saddle and had Scimitar turned into a paddock to await his return in comfort. As it happened, Mrs. Darcy had taken out Boots that afternoon. The horse was behaving more unruly than usual and she was turned into an adjoining paddock to cool down. Regrettably, the horse's behaviour indicated that she was coming into season—something the boy who had seen to her had not detected.

All this was stated matter-of-factly as a man of few words as Edward Hardin might. As if anticipating Mr. Darcy's question, Hardin assured him that it was far too long past to ascertain just which groom was culpable. That was what he said. As to what he thought, that remained under his own counsel.

Thereupon to the scene came Elizabeth, who, having heard about Boots's condition and the ensuing commotion had made her way down the short path to the stables with the intention of enlisting a bit of reason with her husband. She stopped short of the conversing men, listening intently.

"He went and jumped the fence—five boards it was—who would have thought it? Our best hunters would have needed more lead to take that fence," Hardin shook his head in wonder of the feat. "The boys got 'im right out but 'twas too late of course."

Elizabeth had been standing slightly to the side during this exchange and Cressida felt reassured enough by her presence to come and lie at her feet. Elizabeth, however, reached out and pulled at Darcy's sleeve, having the good sense to ask her question out of the hearing of Hardin.

"I am certain I witnessed this event," she said in a low voice.

Cressida heaved herself back to her feet and trotted back to her sanctuary beneath the waggon.

"Did you, indeed?" Darcy replied giving his wife his full attention.

"I am happy to assure you that nothing could have possibly occurred in the nature of what you fear for Scimitar only scuffled with Boots briefly—the merest of moments. I had only feared that she might have received a nip on her shoulder, but there was nothing. All was well."

She stood back in all happiness to be able to reassure her husband that his fears were unfounded. If Boots was to foal, if it was not by Blackjack, it was by another of their own horses.

"A mere scuffle, say you?" inquired Darcy.

If she was not mistaken, she believed that inquiry to be a trifle contumelious. Hers in return encompassed as much resentment as one word could possibly convey.

"Yes."

He closed his eyes and briefly pursed his lips. He then slowly shook his head.

"Lizzy..." he began before apparently remembering himself by saying, "We shall speak of this later."

She narrowed her eyes, but realised that the entire subject of just what horse did what to another horse and how long it took to do it was not a subject that should be broached in company. Hence, glancing at Edward Hardin (who was doing his best not to hear their discourse), she acquiesced. She did not acquiesce with great generosity, but she did acquiesce—but only upon that one point.

With all due reasonableness, she offered, "Is it as abhorrent as all that? I mean to say, Scimitar is a beautiful horse—and of the same line as many of Pemberley's horses."

Poor Hardin stood in nodding agreement to the good sense of Mrs. Darcy's words. He had believed the learning that such a fine animal as Scimitar was the culprit would have appeased Mr. Darcy. For some unfathomable reason, that information only inflamed his ire. Elizabeth's interjection did nothing to soothe Darcy and he stomped about unhappily to such an extent it frightened the grooms to head for the safety of the nearest byre. His pique nearly moved Hardin to do the unthinkable of tugging upon Mr. Darcy's sleeve to bring him back to his senses—for clearly he had left them behind. Of the same mind, Elizabeth actually did so.

Quietly, she asked, "Pray, what is the matter? Certainly it cannot be this matter alone."

He did not answer her directly, continuing to put forth the inadvertent breeding by Scimitar from whence his displeasure sprang. For the first time, he called the horse by its actual name.

"Scimitar was a fine battle horse. I simply cannot bear to have Boot's lineage sullied by the inferior blood of a horse that clearly…" (here he struggled to think of some fault of that particularly handsome specimen of a horse) "…short-coupled. Yes, Scimitar was a U-necked, short-coupled nag!"

It was unthinkable. It would not do.

Elizabeth discretely took her husband's hand. It was an unusual thing for her to do when others were there to see. He took hers briefly in return—an even more remarkable act. He ran his thumb across her knuckles before placing her hand in a more sedate posture upon his forearm and allowing himself to be led up the path to return to the house. As he watched them take their leave, Edward Hardin placed his hat firmly back upon his head. He did not notice that the abuse the hat had taken revealed itself by an absurd crimp in the brim. Had he, he might have thought it fitting—his sensibilities felt a little interfered with themselves.

The Private Struggle of Mr. Darcy

Although he appeared to all the world entirely unaware of the ridiculousness of his obstinacy, Darcy *was* aware. He was aware to a vexatious degree. He should have been proud for his wife's mare to have a foal by Scimitar. Despite his disputatious remarks to the contrary, Darcy knew that he was a fine animal—well-bred and stout of heart. He knew too that Fitzwilliam would forever regret his horse's loss in battle. Perhaps he might even second-guess his decision to take such a fine horse with him to Belgium and into what was to be the gates of hell. Regardless, that was what he did and it was Scimitar, not he, who had died a noble death on the blood-drenched field near Quatre Bas. He had lamented that loss through the haze of laudanum and the clarity of wakefulness. Indeed, during bouts of delirium, Fitzwilliam cursed himself for that judgement. Even when his mind returned to reason, he could not quite make himself quit the subject. He told again and again how it was Scimitar who bore the brunt of the blast that delivered his own horrific wounds. His horse had been courageous, loyal, and true. A hero of the British Empire.

That was quite the opposite in all respects of Major George Wickham.

Yes, Wickham. For Darcy, all other botherations paled in comparison to the sordid realisation of the entirety of *that*. The very repugnance of the name Wickham, much less the heinousness of his deeds, was so abhorrent that Darcy could not bear to think of it. If there was a God, Wickham lay dead in some unmarked grave near Bruxelles. He prayed that was true. He had discreetly discharged emissaries to sort out the matter of whether or not George Wickham was indeed dead or alive, but their findings had been inconclusive. Although Wickham's name was affixed to the list of those who were lost in battle, the resting place for his corpse remained unidentified. That question lying unanswered did nothing to alleviate Darcy's general pique. It only kept it redirected.

As time went on without his wife's amorous embrace to console him (or at least relieve his agitation), Darcy's temper was so compromised that had he been of a less imperturbable spirit, he might have accused himself of despondency. But he would not. For all the vexations he faced, there was much to celebrate. He was a father, Elizabeth was well, his sister was to be married, and Elizabeth's mare was in foal. All things in his life were in order and right. He insisted that to himself repeatedly.

His life was indeed altered, but all for the better—even his love for Elizabeth.

Beyond the gift of an heir, the birth of his children had delivered unto him a renewed appreciation of the woman, his wife and now their mother. He had long thought of her as quite indomitable. Her spiritedness was what had first drawn him to her. He had prided himself upon being the husband to her that he believed she deserved. There was nothing that he would not do, no lengths to which he would not go, no place he would not travel, and no person he would allow to stand between him and her absolute happiness. He had drawn blood in her honour and would do so again in a heartbeat. Being her champion was what defined his manhood. When he learnt that he was away when she needed him most, it grieved him to his soul not to have been by her side. That she managed to weather the entirety of a pregnancy and birth with little help (save for Jane catching the infants as they were expelled) was well and good. Indeed, it was all most fortunate. In his heart, however, feelings of relief and happiness conflicted with those of niggling resentment that she had, indeed, done it all without him. Hence, her enduring such an arduous birth, in a coach lumbering at top speed on the road to Pemberley, left him feeling both aggrieved on her behalf and miffed upon his own.

These feelings lay unacknowledged, however. Such selfish sentiments were unconscionable he thought. But, because they lay nameless, when they provoked strange attitudes about matters quite intimate in nature, those lay free to grow into inclinations that were most unexpected. As time went on and Elizabeth's life revolved around their babies, he supposed that was only right. He began to look upon his wife and their children as his charges—to be guarded and nurtured. To do so effectively, one must observe objectivity at all costs.

He was prepared to overcome any alteration that parenthood wrought upon their marriage. He feared that was inevitable. Although it was not something that had been his constant study, observation had suggested to him that once a child was born to a union, however happy, it is not unusual for the nature of that marriage to alter. Passion was even thought to wane. It had always been a thoroughly abstract presumption, but it was a presumption. He had not had call to apply that presumption to his own marriage.

The time had come, however, for it to be put to a test.

His perception was that when a lover becomes a mother, even in those households where the children themselves are merely marital accoutrements, desires of the flesh may wither. It happened quite often, he had actually heard husbands grouse that their wives found doting on their children sufficient excuse to plead abstinence from marital duties. These men either sought outside company or sat in their studies and sulked. Society not only condoned that response—it was expected regardless from which party such disinterest sprang. If he had ever truly doubted this truth, the philandering of his dear friend Bingley had solidified such a notion. Other than his own devotion to Elizabeth, he could think of no one more steadfast to his wife than Bingley. Beautiful, adoring Jane, who begat four children in five years. Bingley found release outside his marriage, in spite of all the affection within. That was troubling, indeed.

Not that he would ever betray Elizabeth—he would rather submit to celibacy. Yet, neither was he inclined to sulk. In that he would never impose himself upon her, he found himself enduring a feeling heretofore unknown to him—uncertainty.

In all things marital, the Darcys' marriage ran against the grain. In a society that frowned upon marriages formed for any reason other than to unite fortunes, Mr. Darcy had married Miss Bennet for love. Unlike those loveless matches of his peers, theirs had been an extraordinarily passionate union. One would suspect that their proclivities would run contrary to the norm after the birth of their children as well. But, like his peers, Darcy was raised under certain canons dictating the reverence with which one held a mother. His mother had died in childbirth with his sister, Georgiana, when he was but ten years old. It was an impressionable time. His mother had been an ethereal figure to him in his childhood; her early death elevated her memory ever higher. The respect with which Darcy had always held his mother was seen by those close to him as endearing—a leaning to be admired. In this sentiment, as in all aspects of his deportment, Darcy was fastidious. If no one actually determined that trouble brewed because of this tendency, it could be understood. Nonetheless, like most men of his time, when his wife became the mother of his children, he knew she was not actually a Madonna, but she bore a remarkable likeness.

Had his blood not been consumed with adoration for the woman he loved, and hers for him, their story might have gone the way of countless indifferent marriages before them. As it was, it did not.

To Elizabeth's credit, Darcy's desire was not dampened, it was inflamed—extraordinarily inflamed.

Normally a man of incalculable discipline in matters both spiritual and earthly, in this delicate matter, he was lost to reason. The woman whom he had relished with an all-consuming passion was now a mother. The instant he had beheld those young ones, he had vowed that nothing unclean would touch their lives. The unmitigated lust he had for their mother must be quashed at all costs. That portion of their lives must be forever banished. The office of mother was to be revered. Respected. Upheld. He struggled with himself with the same earnestness with which he confronted all things. She was no longer his Lizzy alone, he shared her with the babies now nestled at her breasts. It was an excruciating loss, but one he knew that, as a husband and father, must be observed.

But his will would not serve his conscience.

Hence, he rationalised. He supposed that having her so near, but indisposed, was the culprit. And after long and dutiful study, he concluded that for him to be aroused to such fervour by a nursing mother exposed him as nothing but a libidinous lout. It would not do.

Mr. Darcy's Dilemma

It came to pass that soon after the master had returned, old Mrs. Reynolds was taken quite ill. Although she had been a fixture in the house for as long as Darcy could recall, she was such a sprightly, vigorous spirit, few knew that she was well into her seventh decade of life. She was a bit of a complainer of the evils of others, but never upon her own behalf. Yet it was undiscovered that hidden beneath her skirt, Mrs. Reynolds had taken to wrapping her lower legs to alleviate the symptoms of dropsy. By the end of the day, her feet and calves looked as if they belonged to another woman altogether, for she was a wiry creature and her feet swelled out of the tops her slippers liked two loaves of freshly baked bread.

The protracted expectancy and dread of that summer certainly had drained what little stamina she had. Had anyone been aware of her affliction, they would not have been taken so unaware when her heart seized. Regardless, she was felled by a pain to the chest and she was put to bed. The surgeon was called forthwith. He felt of her forehead, lifted the coverlet, observed her swollen limbs, and shook his head. Apoplexy, he announced to no one's surprise. His simple advice was to gather the family and wait for the end to come, dashing any hope for her recovery.

Darcy did not tell Elizabeth until the end neared, for he knew it would bring back memories of her father's passing. His man Goodwin was her nephew, although had one been unknowing of that fact it would have been unapparent through observation. Goodwin was told and given the duty of notifying what few relatives were still about. Darcy took it upon himself to notify her son.

Mrs. Reynolds had four husbands in the ground and only one living issue. Begotten by husband number two (her least favourite spouse), Cyril Smeads was born within the walls of Pemberley. He had risen to the office of steward in the Darcys' London town house through sheer determination and, although he was loath to admit it, a dollop of nepotism by reason of the affection Darcy's parents held for his mother.

He had begun his career in the dusting-room at Pemberley but felt constrained by his mother's critical eye. At the first opportunity, he travelled to London to work as a footboy. He progressed steadily from thence to bell-boy, to yeoman of the buttery, then on to under-butler and at long-last, butler. He did not, however, return to Pemberley, even for a visit, until he had advanced to steward of the town house. He had hoped against hope that he would be taken on at Pemberley as house steward so as to sit at the far end of the servant dinner table across from, and thus an equal to, his mother, but it was not to be. When old Mr. Wickham died, most peculiarly, he was never replaced.

When word came of his mother's dire condition, Smeads wiped a single tear from the corner of his eye and hastened to call for a carriage. Duty first, he gave a list of instructions to the butler before he took his leave. The two underlings who dared peek out the window to witness his departure could not help but take notice of the beginning of a smile twitch at the corner of his mouth as the coach leapt away. The maids each turned to the other with eyebrows raised, but they were not especially surprised. When the story was spread throughout the house, the only curiosity came from wondering which gave him the greater pleasure, riding from London to Derbyshire in the plush coach bearing the Darcy crest or the anticipation of finally obtaining his mother's position.

That was more than just a possibility. As it happened, Smeads did his job well. He was circumspect, discerning, and dutiful—at least whilst under his employer's eye. Behind the scenes he was tempestuous, egotistical, resentful, and devious. Over time, he became ever more officious. That he kept the house under his command well-ordered was the primary reason he was not dismissed. Mr. Darcy was there but little even prior to his marriage. It had been less a home than a capitulation to convention. Of late, the family seldom came to town, but as it was expected of them, they maintained the house as if they might arrive at any moment. To do otherwise would generate talk. That had been a secondary reason for not abandoning it altogether, but not one to which Smeads was privy. Nor did he know that the paramount consideration for keeping it up was for the good of the retainers—some of whom had been with the family for generations. (Darcy could not in good conscience allow them to be let go.) Provided that Smeads saw to it that he was not troubled by matters mundane to its keep, Darcy was happy to leave the house as it was. Left to one's own devices and judgement over an illustrious Mayfair address was a very advantageous assignment. If Smeads had any notions as to why the house had been all but abandoned by visits from the Darcys, he left them unexpressed to others in the house. He was quite happy to have sole dominion over his staff.

Seasons passed by without even the obligatory Easter trip to town. In the absence of regular visits and inspections by his employer to check him, Smeads had turned the grand Park Lane house into his own personal fiefdom. As with most despots, when given a free rein, tyranny ensues. The only respite those under his thumb had from his dictatorial ways were the day-long jaunts he took from time to time. A few amongst the servants made unsavoury speculations about his doings, but most were so happy to see him gone for even so small a space of time, they were of no mind to care what he was up to.

At Pemberley, crusty old Mrs. Reynolds was not necessarily beloved by those who toiled under her custody, but she was respected. Despite Smeads being of her blood, the initial dislike for him from his underlings had degenerated over the years from scorn into outright contempt. Few could have offered much defence upon his behalf, for his petulance was of legend. Moreover, with increasing brazenness he had elevated what had been merely the pinching of the bottom of the nearest maid into his own version of *droit du seigneur*. Had Mr. Darcy been aware of such debauchery, Smeads would have been tossed out on his ear had his mother been Queen Charlotte. As it happened, Mr. Darcy did not hear of it. Far too many of those offended feared for their positions. It was not uncommon for the men-folk of many houses to employ foul designs upon those in their service. Mr. Darcy, however, was particularly stringent upon this issue—if any man was found to have ill-used another, he was dismissed with malice. The reason for this aberration against his class was often attributed, by those who discussed it, to Christian principles. While the Darcys were no less pious than the average rich person, that reasoning did not quite ring true. A few long-time servants recollected some long past misconduct of that nature, but no one seemed to know the particulars. Regardless, in a house with so many servants of both genders, upon occasion acts of a sexual nature did occur—some even with consent by both parties.

When Smeads hied for Pemberley that day, the happiness his aspect betrayed was roundly trumped by the expressions of unadulterated joy that overspread the faces of those he left behind. Most held no particular ill will toward Mrs. Reynolds beyond spawning the likes of Cyril Smeads, but they were very nearly as pleased as Smeads to hear of her impending demise. Indeed, Cyril Smeads was at last of the same mind of those under his will. All hoped Mrs. Reynolds did at last go to her great reward, and prayed just as fervently as did he for his elevation to head of the staff of Pemberley.

Upon his arrival at Pemberley's gates, Cyril Smeads did have the good sense to contain his unadulterated joy over his mother's demise until she was set in the ground.

But whilst he waited for that to occasion, he set to nosing about the next addition to his curriculum vitae. He had scrutinized Pemberley with a covetous eye in the past whilst under the pretext of visiting his mother when Mr. Darcy had been so generous as to allow him to join his personal servants in the second coach when he last quit London. That had been several years past, and he was anxious to see what alterations the house had undergone. It was a magnificent estate and he was happy to know it soon would be his home as well.

London did not agree with him. There were far too many others of similar rank doing business with the various shops. In Derbyshire, his position would be singular. He would be second only to Mr. Darcy in the succession of orders. He had fretted that when Mr. Darcy married, Mrs. Darcy might intrude upon his finely perfected operation of the house, but her attention had been far too compromised by her husband for her to meddle in his business in London. With two new chicks to keep her occupied at Pemberley, he did not expect that to alter. The only possible impediment for enjoying full rein of all aspects of the Darcy household was his cousin, Harold Goodwin. No doubt, he had Mr. Darcy's ear. Smeads had come to rue every quarrel he had ever engaged in with him. Harold had a puritanical streak that rivalled that of Mr. Darcy's. Smeads feared that he was not above tattling to Mr. Darcy when the opportunity arose.

It was unlikely, but he hoped to uncover an ace in the hole of Harold's deportment—for negotiation purposes, of course.

In the last hours before his mother passed on, Mr. Darcy carried Mrs. Darcy "below stairs" to her bedside to bid her farewell. Mrs. Darcy had still been quite weak from childbirth and Smeads could not fathom why she would take such measures for a servant. And if the lady insisted upon engaging in so sentimental an exertion, one would have thought that a footman would have been called to see to her transport. Mr. Darcy was a fine figure of a man, he supposed, but it was unseemly for a gentleman to perform a duty that a servant could do quite as easily. Were footmen employed for nothing if not their size and a good leg?

At least Mr. Darcy had the good breeding not to weep when his housekeeper breathed her last, but Mrs. Darcy sniffled along with the maids. It was such a maudlin scene, he took it upon himself to place the coins upon his mother's eyes, thus shooing the grieving out of the room. Mr. Darcy spoke to him personally, bidding him consolation on his "loss." Smeads did think it was the ideal opportunity to put himself forth as his mother's replacement.

"I will be happy to stay on and continue on Mrs. Reynolds behalf," Smeads said whilst touching the back of his forefinger to the corner of his eye.

Smeads was not particularly adept at feigning sentiment, but he knew it was imperative to strike whilst sorrow was keenest. He feared that he had overplayed his hand, for Mr. Darcy's eyes, which had an unusual softness about them, suddenly narrowed. He looked to be unready to acquiesce to such a plan, but his wife then called to him and his attention was diverted. He bent and picked her up once more and betook her toward the door.

Over his shoulder, he answered absently, "Do what you must."

Quite suddenly Smeads bethought his distaste of Mr. Darcy's attentiveness to his wife. Perhaps that too could benefit his own designs. Mrs. Darcy's lengthy recuperation would give him time to firmly wedge his foot in Pemberley's door. So smooth would be the transition, there would be little reason for him to return to London. The arrangement he had for supplemental monetary reward would blossom from having the Darcys within his eye-line. He would veritably be the fox in the Pemberley henhouse.

Mrs. Darcy Is Receiving

Two coinciding events did little to improve Elizabeth's spirits. Firstly, Jane's maternal yearnings called for her to return to her own little ones. It had been her decision that her stay with Elizabeth would be without her lovable, if rowdy brood. This absenting bespoke the unassailable truth that even Jane understood just how rambunctious her children's antics could be. Elizabeth knew how very much her sister would miss her young ones and insisted they would be of no trouble, for the halls of Pemberley were vast and servants aplenty. Knowing how important it was to Elizabeth for Jane to stay, Darcy nodded in full agreement, happy to make any arrangements to see that it came to pass. But when Jane declined, he secretly gave a sigh of relief. In truth, he was unwilling for Elizabeth's recuperation and their newborns' care to be anything other than the household's singular objective.

The only occasion that would have bid Jane absent herself from her family for so lengthy a time was that her dear sister needed her. Bingley had taken his leave from Pemberley once Darcy was at home and all looked to be in order. Bingley was known as nothing if not a doting father, but Jane had sent him on his way endowed with the office of mother as well. However, he was not much practiced in making those daily decisions upon his children's care that had come so easily to Jane (who did not choose to escape those matters mundane and untidy as did many genteel mothers). Bingley knew it all fell to him and was quite resolute in his willingness, but fell a tad short in proficiency. Hence, it was not abdication from his duties that bid Jane's return. She was summoned by the sheer number of posts penned in Bingley's barely legible scrawl, each one over-flowing with reports of mishaps and inquiries of procedures. With each week the tone of these missives increased in urgency until they eventually reached the level of out-right panic. Jane knew well the limits of what chaos her husband's sensibilities could withstand. Therefore, when Elizabeth was on her feet, she took pity on him and sent word of her imminent return. Still, it was a parting fraught with doubt.

"Oh, Lizzy," she said, "I had so desired to stay longer, but Charles is quite beside himself..."

Elizabeth, who had helped to birth all but one of Jane's babies (the third coming quite unexpectedly) patted her hand and offered those words of reassurance and gratitude appropriate under the exchange of such services. It was her intent to have Jane leave with nothing but cheery messages and a promise that they would all soon come to Kirkland, but she could not. The carriage awaited and Jane had but to be handed aboard when those feelings particular to those who have shared much spilt from Elizabeth's heart. She wrapped her arms about Jane, holding her tightly.

"You are my port in a storm, dearest Jane!" she cried. "I surely would have not survived had you not been there. We—all of us—would have been lost!"

Embellishment of sentiments was not in Elizabeth's nature, nor were they inflamed by their imminent parting. Jane was too overcome with corresponding emotions to speak and held dearly to Elizabeth's neck, yielding to tears.

Darcy had profusely thanked Jane for all she had done for his family. Hence, he had come to witness her departure only to wish Jane well on her journey home. Witnessing what passed between the sisters threatened his own countenance and he cleared his throat several times before at last Jane's carriage went on its way. Although he remained outwardly stoic, when he and Elizabeth turned to re-enter the house, she still stifling tears, he placed his arm across her shoulders and briefly squeezed her arm before allowing his hand to temporarily rest, then stroke the side of her neck. She was not entirely aware of his unusual public display, for she was so thoroughly distraught over Jane's departure that she did not fully comprehend it and all that it implied.

Jane's coach had no better than cleared the lodge-gate ere meeting an even more lavish carriage approaching from the opposite direction. She recognised the livery, but it got on so fast that she had no opportunity to recognise its occupants. Still, she held little doubt just who it carried. The spattering of gravel in that coach's wake suggested a disinclination by those travellers to pause and converse. Indeed, such was their anticipation of their visit to Pemberley, so near their destination they let nothing slow their progress.

With luggage enough to inflict fear into the heart of the most stalwart hostess, Jane's sisters-in-law, Caroline Bingley and Louisa Hurst, had hied forthwith of word from Jane relating that Elizabeth was much improved. Those words were as good as a personal invitation from Pemberley and they could not contain their enthusiasm (or their curiosity) until Jane returned to Kirkland Hall. They set out immediately to see all for themselves. It was, after all, a feminine duty to sally forth unto that home boasting the newly birthed to apprise the comeliness of the baby and ascertain the degree of disintegration childbirth had wrought upon the mother's aspect and figure. Rarely was one disappointed.

When the sisters were announced, the pocket-square that Elizabeth had used to dry the tears she shed for the loss of Jane's company was still damp. The thought of their fawning countenances did not improve her spirits. In the brief time she had to prepare for their entrance, she then reminded herself of the single virtue of their visit—it would not ruin an otherwise perfectly enjoyable day. As she rose to greet them, she had little more time than to pat her hair and wrap a drooping ear-lock or two round her dampened finger. Briefly, she deliberated on which posture would service her aspect best—to draw in her mid-section or restrain her bosom. So prominent were they, attempting to do both seemed an impossibility. Hence, she abandoned the notion altogether and merely straightened her back—letting her form fall where it may.

Caroline swept into the room with Louisa Hurst fast in her wake.

"Eliza, dearest," cooed Caroline.

She made a bee-line for Elizabeth with extended arms and an expression that threatened a kiss. It was all Elizabeth could do to accept the inevitable and use greeting Louisa to wrest herself from Caroline's grasp. But, Caroline was not yet ready to release her.

She placed the back of two fingers first to Elizabeth's forehead and then to her cheek, clucking, "My poor, poor, dear Eliza."

This solicitousness was offered in a manner that was absent of both congratulations and commiseration. "What you have endured! It is no wonder you look so ill, I do hope you keep mostly to your bed." Then grasping Elizabeth by both upper arms, sought Louisa's attention. "See Louisa, it is *so* true. Childbirth steals one's bloom."

As Louisa was once a mother herself, it might have been expected that she should not particularly care for Caroline's last jibe, but she defended neither Elizabeth nor motherhood in general. As for Caroline, she was oblivious to anything but her own objective. At last Elizabeth wrenched away, but Louisa insisted upon the same affection. When they were finally satisfied to let her go, it was all Elizabeth could do not to draw the back of her hand across her cheek to erase the remnants of their spittle. She motioned them each to take a seat, and settled back in her own chair making one last attempt to resituate her fichu across the bodice of her morning dress.

As always, both ladies were dressed in the latest fashions. Well aware of the fineness of her attire, Caroline sat in her usual grand attitude, one that she had no doubt practiced to better display her ensemble. Elizabeth could not fault her taste, for the gown was an exquisite shade of poppy and, although the enormous girandoles that hung from her earlobes were a bit extravagant for an afternoon call, the coral stones set off her gown to perfection. Louisa had never quite owned Caroline's discerning style, but if her costume was not as splendid as Caroline's, it was not for the want of trying. She too was festooned with ruching, tags, and lappets, and perched upon one shoulder was a brooch featuring the plumage of some exotic species of bird. (Clearly, they were of a mind that six weeks was all the time their wardrobes could spare to mourning the passing of their sister-in-law's father.)

They continued to commiserate her state and Elizabeth made herself to reply only, "I thank you for your kindness, but as you can see, I am quite well."

"And how does Darcy enjoy his return? I understand he enjoyed Brussels and its habitués most exceedingly. I cannot believe that he will be happy once again in such simple company as we can provide here at Pemberley," Caroline said with a sly smile turning up one corner of her mouth.

"Yes."

"And poor Wickham—dead as mutton I'm told?"

Louisa gave a small, but audible intake of air at her sister's last inquiry.

"Oh dear, Elizabeth. Mr. Bennet…" Louisa corrected the priority of Caroline's inquiries. "We were deeply saddened for both you and Jane to hear of his loss."

Remembering herself, Caroline nodded emphatically, signalling at least a temporary retreat, "Sad times these."

Elizabeth could not be certain if it was her sister's nonchalance or audacity that bid Mrs. Hurst's involuntary reproof. Regardless, Louisa was thereupon elevated in

Elizabeth's estimation from the devil's sister to merely an annoying piece of work. An uneasy truce prevailed with Caroline and her sister conversing like two chirping blue tits, oblivious to Elizabeth's inattention.

Elizabeth had thought that she no longer needed her afternoon nap, but the heaviness of her eyelids announced differently. She was uncertain, however, whether it was the day's stress or her guests' inanity that demanded slumber then. Regardless, she felt herself being lulled into a partial wakefulness—able to nod, but not truly cognizant of the conversation.

She was brought to her senses, however, when she heard asked, "Are the babies at hand?" She started, much like a feral creature catching sight of an approaching predator. She also knew that without an impenetrable excuse, it would be unpardonable not to allow her children to be on display. Without adequate notice, however, she was unable to offer anything reasonable. At Elizabeth's reluctant request, a servant withdrew to have the babies wheeled into the room. Caroline and Louisa sat with hands folded on knees, at the ready to enjoy their office of Examiners of Infant Beauty.

Caroline Bingley and Louisa Hurst only stayed the night. Having obtained the intelligence they came to uncover, they were happy to depart the next morning and had thirty miles to belittle and mock her. She believed that as truly as the sun rose each morning. So convinced was she that dispersion was then in progress, as she stomped up the staircase she mimicked Caroline's sing-song locution, "Eliza looked very ill indeed. Her figure suffers dearly. She is certain never to regain it. And the babies! Have you ever seen such unsightly children? How does poor Darcy fare under such disappointment?"

Approximately halfway up the stairs, Elizabeth realised that she might be overheard and ceased. That did not keep her from wishing that she had the brazenness to inquire, "Any chance of a match yet, Caroline dear? No? A pity. We *do* weep for the disappointment that you must *suffer*." However provoked, she knew that she could not bring herself to be that uncivil. The thought was amusing though, and for the rest of that day, she pacified her mind with thoughts of sows ears and silk purses.

Her respite was short-lived.

Initially, few beyond relations were bold enough to decide which event etiquette demanded to be observed—Elizabeth's father's death or the babies' birth. (It mattered not that Mr. Bennet only happened to die at Pemberley, he had lived and been buried in another county entirely—rules were rules.) Hence, the over-riding event should be the happy one. Therefore, general thought upon the matter believed it not at all untoward to combine a condolence call with a quick look at the infant anomaly. If that also happened to sate the rabid curiosity of those who happened to call, it was all the better for politesse.

It was a convention that Elizabeth came to despise however good the inspector's intentions. She knew that Caroline and Louisa's visit was just the beginning of what would be a stream of tittering female well-wishers. All would come to extend their condolences, examine the twins, and winnow out what they could of the suspected scandals that had come to pass within and without the Darcy household. Caroline and Louisa's company had been a trial, but also beneficial for it had allowed her to exercise her discipline and rehearse her non-committal responses. It had fallen apparent with undue haste that such practice would be quite useful.

Although Elizabeth was by nature's design gregarious and had as a rule enjoyed the company of her neighbours, the rigours of childbirth and those difficult months preceding had tried not only her health, but her patience. Her husband bid her stay to her bed—that so soon after the loss of her father she need not suffer the company of anyone beyond her own choosing. But those scandalous events that surrounded the Darcy name (both past and upcoming) conspired against privacy. However distracted she was, and whatever lack of comeliness she felt, it was imperative to present as welcoming a front as possible. Indeed, as Mistress of Pemberley, it was her duty to set aside any inconvenience upon her vigour or disposition and receive those who called with compleat cordiality.

She steeled herself for this daunting obligation by tightening her corset and squeezing her form into what she deemed the less unattractive of her two frocks. She gazed into her looking-glass with no small abhorrence of what she saw, but she had no time for a sulk. When the bell heralded each caller, she heaved a sigh, pinched her cheeks, and patted her hair. It would have to do.

There was a time when there was no need of coaxing colour into her cheeks—she arose each morning in that fine state of blush. That reminder did little to lift her spirits for what would, without fail, be a trying two-pronged ordeal. She had come to be prepared for what each visit demanded of her. Some were actually merely come to see the babies, but far too many had another agenda.

This was no small aggravation to withstand. As a first-time mother, she was all but offered as a sacrificial lamb to the altar of Childrearing Admonishments. She thought with her mother still in deep mourning in Hertfordshire that she would be spared the outrageous cautions, pointless admonishments, and insipid counsel upon the fostering of children. Regrettably, she was not. Even her friend Charlotte Collins came all the way from Hunsford to stand as another holder of the office of Knower-of-All-Motherly-Wisdoms. Whilst she schooled, young Chauncey Charlemagne Collins (still cock-eyed and largely bald) sat by his mother's side screaming for another sweet. (Charlotte's remedy for Chauncey's skewwiff gaze was a special large-billed bonnet. Hanging from mid-most of the brim was a ribbon upon which a small silver spoon was fastened—much like a plumb. It was an imaginative device, but largely unsuccessful.) The sight of so unsightly a child so badly behaved incited within Elizabeth both abhorrence and pity in equal measure.

However, she remained unflappably polite with Charlotte and all others who came to call and only exposed her true feeling upon this one issue to the sympathetic ear of her always-supportive aunt, Mrs. Gardiner.

But much to her exasperation, one axiom was proven again and again. That was The Rule of the Second Guesser—wherein the more disputable the advice and the greater the fervour with which it was delivered, the higher the likelihood that she who rendered it was childless. Increasingly, it was all Elizabeth could do to listen to such twaddle with civility. Indeed, her ear heard very little from feminine discourse other than unsolicited advice and indecorous inquiries. It was these conversations that influenced her that she just might favour the conversation of gentlemen, for now that Mr. Collins was long dead, she had yet to hear a gentleman inquire of the colour of a baby's stool. On the worst of these days, had it not been for Lady Millhouse's continued good sense, Elizabeth feared a compleat loss of respect for her sex.

The elevated regard for two such handsome babes was not without good cause. In a harrowing era for women to give birth, carrying twins to term was quite rare. To successfully carry and deliver both was altogether exceptional. The relative curiosity of twins was reason enough to incite interest. If the story that was told far and wide was any approximation of the truth—that this particular confinement had come to parturition in a *chaise* and four on the road between Wigston and Fleckney—it was all the better for the telling and certainly did not diminish the popularity of their inspection. It was inevitable that not-so-veiled allusions to his potency were made by Mr. Darcy's gentlemen-friends. Just as inevitable was that they were greeted by the very private Mr. Darcy with ill-humour. Mrs. Darcy, however, enjoyed her repute. Although the fulsome commiseration for her labour was a chore to bear, in that she actually bore the babies, Elizabeth allowed herself a bit of conceit for such a singular achievement.

They were handsome babies and the Darcys were prouder than either admitted to have them seen to advantage to the all and sundry. There were, however, precautions.

Despite the assumption of the babies' vigour, all such visitations were not left to chance. By predetermination, the babies were carried in only long enough to allow adequate admiration before they were whisked away. This absenting was enforced lest overly enthusiastic admirers take the notion of picking one up—both their parents were most attentive to the possibility of air-borne indisposition. For had these calls been only those of dear friends, their guard would be no less strict, but they would have been far less trying. Regrettably, such was the Darcys' position, some who called were mere acquaintances. Most of their guests were respectful of the quarter hour limit good society observed. Some, however, did not scruple to overstay their welcome and ooh-ed and aah-ed with far greater determination than decorum demanded. Elizabeth was exceedingly mindful that amongst those mere acquaintances were a portion of gentlewomen who came less to admire Mrs. Darcy's newborns than to find satisfaction in seeing Mr. Darcy's wife looking out of bloom in an unbecoming gown.

Although Elizabeth had believed herself long past suffering vexation by fawning females lusting after her husband, her post-pregnancy throes contributed to a marked intolerance of such discourtesy. She saw no lady daring outright seduction, but Elizabeth was certain this fell less to the lack of trying than to Mr. Darcy absenting himself as a target. With enough notice, he made certain to be away upon such calls. If visitors were absolutely unavoidable, he accepted their compliments politely and bid good-bye.

Mrs. Darcy knew well that Mr. Darcy was embarrassed by, and hence despised fawning women. He despised fawning men as well, but he knew that a well-placed glare silenced them. However, to his great misfortune, when her husband levelled his annoyed glower upon a lady, not infrequently she mistook his glare for some sort of smouldering gaze. As nothing incites feminine passion more than a gentleman simmering with desire, this misapprehension occasionally elevated simple coquetry into outright advances. Thus a small matter fast became unpropitious. Darcy, known as a man of understanding and judgement in all other things, refused to suffer such impropriety with any part of amiability. Indeed, the more obvious the flirt, the greater was his vexation.

If anyone should have been the injured party, Elizabeth thought it should be the wife—yet invariably it fell to her to marshal a rescue. Upon occasions past, she proffered the mischief-maker a kind countenance, a gentle word, and unambiguous redirection.

(And if Elizabeth found amusement both in the array of overtures and Darcy's discomfiture upon receiving them, she was a wise enough woman to have kept it undisclosed.) Not surprisingly, the strategy Elizabeth employed to deflect any coquettes from her husband was not one that had been discussed between them; it was a simple courtesy his wife extended to her husband. It was a courtesy honed to a fine art over several years' practice.

Her good humour in such circumstances, she supposed, had sprung from the fact that she understood full well the allure of a reticent man, particularly one of burnished complexion, dark curls, and ample *italege.* Such a man (who was not only handsome, but rich as Croesus) sent feminine hearts aflutter and their nether-regions aquiver, too. Her own gaze alighting upon him across the room still sent a little frisson through her own heart and parts beyond after over half a decade of marriage.

Although a small part of her heart may once have commiserated the interest of such fisigigs, it did no more. For Darcy's recent design for superintending unmanageable females by absenting himself did not aide hers. For of late, there was an alteration in the conversation of these gentlewomen. No longer did they employ small coquetry. They were given to allusions all arising from what had come to light regarding not only Mr. Darcy's specific whereabouts, but whom were his companions and in what house did he abide whilst he was away. Maddeningly, these were only intimations. No one was quite bold enough to ask directly. Hence, Elizabeth was not called upon to muster a defence. Although annoyed, she was grateful to avoid that bother for she had no true answers to give. She was, however, powerfully unhappy to have to weather such insinuations alone.

When once she might have diverted the offender with crumpets and ices, she was no longer so forgiving. One line of thinking might have supposed that her present state (that of libido agitated to a near-frenzy by her husband's physical capital) would have won them some sympathy from her. It did not. If anything, the general crankiness attendant to hormonally inflamed emotions left her ill-tempered even without good reason.

She knew full well that it was insupportable to fall victim to such womanly weakness as jealousy. Yet, as she sat in company praying that her chemisette did not betray the stains from her leaking breasts, she looked far too meanly upon the elegantly coifed and gowned ladies before her, certain each and every one a rival for her husband's esteem. Whilst bearing an uncharacteristically insincere smile, she self-consciously rearranged her shawl to cover her protruding abdomen, certain her linen cap and the cut of her gown were irredeemably dowdy. It occurred to her for the first time the power of knowing oneself perfectly turned out—it could beget a feeling of inward tranquillity that even religion was powerless to bestow.

She felt it most keenly not sitting in her own parlour amongst a few simpering neighbours then, but a half year before—in the same attitude upon a bench in a park in London. The company she kept that day was far better gowned and far more beautiful than any lady of Derbyshire. Indeed, she was French. Elizabeth would never forget the lilt of her voice nor the litheness of her form. Nor would she forget that lady's intimate connexion with her husband.

There were answers owed by her husband, and she intended to have them. It had nothing to do with her present distress. In no way would she risk the accusation of jealousy. When she spoke the name of Juliette Clisson, he must be both in good humour and unsuspecting. In want of the utmost candour, timing was all.

Through war, pestilence, scandal, and death, Mrs. Darcy's mettle had persevered. More recently, however, it had wavered. It would not come immediately, but she would eventually understand that like most tribulations, those that were not forgotten were endured. And even those that were endured would eventually be winnowed out.

Lady Catherine's Pique

When a post bearing the Darcy seal wended its way to the county Kent, it was taken on the doorstep of the manor-house by the hand of a man wearing the distinctly handsome livery of Rosings Park. It was a magnificent dwelling, and while less admirable than Pemberley, the abundance of ornamentation upon its façade persuaded all who visited of the importance of its inhabitant.

As this post was directed to the lady of this impressive house, it was with great delicacy that it was placed upon a linen-draped silver tray and carried thusly upon the gloved fingertips of a footman through the vestibule. With elaborate ceremony the letter was surrendered unto the similarly gloved hand of the butler, Yewdell, who awaited a few steps down the foyer. From thence, the letter was carried down the corridor through the gallery and into the grand salon, gathering ever more portent as it did.

Once inside the room, the dainty footfalls of the butler ceased. He turned, and with eyes trained dispassionately ahead, extended the tray, wordlessly presenting the missive. Directly in Yewdell's eye-line sat an ancient red macaw (a notorious imperilment to visitors) incongruously mute save for an occasional resituating of his feathers. Hence, there ensued a fierce eyeing standoff, one Yewdell refused to surrender to a cantankerous bird. This little confrontation took place in silence—a quiet absolute save for the insistent drumming of a forefinger of his mistress. So insistent was it, it stole Yewdell's attention from the parrot. The butler did not look toward her, but remained still as a stone (excepting a barely perceptible sneer at the bird) waiting to be beckoned. Yewdell did not presume to wonder why his lady dallied. He only knew that the new velvet slippers that had arrived a size too small hurt his feet. Yet, her finger drummed on.

Customarily, it would be a considerable folly to attempt to sketch a person's nature merely by observing the doings of a single digit. On this occasion, however, it was not. The owner of this particular be-ringed finger was aristocratic, autocratic, and overweening. Indeed, that her finger drummed incessantly on the carved ivory scroll adorning the top of a bleached-teak walking stick seemed quite beside the point.

In any other circumstance such a benignly annoying activity, even by a so ornately decorated finger, might not be noteworthy. But both the stick and the finger belonged to the Right Honourable Lady Catherine de Bourgh, widow of Sir Lewis de Bourgh and Mistress of Rosings Park. Of the importance of rank (hers above all others), Lady Catherine was most sensible. Indeed, pride of circumstance draped itself across her countenance like a veil, snaked down her arm, and initiated the impatient rap on her stick. With all due pomp, she sat pondering the letter and its seal which lay upon the silver tray before her.

All about her, but beyond her notice, Rosings had come to life. It was as if by magic that the news that a post had arrived from Pemberley had spread through the great house. Those like Yewdell who were privy to her ladyship's ongoing and one-sided feud with her nephew's wife held their collective breaths. Lady Catherine was not of a conciliatory disposition. Nor was she used to having her judgement controverted. Every person in her service was aware of Mr. Darcy's visit the previous week. Indeed, everyone in her service, in the service of Pemberley, and a goodly portion of the countryside between the two estates knew the exact nature of his call. It was difficult to decide which was the greater astonishment—what Mr. Darcy said to his aunt or that his aunt made no retort. The poor woman had sat for the whole of an hour in stuttering stupefaction. (Her servants fled behind the baize door, sniggering merrily at their dictatorial mistress's comeuppance.)

Customarily Lady Catherine was happy in the opportunity to interfere in the smallest concerns of her family and neighbours. Indeed, no detail was too small to escape her attention. However, upon the occasion of the letter lately come to her house, she had procrastinated. Her servants' desire to know just what the letter held had reached the level of near hysteria. Lady Catherine's curiosity, however, was not so keen. It occurred to her that it might contain further threats upon her dignity and she needed a moment to compose herself to address them. When finally she did take the letter in hand, however, she wasted little time in ripping open the seal.

The contents of the note (and that it was no more than a note) were quite perplexing to her. Less than a se'nnight after her nephew's mortifying call, here arrived an announcement from him of the most censurable nature.

She gripped the vellum announcing the baptism with such ferocity that the script was literally strangled upon the page.

The History of a Row

The detestable baptismal announcement had not been tossed into the blazing fireplace a moment before Lady Catherine reconsidered.

"Make haste! Make haste, Yewdell! Retrieve that letter!"

Yewdell scrambled for the fireplace, but Lady Catherine had already snatched up the poker and began furiously jabbing into the fire. With his mistress's screeching pleas deafening him into desperate means, Yewdell struggled after the paper which had begun to turn an ominous shade of brown about the edges. Stabbed twice by the poker in her ladyship's hand, Yewdell finally managed to evade both her frenzied prodding and the flames long enough to take hold of the letter. Once it was in hand, he begat a hopping little dance, waving the smouldering letter furiously about before dropping it upon the tile and stomping the smoking remains. When finally the deed was done, it fell apparent that the screeching he had been certain had originated from his mistress actually had been emitted by the bird, which was flapping wildly about its perch, small red pinfeathers wafting down even then.

"Make haste! Make haste!" the bird squawked.

"Silence!" Lady Catherine demanded. "Silence, Henry!"

Yewdell ceased his stomping and stood, dumbfounded, looking at her ladyship as if she, for all the world, had run compleatly mad. It was not until she turned to the bird to again ejaculate her demand that Yewdell recalled that he and the macaw shared the same Christian name. The same did not occur to Lady Catherine, for with no further notice of her butler, she then gathered up the disintegrating remains of the paper and conveyed it, trailing bits of ash, to a table. Thereupon she carefully laid it out, making a few delicate strokes to smooth the edges. Yewdell bowed and asked for his leave.

Said he, "Will there be anything else, m'lady?" praying not, for he eased toward the door to make fast for one of cook's healing balms.

In fortune, Lady Catherine's attention had been compleatly compromised by salvaging the half-burnt letter and she waved him away without looking in his direction. His feet abused, his fingers burnt, Yewdell was happy to be dismissed and bowed only twice before he quickly took his leave, Lady Catherine far too preoccupied to notice his abbreviated genuflection.

It had really not been important to have saved the letter, for there was nothing more to read. Still, she took out a cambric hanky and whisked away any remaining ashes with such care that one would have thought there was something she had overlooked.

It had been merely a customary notification of baptism. Her fit of spleen was not because she had been caught unawares. Well-placed spies allowed her to hear of the delivery of his heir well-nigh as soon as Darcy had.

The baptismal had taken place within a week of the births. This was of no particular surprise. Everyone knew that it was imperative that a baby was sprinkled with waters at the baptismal font, with or without the accompanying naming ceremony, post-haste. Birth and death far too frequently betided newborns in quick succession. Few families waited for the mother to be on her feet lest the child die before being admitted into the church. What the announcement had accomplished was bid her recall the entire history of the double baptism as told to her in minute detail by the agent she had amongst the Pemberley staff. No minutiae was too small to feed her interest. She had heard how Mrs. Darcy had been carried to the Pemberley chapel in her husband's arms; how the vicar bore a ridiculous smile during what should have been a solemn religious rite; Miss Georgiana Darcy and Mrs. Bingley had each held a baby, both bearing equally inappropriate expressions of diversion; Mrs. Darcy reposing on a *chaise-longue*, Mr. Darcy's hand resting on her shoulder in a most immodest fashion… The entire occasion was vulgar and irreligious. She could not think of a display of such sentimentality without abhorrence.

Oh yes. She knew it all. Her outrage that day had been vented only at the reminder. Although she had taken great satisfaction in making herself miserable over all the little details, just as quickly, she had a change of heart.

In that brief time Lady Catherine conceived the nugget of a plan. It took a greater investment to calculate it into an intrigue of cunning refinement.

It had long been Lady Catherine's intention to triple her land and funds by uniting her daughter in holy wedlock with the illustrious Darcy fortune…beg pardon—the illustrious Fitzwilliam Darcy. From their cradles, her nephew, Fitzwilliam Darcy, and her daughter, Anne de Bourgh, had been formed for each other. His mother was her sister. Hence, Lady Catherine's pride in her own circumstances gifted her a very eager interest in the affairs of her nephew. She was of the firmest judgement that everyone connected with him should have an understanding of the highest rank. She held the Darcy name in no less esteem than that of de Bourgh. It was imperative to her that the distinction of rank was preserved. Hence, when her well-laid intentions for her nephew were thwarted by the allurements of a near-penniless young woman of inferior breeding, wholly unallied with their family and of no importance in the world, her ladyship was more than a mite miffed.

When first she learnt of it had she not done all that she could to circumvent such a heinous coupling? Had she not humbled herself by travelling with all good haste to Hertfordshire to beg an audience with the impertinent niece of a *tradesman*? Her devotion to her duty and station were tested beyond measure at such an indignity. Moreover, the necessity of conversing in the utmost privacy demanded the further affront of forsaking the mean little Bennet parlour for their ill-manicured little park. So urgent was her mission, Lady Catherine disregarded such a travail. Soldiering on amidst the supreme indignity of late summer dandelion fluff, she endeavoured to persuade Miss Bennet of the disastrousness of an alliance with a man wildly beyond her ken. Mr. Darcy, she pointed out with all due civility, dwarfed the Bennets in circumstance, property, and family connexions so ridiculously that to think of a match between them was laughable. (If either saw the diversion in such a notion, however, it went unacknowledged by any overt mirth.) Her gentle counsel was refused absolutely! Sincere and selflessly intentioned, she had been categorically scorned. Unfeeling girl!

Rebuffed thusly, Lady Catherine had gathered up her considerable imperiousness, reminded Miss Bennet to whom she spoke, and forthwith introduced her to a hearty dose of intimidation (heretofore quite effective on inferiors). To no avail! *Drat.* Clearly, Miss Bennet was closed to all reason (or had run compleatly mad). Either way, Lady Catherine was most decidedly displeased. Her Ladyship took leave that day with an audible snort and no good opinion of Miss Bennet, the Bennet family, their home of Longbourn and its park, the town of Meryton, or the county of Hertfordshire (nor was she particularly fond of the road leading from thence).

Foolish man to be drawn in by such a girl! But then, by their nature, were not all men fools?

Although she won the admission from Miss Bennet that day that an engagement was not in place, Lady Catherine knew that time was of the essence to rescue her nephew from his inborn irrationality. Hence, she wasted little of it in taking the tale to him, certain Miss Bennet's impudence not in her favour. When he learnt that his loving aunt, sister to his own dear, dead mother, did not look on the match with a kind eye, he would certainly forswear all regard of Miss Bennet.

Customarily Mr. Darcy was a man most misanthropically inclined. Nonetheless her Ladyship's pleas to his better judgement went unheeded. His implacability on having the Bennet girl proved indubitably to Lady Catherine that he had lost the use of his reason. Surely, he had been seduced by arts and allurements of an egregiously libidinous nature. His virtue and the very groundsels of Pemberley had been compromised by a wanton temptress!

It did nothing to salve her vexation to come to know that her little tête-à-tête with her nephew not only did not turn him against Miss Bennet—it bestirred him quite in reverse. Thither went Mr. Darcy to Longbourn to inquire after Miss Bennet's hand!

From that day forward, Lady Catherine sat in barely contained rage, outwardly accepting, but silently vowing that if she could not obstruct that marriage compleatly, she would queer the union in any way at her disposal—and her ways were many.

Regrettably, her nephew was disinclined to allow anything to mar the felicity of his marriage.

It galled her most grievously to admit to a misstep. It was never profitable to expose one's hand prematurely. But she reckoned that when she publicly cut the new Mrs. Darcy at St. James in the first season of their marriage, she had betrayed her true intentions. When her nephew had intervened upon his wife's behalf, Lady Catherine had held faint hope her own humiliation was little noticed by those who were in place to witness it. Even enduring that rather public humbling, she was not truly cowed. The entire ordeal merely steeled her resolve.

Her resolve may not have wavered but her plans did go a bit awry.

With Darcy seemingly lost forever on the war-ravaged Continent, Lady Catherine had thought the time was at hand to banish his wretched wife from Pemberley forever. The intractability that she had encountered from Elizabeth Darcy was most unforeseen. Her headlong flight from her nephew's home at the point of his wife's smoking pistol was not a memory that she relished. She had been inclined to hie to the magistrate and render charges against her, but the entire incident had been far too…*indecorous*. She had chosen not to. Alas, taking the moral high ground did her no service. For having a firearm discharged in one's direction (ruining a perfectly serviceable bonnet) by *that wife* should have sent her nephew the minute he returned post-haste to Rosings bearing abject apologies and the news that he had his wife in chains in the belvedere. He did come post-haste. Unfortunately it was not to render apologies. Rather, she was to suffer under the indignity of a threat by her own nephew with commitment to a mental infirmary! An *indigent* mental infirmary! And lest she forget, he threatened to "send her on her way in a dogcart." In a dogcart! It was not to be borne! The thought of it all incited her into an outright conniption influencing pets and servants to cower in terror (save for Henry the bird, who *never* cowered).

"It is *that wife*!" she bellowed.

Surely, her nephew was under some manner of spell, she reasoned. Yes. Undoubtedly, that wife of his was a sorceress. There was no other answer! He was under a spell cast by a witch!

"It is she who should be imprisoned! No. Pilloried. No. Burned. Her body hanging from a gibbet!"

Unfortunately, under a spell or not, the single person in England (and therefore the world at large) who gave Lady Catherine de Bourgh pause was her nephew, Mr. Darcy. Hence, she was ever so ill-disposed to dismiss his threat of institutionalisation out of hand. (The magnitude of his displeasure had been evident in a particularly nasty expression of countenance.) Truly, she did not believe he could do it. But that he *might*, tried her nerves most exceptionally (even more than the pistol incident—which plagued her in a most grievous fashion come black grouse season). The entire ordeal had nagged at her mercilessly.

Yet, for all her machinations to overthrow his marriage, these five years later, Mr. Darcy was at home in Pemberley, nestled in the happy bosom of his family with *that wife* by his side. Newly graced was he, with the blessing of a newborn son and heir as if there had been no tribulations whatsoever. No doubt Elizabeth Bennet Darcy now spent her days draped in the family jewels and gloating over her victory. Fie upon her!

All this Darcy household happiness had caused Lady Catherine to fall into a despondent sulk, believing all was for naught. So relentlessly did she worry the notion, she was much discomposed. And she remained discomposed until the missive announcing the baptism of the Darcy heirs arrived. Heirs. She made one vow. It would not end here.

Nuptials to Plan

It had been imperative to have the baptismal of the new Darcy infants post-haste, lest the poor babes depart this earth without holy blessings. As it happened, eternal souls were no less imperilled by undue delay in arranging the wedding between Miss Darcy and Col. Fitzwilliam.

The wounds that Fitzwilliam had taken upon the battlefield near Quatre Bas were of a sort that were slow to heal. His leg wound was not only a ghastly sight, but because he had refused amputation, infection had been a serious threat to his life. Of equal concern, because the enemy here was undetermined, was his eyesight. Both eyes had been burnt by some sort of percussion, one irreparably.

However, by the time they wended their way homeward, Fitzwilliam insisted he would walk down the gangway unaided. As it happened, Darcy had not anticipated Fitzwilliam's getting to his feet so soon. Moreover, proper walking attire was hardly part of their luggage. Hence, most unhappy to have reached port only to be forestalled by this last minute hindrance, Darcy made fast work of locating a gentleman aboard who happened to be carrying a walking stick that he used only as an accoutrement of his costume. In fortune, the man was far more in need of funds than of accessories and an agreement was come to with all due haste. It was an outrageous excuse for a stick, having a lacquered shaft and topped with the horn of some obscure animal, but Darcy had disposed the expression of distaste that overspread his countenance upon eying the thing by the time he returned with it to the waiting Fitzwilliam. Initially, Fitzwilliam made no note of the item's disrepute. But when he stumbled ever-so slightly with his first step, Georgiana took his arm to help guide him and he carped the entire length of the gangway that he could have made his way quite on his own if only he had a proper stick.

Fitzwilliam had been so consummate a stoic during the entire of his ordeal that his finally feeling well enough to complain, Darcy understood as a comfort. The colonel's pride, however, was further affronted by finding it necessary to wear a patch over his bad eye. Regrettably, this was as necessary an evil as the stick, for he only had enough sight left in it to keep the other from focusing correctly. Even Fitzwilliam saw that in order to keep himself upright he would have to marshal all available resources, hence he reluctantly tied on the patch. Georgiana looked quite pleased with his appearance and patted his arm with this reassurance.

"You look quite handsome," she announced.

He smiled at her flattery, but to Darcy, Fitzwilliam whispered, "I look like Horatio *Bloody* Nelson," at which both men stifled a laugh.

This was as high a revel as was held during the entirety of their time across the water and such good humour most certainly was heightened by a dollop of giddiness for finally having arrived on English shores.

Those shores beheld far more of a happy homecoming than any might have guessed. Indeed, although Georgiana returned to Pemberley as soon as she saw Fitzwilliam settled in at Whitemore, it would be weeks before Fitzwilliam ventured to hobble his way up the steps to Pemberley House to admire the Darcys' newborns. When he did, his visit was not without its trepidations. He had only lately been advised that he too was to become a father and he had yet to face Darcy's certain wrath. When at last in the same room, he refused to sit whilst he waited to see in which manner he would be greeted by Darcy—sabre drawn or hand extended. All who were privy to the underlying drama witnessed this reunion with bated breath. The disapproving scowl Darcy bore upon entering the room threatened the placidity of Fitzwilliam's countenance and did little to alleviate alarm. After what seemed an interminably long pause, Darcy, at last, began to give a curt bow—thought better of it, and thereupon extended his hand. With a great exhalation of relief, Fitzwilliam grasped it in both of his, inadvertently allowing his stick to topple to the floor. Both men reached down for it and accidentally bumped heads. They both smiled and Darcy retrieved the stick and handed it to his cousin.

When they turned to their company, it was clear that a friendship had been repaired.

Fitzwilliam improved by the day. Providentially, Georgiana's waistline did not expand apace of the reclamation of his health. Although she was slim, fortune saw her tall. It was easy to forget that existing beneath her high-waisted frock was a coming bundle of joy. Hence, the guarding of her delicate condition, which was undertaken with as much the diligence as any state secret, was all the easier.

Once Darcy had resigned himself to the inevitability of the wedding, they needed only await various members of the family to return to their feet before the plans for a discreetly sumptuous wedding were put into motion. Quite expeditiously, Fitzwilliam was ambling about with his stick—indeed, he had insisted that he be able to stand for the ceremony. But although Elizabeth moved in inexplicable bursts of sprightliness, two fortnights after the birth of her babies she was still not so hale as she would have liked everyone to believe. Naps were almost as imperative for her as for her infants. Yet she knew that it was essential that preparations be begun with haste, lest the bride's wedding breakfast serve too as a baptismal celebration. As mistress of the house, Elizabeth believed these arrangements should fall under her direction. Due to her own delicate health, however, Darcy thought otherwise.

"I am quite qualified to make these decisions," said he rather stiffly.

Even had she disagreed, Elizabeth would not have injured him by saying so. Moreover, unspoken in his brief statement was the reminder that he had made arrangements with the utmost rapidity for the wedding of another couple. (Neither Darcy nor Elizabeth, nonetheless, was willing to speak of the Wickhams unless it was absolutely unavoidable.) That occasion, however, involved a detestable groom and a barely tolerated bride. Moreover, that episode was more fraught with urgency in that the groom was in serious risk of flight, hence frills had been compleatly foresworn.

"Yes," she replied, "your abilities are not in question. It is a matter of trespassing upon your time."

"I fancy there no better way in which to employ my time than to assist my sister and champion my wife's well-being."

"I believe you should allow me the privilege of my own mind on the subject," she sniffed.

But she was not truly miffed. As much as she feigned great offence at his over-attentiveness, beyond the felicity of enjoying a doting husband, his stewarding of her health served her purposes. For so long as he insisted upon her rest, she could pretend it was a great bother—when in fact, it was not. Enjoying the luxury of ignoring the duties of mistress of such an enormous estate and curling up in her feather pillows and down counterpane with nothing to do but kiss the tops of her babies' heads was an unadulterated gift. But upon this issue, she was torn. For having been told by her brother that all decisions pertaining to this ceremony would be his, Georgiana was most unamused. Yet, as a compromised maiden, she knew herself not to be negotiating from a position of strength. She was still conscious-stricken over the toll her actions had taken on her brother and therefore, Elizabeth. She loved them both dearly. However, she did not want her wedding trip or her trousseau to be designed by her brother. This would be the single occasion in her life that she coveted as her very own and he would condescendingly overrule her every wish. She would not have it.

With all the major parties in attendance of this discordant discussion, the atmosphere was one of superb temperateness. Regardless (lest anyone think otherwise), Darcy's position remained steadfast. He desired Elizabeth's recuperation to be undisturbed and rejected out of hand that Georgiana take matters under her own advisement. To forward his suit as overseer of all plans, he pointed to his previous experience (omitting the Wickhams, as that name was not one Georgiana regarded, either) and as an example, put forth those he made for his own marriage. Georgiana, however, remained adamantly, if silently, opposed. In that what Mr. Darcy desired, Mr. Darcy generally obtained, Georgiana tested the waters of disagreement with no small caution. Still, test it she would (one might even say that she intended to stick her foot in and waggle it about). But, within her brother's gaze, she neither nodded nor shook her head. She had the good sense to delay any comment until she could speak to Elizabeth in private, fancying a suitable outcome favoured her sister-in-law's sympathetic ear. However, in not giving him every compliment of taste and encouragement in these endeavours on her behalf, Darcy understood that his sister was unmoved. Their discourse had ended in a stalemate. He took his leave, confident that he had been ill-used—the only uncertainty was to what degree.

As he strode from the room, Elizabeth watched his demeanour with careful regard. He made the barest readjustment of his shoulders, a display much like that of a fowl cock settling its ruffled feathers. That small gesture indicated a level of displeasure his countenance did not. Elizabeth did not suppose that it was lost on Georgiana in that he was barely out the door before Georgiana spoke.

Employing every compliment of taste that her brother had expected, Georgiana then offered them to Elizabeth. Flattery did not roll off Georgiana's tongue effortlessly, hence Elizabeth knew she either meant it or was just *that* desperate. She settled on it falling to a combination of both, thus salvaging both their pride.

"I know we must think alike on this, Elizabeth," Georgiana said with no small conviction. "I love my brother with all my heart, but he has not the sensibility for such employment."

Elizabeth was faced with a small conundrum. She was very tempted to explain to Georgiana that when inspired, as a lover her brother was not only attentive and romantic, but of exceedingly tender feelings. His brusque demeanour was but a façade. However, as her premier example of that would have entailed a telling of the fresh rose petals that he had spread across their nuptial bed, she declined to share so intimate a recollection.

Rather, she said, "I think you vastly underestimate your brother's sensibilities."

Georgiana looked at her a bit queerly. In response, Elizabeth only smiled. But they came to an understanding that, while Darcy would be the vehicle, Elizabeth would hold the reins. Hence, to Georgiana's undying gratitude and the consternation of her husband, Elizabeth undertook the central decision-making, vowing to Darcy that she would stay mostly to her bed.

"I am quite well," she insisted.

So insistent was she, no one save her husband challenged her assertion of robustness. Once all decisions were under Elizabeth's command, Georgiana was happy to be at Whitemore many days. Hence, when she happened to be out upon the occasion of an unanticipated visit by the dressmaker, Elizabeth abandoned her afternoon rest for the first time. To toil over patterns and fabrics for Georgiana's trousseau, she took the precaution of seeing the dressmaker in a little-used parlour. To her mind this was not a deliberate subterfuge, it was merely in the name of peace. Yet, her forethought was for naught. For unbeknownst to her, Darcy had been minding her rest each afternoon, and when he found his wife not abed, he went in search of her. When, at last he uncovered her furtive meeting, he was more disheartened than displeased. This is what he was, not how he behaved. Indeed, his exasperation was so very nearly uncivil, one only hearing him vent his displeasure might have thought he had found her *in flagrante*.

"Mrs. Darcy!" he thundered.

So thunderous was his eruption, the dressmaker's assistant was startled. Thus, the stack of pattern boxes she was carrying seemingly exploded from her hands, turning their bits and pieces of odd-shaped tissue into an absolute maelstrom.

Whilst paper wafted to the floor about her, Elizabeth gave no visible reaction to Darcy's rash outburst, merely turning her head in his direction and lowering her chin. The dressmaker had leapt to his feet and into the arms of his helper, both in trembling trepidation. It was Elizabeth's subtle attitude, not the quivering twosome, which bid her husband to recollect himself. (Her gaze always said more to him than any retort.) He had immediately undergone a flush of self-chastisement. It was his study never to allow a discernible show of pique. This loss of regulation, in addition to Elizabeth's small display of censure, influenced him to lower his voice if not his disapproval.

"Pray, should this not be put off until your health is less fragile?"

She knew that although this was couched as an inquiry, it was not. It was now a request. As she was not inclined to entertain self-martyrdom, that she felt quite well was not the question. Clearly, he was still of a mind that she needed cosseting. Because her cosseting was his chief occupation of late, she acquiesced to his unasked appeal. As independent a nature as she had, she still believed that it would be quite impossible to be overly pampered—so long as those which pampered her were the long, pliant hands of her husband.

Hence, she reached out and took in her hand a piece of satin. She turned then to the yet-quaking dressmaker.

"This," said she, "and these." She lifted several rolls of varying widths of ivory-coloured Chantilly lace.

The dressmaker bowed. Elizabeth then rose, placed her hand atop her husband's extended one, and they both majestically quit the room. (It was, however, upon that perambulation that Mr. Darcy made his imprudent, if innocently meant, suggestion to Mrs. Darcy of new frocks for herself, receiving her unspoken reply in the negative.)

The dressmaker and his assistant remained behind and did not witness either that question or the response. They stood a moment, perchance allowing their nerves to settle, before they began the arduous task of gathering up the many pattern pieces and realigning them in the proper boxes.

"I do hope," the flustered dressmaker said, "that Miss Darcy is more congenial than her brother."

Georgiana

Indeed, Miss Darcy was a great deal more congenial than her brother. (Under her present situation, it might be suggested that her brother thought she had been more than a little too congenial.) In truth, she was more agreeable than congenial. At one time, those of her acquaintance would have believed her the most agreeable and malleable of young women, most unhappy to cause anyone undue distress. Consequently, when that most agreeable, malleable, and proper of young women took leave of her home and family without a word *and* in the company of a stable boy of questionable birth to follow the army like a common camp-follower (although there were very few brave enough to utter that slander even in the privacy of their own homes), everyone to a person was utterly aghast.

As assiduously as had this intelligence been guarded, word of it had leaked out. The fabrication that Miss Darcy had merely taken herself upon a scheduled visit to relatives on the Continent was publicly accepted without comment beyond the offering of felicitations for her safe journey. It was, however, commented upon in private. That she returned engaged to Col. Fitzwilliam, a gentleman of the highest calibre and exceptional family was the saving grace on the entire scandalous affair. Had she returned to England under any other circumstances, even the Darcy name may not have saved hers from ruin.

Initially, no one who knew the shy, diffident Georgiana Darcy could believe that she was capable of behaving so rashly. This presumption was most particularly true of those closest to her, for her case was one of the few occasions where public persona was not abused by the truth. She was a young woman whose every word, every gesture, was unassuming and gentle. Her shyness was legendary. Therefore, no one suspected she owned the audacity necessary to behave in such a reckless fashion. Indeed, had there been no other conclusion, her family would have been likelier to believe her kidnapped rather than stolen away under her own volition across the Continent in any attitude, let alone on a chase after a gentleman—whether or not she believed him anything so bathetic as her "one true love." Certainly, that is how her brother saw such a mad enterprise.

Had the gentleman in question been anyone other than Colonel Geoffrey Fitzwilliam, second son of their mother's brother, the eventual outcome of this rashness may well have taken a different turn. As it was, Georgiana's brother held no other man in higher esteem than their cousin Fitzwilliam. Indeed, the colonel initially held joint guardianship of Georgiana with Darcy. All who knew him thought him of superior distinction. As a cousin to the Darcys, his connexions were impeccable. But because his brother was the Earl of Matlock, he was un-entailed, a second son, and had only those connexions to recommend himself.

To be sure, he had led an exemplary life. Rather than living a feckless existence as a bored ornament at the Court of St. James (in no greater danger than to marry badly), he took his commission in the cavalry—the one arm of the military where true expertise was demanded. Although more than a few second (and failed) sons of the aristocracy could take a fence, an inconsiderable number had the gumption or the wherewithal to engage in a cavalry charge.

Fitzwilliam was two years older than Darcy and although not of particularly handsome countenance, his features were regular, his mind well-informed, and his manners impeccable. Upon their initial meeting, Charlotte Collins had considered him for her good friend, Elizabeth. As for Elizabeth, she found the Colonel a most pleasant man, both politic and kind—in every way the compleat opposite of his cousin, Mr. Darcy. Or so that had been Elizabeth's initial impression of the two (she, of course, eventually learnt her opinion of them had been only half-right). As Darcy's friend from childhood, he had been disposed to spend time at Pemberley long before Darcy took a wife. That alteration in Darcy's household did not curtail his visits. Indeed, Fitzwilliam had been quite taken with Elizabeth from their first acquaintance and was quite happy to be in her company. Had she had more than fifty a year, he would have been tempted to court her himself. But he was a second son and knew was he to marry that he would have to barter his good name for a wife with a dowry. He was no more mercenary than the next man—that was simply a fact of the life into which he had been born.

Regrettably, the fondness that Fitzwilliam held for Elizabeth eventually erupted into an esteem that was not entirely platonic in nature on his side.

It would be some time ere he came to the realisation that he was not merely infatuated, but unabashedly in love with his cousin's wife. Unfortunately, in an unguarded moment with her, he blurted the truth—the aftermath of which asked only who between them was the most mortified. It soon fell apparent that honour fell to Fitzwilliam, for although he never spoke of it again, his connexion with the family was forever clouded. His visits became infrequent. Forthwith of the news that Napoleon was re-armed and on the march, he volunteered to lead his regiment in pursuit in Belgium. Only Elizabeth and the eavesdropping Georgiana were privy to his unrequited love, but they both suspected and feared that he might have embarked on a mission of suicidal intent. His rashness set a series of unfortunate events into action, not the least of which involved Georgiana.

For Georgiana had pined for her cousin with considerable dedication in ever-increasing gradations through the whole of her life. However, had she considered making him aware of her esteem, what she had heard clandestinely removed all hope of his returning her regard. Hence, she had feelings unexposed to anyone. Yet, when she was confronted by the possibility that he might actually die without knowing of her love, the shy, sheltered Georgiana took leave of her hearth and home (and possibly of her senses) in daring pursuit of his regiment, determined to save him from himself. Her brother, under the misapprehension she had eloped with a servant, was fast on her trail.

Georgiana, however, found Fitzwilliam first.

Her method of travel was as an army nurse. Regrettably, rather than go to Fitzwilliam, he came to her. He was brought to the little field hospital by stretcher-bearers. Her notice of him only came about through a contentious confrontation between Fitzwilliam and the doctor intent on amputating his leg. In aiding him to stand his figurative ground against the doctors' demands to remove his leg, she thereby won his devotion. And, by his side was she yet when her brother finally happened upon the scene. When typhus beset their filthy field hospital, their only means of rescue fell to a borrowed waggon and the barrel of a pistol. They were relegated to a small cottage on the property of a distant cousin to wait out Fitzwilliam's recuperation and the lifting of quarantine.

The entire impetuous episode culminated (as many an impetuous episode) in an unforeseen alliance of a fertile nature.

But once returned to Pemberley, much to her brother's displeasure, Georgiana behaved for all the world not like a ruined virgin, but as if she had somehow scaled an insuperable peak (so to speak). Contrarily, Fitzwilliam sat about, patch over one eye and gripping a forked staff, with a seriously stupid expression.

The understanding that his sister was with child and by Fitzwilliam due to the intimacies undoubtedly undertaken by *her* whilst nursing him through an extended recovery of battle wounds remained unmitigated for Darcy by the passage of time. For months he continued to take his own personal umbrage with the situation. So distressing was it to him, upon occasion Darcy still pondered the feasibility of calling Fitzwilliam out, saying if necessary he would prop him up to do it. Nothing is less ungentlemanly or more demanding of retribution than having one's sister defiled, he groused. Ruining one's sister is unworthy of a gentleman, said he.

He said that to no one save his wife. After Elizabeth's initial gentle observation that the invalid Fitzwilliam hardly could have seduced Georgiana, she needed not to repeat herself. He would glance in her direction, eyebrows knitted, eyes brooding, with a vein in his temple threatening to explode, but it took Elizabeth only to remind him by means of one upraised eyebrow to cool his rekindled ire.

Despite all the tribulations surrounding her indecorous escapade, Georgiana was truly in love. Whether or not Fitzwilliam had been somehow snared in a web of Georgiana's making remained unexplored. Still, a wedding was demanded post-haste. The Darcy name could weather only so much prattling before it began to take its toll. So far no one knew of Georgiana's condition. She was of tall frame like her brother, that and *empire* fashion would conspire to conceal her pregnancy for several months, but time was still of the essence.

Once she knew Elizabeth—not her brother—would see to the plans, Georgiana waltzed about Pemberley in a manner previously unknown to her. Having experienced the throes particular to impending motherhood, Elizabeth was more than sympathetic. Defending her moods to Darcy was not productive.

"I dare say she moons about with her head in the clouds and feet barely touching the earth! She is quite oblivious to anyone or anything but her everlasting love, Fitzwilliam."

Darcy had spoken with more than a small amount of exasperation and was compleatly oblivious that he had spoken the words "everlasting love, Fitzwilliam" in falsetto—a first for him in Elizabeth's recollection. She had to stifle a smile, knowing full well that he was in no mood (nor often was) to be a target of mirth.

"These, of course, are on the days she is here at Pemberley," he continued to complain.

This was quite true, for as often as not she spent her days at Whitemore, where she lovingly tended to Fitzwilliam's rehabilitation. The one thing that she was not was any semblance of her former self. Gone, seemingly forever, was the shy, reticent, and uncertain girl that they had all known. This turn of events was not included in her brother's wishes.

After the first uneasy conversation about her condition upon her return home, when it fell to Elizabeth to tell Darcy of what had happened (apparently under his very nose) whilst they were stranded across the water with Fitzwilliam, Elizabeth and Darcy rarely spoke of it. Indeed, it was all but ignored. Elizabeth supposed that in choosing to ignore it, Darcy hoped in vain that it might all vanish from the horizon. Elizabeth knew too, that when he caught sight of her in her morning-gown in the parlour looking at dress patterns for Georgiana's trousseau, the truth had been horribly apparent. His distress was as much over her overburdening her strength as in facing what lay ahead.

Mercy Twice Blessed

Although Darcy did not believe himself without fault (in that all God's creatures were inherently flawed), he had rarely found personal shortcomings grave enough to necessitate correction. Due to his elevated station and the resultant lack of reproach, he had once been quite arrogant. He admitted that freely. That arrogance caused Elizabeth to spurn his first proposal of marriage. Although still impenetrably grave at social indiscretions, he had purged superciliousness from his character as compleatly and expeditiously as humanly possible in order to win her. Now that his single failing had been corrected and Elizabeth was his, the agonizing months between her first refusal and her eventual acceptance of his hand were recalled as only a slight misunderstanding between lovers. That now conquered conceit had been his single folly. (His penitence for intemperate behaviour as a lusty youth once had caused him much private grief—now it rarely came to mind.) When he thought of himself impersonally, he knew that he was a loving husband, considerate brother, and now, devoted father.

Few men could call themselves more altruistic, benevolent, charitable, fair, high-minded, righteous, hospitable, just, and kind. He had practiced each and every virtue until perfected. He was Master of his Realm and all who inhabited it. Nothing in or of his life proposed his honour anything other than exemplary.

However, lasciviously eyeing the newly voluminous globes of the mother of his children might pass to do just that.

As it happened, Mr. Darcy, owner of nothing if not his own will, victim of a self-imposed banishment from his wife's comforting arms, found himself prodigiously aroused (to a vexatious degree) by Mrs. Darcy's maternally enhanced...maternal enhancements. As closely guarded as were Mr. Darcy's private perturbations, it was altogether mortifying to him that he was unable to comport himself in a manner befitting his station toward his own wife. As time and libido soldiered on, he was quite powerless to remember that his comely wife and her charming bosom were no longer solely for his delectation. To be driven by desire to have his wife once again was one thing, to be consumed by the need to bury his face between the mysterious, sweet-smelling crevice between her breasts was quite another. Lectures to himself, prayers, exercise—all were for naught. His every desire for her had congealed into this single lust. His notoriously stern will was losing ground and he knew not how to stanch the tide. As he had absolutely no domination over his thoughts, he strove mightily to constrain his conduct.

In this he was marginally successful. Never was he more charged with restraint than those evenings taken in a small, upstairs sitting-room that had long been a favourite sanctuary of theirs when taking solitary evenings together. If company was in the house, they welcomed them in one of the grand rooms meant for that purpose. This room too was exquisite, but much more informal. Just as Elizabeth had longed to have a portrait of their family to hang in the portrait gallery, it had been her particular design that they would continue to betake their evenings here as their number increased. Darcy was wholly of the same mind—or at least he had been when that prospect only included their growing brood of children. It was an entirely different matter when their snug happiness constantly included the personification of his heart's yearning blatantly adorning his wife.

Indeed, if one were unaware of the underpinnings of the scene, nothing would seem at all amiss. The family sat about a typical evening seemingly in beatific calm. Mr. Darcy carefully perused his paper. Mrs. Darcy attended to her embroidery in between loving gazes upon the babies slumbering at her feet—Mrs. Littlepage softly snoring from her perch in the chimney corner. Upon occasion, Elizabeth would fuss with the dainty lace fichu that she carefully draped over her shoulders, resituating it and retying the loose knot to obscure her over-flowing bosom. Each time she made that readjustment Mr. Darcy would glance in her direction then, with great care, turn the page of his paper. Next he would exhibit a fit of vexation over the paper's seeming uncooperativeness, rattling it until it was smoothed to his satisfaction. He did this with such frequency and vigour that a footman inquired if he should require Goodwin. No, Mr. Darcy said, he most certainly did not need Goodwin to re-press his paper and he shook his head once (but soundly) at the notion.

Seemingly unaware of her husband's discomposure, Mrs. Darcy set aside her handwork, leapt from her chair, and strode with broad strides across the room to impatiently rearrange the fire-screen. The footman gasped at this outrage against his office and hurried to assist her. The poor man then retook his station looking terribly perplexed. Mrs. Darcy, however, just as purposefully strode back to her seat and picked up her embroidery. With each and every step, her bosom bobbed, thereby revealing beneath the translucent lace the fleshly hue of her breasts. (The thought had occurred to Darcy that it may well have been that blessed lace stole that was the sole culprit for inflaming his desire for her so injudiciously.) Regardless, Mrs. Darcy could not cross the room (and she appeared to be crossing the room a perturbing number of times) adorned by that infernally thin, lacy mantle, without Mr. Darcy imagining her without it. Then, of course, he thought of kissing her neck and further undraping—whereupon he was driven either to view the dark of night from the window or to be banished entirely from the room lest his...adoration be evident to all.

Not that Elizabeth flaunted herself or her voluptuous figure. He fully admitted that it was quite to the contrary.

When abed, she wore a modest button-front night-dress which was not at all plain, but a lovely pink *peau de soie*, elaborately embroidered, the neck tied with tasselled cords. It was a fetchingly demure gown. However, he had little opportunity to admire it. For when one or the other of her infants were not nursing, Elizabeth fell fast asleep. So deep and peaceful was her slumber, he could not bring himself to wake her. It *was* important she get her rest.

And when she was about, she alternated from day to day between but two frocks. He asked if the dressmaker would call, but her expression intimated she somehow saw that inquiry a criticism. He truly did not mean offence, but those two dresses were beastly tight—she really should have more done up. But he dared not venture another comment lest she take it as a reproach. Far too often, his dear Lizzy took the mildest of observation with ill-humour. He could not fathom what could be the matter. He was doing all he could to leave her in peace.

He thought that the culprit responsible for his unseemly appetence for her bosom was merely her fichu. In truth, that was merely a convenient scapegoat. Like most scapegoats, it did not insist that he inquire more deeply of his motives. Had he, the notion might have occurred to him that he was obsessed with her bosom for the single reason that it was not that more intimate part of her body—the part that he was not to corrupt.

As Darcy was unrehearsed in the politesse of motherhood, he had been of the belief that the fires of lust that burnt with ferocity were only his own. He was certain that Elizabeth's attention was far too compromised by her babies to entertain thoughts of a carnal nature. Yet, he could not forget that she had gone to the considerable trouble of indicating to him that she still wanted him as a husband. It still caused him a palpable pain that in his heated state he had taken her without due caution. Indeed, abstinence even then had subjected him to such a state of arousal that their encounter was very nearly over before it had begun. The brevity of their amour left him barely sated, but it would have been beastly to be at her again so soon. He withdrew from her that day of the opinion that, save for his unquenched libido, all was well and good—only to be faced with the unforgiving evidence that he had caused her great harm. At the time, she had given no sign, made no word of discomfort. Although she had insisted to the surgeon that she was quite well, she had sat in her tub for half a day and walked in strange little mincing steps thereafter.

What had transpired upon that one occasion was a troubling recollection, for she clearly had done that for him alone. She had given herself to him solely to relieve his carnal cravings and then suffered from that generosity. Was there any doubt of her leanings, it was dispelled when she made no more overtures. It should have been no astonishment. Enduring a constitution enfeebled by childbirth, her recuperation was compromised by two infants on compleatly different feeding schedules. He had seen it with his horses. He had once had a mare that had foaled twins and she became so thin and weak they were forced to hand-feed both foals.

Beyond small notice of a certain amount of fretting and manoeuvring over whether or not Mrs. Darcy would or would not employ a wet-nurse, one would have supposed Mrs. Darcy's husband would have remained indifferent to, or outright oblivious of, the entire commotion. Initially, he may well have been neutral. He was not, however, oblivious. He had dared not interject into an issue of which he had no part. Yet, he came to be powerfully grateful that she had acquiesced. At least his Lizzy had not lost her health, much less her bloom. He thanked God above that she relented and allowed for a wet-nurse to assist her. Would that she would allow a second!

"Pray, just how long does human suckling last?" he silently mused.

His best guess was not months, but years, and that was not a comfort.

Another worry plagued him. Either entirely incited by sensual contemplations or merely spurred on by them, an odd caprice had overtaken him. He had begun to find any excuse to lean over her, pass by her in a narrow doorway, anything—just to catch her scent. And, most unforgivably, with absolutely no remorse he had stood gazing at her through the crack of the door whilst she bathed.

Both the act and the lack of remorse bid him know that he had sunk to near depravity. He was ashamed every time he did—which was often. To remedy this final insult to his probity, he alternately fenced to exhaustion and prayed for forgiveness. Yet his desire for her was not quashed. But with every slash of his foil, with every bend of his knee he recalled those heartless, merciless, uncompromising glimpses of seduction—the nape of her neck, the sweep of her hair—and, God help him, the very act of pulling the pins loosing her tresses into an unfathomable cascade of mahogany whorls. Was it any wonder he was driven mad with desire? Was God testing him or torturing him, he knew not. What he did know was that if he could not find release soon, he just might run mad.

It did not take many evenings such as these for the notion of their connexion being forever altered, which had worried Darcy to distraction, slowly but deliberately to begin to crumble. Perhaps it was his inborn noblesse that resurfaced, eventually weaning him from self-flagellation. Perhaps it was that the round of ladies coming to visit Elizabeth allowed him at last to escape to the outdoors, which cleared his mind for some sorely needed objectivity. Regardless, those self-condemnatory thoughts began to be trespassed by others—equally well-ordered and especially practical. He bethought every moment since his return, this time to better advantage. He relived their initial post-natal coming together and considered that perhaps that encounter had not been entirely ill-conceived, but as he had first thought, just a bit premature. Certainly they would eventually consort together again as man and wife, would they not? That would be necessary if they were to have more children. Did not all but an unfortunate few married couples go on to have more children? Elizabeth had endured a successful labour and those fears for her that had once dogged him so relentlessly could be put to rest. She had made it clear that she wanted more children. Moreover, as the children grew, her time would be less monopolised. Perhaps, they might even regain some shred of their previous love-life. It might not be as…enthusiastic as it had once been—after all, she *was* a mother. Certainly a man with his discipline could be discreet in his ardour. Moreover, he would be circumspect in expressing it.

He would promise anything, go anywhere, and endure any strife to be able to love her as he had once again. And if, in time, if motherhood bid that she did not return his passion in equal measure, he would bear that too.

Enough Is Enough

Whilst her husband skulked about in general denial that he was lusting after her voluptuous figure, Elizabeth remained totally insensible of it. Not only was she oblivious to his stalking her, she laboured under a misapprehension quite the opposite in nature.

Although she knew it to be the ideal, Elizabeth had never envied Jane's willowy shape. She was self-possessed enough to be compleatly accepting of her own as more Rubenesque. (And had it not pleased her, her shapeliness had seemed to please Darcy.) Curves, however, were one thing—outright portliness was quite another. It was quite clear to her that gravity's injustice took leave with no great haste. The babies were getting larger every day, but she was not getting smaller with equal haste. Indeed, she felt nothing less than a bloated cow and looked upon her immense mammary appurtenances with, if not disdain, at least annoyance. She supposed their size merely represented the magnitude of the task they had been handed, but that did not mollify her pride. Other mothers nursed and remained quite svelte. She felt as if someone had played a cruel trick upon her and was convinced that her figure resembled nothing if not the forward mast of a battleship. Upon occasion a frown overspread her countenance that was quite persistent.

"Dowager Darcy," she pronounced as she looked upon her reflection in the full length of a cheval mirror, and shook her head in dismay. "Dowdy Dowager Darcy."

Dowdy Dowager Darcy's husband was entirely unwitting that she believed herself decidedly less than fetching, busy as he was endeavouring mightily at every moment to keep from ravishing her. Hence, he was heedless of his husbandly obligation of reassuring her that her desirability had not waned. In that absence, her imagination continued to foster the notion that her figure was objectionable. Had she taken a peek, she would have concluded that she was much on the mend, but she had remained disinclined to take uncensored measure of her own pregnancy-ravaged form. The one thing that she could not avoid seeing was the size of her bosom. She had hoped that it would improve, but it remained so prominent that the extent of her midriff was unknown to her and she supposed it had not shrunk to any degree either. Much desiring to remain uninformed of just how ill she looked, the very nature of her toilette altered.

When once she had cavorted in her tub wearing nothing more than a few suds, she reverted to the dressing-gown draped baths of her youth. The occasional delight of slipping into her husband's tub for him to sponge her back was but a distant memory. Since the birth of her children what baths she took were but perfunctory. She meant to relieve herself of the odour of sour milk and that left little time for a luxuriating soak. When once she rarely wore a cap in their chambers, it became part of her daily wear, for she found it quite convenient to stow bedraggled ear-locks (which had become favourite baby hand-holds and hence, always straggling when loose). Devoid of jewellry, spit-cloth over her shoulder, she saw quite clearly that she was becoming an ill-favoured drudge, but save abandoning her motherly duties, she knew not how to forestall what looked to be her inevitable decline.

Elizabeth Darcy was not mirthlessly inclined. Indeed, she was known to be blessed with a keen mind, frank tongue, and a quick, but not cutting, wit. Through more than one or two entanglements from judgemental lapses, she had become a fairly wise woman as well. Such pessimism was most atypical of her. She despised self-pity in others and abhorred it of herself. Hence, upon this occasion, one must assume that it was not necessarily hers to control but born of those dark forces which are a woman's plight. To her merit, she could often be shrewd in her assessments of situations and those who peopled them. But, as is often the case, objectivity of her own straits was not always at hand. Therefore, her ill-spirits were not deigned by her as such. They were taken as accurate and true. As would be expected, a misconception such as the one under which she laboured could not be improved by frankness for so long as it remains undiscovered.

Moreover, not unlike most persons who were inherently open and artless, she could not make her mind think other than forthrightly. She had used her every wile, called forth all her cunning just to lure her husband to their romantic tryst in the glen. It was her conclusion that because she had invited him to join her there, the next move was his to take. She may not own a fraction of the pride he held, but she certainly had her share. She would not go again to him, he must come to her.

That self-sufficiency was put daily to the test. Evenings were her most interminable trial. In the day, Darcy might see to his accounts or take interviews with his employees. (Without fail, his daily duties included a visit to the stables where he made a point of inspecting Boots to assess her foaling—which invariably cost him a bit of temper.) But come the night they all sat in what had once been her second-favourite room in the house. Darcy sat in his chair reading the paper, Cressida curled at his feet. Each time he turned the page he reached out and gave the dog a pet. Of late, Elizabeth had become ever more jealous of that enfeebled dog. Mr. Darcy's dog certainly received more attention upon those hours than Mr. Darcy's wife. If that slight was not insult enough, he had taken to striding about the room in a most indecorous fashion. Upon these perambulations, his usual costume was a pair of buff-coloured moleskin breeches and his favourite riding-boots. As was his habit, the tops of the boots were folded just below the knee, this particular habit accentuating the muscularity of his thighs. Not since their courtship had she occasion to despise the fashionable tautness of masculine trousers, for a man like her husband they left very little to imagine (and her imagination was then quite her adversary). Was that not injury enough, she knew that he was well-aware of that peculiarity of her libido that endowed his boots (or rather his boots when containing his legs) with an aphrodisiacal quality; still he leapt from his chair and pranced the length of the room in the most provocative fashion. If she had not known his nature as well as she did, she might have accused him of deliberate incendiary behaviour.

An alteration of their daily mode had begun when Elizabeth was well enough for ladies to begin to call. That he gave himself leave to escape for hours upon end when it was he who held their interest most eagerly remained one of her most prominent vexations. When it was announced that he was not about, looks were exchanged and great understanding professed, but it was all quite insincere. Everyone knew it was, indeed, an escape. He sought respite from the unrelenting temptation of his wife, but she saw it as outright desertion—just when she most needed his encouragement to endure what she must on behalf of their station and deserved the sympathy for weathering it.

She had no doubt that he felt he had been entrapped with her. It was clear by the half-cornered expression that occasionally overspread his countenance when she found reason to brush against him. And she had (to slight contrition) begun to brush against him upon every opportunity. She told herself that she did so only to ascertain any alteration in his expression, but in truth, it was not. As exceedingly indecorous as it was to contemplate, she was sorely tempted to reach out and caress him.

"That, no doubt, would alter his expression," she sniffed to herself.

As closely (if surreptitiously) as she eyed his privates, she was certain that upon occasion she detected certain convexities particular to the tumescence of arousal. As closely schooled as she had been in various levels of excitement (and, it must be admitted, the sheer amplitude) of The Master's Unruly Member, that was something he could not entirely hide from her. Despite this noticeable priapism, he neither invited her attentions nor approached her. In her heart, she knew that he awaited her to again propose intimacy, but she steadfastly clung to her demand that, this time, he come to her. Still smarting from certain undeniable physical failings, she knew that was both an excuse and an evasion.

An ugly conviction over-swept her. At one time the thought of her husband not attending her would have been unthinkable—but no more. Upon those occasions her time was her own, he did not join her. It was as if the life they had once enjoyed was no longer. She feared that they had embarked upon a different road—one where they walked side by side, but not hand in hand. It made her heart ache to think of it. So she did not. She saw herself making a life with her children, scurrying from one to the other, rarely allowing Nurse any duties at all. It was as if the hollow in her heart called out for relief and she could only imbue it with the substituted passion of a maternal nature. That may have been keen, but it was not, however…him.

As time marched on and time between the babies' feedings grew, cradles and infant paraphernalia gradually made its way into the morning-parlour. Elizabeth's own disposition had a tendency toward one particular evil of indulgence for her babies beyond those proprietary, and that involved proximity. For convention demanded the nursery be situated on the top floor of the mansion-house, nanny, under-nurse, nurseryman all with adjoining rooms. Mrs. Darcy, however, took her own counsel on that custom like all others—if not actually defying it, at the very least bending it into her own. With them installed across the corridor, she then began to go to the babies to nurse, rather than the reverse. If she had an ulterior motive for this rearrangement, it remained unspoken. Six weeks after their birth even she knew that rekindled amatory rites were in order. Some sort of odd stand-off had been reached—each awaiting the other to open sexual negotiations. Her patience, however, was wearing thin.

Their bedroom privacy restored had not the result she intended. At odd times in the late afternoon, she began to find her husband face down across the bed, still booted, often wearing his frock-coat as if he had just fallen over in a dead faint. But that was ridiculous, he would not swoon. But, so deeply did he sleep, she would have to shake his shoulder to rouse him. She was wholly unwitting that before he had begun to take to the saddle daily, he had recompensed his lack of sleep by taking forty-winks here and there. Now, he had not that chance and the weeks of sleep deprivation had begun to tell upon his vigour. Having no idea how little sleep he was managing each night, how much fencing he was engaging in, and the incalculable strain that his inflamed virilité were subjecting him to, Elizabeth was sorely bewildered. She knew that unavoidable alterations came to a marriage, but the ones that she was witnessing were wildly beyond her expectations. Clearly, something was amiss. The longer their romantic impasse continued the more it became evident to her whence it sprang.

She was not amused, nor was she particularly sympathetic. Indeed, the longer the little seed of jealousy festered in the confines of her bosom, the more deadly it became.

The Inquiring Mind of Mrs. Darcy

As often occurs when two parties are at odds, when they do begin discourse, the topic is not the true issue. As Elizabeth Darcy suspected, what was of great aggravation to her husband did not begin, nor did it end with so simple a matter as a fence-jumping stallion. Her supposition, however, was a bit far afield of truth as well. Her misapprehension lay unchallenged for the length of what was to become a very discomfiting conversation.

When in the course of time those very human events that were once regarded as miraculous gradually transmute to the merely mundane, thoughts occasionally wander to occurrences which, at the time, seemed insignificant. A heart unburdened by concerns of life and limb betimes recollects those episodes with a clarity unbeneficial to any of the parties involved. Such was the case of Elizabeth's mid-pregnancy audience with a personage in London to learn of her husband's fate upon yonder shores. The information came not in letter form, but by way of a woman whose knowledge of Darcy and his doings was not only pertinent but, insofar as yesteryear, scandalously intimate. When her heart was torn by near-hysterical fear for Darcy's life, such an acquaintanceship seemed quite insignificant. At the time, all Elizabeth cared to know was that her beloved was alive and unharmed. It was only with the continuing lack of imperilment to his well-being that her equanimity was eventually restored. But that very calm allowed her to wonder had his virtue remained as unscathed as his constitution.

It only took one particularly trying afternoon with a nattering group of gentlewomen (fresh from the season and rife with London's latest gossip) for her to have had quite enough of intimations and insinuations. If she heard one more female inquire "What could possibly have kept Mr. Darcy so long away?" she thought she might just slap the inquisitor forcefully enough to spin her a full rotation. Her husband had, so far as she was aware, always lived in a way to despise slander. If she could not put the speculation to an end once and for all, she intended to have him answer a few inquiries of her own. Therefore, no sooner had the last carriage betaken its occupants away, Elizabeth set out upon her mission.

She did not have to venture far. She found her husband once again prone across their bed, sound asleep in late-afternoon. Upon this occasion, either he or Goodwin had ridded him of his coat. His boots, however, still bore enough dirt for Elizabeth to know that he had not taken a stop in the brushing room and therefore Goodwin's intervention was unlikely. Doubtless, he had come the way of the postern steps. Although there was a time when she had erroneously suspected her husband was faithless (shockingly enough, it had been Bingley), she had never questioned his love again. Nor did she believe that his odd behaviour necessarily pointed to any deceit on his part then. His strange conduct and her general pique conspired to bid her fear that he was in the grip of some sort of waywardness of heart. If he was, the time had come to find out the truth at whatever the cost.

With great purpose, she crossed the room and demanded, "Darcy!"

He stirred but little.

Seeing far greater measures were necessary, she crawled atop the bed next to him and delivered a firm shake of his shoulder.

"Darcy!" she said more firmly.

That did its duty. He half-rolled upon his back, muttering, "What is it?"

"What is it?" she said, far more loudly than she intended. "What IS it?"

By then, he was fully awake, but clearly unwitting of what was her meaning. His hair was flat upon one side and the bed-clothes had left several red creases across his cheek.

"I fear I have fallen asleep," he said, stating the obvious.

"Asleep? ASLEEP?" she was well aware that shrillness was overtaking her.

"Yes."

"We *must* talk."

"*Must* we?"

The specific tone of this question was not appreciated and she chose to ignore it. He lay upon his back, alternately squinting and blinking, desperately trying to clear both his head and his vision. As if fearing he would flee, she drew up her skirt and straddled him, exacting from him what she sought—his full attention.

She repeated, "We must talk."

He nodded once, but looked to be a bit confused.

"There is something of which I must inquire."

He nodded once again.

She settled herself across his mid-section. His hands settled upon her thighs, thus instilling in her the possibility of the conversation going errant. Still, she persevered.

"Whilst you were abroad," she began, "I, of course, had no word from you."

"This is true," he said sadly.

He answered with genuine regret, but the expression that then overspread his countenance suggested that he was curious as to why this topic was at that moment so urgent as to wake him from a dead sleep.

Regardless, he said, "As I have explained, I wrote as often as I could…the war…the quarantine."

"Yes," she agreed, "there was but one message that found its way to me. It alone was the single word that I received. Only through it did I learn that you were not dead."

She almost began to sniffle at the recollection of those dark days of not knowing, but stopt herself. The letter that she received had not been in his hand at all, but another's.

Instinctively, he patted her reassuringly and then let his hands slide to the narrowing of her waist (a narrowing that she was wholly unaware had re-emerged). She did not, at that moment, want comfort from him. She wanted an answer to the question that had become her constant companion.

"Pray, do you know how I came to have that letter?"

"The post?" he answered reasonably.

"I travelled to London to take it in my own hand."

"In your condition? Lizzy! Whatever were you thinking? Was there no one to keep you from such madness?"

"I am disinclined to be chastised by a person who believes the proper channel for a missive to his wife would be through the benefices of a former lover."

He blinked several times as if he did not hear her.

"You hear what you please. Do not propose to me you cannot hear me now."

He heard her perfectly. They both knew that. His partial deafness had troubled him little in recent weeks. It was abating with each passing day and was only resurrected for his convenience. He heard everything that he wished to hear. He most certainly did not want to be a party to the conversation before him, but he had little choice. His face crimsoned and he closed his eyes at the vision he undoubtedly had of that particular meeting.

For a capricious reason that suited Elizabeth, obtaining some sort of reaction from his usual detachment proved satisfactory. Regrettably, the nature of his response suggested to her that the meeting with his old lover was less than benign. When she had met Juliette Clisson in the middle of a park in the middle of London, she had feared for Darcy so fervently, she cared little for what their connexion might have been before his marriage to her. Now that he was very much alive and well and between her legs, she did not prefer benightedness, she demanded satisfaction.

"What do you have to say for yourself?"

"Am I to understand you to speak from jealousy?" he queried, altering the subject quite artlessly.

"Nay! Never! That is beside the point. You have not answered me."

"You will have to make a more specific inquiry."

He had the infuriating beginnings of a smile and she wanted dearly to smack him across his smirk. Because for the second time in one day, she was moved to near-violence, she bethought the matter. Perhaps, she was just a bit jealous. But that *was* beside the point. She may well have had reason to be.

"Pray would you care to offer the particulars of conspiring with Mlle. Clisson for delivery of a letter to *me*?"

Hearing her speak Juliette's name was exceedingly discombobulating, thus any part of mirth that was tempting his countenance evaporated.

"I had no idea," said he.

"You had no idea of what, pray may I ask?" Clearly, her ill-temper was not abating.

As that was a disputatious inquiry, he chose not to address it immediately.

"It was but a coincidence. I happened upon the lady, Mlle. Clisson, at my cousin's home," he explained.

He did not make the mistake of calling Juliette by her Christian name, but Elizabeth raised a cynical eyebrow at his employment of the term, lady. He, however, persevered.

"She and her party were to sail for London the next day. I was desperate to get word to you. In my haste—in my desperation to reach you—I asked if she might post a letter for me when she arrived. I had no idea that a meeting between you would come to pass. The letter…I believe in the letter, I explained the circumstances…Did I not?"

It fell to Elizabeth to explain to him that Juliette had been compelled to destroy the letter when their vessel was boarded by the French authorities. The insult to Elizabeth, however, was still just as keen.

"I was never able to read your words, but only to hear them through her. And, of course, from her, how eagerly she comforted you."

At last it was out, what had been plaguing her of the entire episode. It was not the insult to decorum, it was not the discomfort of the trip to town, nor was it the sheer humiliation of sitting in a public park whilst great with child. Nor was it taking a meeting with an exquisitely lovely woman from his past who called him "*Darcee*." It was not one thing—it was all too much. A weep of the unbecoming sort threatened her and she was angered at the thought of exposing the depth of her hurt. She attempted to rise from imprisoning him, but she could not do that either for he would not release her. He grasped her elbows firmly.

"Lizzy," said he, "please do not…"

She began to struggle to leave him and he kept his hold on her arms to keep her there. A small tussle ensued as she writhed to remove herself from atop him and he, just as determinedly, clung to her, endeavouring with his considerable might to continue their discourse.

"Lizzy!" he said once again, this time more firmly.

She immediately stopt her struggle—but not because of his exclamation.

Another, more insistent outcry had come to her attention. Indeed, she had become quite cognizant that the genital tumescence (of which she had of late held office of monitor) had reasserted itself. It had reasserted itself in more profound attitude than of her recent memory. The timing of its resurrection, however, was regrettable. She silently announced that to him by ceasing to move about and sitting soundly upon his hips—thereupon issuing him a glare of reproach. Because his passion had not flowered without his notice, he comprehended the grounds for glower immediately. He was somewhat flummoxed, however, over why she was thus offended. There was never a time when she was in such an attitude as she was then that amorousness did not ensue. It only belatedly occurred to him that the nature of their discourse was unlike any other accompanying those past amatory episodes. So thoroughly was he transported, the thought that her wifely instincts might not have remained keen, however, was never once entertained.

Under the continuation of her ill-humoured demeanour, as dearly as he would have liked, he dared not to take liberties with her person. This was a wise choice.

"So," she announced.

The finality of her utterance did nothing to mend his discombobulation. The tightening in his groin was undeniable evidence of his compleat loss of self-discipline. Hence, he saw no reason to deny his passion for her. She, however, sounded for all the world like a scolding nurse—as if he (or at least his member) the errant child. If she was to sit upon him in such a manner (not to speak of gyrating about), he absolved himself of all blame for the resulting genital reflex.

"So," he ventured, smiling happily—certain whatever her pique, she would relent.

She, however, did not. And, steadfastly holding her accusatory manner, inquired, "I am but to speak the name and your ardour returns?"

Her sarcasm was not undetectable.

"Speak the name?" he repeated dumbly.

"Of your former lover," she said tightly. "I credit your honour that she is indeed, only a former lover still."

That explanation brought his attention from the painful throb in his loins. He then did allow her to draw away, but followed her as she fell upon her back, he then lying over her. He bid her to return his gaze, but she would not look directly upon him. Undeterred, he propped himself upon his elbows and cupped her face in his hands so she had no alternative. Initially, she refused, but when she acquiesced, he detected her every injury, her every resentment. In one fell swoop, he realised the enormity of his folly in believing that the sheer boundlessness and ferocity of their love could ever wane.

He kissed her tenderly upon her forehead—if she had supposed that kiss a fatherly one, she would have been egregiously mistaken. Indeed, the next was upon her lips, the very ones that were quivering with indignation. He kissed her more tenderly and lingeringly than he had in recent memory. Beneath him, he could feel her body begin to relax, all resistance draining away. Those passionate longings that she had suppressed broke free at last causing a conspicuous rosy hue to creep up her throat.

Observing this, he admitted, "I have been a fool."

However true, in not specifying in just what manner he had engaged in witlessness, he erred. In fortune, he immediately recognised his blunder.

"Please forgive me," he said, "for I have been insensible of what misapprehension I visited upon you through my single-mindedness. I sought only to reach you and never imagined what the outcome might have been. Forgive me, dearest Lizzy. The only comfort I was afforded was to have found a means to you."

With that, he rose just enough to allow his gaze to take in the length or her torso. But rather than offer exultations to her comeliness as she expected (and was prepared to refuse), he took her hand and kissed it. Gently, he placed his palm against her cheek, his large hand framing her face. She had no alternative but to return his gaze. But, he spoke not. With great tenderness, he drew his thumb across her chin. It was a gesture of such familiarity, she was momentarily rendered speechless. When she regained her voice, she spoke with finality.

"You have returned to me."

As if having leapt an enormous hurdle, she let out a sigh and nestled to him, revelling in his closeness.

She then said, "To have you again by my side is all I ask."

"It is you, dearest Lizzy, and no other, who inflames my ardour," he whispered. "I would never knowingly cause you such vexation."

He began to kiss her—deep, lust-drenched kisses that took away her breath.

When she regained a bit of it, she managed to croak out the denial, "I was not *truly* vexed."

Whether she was or she was not, was not truly in contention. What was affirmed was his desire for her and hers for him. This avowal was buttressed by a continuation of their kisses which had but one end and he embarked upon that culmination forthwith—with explicit delineation.

The release of his long-imprisoned engorgement was a palpable relief, but he managed to contain his urgency long enough to insinuate himself beneath her skirts. Thereupon, she wrapped her arms about his head, burying his face in the ampleness of her bosom. That deed replicated such a deeply seated longing that it was all but he thought he might actually bay with desire. Gathering every fibre of self-restraint, he did not, but with a fierce handhold of her hair, he drove into her again and again until at last blessed relief flooded from him.

He only belatedly became sensible of her cries. In fortune they were born of passion, not pain. When it had once been his constant study to see that she was pleasured before he found his own, he then had not. As much as he would have liked to censure himself for such impetuosity, that did not occur. Some things, he knew, were quite beyond reason. Although he suspected success, had she not found gratification, he knew there would be many days and many nights to make amends.

In the quiet that followed, he once again began to kiss her. This time it was no less deeply and only marginally less lustful, but his eyes began to close.

"You," he said softly, "are God's most beautiful creation."

That he made such a shameless aggrandizement did not decrease her enjoyment of it in the least. She nestled happily against him and he kissed her forehead. In less than a minute, she heard the faint purl of a snore. As she lay and listened to his contentment, she did not question his sincerity. She had further questions to ask, but was not so unwise as to put them forth anytime soon. She would see to it that the occasion would arise when she would proffer them without employing unfair arts. When she did, she would not be disadvantaged by invidious emotions. She did not want to despoil such propitious calm as they enjoyed just then, for much distress had been mollified.

Her only remaining apprehension had not yet been addressed. Carefully, she drew her skirt down over her legs and tugged at her drooping stockings. She did this for two instinctive reasons. Firstly, she was still disinclined to bare all to the husband who thought her "God's most beautiful creation," and, she was quite certain she heard the unmistakable wail of a hungry infant.

Wickham, Alive and on Queer Street Once Again

For all his many failings, Maj. George Wickham was the owner of many an estimable quality. Foremost among his attributes (one of which he took full advantage) was an expression of goodness about his countenance that suggested an open and gentle manner. Too, he was of exceptionally fine figure even when he could no longer claim the beauty of youth. Once he had attained his regimentals, few men could say they commanded a handsomer aspect. Hence, all who had occasion to be in his company were charmed beyond measure. No opinion of him, however, surpassed his own estimation of himself. Therein lay the disadvantage of his character—all his failings were profound, his fine qualities, shallow.

"I have a warm, unguarded temper," Maj. George Wickham was happy to admit (with a simper included in the bargain).

And to excuse his all-too-regular forays into night-life he offered, "Society, I own, is necessary to me. I have been a disappointed man and my spirits will not bear solitude. I must have employment and society."

He also loved schemes and designs of all shades (as the trail of gaming debts he left behind him could attest). But, Wickham had no master plan for his life's path beyond becoming rich. As his birth was less than illustrious, he believed the most direct route to these riches would be through marrying well. When obstruction was thrown in his path, he somehow managed to circumvent compleat disaster by either absconding or lying low. Indeed, he prided himself on landing on his feet with all the stealth of an alley-way cat. Hence, as his prospects dimmed in England, he cast his gaze to beyond the channel. Initially, Wickham's long-cherished hope of making his fortune through marriage abroad was dashed by Darcy's intervention with his illicit liaison with Lydia. But, he had not tossed the notion aside compleatly. Nestled within the most designing recesses of his duplicitous mind remained the merest glimmer of hope. He held on to that hope with the same unflagging optimism that had always kept despair at bay. He clung to that hope with all the tenacity of one who has compleat confidence in his own resolve—however unlikely the ambition.

The oft told history of sad events that comprised George Wickham's particular version of his life was forlorn indeed. When necessary, he could consolidate it into a few sentences, omitting nary an ill-use: Born into the apotheosis of wealth, taken as an infant to live within the hallowed halls of Pemberley, promised a living, cast out, coerced into marriage, dragooned into battle…

To his mind, it was quite true that he had been dragooned into battle as surely as had he been knocked senseless and dragged there by a press gang. His advancement with the military had been sabotaged by Lydia's irredeemable deficiencies as his wife. Had she not been such a screaming shrew, he fancied himself in line for assignment in the Life Guards Green. There, his sole purpose would have been to stand ready to defend the Prince Regent from all would-be assassins cavorting in the West End during his majesty's gambolling forays. Or, if Foreign Service was absolutely demanded, at the very worst, he could have obtained an assignment as an attaché. But the Life Guards Green or attaché demanded an exemplary public presence—not a puling harridan of a wife who was happy for any excuse to cause public scandal. Hence, instead of displaying valorous conduct from the safety of the General's tent, he had been forced to lead a poorly trained contingent of gangly grenadiers into hand-to-hand combat with Napoleon's fiercest battalion. Bugger.

Had he not had the supreme presence of mind under dire urgency of battle to garner a steed and make safe, he would have been a worm-riddled corpse in an unmarked grave in that Godforsaken country still…

Although he would have denied it to the death, an argument could be made that every misfortune he had ever encountered (and their number was legion), was by his own hands.

Greeting the harsh new morn with a headache had become regular as rain for George Wickham. So regular was it that his much-renewed vow of sobriety would be restated before he lifted his head from his lump of a pillow. That resolution was showing more wear than his unmentionables, but as he had no better likelihood of mending his small-clothes than his ways, he chose not to ponder either. Nor was he comforted when he finally reckoned his whereabouts through the squinted caution of half-opened eyelids. Guardedly, he sat up and looked about.

Dissipation had taken hold like Cerberus, and his lair was not pretty.

He could remember a time when he had slept between silken sheets beneath a canopy of damask in the family wing of the grand and glorious Pemberley Manor. Of course, his was not quite as exalted as the bed-chambers inhabited by the Darcys themselves, but yet quite sumptuous in its own right. He longed for that bed. He longed for his position as favoured ward of old Mr. Darcy. He would have been there yet had not old Mr. Darcy gone and died, leaving his prospects in the comfortless hands of his dour and unsociable son.

All of Wickham's misfortunes fell to this childhood friend's abuse—this was a long held and closely nurtured presumption. Clearly, Darcy had been, and was yet, jealous of his father's affection for Wickham. Had he not been cast out without a sixpence, denied the living he should have had…

Wickham retreated from these thoughts. They were unprofitable. If they proceeded, their natural course might bring to mind recollections of a dishonourable nature. He chose not to recall that his own dissolute inclinations resulted in being sent down from Cambridge—those inclinations plagued him still.

It was one scandalous seduction among many that had fully warranted not only censure, but very nearly bloodshed. That little peccadillo with Georgiana Darcy did teach one unalterable truth: never, never trifle with a rich man's sister. Or at least never get caught at it. He should have recollected that simple wisdom when he inadvisably attempted to trifle with Darcy's wife as well. Ah, but that was another story altogether...

Those early misdeeds, of course, were of a lusty youth. Those of his adulthood fell quite beyond the pale. Murder and desertion were hanging offences. Then, they would have to be of public record, would they not? He had covered his trail well; his scheme for re-entry into some semblance of his former life, impeccable. No one will ever be the wiser. Will they?

No, it was best not to ponder the past. The future was grim enough.

The bed on which he lay was nothing more than a cot, one that sagged abysmally even when unoccupied (and all but gave way compleatly when it was). The odour emanating from beneath it suggested that the emptying of the chamberpot was long overdue. A housemaid to see to such things, however, did not come with such accommodations. The only bright spot on a very dark horizon was that if he awakened spitting feathers, he was happy to be spitting them in London. Belgium may have been a bust, but Paris had been a debacle. He wanted not to think of it.

Hence, he looked down and between his feet for the offending pot, but had to get down on one knee to retrieve it. Gingerly, he withdrew it then walked the brief length of the room and swung open the sash. As its contents trickled down the bricks and splattered on the cobbles below, he exhaled an immense sigh of relief at achieving this mean little victory over the foetid air inside. A passer-by had to sidestep the mess, exhibiting the unmistakable signs of unhappiness with a raised fist and proffered several aspersions upon the circumstances of Wickham's birth—expletives Wickham happily cut off mid-squawk by slamming closed the shutter. With that singular triumph, Wickham retreated back to his cot and sank heavily into its depths. He attempted to nestle into a more comfortable position and when situated, rested the back of his hand across his aching eyes. That his pose mimicked the feminine histrionics of more than one novella was lost on him, for his attention was far too compromised by wading through an ever-increasing muck of self-pity.

George Wickham once again on Queer Street would be of no particular astonishment to his friends had he any friends left to surprise, but into this habitat of debauchery and intemperance wafted a most unlikely sound.

From the corner came the soft whimper of a baby, one that threatened to spiral into a wail. More unlikely than the existence of a little one in his exceedingly humble excuse for lodgings was that, upon hearing the cries, George Wickham immediately staggered to his feet and took himself directly to the child's bedside. Once there, he did not scowl or scold. With unfathomable tenderness, he lifted the child from beneath the bedclothes and began a reassuring little shuffle, clucking and cooing like a mother bird.

What Ails Miss de Bourgh

It was not three days after the cursed post from Pemberley arrived that Dr. Brumfitt made his way to Rosings to perform his weekly survey of the health of the ladies therein. As his curricle bumped and swayed along the lane, its forward passage irritated the dry scab of un-metalled road into a blinding storm of dust which engulfed him and his humble equipage as it came to a stop at the lodge gate. He coughed and waved his hand impatiently in impotent hope that the dust would settle back on the road and not upon his freshly brushed suit. Lady Catherine disliked seeing her minions mussed and he knew a man of his position had not the authority to stand in the brushing room. He raised his hat, re-patted his hair, then made a small attempt to sweep his besmudged topcoat with his fingertips. He wanted not to incite Lady Catherine's wrath unduly. Word had it her temper was even more frayed than usual.

Dr. Brumfitt was a florid-faced, potbellied man with more nasal hair than side-whiskers. However, his step was slightly more brisk than the average fat man through the aggrandisement of being the sole surgeon in the village of Hunsford and surrounding countryside. There was a doctor about to tend to ills of the common folk. As surgeon, however, his principal patients were Lady Catherine and her daughter, Lady Anne. In Lady Catherine there was little to see to beyond passing her the latest remedy for her rheumatic hip and listening to her endless complaints. Beyond his eternal mortification at her ladyship's continual inability to insert an essential consonant when she spoke his name, it was an exceedingly advantageous situation. Indeed, having a patient whose unflagging ill-health was only equalled by her mother's ability to fund his services gave him just cause to see to it that her daughter remained alive. Unfortunately, he had little encouragement when it came to Lady Anne's fettle. He was summoned to Rosings with regularity to issue that opinion, one that was little more dismaying to Lady Catherine than it was to his future purse. Hence, his gravity upon those occasions was not an affectation.

Once his audience was approved, Dr. Brumfitt lost little time in scurrying to the small parlour where his inspections were usually undertaken. Surprisingly, Lady Catherine and Lady Anne had preceded him. Both sat in the relative regality of high-backed wingchairs. Lady Catherine still wore her morning-dress. Lady Anne nursed a silent cough.

Whilst yet in nodding genuflection to them both, Dr. Brumfitt attempted to polish the tops of his boots on the backs of his leggings. This manoeuvre only partially cleaned his boots and when he made a quick check, he noted a menacing smudge on the back of his calves. Therefore, he edged uneasily around her ladyship and navigated his considerable bulk into an armless chair, which he then pulled as near as he dared to Lady Anne's knees.

There, all thoughts of sartorial disgrace were forgotten. He once again took measure of her sickly pallor and was truly (very truly) distressed. The surgeon prest his ear to her wheezing chest, and clucked and shook his head as he had each time he called. This day he clucked a little more vehemently. Whilst he did, Lady Anne sat with impassive reserve at his implied prediction of doom. Quite inured was she to being the object of pity.

"Pray, what say you, Mr. Bumfitt?" Lady Catherine said.

Having long past given up reminding her of his correct name, he, with all due commiseration, solemnly pronounced, "I fear every winter steals a little more of her breath, your ladyship."

It was indeed a dismal prognosis. Lady Catherine either grimaced or gave a thin smile (it was difficult to determine which one) at his words. By considerable linguistic pussyfooting, Dr. Brumfitt had already ascertained that Lady Anne's menses troubled her only four times a year. The withered little twist to Lady Catherine's lips lingered just a bit as she gazed upon her daughter's frail figure and pondered those unhappy certitudes. If Dr. Brumfitt's foretelling was true, she knew that the fertility of Lady Anne's unreliable womb would ebb with her lungs.

Unused to abiding disappointment on any front, her motherly concern battled utter disgust quite unsuccessfully. It was essential that feminine frailty not impede her designs. Her daughter may not have yet learnt what her mother knew well: consequence had its debt to generation.

Although initially Lady Catherine had been vexed to distraction when she learnt of Mrs. Darcy's successful confinement, the post from Pemberley was the impetus she needed to take decisive action. Still, she cautioned herself that one must use one's resources efficiently. She had assayed them carefully and pondered the unkind fact that her daughter might not last many more seasons. This one was all but over. She concluded that a suitor must be found with all due haste. But, where? With keen deliberation, she drew up her hand and stroked her chin. Whilst deep in contemplation, her forefinger and thumb located a few stray hairs that abided at the corner of her mouth and twirled them into a single queue. As her thought deepened, her eyes narrowed ominously, imbuing in Brumfitt no small alarm.

Now faced with imminent loss of his cash-cow through sheer attrition, he posed a suggestion, "Perhaps Bath, your ladyship. The healing waters may be the answer."

"Bath, Mr. Bumfitt?" She ceased her twirling, stroking, and squinting, and announced, "The healing waters will be ideal. We shall depart for Bath directly."

She announced this with such resolve, it left no possibility that such a notion originated with anyone other than herself. (She was, by all reports—even some not her own—a most clever and sensible woman.) Although she agreed most heartily with the suggestion of taking Lady Anne to Bath, it was not for the waters. It was for the society. London was the epicentre of the *beau mode* and the shrine of the socially ambitious, but its season was all but over. In Bath the season knew no end. With the answer to just where to commence her behindhand search for a match for her daughter suddenly before her, she would waste little time to set her scheme into action. Her dour mien brightened ever so slightly as to be barely visible to any eye upon her.

However, she was *quite* pleased. Lady Catherine now had a plan in place that would satisfy both avarice and revenge in one fell swoop. Perchance an alliance may have been no longer tenable between her nephew and daughter, but another generation was at hand. Tainted though it might be by Miss Bennet's inferior family connexions, it still bore the Darcy name! It would do quite well enough!

The corners of her mouth creased again, this time into a mean little smile. She knew the springs of Bath drew the titled and the rich (and those with titles looking for those with riches) like flies to honey. It would be little effort to arrange a betrothal most advantageous to all parties. A pregnancy initiated and a baby born. Time was of the essence. A wrong to be righted at last! The de Bourgh and the Darcy fortunes united!

"Yes," Lady Anne's mother announced with finality. "Bath."

To those not of her acquaintance, Lady Catherine's facial expressions were an enigma. As she was a woman not known for her good humour, the one she bore then left the surgeon feeling unsettled. He was not usually offered tea, nor did he expect it this day. He hastened back to his curricle with such rapidity that he did not catch his breath until he was well up the road. Had anyone been watching they would not have seen him turn and look back, for soon a cloud of dust once again engulfed his figure.

Bingley's Betrayal

The near tornadic chaos that embraced the Darcy family in the year '15 excited that of the Bingleys with similar vehemence. There was no travail that Elizabeth had weathered that was not suffered with all due excruciation by her sister Jane. Indeed, were it within her power, Jane would have happily appropriated all of Elizabeth's worriment for herself.

Elizabeth knew that Jane's nature was one of boundless compassion and limitless consolation and had fervently desired to keep her own counsel when it came to her most terrifying fears. But in light of Georgiana's disappearance, Darcy's pursuit of her, Fitzwilliam's battle wounds, their young friend John Christie's death, the typhus epidemic that kept their party abroad, and her own ill-timed and precarious pregnancy, she had been able to shield very little from her sister. Had there not been enough grief to share, those perilous months saw Jane endure an unprecedented imbroglio—but certainly not one of her own making. Although she did not initially apprise Elizabeth of it for it was of a particularly delicate nature, Elizabeth had learnt of it through rather odd circumstances. Indeed, it had been an odd and humiliating business for all parties concerned.

It had come to pass through Lady Catherine's manipulative treachery that Elizabeth had allowed herself to believe that her own beloved Darcy had taken the course of many of a rich man—one that led to a mistress's bed. In retrospect, the thought was absolutely ludicrous, but Elizabeth looked upon her subsequent actions with such abhorrence that she refused to grant herself quarter even in so small a way as describing the accusation. She had absolutely no defence for how she could have supposed that Darcy had been the gentleman seen attending a woman among the cottagers on Pemberley land.

Truth be told, the apprehension she suffered over her continued barrenness influenced her to mistrust not only Darcy's fidelity, but also his theretofore unalterable love for her. To mistrust her husband's loyalty may have been born of her own insecurity, but it was still inexcusable. That she allowed a known asperser such as Lady Catherine to interfere with her marriage begat in her an anger previously unbeknownst to her. She was not, however, merely angry with Lady Catherine. She was furious with herself. Furious and humiliated. Humiliated, ashamed, and abased. When later she recalled how scrupulously she crept about the surrounding countryside searching out the woman with whom she believed her husband philandered, she was mortified beyond words. So humiliated was she, even uncovering that the actual culprit was not Darcy at all, but rather Bingley, she could not allow herself to be relieved.

She had not a minute's respite from fear of the possibility of Darcy's adultery before she turned her indignation on Bingley. Because she was relieved of having to question her own marriage had she found her husband disporting with some other woman, she turned her full fury on her brother-in-law. She was enraged beyond words that her sweet sister would be injured should she learn of it. And she knew it was entirely possible she might. The evidence was irrefutable. The baby was named Charles after the man who fathered him. Therefore, Elizabeth had not revealed Bingley's betrayal to anyone, including Darcy (the scrupulousness with which she concealed this matter served the dual purpose of respecting Jane's privacy and keeping her husband unenlightened of her own insupportable actions).

But, Jane had astonished Elizabeth (to a staggering degree) when she brought the incident to light herself.

As was her nature, Jane's reason for doing so was selfless. The baby's mother expected to succumb from consumption within the month. Far from bearing malice for an innocent child, Jane was adamant that the child be brought up in a loving home. It was her notion that home might be Elizabeth's. Jane had wished to take the baby home with her to Kirkland Hall, but she was loath for Bingley to know that his indiscretion was no longer private.

Elizabeth was inclined to abuse Bingley's backside with a carriage whip, but she had acquiesced to Jane's wishes in the matter. Having walked ever so briefly in what she supposed had been the slippers of a betrayed wife, Elizabeth was keenly solicitous of Jane's wishes and would have done anything her sister had asked of her. It came to pass, however, that the plans that the sisters had so carefully laid out were for naught. They had only just fetched the baby to Pemberley when Bingley happened upon them. He recognised the infant in a trice, leaving Jane and Elizabeth decidedly flustered. Jane's expression was tantamount to having been apprehended *in flagrante delicto*, conscience-stricken as she was to be caught in a covert undertaking. For her part, Elizabeth found herself silently smug, happy for Bingley to have to pay the proverbial piper. Yet, as it was not hers to cast stones, she left them to sort it out alone.

"He who hath sown the wind shall reap the whirlwind," she had whispered as she listened behind the door for retribution to be paid.

When he threw himself upon Jane's lap and in sobbing gulps begged her forgiveness, Elizabeth overheard it all. Bingley was compleatly chastened, utterly remorseful, unconditionally penitent, and wholly self-condemnatory. Such was his wretchedness that it very nearly provoked Elizabeth's pity—but not quite. (To Bingley's good fortune the granting of forgiveness fell to his loving wife, not his infuriated sister-in-law.)

So quickly did other events unfold after that revelation, Elizabeth had small opportunity to talk to Jane about it or what came to pass in its aftermath. Knowing her dear sister's compassionate nature, there was little doubt that she had forgiven Bingley with all the generosity of her exceedingly kind heart. It was a private matter, yet as it was Jane who had brought the issue to the forefront and asked for her assistance, Elizabeth believed enlightenment on the repercussions was absolutely obligatory. Jane, however, was not of the same mind. Thither went the Bingleys with the baby to Kirkland Hall and introduced him to one and all as "their son." Upon that occasion and thence, if anyone dared so much as raise an eyebrow, it was met with benign silence by Jane.

As they were not only sisters, but dear friends and each other's closest confidant, Elizabeth had been anxious to the point of agitation to know what exactly had come to pass between the Bingleys. That Jane was so unforthcoming about it all even to her was highly vexing. Even the supposition that Jane's silence was out of respect for her husband's privacy did little to mitigate Elizabeth's unrelenting curiosity. Curiosity if Bingley's betrayal had damaged the fibre of their marriage was unflinching whilst Elizabeth waited both for her parturition and in unmitigated terror for Darcy to come home to her from across the water. Little did she want to admit that her sister's marital difficulties served her as a distraction, yet that was the only other subject that she could ponder with, if not calm, at least relative composure. Once her own husband was home and she had two babies to dote on, Jane and Bingley's marriage had slipped from the first tier of her concerns. Hence, it was several months before Elizabeth had either the time or the wherewithal for that particular query to resurface.

The time had long passed for the subject to be broached in conversation with any kind of nonchalance. Hence, she sought to ascertain the level of and direction Jane's forgiveness had taken from visual clues. That study was to prove profitable. For, she eventually persuaded herself that all was well in the Bingley house by a means once almost forgotten. Although discourse upon the subject was forbidden, she resorted to what had been, for all intents and purposes, a special language known between themselves as children. A look, a glance, a nod bespoke volumes. Hence, when at last Elizabeth's attention was not so compromised as to overlook a further nuance upon Jane's countenance, she could at last observe that to which she had heretofore been blind. When she did, she was all but taken aback.

For overspreading Jane's aspect was the barest hint of a smile. It sprang from neither amusement nor disguise. It was a smile of a very particular kind. Elizabeth would not have reckoned whence it sprang had she not seen its exact replica each morning in her looking-glass when she arose from her own husband's bed.

The Hapless History of Lady Anne

Lady Anne de Bourgh was not only a bit bird-boned and very plain-featured, she was unobtrusive to the point of insipidity. Good society would not have suffered the tedium of her company if not for her illustrious birth. Still, poor Anne was hardly the first young gentlewoman whose only charms rested in the vaults of her banker.

Beyond her lack of bloom, her insignificant features and soft voice suggested her a bit dull-witted. This was not so. Her predisposition for sniffles and chills kept her away from most engagements, hence society had little chance to exhibit its tolerance or understand it misplaced. The poor girl, it seemed, was always either in fear of coming down with a cold, or in the throes of one. Frail health demanded that she keep mostly to her room. Hence, if she was uncompanionable, it fell to her lack of opportunity to practise being otherwise. It was within this void that the oft observed practise of one who is denied diversion supplied by others was put into place. When deficient in outside amusement, invariably one produces one's own.

This truism was allotted further credence in the draped recesses of Rosings Park Manor and at the hands of its young mistress. However, this came to pass in no such manner as to excite the concern of her companion, Mrs. Jenkinson. Indeed, it was what one might expect from a girl of middling sensibility and not high spirits. For already predisposed to introversion, Anne de Bourgh sought further obscuration between the covers of the nearest book. Regrettably, both her mother and her companion were quite unaware that those nearest happened not to be the most scholarly of choices.

Most correct in her public conduct, Lady Anne de Bourgh was a little less circumspect when under the guidance of her own free choice. When out from under spying eyes, her mind was quite curious. That in and of itself was scandalous, for any well brought up young woman was taught first and foremost that curiosity not only killed the cat, had she been a female feline, she had it coming. Curiosity was a masculine trait—any female exhibiting such comportment was to be branded in compleat want of gentility.

Excused from dance lessons and possessing no ear for music, little was provided but needlework to engage the mind of a girl whose governess was disinclined to tempt her intellect with tutorials. Although she had little taste for wit, Anne's feelings were not insignificant. What her family and acquaintances did not understand was that Lady Anne's dolorous countenance reflected general indisposition rather than a sombre spirit.

Hence, it would have been a compleat astonishment to them all that her taste in books did not favour treatises or biographies. Indeed, the waters of her mind may not have coursed deep, but it was not for lack of stimulation. Lady Anne had become an unadulterated devotee of England's most shameless novellas of romance.

To her great misfortune, her dubious taste in literature could not begin to be satisfied by Rosings's grand library. The tomes that sat so ponderously upon those shelves may have been important, but so were they ancient. Any literature containing the most innocent allusion to the excitation of the senses had been carefully excised. The bareness of emotion upon those shelves led Anne to believe that romance was only lately discovered. Hence, she craved contemporary works. And although she enjoyed poetry, it was novels of forbidden love, mystery, and intrigue that most piqued her fancy.

There was but one place she could quench her thirst for self-discovery without unwanted scrutiny. Her bed-chamber itself would not do (too many maids about). However, she was left to her own devices beneath her bedcovers. There she could escape both her mother's unsparing surveillance and the more easily evaded watch of Mrs. Jenkinson. But then only in the dark of night. She carefully (very, very carefully) took a candle beneath her counterpane and thrust off the shackles of inhibition at last to allow sheer pleasure to envelop her. Emboldened with every passing night she lay undiscovered, she betook herself a little farther, delved a little deeper. So furtive was this employment, no one was wise of it at all.

Books often cost as much as a guinea and even the lending library was far beyond the reach of common folk. For a young woman of title, one would have thought them as available as any trinket for which she might hanker. Surprisingly, Anne was in no better access to ready cash than the next person. Where a young lady of modest means would have had a few coins hid away and tied with a knot in the toe of a stocking, Anne was not so fortunate. She may have lived in a grand house and dressed in finery, but she had neither the coins nor the wherewithal to purchase her own books. Still, she was not without resources. The proffering of a gold eardrop influenced a maid-servant that she was quite happy to dig into her own pocket and take a trip to the circulating library on her mistress's behalf. Anne was not of a deceitful nature, but she reasoned (much like most in want of rationale for a deceit) that if she neither denied nor admitted to squirreling away literature of questionable taste, her honesty was not compromised.

All this hole-and-corner activity was demanded due to her mother's denunciation of any and all modern authors (by her wholesale extirpation of any and all works of sensibility in her library, it was apparent that she was not all that keen on certain authors past, either). Anne knew that such writing was shameful because her mother dictated that opinion to all within her ken.

Indeed, Lady Catherine despised all things *au courant*. Not unlike other aristocrats of a certain age, she was disposed to believe any alteration beyond that with which she was familiar in her own youth was of no good to anyone. Her ladyship powdered her hair with Gowland's no less prodigiously than her face (until it was not freckles she was endeavouring to hide, but age spots). Moreover, she continued to have her dresses cut to the same patterns she had used for her wedding trousseau. She laughed in the face of (or refused to acknowledge) the latest fashion with the abandon that only the very richest could without societal condemnation. The use of a quizzing-glass necessary to peruse their tiny type somehow lent newspapers some credibility, hence they were occasionally tolerated. (Invariably, reading of some Whig outrage would cause her to toss it into the fire, and was she in the vicinity the resultant smoke would cost Anne a coughing fit.) However, Lady Catherine abhorred romanticism in any form. Was not Byron an incestuous Lothario? And that upstart Shelly—expelled from Oxford, his wife a suicide! Blatherings from such men as these were not fit for decent society!

Anne had not dared broach the subject with her mother directly, but she had overheard quite enough as Lady Catherine lectured Mrs. Jenkinson to keep a watchful eye out for such dross lest her daughter be introduced to frivolity and immorality.

Lady Catherine's daughter did not consider herself of a rebellious spirit. In her pursuit of new works, she understood herself merely in want of innocent diversion. *The Castle of Wolenbach* and *The Midnight Bell* were uniformly abhorred by all good society (by her mother's account), hence Anne held them in the greatest esteem. Yet her favourites by far were *The Mysteries of Udolpho*. (The chapter that told of the murderous spectacle behind the black curtain was read with particular relish—the telling of strange and ferocious rumblings sent her into the most tremulous state no matter how many times she read of them.)

Although her mother also looked with equally evil eye upon ladies' magazines, Lady Anne occasionally purloined a copy of *Bon Ton* from Mrs. Jenkinson's knitting basket (Anne was happy to know she was not the only morally compromised soul in the household). Had Lady Catherine actually taken up the magazine, however, she would have been mollified to know that the writers of *Bon Ton* warned their readers that if "women of little experience" read romantic nonsense they would be evermore disposed to "mistake the urgency of bodily wants with the violence of delicate passion." Once Anne read that denouncement, no reasoning could have withstood her determination to read more.

Anne kept these vessels of romanticism deep in the corner of her garderobe and sat in eye-batting, slack-jawed innocence (her skirt-folds not betraying what they hid) whenever Mrs. Jenkinson happened to gain her room unexpectedly. Had she understood that many well-bred young women read such novels without compunction she would have been most disappointed.

Although this sentimental inclination was only gratified in her most recent memory, it had lain inert for some time, only needing a face on which to hang such longings. The countenance that came to personify romantic love to Anne was one that she had known the entirety of her life.

Although she was in his company at least twice a year, Fitzwilliam Darcy was wholly unaware of the esteem that Anne had come to hold for him. Women far more handsome and accomplished than she vied for his attention with indecorous tenacity. He was not only the most eligible, he was the most handsome man she had ever beheld. Beyond this admiration of his person, Anne felt a kinship of sorts. For much like herself, he was not a person in whom happiness overflowed in mirth. Indeed, all the stars were in position for an engagement to be formed: He had understanding and uprightness in figure and form, his station was equal to her own. In her deepest ruminations, Anne may have questioned just why she should be so very fortunate to win the love of such an admirable man. But having been born into untold luxury, she could only believe it fell to God's infinite wisdom—reciprocity for poor health and suffering from an under-abundance of mother-love. Proof, perchance, that she was not so insignificant in His eyes as her mother declared. It did not occur to her that marital love would not be part of the bargain that would be struck.

Anne was well aware of her personal limitations, but so long and so relentlessly had her mother enforced the notion of the unification of the houses of Darcy and de Bourgh through marriage, she eventually accepted it as less a probability than a certainty. Other than general cowardice, the only reason she had never once disagreed with her mother's dictatorial declarations was that her mother had arranged for *him* to be hers. If her mother willed it, it would come to pass. This, above all else, Anne knew to be true. Lady Catherine de Bourgh was never opposed. Time would come when she and Mr. Darcy would be together, forever. Happily ever after—just as in her favourite novels.

Until that time, however, she worshipped him well, but from afar.

Despite the fact of their eventual engagement, she had sat across the room in a mortified stupor upon each occasion she was in his company. She had dared not to speak lest she be sent into some indecorous fit by her respiratory system. Such had been her fate upon the very first time she gathered the fortitude to issue a comment to him. It was a simple inquiry—she had practiced it for days waiting for just the right occasion to approach him.

Voice tremulous, but resolute, she inquired with what she supposed was a note of coquetry, "Do you find the cooler weather to your liking?"

It was not a particularly weighty query, but it was the best she could manage. He gave every intention of answering in the affirmative, but as he began to form a reply he stopt and looked at her with an expression of what could only be described as puzzled revulsion. For she had no more than looked up at him whilst awaiting his response, than an intemperate tickle began in her left nostril. She did her best to alleviate it by what she hoped was an inconspicuous twitch of her nose, but that only enkindled the itch. By that time he had quite forgotten what was under discussion and was staring quite openly at her spasmodic nose. In the absence of comment from Mr. Darcy upon her astute observation upon the temperateness of the day, she endeavoured to renew the direction of the conversation.

"Is it not…not…naahchooo!"

It had not been a sweet, little kittenish sniff—rather it was the trumpustuous snark of a bewhiskered old man, so forceful that it nearly blew the ends of Mr. Darcy's neckcloth over his shoulders.

He had issued only a mild "Pray, bless you," but took out his pocket-square and brushed the resultant droplets of her nasal lubricant from his frockcoat with considerable deliberation before extending it, with all due politeness, to her. She fled in mortification and never ventured a word with him again.

Her yearning, however, could not be stilled. In each novel she read, she saw herself as the heroine, Mr. Fitzwilliam Darcy, the hero. And never once as the heroine did she sneeze in his face.

When it came to pass that Mr. Darcy chose another, Anne spoke of it not. Deep within her tattered heart, she had feared that it had been indeed a notion far too fanciful actually to come to pass. Her mother, however, was inconsolable. Unused as her mother was to interference in the consummation of any of her directives, this was not unexpected. But this time her rage was more severe and unrelenting. As her mother railed and fumed, Anne had little time to find pity for herself. So aggrieved was Lady Catherine, Anne became uneasy. It was as if she, not Anne, were the injured party. During the many of her interminable rampages, Anne had fair time to ponder it all.

Her rumination incited further disquiet as she recalled how her mother had always been most attentive to Mr. Darcy. Very attentive. Almost coquettish. Anne then recalled numerous instances when she had caught sight of her mother's gaze sweeping the length of his figure that, in retrospect, was most unseemly in manner. Instinctively, she wondered just who had been meant for whom.

Anne had ridden in the coach the day her mother confronted Miss Elizabeth Bennet. She was not unaware of the reason for their trip. Initially, she had been hopeful that it was all a misunderstanding—that there was no engagement in place between Miss Bennet and Mr. Darcy. There was not, but that there was nothing official was inconsequential.

Anne had sunk back in the corner of the seat, hoping against hope that her countenance was shielded from the spectacle her mother had become. For, as it happened, Lady Anne was of a pragmatic nature. Although she had known her mother to trample all obstacles by sheer determination, Anne recognised when a cause was lost. She had seen it in Miss Bennet's eyes then, she had seen it in Mr. Darcy's eyes when her mother repeated the particulars of their visit to Longbourn. For Anne, it was time then to move on, broken-hearted or not. It took several years for her mother to come to that conclusion.

Of the grand scheme set forth by Lady Catherine to hie to Bath upon an urgent search for a betrothal for her daughter, Lady Anne herself was unwitting. She knew only that, once again, her health demanded repair.

The Pangs of Love Run Deep

When the dressing bell awoke Darcy that evening subsequent of his engagement in physical congress with his wife, he was perplexed. He was in compleat puzzlement whether he had just enjoyed a particularly convincing dream or his wife, indeed, had afforded him her favours. So deep was his sleep and disordered his recollections, he did not immediately arise. He lay unmoving for a moment to gather his bearings, gazing at the tiny motes of dust suspended in the evening sunlight. He was certain that he recollected a conversation between them regarding a letter—and a misunderstanding over it. If that occurred, so must have the resolution. Surely he could not have slept that soundly—it was far too distinct.

He then sat upright, looking about the room for confirmation that he had not been alone. He went so far as to examine the coverlet beneath him for the tell-tale evidence that it had been only a dream, but there was nothing but the faint remains of Elizabeth's scent.

Whilst he quit the room and made for his dressing-chamber, he remained in that disorder. Mechanically, he lifted his wrists allowing Goodwin to ready him for dinner. He still felt as if he were in some state of fugue, a sleep-walker through his own life.

His head was only beginning to clear when he passed Elizabeth's dressing-chamber. He stopt to determine if she was still within. He heard nothing and made his way directly to the dining-parlour. There he saw himself to be tardy of their guests. Elizabeth sat in her place at one end, Mr. and Mrs. Gardiner were on either side of the table. Although Elizabeth gave him a slight nod, he was unable to look directly upon her, for he had to apologize for his tardiness, insist that Mr. Gardiner keep his seat, and bow to Mrs. Gardiner before taking his place opposite Elizabeth. The Gardiners were newly come to visit and their observations and stories were still new enough to keep the conversation happy without much response from him. Although he was never at ease to make small talk, this evening found him even less conversationally inclined.

Whilst Elizabeth and Mrs. Gardiner grew increasingly animated with conversation, Mr. Gardiner gave himself leave to remark upon them to Darcy, "Do look at them, Mr. Darcy—thick as two inkle-weavers. What schemes do you think they are concocting for us even as I speak?"

It did appear to Darcy that Elizabeth and her aunt were deep in collusion of some kind or another, and he smiled benignly at Mr. Gardiner. That gentleman continued to talk affectionately of the ladies, when from his pocket came an odd sound. It sounded much like the yowling of an imperilled cat. Startled, Elizabeth and Mrs. Gardiner ceased conversing and all turned to Mr. Gardiner in alarm. Darcy went so far as to half-stand, prepared to protect in whatever manner he must. Initially, Mr. Gardiner's countenance mirrored their trepidation, but directly he dug into the pocket of his waistcoat and produced the offender.

Sitting in the palm of his hand was a watch, no bigger than a half-crown, that had clearly gone ill. Its initial screech quickly deteriorated into a buzz, then it clanked twice and fell silent.

"Mr. Gardiner!" declared his wife. "I begged you to not waste your money on such nonsense. It has not lasted a month!"

Mr. Gardiner guffawed at his own folly and held the watch up by its fob, allowing it to dangle a moment ere the entire contents exploded with a dull plonk, springs and tiny gears scattering upon the tablecloth.

"It looks to have been a repeater," Darcy said politely.

"Every quarter hour," replied Mr. Gardiner sadly.

"Yes," said Mrs. Gardiner, "for the entire of a four-week."

She shook her head ruefully, but could not keep her countenance and began also to laugh.

"I should have been more cautious," said Mr. Gardiner. "It was but an English ticker. I thought better of our own countrymen's craftsmanship."

"You, dear husband, thought better of nothing but your pocket!" said Mrs. Gardiner, then to Elizabeth, "I have long fretted him for his economy. A watch deserves more consideration than you give to that man you call your tailor."

Mr. Gardiner endeavoured to explain, "She abuses me unmercifully for the failings of my frock-coats."

"If I would allow it," interjected Mrs. Gardiner, "he would, no doubt, buy them from a rag-man. How can so generous a man to his family be so parsimonious to himself?"

Mr. Gardiner said, "I will answer that, Elizabeth. I do so for the single purpose of caution. I dress to discourage highwaymen—for a thread-bare coat is better than chain-mail in protecting against robbery. Am I wrong, Mr. Darcy?"

All laughed and Darcy raised his glass and tipped his head in recognition of that wisdom. Mrs. Gardiner put a doting hand upon her husband's forearm and shook her head with affectionate acceptance of her husband's idiosyncrasies. He took her hand and gave it a squeeze and they in turn gazed upon each other with all the regard that only a marriage of settled affection could provide. Afore Mrs. Gardiner loosed his forearm, she did the most unexpected thing. She reached out and gave Mr. Gardiner a pinch in the side. Mr. Gardiner's face was turned away from him, so he could not gauge that man's reaction. It appeared *not* to have been an offence.

Darcy quickly looked down at his plate, knowing that he was not to have seen what she had done. His face had crimsoned so that he had no idea whether Mr. Gardiner's had done the same. When he heard the Gardiners once again teasing each other, he thought it safe to look again across his table and to his wife. With almost eerie synchronism, Elizabeth also looked up. Although they had exchanged words with each other and the Gardiners, he had not truly gazed upon his wife since his late arrival. Nor had he given more thought to what just had come to pass that afternoon. In that instant her eyes exposed to him that nothing had been a dream. It had all been as he had hoped.

It was a meal more interminable than any he had endured. So anxious was he to have a private moment with Elizabeth, it was all he could do not to bolt his food and demand the next course. As he sat waiting for the servants to make their way about the table, he recalled a meal that incited in him similar agitation.

It was the last he partook in his cousin's home in Lille. It was the same evening that he imprudently asked Juliette to post his letter to Elizabeth. It had begun badly and went to the worse. He had been seated next to a woman, just a girl actually, who at first glance looked remarkably like Elizabeth. He had only just recovered from that astonishment when he happened to see Juliette Clisson amongst the other diners. It occurred to him that evening ended for him in a remarkably similar state of mind as this one had begun. That one too had come about upon the heels of exhaustion, but added to it was too much wine, too little food, and a melancholy over missing Elizabeth that rendered him all but comatose as soon as his head had fallen to the pillow.

But he was not entirely insensible for he had dreamt—dreams of uncommon authenticity. He had dreamt Elizabeth was with him and that they had begun to make love. But he had awakened to find otherwise. A voluptuous female form had been atop him, but even in his drunkenness, he knew it was not Elizabeth. He had dislodged the offending female, stumbled to his feet and pushed her out the door—furious to have surrendered himself so compleatly to drink. He had been far too much in his cups to have been certain who the woman was, all he knew was that she was not Elizabeth and he would not have her.

In recalling that earlier dream, the reason for his present discomposure fell apparent to him. Upon this occasion, however, it had not been a dream, it *had* been Elizabeth.

At last dinner was over and, thankfully, the Gardiners expressed the desire to take an early evening. Elizabeth had a merry smile upon her face when she kissed Mrs. Gardiner's cheek. She and Darcy stood at the bottom of the stairs as they bid them goodnight. Elizabeth turned to go to the drawing-room, but Darcy, instituting that inexplicable flick of the head (one she had never mastered) bidding his servants withdraw, caught her hand and drew her into a narrow doorway that led to the stillroom. It was narrow enough that a portly scullery maid would have had to turn sideways to make her way through it; hence, as they stood facing each other, there was little room between them.

"Lizzy," he whispered, "shall we take an early evening ourselves? We have no one to entertain but ourselves."

"As you wish," she replied.

Neither, however, made a move from their intimate niche.

"As I wish?" said he. "To be sure."

She dropped her head back and her hands to her sides, surrendering to any and all pleasures he was of a mind to bestow. She was entirely prepared to ascertain if their afternoon amorous combat had diminished his want of her in any capacity. She waited, however, in vain. For, rather than kiss her, he stepped away. When he did, he took hold of her hand, bringing her with him from beneath the shadow of the doorway. He did not notice that frown lines had appeared between her brows, for he thereupon reached behind her and under her, lifting her off her feet and into his arms. She gasped. Darcy, however, had to shuffle her a bit to determine he had a good hand-hold, she kicking a bit in reluctance to allow him his way without her knowledge of his course.

"Pray, be still, Lizzy," he cautioned, "I shall drop you."

The single thing that she did not want to do at this very romantic juncture was to giggle. But she did.

"*Lizzy*," he threatened.

"Forgive me," said she, letting out another giggle, and then with that another, "Forgive me."

He took her then up the stairs to their bed-chamber, he shushing and she giggling until they reached the door. He lodged his knee against the doorpost, rested her upon his leg, and fumbled for the knob.

"Allow me," she said, reaching for it herself.

"I can *do* it," he insisted, as his leg began to lose its wedge.

Finally the door relented, but even with so wide a doorway, Darcy managed to bump her head as he brought her through it.

"I am cruelly used!" she mocked great offence.

"I would beg leave to apologise," he answered, "but I am much occupied with taming this wench to whom I am married."

With that he tossed her in the middle of the bed. She drew herself to her knees and used them to manoeuvre her way to the edge of the bed where he stood waiting. He began to undo his neckcloth, but she took over that duty allowing his hands to move to the narrowing of her waist. He let them rest there, his thumbs strumming just below her ribs. It tickled slightly, but mirth was then lost to her and she did not laugh.

"There was time when your two hands spanned my waist."

"Did they? I do not have that recollection."

"Your memory does you service," she did smile then.

"Lizzy..." he began. He had intended to say more, but his words were smothered for she had taken his face in her hands and kissed him quiet. A small whimper interrupted them, both looking at the other in question from whence it came. Immediately came the clicking and scratching of a large dog's paws as she clamboured from beneath the bed.

Elizabeth said of Cressida, "She must have had a bad dream."

Cressida sat down next to the bed, her big tail whapping on the floor. Darcy said nothing, but did not reach to give the dog a reassuring pet. Rather, he walked to the door and opened it wide in silent directive. Cressida slowly heaved herself to her feet and even more slowly, but surely, swayed her way out of the room. The old dog did not so much as give a start when the big door slammed just as she cleared it. She just kept walking peacefully down the corridor.

The Road to Restoration

That afternoon Elizabeth had left Darcy in much the same attitude as she had found him. So similar was his repose that to a casual observer, it might not have seemed she had been there at all. For her, however, the hours succeeding that brief encounter were a bit indistinct. She undertook her motherly obligations dutifully, but her mind was not fully employed. In that her motherly undertakings at that time could be placed no higher than serving as a spigot, she felt no undue guilt for such a lapse. In body, she cuddled and cooed at the robust child in her arms as he nursed, yet her thoughts still dwelt with her husband. Those were more than dry musings.

She was alternately mortified and exultant—and embarrassed that she felt both of those sentiments so keenly.

It was not that she had planned badly; it was simply that it had not gone as she had planned. She had fully intended to have him account for his connexion with Miss Clisson. Indeed, she had given great study as to how this conversation would ensue and carefully prepared her questions. All was forgot in a trice. She had leapt upon him like some jealous (and possibly demented) harpy. His astonishment was quite reasonable. His answer was quite reasonable. Indeed, the only part of the conversation that was not reasonable seemed to have been hers. Although there were still a few clarifications she would pursue, she was altogether humbled to have harboured such suspicions. She was most particularly unhappy to have presented them with such vehemence.

He had not, however, seemed particularly vexed by her unwarranted inquiries. Indeed, he was wholly forbearing of it all. He could at least have had the good manners to have expressed some sort of pique so she could have justification to employ some part of righteous indignation. In this, he was wholly uncooperative. Not that she maintained any grievance against him. As he was a man capable of superior recompense, it was quite the opposite. Indeed, he had not left a strong impression of disfavour with her whatsoever. Amongst those intimate trappings of love he *did* leave was an impression quite of another sort.

As her office at that moment was the very apex of maternalism, she endeavoured not to think of either his methods nor his means. She endeavoured not to think of them for a great long while. But as her present occupation was of a sort that inspired rumination, she had little success. Hence, the intervening hours between when she left him abed and coming together at dinner did not wear out her disconcertion. She had much to consider.

Several things were proved to her in that brief interlude atop their bed. She had been reassured of his love (although she was disinclined to think herself in need there, as a general rule, one can never quite be reassured of that often enough). Too, she had been convinced of her allurement to him. Moreover, without a doubt, he would soon steal a look under her chemise. She had concluded, however, that if when he did he was appalled at what he saw, so be it. She did not fall with child and birth two enormous babes without explicit help from him. Moreover, she had lately been of a mind that perhaps there was something to all the nudging and winking presumptuousness that her husband's virility alone spawned twins. She was not inclined to place blame, but it was not her feet that were the size of iron firedogs.

She sniffed that she had spent her time fostering such botheration.

Elizabeth had come to all these conclusions solely by her own means. Her Aunt Gardiner was a great and good friend, but such was their connexion, she could never confide her most private perplexities to her. Whilst Jane was her closest confidant in most matters, in the subject of carnal connexions, her ear remained unused as well. This was more for the protection of Jane's sensibilities than Elizabeth's. Insofar as Elizabeth was aware, Jane had never even removed her night-dress in front of Bingley. Hence, Jane's advice regarding the titillation value of the post-pregnancy figure upon one's husband would not be particularly weighty. As she was neither bold enough to risk censure nor desperate enough to endure the embarrassment, Elizabeth was determined to keep her own counsel on the entire vexation.

Soon after Jane had hied to Kirkland Hall, Elizabeth had sent an invitation to the Gardiners. Her aunt was beside herself over their favourite niece's blessed event and anxious to come and see all for herself. It was in all ways a pleasure to have the Gardiners' company. Their happy manners and easy ways always soothed her when she was nettled by some preoccupation. Darcy had always been happy to have them, too. Whether this fell to the Gardiners having been the agents that begat their unification or that, quite simply, they were the only ones of her relations with whom he could bear to spend ten minutes together, she remained uncertain. She did know that both of those elements were pivotal in his regard. The first was simply chance, but the second absolved him of the accusation that he could not suffer any of her relatives at all.

She looked forward to them at their dinner table that night beyond her general esteem, for she preferred a short breathing spell to prepare her thoughts before encountering her husband at leisure.

It all went quite splendidly—although Darcy seemed to be almost as out of sorts as she. Whilst he smiled at the appropriate intervals, he spoke but little. She knew this because she looked upon him slyly, but with undue constancy. Even in the candlelight, she saw that he looked pale. She had noticed that of him before, but thought that loss of colour in his countenance was due only to his having kept so much to the house. Once he began to take to the saddle, she believed that the late summer sun would have tanned him once again to that burnished hue that he bore upon returning from the Continent. But it had not. Indeed, dark half-moons were becoming visible beneath the fringe of his lower lashes—a condition she had not recalled of him other than in the darkest of circumstances. That was most troubling, for he had every reason to be in the best of spirits. She supposed that is what pricked the flight of fancy her own imagination took. Something was clearly amiss.

Elizabeth's preoccupation with her husband's well-being did not keep her from witnessing her aunt's teasing pinch of Mr. Gardiner's ribs. This observation incited within her several emotions—primarily that of happy surprise. Elizabeth was thoroughly pleased to see evidence of a happy marriage improved by a bit of mischievous affection. Second, and soon to overwhelm the first, was that her perception of the occurrence and that of Darcy were not unalike.

The realisation that they both saw and interpreted the incident with exact like-mindedness was a remarkable revelation. When their eyes met with such uncanny synchronicity, a frisson of excitement raced down her spine. Immediately every botheration nagging her had evaporated. She almost jumped to her feet and dashed for the door, thinking of feigning a swoon coming on. But she had hung fast to the mast. With careful planning and Mrs. Littlepage's bounteous bosom at hand, she knew the night would be theirs even before the Gardiners begged an early evening. Indeed, in light of the twinkle each seemed to have adorning their eyes, their predisposition to weariness was not altogether an astonishment.

Nor was Darcy taking her hand and ducking with her into a doorway. She, of course, had no idea what configuration it would take, but she was fully prepared for him to take the initiative that she had so long been desiring. (She supposed was it necessary to name the aggressor in their earlier engagement, it would have been declared as mutually agreed upon.) Perchance it was having her anticipation so delightfully rewarded that set her to giggling like a girl, she could not be certain. She supposed that it was that in combination with a fit of nerves. Regardless, silliness was not at all what she wanted to present just then, but could not bring her giddiness to heel. At least it remained unmanageable until the confines of the bed-chamber and the prospect of his touch at last settled her.

Cressida's interruption had not been invited, but it was not entirely abhorred. Elizabeth was happy for an excuse to gather her wits—and the beat of her heart, for it beat with such fury she felt her ears throbbing. By the time Darcy had taken the few steps back from the door, her wits were in no better order and they were additionally troubled by a burgeoning concupiscence that threatened to cause her to start tearing at his costume. In fortune, their minds were still alike, for he began to discard articles of his clothing ere he arrived back to her open arms. She then assaulted once again the stubborn knot of his neckcloth whilst he began, with barely restrained impatience, to fumble with the buttons at the back of her dress.

Forthwith, he quite gave up undoing the buttons properly and gave a great tug, ripping the buttons loose with enough force to send several pinging across the floor. She threw back her head and laughed at his impetuosity and to once again revel in a compleat surrender to desire.

"You have destroyed my least objectionable frock!" she laughed again.

"They are both objectionable. I shall destroy the other one as well," he retorted.

"Pray, what shall you have me wear? My night-dress all the day long?"

"Of course not. You shall wear nothing and lie with me beneath the counterpane until the seamstress arrives."

His hands began the undulating search of her body that was quite capable of turning her limbs liquescent. She could also sense the lubricant of passion begin to form in the farthest reaches of her nether-regions. She very nearly succumbed to compleat abandon, but his mention of impending nakedness reasserted that niggling little reservation.

Wrapping her arms about his neck, she whispered in his ear, "Pray, put out the light."

She felt only the slightest hesitation before he ceased his caresses, saying, "As you wish."

Before he went to the candelabrum he shed his shirt, hence she had the pleasure of admiring the inverted triangle of his back as he leaned, reached out, and, with firm deliberation, snuffed each candle between forefinger and thumb. When he turned to come to her, she could only see his outline and she immediately realised the disadvantage of him not seeing her when they made love. (Briefly, she considered whether he would entertain the notion of wearing a blindfold, but just as quickly discarded it.) With the apprehension over any disappointment he might have undergone removed, her inhibitions evaporated as well. Hence, it was a glorious and lengthy restoration of marital bliss.

And thus the best sleep either had had since Ascension Day.

Bliss Restored

Having slept through the night without one interruption was always an odd sensation for a new mother. Elizabeth Darcy was no different. The maternal call to flee to her children's bedsides to see if they had survived the night without her personal supervision was keen, but she suppressed it.

Rather, she lay laconically amidst the bed-clothes, pleased to no end to not be awakened through insistent, squalling necessity. To once again have *him* awaken *her*—to be sensible of another type of hunger as his morning pride nestled against her, to suppress a shudder as he drew the backs of his fingers the length of her legs was a savour beyond measure. It took nothing more that those few moments of his burgeoning wakefulness to bestir in her desires and longings that were quite un-maternal.

All this he accomplished before he opened his eyes.

With his fingers, he combed her hair from the back of her neck. She anticipated that he would kiss her there. Instead, he puckishly rubbed the stubble of his beard against her shoulder. Understanding her role compleatly, she gave a small shriek as if of annoyance, then they both enjoyed a quiet laugh.

He nestled even closer, "Oh, how I have missed you, Lizzy."

"But I have been right here beside you every night."

That was more accusation than observation.

"Have you?"

Elizabeth Bennet Darcy was not of uncertain nature. Indeed, the few times she had been confounded, it had been at her husband's hands—sometimes quite literally. She was confounded then and did not immediately reply. Hearing the hurt in his voice was off-putting. After all, had she not all but thrown herself into his arms by luring him to their little outdoor tryst? Perchance that had not ended impeccably, but it had been concocted and engineered entirely by *her* design. He merely followed her lead. She did not think it unreasonable for him to return the favour. After all, he was the husband—she refused to chase about after him as if she were some love-starved Amazon. (Well, in truth, she was no great hand with a bow, but she had been increasingly love-starved.)

Her quiet influenced him to turn her upon her back so he could gain the expression her countenance bore. He half-rose upon one elbow, allowing her to fall back. He was not entirely happy with what he saw. Placing his forehead to hers, he cupped her face in his hand and kissed her lips.

"I think we could find better employment during your brief respite from motherhood than placing blame," said he.

"Well said," she said agreeably before her attention was stolen a by distant sound. "Pray, did you hear that?"

"I hear nothing."

"I am certain that I did," she insisted. "Perchance..."

"I hear *nothing*," he insisted. "All is well. If it is not, Nurse will be here in a trice."

"In a trice?"

"To be sure."

As a deliberate diversionary tactic he began to kiss her neck.

"Mmmm..." said she, "how easily I am beguiled from duty."

It was only when she saw the work of the light streaming through the windows making a chequered pattern upon the opposing wall that she realised the jeopardy in which she had placed herself. Their night's love-making was so all encompassing that she had compleatly lost all inhibition. Those forgotten apprehensions reasserted themselves in the harsh light of morn. She was absolutely naked—in all senses of the word.

As his lips slid from hers and began to nuzzle and kiss her shoulders, she steeled herself for what was to come.

"No," she heard herself say.

He stopt.

"No?" he shook his head slightly as if to reassure himself he had heard her correctly, then his voice altered immediately into his deeper, more formal speech, "Forgive my forwardness."

"I meant not for you to cease," she waffled. "I meant for you to...linger."

Thereupon *she* kissed *him*.

The liberal and meticulous craftsman he believed himself to be demanded that he inquire the specifics of her wishes. "Kiss you? Where? Here?"

He once again began his demarche down her body. Thereupon, she made a desperate feint and grabbed him by the hair.

"No," she said once again.

He laid back, his head propped upon one elbow, his hair askew.

"What?" he said quite impatiently. "Tell me precisely what you desire if I am to have any notion of what I am to do."

"I meant only to forestall the inevitable."

"The inevitable?" his voice was once again deep and a bit starched. Then it softened, he rolled closer, "Lizzy, do you want me now or do you not? You have only to say and I will do your bidding. Perchance, you are still weak. You need to go to your babies..."

"Our babies," she interrupted.

"Our babies," he repeated, and went on, "You have only to speak what is true. Your will be done. Even if that truth is that you do not want me as you once did."

"Yes. I must be honest," she said more to herself than to him. "This is difficult."

"You do not need speak the words," he said, "if they are too difficult. I shall understand implicitly."

"No, you do not understand anything at all," she then was impatient. "It is not about you or my wanting you—for I love you in all the ways I always have. But..."

It was clear that there had been quite enough shilly-shallying about. She threw back the coverlet, exposing herself compleatly. She then lay in abject mortification, but increasingly defiant. Defiantly mortified was no easy posture, but she managed as she bethought the situation. Let him see how altered she was. Let him see his wife as she was then and always would be—forever altered by bearing his children. She did not say the words, but had he looked at the flash of umbrage in her eyes he would have understood her feelings without being told.

"Lizzy, why do you torture me thusly?"

"Torture you? Torture *you*?"

His expression was apparent—as was a rather impressive arousal that she happened to glimpse. Both implied that he was in no way displeased with what he saw. Indeed, he was so pleased that he made what could only be characterized as a lunge for her.

He planted his lips upon hers and grasped her thigh, sliding his hand around and beneath it and wrapping her leg over his hip. He buried his face against her and then smothered her abdomen and any and all adjacent areas erotically inclined with long, lingering kisses. From there, shall we say, nature took its course. However sweetly and fervently they had made love the night before, this was at variance with every part of those couplings.

"Far too long, Lizzy," he murmured. "It has been far too long…"

"Yes," she agreed, although not quite certain to what it was she was agreeing, she was far too compromised by passion.

Admittedly, she found his reaction to her disfigurement somewhat odd. However, his dutiful attention to that and all and sundry kept her in eye-fluttering distraction for so long that the incongruity of it seemed quite beside the point. Rather than off-put, he was aroused—aroused, infused, inflamed, and altogether impaled on the pangs of lust (or to be more exact, she was impaled on the pangs of his lust). And because he was aroused, she was aroused. She was aroused to a vexatious degree. Hence, the whole of his away was very nearly recompensed in the space of that one morning.

When at last the reunification of *mons veneris* and *mons pubis* was compleat, Elizabeth was quite astonished to see that their enormous bed was still standing in the same spot and had not rattled its way across the floor. (She, most certainly, had been turned over, under, and around so many times that they were both lying sideways across the opposite side of the bed themselves—which was why she initially thought it was the bed that had shimmied its way thence.) She lay on her stomach, he on his back, rivulets of perspiration slinking down crevices still quivering in achievement.

Darcy lay so still she thought him once again asleep. She smiled to herself, and closed her eyes re-experiencing the pleasure he wrought. She had betimes wondered if anything could be sublime as those times past—the ones that she had held in her sweetest recollections whilst they were apart. She realised then that her memory had been far too constrained. Whilst she marvelled at his vigour, the man whom she had thought fast asleep rose upon one elbow. They had spoken very little during the previous interlude. (Their intonations had been largely relegated to moans, groans, and the odd whimper.) He did not speak then, but reached out and, sitting up, he bid her turn to him and as he had often done in years past, drew his hand the length of her body, softly tracing his finger tips along her curves. Only the rucking of her nipples announced that even with so light a touch, his hand had wrought considerable disturbance.

She lay back luxuriating in his attentiveness and allowed this scrutiny, tacitly replacing the office of Nursing Mother with that of Desirable Woman. His fingertips and thumb spread wide as his hand made its way across her body, her belly trembling as if it was the first time he had touched her thusly. In the cheery morning light, all inhibitions were gone. When his hand stopt just below her navel, however, she realised then with goodly haste (and no little mortification) that he was gazing upon her sagging, red-streaked belly. Instinctively, she drew her knee and elbow together and half-turned downward in a feeble attempt to keep from his eyes a disfigurement of considerable abhorrence. She shut her eyes tightly, cringing with an embarrassment that was metamorphosing into indignation with utmost rapidity. The first gentle nudge of his hand at her hip was ignored.

"Lizzy," he coaxed.

"Do not," she said. "Please do not look upon me so keenly."

He relented and reposed once again upon his elbow. She scrambled for a corner of the bed-sheet and drew it across her breasts.

"You are as supple as an eel, Lizzy," he smiled, "You have not altered whatsoever."

"How can you speak such a fiction!" she exclaimed. "I despise condescension such as that."

He looked to be puzzled—and hurt.

"Why do you not allow me to say my mind?" he asked. "And impugn my honour as well? I have never spoken an untruth to you."

"The first time you look upon me and that I am so clearly altered, it is demeaning to pretend otherwise."

He said quietly, "It is not the first time."

"Since your return," she clarified dryly, her gaze offering no quarter.

Again he said, "It is *not* the first time."

"Where?"

Quite without her knowing, her eyebrow rose askance.

"Whilst you bathed."

She shook her head, thinking she had caught him in an untruth, "I have bathed of late in a bathing-gown."

"Not," he said firmly, "initially."

"From the beginning," she exclaimed, "I have had no secrets from you?"

He pursed his lips at his dilemma, disinclined to admit to all the unseemly spying upon her that he had been guilty of in the preceding months. He was weighing the options before him, those which would allow him to retain some semblance of dignity, when she offered him escape.

She said, "Accident only could have you discover me thusly. What say you?"

"To be sure," he smiled.

They lay in that posture for a few moments, implicitly exchanging expressions of love and adoration, ere came a scratching at the door, behind which a cry that threatened to turn into a wail was heard. It did not sound to be Cressida.

Lydia Scandalises Once Again

It all came about on the heels of Mr. Bennet's untimely passing.

Elizabeth's beloved father had travelled to Pemberley to advise his favourite daughter of the news of Major Wickham's death on the battlefield near a fly-speck of a place called Waterloo. Little did he expect that he would return to Longbourn the principal in his own cortege. But he had.

Pierced by loss, the family soldiered on those first few weeks of summer in '15. Together they, as their sister Mary so pompously put it, "Poured into the wounded bosoms of each other the balm of sisterly consolation."

Inevitably, Mary's sisterly consolation involved a great deal of Christian recrimination. Indeed, poor, uncompanionable Mary Bennet always seemed to have her hair hanging somewhat out of curl. Those most grievous of circumstances were tailor-made for her tireless proselytization. Although Jane and Elizabeth were not particularly eager to listen, they suffered Mary's pedantic leanings with far more forbearance than did Kitty and Lydia—and for that matter, than did Mrs. Bennet. Indeed, as Mary had little to promote herself as a wife, Mrs. Bennet suffered her not merely little, but not at all.

Mary was plainest of the five Bennet daughters and to suffer by daily comparison to them was mortification in and of itself. But to that lack of comeliness was added the insult of being the middle sister as well. Therefore, it was of no great surprise that her primary employment had been to find a distinction in which her sisters were not her equal. Given that Jane was known as the handsome sister, Elizabeth the wit, Kitty was easily offended, and Lydia simply easy, Mary saw only one alternative. She anointed herself Mary the Pious. In that there was no one more certain than Mary of her own eternal reward, that conceit provoked relentless moralising. Her self-imposed martyrdom was only relieved by one near-catastrophic event. For Lydia had scandalised them all by running off with Wickham to London and living in mortal sin prior to marriage. Thenceforward Mary believed that she no longer suffered in comparison to *all* her other sisters. To her, every other evil paled in the presence of immoral Lydia's multitude of sins.

Lydia, of course, was quite unchastened by such censure. Her attention was far too compromised.

Always an outrageous flirt, during the months following the news of Wickham's valorous death on the battlefield, the trail of officers calling to pay their respects to the widow of a fallen soldier-at-arms quite overwhelmed Lydia's notoriously weak flesh.

Whilst under the exceedingly conscientious watch of Elizabeth and Jane, her unguarded and impudent manner was held in check. But with Elizabeth's impending parturition, Jane and Bingley decamped from their father's house to accompany Elizabeth home to Pemberley with all due haste. Thus, latently lascivious Lydia was left quite at her leisure to ignore Mary's moral admonitions.

As the temptations were many and her mother kept to her room (where she could sit and think with favour of her own ill-use) before taking leave to Pemberley, it was unclear just which officer was actually culpable in sullying Lydia's semi-virtuous honour. Indeed, Lydia had seemed little more interested in specific paternity than would their gossiping neighbours be. Not only was she not discomposed by her predicament, she was very nearly defiant. The single suggestion she was not pleased to be in disagreement with was that she make herself less conspicuous by repairing somewhere other than Meryton.

When Jane received the letter from Mary telling of the latest scandal begat by Lydia, she immediately made for Pemberley with the exceedingly ill news.

"Upon my word!" gasped Elizabeth.

"Forsooth!" cried Jane.

It took near a quarter-hour for them to come to some understanding of what must be done.

The country would have been the most obvious choice to conceal scandalous persons, but neither Jane nor Elizabeth was willing to subject her husband to Lydia's unseemliness. Bingley would have suffered her if he must, for he was a very agreeable man, but Elizabeth would not impose upon Darcy on her behalf. Wickham's name was avoided at all costs in his presence by all who knew their history. Lydia, not surprisingly, was far too dense and far too self-involved to be that circumspect. Added to that inherent discourtesy her present condition and it made for a potentially untenable situation. In London, she would be Mrs. Wickham and others would be unable to take count of the length of her widowhood. The Darcys' London house was a brief consideration, but that notion had been quickly abandoned. Lydia needed supervision. There was no telling what might befall if she were left entirely to her own devices. Reluctantly, they decided to again impose Lydia upon the Gardiners.

Regrettably, this was not the first time that the Bennets had abused the Gardiners' goodness. They had the dubious past pleasure of Lydia's company during decidedly ignominious circumstances. Although Jane offered, Elizabeth thought it wiser that she herself undertake the writing of the letter containing the request. She knew it would take considerable gumption (and a temporary forswearing of conscience) to employ language facile enough to couch Lydia's plight as one of a "war-widow-mother-to-be" rather than "loose-legged-trollop-with-a-bun-in-the-oven." It would all eventually come out (so to speak), but Elizabeth knew too that in the interim, discretion was most imperative.

The thought of London pleased Lydia in all ways. Since the Gardiners were once again willing to take her in and her sisters to fund her time there, she was happy to oblige their generosity. The single objection Lydia had to these arrangements was, however, that Kitty was not invited to accompany her to Cheapside.

The fourth Bennet sister, Catherine (she was for all her life known as Kitty to her family), was the last person Elizabeth thought Lydia should have by her side. It was a long-held truth that Kitty possessed an idle mind. She also was easily led. Although she was a year older, she had always been Lydia's protégé. Hence, Kitty was of a sort much prized by over-bearing Lydia, and the least apt to be a good influence.

Kitty *would* have been quite willing to accompany Lydia to London. However, the summer saw her much in pursuit of her first true beau. Although mourning her father was an impediment to adorning herself with those accoutrements necessary to engage in romance, with Lydia's wily advice, she managed to get on without them. (With such methods as Lydia's loosed, that Kitty remained chaste was a feat in and of itself.) She was fortunate in her choice of beau in that he was a vicar from Shropshire, hence even Mary could not forswear his visits. This imminent engagement was regarded as felicitous by all of her family, but it came by way of Sir Lucas's introduction. Regrettably, the young vicar was a visiting cousin whom Maria Lucas and *her* family believed was meant for Maria. Kitty and Maria had long been the best of friends and had spent the better part of the spring feigning fainting fits and wetting their muslins vying for the young man's affection. Hence, when it came to pass that it looked to be Kitty and not Maria who would receive a proposal, hearts at Lucas Lodge were not happy.

The single person most delighted about the engagement was not Kitty at all, but her mother. Not only would it mean that she would have four daughters married, but she would have the whip-hand over Mrs. Lucas. Their friendship was of long-standing and had been a see-sawing battle of one-upmanship for years. First point went to Mrs. Bennet, who long suspected Mrs. Lucas of envying her Jane's beauty. The Lucas' daughter, Charlotte, was plain and twenty-seven when she became engaged to Mr. Collins, nephew to Mr. Bennet. As Mr. Bennet's bank account and home of Longbourn was entailed away from the female line, Mr. Collins was to inherit his modest estate. Hence, Mrs. Bennet was decidedly disadvantaged. Even successful matches for her daughters did not relieve Mrs. Bennet of that evil. Upon Mr. Bennet's death, had not Darcy stepped forth and made consideration to Charlotte upon Mr. Collins's son's behalf in exchange for her claim against Longbourn, Mrs. Bennet would not have had a home.

This history did little to influence Kitty. Her conscience may have been pricked by triumphing over Maria, but ultimately, the chance to be honourably settled struck her as far greater victory than maintaining a friendship. Therefore, Lydia's inveiglement to come to London gifted her a troubling decision. She was inclined to escape the Lucas' censure, but feared for the loss of her young man to Maria if she betook herself to London. She was much in a quandary—what with Lydia cajoling and Maria looking for all the world like a setter on the point. Had she been of a more discerning mind, she would have realised that following in the wake of flirtatious Lydia was possibly the least favourable road to a felicitous marriage. But she was not. Lydia wheedled and pouted, employing every design to get her way, but Elizabeth resisted.

Although through a momentary loss of reason, the always sympathetic Jane's resolve wavered ("Should not Lydia have a sister by her side in her hour of need?"), Elizabeth held fast to the opposition so long as that sister was to be Kitty. Hence, Kitty was rescued despite herself, for Jane and Elizabeth held the purse strings and eventually forbad the notion absolutely.

Edward Gardiner was Mrs. Bennet's brother. His wife had always been a favourite aunt (even to Lydia, who was oblivious that the affection was not returned in equal measure). Although Mrs. Gardiner was several years younger than Mrs. Bennet and her other sister-in-law, Mrs. Phillips, she was superior in elegance and intelligence to both. As it was, Mr. Edward Gardiner was greatly superior to his sisters as well (granted that alone would not have been considered a great feat), well-bred, and agreeable. Indeed, although he lived by trade, he was an educated and genteel sort of man. Elizabeth knew that parvenu ladies like Bingley's sisters looked upon him contemptuously. She had seen their smirks. Had they not been Jane's sisters-in-law, she would have suggested to them that he was a better gentleman than either of them a lady. But she held her tongue, lending her thoughts to those of pearls and swine.

At one time, the Gardiners' London home was held in some degree of esteem by all their country nieces—Lydia most particularly. As a grown woman, its shine for her had somewhat tarnished. Although she was still happy to spend time in London, the Gardiners' house was on Gracechurch Street. It was handy for Mr. Gardiner as it was within view of his warehouses. That meant, however, that it was not a convenient address. Moreover, her aunt and uncle were much engaged with their own children, hence, their pursuits were not hers. Even was their time not so employed, they could be so *sensible* and their choice of entertainments so *mundane*. Lydia believed that if she wanted to be annoyed by children, she would have been quite happy to remain home with her own brood. Indeed, Lydia was well aware that diversion under the Gardiners' roof would be sorely lacking.

For all that, had it not been for the unhappy fact that an unwed mother-to-be scattered suitors faster than Napoleon's retreat, Lydia would not have been out of spirits whatsoever. The single most vexatious component of the entire plan to them all was that Lydia's stewarding fell once again into the overly abused patience of the Gardiners. Elizabeth despised that it was they who would have to listen to Lydia's incessant whining about "contractions and restrictions." Lydia was put out not only for the sedateness of their comportment, but she was still miffed over Mrs. Gardiner's dour opinion of her infamous elopement. Of late, the only good opinion Lydia had of either of the Gardiners was that Mrs. Gardiner was *not* much of a walker.

However, once ensconced a few months in Gracechurch Street, what Mrs. Bennet liked to call "Lydia's high animal spirits" deteriorated with exactly the same rapidity as her figure ballooned. Always a talker who could not listen to anyone else for more than half a minute, and wrote less than she listened, Lydia began to post several letters a day. Seldom did they differ in style or content. She wrote Lizzy for money, Jane for more money, and her mother to come fetch her.

Which Mrs. Bennet refused to do—a first, it would seem.

Even Mrs. Bennet was hard-prest to excuse this last of Lydia's many peccadilloes. Nor, for once, did she endeavour to do so. Her attention was far too engaged with her own travails. Although Lydia had long been her favourite, she was happy to have her from under her feet in her hour of sorrow. If Mrs. Bennet were to suffer wearing widow's weeds, she would prefer to hold the office of The Commiserated all by herself. She had refused to come to Pemberley to see her newest grandchildren solely because those inhabitants were far too occupied by their own concerns to give proper service to hers.

Indeed, she found little time to console Lydia's lamentable situation in light of searching out the prodigious opportunities for sympathy for her own. In the months since Mr. Bennet's passing, her nerves and headaches had plagued her even more mercilessly. The more her woes vexed her, the less frequently her neighbours called upon her to hear about them—a dichotomy that remained unapparent to her. But then, Mrs. Bennet had always resided in a world seemingly inhabited by no one other than herself. Regrettably, her lack of understanding became more acute and her temper, which was once only uncertain, became unambiguously mean. Her over-bearing nature spiralled into near tyrannical egocentricity. As time went by, only a few of her closest, most tolerant friends (and Mrs. Phillips who by reason of relation had no choice) continued to call. Upon the few occasions that the decorum of mourning allowed her to venture out, all shuddered when the bell hailed her arrival.

Elizabeth had only to suffer her mother's nervous complaints by post. Thus her previous gratitude for her husband's generosity in seeing Mrs. Bennet a home at Longbourn for all of her life was inflated to near worshipful proportions by the aggravation of her mother's poor disposition.

Wickham's Waterloo

Countess Césarine Thierry was an extraordinary woman. Yet, had she had only her looks to promote herself, she would have been pronounced quite unexceptional. It was the second look (which, invariably, they all took) that stole every man's breath.

Her hair was an unusual reddish-gold, but although her figure was voluptuous, it was not uniquely so. Her face was lovely—white powder emphasising her ivory complexion—yet her expression was girlish. Her allure lay in her air. She had a kittenish quality that, when coupled with an earthy little moue of a sulk, made bored men laugh and silly men mute. The story circling about that she was the illegitimate daughter of a Russian prince (and whispers that the flare of her nostrils suggested an unrivalled libido) had elevated her from the shady outskirts and onto the heady heights of Paris's demimonde. That she leapt from milliner's helper to courtesan was not the true astonishment. Nor did that wonder lie in the fact that she arrived in Paris not from St. Petersburg at all. Her exquisite accent belied an English birth.

It was in a little village bordering Donkey's Fen in Cambridgeshire that little Frances was born to Henry and Clotilde Gapp. Having given birth after losing all hope of ever doing so, Mrs. Gapp was nervous of having a toddler about her house, what with boiling pots and china cups. Therefore, it fell to her husband to see to little Frances. Henry Gapp was happy to do so, for he doted on his only child. He had once been a scholarship student for several terms at Cambridge before reduced circumstances denied him his education. Still, he came away very nearly proficient in Greek and Latin and took a situation in the village as schoolmaster. He did what he could to support his family by also serving as tutor to rusticated undergraduates desperate to return to university. Although they subsisted upon the fringes of gentility, Mr. Gapp was a good husband and loving father.

Fanny was a pretty little girl and bright enough to learn well at her father's knee. Mr. Gapp kept her near whilst he tutored, for he was disposed to believe that his daughter being thrown into the company of gentlemen of education would improve her chance for a good match. Yet, when one particular young gentleman took notice of the blossoming Fanny, favouring her with those compliments and gifts that were wildly rich only in sentiment, Mr. Gapp was duly suspicious. The young man seemed earnest and eventually his openness and pleasing address won over Mr. Gapp's reservations. Even had he not such an expression of goodness on his countenance, his finely tailored coat and faultless boots were ample proof that he was, indeed, a gentleman. Mr. Gapp chose not to stand in the way of true love.

It was with profound displeasure that Mr. Gapp learnt that his daughter's honour had been wilfully surrendered not to a gentleman at all, but a cad (he was naïve enough to suppose that the two could not be one and the same). Believing a match was at hand, Mr. Gapp, blinded by the possibility of a marriage that was much in his daughter's favour, had not fulfilled the office of watchful father. Hence, he found himself in the precise position of countless outraged fathers before him. Coughing in the dust left by the fleet feet of a well-seasoned absconder, he looked upon the swelling belly of a newly impregnated daughter.

With hat in hand and trust in his fellow man in tatters, off went Mr. Gapp to the Cambridge provost, to see to it that the culprit was found and made to do right by poor Fanny.

"He's a student here, he is," said Mr. Gapp, demanding retribution. "I have his name. It's Darcy. Mr. Darcy is his name. If he can't be made to marry my daughter, his family can pay. I know they can. They're people of property. I demand satisfaction!"

Righteous indignation had coloured Mr. Gapp's face a frightening shade of red, the intensity of which was not mitigated when he was told that there was but one Mr. Darcy and he had graduated in the previous term.

"I regret to inform you, sir," said the provost, "it would have been impossible for him to be guilty of the heinous act brought here before us. Mr. Darcy is now, and has since Michaelmas been, observing the ruins of Rome and Greece."

This was not the first (nor would it be the last) incident of this nature attributed to a Cambridge undergraduate. Hence, the provost was in no manner astonished at the possibility that one of their students might be guilty of dishonourable conduct. More often than not, the accusation was credible and the culprit was brought either to justice or the altar. Upon this occasion, that was not to be.

"But...but..." stuttered poor Mr. Gapp. "He gave his family name as Darcy, his Christian name, Fitzwilliam. I am not mistaken. He sat in my parlour..."

The provost shook his head sympathetically, but with finality, "It is of no use, sir. I fear you and your daughter have been duped."

Mr. Gapp was inclined to think of a more fitting verb, but chose not to employ it.

The provost, however, had good reason to believe that he knew the identity of Fanny

Gapp's defiler, for the proctors were often in pursuit in the gambling dens and public houses surrounding the college a certain undergraduate. Although he professed to be meant for the church, his attendance had been highlighted by plucked exams, gatings, and rustications. All these offences led to his eventual expulsion. Had he not been under the particular protection of the most eminent family in Derbyshire, he would have been sent down upon his first malfeasance. Until Mr. Gapp's visit, his recent doings had been unknown to the provost. But as that was only a guess and George Wickham was long gone from their institution, he thought it pointless to bring up his name.

However, in the absence of anyone else to blame, Mr. Gapp chose to blame Fanny. Hence, he banished his cherished daughter to a convent in Boulogne to live out her term, praying earnestly for her redemption and eventual return.

When the nuns took Fanny's newborn from her arms, they shushed her tears, telling her that her daughter would have a convent upbringing.

"Your baby will not suffer from your disgrace," the mother superior told her.

As Fanny lay recuperating on the narrow cot in her barren little room, she stared up at a bronze crucifix over her head. It was the single adornment on the wall and, other than her dispiritingly hollow belly, all she had to ponder. She had always blamed her father's interference for her lover's desertion—even when told that she was seduced under another man's name. Like the star-crossed girl she was, she tenaciously held on to the hope that she, her daughter, and her lover would one day be united. She held on to that hope until one day she did not.

In the dark days that surrounded what could only be called a revelation, it was not redemption that excited Fanny's esteem. Nor was it the thought of returning to little Donkey's Fen as a fallen women. Through the agency of that lost lover, she had acquired a taste for wine and the delights of the boudoir. Moreover, in living in enforced poverty in a French convent, she began to believe that she liked money above all else and soon did not scruple how she came to have it.

Whilst still at home, she had spent long hours dreaming of London and eloping there with her lover. Unfortunately, once dispatched to Boulogne, a sizeable body of water lay between her and escape to London. The fare for a channel crossing was quite beyond her means in that she had none whatsoever. However, the governing principle of Fanny's nature was nothing if not autonomy and her spirit was quite indomitable. Hence, she took a look at the lay of the situation and made a judicious decision. Early one morn (and bearing a determinedly innocent expression) she set out on the pretext of herding a bit of livestock to market. Allowing neither muddy road nor stricken conscience to impede her, she walked the way from thence and on to Paris in her bare feet, prodding a trio of geese before her with a stick.

Consequently, hers was not the typical tale of violation and ill-use that drove many a young woman from the countryside into the arms of disgrace as a *fille de joie*, but it certainly was a fair approximation. Fanny had come there with the full knowledge that Paris was where a girl without means could support herself, if not with scrupulosity, at least with style. (It remained unquestioned whether it was actually cruelty that ultimately compromised Frances Gapp, or ambition.) The sale of the geese bought her a pair of slippers, surreptitious diligence of netting purses and feathering hats in her sparse convent room accoutred her to win a position as a milliner's helper. Hovering about the pretty shop, she was soon espied by the husband of a customer who had quickly tired of the office of holder of the purse. When it was evident that she had procured her first protector, she cast out her past compleatly by eschewing the name (however prophetic) of Fanny Gapp. She assumed a *nom de guerre* more fitting the courtesan she meant to become—evermore she was known as Césarine Thierry.

She left Fanny Gapp and all her girlish longing behind her—save one paradoxical desire. As had Fanny, Césarine hoped to see her truant lover just once more. When she gave it any thought, she shook her head at her own capriciousness. It was a compleat whimsy, she knew—perhaps attributable to one's propensity for always recollecting to whom one had surrendered one's virtue. Either that or an obsessive desire for retribution. In the end, she decided to forgo that vengeance. Rather, it was a life lesson that she would fully embrace. For how could she be angry at a man for loving himself more than her?

She would never again allow a man have sway over her heart.

One unfamiliar with the tenets of courtesan society might have believed all disappointment and vexation past. But inherent to success in a realm such as this was a rude predicament. Existing in this exclusive circle demanded not one, but a succession of lovers, each one surpassing the last in wealth. A courtesan who had reached the apogee of her calling was not judged only on the price her time could command, but discretion in the choice of lovers that she could exercise. In attracting those lovers, a display of ostentatious finery was essential—one must feign wealth if one wanted to obtain it.

To look the part was only half the struggle. These potential protectors were lured by way of grand *soirée*s beholding vaunted guests. Moreover, one must have elaborate rooms with a fashionable address in which to hold them. The grander the *soirée*s, the more vaunted the guests, the more lucrative the potential quarry, the more money she acquired. And the more money she made, the more her expenses grew. It fell to her to spend rather than save, for the conventions of the age demanded an extravagant peacock to dress a lover's arm, not a scarlet woman secreted away in a garret. It was an altogether voracious lifestyle, consuming men and their fortunes with rapidity.

So rapacious were these denizens, respectable mothers feared that these *lionnes*—these queens of beasts—would devour their guileless sons. This dread generated an equally lucrative avenue of revenue for a courtesan—that of gentle, but tenacious, extortion. Baroness, countess, and duchess alike would pay handsomely for a courtesan to leave their son's heart and his bank account in peace. (Visiting any *putain* held the substantial threat of a disease that offered not only madness and early death, but the sloughing off of one's virile member—if that was not a deterrent to *amour* for young men, maternal exhortations were all but useless.) Rumours abounded about lovers Césarine Thierry had jilted and aristocrats she had ruined. Occasionally these rumours were spread and slightly embellished by Césarine herself (for one must present oneself as a temptress if one is to tempt). If her reputation was wicked enough, the mothers of endangered sons were quite happy to be extorted.

Despite such embroidery, Césarine was undeniably gifted in the art of beguiling these young pigeons, er, lords. She took great care to procure them fresh from the nest, with only delicate pinfeathers of sagacity clinging to their flesh—ready for the plucking. She lavished them with exotic pleasure until, compleatly picked clean, they fell to earth in a bewildered heap. Ignoring their heartbroken pleas, she quickly turned to her next prey.

Although Césarine told her lovers variously that she had aspired to become an actress, a singer, or, upon occasion (most fancifully) a nun, truth be told, she had none of these aspirations. She aspired only to be rich. One of her earliest protectors was Count Francesco de Nuncio, a landed gentleman of Portugal who caught her eye by dangling an exceedingly enticing jeweled necklace into her cleavage. The count had neither a nervous mother nor a nose for duplicity, hence Césarine convinced him to accept her hand in marriage. As she was no more inclined to sleep with him than he was to settle her ever-mounting gambling debts, their alliance deteriorated with undue rapidity. Other than a new taste for exquisite jewels, her lone acquisition from this union was the title that she would carry the rest of her days and a determination to allow no one to learn that Count de Nuncio's title was as fictitious as her Russian birth.

Vivacious and restless, yet undeniably mercenary, La Complesse Césarine de Thierry, as she called herself thereafter, Césarine settled into a life cushioned by considerable pelf, spending her afternoons dispatching *billets-doux* to her lovers and her evenings in her box at the theatre surveying the crowd for her next armigerous conquest. In her evening *soirées*, she plumped her guest list with poets, painters, and princes and compleatly disregarded the anarchy that was taking place on the very street on which she resided. She feigned great disregard of it all, but it was a hard-fought battle to appear so insouciant when one of her dearest friends was literally dragged from the bed of her lover and with him to La Force prison. (She had heard that Juliette had escaped the guillotine through bizarre circumstances, but the story was so unlikely and was not told with enough certainty for her to hold it compleatly credible.) She most certainly did *not* want to lose her head, but returning to England was not a temptation. She no longer considered herself one of that race. Yet, that someone she knew had stood in a tumbrel was far too close a connexion for her to do other than reinforce her dedication to her own amusement.

To attend her circle, if one was unencumbered by wealth, the alternate currency was an abundance of charm or copious celebrity. For those young gentlemen who had nothing but charm to promote themselves to her, there was always the possibility that Césarine might be engaged in a passing flirtation. Because she was a woman of voluptuous tastes, having a young lover to satisfy her more passionate needs, and a rich one to sate the most fundamental, was the best of all possible worlds.

Moreover, if the young lover's allurement lasted no longer than the bloom of a rose, it was all the more efficient. It allowed more time to pit marquis against duke, racheting up the value of their gifts with a seemingly ambivalent Césarine benefiting from the cachet of duelling paramours. The diamond studded, ruby encrusted choker from the count was a particularly favourite gratuity. It looked to have first been seen adorning the neck of a courtier of Louis XIV, therefore when it graced her exceedingly lovely neck, it was an excellent ambassador to entice lovers to vie for the uppermost position on her dance card. (It was some time before it was missed by the de Nuncio family, and even longer before it dawned upon them where to look.)

By the year '15, Césarine had amassed, and then frittered away, several fortunes. As was her fate, she had not saved a franc. The summer of Napoleon's ultimate defeat, she was peeking into the abyss that represented her fourth decade. Some courtesans kept their looks and their lovers (if price and discretion were adjusted ever so subtly). But those who managed that were women of superior learning and wit. Time had not mellowed Césarine's nature and nothing compromised a lover's esteem more than an aging ingénue with an ill-temper and a persistent cough.

Indeed, dear Césarine had not only done the unthinkable of outliving her funds, she had contracted the courtesan's cliché—a galloping case of consumption. (It was an undeniable scientific truth of the times that the resultant breathiness of a surfeit of erotic spasms resulted in a weakened chest.) Yet even with compleat calamity perched on her doorstep, she did not retrench. So disposed was she to live life, she little knew how to brook impending death.

The particulars of her case were unknown to George Wickham when, with freshly arranged hair, ill-gotten suit, and bearing a pinched invitation, he sidled into one of her *soirées*.

Love Has Its Fashion

"It is a fine day, Darcy," Elizabeth announced pertly.

"Hmmm," was his non-committal reply.

They had long since finished their breakfast and were enjoying a leisurely cup of coffee. History had taught him that a seemingly innocuous statement by his wife could betimes betray an ulterior motive. Hence, with his brief utterance, his cup had stopt short of his lips, temporarily suspended. Ever-collected, he had the presence of mind to blow in its direction as if it was still a tad too hot.

Noting from him a distinct lack of enthusiasm for the weather, she furthered the subject, asking, "Excellent weather to take a turn with the horses, do you not agree?"

With exaggerated care, he returned his cup to its saucer and turned to her. Then, with all due caution, he agreed that, indeed, it was a fine day. He had, however, no further comment as to the appropriateness of the weather for her suggested activity. Time had allowed them a return to easy familiarity that had always attended their private moments. This day they had no guests with whom to contend and hence no propriety to protect. Yet clearly, her last horseback episode was much on his mind. Understanding that probability, Elizabeth had sat looking in his direction, waiting for him to oppose her suggestion. She was fully prepared to rebut. They both knew that it had been proven unconditionally that of late there was little that she could not stay astride—no limit to her endurance. Therefore, he drummed the fingers of his right hand in frustration.

Knowing her husband as she did, she understood his rapping fingers made his point on his behalf. She was not to be so easily deterred.

She said, "You have insisted that I take fresh air. I propose that is done to best advantage from a saddle. The exercise is invigorating. My proficiency *is* wanting. We are of the same mind that one must take the time to practice."

Darcy looked as if he might have liked to have presented an argument against such hearty exertion, but his attention was arrested by a red indention that adorned his drumming forefinger. It was not pronounced, but quite visible just below the knuckle.

Hastily, he stopt drumming and removed his hand from sight.

As it happened, that small injury was a visible reminder of the previous night's amatory exercise. It came about in a manner of utmost privacy and gazing upon the evidence in the very bright morning light was a bit mortifying. For it recalled to his thoughts the entire, unbridled event. The injury had occurred at the culmination however, whilst their love veritably crescendoed. Elizabeth's mention of riding only intensified the memory of her straddling him the night before. She had—or, possibly, he had (the exact perpetrator under such circumstances is not always identifiable) wedged his forefinger deep in her mouth. The impetus was not in question, for it was such a manoeuvre as had often been employed at the very height of their passion. It sated his pleasure and silenced hers (the sheer intensity of her achievement could betimes expose itself through auditory over-exuberance). But lost in the throes of delight, she had inadvertently bitten him. At the time, it had not hurt whatsoever, it had only enhanced his gratification.

He had been uncertain if she was aware that he still bore the memento of that exquisite moment—until he glanced in her direction. The saucy expression she bore was unambiguous. She then raised one eyebrow, a device which could have been construed as over-egging the pudding insofar as his composure was concerned.

Indeed, she also accomplished the unlikelihood of rendering him flustered—this disturbance irrefutably identified by the bright red splotches just then blossoming high on both of his cheeks. Bent on concealing his disconcertion, he first frowned and then coughed, finding great occupation in stirring his coffee. He quickly realised this activity exhibited his rapturously bitten digit and became even more unsettled. His neckcloth had suddenly become a bit constricting and he first tugged a bit at it, then ran said forefinger round just under the edge. He then rose and gave his wife a slight bow as if disposed to take his leave.

She replaced her cup in its saucer and brushed the crumbs from her lap, ready even then to don the riding habit that hung in wait for her in her dressing-room. She had taken the precaution of trying it on and was happy to learn that, with the hooks loosened a bit, she could manage to wear it. But it was not that small triumph that tugged the corners of her mouth into a smug smile. It was the undeniable success of her subtle tease perpetrated upon her husband. It was one of her sweetest conceits to be able still to discompose him so compleatly.

By the time she stood from the table, she was humming with self-satisfaction.

Therefore, her husband standing directly behind her took her quite unawares. As he bent low and whispered to her, she could feel the warmth of his breath against her ear.

"Lizzy dearest, if practice you must, I would much rather you perform to *my* delectation."

"Oh," she whispered.

She sank back in her chair, a small whimper escaping from her throat. He turned as if to quit the room, but then stopt and looked back upon her, clearly appraising the level of mischief he had wrought upon her composure. Satisfied, he strode from the room. She recognised the direction his footfalls took to be heading toward the staircase.

Sitting yet in her chair, Elizabeth had not moved. Nothing changed in her attitude save the crimson that then flamed in her cheeks, crept down her throat, and settled into her décolletage.

"Well," she thought to herself, "the weather will be as fine at eleven o'clock as it is at half-past nine."

As she then scurried after her husband, she also reminded herself that complacency over any part of his inclinations would always be a grievous error.

Had Elizabeth not been so single-mindedly disposed that morning, another observation might have interested her thoughts. It was the first morning since Jane had returned to Kirkland Hall that Elizabeth had not missed seeing her face across from her at their breakfast table.

Never would the Darcys have engaged in such suggestive banter in anyone else's presence, much less Jane's. In reality, had Jane been there to hear them, it is unlikely that she would have been embarrassed. This was not because her sensibilities were not easily ruffled, but because in all probability she would have been compleatly unwitting of their inference. Circumstances had not altered all that much with Jane and Bingley. Even Elizabeth knew that Jane may have at last found sexual satisfaction, but odds were she found it in the *figura veneris primi* position.

Elizabeth and Jane Bennet had always been as different as two sisters could be. This disparity of their natures did not, however, keep them from becoming each other's best friend and confidant. It was only fitting that they married men of opposing sensibilities as well.

Miss Jane Bennet had been blessed with incomparable beauty and graced with a kind nature and unselfish heart. Although she was exceedingly modest, the compliments and tributes she received with unrivalled constancy eventually persuaded her to accept them as true (if only to thank God for His generosity). But it was not for that endowment alone that she had considered herself the most fortunate of souls. Added to her blessings was that she was the first born child of a respected country gentleman. That gentleman, unfortunately, was much in need of a son to inherit his estate. But the unrivalled beauty which graced his daughter's countenance very nearly compensated him for the disappointment inherent to her gender. Four more sisters joined their family circle in rapid succession, and although none were quite so lovely as Jane, their number was sufficient to relieve her of that unwanted distinction. She loved her sisters with all of her generous heart. Indeed, it was not Mrs. Bennet but Jane who doted most upon each and every new baby brought into her family.

Until his most untimely passing, Mr. Bennet had been the most loving and generous of fathers. True, he displayed a distinct partiality to Elizabeth, for she had a lively, playful disposition that endeared her to him. But Jane did not envy her his affection, for she knew he loved all his daughters equally—even pedantic Mary, silly Kitty, and imprudent Lydia. Regrettably, Mr. Bennet was content to laugh at the follies of his younger daughters rather than exert himself to demand less indecorous behaviour. Mrs. Bennet also overlooked indecorous behaviour so long as it forwarded her goal of seeing all five daughters well married.

Despite her father's aloofness, it was well apparent that Mrs. Bennet was the primary instigator of an unpleasing picture of conjugal infelicity their marriage presented. Jane, however, chose to ignore that truth. Rather, she preferred to believe her mother must be of some good distinction, and being unable to bring even one immediately to mind impelled Jane into the severest of self-criticism and dutiful prayers. In the continued absence of any concrete virtues, Jane was then forced to engage in improvisation—for she believed all God's creatures were inherently good. If their goodness was unapparent, the overseer was simply not putting forth sufficient effort. So daily was its proof, all of the Bennet daughters accepted their parents' ill-disposed match in the manner that befitted the sensibilities of each. Lydia snickered, Kitty pouted, and Mary proselytized. Jane and Lizzy vowed to marry for love and love alone. The only thing lacking for Jane to believe hers the most happy life of any young woman in England was to find that one true love and to marry him. When Netherfield was let to young Mr. Charles Bingley, who arrived thither bearing a handsome countenance, happy manners, and five-thousand a year, her prayers (and her mother's) appeared to have been answered.

Charles Bingley was not of illustrious birth, but the son of a wealthy merchant. Neither his birthright nor his pocket mattered to Jane. His single draw-back was that included in the baggage which he carried with him to Hertfordshire were his two older sisters. Louisa was married to a Mr. Hurst, an indolent man more of fashion than fortune. Miss Caroline Bingley had an elegant figure and an air that was decidedly *au fait*, one that she kept aloft through a habit of spending more than she ought of her fortune of twenty-thousand pounds. Both sisters treated those they supposed beneath them with an air of superciliousness and were inclined to think well of themselves and meanly of everyone else.

When Charles Bingley arrived in Meryton society, he was accompanied by his good friend, Mr. Darcy, who had come to advise him on his search for an ancestral home to purchase. Miss Bingley was deep in pursuit of another nature. For the better part of two years she had put herself forth as a match for the imperious Mr. Darcy. Just as diligently, Bingley's sisters forwarded their brother as a husband for Mr. Darcy's sister, Georgiana. Thwarting their plans altogether, Bingley was immediately smitten by Jane and Darcy quietly intrigued by Elizabeth. Jane, with her paltry dowry and fetching sister, Elizabeth, the Bingley sisters saw as matrimonial obstacles on all fronts. When in Jane's company, they only feigned their regard, and lent little civility to Elizabeth whatsoever.

When all was said and done, Louisa Hurst and Caroline Bingley determined on what side their bread was buttered and devoted themselves to Jane. Caroline vowed to pay off every arrear of civility to Elizabeth. That she did so only in lip service was no keen surprise, but the semblance of amiability made Jane and Bingley very nearly as happy as the actuality. As for Elizabeth, she too vowed harmony, but as she had been very conscious of Caroline Bingley's continued disrespect to Jane, she could not find further compliment of Miss Bingley beyond the observations that she "walked well."

It had been love at first sight for both Bingley and Jane, and although the path to happiness had not been without its occasional rut, they had been happy beyond telling. They had even taken a residence within an easy distance to Pemberley (thus a less easy distance from Mrs. Bennet). Despite Bingley's connubial technique being more enthusiastic than adept, to Jane their life was near heavenly. It may have taken several nights of concentrated effort and random prodding by Bingley to accomplish this act of generation, but Jane told herself the primary obstacle had been locating the correct orifice. Further proceedings would go more smoothly. And in practice they had. (Although Bingley had whimpered a great deal, Jane's primary response had been one of puzzlement.) Bingley *had* been thoroughly pleased with the entire business (he had said so repeatedly), but with each successive encounter it had become nothing more than a means to an end for Jane. She was happy to please her husband (and he repeatedly said that he was pleased), but the true end for her was not rapture, but pregnancy. Hence, despite the pleasure she took in his kisses, the nights he came to her bed were for her less an indulgence than a duty.

Initially, Jane had thought herself altogether happy. What she had not been witting, she could not desire. She had learnt, however, that Elizabeth's marriage bed witnessed acts of love-making that resulted in exultations of a most passionate nature. That was somewhat troubling to Jane, but as she did not think herself dissatisfied, she was inclined to let sleeping dogs lie—as it were. At Mrs. Bennet's instruction, Bingley was banned to his own bed except when Jane was actively seeking impregnation. That excluded those times of menstruation, parturiency, nursing, fatigue, and Sundays. Therefore, it was no small miracle that she had birthed four children in five years.

Those who knew how very dearly Bingley loved Jane would have been quite astonished to learn that he had strayed to the arms of another woman. To those of a more cynical persuasion, however, it was of no great astonishment that deprivation drove him to seek that relief. But the reasons men wander from their wives are as diverse as the arms they betray—whether it be in search of love, money, self-aggrandizement, or simply because they can. Bingley did for none of these reasons. His rationale was far too immediate. He was not lustful. He simply sought to relieve a palpable pain in his nether-regions. His may have been more understandable than the average adultery, yet it was no less unforgivable. And that it was unforgivable meant that it had been altogether unknown by even his closest acquaintances.

Although they were quite good friends, Darcy was older than Bingley by nearly a half-dozen years. Darcy was the oldest sibling in his family, Bingley the youngest.

Their friendship replicated that element. Darcy conducted their friendship as if Bingley was a younger, more naïve brother, one in need of his counsel and guidance. Having suffered the loss of his father as a very young man and been compleatly in the company of his two sisters, Bingley was in desperate need of instruction in the manly arts. Darcy did what he could, but Bingley had not Darcy's inherent mistrust of human-kind and his affability and open manner led him to form friendships that were not always in his best interest. With considerable diplomacy Darcy had pointed out this failing to him, but while he may have listened with polite attention, he did not heed those warnings. Those few privy to his fall from grace believed that a lack of discrimination in those he chose to befriend was the one evil that led him into doing a grave injustice to his marriage vows.

Even Bingley was astonished with himself. He loved Jane without measure. How he had come to betray her as he had, he could but shake his head in wonder. As for Jane, she knew her husband well and if he had been unfaithful, she knew that it had not been by design. She did not ask of, nor did he offer, the particulars. It was over. He vowed, and she believed, that he would never again breach her trust. Total unification, however, was not quite so expeditious.

With time, the proverbial silver lining displayed itself in the most unusual of forms within the Bingley marriage. For as keenly ashamed and remorseful as Bingley had been for his adulterous disportment, it had not been without its enlightenments. And there *was* considerable room for enlightenment. Although he had been infatuated many times, however fevered his blood, he had never had the opportunity or the courage to take liberty with a young lady. When he and Jane became engaged, he was still quite young and inexperienced in amours. Hence, he was as much an innocent as his virginal bride upon their wedding night. Moreover, Jane fell with child with remarkable efficiency. He might have held himself with some pride over such immediate success, but he had been relegated to the office of breeding stock almost immediately. As it happened, he was allowed into Jane's bed so seldom that he never really mastered the peripherals.

He had not meant to know any other woman in the Biblical sense. Indeed, he could not recall just how it all came to pass. What he did remember of the young woman with whom he became entangled was quite distinct. While she was by no means a trollop, she most definitely was not a virgin—even his unschooled reasoning knew that. Indeed, when it came to coition, she knew more about what went where than he had ever imagined. That may have been the single reason he saw her after that first grave transgression. Instruction was not a defence he would ever be foolish enough to proffer, but that was what had lured him back. The entire affair had been altogether illuminating.

Waif

At the age of six and ten, Sally Frances Arbuthnot's manner had not altered from the courteous demeanour and modest attitude of her childhood. Although she seldom minced her words, she was never truly rude. But she had an odd inflection to her speech owing to a haphazard upbringing and a travelling nature, which, upon occasion would inspire a listener to reckon from just what part of England she hailed. Upon this subject, she was unusually curt.

"I was born in hell and raised in purgatory," said she with a snap and a dismissive shrug of her shoulder which allowed no room for further discussion.

She could have just as easily said it was Seven Dials whence she came. It was spelt differently but there was not a hairsbreadth difference in their drift.

Born on the wrong side of the vestry in the bowels of perdition to an indifferent mother and a tempestuous father, Sally's beginnings were more than a little ignominious. Inasmuch as those were her beginnings, it did not bode well that her upbringing would improve her straits. The general improvidence of her birth was mitigated by one happy occurrence. For the two features that haunted a propitious outcome for her eventual handsomeness (prominent ears and florid complexion) in her babyhood were ultimately out-distanced with each passing year. Indeed, it may have been tardy, but fate had eventually levelled its smile upon Sally. Hence, in the mere bud of young womanhood she was rendered quite a pretty little snip of a girl. Yet, overwhelmed as she had been with the daily tribulations of endeavouring to remain alive, she did not immediately understand the implication of that favour.

That nature had been kind to her aspect was no small miracle. For few complexions weathered the foetid air of the infamous slum she called home. If they did not begin coarse, they grew coarser with each passing season. Indeed, little could compete with the rancid odour that wafted in with the slightest breeze when the Thames was at low tide. The seven converging streets of St. Giles, however, did give a hefty try, incorporating their own particular congregation of rotting scents from knackers, decaying food, and emptied night jars. So potent was that odour that the stink was actually visible as a gauzy, yellow haze. Perchance it was that grime that preserved Sally Frances's skin tone, for much like all the urchins that littered the streets, she wore a film of dirt like a smeary dusting of face powder.

If her face was soiled, her apron, which would begin the day a bright white, ended as an outright disgrace. As her apron was in no better state than that worn by any other woman or child on her street, her ensemble did not weigh heavily upon her conscience. Hence, she only tugged at it a bit in a useless effort to look more presentable than the scrubby little punnet of whiskered strawberries she hoped to broker for a coin. Her prettiness made her efforts more profitable than most. She was wise enough to know she probably could have been just as lucrative extending a bare palm, but some inborn, but lately arrived, sense of dignity would not allow her to unashamedly beg. There were certainly enough half-naked children pulling at passers-by as it was.

What distinguished Sally Frances Arbuthnot from the mass of teeming humanity struggling for existence in the East End was that she refused to allow her past to define her future.

Sally's mother had decamped without ceremony and seemingly little thought to her little ones left behind. Sally had been barely old enough to remember her as merely a flash of red hair and the odour of gin. She was old enough to know that her mother's name was Abigail, but her image was lost forever—as was her father's. Although rough hands and stagnant breath was all she truly recalled of him, she knew his name well—Archie Arbuthnot. Not only did she know his name, but *who* he was. This was a given in that she and her young sister, Sue, were left in Archie's mother's care by default. Sally and Sue heard it so often they chanted along with Nell Arbuthnot whenever she invoked their father's name: He was Seaman Archie Arbuthnot, The King's Royal Navy's most venerable servant, brave attendant of the ninety-gun dreadnought, *Galatea*.

On a street where working men rarely did work, washer-women never had clothes-lines, and pick-pockets were considered skilled workers, Nell Arbuthnot was considered by her neighbours an upstanding citizen in that she struggled to do an honest day's work. There were so few men of wages about, she had achieved an additional modicum of respect because of her son's occupation. Hence, she announced it with regularity to her granddaughters, no doubt in expectation of their good opinion as well. (In that Sally remembered too much of the sour side of her father's disposition, that was a bit of a folly.)

Nell, however, was not particularly happy about her granddaughters' mother's distinction.

"Worthless wanton whore of the devil" was a frequently heard impeachment.

It may have been an over-statement, but it was hard to argue the facts.

Archie and Abigail had not been officially united in holy matrimony, but they presented a near enough semblance of it for him to beat her without fear of a visit by the constabulary. As unhappy a union as they had (although not unlike many others she witnessed), Sally's thoughts were not often plagued by memories of the two whose carnal rites produced her and little Sue. Indeed, because her regard for her parents was wholly indifferent, had not Nell nattered about Archie endlessly, Sally was quite disinclined to think of either of them at all.

She had a single recollection she cherished. That memory was of her beloved brother, John Christie. He was but a half-brother, born to her mother long before she came to Archie's bed. Nevertheless, from those first lonely nights with Nell when she nestled next to her sister and struggled to find warmth beneath a tatty counterpane, Sally's mind's eye desperately sought a sustaining comfort. When at last she slept, it was of her brother she dreamt.

John Christie was not of Archie's loins and that fact was a hopeless carbuncle on the posterior of Archie's manly pride. Archibald Arbuthnot was but one of the many men who were of the mind that the measure of one's virility could be determined by the production of male offspring. Poor Abigail had the misfortune of presenting him with two daughters after bearing a son by another man. (This, of course, had informed Archie and the world at large that his potency was compromised.) Indeed, he was not at all happy to allow his wages to feed the personification of another man's virility. This affront was made clear unequivocally to one and all, but he never quite drove John off. John was a good earner on the streets. (So long as he was, Archie was not inclined to question just how he came about his contribution to the family's keep.)

Regardless, Archie's displeasure was not compleatly appeased. When he took to drink (which was not infrequently), his rage was vented first on the woman who did not bear him a son and second on the son whom he did not beget. By the time he got around to punishing his detested daughters for their sin of gender, sometimes he was too spent to do much more than curse. Regrettably, oftentimes he was not.

It was Archie's misfortune that he could look upon John with nothing but a jaundiced eye. For the boy who was not his son evidenced a form of manhood foreign to their neighbourhood. Indeed, he was but a long-legged rail of a boy, but John Christie shook an upraised fist in the face of the hulking Archie Arbuthnot as if daring him to thrash him. Upon occasion, Archie did. Upon others, Archie simply fell face-forward upon the bed, wholly insensible to the world and all its contemptible inhabitants.

Once Archie snuffled and snored, Abigail came forward and with her son took to setting upended bits and pieces to right. So diligently did they work that one would have been led to suspect that in and of itself would repair the spiritual damage Archie had done as well. That was not their intent, but restoring their home to some semblance of order was a healing ritual. Sally and Nell always sat in numbing fear whilst John and Abigail made their alterations. As the little girls were far too young to be other than unlearnt about the sheer depth of drunken repose, they sat with their hands steepled, praying that this noise would not awaken Archie. When the table and benches were again at the ready, Abigail sat down to partake of a bit of drink on her own. John looked upon his mother's form with glum acceptance. Thus, his eyes took on a glazed expression, as if only then did he see true defeat. History told him that she would not stop until she was in no greater possession of her senses than Archie.

Sally recollected her brother turning away from their mother's ruin and to them, hiding beneath the bed. His countenance was etched in her memory as surely as if it had been but days rather than years. His eyes had been wide—but not with fear for he was long past that. His expression begged them to him. Humbly, stealthily, like lost little whipped pups, they crawled from their sanctuary and scampered to him. Whilst their mother found considerable interest in the amber liquid before her, his sisters clung to John's legs as he stirred the ashes of the fire back to life. When it began to spit and crackle once again, they all sat. (He folded his gangly legs thereby creating for each of the affrighted little girls a seat.) When they were comfortably situated, he commenced to sing in a low voice so as not to rouse his mother. But not hymns—he vehemently despised hymns. Nor had he sung lullabies. Summoning a ridiculous falsetto, he sang the silly little ditties, the sillier the better. He sang first one then another until they sang all they knew and then they started over again.

John had an endless store of these meaningless rhymes, gleaned from years of carting an ale-pail to and from the public house. (Some were bawdy, but it was some years before Sally understood this.) Each song improved their mood until every time Sally and Sue looked at each other they burst into subdued little giggles. Perhaps satisfied that their humour had been restored, John pronounced it time for bed. When at last they slept, it was to the inebriated rhythm of their parents' snores.

Although her brother had been well aware that their lot was pre-ordained, it would take a number of years for Sally to have that wisdom. But her time on the street explained to her that weathering poverty demanded copious amounts of spirits. Copious amounts of spirits begat violence. It was a circle of sorrowful events from which few had the wherewithal to liberate themselves. Her brother was brave and good but was as powerless to save them from their destiny as was she.

Their only hope was for the morrow. For the sun would rise on a new day and Archie would be back to sea—this her brother promised. And Archie did return to his ship, and as John had promised, all was good again.

Then one day it was not.

Sally forgave her mother for taking leave; she was a weak soul and had her reasons. But what Sally could not forgive was that her mother took her brother with her. Her inconsolability knew no bounds, but she could not fault him. He, good son, had done as their mother bid. Perhaps, she told herself, she would have done the same. It was but the work of ten days for her to find them gone and realise they were not to return. The recognition of that injurious truth made her wail. She wailed until she was sick.

"Hush, girl," she was told. "Yer'll soon ferget."

She hushed, but she did not forget. It was promised to her that the years would fade her recollections. They did not. Time was not a friend. Her brother's face remained so bright in her memory that it eventually was indistinguishable from the halo that surrounded it. Indeed, these intervening years inflated her regard for him from childish adoration to unadulterated veneration.

33

The Weir

There were no hillsides in Derbyshire lovelier than those within the ten-mile perimeter surrounding Pemberley. And in that, in his estimation, no county was half so beautiful as Derbyshire, Darcy saw his home as Eden on earth.

He fancied that he had crossed every dale, picked his way through every wood, and forded every crossing of every brook at some point in his life—either on foot or upon horseback. Even the lake had not escaped his forays. He had whiled away many a youthful afternoon lazing in the sun with one eye in serious contemplation of the cork bobbing suggestively at the end of his fishing line. But, it was his particular pleasure to mount Blackjack and descend the half-mile eminence upon which Pemberley house stood, skirt the lake, and cross the valley. By giving the big horse a bit of his heel, they easily took the steep hill that bore the ruins of an ancient hunting tower. It was not the prettiest of peaks for it was bereft of trees—no more than a craggy escarpment—but of spectacularly good vantage. There he would dismount and allow his horse to graze the upland slope whilst he purveyed all the land and people under his charge. Such a preference of vistas was neither for the purpose of humility or ego—it was merely a reminder of who he was.

He had shown Pemberley's fairest prospects to Elizabeth within the first days of their marriage. He recalled those excursions most particularly—and not merely because they often ended in pleasures connubial in nature (those recollections he kept pocketed in a separate, more exalted, region of his mind). His other memories were not so satisfying, for they involved his feeble attempt to contain his unadulterated pride and his eagerness in sharing Pemberley's beauty with her. He would have much preferred to have remained more composed. He feared that his countenance must have veritably beamed with boyish pride whilst he led her about. To her credit, she had seemed genuinely pleased—not with the grandiosity of it all—but with the natural loveliness of the park. She was most particularly taken with the watercourse as it cascaded and pooled into weirs before the bank surrendered to a profusion of willows. Hence, that had been a favoured destination when they rode.

The weirs had never piqued his particular fancy. True, when the season had been unusually wet, the waterfalls were pleasing. They had been designed with that in mind, but then little within Pemberley's park was put in place without thought to its overall beauty. But the weirs' essential duty was not decoration—they were merely a means to regulate the water. The discernment inherent to his sensibilities did not over-ride the pragmatism necessary for the orderly operation of an estate the size of Pemberley. Hence, it was seldom that he allowed even the delicate lily pads adorning the still backwaters to beguile him. To Elizabeth, however, it was as if the weirs were situated so prettily for no other reason than her pleasure.

It would be the first outing they had embarked upon since the one that had begun with the most romantic of intentions and ended so abruptly. This time, however, was quite different. Elizabeth had no doubt that she was fit to ride. It was pertinent to this understanding to know that her husband could not, in all good conscience, issue any reservations on the venture. She smiled to herself when she bethought the tactfully impish conversation they had had in that regard.

Although not that day, but several days thence, it was an exceptionally handsome day to ride. Elizabeth was so excited to be in the saddle and happy to fit into her habit that she all but skipped down the lane to the stables. Darcy had preceded her, for it was necessary to select an alternate mount for her, as Boots was nearing her time to foal. Elizabeth's good humour was compromised when she recognised that the horse saddled and waiting for her was the brown mare, Lady, a horse nearly as ancient as the hunting tower. Lady was the very horse Darcy had thought suitable to put her on when she first began to ride. She found the horse too indolent then and was most unamused to see that his opinion of her proficiency had progressed so little.

"This horse was not to my liking when first we rode, Mr. Darcy," she said pointedly.

He ignored the complaint and legged her up. It was quite apparent to Elizabeth that there were no wiles her husband would not employ in order to have his will be done. But as they set out, she saw it to be too fine a day to remain in ill-humour.

Darcy let Blackjack have his head and, because it was the direction most often taken, the big horse lumbered up the steep incline to the ruins. So steep was the rise, even Blackjack became lathered by the time they reached the ridge. Even had Blackjack been less indefatigable, Lady would not have kept up. So slow was the horse's progress, Elizabeth considered dismounting and pulling the mare up the hill herself. By the time they made the peak, Darcy had already stopt, dismounted, and loosed his horse's girth. Elizabeth did dismount, but would not allow Darcy's solicitous loosening of Lady's girth for her to dissuade her from her disgruntlement. Hence, she did not scruple to abuse her husband for leaving her behind.

"Lady should be retired to the pasture from which you obtained her. Be certain that when Boots has foaled, you will not be so undoubtful of your winning," said she.

An expression overspread his countenance that bespoke his competitive spirit was not chastened by her censure. Indeed, he did not attempt to conceal his satisfaction, nor did he hesitate to fib.

"I am sure I was quite unaware we were competing," said he.

With that, she made a move as if to switch him with her crop—and then thought better of it. She knew he would not step aside or attempt evasion in any manner. It was not in his nature to capitulate to even so small a thing as his wife's teasing swat. Instead, she watched as he walked to the edge of the precipice and rested one boot upon on a protruding boulder. His right hand still held his crop, it settling on his thigh as he absentmindedly flicked it against the top of his boot. Such was a true indication that he was lost in thought. Even then he stood remarkably erect, his shoulders seemingly incapable of any pose other than majestic. It was a sight that elicited a sigh from his wife of a humbler origin.

For her, imposing peaks, broad shoulders, and the odour of oiled leather was a potent aphrodisiac. Every slap of his crop against his boot was suggestive. Upon infrequent occasion times past, they had engaged in discreet alfresco disportment. But atop this hill she could not entertain such a notion.

She walked purposely to her mare, grasped the reins, and did not wait for Darcy to leg her up. By sheer will (and with an audible groan), she grasped the pommel and heaved herself onto the saddle. He was still lost to his thoughts and only realised that she had mounted when he heard the scuffling of Lady's hooves. He stood and looked at Elizabeth quizzically. She spoke not, but gave her horse a decisive kick. It was but a moment ere he beckoned his horse. As she had a clear advantage, rather than striding toward Blackjack, he put his fingers to his lips and whistled. The horse started at the sound and looked in his master's direction. Forsaking the grass, he cantered toward Darcy, who then grasped the reins and leapt atop him with remarkable agility. Not waiting to take a bearing on her lead, he encouraged Blackjack with a small clicking noise and a nudge in the flanks. Instinct overtook Blackjack and he commenced the chase.

This race was not, however, hotly contested, for the pursuer was no less in want of capture than was the pursued. (Elizabeth saw that the sole benefit of having so ancient an animal beneath her.) Indeed, beneath the brow of the hill lay a meandering stream. The downhill being far less bothersome than the uphill (and with the promise of a cool drink), Lady made good time. Elizabeth stopt beside the stream and once again loosed her horse. The day was not oppressively hot, but it was warm and the exercise did little to alleviate her ardour. She walked toward the edge of the pool that had accumulated below the weir. She took off her gloves as she strode toward it and dropped them carelessly to the ground. She made great work of not noticing that Darcy arrived almost as quickly as had she. She did observe that he did not immediately alight, but watched her with great intensity.

She abruptly sat upon the river bank and commenced tugging at her boots.

"What do you propose to do?" said Darcy—it was not truly a question.

"I propose to cool my feet," said she.

"I must advise you that beck is spring-fed—the water can be quite cold."

If he thought such an admonition would deter her, she was quite certain he would soon learn better, for her feet were already bare and she had begun to tentatively wade into the clear water.

"It is deceptively deep," he added.

"Certainly not. It is so clear that I can see the river stones lining the bottom."

"Beware of the moss."

This he said as he dismounted. He sat down, pulling off his gloves and dropping them into the upturned crown of his hat, which he then sat neatly next to his feet. Although he doffed his jacket, unbuttoned his waistcoat, and tugged loose his neckcloth, he did not seem inclined to pull off his boots after her example.

"Pray, join me. This water is quite refreshing."

"I will do no such thing," he said somewhat gruffly. "Splashing about is the work of children."

At that she threw her head back and laughed—then deliberately kicked water in his direction. It fell far short of its mark, however, and she was certain she detected a smile encroaching upon his sober countenance.

"Come," she inveigled, "there is no one about."

"Elizabeth, that there is no one about to witness an act of frivolity does not render it any less objectionable."

She sniffed at his obstinacy, but he did not hear her for the babbling of the water. Recent rains had caused the water to cascade over the top of the weir with more force than usual, but the swirling water felt good against the calves of her legs. She attempted to venture deeper, but had difficulty keeping the tail of her dress above the water.

"Mind not to venture too far—there is a drop-off when you near the spring."

"You have swum here!" she accused.

"In my youth," he sniffed.

As she was nearly mid-stream and the water was not yet at her knees, she was inclined to believe him over-solicitous, "I can see the bottom—look, there is a fish! A carp!"

Her squeal of delight disintegrated into one of dismay with the utmost rapidity when the slick moss of which he had warned her caused her to lose her footing. She abandoned gripping her skirt and fell flat on her rump with a rude splash, but had no time for indignation before she immediately slid off the ledge upon which she stood. She fell directly into the spring that disappeared beneath the overhanging limbs of several willows. She came to the surface sputtering and shrieking but found quite expeditiously that she had only to put her feet down and that she was not, indeed, drowning. Once she had reinstated her footing, she could hear her husband's laughter. Was her dignity not abused enough by such an unladylike plunge, it was to her husband's amusement. Fie upon him! Could he not be gentlemanly enough to offer her his hand?

All this happened in less time than the telling and she slogged her way to a limb that protruded from the water. A sizable turtle sat quietly sunning itself there until her approach sent him scrambling beneath the water's surface. She pulled herself from the water quite under her own power ignoring the displaced reptile—it would just have to fend for itself as did she—moreover, it was a far better swimmer.

"That looks to be a snapping turtle," Darcy warned.

Instinctively, she looked to see where it had gone before recollecting herself. With great deliberation and compleat lack of notice of her husband, she endeavoured to repin her hair before unbuttoning her spencer, wringing it of water, and draping it across two small branches to dry. Belatedly, she saw her bonnet floating in a gentle circle mid-most of the pond and gave an inward shrug. It looked to be a compleat loss. Then she commenced to wring what water she could from various sections of her skirt. At least her boots were safe on dry ground. She glanced in their direction, wondering how she was going to manage to get back to the other side. It was then that she realised that her husband no longer sat where he had. It escaped her notice, however, that several items of his apparel lay in an orderly fashion where he had been sitting. This oversight came about because her attention was compromised by a slapping sound against the water behind her, which gave her a start. She pulled her toes from the water, fearing that the turtle had come back to reclaim his perch.

Thereupon, a tug substantial enough to unseat her was inflicted upon her person, the perpetrator of this outrage being her heretofore neglectful husband. She, however, was not immediately aware of the identity of her tormentor, for she was compleatly upended. The water was not all that deep, but it was sizable enough for another thorough dunking.

Well aware she had not been dunked by means of vengeful wildlife when she surfaced, she faced another dilemma. Although in that spot the water came no higher than chest-high at its deepest, that was by his measure, not hers. Hence, her endeavours to exact the same indignity upon Darcy were largely unfruitful. In order to dunk him she had to both rise above and overpower him—neither of which she was equipped to do. Indeed, even had she not worn stays, her skirt and petticoat were substantial impediments to water-borne agility. They did manage to thrash about long enough for both to tire—Darcy trying to float whilst his wife clung to his neck.

"You shall drown us both," he said spitting water.

"But you know I cannot swim…" she insisted, wrapping her legs about his.

"Behold, that turtle has returned!" he exclaimed.

"Where? Where?!" she looked about frantically.

He pinched her thigh twice causing her to cry out and flail at the unseen menace before she realised that Darcy was the perpetrator.

"What effrontery!" she declared, desperately treading water.

He reached out and took hold of her, but not without a tickle.

"Belay that! I shall drown!" she exclaimed.

At last, he regained some semblance of his formal self, took her hand, and swam, leading her to the bank. But it was not the bank where their footwear lay. He drew her effortlessly through the water to the shadowed recess of the bower near the deepest part of the pond. It looked a place where a turtle just might lie in wait, hence, she was a bit hesitant.

"Come," said he—it was all he needed to say.

She allowed him to draw her into the shadows. It was even cooler there where the sun had not reached. That chill did nothing, however, to abate the increasing fever in those recesses particular to a woman. Indeed, the water was not cold. All she could feel was his fingertips clasping hers, drawing her into the dusky alcove. The stillness of the spot and the dappled light filtering through the boughs lent it an altogether seductive spot. She did not for a moment wonder what were his intentions—had they been other than erotic, she would have been decidedly disappointed.

Both were still fully dressed, she in the remains of her riding habit, he in his shirt and small clothes.

Upon more than one occasion they had made love in a bathing tub. The warm water and suds lent it a luxuriously decadent air. This, however, was quite different—earthy and untamed. Her skirt billowed from the up-welling spring, an effect of which he took full advantage. She had left her stockings rolled up in her boots, hence her calves and thighs were laid bare for his touch—a touch he offered generously.

"I want," he said, "to do everything within my power to bring you with child again."

That confession stole her breath and convinced her immediately that she was of a like mind. Her hands crept beneath his shirt as he manoeuvred her undulating skirt. Footing, however, became an unwanted issue. The deceptively calm pool hid competing currents, all conspiring against them. They pitched and rolled with such fervency, the once clear water was roiled opaque. It was an insidious torment—nearing consummation but managing to be still long enough to bring their love-making to climax. It was Elizabeth who at last grasped a branch of a fallen tree as a bulwark. He would have congratulated her for her ingenuity had he not been so compleatly otherwise engaged.

As it was all he could manage was a guttural, "Oh…Lizzy."

When at last they came to unparalleled fulmination and then, eventually, their senses, it was he who clung to her. Having personal knowledge of just how very spent he could be rendered after amorous congress, she watched to determine that he kept his chin above water (her own knees now floated quite at their own will). He had made no attempt to climb onto the bank, but rolled upon his back next to her. They were still immersed in the water which calmly lapped at their chins.

"Well," she said with finality.

"Yes," replied he.

He stood. The water was but knee-deep.

She laughed, "And to think that I thought we were sure to drown."

His clothes matted and dripping against his body, he buttoned his breeches then attempted to step onto the bank. His stockinged feet slipped several times before he accomplished it. He sat hard on the ground, used the fingers of both hands to comb his hair from his forehead. Still seated, she did much the same, quite certain her head of wet hair did not look half so alluring as his. He manoeuvred the slippery bank and extended both hands—it took both to pull both her and her drenched ensemble full out of the water—no small undertaking. He then realised what she had yet to determine—they were on the opposite side of the stream from both their boots and their horses. Hence, it was somewhat startling that he wordlessly dove back into the pool whence they had just emerged. He swam the width of the water with an effortless few strokes and when he gained shallower water, splashed through it and up the opposing bank.

"Shall you leave me here in all this state?" she called.

He was busy with the task of drawing on his boots over wet stockings and did not reply. He then retrieved her boots and stockings, rolled them in his coat and whistled for Blackjack who was still nibbling on the lush hillside grass. Upon hearing the whistle, the horse immediately looked toward the sound and began to trot in Darcy's direction. As effortlessly as he swam the current, he lashed the clothing to the saddle then drew himself atop the horse. All this Elizabeth watched with great interest (purely for elucidative purposes and not just to savour the sight of her husband's rippling muscles). He gave Blackjack a nudge in the flanks and the horse leapt into a canter up the stream bed and away.

She sat there knowing full well that he would not leave her, but compleatly flummoxed as to his intentions. In a moment, he reappeared, having forded the current at a shallower point. He loosed the roll of clothing before he slung his foot over the pommel and dropped to the ground.

"Your boots, m'lady," he said with an exaggerated bow.

"I thank you, sir."

He dropped to one knee and took one of her stockings from where it had been tucked in the toe of her boot. He unfurled it.

"Allow me?"

It was a question that could only be answered in the affirmative. Hence, she only gave a small nod in acquiescence. He then began the meticulous process of rolling the leg of her stocking down to the toe in readiness for application to her foot. She offered it. He then unfurled her stocking up the length of her leg with far greater deliberation than she could ever recall of herself. Once it was on to his satisfaction, he smoothed it once again.

"Your garter?" he asked.

She had been so mesmerized that there was a momentary pause before she responded. And when she responded, to her mortification, the first syllable out of her mouth sounded far too much like "Eh?"

"Th-there," she stammered, pointing toward her boot.

"Ah, yes. I see."

By the time he repeated the process for her other limb, she felt so weak-kneed that she was uncertain if she would be able to stand. In fortune, he grasped her under her armpits and lifted her onto Blackjack with such efficiency that her feet never actually touched the ground. He leapt upon the saddle behind her and once again gave Blackjack another small kick. This time the horse did not canter, but carefully picked his way toward Pemberley.

As they made their way in exhausted silence, she wondered if he knew that nursing would belay fertility. And if he did, had he just asked her to forgo that duty? She would seek clarification upon another occasion. She chose then merely to cling to him and think of nothing but the rhythm of his beating heart.

"The mare," Elizabeth remembered, "Perhaps I shall ride her?"

"I think not," he said. "She will follow."

The horse did follow without encouragement. And that her husband chose for her to ride within his embrace as they lumbered back to the stables was a recollection that would stay with her.

Wedding at Pemberley

Besides the complement of his illustrious family connexions, Col. Geoffrey Fitzwilliam was equal parts bold and politic. His courage was that of legend prior to his heroics at Waterloo. As testament to that bravery he carried a lead ball in his ribs from the peninsular campaign and bore a handsome scar on his cheek taken from a cavalry charge. There was little in life that gave him fright. He cared little either for medals of valour or for the celebrity that accompanied such honours. What he did esteem was his family and his own self-respect. The scrupulousness and vigour with which he had come to lead his life was well known to all who knew him.

Hence, when home once more Col. Fitzwilliam sat about with a curiously stupid expression, it was most disconcerting. Yet, ultimately it was also to his good fortune. For had he not, his close friend, soon-to-be brother-in-law, his own father's sister's son, Fitzwilliam Darcy may not have been able to withstand the desire to call him out and do further injury to his battle-scarred person. (Or, more probably, not deign to speak his name.) As it was, Darcy had become almost solicitous of him.

"Do you suppose Fitzwilliam has been somehow addled?" Darcy had asked his wife worriedly after observing Fitzwilliam's unwavering aspect one evening, "I do not believe he has blinked his eyes more than twice together this past quarter-hour."

Elizabeth merely nodded for she knew this was not a query, hence, required no response beyond indication that she heard what her husband had said. She instituted that which she wanted of her husband which was for him to indicate that he had heard her when she spoke. (His hearing was much improved, but upon occasion he was inclined to use his purported deafness to his benefit by ignoring that which he did not care to hear.) But his remark did spark her interest. She observed Fitzwilliam more closely until at last he once again blinked. It was a small victory.

Her husband was quite right. But it was not as if Fitzwilliam had been unhinged by his injuries (although Lord knew there were more than a few heroes of Waterloo who came home in want of some pence in a shilling), he appeared to her to be simply bewildered. Events occurring with the same rapidity of a war-time fusillade had all but overtaken him. In less than a half-year he had volunteered to fight Napoleon in what would ultimately be held as one of the most glorious victories in England's illustrious history, had been grievously wounded in his leg and temporarily blinded, suffered the loss of the finest steed in the history of equines, been secreted out of a hospital rife with typhus in the back of a waggon next to a corpse, sat out a quarantine in France only to wake up from deliriums to learn not only that he had proposed to his demure, and formerly virginal, cousin, Georgiana Darcy, but that she was carrying his child. Considering all of this thrashing about his head and heart, it was little wonder that the poor Colonel was a mite befuddled.

Georgiana's behaviour was quite the opposite. For Fitzwilliam's confusion and the lack of concrete evidence that he loved her had not given pause to Georgiana whatsoever. Moreover, she employed considerable disinclination to suffer from having her virtue sullied. The consequence of her lack of shame and Darcy's having embraced the pretence that nothing at all was amiss all made for a fairly merry household. There were a few trivial travails, however.

High amongst those was that one of the many long-held customs accompanying such a momentous occasion as the joining of two souls was that the bride's chastity be signified by her wearing a pure-white wedding gown. The intelligence of Georgiana's pregnancy had not been shared even with the vicar, thus, the matter of just what semi-vestal shade of white was selected for her gown was not at the mercy of anyone who might think themselves a stickler on the subject. With Georgiana much at Fitzwilliam's side, Elizabeth was quite at her leisure to select the ultimate hue of satin meant for Georgiana's bridal gown. Rather than alabaster, she selected ivory. That colour was concluded as not a compleat abuse of the truth. (In Darcy's eyes, however, it was, and would always be, recollected as nothing if not off-white.) Although the condition in which Miss Darcy was to take her vows was abhorrent to her family, it was not a particular affront to society at large.

Indeed, although the presumption might have been otherwise, in finding herself with child prior to her vows Georgiana was hardly without company. Her circumstances were the same as one in four brides of all classes in Derbyshire (a county whose pre-wedlock natality standing was no greater than any other in England). The ultimate goal was that the wedding took place—as to just how it came about, few quibbled. Even Lydia lived over a fort-night in London with Wickham prior to their vows. But, because when she arrived home she was a married woman, all talk of scandal was forgot. Although it might be another presumption, it was not the fear of the Darcy name being muddied that had Darcy in such a snit.

He undertook the guardianship of his sister with even greater purpose than his duties as the master of Pemberley. After his initial and prolonged outburst over her deflowerment, he remained persistently silent upon the matter. Elizabeth came to believe that it was not his dignity that Georgiana's actions had abused, but his fondness for her.

It was not Darcy's honour that she had injured, it was his well-guarded heart.

It came to pass that Fitzwilliam took Georgiana's hand in a private ceremony in the Pemberley chapel the very moment he could stand on his own. He was quite handsome in his regimentals, an ensemble that included a crimson sash and sabre. Georgiana was a vision of loveliness, with profusion of pink flowers adding just the right touch of colour to her wedding costume. She exuded radiance and bore an unabashedly jubilant expression. Behind Fitzwilliam's outwardly benign mien, however, an expression of puzzlement continued to plague his features. If Darcy still bore any remnants of concern over the marriage, all doubt was cast aside as he stood before the altar and gave his sister away. Ere Darcy placed his sister's hand in Fitzwilliam's, he kissed it. The barest glistening of a tear threatened Georgiana's composure then, but only for a moment.

When Darcy stepped back and stood next to Elizabeth, she believed her own countenance would not be tried again. But her sentimental sensibilities were much abused as she listened to the ceremonial words. They were those time-honoured phrases that inevitably insisted, for better or for worse, that all who listened recall their own wedding.

"With this ring I thee wed, with this body I thee worship…"

Elizabeth ceased hearing beyond those words. All the rest about endowing worldly goods were lost to her. She was transported to that moment in time when Darcy placed the ring upon her finger. Hence the promise she had made to herself not to be so insipid as to weep was put to an even severer test. The only other precaution she had taken so as not to draw attention to anyone other than the bride and groom was proved at least partially successful. Before the ceremony commenced, she had whispered a bid to Darcy

"Pray dearest, try not to glower."

That appeal wavered in its success. For as the morning wore on, she noticed the crease between his eyebrows deepening. She ignored it until they gained their seats at the wedding breakfast, but as he rose to offer a toast she touched his arm and smiled in a manner to remind him to place a more welcoming expression upon his own countenance. With his wife's kind encouragement, he managed a toast of utmost sincerity and genuine affection. This moment was a turning point in his regard of his sister's nuptials. From that day forward he would use his considerable influence to see to it her union was successful. Elizabeth knew that because as the newlyweds stepped into their curricle amongst a snow-storm of rice and confetti, Darcy told her so. Their good-byes were sweet, Mr. Darcy able to breathe a sigh of relief that his sister was at long last safe from perfidy under the mantle of marriage. Both he and Elizabeth stood on the gravel of the drive until they were long out of sight.

The newly-wed Fitzwilliams' decision to take their honeymoon in Bath was long in coming and they undertook it only incrementally. Georgiana had been quite happy to go home the short distance to Whitemore, but the collection of relatives, cottagers, and town-folk standing at-the-ready to pay their respects to the bride and groom influenced her otherwise. For the sake of Fitzwilliam's health, it was decided that they eschew hearth and home and thus avoid the accompanying brouhaha. He needed rest and he needed the restoration of mineral baths.

To be sure, within the county of Derbyshire were several spas of good reputation. Bruxton was but a half-day's journey. But it was merely convenient, not superior. Cheltenham also had healing waters. But, those spas nearby had springs enough only to sip, soaking in them was out of the question. Those men endowed with information of a medical nature believed too that the sea air and bathing in salt water was most beneficial to the restoration of one's vigour and superior to inland spas. Fitzwilliam, however, was disinclined to visit the sea. He had been so off his sea-legs on their return from the Continent any mention of sea-air made him ill. Bath was located near, but not on, the sea and its warm mineral springs met all Georgiana's stringent requirements for her husband's recuperation. The journey was more than she would have liked, but they planned it so as to take rest often.

Be it balm or elixir, there was little that Georgiana did not know of remedies. It was her single conceit. She knew the air so near the sea to be refreshing and the mineral baths superb. Hence their decision was made not upon fancy; it was predicated on good medical sense. She would escort her husband to Bath for medicinal purposes, not because the *beau monde* was there, but in spite of it.

As brothers are wont to be, Darcy remained keenly disapproving of his sister having anticipated the marital vows. Pressed on the matter, he would eventually admit to her that he was not disappointed with whom his sister chose to make the leap. Moreover, Fitzwilliam's brother, the Earl of Matlock and his wife were happy (deliriously so) that Fitzwilliam had taken a Darcy for a bride. Uninformed as to why the wedding took place with such haste, Matlock bore only a slightly less perplexed expression than his brother. When the couple rode away to embark upon their married life together, there was trepidation in no quarter whatsoever save the groom's.

As it happened, Fitzwilliam's unease was altogether misplaced.

Hoodwinked But Not Hornswoggled

The day of their nuptials was a glorious autumn day both brisk and sun-kissed. Such fine weather heralded a propitious beginning for Col. and Mrs. Fitzwilliam. They took leave of Pemberley in a festooned curricle, but travelled no further than Whitemore where they were to transfer into a *chaise* and four, which was already affixed with their trunks. It had been a consideration to take their rest there and start upon their bridal journey the next day, but so anxious was Georgiana to begin her life with Fitzwilliam, she and Elizabeth saw to it the couple's leave-taking was more immediate.

Although it had been at her urging that they journeyed to Bath, once upon the road Georgiana grew ever-more apprehensive. She despised flippant society and she had often heard Bath called a city of great fashion. She expressed her reservations to him and Fitzwilliam patted her arm in reassurance. He explained that Bath had seen its day as the epicentre of all that was wonderful. It was by then populated by middle-ranking citizens, invalids, and aging maidens desperate to find a match.

"Those of fashion have moved on to Weymouth, Brighton, and Ramsgate," said he.

Although he did not notice a visible reaction from his new wife, Fitzwilliam immediately regretted that reference. Ramsgate had been the scene of Georgiana's near-elopement with her mercenarily-inclined seducer, George Wickham. Wickham had only been foiled by a most fortunate intervention by Darcy. In the wake of his blunder, both Fitzwilliam and Georgiana fell temporarily silent.

"If you dislike the society, perchance we should travel on to Bristol," Fitzwilliam offered.

Georgiana shook her head. The reminder of Wickham was all she needed to steel her resolve. She would weather whatever befell her at Bath with good humour. She would not allow her own disorder to sway her from the ambition of hurrying her new husband's return to health. Although she applied poultices and embrocations of all kinds at all times, there was little that could be done but wait for his eye to heal. But his leg needed tending beyond what could be found in a medicinal bag. She repeated their reason for choosing Bath to him then.

"Cheltenham, Bruxton, and even the iron-impregnated water of Tunbridge Wells—none suits our purposes. Your leg must be immersed in warm springs to lift the impurities."

"You should not have to use your honeymoon to nurse an invalid," replied Fitzwilliam.

Georgiana considered whether that remark from him was any part self-pitying, then dismissed the notion. If it had been, it would have been the first of that type she had heard him utter. She knew it might not have been a particularly romantic notion to choose one's honeymoon design as a health retreat, but she was determined to put her husband's well-being before titillating her own amorous inclinations. She would have assured him of that, but her verbal acuity was not sophisticated enough to allow her to form a reply that was not suggestive.

As they travelled, most of their conversation was centred upon readdressing their choice of destinations and reassuring themselves the righteousness of it. All other discourse was stilted, barely more than observing the passing of certain landmarks. Due to the length of their honeymoon trip, they incurred taking their first night as man and wife at a small inn. Regrettably, its only night-lodgings were on the second storey. Thus the exertion of climbing the stairs added to the protracted anxiety incumbent on such occasions bid Fitzwilliam altogether spent—quite unrelated to any activity of an erotic nature. If Georgiana was disappointed, she bore it with composure, shushing his apologies whilst tucking the covers under his chin with motherly tenderness. If this, particularly in relation to his over-whelming air of discomfiture, did not bode well for the future of this nascent marriage, neither dared acknowledge it.

When they did at last reach Bath, the Colonel was once again exhausted from the jostling of their coach. It fell to Georgiana to see to their accommodations, servants, and trunks. He was fast asleep by the time arrangements had been compleated. Hence, her second night as a married woman was passed much like her first. She did ease herself beneath the sheets and as near as she dared without waking him. She lay in that attitude for sometime and gazed lovingly upon his countenance before finally dousing the light. If her dreams were unhappy, it was unapparent, for she awoke refreshed but beside herself in anticipation of escorting Fitzwilliam to the vaunted baths. She had held fast to the notion of the propitiousness of these treatments as if they would render some miraculous balm, renewing both his strength and his spirits. Of more sober judgement than his wife, Fitzwilliam was altogether willing but not so certain as she as to the healing properties of a tub of water.

So anxious was Georgiana to repair Fitzwilliam, they ignored the architecture of this grand city and betook themselves directly to Molland's. By this late hour there were throngs of the quasi-fashionable preceding them. Fitzwilliam was not in uniform and, as they did not make themselves or their circumstances known, the colonel and his wife respectfully stood aside whilst those stricken with gout went before them. In less than part of an hour, either the actual good his soak did or the expectation of it, Fitzwilliam's spirits were revived considerably. He veritably whistled as they made their way to the apartments they had let. His valet aided him into his dressing-gown, but upon this occasion he experienced the considerable triumph of managing to gain the bed on his own. Therefore, he had ample time for reflection whilst he anticipated his new wife's coming to him.

The Colonel was a gentleman, and as experienced as he was with the logistics of physical congress, he was unlearnt in the ways of love. He had led a circumspectly lusty life, not unlike his brothers in arms (and only a little less circumspect than the exceedingly circumspect copulatory life Darcy led prior to his connexion with Elizabeth). In that he held absolutely no recollection of their first sexual congress, he was apprehensive as to just what should be his course on the second. (Or even if there should be a course.) Indeed, the entire situation was most vexing. He was a well-seasoned man who had bedded his share of lovers. It seemed to make no sense how he had managed to impregnate Georgiana without any memory of it whatsoever. Gnawing on this mystery with great concentration for some time, he still remained in compleat bewilderment.

Upon the occasion of Georgiana's apprising him of her condition, she used little in the way of implications. Had she not made it clear that her situation was due to his interfering with her, he would have been seconding Darcy in pursuit of the scoundrel who had. He had not doubted her assertions for a moment. The only possibility was that the copious amounts of laudanum that attended his sick-bed rendered him not only an unscrupulous Lothario but an amnesiac as well. He simply could not, for the life of him, recollect when it might have occurred. Or how.

He knew he must have; Darcy was clearly angry at him. He was sufficiently ashamed of himself for taking advantage of such a delicate flower of a girl. Thoroughly ashamed. Therefore, inquiring the particulars of the act that rendered unto him a wife was absolutely insupportable. When he gazed upon Georgiana in all her blonde serenity, he truly despaired of not remembering. Perhaps one day that sweet memory would return. It must have been lovely.

Whilst he waited in the nuptial bed, he did not ponder these complexities long. He ceased puzzling over them when he felt Georgiana slide beneath the coverlet. He had lately come to the conclusion that he might be exempt from those acts expected of a bridegroom. It was his understanding that many ladies would not consent to connubial affections during gestation—others were happy to engage. He remained undecided on how to approach this dubiety—whether he should put out his arms, or await hers.

Her scent was trifling, but tantalizing—tantalizing enough for that alone to arouse his interest. He turned to her and took her into his embrace. Simultaneously, they realised then that he lay upon his bad leg. She slid from the bed and trotted to the other side. It occurred to him that she was indeed willing for some liberties to be taken. By then he was quite ready to take them. In silent urgency, he bid her hurry—her scent, he wanted again to bask in her scent. Again, she moved beneath the bedclothes and to his side. This time she raised her lips to him to be kissed. It was a timid kiss, so Fitzwilliam kissed her again. He supposed that if it was his duty as a husband, he would do what was asked of him.

They kissed once more, this time Fitzwilliam's eagerness fought a pitched battle with hers. Her alteration from passive to active participant allowed what may well have begun as a duty for him to transfigure into something mightily akin to passion. As his leg was bound and somewhat immobile, thus, his progression was not as he would have liked. But, the small moan that escaped his lips was not born of pain. However, she thought otherwise and arose on one arm in alarm.

"No," said he.

Before she lay back, she employed a small shake and a half of her head, one that loosed her tresses in a very fetching manner. The gaze they enjoyed answered a number of unasked questions. The answer to them all was in the affirmative. The kisses that had begun so tentatively escalated and he allowed his hands the audacity of exploring her sylphic figure. Once satisfied he knew what pleasures lay beneath his fingers, he gently slid his hand down her thigh to the hem of her gown signalling that the time was at hand for carnal union to commence. She lay still as a stone, but he could hear her breath coming in increasing little pants whilst he slowly drew himself upon her. His progress, however, was hampered by his bandages which continued to drag against the covers. He threw the covers back with growing impatience. His bad leg began to throb and his other foot cramped. He leapt from the bed and stood unaided, but swaying as he endeavoured to stomp the spasming into submission. Georgiana sat upright, her countenance awash with concern.

"It is nothing," said he, "just a cramp. All is well."

But he did not think all was well whatsoever. Perhaps all was for naught—perhaps he could not please his young wife. Perchance he was a broken excuse for a man, never to make love properly again. In a frustrated snit, he lay down, the back of his fist to his brows, his resolve wilting with his arousal.

For the smallest moment there was silence in the room save for the tortured breathing of both parties. One might suppose that what Georgiana did next implied a certain degree of impatience with her lover's boudoir resourcefulness. More likely, she simply saw that rescuing the situation fell to her. Regardless, up she rose, casting aside her gown as she did. It was an economical manoeuvre—swift and decisive. So decisive was it, Fitzwilliam's attention was garnered forthwith. (If he was astonished, he spoke not a word of it.) She thereupon pulled herself atop of *him*. She once again gave a shake of her head, scattering her tresses across her ivory shoulders.

He was dumbfounded.

Given that Fitzwilliam had always believed that when he married, unless he had the good fortune to marry a widow who bore him affection, his wife would be a consummate lady. In that he believed she could not be both a lady and temptress, he had held out little hope that his marriage would be sensually fulfilling. Gentlemen taken as husbands under such monetary arrangements were not chosen for the pleasure of their company. They would be used only as the means to procure a future generation. To put it plainly, he would be put out to stud. Some gentlemen found their characters unimpugned by such an arrangement.

When it had come to pass that for whatever reason, his intended was the most consummate lady, Georgiana Darcy, his anticipation was not excited on that account. He believed that fortune had only shone upon him to the point that he knew her to be personable and not some hopeless shrew. He understood that he had somehow compromised a lady and, as a gentleman, was fully prepared to pay the price of that indiscretion through a marriage of duty. However, from his recent vantage, her prospects (and thus his) improved dramatically.

As she sat atop him, totally and unabashedly undraped, he gazed upon her body in all its lithe glory. He did not want to liken her to a horse, but, quite frankly, as a cavalry man there was nothing he held in higher esteem than fine horseflesh—and he saw her as that then. But not as a brood-mare, she was a wild Arabian, long, aristocratic, and wild. (That it was she who rode him was of no concern to his imagery.) Although the voluptuousness of her action was undeniable, she gave herself to him for all that followed. He was most pleased. He was most pleased the better part of the night.

Morning, however, brought back to Fitzwilliam's countenance that same troubling bewilderment. For after their night of nuptial bliss, the dawn brought an altogether new puzzlement. The morn's unrelenting light revealed to him stains upon the bed-clothes. These were unlike those fluid traces of amours past. They looked, for all the world, to be blood-stains. It was he who spied them, not Georgiana. She had arisen before him, slipping carefully from the bed so as not to wake him. Nonetheless, he could hear her as she left for her toilette. She was singing softly, some faintly familiar melody, clearly unbothered by any complaint. Had she not been so carefree, he would have been alarmed that their abandon had done her and their unborn harm. He left the bed still unconvinced that she was altogether well.

However, when he happened to espy her doing the maid's office of pulling those same bed-clothes from the mattress, her gaze met his. She smiled shyly at him before she continued on with her work. She then gave a slight shake of her head, but her expression was one of amused contrition. In that moment his bewilderment lifted. The truth settled over him that until the night before she had been a virgin.

Remarkably, the realisation was one that was not entirely disagreeable.

He knew he should have been angry, but he was not. She looked again upon him with unadulterated adoration so that he could not find it in his heart to be even a little cross. Inwardly, he had a laugh at his own expense. This sweet innocent had compleatly duped him—Col. Geoffrey Fitzwilliam, Cavalry Commander, winner of dozens of campaigns both on and off his horse. Happily, he found being hoodwinked by Georgiana was not at all unfavourable. But, he thought that she should not go unpunished. The single retribution he could conjure was to make certain that if she did not come to the marriage bed carrying his child, he would make it his mission in life to see that she was when she left it. Georgiana was not of a mind to argue that penance in the least.

All of this was concluded without either of them speaking a word.

The Road to Perdition Is Paved with Feathers

George Wickham's undoing had begun long before his nefarious flight from the battlefield. Wickham (the man and the major) was a gambler, a dandy, and a spendthrift of proportions that only a Lord Byron could support without compleat ruination. Although it might be the assumption, Paris was not truly his down-fall. It just happened to be where he had met it.

How Major Wickham, a deserter of the British Army and the owner of, shall we say, more than a lion's share of character flaws, managed to insinuate himself into the fashionable cafés of the *grands boulevards* and become a confidant to one of the most admired courtesans in Paris was a history worthy of *A Winter's Tale*. The single thing to Wickham's credit is that he was not the first, nor hardly would he be the last, to be beguiled by the particular arts of a courtesan. As a practiced habitué of the café class and a man who thought himself above all pure and elevating passion, perhaps he should not have, for it was not in his nature. However, his heart had been fallow for so very long, that it was roused to love-struck insensibility the first time it was unfettered should not have been altogether unexpected.

For a man in a foreign land without a feather with which to fly, Wickham had landed on his feet with much the same facility as would an upturned cat. Still, as one of the race of occupying forces, he had fretted that Paris might just be a brief stop. *Perfide Albion*, the French called their British enemy—Treacherous English. He had heard that invective more than once and chose not to retort. Indeed, he had just chased across the countryside from Charleroi to Paris whilst ground into the corner of a tattered barouche between a particularly squat lady (so uncomely that he was convinced she was the fleeing French Emperor in disguise) along with a one-legged man wearing an over-sized beaver hat. After that little adventure, Wickham believed there was nothing upon which he would deign to remark.

He was, however, most anxious to enjoy an alteration in scenery.

Yet he had found Paris and its inhabitants (insofar as the company he chose to keep) quite otherwise inclined. Life in the demimonde went on as if the country were under no political upheaval whatsoever. Few things appeared to have ruffled the habitués of houses of fleshy commerce. And as he believed that his expertise in the French language very nearly rivalled that of rescuing himself from the brink of unmitigated disaster, he had felt altogether quite at home.

However, was he to be admitted to *chez elle*, Wickham had known that an impecunious gentleman had to have a certain *savior-faire*. Clumsy men were distinctly unappealing to sophisticated women. Compared to the average rich man, Wickham was slick by half, hence he had a leg up, if not over this particular haven of *demimondaines*. Trickery of all kind had always held Wickham's admiration. Regrettably, the single art that he honed most finely was still that of self-deception.

The steps were crowded with over-dressed Frenchman and Wickham had to step around the queue to gain his entrance to what appeared to have the makings of a *grand soirée*. As some talents return with uncommon ease to those disposed to use them, once he gained the room he paused but briefly as he took expert measure. Initiating an air of disdain, he held a tasselled card aloft betwixt fore and second finger and paid little heed to the burly footman wearing Bourbon colours who was then eying him suspiciously. If so insignificant a person as a servant were chary of his personage, Wickham had been loath to take offence. He had his invitation. It was not the *hoi polloi* whose regard he wished to impress, it was the noblesse.

With a twirling motion worthy of a fair *paso doble*, Wickham took off his cape and handed it and his recently purchased hat and sword off to the valet. They were not true to his uniform, but a hybrid; he prayed no one noticed. When it appeared no one had, still wary, he turned to the room. A devilish grin then overspread his countenance as he allowed the familiar sounds of debauchery and vice to wash over him like an ablution.

For his breast coat pocket beheld a treasure—*redingote anglaises* in France, known as a French letter in London. A bit of ribbon tantalizingly protruding from the package promised his ingress to untold delights. He had purchased it from a "discreet" shop in the gallery of *Palais Royal*. That little item provided the little bit of courage he needed when embarking upon seduction of women of a land not his own. He did not truly believe the stories that those ladies of the night were more likely infected with the foul complaint than those in London, but as a dedicated votary of Venus, he had been just uneasy enough to want a little added protection. This linen device would be a severe impediment to his pleasure, but he had reckoned that was better than a case of the pox. He had once had to undergo the torturous mercury cure and cringed at the thought of having to endure it again. Quite unknowingly, he patted it in reassurance as his gaze took in prospective paramours.

They looked to be an enchanting lot. Wickham had seen the gallant women of the époque sitting in the fashionable cafés and strolling the grand boulevards. He thought he would have liked to be the male counterpart to a courtesan.

"Pray, what are they called?" he had worriedly wondered to himself.

His French was not coming to mind as quickly as he had hoped. At that moment, his lack of recall of this particular term seemed to pose an insurmountable predicament despite the dubiety of him attaining such an ambition.

"Ah, yes. *Amant de…gigot*. No, not *gigot*, that is 'leg of mutton.' Something else…" he beseeched his recall of pillow-French and finally produced the term, "'*Le Gigole*.' *Oui*, yes. That is it, dancing partner. Better yet, '*Cavalier*,' companion. '*Amant de cœur*,' lover of the heart," had suited him most keenly, however, and he repeated it softly to himself several times so as not to forget.

Presently, Wickham withdrew his head from the clouds of amour and realised the folly of such a notion. However elevated his self-regard and great his heights of fancy flew, he would eventually find reason. He was ambitious enough and cynical enough, but he lacked determination. He would rather loll about with aspirations uninvestigated rather than endure that humiliation of defeat. Defeat had barked far too assiduously at his heels whilst fleeing Napoleon's drubbing at Quatre Bas. The British may have triumphed, but Wickham's mettle had not. Truth will out, it is said. Truth was, Wickham was not faint of heart but he had a streak of cravenness burrowed deep in his gut.

To his great relief, by the time he landed in Paris, word of Nappy's rout had preceded him, thus allowing the waffling political winds to shift once again. Wickham was fast to sniff out that certain circles were quite happy to welcome the *perfide Albion*. As his situation was, one could say, in a state of flux, he was happy to catch sight of open arms of any persuasion. He began to prowl the boulevards to strike up advantageous conversations and games of chance. Ere long, he had parlayed the few coins in his pocket into a stake. Other than an alteration of scenery, he had reclaimed a fair equivalent of the life he had been leading in London. So similar was it, that it was not long before one of his capers proved particularly lucrative.

Employing no little gall (and, admittedly, one step ahead of a minion of the Prefecture of Police), he had engaged a young gentleman on the *Chaussée d'Antin* in discourse by the pretence of enjoying a previous acquaintance. His attention to his occasionally unreliable French was compromised by the handsome accoutrement which adorned the young man's arm.

Wickham raised his hat to them both.

"Paris in August—abominable is it not?"

That was the single comment that he knew of Paris, and he used it upon every occasion.

Although the young man's costume exposed him of a man of means, his companion was not so easy to peg. When the beautiful young woman turned in his direction, he observed a treble ruff of vermillion curls nearly appropriating a wide white face. Granted, she was an impishly attractive woman and even Wickham recognised the jaconet muslin of her gown and the four full rows of flounces as being the very height of *haut ton* fashion. But whilst her dress was clearly fashionable and expensive, it bespoke a little too much *dégagé* to belong to a true woman of substance. Whilst he endeavoured not to take her too much in his notice, she continually threw the ends of an ermine tippet over her shoulders. (Rather than fetching, it gave the impression that the poor girl was trying to escape being swallowed alive by some wild beast.) Until this time his only acquaintanceships with the women of Paris had been mercenary in nature and, due to his financial straits, did not suit his discriminating taste. He then was happy to be in the company of this handsome couple. Their exact situation remained unclear to him, but he saw it a vast improvement on the denizens of the low culture of the Parisian card-rooms he had kept of late. Hence, he gifted them his most dazzling smile.

With introductions compleated, it took Wickham little time to learn that the young Frenchman was recently of Napoleon's guard. Indeed, hanging from a tri-coloured ribbon about his neck was the medal recognising him as a chevalier of the Legion of Honour. Wickham bowed low, thereby signifying his respect and allowing careful observation of his footwear (no finer gauge of a man's distinction being faultless boots). Admirably impressed, Wickham played his trump card.

Whilst still in genuflection, Wickham's fingers slipped into his waistcoat and grasped a ribbon and medal of similar prestige. With an expression remarkable in its blend of humility and pride, he revealed his own honorific to his new friend. Wickham's, of course, was not his own. It was not even a British commendation, but a Spanish one of similar design. He had bought it from a thread-bare old sot for the price of a drink, never once giving thought to whether the man was a hero down on his luck or just a fortunate pickpocket. Its ignominious origin was unapparent and the young gentleman returned his bow. He then looked upon Wickham with something akin to new respect. Wickham was quite flushed with self-congratulations that he had thought of it.

The Frenchman hastened to introduce himself. He was Viscount Henri Du Mautort, his consort, Mademoiselle Lambert. He was all parts the sort that Wickham liked best in a gentleman—young, guileless, and pockets laden with ready money. Indeed, Du Mautort was gracious to fault, his manners over-riding what little nose he may have had for duplicity. The only impediment Wickham saw to his designs was Mlle. Lambert. It was unmistakable to Wickham that Mlle. Lambert was of a sort who liked Du Mautort for the identical reasons Wickham did. She was all parts Wickham liked even better—wicked ways and easy virtue. She was younger than Du Mautort, perhaps but eight and ten—but that was only her chronological age. Her eyes displayed all the boredom of the most seasoned consort.

The trio walked the promenade with such felicity that Du Mautort would not allow Wickham to take his leave unless he agreed to seal their acquaintanceship with the promise of meeting again. Wickham allowed himself to be coaxed, providentially, to attend a *fête* that very night.

Hence, there Wickham stood gazing across a grand ballroom. It was thick with bodies draped *au courant* and faces caked with powder, but through the melange of richly appointed humanity Wickham managed to espy his *nouveau ami d'honneur*. Again, he raised his tasselled card to catch Du Mautort's eye. In the teeming mass, he had to waggle it several times before he caught his eye, but he was determined that he be bid to join their group, not ask admittance. Once that was accomplished and an upward nod was proffered, he sidled his way through the press of bodies until he gained the edge of Du Mautort's little battery of what could only be described as preening coxcombs. The dandies greeted Wickham with a succession of elegant bows which, without a break in rhythm, he returned one by one. It was only then that Wickham observed that the velvet-coated and satin-slippered gentlemen surrounded a single woman.

Although she was nearly obscured by a collection of admirers, it was difficult to overlook her. Whilst the other ladies stood about, she chose to sit. And sit she did on a sumptuous tuffet of silk pillows all of varying shades of pink. Sitting to the side on a slightly less grand mound of pillows was the lovely Mlle. Lambert, her position clearly of minion status. Had he any designs on Mlle. Lambert, Wickham quickly cast them aside. Perhaps his calculations at that moment were apparent to her for her countenance reflected a certain sagacity that implied she was not unaware that he was making them. It was an effort for him not to give her a wink. He bowed briefly and turned his full attention to the other, more prominent beauty. Wickham gave her an even deeper bow. She, however, refused to acknowledge him beyond a slight dip of her chin. She remained partially hidden behind a sultrily undulating ostrich-feather fan.

Du Mautort cleared his throat as he undertook what he felt were momentous introductions, whispering her name almost reverentially, "Mademoiselle Césarine, *s'il vous plaît,* I present General Wickham."

Being self-anointed a General, Wickham was clearly of the opinion that if one is fabricating a persona, there is little reason to curb one's cachet. Indeed, so thoroughly had Wickham enjoyed the grandiosity of his newly applied promotion, he was listening with far more dedication than looking. Hence, when he finally gazed upon Césarine, she had turned her face whilst stifling a theatrical yawn behind her perfectly placed, be-feathered ivory fan. From thence, all Wickham could catch sight of her was the graceful arch of her neck (and the multitude of diamonds that spiralled round it, dripping tear-drop shaped rubies the size of a toe) as she spoke to Mademoiselle Lambert. He smiled a bit to himself whilst witnessing her little artifice, happy to know himself above his company when it came to the feminine wiles. (It was difficult to ignore that the other gentlemen were much discombobulated by her display of tedium, several all but convulsing into paroxysms of obeisance.)

She lingered in the half-concealment of her fan and a profusion of copper tendrils for oh-so-brief a time before deigning to peer over it in Wickham's direction. Her eyes, half-closed in continued notification of his insignificance to her, batted softly before she raised them to meet his increasingly interested contemplation. Then, she held out one hand and two of her admirers leapt forward to assist her to her feet. It was only when she had lowered her fan to take dainty hold of a diaphanous cerise skirt to stand that her countenance was fully revealed to him. With a three-quarter turn of her aspect, she lowered her chin (a pose so unaffected that it could only have been perfected by many hours of practice in front of her looking-glass). Through a mass of unreasonably dark lashes, her eyes twinkled like penny sparklers and a coy smile toyed with the corner of her crimson lips.

Wickham stepped back stupefied. It was as if Venus had arisen from the foam. Oddly, the first thing that came to his mind was not admiration of her beauty, but that he would have to reassess his recent disdain of his cohorts' sensibilities.

"*Ma demoiselle,*" said Wickham with a slicing sweep of his arm across his extended knee.

He had used the archaic French, "my damsel" quite on impulse. It was a risky ploy and he awaited the rendering of its success with bated breath. It was not to be a long wait. For upon the heels of hearing him, with her chin still lowered, Césarine coyly swept her eyes the length of his figure and stopt when they gained his countenance. Her gaze was penetrating, but slightly amused. Wickham still knew not whether she thought him intriguing or simply a buffoon. He held his genuflection until she fully disclosed her opinion. She withheld it an excruciatingly long time and his weight-bearing left leg began to tremble (not from the strain of anticipating her response, but the extreme abuse of Wickham's sycophantically charged position). His knee set to spasming so profoundly that Wickham began to fear less that he might be spurned by the bewitching creature before him and more than he might literally fall on his face when she did. Finally releasing him (it is highly improbable that she was unaware of Wickham's distress), Césarine acknowledged Wickham's presence.

"*Bonjour, mon Général.*"

His gambit was a compleat and utter triumph!

With little attempt to disguise his glee, Wickham scrambled to his feet. He then delicately kissed her perfunctorily extended knuckles. He was ever-so pleased with himself to have had the audacity to wear the gold sash bearing numerous British military medals that he had found in that same little shop in the Latin Quarter where he purchased the entirety of his uniform *vêtements*. But more importantly, he then employed his own little flirtatious tilt of the head—one he had perfected through long hours before his looking-glass. If he had been a female, he would have batted his eye-lashes and pressed his lips into a sulk, but as he was not he simply puffed his chest, drew in his stomach, and presented his profile.

Although Wickham was neither bored nor any sillier than the average dissolute man, Césarine's charms had still worked their magic on his voluptuous nature with heedless abandon. He had forsaken his plan to lure Mademoiselle Lambert into *le boudoir* without a second's thought. He was knee-deep in a quagmire of quite another sort. He stood stupefied as though struck by a thunderbolt from above. A brief liaison was out of the question now that he had seen Elysium. He truly believed his breast had just been pricked by cupid's little arrow of *amour*. As Wickham was new to all consuming passion, even his burgeoning erection did not persuade him that it was not his heart that was inflamed. He knew but one thing—he must have her.

Whether Césarine was of the same mind was a question he was prepared to spend no small amount of time uncovering.

Love Sings for Jane

It was a bold move on Bingley's part. But he knew nothing less than a decidedly bold move would do to repair the gaping wound that his marriage had become. Moreover, if he was to salvage any speck of the tender love he and Jane had shared, he must make his move with all due haste. Therefore, he waited little more than what passed for a suitable period of penitence before he mustered the courage to go to her.

The night he chose for this matrimonial reparation was not unlike any other save for his own disconcertion and a portentously full moon. His toilette in preparation for this endeavour was elaborate. Once compleat, he patted his hair, licked his finger tips to smooth down his occasionally errant sideburns, and then nervously rendered the same to the front of his night-shirt. Whilst engaging in these preparations, he knew that just beyond the heavy door separating their respective beds, Jane slept quite unawares. Still, he took the precaution of peering into the keyhole in reassurance that all was as he anticipated. In the moonlight sweeping across her counterpane, he could make out the outline of her form. Only then did he manage a hesitant knock upon the door of his wife's bed-chamber.

Although he did rap upon her door, it was in actuality little more than a scratch. This light touch served the dual purpose of obeying decorum without actually awakening her—this because he designed not to offer her an opportunity to thwart him either by an out-right rebuff or feigning sleep. He opened the door forthwith and stepped into the room. (He would have liked to think that he entered with great manly condescension, but in fact it was more of a sidle.) Not wanting to cause her a fright, as he neared the bed he whispered her name once more. Still, she did not stir. He could observe the counter-pane continue to rise and fall with the deep respirations of her sleep.

With more conviction, he called, "Jane, dearest."

She sat bolt upright, but her eyes were still half-open.

"Pray, who is ill?" she asked worriedly, thinking of no other reason than an ailing child to be disturbed after she had retired. Those instructions were implicit with Nurse.

"No one, save me," said Bingley.

He made for her bed with more haste than the mere chilliness of the floor might have influenced and, once arrived, slid beneath the covers with the same remarkable dispatch. By that time, Jane was not only compleatly awake, she was in high alert (as much at the introduction of his cold feet as the intrusion itself). The shallow indention even her slight frame made in the soft batting of the mattress was excuse enough for his forward motion to propel him directly into her embrace—had she held out her arms to him. But she had not.

She had, however, understood then that no one was ill. But that did little to alleviate her apprehension. From her expression of heightened alarm, she not only did not move to embrace him, she looked upon her husband's form with compleat incredulity—almost as if some sort of feral creature had made its way into her bed.

Now near enough to feel his breath upon her cheek, she inquired mildly, "Are you, sir, unwell?"

"It is only my heart…"

"I shall get my salts…" said she, but she made no move for them.

Had it been any other who spoke those words, Bingley would have believed himself the victim of sarcasm. As it was dear, sweet Jane who said it, he knew better. Rather, she brought her hand from beneath the bed-clothes as if to press the backs of her fingers to his fevered brow, but he caught them and pressed them tenderly against his lips.

Then he said quite fervently, "I need only your forgiveness."

In a comforting tone (if one was perfectly frank, it could be described as the precise accent she used with their children), she said, "Have I not sworn my forgiveness?"

"You forgave my weakness. I fear you have not forgiven me—for I cannot forgive myself."

With this last, he gave a small hiccupping sigh. But Jane found all untruths unpalatable, even those necessary to salve the wounds of those most dear to her heart. Hence, she could not in all good conscience declare her husband unequivocally absolved of his monumental betrayal of his wedding vows to her.

"I see," said she.

That was not untrue, for she did see. She saw quite a lot. As his hand loosed hers, he found it new, if tentative, employment in drawing her nearer. She understood then that he had come to her in want of resuming their intermittent and somewhat indifferent love-life. She not only saw that, she also felt it. Indeed, their bodies now perfectly aligned, she felt a stiffening that was not just his resolve. Thereupon an expression of obligatory acceptance overspread her countenance—one the dark mercifully did not allow him to behold. Hence, he was spared seeing upon her aspect what some might have mistaken for a grimace. That he did not see it did not suppose he did not know it was there. He understood well that Jane knew her duty to her husband and that she was fully prepared to accept any and all attentions he paid her without complaint. She lay quiet, her hands folded across her bosom in wifely subjugation for him to do with her as he wished.

She had forgiven him and time was at hand for her to prove it both to God above and husband beside her.

As bold as Bingley's entry into her bed-chamber had been, the redesigned path he was about to embark upon held even more risk, this he knew. However, in his enthusiasm to return to her bed as well as her good graces, Bingley had found himself very nearly lapsing into his previous habit of heaving himself upon her recumbent form and having his way with her female parts. And she, as was her habit, lay quite still. Her only rearrangement of her person was to move her hands shoulder high and palms up in an attitude not unlike one might find oneself in if beset upon by highwaymen. Their amorous encounters had always taken place thusly. Jane had always found this discreet placement of her hands reassuring, since that most unsettling night when she had inadvertently grasped her husband's member and the resultant fright to them both was not easily forgot. Since that occasion, she had also always kept her eyes tightly shut during physical congress, certain she did not want to behold this appendage or accidentally gaze upon any indecorous activity it wrought. She did so not like being caught unawares.

In truth, it was reassuring to Jane that their love-making never altered. When Charles slipped between the bed-sheets, she knew the preparatory foreplay would consist of a kiss upon each cheek and twice upon her lips. This entire frolic would inevitably culminate with a tweak to her left breast. That signalled the commencement of what she knew must be an arduous husbandly duty. (She knew it was quite arduous for him because of all his grunting and sweating.) Indeed, his mission previously had been to get the job done in all due haste lest any tarriance was imposed upon his good wife's privacy unduly. And in respect for this privacy, four children had been conceived without once drawing his wife's night-dress above those component parts absolutely necessary to accomplish this feat. His measures had always been great on the side of efficiency and light in the area of any pleasure other than his own. For that, he was ashamed almost as keenly as for his adultery.

This conclusion was not reached with particular ease.

Initially, his remorse had a Calvinist bent under which he understood to believe that anything pleasurable was suspect. The black waistcoat he took to wearing, however, was soon abandoned. For although Bingley was naïve, he was not stupid. Contrition was well and good, but self-reproach alone was not the only answer to his marital woes. Yielding to temptation in the arms of another woman (one in the habit of enjoying liaisons that were not only passionate, but very nearly raucous), had rendered him soiled of virtue perhaps, but also considerably enlightened about the delight that mutual gratification could bestow. He was eventually able to escape the shackles of guilt long enough to imagine a more passionate congress with his wife.

Indeed, he had worried that notion relentlessly, desperately wanting to share such pleasures with the one he loved best, but fearing he would injure his demure wife's sensibility irreparably. In his deep and lengthy deliberation, he recalled certain sultry looks that he had observed pass between the Darcys. His new enlightenment suggested to him that their marriage bed was far more lusty than his own. He had always known that Darcy was a man of experience. It was not a great leap for his ruminations to wonder if Jane and her sister spoke of such matters—then as quickly as that, he dismissed the possibility. He reasoned that even he and Darcy did not discuss such intimate matters; certainly ladies were no less circumspect. With no other avenue of enlightenment to pursue, he eventually concluded it better to risk Jane's sensibility than her heart. He would not rest knowing that he had not pleasured his wife with the diligence he had another.

Hence, he had come to Jane with only one ambition and that was to reward her for every moment of gratification that she had allowed him. Although it did not commence with particular finesse—for he chose to allow his hand to traverse her person via marching index and middle fingers, causing Jane to stifle a nervous giggle. As he expected, she was initially hesitant to allow him to make free with her person. Yet, sometimes playfully, sometimes seductively, he persevered. Indeed, with his gentle diligence (and fingers joined by the palm of his hand in fetching undulations), she allowed her night-dress to make its way upward. Indeed, so far was it raised that it was discarded altogether. Blessedly, the room was dark, hence the crimson of her countenance was known only to herself. She lay motionless, but a susurration escaped from her lips quite unlike any other he could recall.

"Charles, pray is this..." she began a question that she knew not how to form.

"Hush, my sweet," he reassured her, "all is well. Allow me to stroke you," he implored.

To him she agreed that his stroking was most comforting. But, in point of fact, it was not. She found that it was most...invigorating. So invigorating was it, her recently complacent hands located and took hold of various makeshift knurls upon his body—in fortune, for the manoeuvre upon which they embarked required a firm handhold on something (or anything). The progression of their venture was quite familiar, but her response was not. From the deepest reaches of her throat wafted a moan heretofore unheard in their bed-chamber. In that instant two illuminations unfolded. Jane understood without reservation the romantic rapture that Lizzy had tried to explain to her lo those many years ago, and Charles recognised what had been missing from both his marriage and his extra-marital encounter. With Jane, it had been passion, from his illicit paramour, it had been love. He then recognised the confluence of both in the woman who was his wife.

Passion overdue was merely passion delayed. No, Bingley would not stray again. Jane would see to it he had not the strength.

Small Worries Loom Large

Sitting in comfortable resplendence in the corner of Mrs. Darcy's dressing-room was an over-stuffed *chaise-longue.* It was well-used, the worn damascene along the arms mute testimony to its popularity with its mistress. She had refused to surrender it to the upholsterer for refurbishing because she rather liked it as it was, threadbare and fraying. Upon this occasion, she reposed there in an obvious state of discomposure. Hannah inquired if she needed anything and she shook her head impatiently, hence the maid withdrew. Closing the dressing room door behind her, Hannah was startled by the spectre of Smeads in the shadows of the corridor. She had been finding him in odd places at odd times and, because of it, she was becoming increasingly disconcerted herself. Hannah was a simple young woman—schemes and schemers were not her forte. Her unease as much as her mistress's bade her remain at sentry outside the door until Smeads betook himself down the hallway. Once he had withdrawn, Hannah peeked inside the room once more just to reassure herself that all was well within. She saw Mrs. Darcy restlessly tossing about upon her *chaise* before settling herself.

Upon most occasions the simple act of lying there and fingering the fraying kindled sweet remembrances for her. On other occasions when she had reclined thereabouts, she was in the company of her husband (whose massaging of her feet betimes resulted in the dispensing of favours of voluptuous nature particularly suited to the chair's recumbent form). Indeed, this oft-used chair in which Mrs. Darcy reposed had been the place of many comforts, which was perhaps what had enticed her to retreat to it.

As she had plumped down this day, however, those much cosseted feet had impatiently flipped her slippers half-way across the room. (Such abuse of carefully embroidered footwear was an indication of the vastness of her displeasure.) The window to the right of the *chaise* would have emitted a soft glow of the late afternoon sunlight had it not been obliterated by what appeared to be an over-venturesome closing of the velvet side-drapes. Indeed, it was a lovely afternoon, yet Mrs. Darcy enjoyed it not.

So little did she enjoy it, she attempted to further herself from it by a tri-folded piece of damp cloth dipped in chilled water and placed over her eyes. Hannah had attempted to arrange it for her, but in a fit of pique Elizabeth had shooed her away. If she was to sulk, she wanted privacy in which to pity herself.

Alas, there was much to grieve Mrs. Darcy that day and she felt especially ill-used by events.

As she once again refreshed her wet cloth and strung it daintily across her furrowed brow, Elizabeth mulled over the latest of the obstructions to the happiness of their household. It was particularly vexatious to have to accept that having her husband once again by her side, her babies healthy, Georgiana married, and the wet-nurse dispute with her mother resolved, that all bothers could not be banished. Contentment always seemed somehow at bay. An entirely new disturbance to their peace had been provoked, and upon this occasion she knew herself to be, if not compleatly blameless, not the primary culprit. Nor would she reproach her husband as intractable (although he could be at times *quite* intractable).

No, they were equal partners in this dilemma.

Why, O, why were they the only parents in the whole of England who could not find a suitable nurse to help care for their beloved children?

They had auditioned, appraised, tested, scrutinized, and evaluated seven consecutive candidates. All were miserable failures (one Mr. Darcy had to be cajoled from having the bailiff set upon). Perhaps it was too much to ask that but one woman see to both the babies, but she so did not want to have two compleat sets of nurses, nursery under-nurses, nursery-maids, and odd-men all bustling in and around their babies' bed-chamber. They feared there was too much bedlam surrounding their children as it was.

She supposed in those long days waiting for her husband to return that she should have used her time more efficiently since she knew well of the coming of a child. But her thoughts had been so contaminated by fear that she could barely face each new day, much less make detailed preparations for an event she had difficulty facing alone. In the back of her mind, it had been her belief that if the worst happened, she would tend her child by herself. She had no other accounting for being so ill-prepared. But she stopt castigating herself early on for the double birth that she could not possibly have foreseen. There was enough bother to keep her mind occupied without dredging up past lapses.

Although between Elizabeth, Hannah, and Mrs. Littlepage, they were managing to keep the babies both fed and dry, other duties were going wanting. She knew it was unreasonable not to make arrangements for more help, but she dragged her feet on the issue, truly reluctant to bring someone else into their family fold. Mrs. Littlepage had been test enough.

"It is pointless, Elizabeth, to be of such agreeable means and not make use of them for our own benefit," Darcy insisted.

So very weary was she becoming, determined as she was to see to the babies and the running of the house, she barely had the energy for love. Whether this was the impetus for his putting his foot down on the matter remained undetermined. Regardless, Elizabeth happily allowed herself to be persuaded.

Their search commenced in quite an orderly fashion. Mr. and Mrs. Darcy were of the same mind that casting about for additional help should commence with a survey of those within whom one held in the greatest trust. Hence, one would have expected Elizabeth to inquire of the single person she held in the highest esteem, her sister Jane. However, Elizabeth knew (as well as should have Darcy) that whilst Jane was the happy mother of four, her repute as mistress to Kirkland Hall was compromised by an artless disposition and irresolute husband. The ruling of their household had come to pass just as Mr. Bennet had once foretold—Jane and Bingley were each of them so complying that nothing was ever resolved upon and so easy that every person in their service cheated them.

The Bingley children were adorable but ran compleatly at their own will. Their children's nurse was dignified in bearing and kind in deportment, but always looked frazzled and bore a perpetually abused expression that was singular only to one whose injury was long-suffered. The children ran wild with nurse in their wake, whilst both Jane and Bingley sat and listened with pleasure to the havoc they wrought.

Mr. Bennet's sage observation was never more expeditiously demonstrated than when one looked upon the officious spectre of Jane's lady-maid, Mary. After lo these many years Mary was still compleatly contrary and still in her service. Jane was all but timorous in her presence. Elizabeth was somewhat intimidated herself, but believed she could muster the wherewithal to let her go.

"But, Lizzy," Jane objected, "I could not. It would wound Caroline, for she selected her particularly for me."

Although Bingley's man had been with him for years and was therefore quite dedicated, Jane was not so fortunate. Caroline Bingley had happily supplied Jane her maid and Elizabeth suspected that the maid's insolence was directly related to that connexion. Seeing Jane quake in the presence of the very person whose life was to be dedicated to her benefit had long been a pin-prick in Elizabeth's side. Moreover, she knew that Mary was upon her best behaviour when in company and that did nothing to mitigate her vexation. She had faced the fact that in the Bingleys' house, orders were requests and instructions were guidelines—all open for debate. Upon the occasion of an open slight, Elizabeth had had enough and told Jane so.

"Ungovernable girl!" she said before Mary had quite withdrawn from the room, "Jane, you must do something about such abuse!"

But Jane only repeated her previous excuse of not wanting injure "dear Caroline."

"If Caroline is so happy with her, why not have Mary tend to her?" Elizabeth said, then was instantly sorry for her sarcasm.

Jane always took the good in everybody's character (no matter how deeply imbedded) and made it still better, ignoring the ill-traits altogether.

"Oh, Lizzy! I know as a mistress I do deserve reproach. Mary means well, she is just plain-spoken."

"But she behaves abominably to you."

"Nothing that I regard," assured Jane.

"Pray, I cannot believe Mr. Bingley would have you sacrifice your own happiness to serve the caprice of your lady-maid."

In invoking Bingley's name, Elizabeth realised her argument had faltered, for Jane and Bingley's tempers were by no means unlike. They were both of sweet nature and generous heart. Although she continued to question it, Elizabeth knew Jane would never take another course. Because she inherited Mary from the Bingley family she would sooner leave his house altogether (and she would rather die than leave her beloved Bingley's house) than question whom he chose to serve it. That Bingley's wretched sister Caroline had employed her and, no doubt, had a hand in keeping her on just to spite Jane, she did not choose to point out. Had she, no doubt, she would have had to suffer a recitation of Caroline Bingley's little-exhibited virtues. Hence, she had allowed the subject to drop.

Servants in general remained out of topic until upon a visit by the Bingleys, the urgency of the Darcys obtaining a nurse was brought into their discourse. When this discussion arose, to Elizabeth's surprise it was Darcy who initiated it. Moreover, he specifically named Jane to be consulted on the matter. In that Jane's single conceit was that she knew well of babies and nurses, she was quite delighted to be invited to be of service. Thinking that he had solved their problem efficiently, Darcy was well-pleased with himself to have been her agent in the matter.

Straightaway, Jane proudly proposed the sister of her own children's nurse, for that woman, Mrs. Biggs, was then much at liberty. In that Elizabeth's belated nudge to her husband profited nothing but a bewildered expression, Elizabeth smiled and murmured her thanks to Jane.

"I shall have her sent round directly," said Jane, exhibiting more self-satisfaction than Elizabeth had ever recollected of her.

"Pray, do so," said Elizabeth, with a smile of exceptional cordiality.

As to Darcy, however, she waited until the Bingleys had taken leave before addressing his…impedance (she refused to use the word meddling, but she thought it). Elizabeth knew what Darcy did not—that this Mrs. Biggs was not only sister to Jane's nurse, but to her lady-maid Mary as well. As to which particular family lineament Mrs. Biggs would tend was not a question Elizabeth particularly cared to explore.

"Pray husband," she said with all reserve of temperament, "have you not expressed your belief that every disposition has a tendency toward some particular evil?"

"I am free to confess, I have."

"Even my beloved sister, Jane's?"

"I take leave to observe that I hold your sister in the highest of regard. Yet, even Mrs. Bingley must have some faults in her nature. Lo, I have yet to uncover one," was his diplomatic reply.

"Pray then," she continued in a carefully modulated tone, "I suggest to you one."

He did not speak, only nodded once. This was in acknowledgment that her level articulation indicated the high probability of the culpability of his own character being delineated soon after.

"Jane is good. There is no one beyond you and our children that I love more. It does not follow, however, that one who is much beloved is wise in all things," said she, "present company excepted."

She then nodded graciously toward her husband.

"Present company excepted," he echoed, nodding warily in return.

"My sister's single indulgence is that of her children. I suppose one must enlarge that to include everyone Jane loves, for I fear she indulges us all," Elizabeth chortled happily at that unassailable truth before continuing. "She is too kind to be as severe as she must with everyone including those under her direction. Every person in her service is either utterly lackadaisical or outrageously recalcitrant. Her nurse is a twit, her maid a shrew. That does not bode well for us in employing a relation of someone she has in service. Do you not agree?"

"Your point is well taken," Darcy said.

It was not an admission that he had blundered, simply that she was not wrong.

"I do hope," she added, "that were we to err in this matter, it is to that family's simple-minded side, for both Jane's nurse and lady-maid are Mrs. Biggs's sisters. I know a nurse must not be a compleat gull, but I should like to observe some small tenderness when dealing with wee-ones."

"All will be well," he assured her.

As he did so he reached out and patted her hand in, to his mind, a reassuring manner. To Elizabeth, it was ever-so slightly condescending. (It was quite remarkable how that hand-pat took on a definition quite unintended by its provider.) Did her own good husband think that Jane knew better than she what was best for their children? Had she not yet proved her proficiency as a mother? These thoughts and others like them continued as they attended to their respective toilettes. But when they climbed atop their bed (she predictably via the bed-steps, he by swinging first one long leg then the other—not unlike stepping astride his horse), he gazed upon her with charming allure. Hence, with very little effort she ceased seeking to find offence in this small (but painfully compleat) disregard for her opinion upon the nurse issue. And despite a magnificently employed device occupying the better part of an hour, he altered her thoughts only temporarily. Such was her admiration of his endeavour, he was blissfully unaware of its only partial success. They both nodded off into beatific sleep, yet when the next morn dawned the insult to her motherly *amour-propre* still gnawed at her quite unrelentingly.

And with the dawn and a half-day more came the unsolicited Mrs. Biggs. It was with colossal determination that Elizabeth looked upon her with unprejudiced eye and impartial words, yet she could determine immediately on which side of the family tree Mrs. Biggs's apple fell—and it was not to the side of the irresolute. Indeed, she was not of faint-heart, but rather, a martinet. A martinet possibly worthy of Wellington's adjutant, Elizabeth observed, but only to herself—if she was to be proven wrong, she meant to keep her misjudgement discreet. Hence it was with charity and all good will that Elizabeth showed her to the nursery.

Mrs. Biggs was all deferential compliance but held with her an air of superiority—that in and of itself a remarkable feat. Of no particular reassurance as to her suitability, Elizabeth still persuaded herself to reserve judgement until this Mrs. Biggs was given an opportunity to display her proficiency, or lack thereof, before making a determination out of hand that she was unacceptable. Elizabeth remained overtly agreeable, but eyed every move the woman made with suspicion, awaiting a wrong move—in an attitude remarkably similar to that of the spider with a fly.

As the afternoon wore on Mrs. Biggs was, if not particularly exuding warmth, at least efficient, and she seemed unfazed by tending to two infants at one time. Still, Elizabeth weathered a curious hesitancy in embracing not only Mrs. Biggs, but also the notion of her. It occurred to her that her seemingly irrational ill will might be the emergence of a fledgling appearance of mother's intuition. As it was either that or a nonsensical obstinacy, she was not disposed to reveal it to her husband until she knew it was truly honed. Hence, when he asked how well Mrs. Biggs got on, she answered as inconclusively as was within her command.

By late in the day, dislike was sharpened into particular abhorrence and it was fortunate that Mrs. Biggs revealed her true self when she did, as it saved Mrs. Darcy a great deal of snooping. As it was, the unparalleled regard Elizabeth held for her children's well-being demanded a surveillance of considerable stealth. Compleatly oblivious to this study, Mrs. Biggs took her tiny charges in hand with capable authority. This she did unaware of her employer's circling her with a cunning that had elevated from spider and its lunch to that of a tigress protecting her cubs. Under such tense scrutiny, it took very little time for the woman to betray herself to be the scolding and ill-tempered shrew Elizabeth supposed her to be.

For little Geoff was lying in his cradle, chewing happily on his coral teether (with silver bells—one that had once been his father's) whilst Mrs. Biggs had been dutifully, if perfunctorily, rocking him with one foot. Geoff was a restless sleeper, difficult to lull to nap, difficult to arouse. Of this Mrs. Biggs had been apprised. Elizabeth had explained the precise methodology that she and Mrs. Littlepage used to soothe him. When he began to fuss, however, Mrs. Biggs was disinclined to indulge him. Rather, in a harsh whisper, she demanded he hush and commenced pumping her foot faster. Not unusual for an infant, the boy's vocabulary was limited and did not include those words she employed to command his silence. Therefore, they were ineffective and he continued to cry with ever increasing vigour. Through the keyhole (a position she did not divulge when the story was repeated) Elizabeth observed it all and gasped in outrage. This outburst was unbeknownst to Mrs. Biggs due to the baby's distress. Hence, she was taken in all astonishment when she then wrested the teether from his little fingers and cast it aside only to find that Elizabeth had flung back the door.

"Aha!" Elizabeth veritably cried out at her, startling the woman senseless.

Mrs. Biggs recollected herself with surprising haste, having a justification on her lips whilst Elizabeth still stood in speechless fury unable to put two words of indignation together that did not include an invective or blasphemy. Calmly, Mrs. Biggs issued a much-used explanation that addressed the issue of recalcitrant children and her belief of how they should be governed.

"I believe, Mrs. Darcy," said she, "that children but come into the world of a corrupt nature and evil character. They are in desperate need of being slapped into quiet."

(Mrs. Biggs did not actually say those last words, but that was what Elizabeth understood as her meaning.)

Mrs. Darcy replied, "I believe children to be innocents whose small transgressions want kind correction, Mrs. Biggs. And *you* are not well-suited to our needs here."

As Elizabeth retrieved the teether and returned it to her son, murmuring soft apologies to him, he took it again in his hand, kicked both it and his feet in unison, and giggled at the jingling noise he made. The happiness then reinstated to her child allowed Elizabeth to turn and glare once again at Mrs. Biggs. That woman wavered no fair amount before succumbing to the mistress's withering gaze.

"Beg pardon, m'lady."

Without further comment, she hastily gathered up what little tattered dignity she could muster before quitting the place by way of the nearest footpath leading away from the premises.

Her mother's instinct now fact not fiction, Elizabeth meant to share with her husband the news of the woman's absurd Scottish-Calvinist leanings and the due care they must observe in future interviews (if somewhere in this recitation was an implied "I told you so," that was quite beyond her control). Off to Darcy went his wife with her son upon one shoulder and the not-quite awakened Janie stirring in the cradle of one arm. As this little trio made their way up the hallway, Mrs. Littlepage joined in behind them. Elizabeth issued whispered assurances to her recently endangered children of the unlikelihood they would ever leave her sight again whilst Mrs. Littlepage scurried from side to side in vain hope she might be handed at least one of the children.

With Mrs. Littlepage determinedly on her heels, Elizabeth scurried up and down the grand corridors of Pemberley in this manner until at last she located her poor, beleaguered babies' father. There, she unceremoniously released the heavy bundle that was Geoff unto his father's arms and reshuffled Janie, who had finally aroused from her slumber. Her husband was more impressed with his wife's ability to subdue two squirming infants at once than curious of how it happened to be necessary.

"Lizzy! Where is Mrs. Biggs?" he gasped out as he juggled his son into an upright position.

"Mrs. Biggs, indeed!" she veritably harrumphed. "I have come to learn that Mrs. Biggs's nature would be better served levelling lashes upon the backs of the men walking the treadmill in Newgate Prison than to tend a baby."

This announcement was accompanied by a recitation (compleat with all due expository commentary) of Mrs. Biggs's evil-doing. When she had concluded, Darcy issued but one mild inquiry.

"The woman has left this house?"

Elizabeth and Mrs. Littlepage both nodded their heads in unison—Elizabeth bore an expression of satisfaction. One unacquainted with Mr. Darcy might not have understood how little prone he was to discomposure and thus not realise that he was no less outraged than his wife. She knew that his nature was more subdued, hence, his "aha" may not have been so loud, but it was equally heartfelt. Indeed, her vindication was so apparent that it was quite unnecessary for her to issue any sort of recriminatory comment in defence of her instincts. Darcy then inquired where Mrs. Biggs was domiciled and how long before the constable could apprehend her. This, of course, impelled Elizabeth's fully flowered self-righteous indignation into retreat so she could suggest his reaction might be a bit excessive (but just a bit).

"I am uncertain if the magistrate would consider her actions as felonious as do we," she replied.

As much as they were alike in their distaste for undutiful children, they were never quite happy that they gave up the notion of having Mrs. Biggs in stocks on the Lambton green.

So went nurse number one.

Now on compleat alert, the subsequent applicants fell to Mr. Darcy's strict measure one by one. The second one he saw as too slovenly, from the third he detected a peculiar odour, four looked a trifle gluttonous (she was large, but hardly the five and twenty stone he proclaimed). The fifth one Mr. Darcy reckoned was a trollop and he would not have her influence near his children. Although Elizabeth had initially stood by each dismissal in nodding approval, as each one was banished for increasingly obscure reasons, she grew alarmed that they would never find adequate help without someone relaxing *his* criterian in some small way. When the next he pronounced as far too pleased with herself, Elizabeth was compleatly exasperated.

"Upon my word, sir! If a covetous applicant comes before us I believe we can actually boast of having seen one for each of the seven deadly sins. I truly believe you above being pleased in this matter!"

He smiled as if somehow satisfied to have reached some sort of pinnacle of selectivity, but it was that conclusion that drove her to her *chaise-longue* in a dolorous funk. Upon reassuming her other duties of the house, she knew that she was much in need of additional help. Whether it was admitting this failing to herself or her husband's demanding nature that was most bothersome, she knew not. She just knew that if the babies gained much more weight, she was going to have to pull them about in a cart if she was to get any of her duties accomplished whatsoever.

In time, Hannah came to her despondent mistress with a cautious suggestion. She had a cousin (a relation of Hannah's should have been inquired of in the first place), who had a number of younger siblings who had grown up healthy and happy under her custody.

"She is just a simple girl, but very good with wee-ones. Pray; would mistress like to speak with her?" queried Hannah.

Yes, mistress would. Mr. Darcy was no less pleased than his wife with the sweet-natured Margaret Heff and she was in place by the end of the next day. It all ended well, but it was with a sigh of relief that Elizabeth patted her cherished chair, perhaps reassuring herself of its longevity, for she rued the day when they would have to obtain the services of a governess.

39

Basking in Love's Tepid Arms

So it was, for whatever quirk of fate that intervened, George Wickham had been allowed admittance into the elite circle and selective boudoir of Mademoiselle Césarine Thierry. That this coterie was becoming less and less exclusive with each passing day, Wickham was quite unwitting.

This misconception was a blunder, but an understandable one for an *étranger* to those swells who inhabited the Parisian demimonde. Had Wickham been more familiar with actors in this little theatre, he would have known that, while seemingly prosperous, Du Mautort was living in Paris on a stipend not much larger than Wickham's army pay, but one day would inherit. When it came to the elite of this terrain, Du Mautort was merely a hanger-on and more love-struck than Wickham. Still, the one truth Wickham knew was that a courtesan had an infinite number of aspirants from whom to pick. If his Césarine thought his own company was acceptable, it could only fall to his undeniably superior mien and unrivalled handsomeness.

Yet Wickham knew that her time was not his exclusively. He may have managed to feign an elevation in station, but he had not the wherewithal to produce the funds to support it. Through considerable cunning he did manage to concoct an elaborate scheme involving a forged letter of credit and a fictitious bank account. He used this subterfuge to influence Viscount Du Mautort to advance him five hundred francs. (This was the whole of Du Mautort's monthly budget and put the poor man in quite a pinch, but so desperate was he to abide within Wickham's, and therefore, Césarine's good graces, he somehow ferreted it out of his own paltry purse.) As Wickham's conscience was already severely burdened by previous indiscretions both morally and criminally reprehensible, this arrant fraudulence was insignificant by half.

If he thought of it, he did so only briefly, for *Général* Wickham was in the throes of pure adoration. He had fallen hopelessly in love with a woman who was as handsome, graceful, alluring, winning, sociable, and cunning as himself. Moreover, she had succeeded in supporting herself quite admirably solely by the employment of her charms. She was the best parts of all things he regarded. (That she, as he, was shallow, narcissistic, dishonest, and promiscuous somehow went if not undetected, at least unacknowledged.)

Césarine did not invite him to her boudoir that night of their initial meeting. She remained aloof, but managed an expression upon her countenance to suggest that she, in spite of herself, just might be susceptible to his charms. With exaggerated nonchalance, she told him that she would not oppose a visit should he come round the next day.

"If I am not otherwise occupied," said she.

As one who had employed the manoeuvre himself more than once, Wickham certainly should have recognised a game of cat-and-mouse as the artifice that it was. Regrettably, he was far too deeply enthralled to catch his breath, much less suspect her of such a hoary gambit as that. Hence, he was upon her doorstep before the stroke of noon bearing an enormous bouquet of lavender, foxglove, and white Dutch hyacinths. (Finding a flower shop stocked with these embargoed bulbs was more difficult than inducing the proprietor to extend him a line of credit.) The flowers had been an extravagance, but seldom was Wickham mean with funds if he was endeavouring to impress a lady—particularly if the funds were not produced from his own pocket.

As Mademoiselle Thierry did not arise before two, Wickham sat playing an unrewarding game of mental twiddle-thumbs whilst his perspiring hands rendered his costly assortment of flowers progressively more wilted until nigh four o'clock.

When finally she did appear, Wickham judged it well worth the wait. For not her maid, but Césarine herself threw open the door to greet him. She was wearing little more than a dressing-gown, albeit of expensive fur-lined, red brocade festooned with plumage from some unrecognisable, but suitably exotic bird. (She was also wearing the ruby and diamond necklace from the other evening—it was an adornment that he would often see again.) Wickham, who prided himself on being informed in such matters, was clearly quite taken with her fashionably seductive *ensemble*. He stumbled a bit when he entered the room, crimsoning his face as if he were a virginal schoolboy. (This was highly vexing to Wickham; the appearance of sophistication was imperative.) With a graceful wave of her hand she bid him take a seat. He found himself, however, seated on a tuffet so tiny that his legs protruded like some flannelled grasshopper. From his disadvantaged position, he thought to offer up his floral tribute. With elaborate condescension, she took it from his hand and airily tossed the twenty quid of flowers on a side table in a limp heap.

As swiftly as she appeared, she quit the room. She exited through another door, trilling flirtatiously over her shoulder that she would return forthwith.

He noted several urns of flowers all more impressive than his and he winced at how paltry his offering was by comparison. (From his ridiculous attitude, he was still too beguiled to discern just how keenly he was being manipulated—had he looked more closely he would have seen that although they bore all the signs of being from other suitors, they were of similar flowers and arrangement.) He refused to be thwarted. A fit of pique at such humiliation provoked him to move from his perch on the tiny stool to a more commodious arm-chair. If he was to be spurned, he refused to weather it with his knees foremost.

Indeed, when in time she did return, it was to the sight of Wickham, cigar in hand, puffing away in the most audacious manner. In that all good company knew it exceedingly ill-mannered to smoke in a lady's presence, Césarine scowled. When he deliberately blew a cloud and thereupon tapped some non-existent ashes into a vase of flowers next to his chair, she thought better of her disapproval.

She turned her chin just enough to display what she fancied was her best side and simpered, "*Très vilain, mon ami.*"

Harsh Streets

The day fate officially announced itself as truly cruel, little Sue Arbuthnot's cheeks still bore the lingering traces of baby-fat. Her big sister, Sally Frances, was but ten. Both were far too young to be forced into pitched battles with life's atrocities. The specific brutality life chose to throw in their path was the loss of their mother. Had she merely died, that would have been a kindness compared to the bewildering fact of outright abandonment.

Indeed, she had simply vanished—no kiss upon their foreheads, no word of good-bye.

It had been an abrupt departure. There was no foreshadowing or omen. One day her brother was watching her mother stirring pottage in their lodgings on Bucks Row, the next both were gone. Gone like ghosts. When Sally recalled it, the only thing that pointed to such a disruption was that had been the first breakfast they had seen for days. Sally recalled it particularly for she had sat quietly at her mother's knee hoping against hope there would be enough left for her. She only got the spoon to lick, but to her mind that was fortune enough.

Although she remembered how that day began, the rest was lost to her. Whether they were brought or made their own way thence, she knew not which. She only knew that they found themselves standing before Archie's mother's lodgings. Barefoot and unkempt, Sally clutched a meagre bundle of belongings wrapped in a piece of broadcloth and tied with a string. Sue, looking just as forsaken, clung to nothing but her sister's hand whilst Sally stood there several moments, rubbing one foot upon the back of her other calf whilst determining what to do next. She had been far too timid to rap upon the door, so instead, they found themselves a seat and patiently waited to be found. They had seen their grandmother before and she had seen them, but some innate sense of survival told Sally that this was an impression that might prove important. Therefore, forsaking her own hair, she used her fingers to comb Sue's forelock from her face, spit on the hem of her skirt, and went to work on her besmudged face. Turning her head a bit askew, Sally gauged the effectiveness of her work.

Sue inquired. "Do I look pretty now, Sally?"

"You always look pretty," Sally replied matter-of-factly.

Satisfied, they both sat in solemn wait until their grandmother happened upon them several hours later.

Nell Arbuthnot had been widowed by Ollie Arbuthnot since the year '06. They had been legally wed and as she only lifted a glass when one was given to her, she was known as a woman of steady character. Ollie had been a hard drinker, but as he had been mostly at sea and was now long in his grave, that failing no longer grieved her. Nell had but one living issue, Sally and Sue's father, Archie. Ollie and son were like-minded men—both loved a drink, the sea, and a good fight—in that order. Both were members of His Majesty's Royal Navy. But whilst Archie had signed on of his own volition, Ollie had been slapped into service by a press gang. (Nell had often nagged her husband against falling victim to drink near dark alleys, but when he returned that reproof had been compleatly forgot as he was gone for better than a year.) After Ollie's untimely passing (also through the agency of a drunken binge), Nell managed to fend for herself through a steady mending business. These fortunate circumstances saw it unnecessary for her to suffer under the yoke of a second marriage. She was independent and did not want for food on the table—a handsome living in that section of town.

That small leverage against want was obliterated the morning she found Sally and Sue sitting patiently upon her stoop. One mouth to feed on her scant income was doable, three looked to be a catastrophe. Still, when faced with her duty, pragmatic Nell shouldered the responsibility with little more than a shrug of her bony shoulders and watched helplessly as the careful balance that she had kept between want and need was upended. Indeed, within months after inheriting her granddaughters, privation crept into their simple lodgings like a noxious tenant. Many an evening was entertained by Nell explaining just how little happiness befell a poor working-woman like herself.

Young as they were, they recognised the storm-clouds building. Archie's ship would soon return to port.

"Archie'll be madder'n a wet 'en when 'e gets 'ome and learns his woman be face-making with some scoundrel," she solemnly promised his daughters. And for good measure, she lamented, "If it weren't fer bad luck, your Grannum would have no luck a'tall."

"We're sorry, Grannum," Sally sympathised, for they *were* truly sorry.

Nell had been fond enough of a son who was gainfully employed. Still, Archie had his father's predisposition for splenetic fits—episodes made worse when fuelled by drink. He was not parsimonious of sharing this bent with those in his household. As he entertained no scruple to raise his hand against his mother either, Nell had been well-nigh as happy as Abigail that he was at sea most of the year. That, however, was the only thing she shared with Abigail. Despite his intemperate ways, Nell did not suffer Abigail's carousing behind Archie's back with much tolerance and kept her ear to the doings of her son's family. She made it her business to stop by their lodgings just to raise an occasional objection. Early morn or late, invariably, she would only find Abigail's son, John, looking after the little girls. When confronted over her faithlessness, Abigail had protested her innocence offering a long, winding account as to why she was so often out all night. Nell was not the sharpest knife in the drawer, but she knew a bald-faced lie when she heard it. Hence, she was not only well aware that her son's wife had a penchant for libations and adultery, she was quite witting that she was also high in the belly again—and not by Archie.

"She's got another's bye-blow up the spout, she do."

For if Nell was not a regular kneeler, she still believed in the sanctity of marriage. She may have had no good thing to say about a left-handed alliance, but it was, after all, an alliance. Hence, breaking such was evil at its worst. Everyone knew that the loss of virtue in a woman is irretrievable—and virtue was often the only possession a woman could call her own.

Rightfully, Nell held the conceit that her son would be a good catch for any woman in their society. She admitted that Archie *was* a bit of a drinker, but he was a god-fearing seaman—stout-hearted and hardy. That girl, Abigail, was already burdened with one misbegotten child—that tall lad—when she took up lodgings with Archie. That was one strike against her so far as Nell was concerned. Increasingly, when Nell was offered a glass of ale and a chance to complain, Nell was happy to announce that her son could have done better than a round-heeled barmaid. Moreover, Abigail's new occupation of child deserter had not improved Nell's poor opinion.

Quite precipitously, the toll of little ones to see to and unremitting poverty overtook Nell. This dolor was accompanied by an extended affair with a bottle of gin—one that instigated a tremble so persistent it put an end to any hope of using a needle and thread. All this came to pass before Archie Arbuthnot's feet had once again touched dry land.

His beloved mother or not, Nell still had fully meant to lay low when Archie reappeared. She could see him then, sea locker perched on his shoulder and his hat cocked at a dangerously acute angle—thus announcing he was expecting forthwith to be rewarded by his woman's faithful embrace (few male libidos bore a year at sea with any part of impassivity). At one time, Nell rejoiced that her son returned from sea. Once he had been a source of pride, bringing her trinkets from some far-away lands. Now that it was she who would answer to his temper, her heart grew cold at the thought of him.

When at last she heard word that the *Galatea* had docked, Nell had cowered in wait, a healthy sized drink before her. In doleful, if resigned, anticipation, she awaited what Abigail's unsuspecting consort would bring down upon their heads. That hell would be unleashed was not in question—all that remained was to determine which form it would take. Across the table from her sat her two solemn granddaughters. (Well, in truth, little Sue was solemn, Sally Frances was absolutely sullen.) The older girl sat with her chin thrust outward, one bare foot banging the table leg and a protective arm about her sister whose wide, sad eyes periodically welled up with tears. It was a portentous time. As young as they were, both of the sisters had just accustomed themselves to their grandmother and another upheaval was not looked upon by either with a kind eye. Although Sue still cried for her mother, Sally had realised that her mother and brother were not to return. They had listened as their grandmother had taken to engage her neighbours in incessant, if hushed, conversations (fuelled by drink and vituperation) over the specifics. Anytime adults went to whispering, the girls knew well that the winds of change would not be blowing softly. Because their recollections of their father (and their father's temper) had not altogether faded, they had a good understanding of the coming Armageddon.

Even the neighbours knew that after Archie was released from his ship only to learn that his wife had taken surreptitious leave (and wags snickering that she left heavy with another man's child) he would need someone not only to cook his meals, but to endure the rage of his injured pride. It was to be a precipitous fall in spirits. He had come ashore happy to celebrate in the bosom of his family his elevation from Seaman Third Class to Boson's mate (having leapt a rank or two due not to the carnage of battle but to the crew's rout by way of an extended encounter with the scoots). He betook himself directly to the rooms he kept, celebratory bottle in hand, and found no one there. As expected, he made his way with some haste to his mother's small house. There, beneath the shadow of his menace, he persuaded her to relate to him the full and woeful history of recent events. (Forasmuch as Archie's lack of inherent maternal respect influenced him to take his belt to the bearer of these ill-tidings, all tender feelings on his behalf had altogether wavered.)

In the flailing about, Sally and Sue managed to scramble for the safety of the woodbox, but had only just found shelter when the ruckus ceased. For this set-to was fierce, it was also short-lived. To Nell's fortune, Archie's arm was weary from hoisting home his locker, and he soon gave up his lashing. He fell away, spent. He flung his belt to the floor, but caught his bottle of gin in his hand and took unceremonious leave. No one he came across, however, had the nerve to point out that his breeches were creeping down his hips.

Seven Dials was thick with wives, mothers, and daughters beaten more commonly thrice a day as thrice a week. Archie's thrashing his mother was not, therefore, an uncommon occurrence. The exact reasoning behind what was to unfold remained unclear to Sally many years hence. It was all quite out of character.

Nell Arbuthnot was blustery when speaking with others across the yard fence, but few would have ever accused her of possessing much courage. Still, as the little girls had not weathered many frosts, she knew what they did not. Archie would not be recalled to his ship for many a fortnight. So perilous an intelligence as that inspired a second leave-taking. Late that night the old woman stole away in the dark. She did not, however, take her leave alone.

She took Sally and Sue with her.

There was little time to devise a plan, leaving it light on design and heavy on risk. Nell had but a few coins to her name and the street and all its plagues were to be only a bare improvement from the sting of Archie's belt. But she had endured Ollie's wrath for far too many years to allow herself to be beaten by her own son. If it had been another man, she might have poisoned his food, but she could not, in all good conscience, murder her own son. Hence, without a roof over their head, the little family huddled together that first night for warmth, their toes tucked beneath them lest the rats took interest. With a little stealth (and the imposition upon several friends), Nell found them enough money to keep lodgings a half-mile (and several eons) away. Accommodations, however, were not particularly deluxe. Making their way along the dusty walkboards, the unhappy situation was apparent. When once they were merely amongst the poor, now they would abide in the absolute bowels of hell. It was the one place that Archie would not venture to find them.

She did find one small room up-wind from the knacker's, but it was cheap and they could not quibble with the amenities.

"What's that smell?" asked Sally, curling her nose,

"It's the knacker. What d'yer think?" Nell answered impatiently. "We don't got money fer no inn.

"The knacker?" Sally repeated, peering round the corner. "Isn't that where the dead animals go…"

Nell grabbed her by the nape of the neck and slammed the door, refusing to answer further. Sally and Sue exchanged sidelong looks and Nell shook her head at their sensibilities.

"It won't be no bother till come summer," she assured them.

Nell found ways to make what little resources she had profitable. Her tremble still bothering her, she had to look for less detailed employment. Work was plenty if one's sensibilities were not easily bruised. Mothers were taken to the straw regularly, and when they were not, there were plenty of dead in want of lying out. Be it bringing in the newly arrived or washing the dearly departed, nothing was beneath her. Truth be known, she had far fewer qualms over ushering out the dead—they were at last at peace. She saw it far more unkind to smack the bottom of an infant to force his first breath of life, knowing as she did what lay ahead for him. Times were hard and getter harder.

Nor was it beneath her to pinch the occasional apple from a cart for a little sleeve-polish resale. Nell was not proud of this petty thievery, but so long as it was petty and put food in their mouths, she did not lose much sleep over it. Yet, she did not dismiss it easily enough to let Sally see it. (But Sally knew all the same.) The greater evil as Nell saw it was not so much that theft was a sin, but that the bustling street was thick with beggars and thieves all more adept than she.

"Drat 'em gerls. I'll be playing rabbit-catcher fer these mothers afore I can keep up with thems that's runnin' smobble."

Although Nell expected Sally was insensible to the remark, she was mistaken. Like most children, the precocity of poverty allowed her to pick up street cant quickly. She knew the term was meant of those who thieved from counters. Indeed, Sally had gotten her bearings no less quickly than had Nell. She innocently offered up some of her recently garnered intelligence for Nell to admire.

"A bung-nipper is a pickpocket," she announced proudly.

Nell gave her an exceedingly displeased look.

With the same resolve as Nell kept her pilfering from the girls, the girls kept their begging from Nell. As proficient as they became at tugging at the sleeves of strangers, they became equally adept at making up tales for Nell's benefit as to just how two so young were so frequently the beneficiaries of great luck. Sally explained it patiently to Sue as "weaving crammers."

"Everyone does it sometimes," was her sage rationale.

With a wink to Sue, then to Nell, she said in all earnestness, "We found it right here on the street, we did."

It was not a poorly constructed falsehood, but it was not one that held up upon repeated uses.

Some of their schemes were more lucrative than others. One of particular merit involved an adorable trio of kittens the girls found beneath some broken boards of a walkway. The kittens were a white-faced and brindled lot, seemingly abandoned by their mother. They gave them a bit of a chase, but the girls eventually cornered them and placed them in Sue's apron. Holding the corners up daintily, Sue beamed with pride, even then practicing the whine she thought was necessary to negotiate keeping one of them as a pet. Quite unceremoniously, she was beset upon by an exceedingly affronted mother cat. The rangy feline took a clawing trip up Sue's skirt to remand her kittens, causing the little girl to shriek in indignation. Although Sally detached the cat's claws from Sue, Sally had not the heart to shoo the mother cat away. It was a gaunt thing and it would have taken little more than a well-placed kick from even her small foot to be rid of it. Instead, she took the kittens from Sue's apron and placed them on the cobbles.

"Have yer way, Puss," said Sally, pushing the kittens toward their mother.

She watched as the mother cat seized the first kitten delicately behind the neck and dragged it away. Diligently, the cat returned twice more. Sally watched with pleasure, but Sue threw a fit, hopping up and down, crying and begging to keep at least one. Sally firmly shook her head. Sue wept openly at the loss and in tears and despair, buried her face in her sister's apron. Although she stood quite tall, tears too began to fall upon Sally's cheeks as she watched the last kitten disappear between the same broken floorboards whence they were found. Although the sisters both wept great tears, theirs were quite disparate emotions. Sue's were the simple tears for the kitten she could not keep. But Sally's betrayed a sorrow of a far deeper loss. Indeed, the sight had begged her think of her own mother—a recollection that she did not often entertain.

Both girls gave up their enterprise for the day. Sue snuffled crossly all the way home. Sally, however, did not cry further—whatever the temptation. The realisation that their mother was less dutiful than the average, emaciated, flea-infested feline was cruel, and it stayed with her for some time.

From that unpromising beginning sprang an unlikely turn. Sally had grasped an odd notion. Dignity had not been a word that she knew, but an understanding she learnt. Rather than looking upon that cat's deed as a symbol of the mother-love they lacked, she chose to see it in a more providential light. For, if a hollow-bellied, heavy-teated cat had the discipline to demand what was hers in life, Sally did not see how she should ask any less. "Come along, Sue," said Sally Frances Arbuthnot. "Law, gerl, we ain't no jingle-brains. There's got to be better for us."

When her granddaughter made this life-altering resolution, Nell was quite unawares. Busy was she with her own pursuits, most of which might have injured Sally's new-found honour. Despite her lowered circumstances, Nell defended her own honour with no small vehemence. So much so that her pride made her a bit a of a pest to what passed for neighbours, never letting them forget that she had once owned her own house. She told anyone who stood still long enough that she and her granddaughters were quite above their current situation. Believing oneself above one's company whilst pinching fruit was an uncomfortable contradiction Nell chose not to address. Hence, Sally left the subject alone as well.

Affaire d'Amour

There unkenneled between *ma demoiselle* Thierry and *le Général* Wickham an affair of absolute love and utter devotion. This union was sheltered by the compleat and impervious non-existence of forthrightness upon any matter. Their match was superb—if one did not take into account that it was built on dishonesty and was fed by lies. In the recesses of his mind, the authentic self he seldom addressed, even Wickham knew disaster loomed.

Wickham recalled a quote from his time at Cambridge where Plato was in agreement. "Everything that deceives may be said to enchant," wrote the old philosopher of some long-lost love.

Wickham agreed whole-heartedly. And enchanted he was as Césarine addressed him as "*tu*" and expelled erotic susurrations against his ear. Later, in recollection, he believed himself to have been merely bewitched. But it would take the passing of several frosts to come to that understanding.

True to the wiles of any accomplished seductress, Césarine did not allow herself to be lured into Wickham's grasp with any haste. It took more than a fortnight of cavorting upon a tufted sofa in her powdering room before he was granted leave to stay the night. It took even longer for her to allow him leave to keep a toilette bag in her apartments. Until she relented, it had been a bruise upon his ego to depart from thence in the wee hours of the morn unshaved and unkempt. Eventually however, his perception of doing so altered. He realised that to be observed taking his leave *dégagé* was testimony to his success within her apartments. Therefore, once he gained the pavement, he loudly called for a coach, looked about to see if anyone took notice, and partook of some happiness when anyone did.

Césarine's rooms were at once grand and exotic—a giant urn of ostrich feathers stood in one corner and a bidet was partially hidden in another. The mystique of her accommodations was enhanced by a blue velvet curtain, which shielded a door leading to a side street for those guests whose desire for discretion was absolute. Whilst he sat in awe and wonder of the sights and scents that permeated her chambers, Wickham reminded himself that he grew up in more impressive, if decidedly less uninhibited, circumstances at Pemberley House. Ignoring her distinct disinterest, he took great delight in detailing that mansion and its accoutrements as his own. So detailed was his reverie, his paramour eventually ceased to nod at appropriate intervals and flung a slipper at him.

Césarine's attention was often compromised. The hours she had to spare for Wickham's company were limited and she had little surplus for him to wax eloquently about charms other than her own. Oftentimes she banished one and all from her chambers and dedicated herself to an elaborate eye-mask meant to blot out any vestiges of daylight that seeped beneath the heavy drapes. When she did arise, it was seldom before noon. From thence until six she submitted to the daily ministrations not only of her *corsetière*, but her *couturier*, her *coiffeur*, and *cordonnier*, nattering with them all for hours on end. When at last she submitted to take tea, she bid whatever lover proved most ardent to bring it to her. Thereupon, she listened to the latest odes to her beauty composed by her most infatuated admirers as they were read to her. Initially, she had endowed this duty to Wickham as a torment, but he was surprisingly happy to oblige. Indeed, he took the opportunity to mock the writer and the writings by using a ridiculously sing-song voice thus compelling Césarine to toss him out on his ear. (He thought it was a fair exchange and was not asked to undertake that office again.) When he had not been ousted, she spent the better part of two hours unrepentantly answering *billets-doux* from past, present, and future lovers.

Of this particular wile Wickham was not so forgiving. He suffered all such abuse sprawled upon a purgatorial *chaise-longue*, cooling his heels and glowering. His displeasure at being denied his way with her was of no interest to Césarine. Indeed, she did not even dismiss Marie-Therese Lambert whose main purpose, it would seem, was to whisper the latest gossip in Césarine's ear. Whilst Césarine primped, Marie-Therese was as often as not in repose upon Césarine's bed partaking from a box of expensive chocolates. That the morsels that she so daintily dropped in her mouth were bought by Wickham's fast-depleting pocket did not grieve Marie-Therese's conscience. Indeed, she took each one with such relish, it was remarkably obscene.

Wickham could not account for the intimacy of her connexion with Césarine. He had been privy to the silly camaraderie of the ladies, but this, this was of another ilk altogether. It was of a sort that had initially made Wickham curiously uneasy. Unfortunately, in time he came to lose that disquiet and to view her as a usurper of Césarine's time of no greater evil than her *manucuriste*, her *couturier*, her *coiffeur*… He saw her as but another fawning minion whose sole purpose was to keep his lover diverted. Eventually, he would learn his instinctual prejudice of her had been just—but that would not come to pass until first every other instinct he possessed was compleatly compromised.

Césarine employed every gambit at her disposal to have Wickham veritably panting for her company. It was apparent even to him that she was abusing his affections, but when more evenings brought further excuses to keep him from her bed, he still did as she bid. She took his arm and had him escort her and her ruby-encrusted neck to her chosen entertainments—*opera bouffes* that involved farces so unsophisticated that even his *amour-propre* was injured. When Wickham realised that his urbane Césarine had a soft spot for low comedy and could explode with raucous laughter at the least provocation, he thought it endearing. He thought it endearing even whilst trying to find their seats through the agency of his walking stick sweeping to and fro through the riff-raff to clear their passage. At long last his indulgence was repaid. She gifted him with a night of passion he had heretofore not experienced. Indeed, his little flower knew things—secret things—that kept him at a crescendo for what seemed an eternity. He was so spent after these ministrations that he lay in a perspiring heap unable to respond whilst she entreated him to please her again. These pleasures were repeated night after night so rapturously, that being unceremoniously evicted from her bed before sunrise was endured without complaint.

Or at least initially he complained, but that begat a row of such vociferousness that it surpassed the worst of those with Lydia. (Indeed, she hit him across the face with a riding crop and threatened to poison his cat—had he a cat he would have been truly alarmed.) But unlike Lydia, her revenge for his insolence included taking in other lovers, bedding them right under his nose.

In the end, he slunk from her room without a fuss and counted himself lucky to survive with his manhood unimperiled.

They settled into what would pass for a sensible little affair, punctuated by occasional ménage á trios with various female friends. Strangely, Marie-Therese was never one of them. (He supposed Marie-Therese's boat did not float in those waters, but it was only a conjecture.) Wickham had long thought of himself as quite the roué, but never, in all his many escapades, had he made "the beast" with more than two backs. His favoured position had always been *figura veneris primi*—this only partly because from the superior position he was most sated but because it also favoured a quick escape should a jealous husband or vengeful father chance upon him mid-coitus. Upon the threesome occasions, Wickham found himself allotting a far greater amount of time to looking than to putting, and despite its essential licentiousness demurred this next time round.

Césarine teased him merciless for being a puritanical Englishman. Of the many insults that had been hurled at him, he thought that one quite the most ludicrous. He, Wickham, puritanical? Why, was that not the exact opprobrium he had once heaped on Darcy? It was Darcy who was the prig. He, Wickham was the consummate Lothario—game for anything…except, well, this.

"Pray, did not your own Voltaire say 'Once a philosopher, twice a pervert'?" sniffed Wickham.

"Voltaire," intoned Césarine, "was an impotent, old agnostic."

"And you would be of that information, because…?" Wickham retorted sarcastically.

"*Mon ami*," she answered.

"Your friend?"

"*Oui*."

"Pray, how would your friend know anything of Voltaire—he died before you were born."

"*Oui, le marquise de Pompadour*," she said with finality, effectively ending the conversation and dismissing him.

"Whatever do you mean?" Wickham inquired helplessly.

As he said it, he simultaneously began to gather up his belongings for the onslaught of perfume bottles, shoes, and errant pets that he knew would be flung in his direction, thus announcing his temporary banishment from her sight. It was another of her maddeningly alluring quirks. She would make either an absurd non sequitur or statement fraught with expectancy and leave him hanging precipitously for the rest of the story. Unfortunately, his refusal to submit to her particular choice of boudoir games meant she would find someone forthwith to take his place. That vexed him no end. But he dared not provoke her. Their past riotous frays incited by passing flirtations had nearly cost them a visit by the gendarmes.

Alas the fires that burn brightest fizzle fastest. When at last their affair began to ebb, it was not love's flame that was the actual betrayer.

Indeed, it had come to Wickham's notice that Césarine took no precautions after love-making. He supposed that whatever purgatives she undertook to avoid pregnancy were administered privately. Unlike most gentlemen, this was not a subject that he usually left to chance. His usual methodology was to confine his affairs to wives whose husbands were not too long absent. If said paramour happened to turn up with child, the husband would not be suspicious. Falling with child was a profound danger for his lovers, of this he was certain. His seed had borne fruit far too prolifically in the past.

He was well aware of his potency. It was one of his greatest conceits. His seed was unrivalled in not only begetting, but also begetting the most prized of offspring—the male child. Had not he, George Wickham, fathered three sons by Lydia and at least one other by some long-lost lover? Four sons. What had Darcy done? His bed was fallow, his wife barren! Aha! Who was the better man now, Darcy? Wickham may have daydreamt about throwing that in Darcy's face one day, but that was not truly a confrontation he longed for. What he truly wanted was Darcy's money, Darcy's house, Darcy's position, and Darcy's wife—in that order. What he did not want was a confrontation the result of which he could not be certain.

Wickham had nothing to prove and a great deal to lose when a woman he bedded got herself with child. Children were of no good use in the world. But as a veteran observer of female fecundity, he recognised the subtle signs of impending confinement when he saw them. And Césarine had become a veritable signpost of parturiency (up to and including the occasion upon which he had witnessed her rudely upended and heaving her breakfast with the utmost indelicacy into her chamber-pot).

"*Mon saucisson*!" he commiserated, "My poor little sausage, are you unwell?"

"You fool! Do not speak to me of food!" she squawked.

No other words could have spoken the truth of her condition to him more plainly.

In the past, it would have been his inclination to take his leave with no compliments and the utmost rapidity—if at all possible without leaving a detectable trail. However, the circumstances in which he found himself were unlike any he had known before. At long last he had found a woman both worthy of his seed and willing to take it. But, with ever-increasing tightness in his chest, he watched her ever-increasing waistline for what it bespoke was a cruel blow.

His sweet little dew-drop of honey, his *inamorata*, his darling, most adored, *sa petite saucisson pauvre*, Césarine was indeed with child, and she told him it was not his.

The Col. Fitzwilliams Meet Lord Beecher

The autumn following the glorious defeat of *Le Petite Usurper*, all of England had recognised the folly of their initial belief that it would be not only an expeditious victory, it would be relatively innocuous. When it came to pass that although the victory was compleat, its toll was extensive, few citizens did not feel an obligation to those who fought. Indeed, it was as if all of England had embarked upon virtual idolatry of any and all veterans of the Napoleonic campaign—the degree of their adoration relative to said veteran's rank. If the soldier was both an officer and an actual military hero, society's aspiring generals, phrenic camp-followers, and fashionable battle-mavens were thrilled beyond all reason to behold his company. There were no lengths they would not go to fête him, no compliment was too grand, no admiration too adulatory.

For a man like Fitzwilliam, any recollection of the rigours of battle was something he would have liked to consign to oblivion. For him, the brouhaha was altogether vexing. He had thought to escape such talk by retreating far from London. As it was, absolute avoidance was impossible. In Bath, the war and its heroes were very much the topic of discourse, but no one wore the black of bereavement. The triumph was still new and no one spoke of casualties. In the pump room it was still the season of victory and to those who sipped there, regimental losses were merely a statistic. It would be some time before the full cost was felt by all classes. The fathers of the dead who had betaken themselves on the brief voyage to Flanders to pay witness to the soil that bore the remains of their sons were only then making their way home.

Therefore, for those still in the heady riot of conquest, no detail of those victorious engagements was too small to entertain their imaginations. Hence, there were few men in Bath more in demand to grace various *soirées* than an officer who had been in the thick of battle. Of those choice men, one who served a cavalry regiment was elite again by half. As colonel and commander of his regiment, Fitzwilliam's service had not only been notable, it had been chronicled in the *Gazette*. (This put those persons of society in a quandary—they, to a person, had read with zealous fervour every word written by the low publication, but were loath to be the first to admit to having been a reader. Ultimately, curiosity prevailed.) Col. Fitzwilliam was unaware both of the excited temper of the pump room and his celebrity, hence, when he and Georgiana endeavoured to make an inconspicuous entrance that morning they were unsuccessful.

It was but their second day in town and they had deliberately made an early start to avoid the crowds. News that the good colonel was about town had preceded him. Indeed, upon his entrance, the orchestra's soft strain ceased and was replaced forthwith by the regular beat of a march. As the music altered, the milling people ceased their gossip and looked about accordingly, straining to see what personage inspired the triumphant sounds. Intending anonymity, Fitzwilliam had purposely not worn his regimental garb—to no avail—he was immediately recognised. Fitzwilliam, appalled, slowed to a stop at this notice. Georgiana clung fast to his elbow and could feel his indecision. She waited for him to resolve whether to go on or turn back.

His hesitation was quite brief. But, in the end, he moved on—all in the room conspicuously aware of his stiff-legged gait. Moreover, due to the crowd and his limp, the Col. Fitzwilliams could not cross the room to the tap expeditiously. Therefore, they were laid open to a number of undesired salutations. None were more imprudent than that of an old man with an ear-horn, himself a veteran of Yellow Fever in the West Indies, who believed that suffering that malady that he was a military peer to one who fought hand to hand with Nappy's *Vieille Guard*. Indeed, so certain of that was the old man, he stepped forward with out-stretched hand.

Said he, "I am proud to offer my hand to you, sir. Your name will be the first mentioned whenever English courage is ballyhooed."

Regrettably, that single overture served as the finger removed from the dam—and Fitzwilliam was immediately assaulted by a little bevy of adorers with a torrent of inquiries of the particulars of his engagement which were far more exclamatory than interrogative.

"Pray, were the Belgians compleatly disaffected?"

"There is nothing like old blood if one is in want of gallantry in battle!"

"Is it true that the German militia were without shoes?"

"Pray, did you not ride by His Grace the Duke of Wellington's side up the hill of St. Jean?"

"Word has it that infernal Bonaparty stole away dressed as his servant. Pray, did he?"

With the onslaught, Fitzwilliam had cursed his lack of two good legs, quite certain had he been able he would have liked very much to flee. As he did not, he strove on to the taps. Because he was hobbling, any indication of the notion of flight was unapparent. True to his breeding, he murmured thanks to those compliments of his service, shook his disapproval to those more outrageous suggestions honouring him, and forged on past the hullabaloo. All the while, Georgiana's grip on his arm became evermore fierce, her mortification over suggesting they come to Bath compleat. She had in no way meant for him to be put on display, but undeniably, that was exactly what had occurred.

After someone shoved a tri-colour flag into Fitzwilliam's hands (for what reason he could not fathom), they gained the taps and in turning their attention to them, the mob of well-wishers began to disband. As they dissolved back into their previous cliques, one party stood their ground. It was a threesome that Mrs. Colonel Fitzwilliam could not ignore.

Lady Catherine de Bourgh stood mid-most of Lady Anne and a young gentleman heretofore unknown to either Georgiana or Fitzwilliam. Witnessing the pompous Lady Catherine literally rubbing elbows with the middling society of a public pump house was unprecedented. So taken aback was Georgiana, her countenance could not decide which expression to engage first. Forthwith, however, it settled upon gaping in amazement.

Even more extraordinary than seeing Lady Catherine was that she seemed all too pleased to behold them. Fitzwilliam was no less apprehensive than Georgiana. For Fitzwilliam's manners had once bid him a favourite of Lady Catherine's, but his continued alliance with Darcy and Elizabeth in the face of her displeasure suggested that his place in her warm regard may well have waned. Since Darcy's marriage, he had not had cause to travel to Kent to discover her sentiments on the matter and had been happy to remain unenlightened. However, circumstances had altered of late. As he and Georgiana were both quite witting of Darcy's most recent visit to her, they were prepared for the possibility of a cut. Indeed, her ladyship's intractability was of legend.

Therefore, Col. and Mrs. Fitzwilliam froze in their tracks. Colonel Fitzwilliam, leaning heavily upon his stick, bore an expression of apprehension that exceeded the one he wore upon his last cavalry charge; Georgiana's eyes resembled those of a trapped rabbit, wanting, but daring not, to look for the nearest burrow.

Lady Catherine de Bourgh erupted into a gesture of welcome that was as obscene in its insincerity as it was in enthusiasm. She walked a full ten foot with arms extended, fingers waggling until their serpentine grasp entwined Georgiana into an embrace before endowing each of her niece's cheeks with an enormous, wet kiss. Both of these kisses were planted with an emphatic "mmm-ahh!" Her arm-clinch was so assiduously applied that it lifted Georgiana upon her tiptoes. Thereupon, her ladyship quit her niece and attacked Fitzwilliam in similar fashion. Lady Catherine released Georgiana with such haste that she nearly toppled and she stood weaving for a moment, stunned as much by the effusiveness of the affection as from the unlikelihood of its source. Already discombobulated, as it was viewed over first one then the other of his aunt's shoulders, Fitzwilliam's countenance betrayed an inclination toward panic. Although Georgiana had squirmed in her turn a bit, Fitzwilliam had stood still as a stone. Nonetheless, her ladyship continued her hold on him for a full minute, all the while gushing compliments upon their marriage—tidings that they only accepted with a noncommittal nod. They dared not do other, they were far too perplexed. To have Lady Catherine de Bourgh's congratulations extended in so eager a fashion was a far more frightening event than had she taken to them with a horse-whip.

When Lady Catherine finally stood back, her countenance was afflicted with a smile of such malicious ambiguity that it sent a small shiver down Georgiana's spine. She felt as if the woman had somehow thrown down a summons to a contest—of what sort, Georgiana had not a clue. As for Fitzwilliam, of the many disconcerting confrontations he had weathered of late, he thought one with this aunt was less preferable than all by half. Yet, so little did he want to give her any excuse for offence that he undertook the extraordinary risk of taking a low bow whilst using his walking stick as a pivot.

"It is so good to see my dearest nephew looking so well!" Lady Catherine trilled.

Dearest nephew? First in deed, now in word, her aunt's design was lost on Georgiana. She endeavoured mightily to determine what it all meant, but alas—intrigues other than by her own design were opaque to her. More acclimated to such manoeuvrings insofar as battle logistics, Fitzwilliam entertained the probability that it was simply false diplomacy. Indubitably, his aunt was labouring under the supposition that in incurring Darcy's wrath, she could recoup family disfavour through him. If that was her design, her terriers were barking up the wrong tree. His allegiance was to Darcy. His marriage to Darcy's sister merely sealed any cracks that fealty may have weathered. Hence, he looked no less warily at her ladyship than Georgiana did.

If she sensed this mistrust, Lady Catherine gave no indication of it. Indeed, she prattled on like a Folkestone ferry-woman, eventually returning to her more officious self. Nor did she scruple to inquire of her beloved nephew, Darcy and his "precious newborns." In omitting Elizabeth's name in her inquiries after the health of the Darcy family, Lady Catherine inadvertently exposed the weakness of her family reconciliation. (This omission was not over-looked by the Fitzwilliams, but neither betrayed their notice.) It was only after remarking upon the fineness of the weather that her ladyship introduced the de Bourgh ladies' consort, Lord Winton Beecher "of Trinidad." Although Anne was neither addressed nor alluded to by her mother, Col. Fitzwilliam had given her a curt bow all the same.

Georgiana smiled amiably and curtsied to Lady Anne. Although they had little in common, the timidity of each had made any intimacy between them challenging. Therefore, they were not fast friends, but neither had they entertained any particular animosity. Hence, Georgiana looked upon the young gentleman who accompanied Anne with interest. Indeed, it was difficult for her to ignore him—Lord Beecher's fingers snaked around Lady Anne's fore-arm with possessive determination. For her part, Lady Anne's long countenance bore an expression of unmitigated pleasure. (Clearly, she was only a little less happy to encounter her relatives than to have an occasion for Lord Beecher's interest in her to be on display.) Try as she might, Georgiana could recall neither Beecher's name nor his face. Clearly, he was not of the Darcys' acquaintance. She covertly took what measure of him she could for she knew that she would be called upon to relate the particulars. In fortune, he was somewhat short, hence, her powers of observation could be employed from a lowered gaze and still keep him in her eye.

Her initial surveillance revealed little beyond his youngish appearance and well-tailored coat. Further study saw him as not particularly strong-featured. From what she could see of his cheeks (which were half hidden by his starched collar), they were florid enough to insinuate a predilection for spirits. It took little time for her to sniff out a pronounced superciliousness and more West End airs than any pink of the ton. As they conversed politely about the weather, Lady Anne looked upon him with such simpering approval—neither his swagger nor his pomposity drew her censure. Lo, there was little left to the imagination that, was one in a mind of matches, love (in some form or the other) was ripe.

It could be said that upon Beecher's introduction, Lady Catherine's carefully arranged attitude of charity for all and sundry wavered. Although it was not readily apparent, Georgiana sensed that Sir Beecher was less in Lady Catherine's favour than he was in her daughter's. Hence, when her ladyship spoke of and to him, her voice was a bit pinched. Still, she tendered him the reins of the conversation (an unusual capitulation for her) allowing him to inquire of Fitzwilliam the telling of every skirmish, every cannonade, and every French soldier he witnessed taken down. Save Georgiana, all stood transfixed in wait of his retelling of those horrific events. Such inquiries as this, of course, were sheer torture for Fitzwilliam. Therefore, what he did recount was told in so succinct a fashion that had one not known otherwise, it was a tale indiscernible from one who had not set foot in combat. This spare telling was met with disappointment, but he politely refused to elaborate.

Georgiana had grown as discomfited as Fitzwilliam by then and begged their leave. Only after several such entreaties did Lady Catherine relinquish their company—and allowed their leave-taking only by issuing several admonitions of questionable medicinal merit. (One included viper flesh and wood lice.) Whilst Lady Catherine advised, Lord Beecher stood by doltishly in nodding agreement—an attitude most desirable in a future son-in-law.

As the threesome moved on, Beecher bade, "Cousin Georgiana, do have the Colonel submit to a tar and seaweed scrub, for it does wonders for the complexion. The sun, you know—it steals one's youth."

They turned to leave and Georgiana gave him a curt nod—but under her breath, she hissed, "Did he call me Cousin Georgiana?"

Fitzwilliam allowed that, indeed, he had.

By then they were far enough from their recent company for her to further fume, "Call me by my Christian name? Jumped-up midge of a man!"

Fitzwilliam was just happy to be rid of their company, and sought no insult, "There, there. Lord Beecher…"

She interrupted, "If he's a Lord, I'm good Queen Bess!"

At that, Fitzwilliam turned to her and when he did, an expression overspread his countenance of absolute incredulity. He thereupon slapped his good knee and threw his head back in an enormous and extended guffaw. It was the first good laugh he had had since…well, he could not remember the last good laugh he'd had. It certainly predated Quatre Bas. Georgiana was most pleased at this return of good humour, but not entirely content to be the brunt of it.

"Am I not Mrs. Colonel Fitzwilliam?"

Fitzwilliam's burst of laughter was less at her indignation than at her means of expressing it. He petted her arm and shook his head still smiling. They walked on.

Notwithstanding Georgiana's umbrage and Fitzwilliam's improved disposition, the incident at the pump room was notable on several levels. It revealed that Lady Catherine meant to repair the considerable rent she had caused in the fabric of her family's unity. Also apparent was Lady Anne's understanding with Beecher, for who would dare speak in such an intimate manner if not a cousin (even if he was a jumped-up colonial). As for Fitzwilliam, it forever supplied an endearment for his wife that would have puzzled all who knew them. Alas, the world at large would not know of it for only in the closest of company would he call her Queen Bess.

Bath

As with most great families of the day, life for the de Bourghs centred on their estate of Rosings Park and surrounding villages. Although Lady Catherine had enough guineas with her banker to keep that man eager to attend her, her primary wealth, as was Pemberley's, was derived from the land. As preoccupied as she could often be in preserving the distinction of her rank, Lady Catherine's obligations to her tenants knew no season. Indeed, no dispute between cottagers was too minute, no disharmony too insignificant that she did not sally forth into the village to scold them into mediation. Not every person who called themselves a member of the fashionable elite were entrammeled by the niggling botherations of a great estate, thus they were free to spend their time on the move from one spa to the next. The usual whereabouts of these people of title and fashion was not intelligence of which Lady Catherine was unawares. Many a day in her youth was spent within the beautiful city of Bath happily attending balls and tea parties given by the most distinguished of families. Indeed, it was there that her engagement to Sir Lewis was formed.

Consequently, when in want of the most fertile grounds for a husband-hunt for her daughter Lady Catherine selected Bath to set up her traps, she was under the supposition that it was still the primary playground of the *haut ton*. Her ladyship's knowledge of the latest fashion in resorts, however, was no more *au courant* than her powdered hair or hoop-skirted frocks. Once the epitome of elegance, Bath had endured a gradual, but decided, decline in status. By the year '15, it was dismissed as the vulgar lair of opportunists and fortune-hunters by the *crème de la crème* of English aristocracy. It had held its cachet only with the oldest of families who had frequented it with dogged determination not only for generations, but centuries. Her ladyship's dilatory attention to society did not bode well for the quality of her future son-in-law.

That autumn Bath was bustling, but it was awash with cashiered officers on half-pay looking for employment as riding or dancing masters and naval officers who found themselves newly rich through the capture of cargo-laden enemy ships. If added to the mix were a few failed sons of the aristocracy, one only needed chancers and free-booters to have a sorry mélange from which to troll for a suitor of any kind, much less one of the proper timbre. Ere she set foot from her coach, Lady Catherine announced her disinclination to rub elbows with those visitors who sallied forth to spas only to paddle in the sea, take an elixir, and attend card parties to gossip. (That sort found its own level, she sniffed.) She set off in all vigilance of societal interlopers, but missed the one who landed right under her nose.

Gatherings abounded and the de Bourgh ladies did not want for society. Lady Catherine had only to send her footman with her cards before invitations accumulated more rapidly than they could reply. Regardless of the quantity of occasions to demonstrate otherwise, Anne's inherent lack of effervescence at these balls was not off-set by word of her fortune—at least not expeditiously enough for Lady Catherine. Hence, that good lady took it upon herself to ferret out the best prospects with all the dedication of a scent hound. At each and every dance and evening card party, her ladyship's eyes coursed the room with all the cunning of a jackal after a rabbit as she looked for a suitable match. All the while, Anne stood about wearing her usual dull expression. Lady Catherine had seen to it that her daughter was adorned in the finest of costume that Bath's shops afforded. Hence, Anne was set out with enough tags, bobbins, laces, and fallals to make movement a serious threat to her company. However, few gentlemen beyond those on her card asked permission to engage her in a dance. The only names on her card were titled but aged contemporaries of her mother's. (Her ladyship was not opposed to an elder suitor, but as a grandchild was her primary ambition, she did not entertain the notion of a son-in-law in his dotage.) Hence, when Lady Catherine made her wishes more widely known, many a mother set off to round up their sons—by the ear, if necessary. In time, several candidates stood at the ready—but none looked particularly promising to her. Lady Catherine was unamused and continued to scour for better prospects.

Amongst the frivolous of their class (Lady Catherine did not openly admit to this failing of her peers—but accepted there were more than a few feather-brains dotting the assembly rooms of Bath), one particularly caught her eye. With the smallest of inquiry, she learnt that he was the son of a West Indies viceroy. He had all the requisites of a respectable man having inherited a fortune from his father who had interest in numerous privateers. Lady Catherine presumed that young Lord Beecher was in possession not merely of a title, but she was unacquainted whether his wealth was in plantations or cash. Ready money was advantageous in a gentleman, but not a requisite to her. Indeed, Lady Catherine might have preferred otherwise. A son-in-law who was landed but without funds of his own would be far easier to manipulate.

Quite new to the country, Beecher was ill-informed of just who amongst the guests were most prosperous. But as he was the sort of man for whom obtaining this intelligence was a priority, he made for the dowager-hostesses with all due haste. From them he learnt that the de Bourghs and the Darcys owned a fairly large chunk of England and Miss de Bourgh was much in want of a partner. Although he found the narrow countenance and meagre bosom of Lady Anne quite unappealing, his opinion improved upon hearing that they came with twenty-five thousand pounds. He wasted little time in making his way to her side to inquire of her the next dance.

Young Beecher had his choice of partners that night, for along with his title he was adorned with a tastefully arranged mass of blonde ringlets and a scarlet waistcoat. His countenance may have borne both the nose and sneer of a true patrician, but the smitten Anne only took notice of the curls. They were vast and she was well impressed.

Lady Catherine looked upon their acquaintance favourably. Quality of breeding was not her ladyship's first consideration. Nor her second. What she was looking for was availability, malleability, potency, and title. And a carriage. The gentleman in question must keep a carriage. No trait of character surpassed the necessity of a gentleman keeping a carriage. Given that Lord Winton Beecher had a *chaise* and four whose livery was of the most triumphant shade of mustard, his desirability improved. Whether her knowing that he was a dandy and a gamester with a great propensity for running into debt would have polluted her regard must stand unexamined. That small matter was over-looked, for it was readily apparent that he had much in common with Lady Catherine. For, was it truly possible, his esteem for rank and connexions rivalled hers.

Before the week of his introduction was out, Lady Catherine had winnowed out that he belonged to White's and Boodle's, had an opera box on Drury Lane (and one in Covent Gardens). She also observed that he did not look to advantage in a saddle and had ascertained through diligent snooping that before he departed Trinidad he had kept a mulatto mistress and had fathered a child. Rather than off-put, that information bade well for the match in Lady Catherine's eyes. (A mulatto child would be of no bother so long as it stayed in the West Indies.) All her ladyship saw was that he was titled and he was generative. He may not have been particularly pliable, but she had her own particular ways of persuasion should he want to keep his coloured bastard from public knowledge. She knew it all save for the extent of his debt, for that was intelligence he kept very close to his vest. The only obstacle was the unlikelihood of her daughter being at variance on the matter.

As it happened, Anne did not prove to be much of hindrance. Indeed, she could but wonder at his beauty and had been almost fluttering in admiration for the sheer luminousness of his golden ringlets as they circled the dance floor that night. And as their romance progressed to afternoon promenades, the subsequent attentions of an Adonis such as Lord Beecher flattered Lady Anne most agreeably.

Upon particularly fine days, they drove out in his gig to take the likeness of nearby landscapes, for Beecher fancied himself a water-colourist. Anne spent hours in his company adoring his brush-strokes (whilst Mrs. Jenkinson sat under a parasol in vain attempt to keep her freckles at bay). Upon foul days, he delighted Anne by escorting her to the new circulating library and they sat in the communal rooms drinking coffee, he with his newspaper, she with a novella hidden beneath Fordyce's Sermons. She believed it to be a prelude to what their marriage beheld and was in no way disposed to question either the match or his character.

New as he was in town, gossips were not privy to stories of his ruin of several fortunes and that his gaming debts were a disgrace. (His match was the better for that lapse, for Lady Catherine was violently opposed to games of chance.) As none of his shortcomings and all of his advantages were in play, an engagement was formed before the year was out.

By the time their paths crossed with her newly married niece and nephew at the pump room, a portion of Lady Catherine's scheme was underway and she was well-satisfied to engage the remainder.

Life As It Is

The Arbuthnots lived in an oddly thriving neighbourhood. A few tradesmen were about, but they were not the predominant merchants. The most lucrative vendors of their community were gaudily painted women sitting in the windows of "boarding houses," presenting their "wares" to passers-by. Pretending a lack of candour that was, at best, a feeble attempt at forestalling Sally's inevitable indoctrination in the baser ways of the world, Nell told her granddaughters that these ladies of commerce were "washer women." In that many of them were fairly falling out of their wrappers and did not appear until late in the day, Sally looked upon them a bit suspiciously. This suspicion was passably close to curiosity, which caused her to eye these ladies surreptitiously. It took very little time for Sally to conclude that Nell's explanation of the finer points of street life had been of the cock-and-bull variety.

As the years enlightened her, Sally ceased being innocent of the meaning of it all. By the age of twelve, it was not unheard of for girls of the street to be girded to go forth into whoredom. Even had Nell not kept keen watch over her morals, Sally still would have been disinclined to harbour ambitions of a prostitutional nature no matter how tempting a steady source of income might have been. It was not a matter of Nell's preaching (Nell had lost all religious credibility by eschewing the Church of England for a daily sacrificial to the altar of Bacchus), Sally simply could not fathom renting out one's bodily crevice to some grunting sapscull of a man. The notion was absolutely appalling to her. She would rather live on alms than that—and she despised the notion of living on alms. Sally was determined that if she sold herself, it would be for skills of a non-carnal variety. Even the nights all they had was their zealously guarded cubby-hole of a room and stomachs that ached from hunger, on this personal canon Sally did not waver.

Having denied such a life to herself did not suppose Sally sat in judgement of others. She made many a friend amongst the hussies, trollops, and tarts of their street. One was of particular note. Although this lady-of-the-night appeared to be no more than a girl herself, she held young Sally compleatly in her thrall. Like many another face in St. Giles, hers was Irish. But the people of Little Daisy Mulroney had emigrated a generation before and she had not a hint of a lilt. Unlike Daisy, most of the loose women did not answer to their Christian name but employed a descriptive, often colourful, alias. The sobriquets were usually bequeathed by reason of some peculiar physical characteristic or, occasionally, criminal preference. Daisy Mulroney, however, swore on the soul of her dead mother that Daisy was indeed her Christian name and not a street moniker alluding to her straw-coloured hair. "Little," however, she was. Yet, she was not merely of short-stature. Daisy had an oddness about her that, although she would have denied it, was undoubtedly what fascinated Sally.

Although Daisy was three and twenty years in face and understanding, her body was that of an over-sized child. Her bosom had not developed nor had her menses coursed. Her form was compleatly unfledged. Indeed, it did not appear likely that her body would ever mature whatsoever. To another such a mean slap by life might have turned one's disposition a bit rancorous. Daisy's, however, was of a peculiar sort and rather than believing herself disadvantaged by nature's carelessness, she chose to appropriate it as leverage in her chosen occupation. From the very beginning of her career she was introduced to an ugly, but lucrative fact of street life. That understanding was that no act of prostitution paid better than an alleged deflowerment—the younger the deflow-eree the better. Daisy's introduction into the many aberrant ways of debauchery was no more expeditious than most, but her perpetual pre-pubescence earned her hefty fees. Indeed, with wide, flat, and freckled face, plump figure, there was no woman more celebrated or in greater demand than Little Daisy. Ten years after her introduction to the carnal trade, she was still allowing herself to be deflowered on a daily basis.

One might have supposed that in presenting herself as a child that she should have dressed in a girlish manner. She did not. Amongst these debased doings was more than one fully developed harlot dressed as an innocent. Despite the advice of seasoned veterans of the night upon the error of her modus operandi, she adorned herself not in ribbons and bows or childish accoutrements. She traipsed around in pink half-boots with a scruffy rabbit tippet thrown over her shoulder. The incongruity of her costume and her aspect was clearly unobjectionable to her clientele. For Daisy stood with one hip cocked, blowing a cloud off a cheap cigar—and business could not be better.

Although Sally was full young and had yet to experience her own carnal tendencies, she was not unlearnt in the ways of the most wayward denizens of society. Still, this sort of degeneracy was troubling to her. Daisy thought little of it.

"Sally-gerl," asked Daisy, "Will they burn in hell any hotter for one sin more 'n the other?"

Sally allowed that she thought not. She certainly did not think of Daisy as a sinner. Daisy was a survivor.

Indeed, as her eidolon of survival, Sally shadowed Daisy's every move that did not involve a prone position. (It was actually necessary for her to stand with head averted for a few vertical ones—a three-penny upright Daisy called them.) As Daisy owed her allurement to the prurient interest of strangers, one might have expected her to find little amusement in the curiosity of this little street snipe. But she was amused. Indeed, at odds with both their professed inclinations, theirs was friendship quite without reason.

This singular attachment pleased Sally to no end. There was little enough mirth to be found during a hand-to-mouth existence that defined a good day as one in which she had more than one meal. To her credit, Nell saw to it that they began each day with clean aprons and caps. For better or worse, she also clung to the fiction that they had not sunk to the society that they had with tenacious determination. Therefore, Nell was most displeased that Sally deigned to entertain herself by passing her time with a fallen woman. Undeniably, it was an enthusiasm that Sally could not reconcile within herself. There were far greater vexations upon which to ponder than ones of introspection.

Invariably their most prosperous days were those of fair weather. Indeed, the rainier the day, the fewer people out, and those who were out were much in want of being in—therefore multifarious sales were a bit distressed. Only Nell could count on profitable foul-weather days, for folks died come rain or come shine. Regrettably (for Nell in any case), they did not die with the frequency necessary to retain regular shelter and it was not unheard of them to be locked out of their meagre lodgings. Hence, as the three of them cowered in the rain beneath a scant piece of tarpaulin, Sally meditated upon her grandmother's audacity for taking leave of a perfectly good home owing to Archie Arbuthnot. When she did, she recalled the time she had gathered enough courage to suggest to Nell that it might be safe to return to Dyott Street. Nell wouldn't hear of such nonsense.

"He might still find us, gerl." She warned, terror flickering about her eyes. "He might still find us."

"Donna you worry fer us, Grannum," Sally assured her, "he's long gone."

But her grandmother's countenance bore then a strangely unsettled expression, one that Sally was seeing with increasing frequency. Sally did not know if it was the drink, or something far worse—something that she could not fathom. Regardless whence it was derived, this foreboding grew ever-more prevalent over the months. They never knew when Nell might fall victim to paroxysms of fear so intense that betimes led her to hide beneath the bed. Occasionally these fits were witnessed by those other than her granddaughters, which gifted Nell with the unwanted stigma of dementia—a conclusion not conducive to generating new employment. She was called less and less frequently to attend the sick, the parturient, and the dead. Indeed, all but Daisy began to avoid them like the plague. After one particularly unfruitful spell, even Daisy Mulroney began to worry for them. Therefore, despite Nell's obvious dislike of her, Daisy proposed that they share her own rooms.

Said Daisy, "You can lay up here if yer want, it's nothing to me."

Even Sally could see that the exaggerated indifference with which this suggestion was clearly a ruse. Daisy had a heart after all. But Nell refused absolutely. So adamantly was this refusal issued, it plagued Sally's conscience. Daisy, however, appeared not to have found offence. With a shrug of her shoulders, she withdrew her offer with the same indifference in which it was tendered.

"Suit yerselves," said she.

Daisy Mulroney

Daisy Mulroney's life was not particularly kind, but she was never over-much hungry. She had two dresses, all her teeth, and a small room all to herself above a rag and bone shop. Although her occupation was not the first she would have chosen in another life, business, such as it was, was good. Moreover, her anatomical peculiarity required of her nothing in the way of purgatives. (That was no small expense.) Depending on how successful a woman of the street was in her encounters, avoiding pregnancy was far more expensive than the alternative. The professional woman either anted up for tansy, quinine, or pennyroyal first, or ended up on the foul end of a stick. As this bother was not her lot, Daisy was of the nature to be thankful for small favours.

Little Daisy Mulroney wasn't born to The Dials. The story that she had once been told was that her father was a tobacconist who had a shop on Holborn Hill. Whether that was true or not, Daisy had no independent verification. What she knew to be true was that, after her mother was widowed, their meals came with increasing irregularity. In time, she was loaned out to a consumptive aunt to help her with what chores she could. It was not an unusual arrangement. Daisy was paid with her keep. But when her mother died almost simultaneous of the aunt, there was no one around to reclaim her. The rooming house in which she had long resided with her aunt had gradually taken on the distinct odour of ill-repute. Daisy had already begun to suspect that she was not a late bloomer at all, but one who would never bloom, when she befriended several girls who lodged there. Because she was as small as a child, others often assumed that she was not of adequate wits—a profound misapprehension. She was both clever and resourceful. Indeed, in that she had nowhere else to go, she saw an estimable advantage to be allied with the worldly women she found herself amongst.

Unasked and unpaid, Daisy began to run errands and do other small services for those ladies of evening who disported within the house. Gradually, they became her friends and thus were happy to school her on the finer points of selling oneself. Moreover, they found themselves delighted to reap the benefit of one as singular as Daisy in their midst. They dusted her with powder, daubed her with rouge, and then set her out on the stoop more decorated than any maypole on May Day. All in all, Daisy was quite pleased with herself and her new best friends. She remained pleased even after she learnt what it all meant.

As Daisy was also of the nature to find benefit in all adversity, she did so then. It took a bit of study, but finally she found it—she reckoned with her mother dead and no family to speak of that she did not have to suffer from anyone's disappointment in her lack of bloom. Life, she believed, was quite fitting. For where else but in her chosen profession could someone be rewarded for what she did not have.

Before Mother Mulroney was called to her great reward, she had birthed a succession of children by a succession of men. Moreover, she had done the remarkable of marrying them each and every one. Understandably, as the last surviving child, Daisy was uncertain of the particulars of all her mother's connexions. Daisy did know that of eight children born to her mother, only three grew to see their majority (which was actually a fair percentage for their purlieu). The three who survived consisted of Daisy and two older boys. Her half-brothers were both born of a bald man named Reed. When relating the intelligence of her first husband's most prominent characteristic, Daisy's mother had been quick to note that his was an early loss of hair due to rheumatic fever—the burden of which undoubtedly caused his subsequent demise. That had been her mother's account of his death, but Daisy had heard otherwise. Whether it was a bad heart that actually did him in remained undetermined, but she learnt that he had lived long enough with it to die picking oakum in Newgate Prison. The crime he had committed had been only some sort of chicanery. However, the butt-end of his misdeed had a brother. That brother was a lawyer and that meant jail. When confronted by Daisy of the particulars, her mother shrugged her shoulders.

"'Twere a bad bit of business all-round," she replied.

Life went on for Widow Reed, for she was not a woman who allowed her own goodness to be blighted by her husband's malefaction. Still only five and thirty years old, she did not intend to remain a widow ere long. Directly after learning of her husband's passing, she united with an Irish Catholic named Mulroney, the proud owner of a respectably unprosperous tobacco shop. Alas, Mulroney may have been a better husband than Reed, but he was no less unreliable so far as being mortal. As it happened, not a ten-year after they were married he ran afoul of a brewer's dray and came to an untidy end. (He was fond enough of ale that the irony of this particular misfortune was not lost upon his survivors.) Due to the precarious nature of his finances, the bailiff and his man ransacked his shop before Mulroney's body was laid to rest. Her sons by Reed having long flown the coop, Widow Mulroney had only Daisy (and the tin of coins she had kept behind a broken brick) at home to help mourn him.

Upon occasion the two boys born of the oakum-picker (as Daisy much liked to call him) happened by. It was always a fascination to her to see them. Due to their differing parentage neither of her brothers much favoured her. Tommy was a big bear of a man, short-tempered and often as not in want of hiding over some malefaction or the other. Frank was older and smaller than Tommy. Daisy did not remember much about him except that he was pretty and pious with the additional credit of a quick mind. These traits caught the eye of a particularly benevolent priest. Knowing Mulroney was dead and gone (and oblivious to the fact that Frank was not Mulroney's blood son, or therefore, even Catholic), he saw to it that young Frank attended a day school. Frank liked school and frantically set to learning the catechism hoping not to be found out. Meanwhile, Tommy's penchant for drinking and brawling got him a murder sentence on the Newgate treadmill. Mrs. Mulroney could not help but see the resemblance to his father and refused even to stand outside prison on visiting day. After Mrs. Mulroney's passing, Daisy's curiosity betook her there to determine if he still abided within.

She heard so many varying accounts that she knew not what to make of it. He was said to have either swung on the gallows months past, garrotted a guard and escaped, and that no one by that name had ever been sentenced. Thomas Reed was a common name. She discounted that he had never been there, but was altogether uncertain how to regard the other two stories. In the end, she reckoned he was either dead or as good as, and took her leave.

Frank's prospects had been much better. The priests had influenced him to take Benedictine orders. Hence, by the time their mother called herself Widow Mulroney, the Reed brothers had embarked upon remarkably divergent paths in life. Ultimately, however, they reunited in a most unhappy fashion. This, however, would come to pass long after their mother was alive to care. The last living issue of her unions, Little Daisy Mulroney, as the history of her kin suggests, had many influences that held sway over her predilections. Regrettably, like many folks, her future was not decided by free will.

Mid-morning was Daisy's favourite time of day. The drays had cleared the street; fresh bread had cooled and was no longer a temptation. Moreover, she could cross a side street without fear of tripping over a corpse or worse, chance someone bent on interfering with her person. Few of her profession attempted legal retribution upon those occasions—convincing the authorities that she had not simply been refused payment would be a bother (a shiv in her boot was far more efficient than the law). The early hour also meant there was little chance that she would come across an actual customer. By that time of day, most men's heads still ached from the past evening's merriments, hence any morning pride had either been taken down by a friendly hand or had not been worth paying for in the first place.

As she walked along, the foot-path was soon bestrewn with tiny street Arabs and she espied a vagrant enjoying his first crotch-scratch of the day. Publicans threw back the sash to air out whatever disturbance had been wrought the night before and shopkeepers began to lay out their merchandise. One, with dearest goods already in place, eyed her warily as she passed. She took little notice of him—all shopkeepers were by nature a suspicious lot. The only amusement she noted during her stroll were those self-proclaimed decent folk passing through St. Giles, their coaches closed tightly to ward off the stench of the street. Everyone scrambled when one of these grand carriages rumbled by, for seldom did they pause for pedestrians. Orders to their coachman, she supposed. If gentlefolk found themselves in St. Giles, they were either lost, looking for bargain entertainment, or out to save souls.

Daisy did not mind the occasional barouche come lumbering by, but those impassioned altruists could be a trying bunch. They were out to save the world one sinner at a time, they were—and a fair number wanted to start with her. A person of her leanings could not move through the street for them—thick as thieves they were—employing manners too meddlesome for a Billingsgate hawker. Early on she simply ignored the zealots and pushed by them. But so persistent were they, Daisy's curiosity eventually got the best of her. When one little bird of a woman grasped her arm, she turned and faced her. The woman was so delighted to have an unadulterated trollop (and but a child!) within her grasp, Daisy feared the woman might just weep.

"Say yer piece!" Daisy barked at the woman.

Wasting neither time nor tact, the woman gathered herself together and explained how she, Daisy, was a disgrace to all of humanity, an insult to Christian virtues, and without a doubt would burn in hell for all eternity. Daisy blinked at her repeatedly, flabbergasted as how to respond. This gap in the conversation led the small woman to announce Daisy's ultimate damnation.

"Repent, young one, repent! Do you not, it is at the cost of your immortal soul!"

Daisy looked the woman up and down considering how to explain to so hopeless a case the realities of street life. Thereupon, she had a change of heart.

"Piss off," sniffed Daisy with the air of an habitué of Regent Street.

The woman's expression left Daisy suitably happy that she had made her point. Whilst Daisy may have declined to fall to her knees in repentance of her sinful ways, she was still leery of refusing such holy shenanigans out of hand. Although she was raised in the church, what little religious belief she held was wavering. Indeed, she held off from walloping anyone of them with her furled parasol for that reason alone. She may no longer have been a devout Catholic, but she was not so hasty as to declare herself an atheist. Her religion now dwelt somewhere between utter disbelief and superstition. She disliked the notion of a deity who would allow babies to starve in the streets, but was roundly afraid that if there was one that cruel, she did not want to offend Him.

It was a healthy fear. Beyond just dead babies, she had seen first-hand what He could do. Her brothers had been unwise in their choice of vices and they had come to a grisly end. Even Frank, God rest his soul, who was unceremoniously tossed out of the seminary on the allegation of being "overly indulgent to the whims of nature"—whatever the deuce that meant. But Frank's good fortune did not end then and there. For through some fortuitous connexions, he managed to obtain a place on the grounds of a rich man's house in the most prestigious part of Mayfair. Once she heard that, rarely did a *chaise* and four pass by that Daisy did not look to see if she saw Frank clinging to the footboard. She did so even long after she learnt that he was dead.

Although Tommy had a mean streak and had repeatedly fallen victim to it, Frank was given life's luck-penny. Hence, when Daisy heard tell that both had been killed dead as Dooley's doornail by a rich man's hand, she was not particularly astonished. However, when told the name of the man who killed them—Darcy, she believed they said—quite surprisingly, she did not cry out for retribution. Nor did she bother to inquire just what larceny her brothers were exacting that demanded the ultimate penalty. The only question that grieved her whatsoever was simply one of curiosity. She wondered just how Tommy roped Frank into it.

Hence, when it came to pass that Daisy's little friend Sally had business at the Darcy country home in Derbyshire, she thought it a small world indeed.

To Bathe or Not to Bathe

"Pray, do you think this is a wicked indulgence, husband?" Elizabeth asked, a one-sided curl of a smile suggesting the question not truly ecclesiastical in origin.

Mr. and Mrs. Darcy sat luxuriating in a huge copper tub, their heads resting on opposing ends, their limbs overlapping mid-most. Elizabeth's hair was pinned upon the top of her head, but the steamy air had influenced a few strands to cling to her face and neck. Mr. Darcy's head was partially submerged allowing his hair to float about his head like wings. He had one ankle hooked over the edge of the tub, but beneath the remnants of the ever-dissipating soapsuds his other foot was intent on making mischief where his wife sat.

"Whatever do you mean?" he asked with all due innocence.

With a little yip, she shook her head as if he had, for all intents and purposes, answered in the affirmative. She took hold of his big toe and, with some effort, pulled it above the water-line. The saturated wrinkles thereon made it look more akin to a stewed prune than a human digit. It announced that their sojourn in the tub had been a lengthy one. She raised an eyebrow.

"Is it not dissolute to languish as we do?" she asked. "I certainly *feel* wicked."

Mr. Darcy had gone to a great deal of bother to find a Slav coppersmith lately of Prague to fashion the enormous vessel in which they luxuriated just then. It did not improve his temper to have the morality of the entire venture questioned after he had invested half a year and seventy-five guineas to obtain it.

He sat up quite abruptly and gave a quick toss of the head thereby flicking back his dripping forelock. An expression overspread his face that suggested he thought himself chided. Elizabeth recognised the expression. It was one increasingly familiar—but not from her husband. She witnessed it upon the countenance of her husband's son. That occurrence usually happening when something he should not have was taken from his determined little fist. Any moment she expected her husband's lower lip to protrude as well. She wanted to laugh, but managed to avoid that blunder. Under no circumstances would he enjoy himself being an object of mirth.

"Surely no one bathes as often as do we," Elizabeth announced (the word "together" was implied but unspoken).

"Pray, do you believe that an activity is inherently wicked because it is not commonplace?"

As he often did, he took her idle musing as a grave deliberation.

Said she, a little too testily, "I do not. I only suggest we over-indulge..." (here her own toes embarked on mischief of their own) "...the blessing of cleanliness."

"Pray, do you recall," he said, catching her foot, "the first time you occasioned my bath?"

She was not given time to reply, for he clasped her ankle and gave it a tug. This time, she was alert to such business and, with a quick feint of her foot, wrested it from his grasp. She then drew her knees beneath her and threw herself atop him, displacing a large amount of water that sloshed over the side.

"Mmmm," she recollected, pressing her body to his. "Indeed, I do recall it. The mortification *and* the reward."

The incident that he alluded to was well within her memory, for it had occurred quite early in their marriage. On that propitious occasion, although her egress into his bath had been unpremeditated, she had been treated to favours of unrivalled eroticism by her husband (whilst in, out, and around the tub) that remained quite singular in her recollection. Therefore, when brought to mind it never ceased to inflame her cheek and her libido. If her husband knew that and used it as a ploy of arousal, she could have saved him the bother. With nothing between her breasts and his chest but the slight surge of the warm bath water, she was quite aroused without such reminders.

Indeed, that evening had prompted a proclivity between them of enjoying water-borne delights. So predominant was this leaning that Mr. Darcy had not only engaged a coppersmith for an over-sized tub, he brought about the renovation of one of the smaller of Pemberley's many rooms in which to place it. In those many hours he remained steadfastly within the walls of Pemberley at Elizabeth's request, his mind needed employment. He had drawn and redrawn plans, engaging the finest artisans to carry them out. The flooring was of particularly high quality white marble, bearing fine blue veins throughout, and the walls were lined with blue and white Dutch tiles. He managed to keep the project a surprise from her until the waggon carrying the tub arrived.

As would be expected, the delivery of an apparatus of such magnitude drew an audience of servitors who snuck away from their duties just to witness it. It was contained in a wooden crate, one not dismantled until it was brought inside. It had been by his own design that Darcy had not personally overseen the unloading of the tub, but watched from a window above. It had fallen apparent very quickly that removing himself from the process did little to reduce the level of curiosity surrounding it. Indeed, that it was camouflaged in a box seemed to pique interest rather than the reverse.

"Smeads," Darcy called. "See to it that those not directly involved return to their own duties."

As Smeads had been a fixture in his family for as long as he could remember, Darcy paid little attention to him so long as the house ran smoothly. He suspected, however, that Elizabeth did not care for him. She had not said as much. Indeed, he had asked her obliquely if she was pleased with Smeads's elevated position, but she had demurred—possibly not wanting to cause her husband additional upset. Her reservation, even unspoken, had bid Darcy to eye Smeads more keenly than he would have otherwise.

At Mr. Darcy's order, Smeads bowed smartly and began dispersing unnecessary staff. Such a brisk response should have made Darcy happy, but it did not, although he wasn't sure why. A little ruffled by the suspicion that Elizabeth's every reservation had such an effect upon his own opinions, he dismissed the notion, happy to have his mind occupied with the work before him.

And it was very much a work in progress. He fully intended to have the room equipped with towers for hot and cold water, but for now they could only wait for the tedious business of filling the tub with buckets. Once the bearers of the buckets retreated and they had immersed themselves within, they had agreed that it was worth the wait.

And now, as if by foreordainment, Mr. and Mrs. Darcy prepared to enjoy every facet of their tub. Wordlessly, Mrs. Darcy rose slightly from her husband allowing them both to sit. (Much like a conductor had rapped upon his podium for the orchestra's attention and raised his baton.) For a moment they did so, only gazing into each other's eyes. Simultaneously, she manoeuvred her ankles around and behind him and he grasped her rump, drawing her near. Placing her hands upon either side of his face, she expected only to exchange loving gazes, but she was thwarted. His gaze was loving as well, but it had been arrested by a dual sight other than her eyes.

"You, sir, are not looking at me," she accused.

"I do so dislike to contradict you, but *au contraire*," he whispered.

He placed his hands on either side of her torso, just above the waist. Pensively, he stroked her there with his thumbs. She did not truly want him to stop, but it was a considerable feat not to laugh or clamp her elbows against her sides as she was quite ticklish. From a sensation other than being exposed to the cool air, her nipples cockled. Whether or not it was that which arrested his attention, fortune saw him quit that stroking forthwith and draw a hand up to cup each breast. He held them thusly, almost reverentially, for a moment before bending forward to kiss them each. She was so taken by the tenderness of his enterprise, that she enfolded his head in her arms and ploughed finger-furrows through his hair. So lengthy was his idolatrous attention, her head rolled to the side, revelling in the grandness of it all.

But as such applications rarely are sustained, these were followed by further, greater rewards—at her instigation.

Feeling his arousal, she begat a gentle, but insistent undulation—one undeniably successful in encouraging a specific response.

"At your command, Madame," he said still whispering.

His response was precisely what she desired. But to have her will be done, he lifted her upwards out of the water and, with a gingerly bit of positioning upon his part and small wriggle upon hers, success was met. (As he *was* much favoured by nature, she smiled inwardly at just how very far out of the water she was drawn in order to be engaged thusly.) Thereupon, true undulation began, and she was of a mind to wrap her arms about his neck and draw herself nearer. He, however, was of quite another mind and held her by her shoulders before him. With each surge and withdrawal, he watched her so intently she could but return his gaze in equal measure. Their breaths were becoming more ragged, but he reached out and placed his palm against her cheek.

"Lizzy, Lizzy," said he. "When I thought you could never become more beautiful, still you gain countenance."

There was nothing particular she wanted to say just then (if, in fact, she had the capacity to speak), but she turned her head toward his hand and took his thumb into her mouth as she reached achievement. The engagement that ensued to Mr. Darcy's ends was not a bit evil, but definitely rambunctious—Mr. Darcy ultimately of the opinion his money had been well-spent.

After a spell of quiet, Darcy pulled himself dripping from the tub and walked the length of the marble floor to where his dressing gown lay. Elizabeth rested her chin upon her folded arms upon the edge of the tub, enjoying the pleasing vantage of her husband's naked form.

To his broad back, she said, "You take to the water so happily, should we not sample sea bathing?"

This was spoken entirely in jest. Now luxuriating in post-coital recumbence, she was as happy to bedevil him as he was to be teased. Still, she treaded lightly, his small regard for this newly fashionable activity and its attendant accoutrements of dress were not unknown to her.

"Harrumph," said he, "I should not like to think of myself wearing a bathing costume. I should not like to think of my wife wearing one either."

"Nor do I," she agreed, "I quite like what I see at present."

At that he turned and gave her a cheeky smile, one quite unlike him. She thought that perhaps she had disturbed his composure. She hoped that she had—it was only fair in that he had done the same to her with such regularity. She also knew that it was unlikely that either would have themselves winched out into the sea in a waggon wearing little more than their small clothes, but she had her reasons for betaking themselves to the seaside. Little Janie had a suspicious cough and the sea air *was* the surest restorative. The larger question would be whither they go?

Brighton was the most famous seaside resort and Ramsgate most fashionable of the Kentish seaside bathing places. But Ramsgate inspired memories Darcy had long been in want of forgetting. (It was, after all, the scene of Wickham's barely aborted seduction of the then fifteen-year-old Georgiana.) Only those who dared ignore rank were those at its pinnacle. The Darcys were at its pinnacle. And for them, they would not season this year in London. Brighton, Elizabeth had heard, had a lovely pier upon which to stroll—perfect for a carriage. Brighton, she decided, it would be.

A Blow to the Unused Heart

A courtesan is vastly inconvenienced when falling with child. Such a bother suppressed not only Césarine's merriment, but her income. Her confinement was even more ill-timed. Her capital was depleting with no small rapidity owing primarily to her inability to engage in any part of pecuniary restraint.

At one time the throes of a "delicate condition" might only have caused her an inconvenience. She might have announced a retreat to the country to take a cure, or possibly, embarked on a Mediterranean excursion. But she could no more. It was not her health, but her wealth that impeded such ploys. She lived as if each day was her last, sending Marie-Therese upon regular trips to the pawnshop bartering with jewels of ever-decreasing value. The one piece she refused to part with was her ruby necklace, saying that she would be buried in it rather give it up. (Increasingly, that became a possibility.) There were added worriments beyond her lavish lifestyle to deplete her funds. Indeed, they were further taxed by bills from various doctors and apothecaries, the stack of which was accumulating in reverse proportion to her *bijouterie*. She should have known better than to make her predicament public, but Césarine was not, nor had ever been, discreet. Although it had not been important upon her ascension to the apex of the demimonde, once there, impending poverty created a stench of failure. There were few men of her acquaintance who wanted to be associated with a decline. Hence, her influential lovers scattered like rats abandoning a sinking ship. For all purposes, Césarine was, indeed, sinking.

Bearing a child over-taxed her already compromised constitution. She was soon assigned to her bed—the very same bed in which she had transported rapturous lovers to forbidden ecstasies—and no one, save Wickham and the ubiquitous Marie-Therese, was there to watch over her. Viscount Du Mautort was still devoted to Césarine, but could come but seldom. For having been alerted to her son's irresponsible love-life, his mother, Countess Du Mautort, had hied to Paris intent on interfering with her son's allowance and, thereby, his friendships as well. Du Mautort's woes, however, were of little concern to those who attended Césarine's bed.

It would have been to their utter amazement had Wickham's acquaintances seen him then—love-struck and morose, pining over a woman. Through marriage, intrigues, and liaisons, he had never once fallen in love. It was not that he was without those inclinations that drove men to move mountains and slay dragons, for he believed if the stars were aligned to perfection, he might one day fall under a woman's sway. But he struggled against that possibility all his life, for his heart was very dear to him (being tolerably near his stomach) and once it was lost to another he feared it might never be retrieved. It was much more agreeable to be the betrayer rather than the betrayed—and if he did not put his own heart at risk he would not be betrayed. He believed it was entirely an issue of mind over matter. His heart was under strict regulation: if he chose not to fall in love, he would not. He had other fish to fry.

He was drawn to Césarine for many reasons—not the least of which were the charms of her bed. There was, however, a greater force at work. Wickham admired beauty, the pretence (rather than the actuality) of breeding, a coquettish manner, and a gaming spirit above all other qualities. That these were those most prominent in his own character remained unexamined. Indeed, such was his ego, no love, no matter how exceptional, could have rivalled that which he held for himself. That is, until he found himself under Césarine's spell. For, although it was unapparent to him, in all ways save her aspect, Césarine was his mirror-image. He had reached the pinnacle of narcissism—he had fallen in love with himself. Not that he realised it. Through childhood, youth, and manhood, introspection had never once plagued his thoughts.

He truly believed that with her *savoir faire*, his ingenuity, and their combined beauty, nothing was beyond their grasp. They would parlay their talents at the gaming table into a tolerable stake, whereby they would travel to the four corners of the earth until at last they tired. Thereupon they would purchase a grand chateau—grander than Pemberley—and live out their lives in untold splendour. He smiled as he thought of it.

Had he attended his catechism with more dedication than his seductions, he might have remembered the admonitory proverb that said there was more hope of a fool than a man wise in his own conceit. As he did not, when at last he was careless with his devotion, the fall was extraordinary—but not compleat.

He loved Césarine more than anything in life with the exception ultimately, of himself.

Not once had Wickham sat in a sick-room. Not for his mother, his father, his wife, and certainly not for his children. (He did slouch about a bit outside old Mr. Darcy's death watch daubing a suspiciously dry pocket-square to the corner of his eye—but if one were perfectly frank, those tender feelings that had been awakened in him were far more on behalf of that man's bequests than undying affection for him.) Indeed, the single sick-room he had reason to inhabit was one he fashioned for himself after contracting a nasty case of gout—one that had kept him off the dance floor for most of the season in the year '12 and thereby convincing himself he knew something of suffering. Hence, bearing the particular burden of that horrific disorder, he believed himself quite commiserative to others who had fallen ill (although Lord knows, nursing the ill *was* the work of women).

When it came to obliging expectations, Wickham was a rapid study. As Césarine's condition grew worse, he grew morose with unusual synchronicity. He clutched her hand and issued every sympathy, commiserated every pain. The more weakened she became, the more his love flowered. By the time her labour commenced, he had somehow transfigured into his own cranky version of the most lovelorn lamenter that ever prest tear-stained cheeks against a suffering brow. Given compleat understanding of

Wickham's narcissistic nature, one might have been led to wonder if his utter devastation was less for her suffering than his loss. (If Césarine was of that opinion too, one can only conjecture.) As it was, he was the only lover still faithful to her side; hence, Césarine avowed her love was returned in equal measure.

Wickham most fervently desired to believe that true, however in the deepest reaches of his heart was not altogether persuaded. He was tempted to call for a Bible and demand a blood oath, but in some situations even he knew that questioning veracity is indecorous, so he did not. He renewed his profession of undying love and translated that love into pages of melancholy script describing the depth of his devotion (often in iambic pentameter and purple ink). He read them aloud to her with such heartfelt, singsong reverence that when Marie-Therese inquired of the doctor if he knew of some potion for sedation, Césarine was not whom she had in mind.

Showing remarkable pluck, Césarine Thierry, unmarried woman, delivered a living, breathing, and thoroughly bastard daughter before she succumbed to the collision of childbirth fever and consumption.

Inconsolable, Wickham lay prostrate across her body begging God to take him too. Marie-Therese took him by the shoulders and urged him away.

"There, there, my little kumquat," she cooed. "There are things that must be attended to."

Wickham only moaned and clutched Césarine's body more diligently thereby impelling Marie-Therese to call for Cook. (Cook was the last remaining servant, and although not particularly devoted to Césarine, she was a sensible enough woman to know that if she took her leave there would be even less chance of obtaining her back wages.) Cook was not happy to have to man-handle a grief-stricken mourner, but once accepting a duty, she did not shirk it. Cook, whose meaty forearms were not less slight than a smithy's, took hold of Wickham and rendered him to his feet—but regrettably not to his senses. She caught him under the armpits and hauled him yet be-wailing out the door whereupon she sat him (still weeping) into a side-chair. But so flaccid with grief was he, he slid immediately to the floor.

As a woman not over-burdened with patience, Marie-Therese could suffer Wickham no longer. It was not that she was not bereaved, for she was—in her own way. She was only mercenary, not heartless, and sentiment was one luxury she could not afford. Time was of the essence.

Money-lenders were even then gathering to pounce on Césarine's belongings not yet at the pawn-shop. They were intent on dividing what spoils remained against her promissory notes. Not only were tradesmen owed, but invoices from doctors had been stacked in a neat little pile on the dressing table. Creditors would be swarming through her drawers forthwith. Marie-Therese was uncertain but believed the last of the most precious jewellry had been stowed in the cotton batting of the mattress where Césarine's corpse lay. But she made no move to help Cook to lay out the body. The beefy woman gave a great heaving sigh at the obligation of further work outside her culinary domain. But as help was unforthcoming, she went to work—supposing, heavens knows, she had the wherewithal and experience to put together even this tart.

The deceased Césarine's jaw drooped in the distressingly familiar yowl of death and Cook twirled a pocket-square she had wrested from Wickham into a sling to bind it up. Marie-Therese oversaw her activity from the corner of her eye as she methodically scavenged the room. Nothing was left to chance. All the while she worked, Wickham continued to weep from his heap on the floor. A great hiccupping keen had commenced, but he quieted himself as he pulled up and onto the seat of a prayer-desk. He looked briefly at the object upon which he sat (as ornate as it was little used) and then began to weep once more.

Wretched was he. Wretched, disconsolate, and confused. Confusion did not lift when the bell tolled a caller. As if an automaton, he drew himself to his feet and, whimpering all the way, walked to the door and threw it open.

"*Quoi*?" he rudely asked.

Before him stood a solemn, portentous, and not a little censorious trio of nuns. The older one was forefront, the other two at her elbows. Instantly, Wickham regained a diplomatic demeanour. He bowed, and as they gained the room, he made a quick look about the corridor. His inspection was two-fold. Firstly he wanted to determine if there was an accompanying priest, and secondly if there were any lurking creditors. When he observed no one, he cautiously closed the door and turned to the threesome who stood looking at him balefully. Recollecting his recent disconcertion at the prayer desk, he instinctively drew back and called to Marie-Therese to sort it out. He wanted nothing to do with those of religious persuasion at this juncture—suddenly quite aware that Césarine's soul had been grievously ignored.

With an acute lack of forbearance, Marie-Therese appeared and, with a wave of her hand in the direction of the far corner, indicated the temporary repository of Césarine's child. Cook, more sensible of all that had transpired than anyone else in attendance had judiciously placed the newborn in a make-shift bed in the bottom drawer of a highboy. The baby had lain perfectly quiet for so long, it hadn't occurred to Wickham that she was still alive. Whilst Marie-Therese hurried back into Césarine's bed-chamber and began to rummage over, under, and beneath the bed, Wickham heard her grouse. She complained quite bitterly and relentlessly that men, and particularly *perfide Albion*, were the most impotent, incompetent, unlettered, improvident fleas on the back of a dog that ever the world had seen.

Marie-Therese's French was far too quick for Wickham to make out what she said beyond the aspersion of his nationality, but he still became incensed. It was all moving too quickly. It was as if the pretty little fable which represented his mind's-eye version of his life was being ruthlessly dismantled. Soon there would be nothing left of either Césarine or their love.

He could not quite grasp the meaning of it.

And then, he did.

The nuns had been summoned to take the babe to convent and Marie-Therese was pillaging any of Césarine's chattels that she could stash in a portmanteau. Her possessions stolen and the child, *their* child taken! This was an outrage. He would not have it!

It came to pass that Marie-Therese did well scavenging all of Césarine's earthly possessions (or at least those she uncovered). The one thing Wickham knew was that Césarine did not go to her great reward adorned with anything about her neck but a simple gold cross—a present from Du Mautort. That gentleman wrenched loose of his mother long enough to pass the hat to pay for poor Césarine's funeral expenses. Fortune had it that the mistress of a scion of the sugar beet industry had died the same day and services were held at the Church of the Madeleine with only an hour separating hers from Césarine's, in fortune, the flowers remained unwilted long enough to honour them both. However, Du Mautort assumed they were Wickham's doing and wept with gratitude when he saw them. He would have been happy to have stood that cost himself but his pockets were all but played out from hiring a trio of troubadours to sling rose petals before their meagre little procession as it travelled to the burial site. Marie-Therese did not deign to grace the procession with her presence at all, but Du Mautort walked with one hand placed reverently atop the coffin, his other over his heart.

No one stood in the position of bereaved husband. As profuse as had been his possessiveness of her time and despair over her death, it would have been expected that Wickham would have led the cortège. As it was, he did not. Marie-Therese went to great lengths to search him out, for she had something which she would take great pleasure in presenting him. But, alas.

Indeed, once again Wickham had gone missing.

Wickham, much like all gamesters, knew that the height of cleverness is to be able to conceal it. While he did not hold the aces, he had one very valuable one in the hole. However, it was not the one he thought it was.

Mrs. Darcy's Horse

Elizabeth's sleeping habits had altered but little since her marriage. She had always slept deeply and relished in doing so. The soundness of her sleep and that she awakened so refreshed betokened the gratification she was rendered by her husband's robust attentions beforehand. As would be expected, once she became a mother she had never slept again with the same depth. (Darcy had teased her that so lightly did she take her sleep that she had come to do so with one eye open like some fugitive from King's Bench.) Hence, when her children's sleeping through the night coincided with a replenishing of their nightly vigours, she once again began to enjoy a most satisfying rest.

Therefore when Darcy knelt next to her well after midnight one chilly night in early spring, his attempts at awaking her were, beyond a few loving murmurings of her absolute willingness to comply with whatever he wanted of her, unfruitful.

"Lizzy," he gently shook her shoulder once again, "Lizzy!"

"Yes, I am quite awake," she said, the truth of her statement impugned by the lack of her eyes being open.

"It is time," he said.

"Time?" she opened one eye, sat bolt upright and threw back the bed-clothes. "Time! It is time?"

"Yes," he assured her.

Once her eyes were open, she saw that he was fully dressed—at least insofar as boots, shirt, and breeches. He had foresworn proper coat and neckcloth for his great-coat. Over his arm was a cloak for her. By the time she saw all that, she was fully awake. She was on her feet in an instant, grabbed her cloak and was swinging it about her shoulders all whilst heading for the door.

"Wait," he said. "*Wait!*"

Their exchange had been made in stage whispers, for the house was compleatly asleep. Both understood their undertaking may well be lengthy and she under no circumstances wanted the babies to be roused.

"Sshhh!" she reminded him, turning to see what was the matter.

"You must wear your slippers lest you catch your death!"

In one hand he held a candle and in the other her slippers. They were daintily hanging from the tips of two of his fingers, which he then extended to her. Knowing the wisdom of his insistence, she impatiently allowed him to fit them upon her feet by balancing one hand on his back as he bent before her.

"Lizzy," he implored, "if you would just be still…"

"I cannot help it," she said. "Time is of the essence!"

"I beg to differ, my dearest; it is not."

She cut him a look that suggested he knew little of what was or was not imperative but kept still enough to be compleatly shod ere she made for the door.

"Wait, Lizzy! Wait!" he said helplessly as she bounded down the stairs.

He had caught up with her as they quit the house, but he slowed momentarily to trade the candle for a lantern from the footman by the door. In that brief exchange she again out-distanced him, but before she gained the courtyard he had caught up with her and grasped her elbow.

"If you insist upon making such haste in the dark you are certain to turn your ankle," he admonished, adding for good measure, "then who shall see to your children?"

She turned to gift him a glare at that overt abuse of her motherly instincts, but attempted to rein in her ever-increasing excitement all the same.

"I can see perfectly well," she insisted, only to be blessed by the God of the Wilful with a stumble.

He, however, had the good sense not to speak the words "I told you so" when he caught her before she fell, but the expression upon his countenance said it quite well. Her dignity slightly bruised, she altered their discourse from her haste to the reason for it.

"How does she fare?" she said. "Is there any way to know how long it shall be?"

"Not a method yet known to mankind," he assured her.

The entire of their employment at that hour was due to the impending foaling of Elizabeth's horse, Boots. Although some would have considered it indecorous for a gentlewoman to attend a birth such as this, it had been the Darcys' design since they first learnt of Boots's condition. But fortune saw when the time was nigh that it was nightfall and there would be few people about to be offended by their unseemliness.

It was the event around which they had set their plans to decamp for Brighton. Elizabeth had wanted to await Boots's foaling. As time grew near and Boots's belly grew ever-larger, Darcy had twice-daily appraisals of her progress. Until this particular event, he only came to a foaling when it was convenient and never in the middle of the night. But on the advice of Hardin that Boots appeared more restless than usual, he had come to the stables late that afternoon directly to see for himself. Although not as practiced as Hardin, he recognised the signs in Boots immediately and gave Hardin leave to awaken him if it became necessary.

The horse barn was a huge edifice made of stone with a gabled roof. With the lantern before them, Darcy escorted Elizabeth down the passage, picking their way carefully along as if it had not been swept clean of any trace of droppings. She was happy to take her husband's arm, but it would have been truly no great feat to have found her way on her own for the place was well lit by six lanterns hanging from various posts around the stall. Moreover, Edward Hardin sat upon a stool outside the stall door, carving knife in one hand and a piece of wood in the other. A large pile of thin, yellow coils lay between his feet attesting to the length of the wait. He stood up directly upon seeing the Darcys approach and took a deferential step back. Then, he seemed disconcerted, clearly uncertain of the exact protocol; he had never encountered a lady under these particular circumstances. He bowed, figuring if that be decorum when met in daylight hours it would suffice quite nicely for night.

Elizabeth returned Hardin's shy bob with a smile, asking, "How does she fare, Mr. Hardin?"

"All's well, Ma'am."

She stepped up on the first rung of the stall door and peered in. Boots was then standing, but was clearly distressed, nickering and throwing her head about. Elizabeth frowned as the mare turned several revolutions before dropping first to her knees, then gingerly rolling onto her side.

"Pray," Elizabeth whispered, "is it imminent?"

"She has been doing this for some time," Darcy said, "but may well proceed as you see her for some time more."

She looked upon him with true trepidation. "Do you truly think so? She is lying down, I understood you to say that was done only at the last."

Darcy put his arm around her shoulder and gave a small squeeze, saying, "Fear not, she will take what time is needed and we cannot hurry her."

"Coffee, Mr. Darcy," said Mr. Hardin, holding out a cup of steaming brew.

"Ah, yes," Darcy took it from his hand, and then held it out to Elizabeth. "Lizzy?"

She shook her head and neither made any note that he had called her his pet name in front of Edward Hardin. In the night air, with the smell of hay and muck about them and wearing nothing but little to cover their *déshabillé*, it seemed altogether fitting. Darcy and Hardin leisurely sipped from their cups and warmed their hands simultaneously. After a few moments Darcy upended a wooden bucket.

"Your throne, Madame," he quipped. "Truly, you may as well sit, Elizabeth, for you know what they say of a watched pot."

As if to prove that point, no sooner did she sit, than Boots sat up, dragged herself to her feet, and again commenced to circle restlessly, nickering and occasionally attempting to bite her stomach. When at last she went down once more, she lay back upon her side straining.

Hardin and Darcy stood, but did not move nearer.

"Is the time nigh?" she asked anxiously.

"Perhaps," Darcy said cautiously.

Elizabeth leapt to her feet, but feared to go nearer if the men did not. Darcy put his hand out as if anticipating her moving too fast and startling Boots. They watched for a small time before Hardin nodded once to Darcy and moved toward the stall door, then swung it open just far enough to allow them to enter one by one. Elizabeth sidled in last and hung back against the wall, holding her breath.

Boots by then got to her feet no more, but she did keep lying out full and then sitting upright several times. Then she lay upon her side once again and began shivering and giving low, shuddering moans. Hardin had inched his way to her haunches in a half-crouch, shushing her all the while. Elizabeth dropped to her knees watching closely as he slid his hand across the horse's rump, soothing her in both word and movement. Boots began to strain even more fiercely and liquid began to drain from her hindquarters.

"See there," whispered Hardin. "Do you see?"

"Yes," gasped Elizabeth, not noticing that this inquiry was not of her. "I see. Is it the foal?"

"Yea," said Hardin, "'tis."

"I can see something," she said, still whispering. "Is that the nose?"

He shook his head, "Nay. 'Tis the feet."

She inched her way forward upon her knees until she was almost even with Hardin and touched his shoulder. He looked at her and nodded his approval.

"Is all well?" she asked.

He nodded, "'Tis."

In a moment, she could see indeed two small feet protruding. Nothing further happened for a full half-minute and Elizabeth felt herself becoming alarmed, recollecting all that she had heard that could go wrong when foaling a highly bred animal. She knew that her own breath was hasty, but could not hear it for Boots's. Then Boots again sat up. Hardin reached out and grasped the foal's protruding feet. Thereupon in one swift movement, Boots stood—simultaneously delivering the foal compleatly. It came slithering out in one gush and Elizabeth leapt to her feet, backing hastily away. Hardin stepped back as well, but not half so hastily. He picked up a handful of hay and wiped the birthing residue from his hands, again shushing Boots who stood unsteadily. Directly, Boots turned about to the mass of mucus, blood, and wet hair and began meticulously to pick at the surrounding sac. At the same time a head joined the feet as discernible body parts and the foal in its entirety began to struggle free of its translucent jacket.

With the collaboration of Boots's licking and the foal's kicking, ere long the newborn got unsteadily to its feet and stood in all its knobby-kneed glory. It stood there, legs akimbo, and allowed Boots to continue her motherly licking. That encouragement propelled the foal forward and it began to hop about with all the finesse of a drunken lord, lifting up each foot high as if trying out its new hooves. Forthwith, it nosed around upon Boots, first behind the front legs and then in front of the back legs until at last it found the proper spigot and began to nurse hungrily.

At this, Elizabeth clasped her hand to her mouth in awe, exclaiming, "Darcy, have you ever witnessed anything so remarkable?"

She turned about to see if Darcy exposed any of his tightly held emotions upon this momentous occasion, but she saw him not. The stall door was ominously agape and she went through it into the pathway separating the stalls on either side of the barn. She quickly looked both ways and saw his lone figure against, but not leaning on, the frame of the open barn door. He stood quite erect, his forearm resting against the door frame, the back of his hand seemingly prest against his lips. She could see him momentarily drop his head and then throw back his shoulders as if ridding himself of some burden. Something about his attitude made her uneasy.

"Darcy," she said quietly, walking the short length of the pathway, "are you well?"

He then turned, the moonlight backlighting him with a mysterious aura. She could not see what his countenance beheld, but she sensed it. She could tell that he was struggling to maintain his emotional equilibrium, but she could not fathom why under such celebratory circumstances. She walked briskly to his side in order to ascertain just what it was.

Before she could speak, he cleared his voice and admonished, "Lizzy, come. It is far too cold here."

He reached out and protectively drew her cloak closer around her. However lovingly meant, that did not thwart her.

"She has foaled," she said.

"Good," he said, then, twice more. "Good. Good."

It was even more clear to her that something was amiss, "Pray, why did you leave?"

He did not look at her, but still fussed with her cloak, saying, "I felt of a sudden…constriction. I desired fresh air."

"I see," she said, but truly she did not, saying dryly, "I thought you invulnerable to the stench of animal husbandry."

Upon the rare occasions that she found him out of sorts, it was seldom that he confided in her whence such melancholy sprang. Hence, she did not expect him to then in so unlikely a place as they were and amidst the shuffling feet of the horses and the aromatic odour of the hay. She took his hand, however, to lead him back to admire their newest foal. He stopt abruptly, thereupon she did in turn.

"Abide with me," he said softly.

She turned to face him and he nestled his hand on the side of her neck beneath the collar of her cloak. Thoughtfully stroking her chin with his thumb, he laid first his chin then his cheek against the top of her head. Drawing her near, he gently began to sway them both. She was truly puzzled by this tenderness, but spoke not a word. She felt that if she made a sudden move that he might bolt from their intimacy like some frightened animal.

"I know why," he said finally, "the female of the species gives birth."

"Do you?" she answered.

"Yes, we men have not the mettle."

She did not for a moment think he spoke of her mare.

"It is our lot, I fear," she agreed, "yet, you must agree that as a rule, all goes well."

"As a rule," he repeated ruefully.

Increasingly between them came small patches of conversation where words were not spoken, phrases omitted, entire subjects avoided—but all was deduced. This was such a time. Hence, he was not called upon to repeat those fears that he had endured—that he endured still. She understood it all. In suggesting that, she took his hand and brought it to her lips. That was a rare gesture for her, for if hands were to be kissed they most often were hers.

"Come," she said, turning, "We must learn the gender of the foal and I am not so happy to ask the favour of determining that from Mr. Hardin."

"As you wish," he said. "As you wish."

49

The Pleasure of His Company

The antics of the gangly new foal entertained them for some time, but soon the lateness of the hour made Elizabeth yawn. Therefore, it did not take much coaxing from her husband to persuade her to return to their bed. She took his arm, and they strolled languorously back up the path to the house. It was her design that their languidness be celebrated through connubial congress, for though she was tired in body, her heart was quite inspirited. Regrettably, he only escorted her to the base of staircase. There, he kissed her hand.

Said he, "You will forgive me, for there are arrangements that must be made for the foal."

She did not want to be sent up to bed without him, but she inadvertently yawned once again—which was not the message she meant to deliver.

"Cannot Mr. Hardin see to them?" she asked.

He shook his head.

"You shall not be long?" she said wistfully.

Her disappointment was apparent, hence he said reassuringly, "I will return directly."

Elizabeth dutifully ascended the stairs. After a quick look in at the children, she situated herself upon the bed to await Darcy's return. As time went by and he did not appear, "directly" began to feel more like an eternity to her. Still, she was determined to wait for him. Restlessly, she took up a book that she had been intending to read. But once she realised that she was reading the same sentence again and again without comprehending a word of the text, she tossed it aside. When she did, her attention was arrested by the light shining in through the doors leading to the balcony. The moonlight had illuminated the stone of the balustrade as if it were day. It was an eerily lovely sight. She sat up, put out the candle next to the bed and wrapped her arms about her knees. From the darkness of the room, the spectral show lured her from beneath the bed-clothes and out through the doors.

It was chilly and she scampered to the railing. Looking up to the glittering stars and waning moon that seemed to hang like a lantern from the heavens, she stood first upon one foot, then the other, endeavouring to keep her toes from freezing. It was far too cold to stay for more than a few minutes, but she took a longing look toward the stables, straining to see if there was any sign of her husband coming up the path. Regretfully, all was dark. But just looking in that direction and picturing her husband as she supposed he was just then—talking to Mr. Hardin of the foal and Boots—filled her heart with adoration.

Dreamily, she rested her arms across the rail and allowed herself to bethink his attire—for to her it had been quite noteworthy. Indeed, it was a rare occasion that she saw Darcy thusly—eschewing his waistcoat and neck-cloth and wearing only his shirt and breeches beneath his great-coat. He rarely left their apartments without being fully attired. Her mind had been too preoccupied, first with Boots and then with her husband's unexpected melancholy to have given it much thought. It was only in the sparkling chill of the night that she allowed his figure the full attention it deserved. Unfortunately, she had to enjoy the sight only in her thoughts.

She recalled most particularly how a bit of chest hair had peeked above the unbuttoned neck of his shirt. His great-coat had been tossed on without his usual meticulousness and had remained unbuttoned, so she had an advantageous view of his breeches as well. He had mis-buttoned them. Odd how that came to her then, she had barely noticed it at the time. Neither had she paid proper due to his boots.

Yes, his boots.

They had been turned down at the knee. She had never quite conquered the libidinal interest she had taken over Darcy's boots—or rather, Darcy in his boots. It was fortuitous that her mare bore knee-high stockings on her feet, or it might have been surmised by everyone that the mare had not been named for her own markings. Rather, she had been named on behalf of the ridiculous fixation her mistress had over her master in his riding boots.

It was peculiar that she only just then thought of that singular lust. It brought back the fond memory of the night he presented Boots to her. He and Fitzwilliam had purchased her in another county and told her that her name was Dulcinea. That was a lovely name, but her husband stood next to the mare, his long legs next to hers, her white stockinged feet next to his tall, black boots—the name was as impetuous as it was inescapable. Elizabeth had repaid her husband that night for her wonderful birthday gift—several times in fact. She remembered most particularly because when he had undressed that night, she had asked him to wear his boots when they made love.

Not surprisingly, he had looked at her most peculiarly. She could not recall the event without thinking of his confused expression when he had asked, "Only my boots?" as if he had not heard her correctly. After she had nodded emphatically, he had made no further query. He retired to his dressing-room and returned as she had asked. The sight of him—toned limbs and, of course, turgid member—had never quite left her thoughts.

Just then, she was startled back to the present by a sudden gust of wind that whirled through the pillars and came up beneath the tail of her night-dress. At the incursion of cold air against her legs, she gave a tiny squeal. She did not, however, retreat to the warmth of her bed. Since her husband's away to the Continent the year before, she abhorred sleeping without him—even when he was within the sound of her voice.

"Lizzy."

His voice had been quiet. It drifted to her as if upon the wind.

She turned.

He stood in the doorway, one hand resting against the frame. He had not removed his great-coat.

"Come dearest Lizzy," he said softly. "You will catch your death."

She had taken a step in his direction, her arms outstretched. She stopt. Her arms, however, did not fall to her sides, but remained extended, beckoning.

He took the expanse of the balcony in three long strides and took her in his arms with such ferocity that she gasped. He covered her mouth with his and kissed her hungrily. Briefly, she puzzled over how he managed to read her mind so remarkably.

With a sharp intake of breath, he drew his lips away, whispering, "When I saw you here…as you are…in this attitude…the wind…"

His voice trailed off, leaving her absolutely no idea what he meant—that he had seen her then as the embodiment of his earlier dream. Little did she care what inspired his kisses, for they had recommenced. She pressed herself against him, lost in his love. So lost was she that she hardly noticed when he put his hands beneath her armpits and abruptly lifted her upon the wide, stone railing. (However, the cold stone against her nether-end was a bit of a jolt.) She certainly did not fear falling for he held her firmly, but the chill of stone caused her to burrow beneath his coat, her arms and legs wrapping about his body. When he cupped his hands beneath her rump, she thought he only meant to cushion her against the surface of the rail. But he did not.

He lifted her up and against him and turned about, carrying her thusly through the doorway, then set her down upon the end of the bed nearest the fireplace. Warmth from the remains of the fire still emanated from the hearth, rendering the rumpled bed warm and inviting. Still, he did not hasten her beneath the bed-clothes. He stood before her with his arms to his sides. It was a tall bed, but he was taller still and she drew herself to her knees. They remained in that attitude for a moment. As they faced each other, all that could be heard was the rustling of the wind and their laboured breathing. He ridded himself of his coat and impatiently kicked it aside.

"Darcy," she said, reaching out for him.

Embracing her, he bent down, nuzzling her hair with his lips. Then, he cupped her chin in his palm to draw her gaze to his, saying, "You should be imprisoned."

"What?" she asked dumbly.

"It should be unlawful for any woman to be so alluring," said he, his words no more than a susurration.

When she gulped, it was unpardonably audible.

He kissed her lips once again and her arms fell weightlessly to her sides—her surrender was compleat. With great deliberation, he reached out and released the ribbon at her neck. Her gown fell capriciously to one side. By his design, the moonlight cast its glistening spell across her ivory shoulder. With the same purposefulness, he kissed her there. Hitherto, his motions had been attentive, but circumspect—even as his kisses proceeded up the side of her neck. His restraint was not soothing to her, however. She sensed that beneath his composure, every sinew in his body lay coiled. Hence, she should have been prepared when he took each side of the placket of her gown and ripped it from her body.

She gasped, but she did not shrink from him.

Just as it had done to her shoulder, the moonlight cast a shimmer across her exposed bosom. Although his breath had become ragged, he did not immediately touch her. When he did, he placed his hands lightly about her waist. Her skin trembled uncontrollably beneath is touch. She endeavoured mightily to keep still, but to no avail. In her defence, he did little to abet that quest. For his fingers did not linger upon her waist, but made their way up her sides. He took a devilishly long time getting there, but when he did, he cupped her breasts in his hands. Thereupon, he bent to kiss first one, then the other.

By the time he had compleated this adulatory demarche up her torso and was giving his full attention to her bosom, she had ceased quaking. Indeed, all thought of governing her own body ceased and she began to contemplate what acts she meant to perpetrate against him. It would have been a temptation to rend his shirt as he had her gown, but she knew she had not the strength. Still, she wanted him rid of it. She wanted him rid of it immediately and hastily began to tug it from his waist-band. Gallantly, he forewent the pleasure of her lovely bosom to extricate himself from his shirt. Thus abetted, her lips were free to linger upon his chest, until, tossing his shirt aside, he grasped her hair and drew her head to the side and began to kiss her neck once more—this time quite hungrily.

She allowed that, but only because she was greatly occupied by foraging past the buttons of his breeches to reach the virile member within and free it. As his manhood was much in need of freeing, he returned the favour by gently seeking the recesses of her womanhood. She pressed her knee against his thigh, writhing with the pleasure he extended her. Her reluctance surpassed his when he released her. But his reason was a noble one—he meant to rid himself of his costume entirely.

As he began to hop about, tugging at the heel of one boot, she bade him otherwise.

"No," said she. "No!"

He stopt. And when he did, he looked upon her with an expression of confused perturbation. Providentially, she managed to modify her admonition, "Not your boots!" Insofar as his breeches were unbuttoned, he forewent the nicety of further disrobing. She fell back across the mattress drawing him down upon her—breeches, boots, and all.

As it happened, his urgency disallowed further foreplay. Not unexpectedly, he reached achievement far too quickly to satisfy her fully flowered cupidity. Still, she gave him a smile that implied greater satisfaction than she felt. But he lay with her only long enough for the perspiration to evaporate from the furrows of their bodies ere he sat up and resituated his manly apparatus as if to leave. What was this? Perhaps she had erred in smiling. Had she left him to think her ready for sleep?

He did leave the bed, but only as far as the doors to the balcony, which he soundly closed. She turned upon her side, watching him closely as he did so. Without looking in her direction, he went to the fireplace and stirred the fire. It was whilst she watched him that she first caught the scent of roses. As the fire began to glow once again, her gaze was arrested by the sight of flowers lying across her pillow. She was astonished. Whether he had gone to the trouble to pluck them from the greenhouse or merely taken them from an arrangement on the mantle, she cared little. He had laid them across her pillow. She reached out and picked one up, holding the petals beneath her nose and taking an aromatic whiff.

Only then did he return to her. But rather than lying beside her, he sat upon the side of the bed and pulled off first one, then the other boot and set them in precise order next to the bed. He stood and withdrew his breeches and sat upon the side of the bed.

"I thank you," she said, holding the rose aloft.

He gave a slight nod.

"Shall we sleep?" said she tossing the flower aside.

It was clearly a facetious question, for he bore a certain accoutrement that suggested sleep was not an option. She knew he bore it, because it was difficult to ignore as he crept across the bed in her direction.

"Come to me, Lizzy."

It was both an invitation and a promise.

How Low Is Bottom?

In declining Daisy Mulroney's offer and others more respectable, it took very little time for unrelenting want to take hold of the Arbuthnots. The only avenue remaining to their little family was the one that lay up Ayliffe Street. That route led directly to the Whitechapel workhouse. To betake themselves upon that long walk through Goodman's Fields to such an austere edifice was a decision born of practicality. Nell was still of enough mind to have resolved never to employ such a desperate measure for herself alone—she could still manage quite well in those mean rookeries patching clothes and minding the dead, thank you.

"It's ye little ones, it is," she insisted. "I canna care for us all."

She told them that it was not difficult to find a spare cot for one but not for three. She could do without over much to eat, but she simply could no longer endure putting her granddaughters to bed only to hear their hungry whimpers. She was used up.

Because Sally was even then old enough to be lured by the quick money particular to the immoral trades, she knew Nell worried for her of that. Although the workhouse was an institution whose sole occupation was the housing of the ill, or vagrants and parish children brought thither by want, it had its advantages—even Sally recognised them. There they could look forward to bread and milk three times a day and, if luck shone upon them, suet dumplings and butcher's meat once a week. They would have a roof over their heads and even a cot upon which to sleep—there was little not to like but for the unspoken fear that their walk thither would be but in one direction.

Wrapping all their worldly goods was the work of a minute. Hence, with each child's hand firmly clutched in hers, Nell heaved a sigh before commencing their descent into the ultimate bastion of poverty. Sally was inclined to think herself too big to be taken by the hand, but she had not the heart to pull away from her grandmother then. Neither Sue nor Sally said a word as they trod along. But, as they crossed each street along the way, Sally took a longing look down through the haze of each cobbled way and fancied that she caught sight of her brother's lean figure coming to rescue them all.

Once a handsome building, the Whitechapel Workhouse now stood in oppressive consequence. It was a three-story dark-brick edifice, which, in Sally's eyes, seemed a quarter-mile long. About the door milled a mishmash of downtrodden humanity. Overseeing the lot stood a man bearing the aspect, if not the robes, of a true martinet. His countenance was so cross, Nell held both the girls in an iron grip and hung back a bit, perhaps to give herself time to take a lay of the situation. Directly Nell ascertained that, despite their seemingly unconsidered positions, the people there had method to their grouping. To the left stood a smattering of youngsters, mid-most those crippled or otherwise infirm. To the right were a few that looked to be a bit narrow between the eyes and one or two seriously unhinged. The outer-most quadrant appeared to be reserved for the bulging stomachs of fallen women. (Soon those unfortunates would be wearing a telltale yellow badge.) Nell studied the situation, uncertain just which queue was theirs for, to varying degrees, their little group represented each. The officious man waved his walking stick over their heads like a Cardinal invoking divine unction, driving some away altogether. Before they knew it, the man barked orders for them to enter and they were somehow thrust through the throng and then to the doorway.

"See the board!" he bellowed.

Inside, Nell and her charges observed a long wooden bench. A bit discombobulated in the uncertainty of just what board they were to look upon, she endeavoured to hide her disconcertion (yet of a mind to continue the ruse of her superintendence of their destiny). She concluded it was unlikely that they came in all this way to gaze upon a bench and she motioned to the girls to sit before taking her place between them. Time proved this a proper disposal of their persons, for within the quarter hour a fierce looking matron appeared, assuring them of their good fortune arriving on the very day and hour the Board of Guardians sat reviewing admissions. Nell was disproportionately happy at the news, not anticipating biding their time in a louse-infested probationary ward amidst the lunatics for a week (the fleas less a bother than those whose minds had wandered). She knew they would have to qualify for entry and had prepared answers for the anticipated questions. She would have to vow their residence in the area and the bastardies of her granddaughters. She assumed their destitution was evident by the rags they wore. Through all of this, Sally sat still as a mouse, a warning glare from Nell unnecessary, as the general oppressiveness of the place was enough to render her mute.

The matron led them through their paces before a solemn conclave of dour-faced men who proved to be "the Board." As Nell and the girls were in reasonably good health for their situation, the medical officer found no reason to put them in quarantine. (This was a relief for Nell had a bit of cough, which she suppressed as best she could.) The girls were no more disposed than Nell to be separated, for word did have it that that place was less a sick ward than a death house.

Their dignity was further affronted by having to stand naked as God made them for a de-lousing before being handed grogram gowns and calico shifts, day caps, worsted stockings, and woven slippers. To their surprise they were allowed one Linsey-Woolsey petticoat apiece—which suited little Sue as she had not owned one of any fabric afore. She twirled about, proud as a peacock and would have made herself dizzy had not she been roused from her reverie when a bell heralded dinner. It was all her sister could do to catch her by the collar before she took off head-long toward its sound.

"Recollect yerself, Sue," admonished Sally, suddenly quite aware they were about to enter unaccustomed domain.

As food went, the fare was poor by almost anyone's standard. To this threesome, however, regular meals were a luxury and they were contentedly chipper about anything put before them. Adults were meant to receive seven ounces of dressed meat a day, but that seldom happened. All the same, a scale sat at one end of the dining hall, supposing to visiting dignitaries that anyone had the right to challenge the weight. Upon occasion, there would be a bit of grumbling. However, even when no meat (and very little cheese) was in evidence, no one dared take plate in hand and brave the lonely walk to the far end of the dining hall to challenge their portion. Much affronted by this contradiction, Sally inquired (far too stridently) as to how this came to be.

"For God's sake, child, shush! Eat yer porridge and be happy to have it!" said Nell.

She hushed, but did not cease her speculation. And in her quiet, Sally came upon the realisation of what she should have understood beforehand. The illicit trade in inmate commodities improved the paltry pay of workhouse employees. Pecuniary advantage it was called. It was the way of their world.

They were settled into a dormitory that ran the length of the building. It was a wooden cot with a straw pallet that they would have to share, but Sally looked up to reassure herself that there was, indeed, a roof over their heads. She was inordinately pleased to see it was quite sturdy. The only failing of their accommodations was the particular affront Nell assumed when learning one half the floor was dedicated to the expectant unwed. So dedicatedly did she grumble and grouse about her granddaughters being exposed to such riff-raff, one aware of their history would have found it quite odd indeed. Sally said nothing. If Nell was affronted that meant that she was not falling into one of her frightening spells. Besides, gossips had long since exposed her to the indecorousness of her parents' alliance. Nell's pretence otherwise was a bit of self-deceit that Sally chose to humour. When she could without Nell noticing, she sneaked long looks at the woeful inhabitants of swollen bodies reclining uncomfortably on the hard cots. She could not bring herself to despise them. It was a struggle to choke down outright pity.

Before they were allowed in, the matron announced the single rule within the house: no refractory behaviour. Not exactly certain what refractory behaviour was, before Nell could stop her, Sally dared to inquire. Her question was met with a hard stare, suggesting to Sally that she may have just committed a refractory act. In due time, it became clear. There was to be no foul language, assaulting of other inmates, or indecency of any kind. These were all simple enough. However, there was an absolute rule against drunkenness. This was a cruel dilemma for Nell, but after an initial infraction that resulted in a day's solitary confinement and incited howls of anguish from Sue, she managed to keep to a sort of white-knuckled sobriety. Sally watched over her most keenly, knowing that if she did not refrain from drink, the terrors might come back upon her and send her forever to the ward of the unhinged.

They were not taken on a tour of the place, but in due time, curious as ever, Sally managed to take measure of every room. The main floor housed a dining-hall, kitchen, bakery, laundry, and chapel. The second story held the casual wards which bore low-slung hammocks for those who betook themselves out for work and returned each night to sleep and eat. Sharing that long room and divided by a partition was what was known as the foul ward inhabited by those in various throes of disgraceful disorders. Female dormitories were on the third story, above them a loft that housed those with a touch of the March hare (and those with absolutely no seeds in their pumpkins), to the importance of which Nell seemed oblivious and from which Sally recoiled. There, too, was an area reserved for young mothers with infants and other "refractories." The huge yard behind the house was used for vegetable gardens and orchards, and even a milk house and piggery.

It was a self-sufficient place, all duties were entailed toward that goal. They would have to work. Some of the women were set to spinning wool and flax, some to sewing. Others knitted. One look out the back window at the plethora of green enticed Sally unlike any treat she had ever been offered leading her to volunteer for the only outdoor work available, the piggery. She was up to her ankles in muck, but she cared little. Somehow she felt more besmirched with far less grime when the dirt originated from the street.

Inasmuch as Nell committed herself to teetotalism, she was freed from her tremor and thus her fear-driven fits, allowing her to join the retinue of seamstresses. Sue was too young to do a true day's work, thus she followed Sally lest she be farmed out as a charity case. Other than having a certainty of food on the table, the one positive in the dank, depressing walls was that when not at their chores the children were rounded up and taught to write, read, and cast accounts—not only the boys, but the girls as well. Therefore, it was Sally's great fortune to have learnt to read in the year prior to receiving an actual letter.

It was not just one letter, but, miraculously, two. Both were posted from Derbyshire. The timing of their arrival was exceedingly propitious. Six months before, Sally's little family had no firm address. Six months before, Sally could not have deciphered her brother's letter herself.

For the Love of London

The first year after that of Waterloo, the Bingleys prepared to hie once again to London. They would travel with their children, their children's nurses, governesses, maids, man-servants, and baggage in what was a caravan worthy of any eastern potentate. It was with even greater regret that Jane would take the season in town. Leaving her sister after such a tumultuous year for them all was a particular trial.

From the very beginning, Jane's serenity and unceasing love had been a calming influence upon Charles Bingley's ebullience. Yet, having purchased a country estate did not suggest to him that he must become only a country gentleman. He had never been one of the coarse bloods cutting a swell in the West End. Bingley was a gentleman in all that that implied. But, his essential nature was gregarious. He loved the conviviality of company and the bustle of town—and he most particularly loved to watch sport. Regrettably, there was precious little sport to his taste to be had near Kirkland Hall and no suitable society in under a half-day's ride. But, one of the few promises Jane had ever extracted from Bingley was to reside near Elizabeth. As it had been one of her few requests, Bingley did not hesitate to do that which made his beloved wife happy. But, as the Darcys were seldom in town, the Bingleys had to compromise Bingley's need for society and Jane's need for her sister by wintering in Derbyshire and spending the season in London. How much, if any, this half-year lack of diversion influenced Bingley's adulterous behaviour would be a subject for debate. Also up for conjecture would be how much regret Jane held for insisting upon that arrangement and whether that remorse held sway over her forgiveness.

Although Bingley had not spent the time in it he would have liked, he was quite proud of his house in town. It was one of the stateliest houses of the very fashionable Belgrave Square and was but a short distance from the Darcys' house in Mayfair. Of the two, the Mayfair section was the more esteemed, but the difference was so small that it was only discerned by the reckoning of those who monitored such important nuances of station. Regrettably, Miss Bingley and Mrs. Hurst were of that ilk, hence they badgered their brother with all the dedication of the most determined social climbers to find a house that befitted their ambitions. For Jane, however, any house was acceptable so long as she was within the bosom of her family. She was truly willing to be happy wherever her husband chose to domicile them. (As no one is happier to point out one's defects than one's relations, such selflessness alone was enough for Caroline and Louisa to despise her.)

Whilst Caroline nodded emphatically, Louisa sniffed behind Jane's back, "Jane is known as a charming woman simply because she has a smile and manages a civil word for everyone."

(As a professing Christian, Jane's devoutness demanded she overlook her sisters-in-law's multitude of imperfections. She continued to give them both a smile and a civil word whilst they continued to be parasites upon her household.)

Despite the presence of an entourage of sponging relatives, Jane found much in London that was charming. Perhaps because of her country up-bringing, she was partial to its parks and demesnes. This multitude of lawns and gardens was not only aesthetically pleasing, it was mandatory for part-time city-dwellers. For the Bingley's London home was as its neighbours—magnificent but narrow, with little more than a courtyard separating it from the coach house. Their home's specific lack of grounds was highly recompensed by its easy distance to Kensington Gardens. There, the children had room to run and shriek to their hearts' content—and there were lovely gardens for Jane to admire whilst she listened to the happy sounds of her children playing. Such luxuries of the senses made a happy season for Jane.

Bingley and his sisters esteemed London in equal measure. But unlike his sisters, Bingley liked it for diversion rather than rank. One could not call oneself a member of the first set without admission to Almack's. Much desiring that appellation, Caroline and Louisa insisted Bingley oblige them all by purchasing tickets. Used to obeying his older sisters, Bingley did as he was asked. (Not having to listen to his sisters' complaints made a happy season for Bingley.) Despite his disinterest in society's demands, his membership in White's and Boodle's brought him both amusement and cachet. Jane and Bingley were such a handsome, likable couple, they became members of the first circles strictly on the merit of their happy dispositions. Indeed, many a hostess vied to have them grace her *soirées*. His sisters were always of the first fashion, but Louisa's husband, Mr. Hurst's standing was dwindling in reverse proportion to his gambling debts. Hence, the trio was left to grace certain affairs by riding in upon Bingley and Jane's companionable coattails.

As Almack's was not entirely to Bingley's taste, he kept opera boxes on Drury Lane and Covent Gardens. The Bingley sisters despised entertainments there for those venues allowed the general riff-raff within elbow-rubbing distance of those of the first circles. (Caroline and Louisa were not exactly of the first circles, but within clawing distance, therefore exceedingly watchful of intrusion from their lessers.) They cast their sights upon obtaining an invitation to the Carlton House—a residence neither Jane nor Bingley had any aspirations to visit. (Bingley disliked the Prince's fast set for their pomposity, Jane because Charles did.) Upon one occasion, they found themselves seated behind the Prince Regent and his retinue at the Argyll Rooms, an event that sent Caroline and Louisa pea-green with envy. Bingley's sisters, however, reassessed their contempt for the amusements of the *hoi polloi*.

Until the spring of '15, they had settled in to London quite nicely each season, Jane busying herself by visiting the merchants on Bond Street and Piccadilly. There were found the finest shops and the smartest streets in which to stroll. Not surprisingly,

Jane was not intent on being seen, but on searching for fabrics and trim for her children's costumes. At home, she was content to receive callers and confer with her seamstress. But, Bingley absented himself to engage in less mundane endeavours. He favoured the race park or clandestine forays to boxing arenas. He occasionally enticed Jane to join him to watch his horses run, but he kept his continued involvement with pugilism a closely guarded secret. That concealment was the only one he kept from her, and he did so (he told himself) only to protect her sensibilities. (There had once been a bout that ended untidily.) As Darcy was unwitting of Bingley's small marital transgression as well, Bingley was saved from having to defend his selflessness. Had Darcy been with him in town, Bingley would never have been able to keep his boxing forays from him. That he was not forced to forgo that which he keenly enjoyed was the single inducement to forgive the Darcys' refusal to join them in town. Jane, however, had nothing to salve the loss of her sister's companionship.

Was it not for that lack, Jane would not have disliked London whatsoever. Bingley sisters had long-professed their ambition to become her closest confidants, but even sweet, credulous Jane saw the futility in expecting that. (Moreover, she was even less convinced that would be to her advantage—an understanding that showed tangible decrease of her gullibility.) Once she and Bingley had wholly reconciled, Jane's desire for the Darcys to join them in town would be one of the few to remain unrequited.

The Spoils of War

The Darcys had long eschewed travelling to London for the season. They had never given an absolute reason as to why they had stayed away. Bingley knew that the ladies had once been attacked by a band of brigands, and Elizabeth abducted on the road from London. Darcy's rescue of her had been swift but deadly. Their reluctance to undertake the journey was understandable.

In time, London had been tolerated, but there were absolutely no circumstances that would lure the Darcys once again to attend court. St. James and its attendant pomp would just have to do without them. Of this specific, even Bingley was unwitting. It had been an unspoken agreement between Darcy and Elizabeth. That covenant came about because he had had to inflict ultimate injury upon Elizabeth's kidnappers. Darcy knew nothing would ever again tempt him to strap on a sword.

After the birth of Darcy's children, the Bingleys hoped that alteration in situation might herald an adjustment in habits that would include joining them in London.

With uncharacteristic boldness, Bingley dared to inquire of Darcy if their minds had altered in the matter of returning to town. Although Darcy replied in the negative, Bingley chose not to let the subject drop. His tenacity in urging them to London did not originate entirely from his own desires, but Jane's. If it fell only to him, he would not have presumed to alter Darcy's resolution (however happy he would have been to have his friend's company). But he was never more devoted to Jane and determined to do whatever necessary to see her happy. (If this new enthusiasm for ensuring his wife's wishes was birthed in part by guilt, it remained undiscovered.) Bingley was typically quite forthright in his inquiries, but upon this occasion his remarks were indirect. He spoke not of what possible reason the Darcys might want to leave Derbyshire, but tendered his own complaint with country life.

"I say, if one does not ride to hounds, there is no sport to speak of in the country when the pheasant is not in season."

This was an exaggeration, but just barely. The only competition Bingley enjoyed were contests of the spectator variety, hence, Darcy smiled benignly and did not suggest that his friend ride to the hunt. This agreeability did not stop Bingley's design. Indeed, that the implication of silence was agreement was a notion he wholeheartedly embraced. Therefore, he soldiered on quite without encouragement.

"Granted," Bingley conceded to himself, "there is the occasional bear-baiting, but that is absolutely barbarous!"

"And fisticuffs are not?"

Darcy's retort bid Bingley bethink his belief that Darcy was unwitting of his continued interest in pugilism, but he was not entirely thrown off his subject. He even bristled (or as near to it as Bingley's amiable nature could manage) at his friend comparing the two proceedings.

"The two could not be more dissimilar! Pugilists perform before gentlemen in a Boxing-Garden."

"Bear-baiting takes place in a Bear-Garden before more than a few who call themselves gentlemen. I must take leave to observe the two bouts far more alike than not."

Darcy was well aware of the abject cruelty of bear-baiting. It was a contest both ancient and bloody, whereby a tethered bear was attacked by dogs trained to do just that. The outcome was never in question, the only contest was how long it would take the dogs to tear the bear to bits. Bingley was city-bred, but Darcy had heard of such events all of his life. When Bingley had put the questionable opportunity of attending such an event before him, Darcy had refused out of hand. Moreover, he had strongly advised Bingley against attending as well. But Bingley had been regaled by acquaintances with the curiosity of it all. Not having the opportunity to witness any kind of fight to the death, Bingley had simply been caught up in the adventure of such a notion. He had returned, however, altogether sickened at what passed for amusement to certain men. He had also been sorely unhappy not to heed his friend's advice and not too proud to admit it. Most probably displeased for Bingley to have followed another's counsel rather than his own, Darcy had been disinclined to let the matter drop without chastisement.

Said he, "I say, understanding the nature of the event, how could you have expected other, Bingley?"

"In my defence," Bingley explained, "that it was called a sport and I anticipated other than a blood-letting. Indeed, I found it altogether unchristian. It was not the inhumanity of it that gave the greatest offence, but that it was called a sport."

Darcy nodded his head in agreement, then added pithily, "I understand our Puritan brothers hate it as do we. They despise it not, however, for the injury to the animals, but for the pleasure it gives the spectators."

"Perhaps that is so," replied Bingley, oblivious to the bit of jest. "But they have a petition to ban it put before Parliament and I fully intend to sign it."

"There is little hope for that passage so long as there are taxes to be gained."

They both nodded their heads in unison at that incontrovertible fact.

Bingley most assuredly did not want to revisit that reviled event, but did not scruple to employ the recollection of such savagery to lure them to town. Darcy did not succumb to his design, but did promise to join them in London. There was a proviso, of course. Elizabeth's approval would be needed for such a plan—and Darcy knew it was unlikely to be forthcoming. It was a barely transparent avoidance. Darcy looked to be agreeable and Bingley could go to Jane and tell her of his success. Nothing had actually changed, but neither had there been a disagreement. That outcome was always the happiest for friends, but this eve Darcy had an ulterior motive for remaining upon the most amiable of terms with Bingley. There were subjects that he needed to address with his friend. Those matters had little to do with the calm pursuits of the country that bored Bingley as provincial.

Much unrest was afoot—both politically and economically—of importance to all landowners—and would affect Bingley most particularly. For Darcy knew well that Bingley's finances had been strained during Napoleon's embargo. That situation was not singular to Bingley. Many merchants were precisely in the same precarious situation. Bingley's merchandise had lain for months at a time upon the wharfs, decimated by pilfering and decay. As his closest friend, Bingley had confided to Darcy that he had borrowed heavily against those goods. Once the war had been won, Bingley had been as jubilant as any citizen to know at last that his goods would once again pass freely across the seas. Bingley had a man charged with these negotiations. He had assured him that all financial spleen was at last behind them all.

Bingley could be accused of naiveté in many ways, but he was not uninformed. He knew in just what straits his finances dangled. One of Bingley's most admirable qualities was his honesty. Regrettably, he often assumed those he dealt with were of similar scruples. Without the appearance of doing so, Darcy had always tried to look out for Bingley's welfare. It was a delicate matter to inquire of another's business without appearing a meddler. Still, Darcy felt a moral compulsion to do so.

It had been thus from the beginning of their friendship.

Although Bingley was younger than Darcy, they were alike in mindset and morals. Their politics and scruples ran concurrently. Unquestionably, Bingley looked up to Darcy. Yet, that esteem did not render Bingley an admirer of all of Darcy's traits. Bingley was the only friend who dared criticise Darcy's compleat lack of congeniality. Their ethics may have been alike, but their natures could not be more dissimilar. Whilst Bingley was open and optimistic, Darcy was dour and pragmatic. Darcy's pragmatism was often tainted to an unhappy degree with pessimism—and Bingley liked more than anything to be unbothered.

Had Bingley asked, he would have attributed their opposing temperaments to a single difference in their situation. They both were only sons, but he was the youngest sibling and Darcy, the oldest. Darcy was decidedly richer, but they were of the same class. Although Bingley was not entirely unwitting of other factors that separated them, he did not lend them proper due. There was far more separating them than sibling placement.

For Bingley was only one generation landed gentry. His land was purchased, not inherited, making him the first of his family to be master of an estate. Bingley was not of the first, but of the first of his kind. Times were evolving in England, an ever-increasing number of untitled and lately rich were purchasing their own legacies. Darcy's family was not ancient, but it had owned Pemberley and surrounding lands for hundreds of years. Those new to the land saw it only as a business. Men born into Darcy's landed class felt an obligation to make the best use of their assets to retain not only wealth, but also prosperity for future generations of their own and those whose livelihoods depended upon them. Continuing his line was a fundamental occupation to Darcy. He cherished Pemberley not only upon his behalf, but also upon those who came before him, and those who were yet to come.

Another dissimilarity in their nature was Darcy's bent for brooding and Bingley's total want of introspection. These traits were part and parcel of how their estates were managed. Bingley was a kind employer but he had not the sense of obligation to his roots as had his friend. Hence it was unlikely that he ever would. That void did leave Bingley adequate time to pursue entertainment. Once settled into a loving family life, he was free to compete his own horses at the race parks and back his favourite pugilists in the boxing ring.

As did Darcy, Bingley had an overseer in whom he had compleat trust. Regrettably, Bingley's overseer of Kirkland was not a son of the land, but a man of the bottom line. Darcy had found fault with Bingley's man's advice on any number of matters, but was disinclined to criticise without invitation. The intelligence passed to Bingley by the supervisor of his investments was of no greater wisdom than that of his overseer. The recently passed Corn Laws were thought by many landowners to be a panacea for all their losses. Darcy, and even Bingley, understood their agricultural limitations. Derbyshire was largely wool-producing and would benefit but little. Therefore, when Bingley's man had enticed him to turn the hills of Kirkland into coal, Bingley saw it as a lucrative decision. Darcy knew coal to be an ugly, dangerous business. If not closely watched, abuses were rampant. Bingley did not keep close watch over his land. Indeed, he liked to spend the lambing season in London.

So critical was such a venture to all in the townships surrounding Kirkland Hall, Darcy was moved to do the unthinkable—he offered Bingley unsolicited advice. With great deliberation, he recounted every drawback to the plan and general caution in all his business ventures. It would alter the entire character of the countryside. Darcy trod carefully however. Bingley's interests were diverse. The very Corn Laws that were seen as all and good to the landowner foretold stagnation for manufacturing. It was a dicey time for every class and men who were unreliable had Bingley's ear. It was Darcy's opinion that was he to put his eggs in one basket it should be in his land. Goods could be pilfered, decayed, or seized. Land was eternal.

"Beware, Bingley," Darcy succinctly concluded, but Bingley heeded not.

"Life goes on in the country, Darcy," replied Bingley sagely, "whether we are here to see it or not."

Disinclined to waste his words upon closed ears, Darcy did not respond. Neither did he choose to go to London—unrest there was insidious. Newspapers were rife with tales of marauders. But, Darcy could not persuade Bingley against town either.

"I fear," he said at last, "that you may find the dogs in London these days no less savage than those at that bear-baiting."

At this, Bingley laughed heartily, certain his friend had exaggerated the dangers.

Embroidery of the facts, Bingley forgot, had never been Darcy's pursuit.

The All-Knowing Mother

In having only to sit and watch for five years as her two sisters, between them, birthed seven children in that good time was not, however meagre, without its advantages for Elizabeth Darcy. Her mind had not been at all idle. In such close proximity to Jane's children, often having them stay with her at Pemberley, she was privy to their every sneeze and wheeze. (By her own design, Elizabeth was much less in Lydia's company, but there her learning was keen as to what methods to eschew.) This close scrutiny birthed in her no small conceit of what her own abilities would be when she became a mother. She was happy to admit (even if only to herself) of knowing every particular when it came to nurturing offspring. What with the little waggon she and Georgiana had gone out in upon the lands surrounding Pemberley nursing the ill and the down-trodden, when it came to afflictions she fancied herself an equal to Georgiana as a well-spring of curative knowledge, but it was not, of course, an opinion she would dare share with her. (Stealing her thunder, she supposed, would not lead to a felicitous sisterly bond.) Still, when at last she had children of her own, she thought herself better prepared to weather the storms of their indisposition more readily than any other mother in the county.

But then it is said, when the flight is not high, the fall is not heavy.

By the first remembrance of their day of birth, Janie Darcy was sporting a summer cold. Geoff's constitution fared better, but his favourite coral teether was being worked on with such regularity it kept the front of his gown perpetually damp with drool. These small tribulations caused their mother little concern, although their father's fastidiousness did keep him somewhat nervous of taking hold of either of them. His abhorrence had commenced upon holding little Janie when she issued a sneeze. She had given such a sweet little shiver in its aftermath that he had been amused and looked lovingly upon his darling daughter.

"Lizzy," he said, "did you hear that? Our brave Janie has just sneezed!"

He then lifted the baby triumphantly before him and only then realised that with her sneeze she had expelled a string of mucus extending half-way down his waistcoat.

"Oh dear God in heaven!" said the fastidious Mr. Darcy upon this realisation. "What the devil is that?"

Elizabeth rushed forth to rescue little Janie who had suddenly become to her father an object of danger, for she was crinkling her nose as if ready to explode once more. However, as her nasal passages had been cleared the first time, this one was less lethal. In that annoyingly knowing way that only seasoned mothers could enlist, Elizabeth took her from her father's arms and gave her to Margaret, then rather coyly took his pocket-square and brushed away the offending slime. He stood still as a statue, arms extended and a look of utter disgust upon his countenance whilst she attempted to remove all evidence of the impudent discharge.

"I have never witnessed anything so ghastly in my life!" he announced.

"Stay close, dear husband," she laughed. "One may yet upend their breakfast—or worse."

"I fear I will not be disposed to witness that," he sniffed. "I must hasten to have this waistcoat burnt."

She continued to work on his waistcoat long after any residue remained, finding amusement in how brief a time it took to render his expression from indignantly appalled to unabashedly amatory with only a saucy gaze from her upturned eyes.

"I pray we will embark soon for Brighton? I fear our children are much in need of a sea remedy," said she.

Elizabeth continued to blot at his waistcoat as she spoke. Darcy found her newly acquired motherly self-possession exemplary (and not a little inviting). He retrieved his pocket-square and then looked upon it before changing his mind, holding it by two fingers a half-arm's-length away for her to take.

"We have only to fasten the trunks on the coach," said he, dropping the offending cloth into her out-stretched hand. She took it and almost stuffed it in her bodice for future use before thinking better of it and tossing it aside. (He looked relieved that she had.) He took his leave and Elizabeth turned her attention back to her children. As she did, she gave a small, self-satisfied waggle of her shoulders, but of this she was compleatly unaware.

Inasmuch as Miss Margaret Heff was in great awe of the Master of Pemberley, she did not observe either the waggle or the Darcys' exchange. She had done the considerable feat of being handed off Janie whilst keeping her eyes compleatly averted. She was a simple girl, come to the grand house with much the same veneration as had she entered a cathedral. Her introduction to the gentry had been the single winter she helped in the house of Squire Thorne. He had been a plump, rumpled man with thin legs, straw hair, and no good word to say to anyone. She did not much like him, but she did not fear him. Although he had yet to speak directly to her, she feared Mr. Darcy. Some called him handsome. She did not observe him to be so. Granted, he was fit and his features were agreeable, but she saw upon that proud countenance an expression of most unambiguous dourness that affrighted her quite beyond all good reason.

Before she had set foot in what she knew must be the finest house in England, her sister Hannah had assured her that Mr. Darcy was not quite as forbidding as he appeared. But that was little comfort in that he could have been half as forbidding as he appeared and still been a very forbidding man. Then again, Mr. Darcy's disagreeability was compleatly redressed by Mrs. Darcy's kindness. That good lady was quite easy. Indeed, she was easy and kind and clearly devoted to her children. Moreover, Mr. Darcy seldom came into the nursery. Not unlike the houses of other gentlemen, when his children were to be seen, they were brought to him. In other houses, however, custom had it that children were brought not only to the father, but to both parents, and then but once a day. In Pemberley, mistress was in and out of the nursery all the day long. This, of course, was in addition to the numerous times each day they were brought to see their father. It ran Margaret quite ragged, all this bundling about of babies, but she dared not quarrel with the arrangement.

The other peculiarity about this arrangement was that once the children were brought to their parents, who seated themselves in the salon they favoured for such meetings, Margaret was dismissed. Hence, Mr. Darcy's conduct toward those children behind closed doors was unbeknownst to her. Moreover, Margaret knew enough not to be inclined to inquire. Regardless, it was a curious thing.

That particular day, Margaret had been taken quite unawares when the apparition of Mr. Darcy had invaded the nursery. If she had not known better than to think such a thing, Margaret might have believed that Mr. Darcy's tarriance there was solely to visit his ailing children (for they had been kept much to the nursery). But they were not all that sick and that would have been an exhibition of fatherly concern that some might believe untoward. Hence, she dismissed that notion out of hand. As forbidding a man as Mr. Darcy would not be subject to the sentimentality of a display of paternal affection. The fathers of her acquaintance may have been fond of their children, but they knew enough not to display it.

"Fine notion, mistress," said Margaret once Mr. Darcy's bootsteps had faded off down the hall. "Brighton is a fine place, not like I hear Bristol. Bristol's waters are rotten with the leavings of the cess-pit. Fancy that! All those fine folks, swimming in...," here Margaret stopped and reconsidered her remark, "swimming in with Lor' knows what!"

She laughed a small laugh at the folly of gentlefolk. She and Mrs. Darcy had quickly fallen into such an amiable camaraderie that she often had to remind herself to whom she spoke. For her part, Mrs. Darcy encouraged this intimacy, believing a kinship with her children's nanny an advantage to them all. Hence, Mrs. Darcy endured this small accident of language and any others in all good humour.

To her credit, Margaret Heff was an unerringly good judge of what was and was not an illness, Mrs. Darcy her acknowledger and supporter. However, Nurse's unerring disadvantage, at least insofar as her current employer, was that this repository of information brought with it elucidative intelligence inflammatory in nature. Indeed, when a disorder had been determined, Nurse's single evil increasingly exposed itself as a penchant for prattling on about the accompanying terrors with relentless enthusiasm. This was, of course, much to Mrs. Darcy's accelerating chagrin.

Margaret returned Janie to Mrs. Darcy and took little Geoff into her arms, then sat down to wipe his chin clean with the hem of her initially spotless apron, saying, "I do dread the babes' teeth working through. It is a cruel time for them. It's a sad truth that more wee-ones die from a fever at this time more than any other—that or the small-pox. It can sneak up on them when they are in such a state."

Mrs. Darcy abandoned the wise, all-knowing nod she had been affecting and an expression overspread her countenance of alarm and shock. This alteration upon her employer's countenance was heeded late on, and Margaret silenced herself, allowing the recently lost colour to return to Mrs. Darcy's cheeks. Without Jane at hand to reassure her, Elizabeth was fast in the grips of near panic.

Whether Elizabeth was dragooned into action in the face of such danger or her mind had already been settled in that favour is of little concern. As it was, the sea air was beneficial and Mrs. Darcy was happy to set up house there until each and every tooth in her children's heads worked its way free. Although she knew she must report the intelligence of their children's perils to her husband, she vowed to do so with the utmost discretion. It would not be helpful to alarm him unduly. It would just be additional excuse to escape London without comment from the all and sundry. But as she gained the corridor and started for his study to tell the tale, she compleatly forgot herself and her promise.

"Darcy, dearest!" Elizabeth called, then louder, "Darcy! We must make haste for Brighton!"

Death Is a Fair-Weather Friend

Nell Arbuthnot sat with her hands folded in her lap, eyes shut tightly, and feverishly whispering a prayer to God above. Nell knew, if Sally had not yet learnt, that no good news came by post. More excited than frightened, Sally Frances retreated to her allotted cot before daring to determine what news her letters beheld. She pulled her legs beneath her, settling into a position of anticipation. She laid first one, then the other before her and ran her fingers lovingly across the lettering of her name. Taking a deep breath, she took the first one in her hand, her young fingers trembling as she prodded loose the wax that sealed it.

Clearly, it had made its way through many hands, but the seal was still intact. That it had found them had been very nearly as great an astonishment as that someone had actually taken pen to paper and written to her at all. Although Nell was incredulous at such a mystery, Sally instinctively knew who it would be from. Much like her grandmother, Sally's devoutness had been more in lip service than active pursuit. The single faith she had religiously clung to was that her brother would one day reappear. Here, in her hand, was the answer to her prayers.

When she began to read, it was haltingly. This fell less to her anxiety than by virtue of the limited experience both in the letter writer and the reader.

"Dear Sister Sally," it began, "I hop this leter finds you wel."

By happy chance John Christie's grasp of letter composition did not exceed hers in comprehension. In careful hand, he inquired of the health of the members of their family (notably excluding Archie Arbuthnot). The remainder of the letter was short, almost brusque. He admired the local militia and said he hoped one day to curse Bonaparty's corpse himself. Upon reading the second letter, Sally understood that it had been written first. For although it began much as the other by inquiring after their health, he told of acquiring a fine situation at the estate of Pemberley in Derbyshire County. Sally had to stop and carefully spell aloud those names of places, for she was much unacquainted with counties beyond her own. The name Derbyshire was a bit of a struggle as was Pemberley, but the name of Darcy, however, she made out for herself. She read on to learn that he was employed to look after the horses and found that such work made him feel good in his bones. His lady, he said, was beautiful and she smiled at him when he brought her horse to her. He sometimes took his meals with a Mr. Hardin and his wife, saying that more than once she had made him sweet biscuits. He then bid them good-bye and promised to write again soon. Almost as a postscript, he noted of the long-past death of their mother.

"May she rest in peese," wrote John Christie.

Of the entire letter, that their mother was dead and buried was the very last of Sally's concerns. Nary man, woman, nor child was unaware that war of a significant nature was certain to take place across the waters. She despised the thought of her beloved brother leaving his horses for the company of men bent on war. She prayed it was but a young man's curiosity.

Although Sally had immediately taken pen to paper and posted a letter in return, in the months that followed she received no reply. Rather, another arrived penned by him and posted from Dover. This missive bore information that was grievously unsettling. For in it John Christie announced his enlistment in the Regulars as an infantryman and his deployment as a grenadier. As he wrote his letter then, he sat upon a sack of flour that was soon to be loaded onto the very ship that would take him across the channel to battle. Most oddly, he referenced some sort of "unhappy" business that prompted his enlistment—but did not elaborate. But it was not merely the intelligence of his enlistment alone that troubled her. Behind his spare words, she sensed a sorrowful history. She had long hoped against hope that although far from her, her brother had been happy. Now she believed that was not the case. She winced at the notion.

Nell, however, was impressed, "Grenadier? A grenadier canna be all that bad—can it?"

The newspapers that had once been alive with war's alarm were filled with tales of battles that had been fought and won. Soldiers were even then streaming into London, some of the over-flow of wounded had been placed in the White Chapel infirmary. Sally began to skulk about the ward under the pretence of writing letters home for the injured. But her true reason was to ask if anyone there was from Derbyshire or was a grenadier. No one was, but more than one veteran was happy to relate the casualties of such stout-hearted souls as the grenadiers.

"They be tall. They be taken out first," said one grizzled soul who would never walk again. "Nay, grenadiers don't last long fer it."

After hearing that damnation one too many times, Sally returned to her belongings and reread her brother's letter. "Grenadier" he had said—because of some "unhappy" business. She crumpled the letter in her hand and fell forward into the coarse straw, commencing a soundless sobbing. Although nothing in the missive indicated it, she knew in that instant that her brother was not just gone, but dead. Nell was appalled as much at this histrionic spectacle as the gross abuse to a letter that had come all the way from Dover. Carefully, she uncurled Sally's fist and took it from her, smoothing it out on her lap.

"There, there child," she soothed with just a little condescension. "What words can want all that?"

Reading this letter, there was no mention of Abigail, but Nell still came to the conclusion that Sally's despair was for the reminder of her mother's fate. (She may not have said a word all this time, but Nell suspected where Abigail had gone, for she used to boast about having once worked at a fine house in Derbyshire.) Did not every lass pine for a mother lost?

Although at seven years old Sue was too young to comprehend the contents of the letter and all that it implied, her dear sister was wretched and she was old enough to understand that she should be too. That she was insensible of just why she was inconsolable in no way mitigated the level of her distress—Sue wailed loud and long. Nell drew the tear-stricken Sue onto her lap with a series of shushing sounds meant to be reassuring. But Sue had long ago learnt her own remedy and employed it then by putting her thumb in her mouth. She continued to snuffle but ceased sobbing. Nell believed her five years past that sort of failing.

"Belay that, girl!" she said crossly, catching her by the wrist. "Yer too old to be on the teat!"

Having had her single comfort snatched away, Sue begat another wail, this one threatening to arouse unwanted attention, hence Nell relented.

"Have yer way then," said she and turned loose of her hand.

Sue's thumb popped back to her mouth as if tied with a string, but she continued a hiccupping cry regardless.

By the time this ruckus abated, Sally had regained her own senses. She ceased to cry but turned her face to the wall and refused to listen to Nell explain how the death of her "dear mother" should not be of any particular bother in that it happened so long past. Sally was disinclined to explain herself to Nell. Indeed, she told not a soul. She did, however, make another vow to herself. Her brother deserved all that was good in the world. If he received otherwise, that offence fell at someone's feet. She would travel to this place called Derbyshire and venture to this house of Pemberley. She would uncover what befell her brother that drove him to join a battle clear over the water. She would if it took all the rest of her days.

The promised vengeance was not to come to pass with any haste. Little Sue did not survive another frost. The only solace found in her passing was that it was gentle. Or at least as gentle a passing as the shivers of pneumonia would allow. Always amongst mourners was an optimist, this one reassuring Nell and Sally that it was fortunate Sue did not succumb to a death by more violent means.

"Yes," said Matron with the logic that only one determined to be a comfort might employ, "to be shure. Poor gerl could have been brained by a lunatic inmate."

Although that calamity was not the first one that came to mind, Sally still knew that was not an impossibility. The single relief the notion brought to her was that thinking of the various potentialities for death in the workhouse ate up the time it took for someone to find Mr. Summons. It was he who must come round to collect little Sue's remains. As Nell keened, Sally sat wretchedly fingering the ragged remains of her sister's petticoat and distracted her mind by continuing to enumerate the many ways little children went dead in the workhouse. There were fires, of course. Fires of all sorts were of particular danger—scalding from upending a wash-pot or burnt whilst hovering for warmth before the fireplace. They fell, too. She had seen the body of a little boy who fell from the roof that previous spring. Of course, he had been fleeing the place, so she was not quite certain that should be counted. She did not want to consider it, for it was an ugly death. Not like Sue's.

Sally glanced over at her sister's face. Just the day before, Sue's countenance was flushed with fever as she struggled for life. She no longer looked like a living being. Death had crept over her countenance with its icy hand, leaving her skin grey, her eyes sunken.

The single good of this particular parting was that little Sue dying in her bed from unsuspicious circumstances relieved the workhouse staff the burden of an inquest. If a funeral was desired—well, shoulders were shrugged and toes dug circles in the dirt. Matron saw to a wooden box (one that look remarkably similar to the beds laid out for the casuals) and a chalk-rock to scratch her name upon it. Anything beyond those meagre arrangements was extraneous. Flowers, mourning bells, or a vicar to recite a verse fell to the family purse—however empty.

So it was that Nell was not inconsolable forthwith of little Sue's demise. She reclaimed her previously intimate relationship with a bottle of gin, forsook her sewing, and forsook Sally.

"This be it," she slurred. "Yer don need nothin' else. Sweet relief, Sally. Don't bother me no more."

It fell to Sally to wash her sister's body in preparation for interment. She thought then she had done for her sister, but when Summons attempted to lay Sue's little corpse to rest in the coffin, she would not quite fit. It fell then to Sue to rearrange her sister's body at an angle—Summons stood by with his lower lip agape as if he had no clue as to the remedy for such a situation. Sally was inclined to want to brain *him*, but as he was clearly in want of a few pence in the nob, she gave up the notion. Despite all the disconcertion, Sally did have the presence of mind to run and find the piece of flannel shirting that Sue refused to sleep without and place it next to her before they nailed the lid in place. Had she forgot that one last kindness, Sally thought she might have actually run mad with grief.

Even without Nell to remind her, she recollected enough of the Lord's Prayer to serve Him. Thereupon, with all due deliberation, the old man who was on burial detail took one nail at a time from the confines of his mouth as he hammered the lid in place, hence Sally had a great deal of time to ponder the compleat absence of tender feelings in this entire heartless ceremony. It was an understanding that grieved her quite unreasonably. If the rent in her heart was in anyway mended by the seething rage she held for all who represented their guardianship, she felt it not. Sally asked for the chalk from Mr. Summons and with it carefully sketched a flower beneath Sue's name.

Before the cock had crowed the next forenoon, she slid from her bed and without loss of life or limb climbed out a window, shimmied down the brick outcropping, and ran like thunder.

She never once looked back.

The Indecisive Confinement of Mrs. Col. Fitzwilliam

Fitzwilliam and Georgiana had been home to Derbyshire County but briefly in their year-long tour of England's spas. Their travels took them to the chilly coast of Kent and Margate then they skirted Ramsgate altogether and strove on to the smaller Sussex towns of Littlehampton and Worthing. Whilst they journeyed, Fitzwilliam resolutely dragged his game leg from site to site, insisting it was no bother whatsoever. For Georgiana's part, she assured him that he looked quite dashing driving a gig rather than on horseback—and as the double-vision that had long troubled him had abated enough for him to at last toss aside his eye-patch she could compliment him on that as well.

Still, it was evident he yearned to be able-bodied enough to return to the saddle and enjoy the long rides that he and Darcy were accustomed to taking of a morning. He missed them less for the reassuring sensation of a brisk mount beneath him and the scent of saddle leather as for the company of his good friend. Hence, when they finally made their way to Brighton, he was quite unhappy to find that they had arrived before Darcy and Elizabeth. When at last he espied their arrival, he betook himself directly to their apartments—only to find the new parents still all in an uproar having not made a great deal of progress in situating their retinue. Fitzwilliam had to laugh at the throng of beings their first trip from home required. For the number of trunks still sitting on the landing told the tale of just how many were in their entourage of babies, nurses, and maids. His own quite simple situation in Georgiana's able hands meant Fitzwilliam was quite at his leisure to ridicule Darcy's.

"I say Darcy," Fitzwilliam said, endeavoured to disguise a grin, "you are laden with more provisions than required by both Wellington and Blucher together!"

Darcy stood amidst the mound of baggage that had barely dwindled from the day before. He looked about him as maids and footmen heaved and pulled them about. "Such disorder looks to be indefensible, indeed. But you cannot imagine what folderol two so small can demand."

As he spoke those words, it occurred to Darcy that Fitzwilliam's understanding of such matters would soon be tried. He had finally accepted that his sister was no longer a deflowered virgin, but a mother-to-be who would soon bring forth a living, breathing infant. Indeed, once his sister's marriage had taken place, the sense of betrayal Darcy had felt toward Fitzwilliam had all but vanished. To see his sister happy at last had done wonders to return him to good humour. But as the months had worn on and the Fitzwilliams did not return to Derbyshire, sending only brief letters admiring the landscape of their latest holiday vista, Darcy had become alarmed.

"Pray should not they make their way home for Georgiana's upcoming…event?" Darcy inquired, as if to reassure himself that his mental calendar had not failed him.

"One would think…" replied Elizabeth cautiously.

She had no more clues than did Darcy why all their carefully phrased letters inquiring of Georgiana's health had been ignored. The return letters, written in Georgiana's precise script, said nothing but of the excellence of their happiness, the fineness of the vistas, and wishing the same for the Darcys. There had been no announcement of a child born dead or for that matter, alive. They did, however, enclose an itinerary. Hence, the Darcys' trip to Brighton was designed to coincide with that of the newlyweds. Because of all that lay untold, any riposte he would have liked to have employed in response to Fitzwilliam's gentle teasing remained unspoken.

They quickly made arrangements to meet for dinner, Darcy quite anxious to see his sister and endeavour to determine just what her condition was. Their astonishment was compleat upon their reunion with the happy couple. For upon the nine-month anniversary of their nuptials, Mrs. Col. Fitzwilliam sported a pregnancy that could at the most be only of six-month maturation. Darcy frowned, uncertain what to make of any of it. Had his sister in this short time miscarried, then conceived another child? Elizabeth was better at hiding her disconcertion, and offered hugs and kisses all around. When at last they were seated, Darcy repeatedly looked to Elizabeth with the question in his eyes he dared not put to his sister. Elizabeth was less concerned than simply curious. Her husband's glances told her that it would fall to her to learn the particulars. Georgiana, however, was not forthcoming with those particulars. As Elizabeth had been the original conduit of Georgiana's notification of her quasi-defilement, she thought she was owed some sort of explanation, but knew she must await until they were alone before pressing the issue.

From first they met, Elizabeth and Georgiana had been fast friends. There had been little that they were not eager to share. Georgiana had confided in Elizabeth some of her very deepest feelings. Or rather, they had shared their most intimate longings until Georgiana had fallen in love with Fitzwilliam. Other than providing the confidence of her pregnancy, Georgiana had reinstated the reticence of her girlhood. If that was because Georgiana was aware of the unsuitable regard Fitzwilliam had once held for her, Elizabeth could not determine. She very much wanted to return to their easy company and affection. If she had to spend the rest of her days in pretence that no profession of love for her had ever passed Fitzwilliam's lips, so be it. So long as only she, Georgiana, and Fitzwilliam knew of it and Darcy did not, all would be well. It would be as if it were never spoken and Darcy and Fitzwilliam's friendship would remain unimpaired. Elizabeth cast aside all thought of such worries and attended the one at hand. However, her endeavours were a bit dull-witted.

"Pray, are congratulations in order soon?" she asked Georgiana.

Georgiana answered without resorting to artifice, "Yes. Yes, they are."

Now that the obvious had been established, Elizabeth meant to delve further, but did so with all due caution. She chose her time carefully. When she found Georgiana cooing and admiring Janie and Geoff, the time was ripe. However, Georgiana avoided looking directly at her. Elizabeth knew a subterfuge when she saw one, and devoted an aunt as Georgiana was, she did not think interest in her niece and nephew supplanted her own condition.

"When do you expect to be confined?" Elizabeth asked innocently.

"Martinmas?" was her reply, less a statement than a hope.

"Am I to understand that...you have suffered a disappointment prior to this happy news?"

At this direct query, Georgiana stood and looked directly at her interrogator.

"No, I have not."

Elizabeth could not let it go. She feared that in being Georgiana's informant to Darcy and then subsequently successfully persuading him to support her marriage to Fitzwilliam that she had been an unwilling agent of Georgiana's deception of them all. She did not look upon that office with a kind eye. It briefly crossed her mind that Georgiana meant to recompense her for the compliment of Fitzwilliam's regard. If she had then—*touché*, Georgiana. But she could not think so meanly of Georgiana or her motives. She remained dogged, however, in determining what had come to pass.

"No?" she repeated, determined to be blunt. "All has been well? You have not miscarried?"

"No, I have not." With this admission, Georgiana did not look particularly chagrined, nor did she sound particularly convincing (nor did she appear in want of it) when she said, "I was initially mistaken."

"I see," was Elizabeth's only reply, knowing it was an understanding between them that, indeed, see she did.

There was no further word on the matter from either of them. But Elizabeth did repeat the conversation verbatim, and with all due inflection, to Darcy. Once she convinced him that she was not a conspirator in this matter, he was even less amused than was she. But as a new child was expected, they believed it to be in the best interest for all concerned to consider the subject a *fait accompli*. That this adjustment was right and true was reinforced by Georgiana's evident bliss and the return of reason to Fitzwilliam's countenance.

Re-acquaintance

It had been Elizabeth Darcy's inaugural trip to Brighton and she was most anticipatory in the prospect of it. Everyone else in the first tier of their party was quite familiar with its roadways and façades, but fortune saw them happy to rediscover its charms with her.

The Darcys and the Fitzwilliams took their first turn about the town in a splendid barouche. It had been taken to accommodate all of their party. Elizabeth certainly did not complain, but would have liked to have been shown the sights by her husband's side in a curricle. From her introduction to that equipage, she had decided it the most felicitous of conveyances imaginable. That, of course, was not to the merit of the curricle, but to her husband's meritorious driving. (Indeed, it was second only to dancing with him in her estimation—at least of those occupations suitable to speak of in company.) She needed only to think of those splashing-board, lamps, and silver moulding to recall the giddy exhilaration of taking a corner and very nearly having themselves upended. But she reminded herself that the sea-breeze was exceedingly pure and their sojourn extended. There would be many days for them to take to the open road alone.

They had arrived in good stead, but their journey had been lengthy, dirty, and tiring. Yet when they first arrived and their trunks were only just being unfastened, they could smell the enticement of the sea air. On a whim, each took a baby in their arms and strolled in the direction of the shore. At a word from Mr. Darcy, Goodwin began directing their retinue of servitors to unburden their carriage of three months worth of trunks, boxes, and cases. As the Darcys strode off, they heard Hannah wrangling with Goodwin over whose trunks would be the first to be taken down. It was an odd comfort. Rather than being irksome, the interminable squabbling was a reminder of home. It was but a short stroll to the esplanade, but so healthy the size of their children, by the time they gained the sea-walk, Elizabeth had tired.

The rush of the surf, the burst of sea air, and the sound of the gulls squawking overhead instantly invigorated them both. They silently shared the recognition that their visit would be a rejuvenation not only of their vigour, but of their spirits as well. That night, the combination of the fatigue of the road and the salt air had Elizabeth sleep more soundly than she had in some time. Indeed, by the time they arose, their morning tour had become one of the afternoon. Having been in Brighton for a week, Fitzwilliam and Georgiana were impatient of them, however. But a late start did little to smother their high spirits.

Upon Darcy's instructions, his driver turned to the outskirts of town and toward Devil's Dyke. Always the meticulous planner, Darcy designed for them first to observe the outskirts of Brighton and from thence, to hie the town's centre. They must see the panorama from above if they were to fully appreciate it.

"Pray do you recall when first you and I came to Brighton?" Fitzwilliam said to Darcy. "Merely boys we were."

"Indeed," replied Darcy. To Elizabeth he explained, "It was the year after I left Cambridge. We stopt here before making for London, and from thence we departed upon our tour of the Continent."

Elizabeth and Georgiana smiled at each other at their husbands' remembrances. They had spent many an evening hearing them relate tales of their travels—at least the ruins visited and the vistas admired. Either nothing of a romantic or adventurous nature occurred on that year-long pilgrimage, or both gentlemen were far too circumspect to talk of it.

Fitzwilliam, still recollecting that long past Brighton visit, said, "When last we were here, Brighton was still just a small fishing village—but one in a state of alteration."

All nodded knowingly, for that was just after the Prince Regent discovered Brighton's charms and begun to build his pavilion, thus besetting upon the quiet village the nation's most fashionable society. Their attention was then arrested by the sight of a smattering of tents upon the far down. With a scholarly tone quite new to him, Darcy explained to the ladies that prior to the end of hostilities, Brighton had been the most vulnerable of seaside towns. It was the port most expeditious to France and the shortest overland route to London. Pointing them out with his stick, he added that the downs had once been thick with tents that stretched forth in long, narrow rows and served as the temporary encampments of militia.

With that last word, Darcy quit his commentary. This cessation was abrupt. So abrupt was it, it did the very thing he had sought not to do—it reminded Elizabeth that Brighton was where Lydia and Wickham were first thrown together. The regiment, which had all wintered near Hertfordshire and kept Lydia and Kitty atwitter for that duration, was sent to Brighton come summer. Ostensibly Lydia had come to Brighton to keep Col. Forster's young wife company—in actuality her motives were less benign. For it was not Mrs. Forster's company, but that of the scarlet-coated officers that excited Lydia's esteem. And they came not in pairs, but by the half-dozen to sit in the Forsters' parlour. Even under so watchful an eye as the Colonel's, Lydia and Wickham had formed an immoral alliance.

Forsaking her family and all her friends, they had run off like bandits in the night to live in mortal sin in London. As it was, Darcy located them and reached an understanding with Wickham that had him make Lydia an honest wife. Had not Darcy used his considerable connexions, the entire Bennet family would have had to partake in her ruin. But they were saved. And that they were saved and Elizabeth eventually married to her saviour improved her opinion of Brighton considerably. It had been a harrowing experience, but one Elizabeth seldomly recollected.

However, Darcy believed the memory of her sister's near ruin grieved Elizabeth to the same degree that the name of Ramsgate lived in infamy within him. The similarity lay only in the odd fact that both seductions involved the same cad. Other than that, their outcomes were very different—Wickham was thwarted from eloping with Georgiana and he was gently forced into marriage with Lydia. Elizabeth's contempt for Wickham was considerable, but she was long past fretting over what had come to pass. Hence, the disconcertion Darcy felt on her behalf was misplaced. It was his alone. He could not bear to think of Wickham at all. Indeed, he allowed that memory to cast a pallor over his mood—one that he did not expect to lift with any haste.

In his obvious discomfiture for having broached the subject, Elizabeth took his arm. She was certain that whatever ill will she still endured over that entire escapade paled in comparison with his. For any mention or thought of Wickham grieved him still. Ubiquitous as Wickham had been, there were very few places they could escape his memory altogether. She patted Darcy's arm with kindly meant reassurance.

"Let us not think of the past," was her wise counsel.

It was wise, but she knew how far was the chasm between doing and not.

Darcy chose simply to alter the subject of the conversation and addressed Fitzwilliam, seated across, "What say you, Fitzwilliam, to the Prince of Wales's invitation?"

Upon hearing this, Elizabeth's mood brightened. Fitzwilliam had already been weighted down with medals for service to his country, but she had only just learnt of his invitation to join the Prince's favourite regiment, the 10th Light Dragoons. The unspoken question was not so much if he found favour with such an honour, but whether Fitzwilliam would ever be fit enough to join such a regiment.

"My military service is compleat," said he quite solemnly.

Although it was clear to his other listeners that his conclusion was a melancholy one, Georgiana appeared relieved.

"He has given enough in service of the crown, I should think," she opined.

Still Fitzwilliam's countenance just then was not a happy one. It was difficult for Elizabeth to witness his dispirit, hence she could but imagine how Darcy must suffer for him. She took her husband's hand and, synchronously but more in mercy of their own discomfort than Fitzwilliam's, they both looked away, Darcy to the left, she to the right. Hence they did not observe Georgiana's own form of comfort—she turned so as to allow her flowering belly to rest against her husband's side. Elizabeth glanced back and caught sight of this unspoken comfort as it bid a small smile tempt the corners of his mouth. It was not something she thought that she would disclose to Darcy. It was far too intimate an exchange.

They had no sooner returned from their tour than their party was improved by the Gardiners, who, having been secluded with Lydia for the whole of the winter, had lately arrived from London. Indeed, they had accepted Elizabeth's invitation to join them at Brighton without discussion and in no little haste to enjoy the relaxation the sea air could provide. Verily, they were anxious to the point of being ready to flee to the sanctuary of any abode uninhabited by their youngest niece. This state of disturbance upon their part was painfully obvious and, as she was the agent of that particular affliction, Elizabeth felt exceedingly guilt-ridden. She was, therefore, even more inclined to do whatever she could to make it up to them (lest someday, someone repay the compliment).

It was not as if they were taken unawares by Lydia's own special form of conceit, for they were not altogether surprised. Lydia had resided in their home during the days it took for Darcy to barter and coerce Wickham into taking her hand in holy wedlock.

Although Mrs. Gardiner had no kind remarks for her behaviour then, she soon understood that Lydia in want of a wedding was not half so ill-mannered as Lydia in want of everything. Although she had come to them in all-appreciative obligation, her ingratitude expanded with the same rapidity as her waistline. Elizabeth and Jane had intended her stay to be temporary, but kind Mrs. Gardiner insisted upon standing by her through her term. Yet by the time Lydia delivered her first daughter, she had availed herself of every kind of rant and demand. Had Mrs. Gardiner been of less hardy stock, she might have taken to her own bed.

With the Gardiners came the first Elizabeth had learnt of Lydia's successful parturition, and they related to her the single celebratory aspect of Lydia's confinement. On her fourth attempt, Lydia had finally produced a child worthy of her attention—one cast in her own image. She, at last, had a daughter—a baby she could swath in pink ribbons and frilly lace to her heart's content. (The little attention Wickham gave his sons was to insist that they be encrusted with those accoutrements particular to the masculine sex as soon as they left the breast.) As there was nothing Lydia liked better than her own contented heart, she was momentarily most inordinately pleased. Regrettably, the poor child had lost her novelty within the month and Lydia turned her notice to a more lucrative project.

Much to the Gardiners' dismay, she embarked upon a mission to interview the specific suitor she had deemed father to her child. As their number may not have been legion, it was large enough to engender a project intricate in contemplation and manipulation. It also involved wiles unworthy of the most unprincipled of women. The Gardiners were a little less inclined to subject their children to Lydia's machinations than they were to witnessing it for themselves. They left Lydia to their home, Cheapside, and the whole of London with which to have her way, only taking time to bundle into their trunks whatever clothing was handy before taking leave. It was with a deplorably mismatched ensemble that Mrs. Gardiner apprised Elizabeth of the specifics of her sister's latest roguery.

"Bless me, Elizabeth! Mr. Gardiner and I did what we could, but she was in no greater means of listening to reason than she was lo those many years ago..."

Leaving Lydia to her own devices was the single incautious decision that good couple had ever made. Yet in the end, no one, least of all Elizabeth, would have quibbled with the necessity of divesting themselves of Lydia's daily fits and indecorous behaviour. So great was her own culpability in subjecting them to Lydia in the first place, Elizabeth patted her aunt's hand and shook her head in consolation (doing so without actually "tsking" aloud with only the greatest of discipline). Simultaneously to her commiseration, Elizabeth was hastily apprising and discarding what next to do with Lydia. She veritably scratched her head with perplexity, for, now that nunneries were obsolete, she truly had little notion which way to turn. That unprofitable employment she gave up in favour of one more to her liking.

All Lydia's schemes and deception might have taken their toll on dear Mrs. Gardiner's spirits. Hence, Elizabeth inveigled her to take a turn round the shingles that lined the waterfront with herself and Darcy. Since Darcy's rescue of Lydia's honour and insistence on bearing the burden of the remuneration Wickham required, the Gardiners held few in higher esteem than he. Aware of her discomposure (but not necessarily its origin), Darcy offered Mrs. Gardiner his arm. The fondness and admiration she held for her niece's excellent husband sent Mrs. Gardiner into a bit of a flutter. Elizabeth and Mr. Gardiner exchanged amused expressions as she took his arm in turn. Thereupon the two mismatched couples led the entire party out that day upon a stroll. Such walks became a daily pleasure—each one a new adventure.

Upon one such walk Darcy had inquired which direction they favoured their path to take. The sight that the Gardiners were most in want of viewing that day was the Brighton Pavilion for it was still in the throes of the Prince Regent's ever-altering design. Regrettably, when their walk allowed them at last to gaze upon its opulence, they stood for the whole of ten minutes before they realised how little amused they were by its general gaudiness. But it was there that Mr. Gardiner espied a curiously built ramp that, word had it, was fitted particularly for the prince.

Mr. Gardiner was not one whose bent was much to gossip, but as a man in trade he could not help being privy to idle talk. It was quite seldom, however, that he had occasion to observe firsthand the mad doings of royalty; hence, upon this occasion he was a keen observer. As a gentleman, he believed it only courteous to share what intelligence he carried with his companions. Whilst Darcy pretended disinterest, Elizabeth and Mrs. Gardiner wanted to hear it all.

"See there," he said, "that must be it! It is a chair on rollers!"

Indeed it was—a chair constructed specifically to aid the increasingly adipose prince in mounting his beleaguered steed. They eyed the bizarre contraption most particularly, but it appeared to have been abandoned. That gave credibility to further gossip that, to his misfortune, the prince had become so obscenely obese the chair had been rendered unusable. Mr. Gardiner had great interest in machines of all sort, thus, its obsolescence did not lessen his enjoyment in seeing it at firsthand. He and Mrs. Gardiner marvelled upon it for some time. By then Darcy feared they might be taken for common sightseers if they lingered and he retrieved Elizabeth's arm. In good time, the Gardiners and their frolicsome children fell in behind, and Elizabeth and Darcy, arm in arm, strolled behind Margaret as she pushed the babies a little ahead of them in their carriage. They led their entire party on the walkway tracing the edge of the waterfront. As new lovers often do, Georgiana and Fitzwilliam trailed them all, seemingly lost in their own conversation.

Pointing down the beach, Darcy drew their attention to the unwieldy bathing machines being cranked out to the surf, allowing flannel-clad bathers to cautiously dip their toes and gauge the temperature of the water. Sea gulls dived and children shrieked and Geoff and Janie sat in wide-eyed wonder at the sights. So much did the twins attract admiration from passers-by that Elizabeth remarked that they might do well to put them up in a booth for a penny a look. As the Gardiners stopt and took notice of the bathers, Darcy could not resist calling out.

"Mrs. Gardiner, pray shall you take a swim?" Darcy teased.

She blushed. "I think not. Perhaps just an ablution of sea water."

"I'm told it should not be taken without a mixture of crab's eyes and wood lice. I understand milk may be added to make it more palatable," Darcy said with unexpected drollness.

Everyone laughed. Elizabeth remarked that they lacked only the Bingleys to make their holiday compleat. Regrettably, they had yet to arrive. For such was the size of the Bingleys' brood and the laxity of their resolve, they always arrived a fortnight behind everyone else. Still, Elizabeth was pleased to hear her husband in such uncommonly tranquil humour. She almost said as much but her attention was taken by a voice calling out. It was a voice that was so familiar that she stood motionless, attempting both to locate and place it. When she did, her reaction was visceral. She cringed both figuratively and literally in recognition.

"I say, nephew!" trilled Lady Catherine de Bourgh. "Too-roo! Nephew!"

At this their entire party, almost as one entity, stopped in its tracks. But only Darcy turned to Lady Catherine as she approached. Elizabeth found it necessary to rearrange the blankets around her children. So busy was she, she was quite unable to take notice of anything else. Her own ploy, however, was unsuccessful. For much to Elizabeth's astonishment, Lady Catherine hurried toward her. Elizabeth turned to face her—arms folded. In defence of her children, she was quite ready to do battle. That proved to be quite unnecessary.

For as it happened, Lady Catherine (or the amiable spirit that had taken over her body) was quite happy to see them all. They knew this to be true because she briefly stopt her advance to extend greetings and good-day to all—several times—with great emotion. As Darcy insinuated himself between Lady Catherine and his family (whether to protect them or keep his wife from doing her damage, one can only conjecture), all the others in their little band stood still as stones. Mrs. Gardiner, having heard a great deal of Lady Catherine's numerous ill-deeds, stood with her mouth slightly agape.

Said Lady Catherine, "My dearest nephew! Dearest Elizabeth! Do we have the good fortunate to admire your new family?"

Lady Catherine inquiring after her children was more alarming to Elizabeth than anything else she could imagine and she was loath to allow it. Nonetheless, Lady Catherine endeavoured mightily to look over and around her nephew at the small charges in the baby carriage. Elizabeth truly wondered was it a ruse to get near her children and do them harm. Possibly of the same mind, Darcy stood his ground, walking-stick held lightly in his hand (seemingly at the ready) as his aunt approached. He tipped his hat ever so slightly but said nothing. In the absence of an invitation to do so, Lady Catherine sashayed around him and over to the carriage. She then bent low to peer in at the babies. It was all Elizabeth could do not to throw herself across them in their defence.

After a scrutiny that bordered on the untoward, she announced, "Handsome children are they not!"

It was only then that it became apparent that Lady Catherine was not alone. Although the Gardiners had never met her and Elizabeth had seen her but little and could be forgiven, Darcy should have recognised Lady Anne. She certainly had recognised him. She commenced a simpering, eye-batting giggle—from whence she quickly retreated behind her fan. It was a display worthy of Lydia at her most inane and Elizabeth had to make herself not look over-long at her. Such as it was, it managed the considerable feat of stealing Elizabeth's attention from Lady Catherine. When it returned, it was only with the severest self-discipline that she kept from wheeling the carriage and making for the nearest shop for sanctuary.

Whether Anne was in such a coy state due to the opportunity to exhibit her new husband, no one there could fathom. But her attitude did the considerable favour of arresting Lady Catherine's attention from chin-chucking of the twins to introduction of her new son-in-law, Lord Beecher. Beecher bowed from the waist with ingratiating depth, this time avoiding the error of addressing anyone with too much familiarity. Through their astonishment, Elizabeth curtsied politely and Darcy managed to return Beecher's bow (if by half in depth).This round too Lady Catherine honed her newly acquired office of doting aunt by employing a smile that revealed more than only her jaw teeth.

When there was a moment of quiet, her ladyship found better use of it by booming, "I must see you take to the sea, Darcy!"

Because Georgiana had thought it imprudent to share with Elizabeth the queer meeting she and Fitzwilliam had had with Lady Catherine in Bath, wisely surmising it was not a pleasant subject, Lady Anne's engagement, and hence her marriage, took everyone else compleatly unawares. Moreover, Anne's thin frame looked to be sporting a fecundity rivalling that of Georgiana. Nothing, however, was more astonishing than Lady Catherine's compleat and utter reversal of deportment. It remained entirely altered until she commenced upon a recitation to one and all of her own bathing ritual. It was once again the Lady Catherine of yore.

"At first light twice or thrice a week I betake myself to my bathing machine and put out to sea. There one is free to disport in the water. Of course, a flannel gown is worn—although I understand there are others who eschew such modesty for a bathing costume. The dip is quite refreshing and has done wonders for my rheumatism."

This entire monologue was uninterrupted either by question or exclamation. She then bid Darcy and "his delightful children and worthy companions" a good-day.

It was uncommon for Elizabeth to be struck speechless, yet she was struck speechless then. Which was just as well, for there was no comment that anyone of their party could deem to make for the better part of a quarter-hour. Only then did Georgiana volunteer a recounting of their meeting in Bath.

"How could we have over-looked a wedding of such merit?" Elizabeth mused.

It was less a matter of them over-looking any such announcement than that no announcement had been made. It was abundantly clear that Lady Anne had reason, if not to hide her condition, at least to camouflage its maturity. She was hardly the first, nor would she be the last, lady who took her vows with a bean up the spout. It would remain out of topic until the baptismal announcement arrived. Until then, no one would ever be said to have been with child.

57

Lydia Takes on As Maid a Character Familiar to Our Story

As the Gardiners hied for Brighton in want of asylum from Lydia Bennet Wickham's company, the dust from their carriage had not time to settle ere their least favourite niece arose upon her high-horse and commenced to issue orders in rearrangement of their household to suit herself.

She had been lying in wait for the opportunity to play mistress of the house. Indeed, she had little of late to keep herself amused and had been quite out of humour. Aside from the aforementioned letter-writing campaign to her sisters asking after an increase in her allowance, poor Lydia lacked any resources for solitude. Hence, the dearth of diversion demanded by her confinement encouraged her already indolent mind to imagine that the Gardiners' servants were plotting schemes against her. That they were not was not to her credit, for she was easily the least-liked personage ever to cross the Gardiners' threshold. An uncommonly generous observer such as Mrs. Gardiner might have attributed this general unpopularity with the help as owing to Lydia's being unaccustomed to delegating chores, for the Wickhams seldom had funds to hire more than a single servant.

Indeed, that was what a generous observer might opine. One more objective would undoubtedly note that had she one servant or ten, Lydia was not a kind employer. The wages she paid were mean and her expectations high. The Gardiners were generous to their house-maids and were repaid by their servants' devotion. Lydia believed any kindness extended to those in one's employ was a serious character defect, one that would be but repaid through disloyalty and theft. Hence, she watched those servants like a hawk and complained regularly of their laziness. Indeed, Lydia was uncivil and demanding to all the help, particularly when she thought Mrs. Gardiner was beyond ear-shot.

All the maids weathered Mrs. Wickham's presence with a forbearance found only in very happy households. They all knew that Lydia's tarry there would be but for the length of her confinement. What they did not know about the particulars of that confinement, they conjectured. After they conjectured, they snickered. Of this, Lydia was well-aware. Hence, Lydia was nigh as delighted for the Gardiners to take their leave as were they. If all went well, she would be out of their house before they noticed anything amiss.

Her first item of business was to tell the Gardiners' long-time house-maid, Clemmie, that she was to have her duties reduced, rightly supposing the woman would relinquish her situation. That poor woman had been the primary sufferer of Lydia's wayward acts and principal bearer of those tidings to Mrs. Gardiner, therefore Lydia was most anxious to have her gone. Having little intention of anything but a temporary leave-taking, Clemmie removed herself from the Gardiners' premises with a raised fist at Lydia and a vow that Mrs. Gardiner would hear of this outrage forthwith. Any reasonable person would have been intimidated by such threats. But Lydia had never been accused of reasonableness, therefore, she gave it little thought.

Although impetuosity was one of Lydia's most prominent traits, upon this occasion she had not acted with absolute rashness. Elizabeth and Jane had funded a nurse-maid and wet-nurse for her new daughter and she intended to have her own help in place long before the Gardiners' return. If (or rather, when) they reinstated Clemmie, she would be well-advanced toward situating herself in her own lodgings. Elizabeth had held firm in opposition to her pleas for money, but Jane's resolve was notoriously weak. So certain was she of Jane's capitulation, she had located a handsome house just over the way that was soon to be let. What lustre its address lost in being in Cheapside, it was near enough to the Gardiners' house for convenience's sake. In the meantime, she was inclined to enjoy the freedom of having her way in the Gardiners' house and free to impose upon their help for her immediate needs. Indeed, in an unusual fit of forethought, she had put out notice that she would be interviewing for a new house-maid before forcing Clemmie to take her leave.

Unbeknownst to Lydia, Clemmie had seen to it that the neighbourhood was well-apprised of by whose hand she had lost her situation. Amongst the maids-of-all-chores there was a quiet but efficient channel to both inform and warn off potential help from certain households. Regrettably, under Lydia's command the Gardiners' home was the recipient of a general shunning by any potential servant regardless of race, religion, sex, or national origin. Hence, it came to pass that as the most recently employed baby-nurse both took umbrage at Lydia's abuse and took her immediate leave by means of the nearest door, Lydia was in pursuit waving a monstrous hat-pin and venting curses heretofore unheard on this street emitted from a supposed gentlewoman's mouth.

As this last baby-nurse hastened up the street, Lydia could not keep herself from discharging a somewhat pointless parting shot, "If you cannot do a simple chore, pray never cross my doorstep again, Polly!"

The departing servant gave a look over her shoulder that suggested the unlikelihood of her returning anywhere near Gracechurch Street again.

She, however, issued one qualification, "This doorstep won't see my foot so long as the likes of ye are about!"

At this last impudence, Lydia stomped her foot and invoked another curse, this one decidedly less blasphemous that those previous. As she turned to re-enter the door, her eyes lit upon what to her was a most trifling personage. There stood a slight bit of a girl with eyes trained upon her and appropriately aghast. Lydia looked at her from forehead to toes taking note of her small stature and sooty face. Two eyes, quite appropriately black as coals, peered back at her with unusual keenness. The reason for the young woman happening to be upon the stoop was partially explained by the offering of assorted threads she carried. Although Lydia's fit of spleen had been vented, the turn of her countenance still bore traces enough of her recent wrath (and her hand still grasped the hat-pin) that the poor peddler-girl took an instinctual step back.

Contentiously, Lydia inquired, "Who might you be?"

"N-n-o-body, m'lady," said Sally Frances Arbuthnot, at that moment bearing no ingratitude for her lack of prominence.

"You are not some chit come here to spy for a dun—what say you? Speak up, girl! What say you?"

"'Pon my honour, m'lady, I come from a shop just over the way. A servant at this house is in want of these notions. I was told to ask for Clementine."

By then, Lydia had lowered her weapon and unmindfully jabbed it into her topknot. She looked again at Sally, this time in thoughtful consideration. After a moment's observation she determined that the girl was neither a bill-collector nor his agent (so often had she been frequented by such, she could make them out at twenty paces). Hence, when she responded, her tone lost a full octave along with its belligerence.

"She is no longer in my employ," said Lydia calmly.

Now that reason had reclaimed her, Lydia glanced both ways up the street, suddenly aware of her very public indecorousness. Age had not yet gifted her with much circumspection, but she had come lately of a mind that did she not redeem herself in some manner that the Gardiners might send her packing back to Longbourn before her own design had been set in place. Satisfied there were no overtly prying eyes, she returned her attention to the insignificant girl on her stoop. She looked upon Sally first one way and then the other as if sizing her up for some unknown duty, then idly tapped a forefinger upon her chin. At that moment, societal disapproval was of small concern to Lydia. She had a far more pressing one. For, if one discounted the woman who had her infant daughter even then attached to her teat, she had absolutely no household help. The enlightenment that overspread Lydia's countenance then suggested the appearance of the girl before her was providential.

"Girl, can you do a maid's work?" she demanded.

Sally was nothing if not alert to a situation that might offer pecuniary advantage, hence, she replied without hesitation, "Yes, m'lady."

"Come," Lydia announced.

Silently, Sally followed her across the threshold into a house that, to her disadvantaged eyes, appeared quite grand.

"Can you see to a child as well?"

"Yes, m'lady."

Upon this particular occasion Sally's affirmative answers were honest. It would be fair to suggest that had Lydia asked her could she balance a tri-coloured ball on her nose whilst standing atop the back of galloping horse, her response would not have altered. For a girl like Sally who had a biscuit in her pocket for lunch but to whom dinner was still only a hope, to have a chance for a situation in the house of gentlefolk meant she would have said yes to most anything. That these duties were, indeed, within her sphere of capabilities was of particular good fortune. Still carrying her basket of threads, she followed Lydia through the vestibule and up three sets of stairs to the nursery. In one corner sat a grey-faced woman wearing a faded pink shawl which was loosely thrown across her shoulders. The woman looked upon Lydia with all the apprehension one might invoke had a snake trespassed across a footpath. Lydia returned the compliment.

"She," said Lydia, pointing directly at the woman, "is bloody worthless!"

The woman's countenance bore an expression so benighted that an observer might infer, indeed, she was. She did, however, begin a small undulation influencing her rocking-chair into motion. The implication was that she was rocking a baby, but her arms were empty. At the intrusion of her mother's discordant voice, a baby begat a thin little wail from the opposite side of the room. Lydia strode to the cradle and looked down. Sally still stood just inside the doorway—her instinct for survival insisted she keep a means of escape at hand. But, Lydia snapped her fingers in her direction, bidding her come. With some reluctance, she did.

Standing over the cradle, Sally looked down at what was to become her ward. She was quite a pretty little baby with delicate features and thin limbs. Although her gender was apparent by her white cap with pink streamers, had she been otherwise adorned Sally still would not have taken her for a boy. She looked quite fragile lying amidst a crocheted shawl bearing small pink flowers—so fragile that Sally was instantly taken with her. She thought she had never seen any baby quite so lovely. Wafting up from the child, however, was a familiar odour—one quite incongruous to her genteel surroundings. Sally detected the unmistakable stench of excrement. The baby was by then kicking furiously enough to loosen its coverlet and Sally saw that the remnants of baby-waste had seeped up her back and beneath her extremities so ungovernably that the poor child looked to have been bathed in it. Less accustomed to filth than most of her class, Sally immediately went to repairing the situation, Lydia pointing out the location of the proper provisions.

"There, there, little one," Sally cooed, when at last the baby was put to order. "There, there."

"Well," Lydia announced, "you did well. Your bed is in that far corner. Please spare me further bother until after supper. Then bring my daughter to me after she has been bathed once again."

With that, seemingly satisfied with the turn of events and evidently unworried about Sally's lack of proper references, Lydia quit the room, closing the door solidly behind her. Sally's countenance remained placid, registering no reaction from Lydia's abrupt departure. Rather, she returned her attention to the small bundle before her and wondered should she lift her from her cradle. The baby returned Sally's earnest gaze with an expression that was both familiar and unsettling. Sally was torn from that perplexity when she recalled she was not alone. The poor woman who sat in the corner still rocked with eerie determination.

"My name is Sally," said she. "Pray, how are you called?"

"Malmsy," said the woman, rocking with renewed vigour.

"How'd y'do, Malmsy. And the baby," Sally continued, "how is she called?"

"Her name be Susanna."

"Susanna," Sally repeated. Then with a great intake of air, she asked, "Shall I call her Sue?"

"Suit yerself."

Brighton Charms

In their months in Brighton, the Darcys found a multitude of pleasures—not the least of these accompanying their children to the seashore. Frolicking amongst the lapping waves with a tiny hand in each of hers was Elizabeth's heart's bliss. Darcy stood by with parental reserve and watched as their children first beheld the water as it lapped against their feet, then, hanging onto their mother's fingers, falling down, only to be lifted up and swung about—laughing and giggling with delight. Darcy's refusal to venture further than the beach chairs (hat and frockcoat in place and determined to remain aloof from such a public spectacle) could not lessen Elizabeth's spirits. It was not infrequently, however, that she would look in his direction and see him smiling at their antics. She knew were he truly offended, he would not have accompanied them in the first place.

When the Bingleys finally arrived, it was quite a parade when they all departed for the seaside—children, nurses, blankets, and wicker lunch-baskets required several carts to deliver them all. Of course Bingley had not Darcy's reserve and ran and played tag with the wee ones with all the enthusiasm of an over-sized child. But, soon the diversions of Brighton called to his restless need for diversion and he began to inveigle first Darcy and then Fitzwilliam to join him in attending one of Brighton's boxing competitions. When first he broached the subject, Jane was altogether miffed. In an attitude quite uncommon of her, she put her hands upon her hips.

She said, "Charles Bingley! Did not you swear upon your very honour that you would no longer attend such a cruel entertainment?"

"Jane, dearest, I sold my portion of the boxer as I promised. I did not say I would never again look upon a bout. There can be no harm found in the mere observation of one."

She was not compleatly appeased, but was unable to deny her husband diversion and gave her blessing, for Bingley could not have enjoyed himself had she not. In the end, the gentlemen did attend one bout, but as both Darcy and Fitzwilliam had seen far too much of war, blood sports were not to their liking. Hence they persuaded Bingley to exchange that enthusiasm for the race course—indeed, horse-racing was an entertainment where the ladies could accompany them. It was at one of these events at Brighton's lovely new racing courses that they happened upon two of England's foremost horse enthusiasts, Lord and Lady Millhouse. Lady Millhouse's first inquiry was not of their family but how Elizabeth's mare's first foal was doing.

The Millhouses, aside from being Pemberley's nearest neighbours, were friends of the finest sort—good-natured and gregarious, they made every day into a celebration of sorts. They had been there but for a day and Lady Millhouse had already dipped her toe in the sea. "Hah! Watch us, Darcy and see if we do not put on our bathing costumes!" she proclaimed.

Quite soon, Lady Millhouse's enthusiasm for their own sea-bathing transmuted into insisting upon Darcy's. With Bingley joining their refrain, they spent most of the afternoon in belabouring that notion. But Darcy steadfastly refused even to entertain such abhorrence despite how determinedly Bingley coaxed him.

He extolled the breeze, the surf, the fine, hard sand, and the deep water not ten foot from shore, "The machines take you directly there and back—you would be in no one's eye."

"I think not," was Darcy's terse reply.

Elizabeth controlled a smile during these exchanges, for she was entertaining a small secret.

It was true that Mr. Darcy refused to put on a bathing costume and be cranked out to sea in a bathing contraption. But there were many hours in the day and they had found their own particular diversion.

It all began within the week of first arriving in Brighton. Early risers, Fitzwilliam and Georgiana always took their rest early, leaving Darcy and Elizabeth quite to their own devices after dinner. The beautiful, warm night air and moonlit paths beckoned them from their drawing-room. After the children were put to bed and all was quiet, they betook themselves in an open gig along the winding roadway to Devil's Dyke and from thence back down along the esplanade.

After repeated forays into the night, they gradually grew accustomed to making their way about by the moon. Ere long, they tired of the same byways and found themselves above the cliffs overlooking the shore. The night was balmy and their blood was stirred by the sight of the black waves as they lapped, then expired onto the beach. They were farther than the esplanade, but a trail was clearly visible from the road down to the beach as if inviting them to take themselves upon it. The incline was a bit steep and Darcy went first, Elizabeth reaching out to steady herself upon his shoulder as they crept their way to the water's edge. They strolled there for some time, then simply retraced their steps and returned to their apartments, never speaking a word of their adventures to anyone else in their party. In time, seeking new explorations, they ventured farther and became bolder, taking off their boots and wading in the surf. It was delightful, with no mud, no weeds, and no slimy rocks to impede their enjoyment.

To splash through the waves was a freedom neither had ever discovered for themselves until then.

"This is superb!" Elizabeth exclaimed.

She had grown ever more daring, grasping her skirt tail above her knees. A wave would come in and douse her to her hips, but she would only laugh and tease her husband to join her. He had folded his coat, gloves, and waistcoat into a tidy pile beside him, his hat and boots in a neat row, and adamantly refused to enter into such frivolity. The farther out she went, however, the more disturbed he became (which, no doubt, had been her design).

"There is deep water not ten-foot out!" he called, echoing his caution when they had swum in the weirs at Pemberley.

But, she did not heed his warning and a huge swell threw down upon her, washing her off her feet and rolling her onto the beach before its rush began to sweep her back out again. In that brief time, he had raced toward her, but was washed from his feet by the same rush of water that upended her. The mischievous upsurge drew them both back into the ocean's grasp momentarily, but he managed to take hold of her skirt before she was washed far away from him. When at last they broke free of the water's clutches and the wave receded, she was gasping and indignant—both at the ocean's impertinence and at her husband's being right about it.

They were both wet, sitting side by side on the wet, packed sand, with only an occasional teasing breaker passing over their feet.

"It is quite evident," she said, "that moving waters dislike me. They attack me at every turn."

"This I cannot deny," he teased. "Had I not been here, you no doubt would have been food for the fish."

To her chagrin, he then stood. She thought they were meant to leave, but he began to scavenge for dry tinder, stacking it in a pile. She saw his intent and joined in and soon they had a tidy bit of fire-fixings. He strode off toward the coach to retrieve a lantern to set it alight. They removed their outer garments and hung them over sticks to dry. When all was done but the waiting, they lay down side by side and stared at the sky as bits of disintegrating sparks flew heavenward. Her attention was arrested from that mesmerising vision by a husband who was inclined to want all her attention for himself—attention she was only too happy to supply. In fortune, they were not too long upon this engrossment when they were interrupted by the sight and sound of a boat coming ashore up the beach. Still prone, they lay still for a moment to determine who it was. From that distance, Darcy determined it not to be benign activity and quickly began dousing the fire with handfuls of sand.

"Quickly," he demanded, "dress yourself."

Keeping to a low crouching walk, he made his way over to where his boots and coat lay. Whilst she understood the necessity of clothing herself, she thought it a bit ridiculous that he worried for his own lack of decorum. She would have told him so had she not then seen that he had made not for his frockcoat, but for the pistol that lay beneath it. She was aghast. Never once had she seen that upon his person the entire of their trip.

"Where did you…" she worriedly began whispering, but he put out his hand to hush her, and employed the same crab-like walk back to her side. They sat quietly huddled together for a few minutes longer watching through the now ominous moonlight as men climbed out of the dory and began tramping toward the cliffs.

"We must away," he whispered. "Quickly."

That was an observation that was unnecessary for him to have issued, and in bare feet they began to climb up the incline toward their gig. Darcy veritably tossed Elizabeth into the seat and leapt in beside her, not scrupling to take the whip to their horse to encourage it begone. Taking more than one turn perilously, they then rode pell-mell toward town. When they reached the outskirts of Brighton, they slowed to a trot, then stopt. Both turned and looked behind them to see if they were followed. When it appeared that they had not been, Darcy retrieved the boots he had hastily thrown in the floorboards and put first one then the other on by bracing each foot against the splashing-board. Only then did Elizabeth dare to take a breath. Although she saw the pistol-butt protruding from his waistband, she made no inquiry. The reason for such precaution was evident. It would be only upon their journey homeward that she would see that he still wore it, as he probably had upon their coming as well.

Although Darcy made discreet inquiries with the constable, they did not find out who it had been or what matter of misconduct engaged them. "Smugglers," Darcy surmised, something that at one time was seldom seen along those shores. They were quite satisfied not to have been again beset upon by highwaymen. Although it was not openly discussed, both concluded that if they were to disport in a water-borne fashion, they would do so only upon their own property. They would keep by the sea only in the broad daylight. They did not regret their escapade, but neither did they repeat it.

It was only a few days thence that a post arrived for the Gardiners from their maid of long-standing. She informed them of her dismissal at the hands of Mrs. Wickham, who outrageously had hired a girl of her own choosing to replace her. Beholding that information, the guilt which had been abating with every smile she brought to the Gardiners' countenances resurfaced within Elizabeth with a vengeance. The only remedy available to her was the one she employed that evening, pledging the entirety of her father's small annual legacy to obtain Lydia new lodgings forthwith. It was not a lofty sum by Darcy standards, but what with Lydia's own inheritance from their father and Wickham's pension, she should be able to live quite well on it. That is, one could—whether Lydia would remained to be seen. It was all that Elizabeth had to give for she was still adamant that no funds from Pemberley go to the wife of Wickham. While Darcy had set up a generous trust for Wickham's children, it was, much to Lydia's consternation, inaccessible to her. Elizabeth had little hope that her small contribution would be of any further satisfaction.

Her generosity, however, the Gardiners were disinclined to accept.

"She is our niece," Mrs. Gardiner had insisted.

"But she is my sister and therefore more my responsibility," said Elizabeth, not wanting to point out the obvious disparity of incomes.

They closed their eyes, pursed their lips, and shook their heads in continued refusal of her offer. Hence, when they took their leave it was with genuine sorrow and no little self-reproach that Elizabeth bid them farewell. She vowed, however, that she would hie to London as soon as her children's health permitted to see Lydia settled into a house of her own. Darcy found this notion much to his disfavour. But as he remained vague about the reason for his disapproval and did not truly take a stand absolutely against her, she forged on with her plans.

As a man who seldom waffled on any issue, Darcy was uncertain how firm a stand to take against Elizabeth's going to London. As he was disinclined to take his family to bide in Mayfair, he could not make himself believe that Cheapside was in any less danger. What they had witnessed upon the beach told him there was much malfeasance afoot in England and he was not about to allow Elizabeth to travel there alone. Loath as he was to insinuate himself personally into Lydia's doings, he was becoming increasingly aware that it might become necessary. His disposition exposed this abhorrence and as he chose not to explain himself, he left himself open to the allegation of imperturbability from his wife when in fact his hesitation sprang from quite the opposite emotion.

Perhaps to alter the subject, Elizabeth asked Darcy what he made of Lady Catherine's reversal of opinion. His mind was still otherwise employed and he gave a slight shrug of his shoulders, dismissing the entire mystery out of hand.

Said he, "Perchance she has thought better of her opposition. She has little to gain by remaining so very obstinate."

This was undeniably true, but Elizabeth was not so inclined as her husband to accept this particular hand of friendship without a glove sporting a healthy coat of unslaked lime.

Elizabeth's discomposure from her continuing consternation over Lydia's imprudent conduct and Lady Catherine's newly invented family affection would have waned eventually through sheer determination. It would have had she not, through the bustling street filled with private carriages, hackneys, drays, and assorted children, nurses, maids, and gentlefolk, been certain that she spied stepping out of a shop and sauntering off down the street, the unmistakable aspect of the late Major George Wickham.

Quittance

George Wickham knew that was he to return to his homeland a free man, it would be a tricky business. Beforehand, he must concoct a story of sufficient cunning to hoodwink the notoriously sceptical military authorities. Moreover, it must serve to acquit him of misconduct in society's eyes as well. The latter gave him greater pause, for although those canons set down by military tribunal were unsparing, those of society were absolutely pitiless.

The convoluted fallacy Wickham meant to inflict upon his wife, kinfolk, and general acquaintances went through several alterations before he struck on one of sufficient melding of fabrication and truth as to be believable. However, as he wended his way homeward aboard a transport vessel, he had little opportunity to ponder that unhappy truth clinging as he was to the ship's rigging whilst the shifting deck heaved and bobbed its way through the choppy waters of the channel. It was only when they found calmer waters along the English coast-line that the discomposure of his innards subsided long enough for him to ruminate over his knotty situation.

Wickham's prior crossing had been even less agreeable to his constitution than his current one as on that occasion it had been on a British troop ship taking him directly into harm's way of Napoleon's army. That passage had been characterized by white-knuckled apprehension of the ensuing battle and an ill-timed bout of the trots. He had always been uncertain whether the roiling sea alone or the up-coming fight instigated his intestinal disturbance. Regardless, it had been a relentless seizing of his bowels which demanded he observe the whole of the crossing through a water-level porthole. Attached as he was to the slop-bucket, he had little to divert his thoughts beyond wrestling with his finely honed sense of self-preservation (which prevailed quite handily over honour and duty). Indeed, it had nagged with pertinacious determination that he fling himself over-board and swim with all due diligence for the safety of British soil.

But he had not. He had held tight to the mast and sallied forth into a battle that still haunted his sleep. That, however, was a time and place he and his little-employed conscience endeavoured mightily to avoid.

The ship upon which he returned was not of His Majesty's Navy, but similar in size, design, and purpose. However, this one did not ferry soldiers. It carried a collection of citizens both French and British, all bent (for considerations as disparate as their identities) on making their way to England. After finally releasing himself from the security of the jib, Wickham took solitary, off-kilter walks on the gunwale whilst perfecting his version of recent events. It was imperative that he account for his time abroad.

His foremost concern was that this retelling place him in both a well-disposed and heroic light. After careful deliberation and no small calculation, he thought his rendering plausible and made for the well-populated forward deck to assess its viability amongst the general public. Effecting a discernible limp (the better to draw sympathetic attention to himself) and employing a pseudonym, he engaged first one, then another passenger in conversation, honing the tale of his whereabouts after the war to a few brief assertions—as any good liar knows, it *was* imperative to keep his lies to a minimum. The little decoration he added was professing great anticipation in rejoining the bosom of his fictitious family. After this tender proclamation, he would pause and gaze about, calculating which listeners were most amenable to further exposition. To them he would direct a most dazzling smile which, embellished by a small furrowing of his brow, would falter ever so briefly, thus exposing both the disquiet lying deep within his poor, troubled breast and his bravery in weathering it. With unfailing regularity, this ploy would rouse the more sympathetic amongst his audience to demand further elucidation of the vexatious events he struggled so courageously to conceal. Inevitably, these gentle-hearts beat in the bosoms of the female species.

"Come, come, sir! Forbear not! It is best to unkennel what plagues you and allow us to lend our condoling hearts."

"Yes. I suppose that is best," said he, lowering his voice and his countenance, the better to bespeak the terrible ordeal he had endured.

He then told, with compleat humility and very little truth, a fairly graphic battle-wound fable—one remarkable for emphasising its severity without actually identifying its exact whereabouts upon his person. It should not have been his foremost concern, but he was predisposed to employ this obfuscation so as not to imply to any lady paying heed that his vigour was in any way compromised by bodily trauma. However, in light of no noticeable damage to his extremities, this ploy did not do justice to its intent. Indeed, it begat whispers regarding the exact nature of his limp and the speculation of those few whose interest was excited was not complimentary to the well-being of his manly organs. Had Wickham been aware of these conjectures, he would have been highly unamused. As it was, he mistook their expressions as enthralled admiration rather than appalled curiosity and, never one to relinquish so rapt an audience, he thought to further detail his recuperation from battle-wounds.

To the increasingly aghast listeners, he told how he had lain in excruciating pain and squalid conditions for months in the *Hôtel des Invalides* on the west side of Paris—his purported recuperation coinciding precisely with his leisurely abode in Césarine's bed-chamber. Initially, he had thought actually naming a hospital in Paris a particularly rich touch and congratulated himself for recollecting that edifice for his story in the event he had been espied in the area by someone who might subsequently cross his path. Regrettably, a gentleman who stood at his elbow for the entirety of his monologue revealed himself a Parisian *intime*. His costume was one of a proper gentleman, but he was on the short side. Hence, when Wickham looked down upon him he obtained a clear view of the gentleman's vain attempt at obscuring his bald crown with a generous forward feathering of what was left of his hair. Wickham took immediate measure of the man in a single glance before his attention was stolen from appraising his station to what he had to say.

Apparently familiar with the hospital Wickham had referenced, an expression of puzzlement overspread his countenance. He had a French accent, but his English was superb.

"*Hôtel des Invalides* you say? Are you not mistaken? I was of the understanding that hospital lodges war veterans of the French—and is one of France's finest infirmaries. I cannot imagine the conditions you describe. And why," he added, "pray, would you, an English officer, be sent to recuperate amongst his enemy?"

"Ah, yes. Er, no. Of course. Of course. My French is abominable, my recall even more dreadful. And I *was* quite ill when taken thither—out of my mind with fever. It may have been the infirmary of *Salpêtrière*. I was *quite* ill you see…"

Wickham knew well that the height of cleverness is to be able to conceal it and he hemmed admirably. He had learnt well and he had learnt early that one confesses to little faults to prove that one has no large ones. Although Wickham continued to engage in self-censure, the inquiring man continued to look oddly at him. Even Wickham knew it was quite peculiar to have been so long in a facility that he could not correctly name. But the man soon toddled off twirling his walking stick, seemingly heedless of Wickham's blunder. Not allowing his gaze to follow the man's leave, Wickham turned to the others and was happy to see that the Frenchman's questions did not divert anyone else. It was a reminder to him that elaboration could be dangerous. His smile, however, remained genial and his new friends were disinclined to be suspicious. He continued his story, but with caution.

Those who were not instantly sympathetic to his heroic sacrifice for England (his limp had become increasingly conspicuous) could not admire enough his modest admission of having rescued a baby girl he claimed to have found in the arms of her dying father.

"I cannot imagine what such a small child was doing there at all let alone survive in such carnage!" he exclaimed. "Yet, I should not be entirely surprised. More than one wife followed her husband through Belgium taking in washing and riding after his regiment in a baggage waggon."

"Pray, was her father a French soldier, or British?"

Wickham had spent less time than he ought to polishing the reason for having a child in his possession. He preferred not to have to improvise, but knew that he could feint or parry with equal ease when called upon. Hence, a quick contemplation suggested to him that sentimentality would be better served was she of English blood.

"Her father wore a red coat," said Wickham.

In response to his words, there was much clucking and even one half-sob. He had chosen well.

Indeed, his tale was told with pathos of unconscionable amplitude, and by bringing to mind poor Césarine's protracted demise, he even managed to elicit a well timed tear on behalf of that poor, non-existent son of the British Empire. His disclosures, to be sure, succeeded most uncommonly well with the feminine gender. Indeed, had he not actually had an infant in his possession, seeing how very ably this artifice went over, he might well have been compelled to go out and procure one.

For all his exalted schemes, returning very nearly penniless whence he came was a virtual admission of a compleat drubbing. He, however, refused to acknowledge that truth. When he had fled the battlefield, he held the highest of hopes. From the back of that galloping steed speeding away from certain death, scheming notions had flitted wildly about his head; those reverberating most prominently was the succulent Shakespearean metaphor suggesting the world as his oyster. He need only find the sword with which to open it. Although at the time, he thought little could be more simple, he had never actually found that sword. And while he had not come by it honestly, he was returning with a very lucrative treasure. Had he managed to have escaped with Césarine's treasured necklace, he knew of several money-lenders in London who would have been happy to do business with him. Regrettably, he had been a step slow of Marie-Therese. She had taken that jewel-encrusted ornament without a second thought, just as he would have. Seldom had he ever lowered himself to outright thievery (he vastly preferred chicanery), but this time had been of a singular nature. Alas, for that loss. Why should some faceless creditor make off with a treasure that had once hung so fetchingly about the neck of his true love? (May she rest in peace.) It would have served him far greater benefit than Marie-Therese. She was still young, France in tumult. A woman such as she would thrive in such an atmosphere. He was exceedingly happy to have gotten away with what he had. As to why he had absconded with Césarine's child was a scheme he had not compleatly worked out. With her parentage, the child was a valuable commodity. Once he had her safely out of France, his bargaining position would be most advantageous.

He came home by way of Brighton, for that was the most accessible port and it would have been suspicious to come a more circuitous route. Since 1802, it was the busiest exchange of French refugees fleeing Napoleon and Englishmen flocking to Paris to be presented to him. Amongst the surging throng of the disembarking that day, Wickham bounded down the gangway onto the Brighton dock with a bit of a strut, but his swagger was compromised by the gnomish-looking woman pulling a goat who dogged his side. He had hoped to find a suitable wet-nurse, but this woman and her nanny-goat was the best he could do for the few coins he was willing to pay. She was so disreputable-looking that he had considered just taking the goat, but was loath to have to milk it. Indeed, he quickly saw his enterprise being threatened with collapse under the sheer weight of peripheral nuisances demanded by travelling with a child. Had he not been so determined not to leave France without some sort of booty for his trouble, he might have left the child upon the first church doorstep.

He looked down at the basket and the girl-child therein, observing her fast asleep. Thereby he was gifted an inward sigh of relief. He had a brief reprieve before he would need to befriend another motherly benefactor. The horrid goat-nurse of a woman he had employed had been absolutely disgusting. He had despised the necessity of being seen in her company, but he was low on funds and knew not what else to do until he obtained proper lodgings.

He looked about the familiar landscape of Brighton without apprehension but with what might have been a bit of melancholy.

The town was much the same as he remembered it, but those recollections were not particularly sweet. He recalled it still as thick with militia as it had been that injudicious summer of '09. It was that most foolish summer that he plunged into that imprudent romance with Lydia Bennet. Had he given it any forethought, he would not have. He would have seduced a girl who was not so eagerly protected. Still, it had been an astonishment that everyone involved in the entire mad-cap affair was most uncompromising about such a portionless creature as Lydia Bennet. But as most men were aware, a stiff prick has no conscience.

From the relative wisdom of hindsight, he allowed that it was a profound ill-judgement to have stolen away with Lydia as he had. But she had been ripe for her age, a wild, flirtatious girl, her character marked much more by volatility than virtue. Had he not been so bloody bored with tiresome militia duty, he would not have been so unguarded as to abscond with an empty-minded school-girl and hie with her to London. He may have intimated to her that they would eventually be wed, but he would never be convinced that she had been wholly seduced. To Lydia, immediacy was paramount to convention. Had she not been so bloody miserly with the ultimate affection, the entire elopement charade would have been unnecessary.

Indeed, the first bloom of infatuation had worn out almost as soon as he had thrown her across the bed and tossed up her skirt. He had been making preparations to take leave without her when Darcy had shown up unceremoniously at their door. However, as he was deep in Queer Street with creditors pressing him on all sides, Darcy's proposal for him to take her hand in matrimony had been far too lucrative to reject. He had hoped to make away with the money and forgo the wedding. Perhaps suspecting he might abscond, that bloody Darcy had watched his every move (and had his man mind him whilst he slept). When he stood up with Lydia, he may as well have had a pistol prest to his spine.

"Whatever happened to the notion that a runaway match was something romantic?" Wickham had lamented to Lydia. "Certainly Darcy's understanding contains not an ounce of true passion."

Always prone to hasty judgements, Lydia Wickham could but sniff in agreement.

He was reminded of that trip to London then for another reason, this one more immediate. The one who was instrumental in aiding them to elude Lydia's family for so many days whilst playing at being love-birds was whom he would again seek out. He needed a place to recuperate from his ordeal and time to contemplate his next action. He would also need someone to help him with the baby. Looking after a child was quite new to him. He had never so much as taken a babe in his arms. His own children he had admired from across the room. He had wrangled assistance from any number of ladies sympathetic to a bachelor with an orphan on the crossing (one even culminating in a bum-tickle—which might have alleviated some of the coarser conjectures regarding the nature of his "wound" had the lady in question been less circumspect), but he would have to find more permanent aid if he wanted his steps to cease being haunted by the loathsome milk-crone.

After stopping in a shop for a replenishment of his favourite cologne, he went straightaway to inquire of the next post-*chaise* to London. It was a seven-hour trip and if they did not leave forthwith, they would be delayed yet another day, for travelling on Sunday was not done. The agent was busy with a young woman who wore what appeared to be her best travelling clothes. She was told that the next post's departure was imminent and she was to make her way down the footpad without delay was she not to be left behind. Wickham hastily purchased his ticket and took his place next to her as their trunks were loaded into the boot. He could sense it when she looked to him, but he did not return her interest. She looked inquisitively at the bundle he carried and only looked a little puzzled as he over-saw the goat being loaded. The crone first objected at how the nanny's feet were being tied and then fussed as it was pulled up onto the top of the coach.

"Take care!" said she in French. "*Faites attention*!"

When at last that troublesome pair were both settled (the goat's bleating no worse than the old woman's), Wickham turned his attention to the cumbersome task of gaining the coach with the baby basket. Only then was he forward enough to tip his hat to the young lady. She turned her head away from his impudence, but he observed her to smile coyly as she did. Once all was ready, with gentlemanly grace, he handed her into her seat. He took his place across from her and perched the baby's basket on his knees. From thence came stirring noises. Wickham affected a look of concerned discombobulation as he fussed with the baby's shawl. The carriage lurched forward.

On the door of the coach just below the window was stencilled the name "Lightning." How fitting thought Wickham. He believed he would be quite happy to see London once again.

Lady Millhouse Interjects

Lord Millhouse was a genial soul, but Lady Millhouse was a long-time Darcy family friend and was, in all ways, quite formidable. Lady Millhouse's true occupation was that of horsewoman, but she was a devoted wife and excellent friend to the few amongst her peers whom she respected. Bombastic as she was kind, her cheerful exuberance belied her sad history of enduring thirteen pregnancies with not a single child surviving beyond a fortnight. Successive blows of such strength and number would have felled a lesser being. Yet, so little did that burden trouble her bearing, those unacquainted with her tragedies would never have guessed that she had suffered as grievously as she had. Indeed, quite the opposite. For the entire of her life she had presented herself as nothing if not indomitable. Belying those blows of unendurable loss, Lady Millhouse did not begrudge the happiness others found in their own children. Indeed, she heartily joined in, bestrewing not a few of her nieces, nephews, and the offspring of close friends with motherly love and unswerving attachment. Although she was of no blood kinship with the Darcys, she was in deportment and affection as much an aunt to Darcy and Georgiana as Lady Catherine could ever have wished to be. Whether her dauntlessness was inborn or learnt in trial by fire, Elizabeth was wholly unacquainted. She did know, however, that in her own darkest hours, Lady Millhouse had come with words of uncommonly good judgement—horse sense, Lady Millhouse called it.

Her bond with the Darcys had fastened ever more tightly subsequent of the ill-fate of her adored nephew, Newton Hinchcliffe. When told that young Hinchcliffe was felled on that vast graveyard known as Waterloo, Lady Millhouse took the news with unyielding stoicism. However, she had been determined to have Lord Millhouse accompany her to Belgium to find the exact location of Newton's final resting place. As any notion upon which Lady Millhouse became attached was as good as done, they sailed within the week. After hours of searching the graves he was at last found, but Lady Millhouse was not happy to leave him there. It was her wish for him to take his last rest not in some foreign soil, but within the earth of her beloved Pennyswope, to lie forever amongst those graves of her many departed infants. Although Lord Millhouse insisted on the folly of doing so, she was adamant on this point.

"I shall take him home if I have to swim the channel with his corpse on my back!" she said defiantly.

Hence even a phalanx of gendarmes and her husband's disapproval could not sway her from disinterring his body and carting it back to England.

Her time had not been misspent, for Newton's reports from that battle had won him great, if posthumous, acclaim and there were those who clamoured to pay him respect.

"Would he not have been pleased?" said Lady Millhouse upon hearing of it, bringing a linen handkerchief to wipe a tear from the corner of her eye. Proudly she said, "And to think that he might not have been here to know of it."

As no one was of a mind to question whether in having shuffled off the mortal coil, Newton would have been less cognizant of his acclaim had he been dead in the ground of France rather than England, that determination remained Lady Millhouse's to pronounce. Her friends merely shook their heads in perplexity, far too troubled by the sight of one who was so seldom discomposed falling victim to a weep. All stood ready with limitless sympathy, but most stood helplessly about and said, "There, there."

Despite his affection for her, certain familiarities from Lady Millhouse upon occasion had driven Darcy to distraction. Although his dignity was occasionally battered, he could never bring himself to be truly vexed by her earthiness. In consequence of her sorrow, the Darcys encouraged her to visit Pemberley at every opportunity. Their object for such generosity was the two-fold kindness of cheering Lady Millhouse and relieving Lord Millhouse of the office of sole consoler.

When her ladyship did occasion Pemberley, the directness of her address was weathered by the master of the house with even more forbearance than ever known of him. Although it remained unspoken, her visits were encouraged for a consideration other than simple kindness. Whatever their friendship offered Lady Millhouse, hers recompensed them several times over. For rich as the Darcys were in family, love, and property, there was but a single commodity in which they were poor. Their children had no grandparents to bestow those particular indulgences that are peculiar to that race of second-season parents. Both Darcy's mother and father were long in their graves, Mr. Bennet more recently so. As for Mrs. Bennet, as a grandmother she was even less devoted to her grandchildren than she was to her daughters. From a woman whose regard for riches and those who were rich was unparalleled, this lack of devotion for children in so coveted a pecuniary position appeared quite extraordinary.

It was of no surprise that she did not hie to Derbyshire to gaze upon her newest grandchildren. For after betaking herself to the first several of her daughters' childbirths, weathering their ordeals to bask in the joy of grand-motherhood grew steadily more tiresome. Before long, her nerves had suffered quite enough.

When time came for Jane's most recent lying-in, she had said, "I am well content to abide here and look upon the wee one once uncertainty has passed."

Her meaning was not ambiguous. Nor was it challenged. For the single pragmatic quality Mrs. Bennet owned was that of affection. She was not without feeling, hers was simply finite in nature. One child in four would not see their first birthday, the odds were not good and she had not excess to invest in those tiny souls not long for the world.

Elizabeth had her own answer for this seemingly paradoxical behaviour.

She said cryptically, "One of my mother's greatest wisdoms is to know when the pot no longer needs stirring."

Indeed, Mrs. Bennet's interest in her daughters' well-being had waned precipitously once they were advantageously married. As it would be fully a year before mourning would allow her to enjoy the benefits of society, was it not for her exceptional regard for her youngest daughter, Lydia, the woman would have had little interest in her family whatsoever. She found her time better employed at Longbourn concentrating on the thing that most caught her fancy—herself. Now that she was a widow, it took every hour of every day to adequately see to her own needs. As much as she enjoyed her own nerves and fits, she could little weather the cries and unseemly discharges inherent to those miniature beings, her offspring's offspring.

"There is ample time to be in their company when they are proper young ladies and gentlemen," she had announced.

Jane had long since ceased to cajole her into grandmotherly affection. The only children she would tolerate to visit Longbourn were Lydia's, and only then when Hill kept them out of her sight. Although there was no grandmother who warbled on with more enthusiasm of the advantageous situations of her grandchildren, her affection for them was of a particular kind—that which was displayed best at a distance.

Therefore, it was by absences either in spirit or in the flesh that Geoff and Janie suffered a dearth of grandparental attention. Hence, it was to the Darcys' additional fortune that Lady Millhouse was particularly happy to undertake the office of Provider of Grandmotherly Effusion. Yet, as with every silver lining, there comes a cloud—and, insofar as Darcy was concerned, even this one.

The Lady of Pennyswope Manor had been a most cherished friend of Darcy's parents and therefore privy to their most closely guarded secrets. Although her connexion with her Aunt Gardiner was very dear to her, Lady Millhouse was the single visitor with whom Elizabeth could be compleatly unguarded. Although her trustworthiness was unquestioned, this intimacy and her lack of discretion could occasionally exasperate Darcy, particularly when she was sent to rhapsodising whilst recollecting his childhood. Unfortunately, every achievement celebrated by the twins provoked her remembrances of the young Master Darcy which were not necessarily those that he enjoyed in recapitulation.

"Yours is a strapping boy, Elizabeth," Lady Millhouse said admiringly—and repeatedly; "if only your mother were here, Darcy. There would be no end to her delight!"

Darcy's mother had died whilst giving birth to Georgiana; he then was but ten years old. Although Darcy thought of his father with nothing but the highest of esteem, he was his mother's son, inheriting both her aspect and temperament. He admired his father, but it was his mother he had adored. Lady Millhouse had been her lone confidant. Because of that, Elizabeth was pleased beyond measure to hear her applaud young Geoff. Darcy's countenance remained passive whilst she laid out her compliments, but even Elizabeth could detect a small swell of pride in his attitude.

With goodwill and happy thoughts flooding their bosoms, Elizabeth and Darcy nodded and smiled with approval. Although he always steeled himself for Lady Millhouse's occasional inexplicability of discourse (as his dignity often bore its brunt), her conversation that day in the sitting room at Brighton had been so benign he had been lulled into a truly genial mood. Lady Millhouse, however, made an addendum.

"But wee Geoff is not half so enormous as was our Darcy here. Now there was a child of goodly bulk!"

That comment in and of itself was not alarming. But having heard this particular recollection many times before, Darcy's pleased expression evaporated. Elizabeth had not, hence her ears perked up.

"Indeed?" was Elizabeth only response, not daring to glance at her husband, for she could sense his glower.

"Yes, indeed! So fat was he that he could not walk until well into his second year," she said, smiling at the memory—as if she could behold his plump little person even then. "He had rolls and rolls and *rolls* of fat—so fat that when at last he stood, his little legs bowed under the weight! His mother was beside herself in fear that they would never straighten out!"

The one truth Elizabeth knew was that Darcy did not suffer a pricking of his pride with any part of good humour. She knew it probable that even good Lady Millhouse could try his patience. This subject was of particular mortification in that of his many conceits, foremost was the well-proportioned muscularity of his figure (one of her particular pleasures as well). In a time when men did not scruple to wear a corset, even at five and thirty years he was justly proud of his trim physique and not of a mind to recollect himself otherwise. Elizabeth knew that likely. But what with Lady Millhouse's descriptive powers thoroughly employed (and possibly embellished), Elisabeth had to bite the inside of her cheek to keep from laughing whilst imagining that long-past roly-poly baby.

"Thank you, Lady Millhouse," said Darcy, "for those reminiscences. I am certain you overstate my early robustness." Then in a change of subject stunning in its facility, he said, "I understand your favourite hunter threw her first foal, does he look promising?"

"Yes, he is a fine one," said the lady, not taking the bait, but rather, immediately returning to her previous topic. "And what trouble Darcy's mother had getting him to make his water in the pot! His breeching was put off for an embarrassingly long time. Had his father not had the superior notion to tell him he could not sit a horse until he was out of petticoats, I fear he would be wearing them still!"

Darcy scowled that his attempt to reroute the conversation was in vain, but nonetheless gave another attempt. "Are you here to see to his prospects at the Brighton race-course?"

Before Lady Millhouse could respond to Darcy's question, Elizabeth, who had been endeavouring greatly to keep her countenance, burst out with laughter, then quickly covered her offending mouth with both hands. Lady Millhouse looked at her, but Elizabeth did not dare look to Darcy. He had stood abruptly and strode to the window, his dignity clearly bruised. She was chagrined—but only by half.

Lady Millhouse continued to talk on in the same manner and Elizabeth was uncertain whether she was oblivious to, or insensitive of, Darcy's dislike of her subject matter. But Elizabeth did observe her give a momentary glance toward him before retuning her attention back to Geoff, whom she had been entertaining with an assortment of faces and noises.

"Yes, young man, you are your father's son. No doubt that will be your enticement for good behaviour for him. Just lay out the chance of a horse in front of him and he will do your bidding," she poked him in the ribs and sent him to squirming and giggling.

"Darcy was on a horse by the time he was three. Did he tell you that, Elizabeth?" she continued. "I think not. That is the only accomplishment of his that exceeds his way with a horse—his reserve!"

Of her husband's many favourable attributes, his way with a horse and his taciturnity were not even in the top three, but on this point Elizabeth remained silent to her company. Initially she did not dare a peek in his direction, but after only a trice, did. He caught sight of her then and, for the briefest moment, returned her gaze. She made no response but to raise one eyebrow. That small expression had become a secret communication between them. When employed, it was a reminder of the intimacy of their connexion and, upon this occasion, of those virtues he owned known only to her. He then turned an ever deeper shade of crimson than the one that Lady Millhouse's reminiscences had provoked.

But as his horsemanship was the single conceit that Lady Millhouse could have invoked to return him to good humour, he lost his previous air of displeasure and did not quite smile, but made a small attempt at it.

"I am certain you exaggerate on that point as well on all the others you have employed today, Lady Millhouse," he said picking up Geoff.

To him, he said, "You shall out-pace your father in all things. Will you not, my boy?"

"Yes," said Elizabeth, "he will be repeating all the Responses by the time he is three, a full year after he takes a four-foot fence. But what of Janie? She may well be the one who inherits your horsemanship. What then?"

Darcy gave Geoff to Lady Millhouse and picked up Janie. To her he said, "You will learn to dance and play and sing and speak French. If you take a fence before your brother, I fear I shall never forgive you."

Lady Millhouse, now with Geoff attempting to stand in her lap, was in great satisfaction.

Said she, "I am certain if I have my way, young Geoff here may be the first on a horse, but Janie would not be second in proficiency."

With that both Elizabeth and Lady Millhouse shared a momentary gaze. Within that look was the understanding that they both felt alike in that sentiment. Darcy missed this exchange, for he had begun to take his daughter upon a turn around the room to a strain of music that only he could hear.

61

A Season Ignored

When love is strong, yea, even when love is not, the birth of a baby is both an inestimable blessing and a thankless bother. When into the lives of parents longing for but one child there are born two, it is reasonable to expect both labours and adulations to increase two-fold. As the Darcys' circumstances were more fortunate than most, little were they bothered with labours they did not solicit, hence they had ample time to enjoy their generative windfall. Regardless how often their father insisted their babies consisted of nothing but caterwauling at one end and unexpected discharges at the other, it was clear to his wife that he was absolutely smitten with them both.

Wisdom had told the Darcys that in face of the whispers surrounding the actions of various members of their family, they should hie unto London immediately after Easter to draw as many eyes, incite as much gossip, and disturb as many sensibilities as only those with incalculable wealth were given leave to do. Thanks to their new family, a compromise had been struck upon where to summer. Yet even without their presence in town, word had made its way to the *haut monde* of their double blessing. (Indeed, both Archbishops had sent congratulatory notes.) Darcy had told Elizabeth that in having birthed twins she had done the single service possible that could over-ride the speculation swirling around his and Georgiana's mysterious leave-taking across the water.

Once back at hearth and home, the Darcys were happy to bask in the glow of new parenthood—or at least Elizabeth basked; Darcy employed all his considerable resolve to appear aloof. Although she was not fooled by his ostensible reserve when it came to the pleasure he took in his children, neither was Elizabeth fully aware of just how foremost they were in Darcy's every reflection. It was unfortunate she was unwitting, for had she been, she would have been both pleased and uneasy. For he was uneasy—uneasy and apprehensive.

Darcy's world had once been inert, stubbornly fixed, revolving around Pemberley, its wants and needs, its consequence. Now his world was moveable, seemingly from day to day. It had fast become a wonder to Darcy how very quickly two separate souls could so compleatly redefine his interpretation of family. When once it had been embodied in but a single word—Pemberley—now that great estate was merely a single leg in his particular holy trinity—Pemberley, Elizabeth, children.

But just as marrying Elizabeth brought both unalloyed happiness and palpable fear that some misfortune might befall her, fatherhood brought the additional alarm that attends one who has much to lose. This alarm had, in that single heartbeat of a moment when his children were presented to him, increased three-fold. If Elizabeth doted on, and in turn, feared for, the well-being of her offspring, he did so in remarkably similar fashion. Elizabeth was much on the alert for immediate dangers; his worries only began there but scattered onto those eventual. Soon, his children would not keep to the nursery; they had taken them upon the road to Brighton. He had not meant for Elizabeth to learn that he was armed upon their journey. He had kept his pistol at hand, but out of sight. But he could, in no way, ever again take to the road with his family in any other manner. As husband, father, and master of his domain, he was not inclined, however, to expose his apprehension. That was unseemly. It was the duty of a man to weather the daily perturbations of keeping his family alive and healthy with all the aplomb he could collect. As a man confident in his manhood and bearing no small self-possession, anything less was unacceptable. At whatever cost, he would not give in to public disquietude. He would apportion that to Nurse and his children's mother. He would stand in silent watch over them all.

His ability to contain such cares, however, suffered inversely to the degree of his family's growth. As much as he admired the notion (indeed, to an unseemly degree) of fathering more children by his beloved Elizabeth, the thought of such a happy prospect occasionally unsettled him. It would be another soul to fear for, another heart to protect.

Highwaymen and disease were not the least of his worries, just the foremost. Although they paled in comparison to those ostensibly trivial ones of his intimate household, there were additional bothers that threatened—for all of the countryside was in general upheaval in the aftermath of the war. As Col. and Mrs. Fitzwilliam had witnessed at Bath, tens of thousands of former soldiers were returning to the labour market which quite overwhelmed the Tory government. Most of these men were not officers and not looking for work as dancing masters. They were labourers.

As a major landowner, the Darcys were, by obligation to their class, of Tory persuasion. The exceedingly poor harvests over the past few seasons had largely escaped them as their income came from some mining, but primarily from rents for sheep and other grazing. But it created a severe economic downturn in most of England and what with several decades of war, the interest payments on the national debt were so high that the government could do little to alleviate the suffering. The single decisive step Parliament took was to enact the Corn Laws designed to regulate the price of grain thus profiting those whose land grew grain. Regrettably, this decreased the price of everything but bread, the staple of the poor. And at this, the poor were unamused. Unamused and out of work, they rioted. They rioted most frequently and most vociferously in London and they did not wage their war against their own neighbours. They sallied forth into the West End and toward the homes of those who made their fortune from their land.

No, Mr. Darcy was happy not to take his family to London for the season. The season, it is said, knows no season, but to him, the season was as good as dead. He had only suffered it as such in the past to see Georgiana find a suitable match and be married. Now, smugly, he realised that he would have a nice, long respite from society. He would not have to weather it again until his children were of marriageable age.

Of the many weighty matters that were his to attend, one of particular repellence had remained unaddressed. Indeed, he had spent a great deal of time locating pressing matters to which to attend for some months until he could put off the most repugnant one no longer.

He had been forced to the conclusion, since independently verified through Lady Millhouse, that the despicable Wickham was the…yes he had to speak the word, to himself if to no one else…Wickham was the bastard son of his father. Wickham was his half-brother. (Repeating it silently in his mind did nothing to remove the unmitigated repellence of that fact.) He had accepted it with his understanding, but not his heart. Never in his heart.

Returning to Elizabeth compensated that ignominy amply. To have returned to her as mother of his children made all other worries tolerable. He struggled to keep that perspective. Wickham was, if there was justice in this world, lying in an unmarked grave in Belgium, noble warrior to the world, murdering maggot to all that was holy. After disclosing the entire sordid affair to Elizabeth, together they had decided a course. They would speak neither of Wickham's dishonour in battle nor his humiliating connexion to the Darcys to anyone. Ever.

It may have been thought that Darcy would perchance have had to reconsider his place and heritage in light of the revelation about Wickham being of his blood. And in doing so that would have been reflected in a lessening of his arrogance rather than the reverse. However, it did not. He now found himself obliged to make up for Wickham's degeneracy by his own comportment. When once his consideration of his hallowed position had softened under Elizabeth's influence, his hauteur was reinstated. At least it was reinstated insofar as his outward mien. He had the spectre of Wickham's degenerate nature to overcome and two children to guide by example. He would begin the reconstruction of his family's dignity forthwith.

Mrs. Darcy's Duty

The Darcys returned to Pemberley before their children turned one. That approaching anniversary brought other, more sombre recollections. The remembrance of Elizabeth's father's passing was one of considerable sadness, but it meant that their official mourning period would end, giving them leave to open Pemberley once again to one and all just in time for their children's first birthday.

Although he did not share them with her, Mrs. Darcy was not entirely unaware of her husband's concerns. But she was much occupied at the moment in her office as hostess under whose watch visiting ladies were not in want of coffee and muffins. As the lady of the manor, it was her habit to make herself the proprietress of hospitality. But as there was a great deal of disorder within England, upon the right occasion she would have been happy to find an excuse to enjoy the talk of gentlemen. Pemberley received newspapers from London regularly, but in the far county of Derbyshire any news of Parliament was sorely behindhand. Although intelligence was sparse, additional details could often be gleaned within the discourse of the landed gentry surrounding her husband.

Her forehead crinkled slightly as she thought of what she might be missing. But, as was her duty, she sat amongst the ladies reminding herself that it was Sunday, so even the talk of men must be mundane. Albeit, this Sunday was one of particular note. It had been especially set aside to officially introduce their offspring to the neighbourhood. Elizabeth had planned for the event with extraordinary care. So keen was her desire to present her children to their greatest advantage, she secured an over-sized wicker carriage from London in which to display them. Satin ruching covered the cowl and Austrian lace strewn with salmon ribands was so abundant about the edges, it was clear that Elizabeth found herself much more pleased with frippery when it promoted her precious ones. But despite the fuss and bother, like all best laid expectations, things did not go according to plan.

Janie was, as usual, quite placid, but Geoff kept crawling about and spoiling the well-thought-out arrangement. This, of course, provoked no little tsk-tsking from the grey-haired fusspots long past embarrassment by their own children's misbehaviour. It was not a matter of forgetting herself, Elizabeth simply could not stop herself from gifting a glower in the direction of the scolding noises. Thus chastened, the audible disapproval ceased. Satisfied, Elizabeth resettled her son and straightened the bow under Janie's chin. Nothing so insignificant as small-minded matrons could dampen her pride in them, or her spirits.

As any parent could guess, however, on the one day when the most eyes were upon them, the Darcys' usually amicable children were not inclined to suffer company. Geoff's attempt at escape was but the half of it. For every chuck under their chins became an ever escalating pique. More might have been made of their ill-temper had not by happy chance the Darcys been of such fine repute. Hence, this lack of friendly compliance by the tiny guests of honour did nothing to quash the admiration the twins garnered save for those few who were determined to find fault on general principle. Having silenced that small group with her disapproving look, Elizabeth stood over the carriage and basked in the singular pleasure of hearing nothing but compliments for her children. She would have liked to know her husband took note of their success, but his mind seemed otherwise engaged. She could not catch his gaze once.

Even with Nurse's help, Elizabeth had her hands full keeping the twins' costumes straight and their chins wiped. Eventually, she altogether gave up her attempt to keep them settled in the carriage. She plopped little Janie into the nearest friendly lap and looked about to see where young Geoff had crawled. She quickly spotted Margaret in an all-out pursuit of him across the lawn. He was in petticoats and occasionally tangled with the hem, but was making good time in that he had all four appendages in full use and Nurse had but two. With great dispatch her charge managed to reach, and thereby trespass, into the gentlemen's sanctuary. Much to Nurse's horror, she could not quite catch hold of the tail of his frock to haul him back—he was far too quick.

Indeed, quite without warning Mr. Darcy was assaulted from behind by way of a colossal yank upon his coat. It was a sizeable enough tug to cause him to take a step back just to offset it. Fortunately, Darcy was nimble enough to regain both his footing and his composure without trampling his son, but this insult caused a collective gasp of astonishment to erupt from the witnesses. Mr. Darcy, however, gave little notice of this violation of his person beyond resituating his lapels. Without comment or a downward glance, he then resumed his office of the recipient of generalized obsequiousness. To the delight of those few brave souls who dared venture to look, a peek revealed the culprit of this *lèse majestè* as a dark-haired babe standing tenaciously by clinging to his father's coattail. Still in leg-swaying triumph, the baby grinned happily, wholly unaware of his colossal breach of decorum. He clung determinedly to the tail of his father's frock-coat, seemingly disinclined to loose himself from the means by which he had struggled to his feet. As Darcy refused to acknowledge this new accessory to his costume, a few gentlemen found need to scratch their noses or cover a small cough, but not a soul dared to laugh.

And because by then Margaret was so wholly mortified, she stood in a hands-extended dither, uncertain just how to rectify the situation. Geoff remained attached to his father and his father continued to ignore that he was, indeed, there. It thereby fell to Mrs. Darcy who had come lately upon the scene of this felonious behaviour to daintily extricate her husband's frock-coat from their son's clenched little grasp. Although he was the perpetrator, Geoff was most displeased to be rescued from this ignominy and began to bawl. As Elizabeth hustled him off, she explained to those still taken with interest of the incident, as only mothers are wont to do, that the child was much overdue for a nap.

"Shall I take him, m'lady?" said Nurse.

She did not wait for a reply before taking him into her plump arms. And as his howls of outrage faded into the distance, those ladies not previously under Mrs. Darcy's custody re-shouldered their sagging parasols and with heads together formed a small pavilion where they could natter about unruly children without fearing for their complexions.

With Mr. Darcy's imperiousness fully re-employed, the men resumed their talk. And again, without ever altering his expression, Mr. Darcy occasionally offered a contributing nod.

As for Mrs. Darcy, as Nurse swept her son away off to his nap, she returned to Janie who was behaving herself in a manner befitting one who even at that tender age knew that she was a Darcy. Upon gazing at that tiny, decorous countenance, Elizabeth rewarded her with a quick but tender kiss. Janie's expression was so solemnly familiar that she gave herself leave to steal a backward glance at her husband. There seemed to be no lasting havoc from her son's little adventure. Once that had been determined, her gaze lingered. She admired the broad expanse of her husband's back with some leisure. She had no fear she would be caught by him in this open veneration for his figure, knowing full well that he would not return her gaze. But that was of little consequence. He was in company. He did not expose his private inclinations to others.

That her pleasure at that moment was singular did not diminish it in the least.

It was long understood that when Mr. Darcy sent his cards out for an afternoon's entertainment, unlike some more convivial hosts, the invitation did not extend beyond dusk. The shadows had by then lengthened ominously and the air grew chill. The looming night would drive even their most diligent friends to call for their carriages. Although she was far more sociable than her husband, Elizabeth was quite happy for their guests to depart. As she gave one last pert look over her shoulder, she betokened a generous, if subtle, sigh. But then, she seldom looked upon her husband's virile figure with other than unadulterated adoration.

As for her son's modest insult upon his father's sizable dignity, Nurse may have, but she fretted not. She knew that had her husband been truly displeased, he would have bowed with exaggerated courtesy rather than appear oblivious. Unlike his wife, who delighted in anything ridiculous, he was excruciatingly grave when confronted by indecorous behaviour even when it involved his children. The thought of it all made her laugh—but only to herself.

On this occasion her laugh was accompanied by a regret. To behold her son's first wobbly attempt to stand had been a treasured moment and yet she only shared that instant with Nurse. Although Darcy was the means by which it was exacted, the moment was forever lost to him. She lamented that loss on his behalf and then wondered if to do so was maudlin. Were fathers to take sentimental note of such milestones? Or more to the point, did Darcy? His moods were of late so unpredictable that it could be quite perplexing to endeavour to determine just what turn his inclinations might take.

As she gained the shade of the loggia, the increasing chill gave her a shiver. Elizabeth longed for the night with even greater anticipation. It would only be with the dark that the tender feelings Darcy spent his days endeavouring to deny would have any opportunity to be coaxed forth. Their history suggested that the more repressed his emotions, the more explosive their release. This day had required far more than even his accustomed reserve. That was a tantalizing prospect.

She would enjoy what time they had in quiet, for it would soon be a precious commodity. She had received a post from her mother say that she would be arriving within the week. And she would be bringing Lydia with her.

A Momentous Event at Rosings

Sitting quite erect, Lady Catherine occupied a well-used wing chair that rested in the precise centre of a long corridor. The chair was upholstered in crimson caffoy and amongst the other rather splendid furnishings, it alone looked a bit worn. Although it sagged, it did so with a kind of withered majesty—one of the same sort that graced the countenance of its distinguished occupant. But as the chair appeared quite comfortable, there the similarity ended. For so forbidding was the lady's figure, the opulence of the room strewn with statuary and ormolu struggled to maintain its impact.

Her finger drummed with great determination. And if the drumming did not, the look of unamused apprehension Lady Catherine bore betrayed her usual hauteur. Clearly, her ladyship awaited an event of some import. But, one of a particular nature. Hence, curious of the outcome they may have been, every soul within the walls of Rosings was of the discipline to make no acknowledgment of the event. This was no small tenacity, for the portentous proceedings unfolded just beyond the enormous oak double doors directly in front of Lady Catherine's chair. A tall clock stood in an alcove, chimes silenced. Even mice cowered in the crevices, none having the brass to dart across the edge of her carpet. It was as if the house itself was as transfixed as was her ladyship. Indeed, the shadowed niches of the cavernous hall revealed several servants practicing the art of unobtrusiveness with meticulous care.

Henry, the parrot, sat on his perch in the corner maliciously eyeing the gathering—but even he was silent. The single exception was an otherwise undistinguished footman who cleared his throat of an annoying tickle. When he did, Lady Catherine did not turn in his direction, but her drumming finger stopt. Then, it recommenced, giving the footman leave to understand such insubordination would not be tolerated. His rasping throat, however, threatening to erupt into a cough, he subtly began pulling a pocket-square from his sleeve. With even greater delicacy, he stuffed the whole of it into his mouth.

All quiet once again, shadows slowly marched across the floor. So deeply did they intrude, a skulking figure broke rank. Yewdell drew his resin torch like a sword, pranced the length of the room as if a lancer of the 17th addressing each candelabra as he went. Grand as Rosings was, its mistress bore a parsimonious streak. Hence, the renewing of light that was burdened by the candle tax was not a good sign to those servants who had begun to admire the thought of their beds. Returned to his station, Yewdell stifled a yawn. There may have been an inward sigh from the others, but little more. Although the night looked to be long, nary a head dared droop so long as her ladyship was still at her post.

Lady Catherine had no, nor did she expect, company upon this watch. Irritably, she looked about and saw amongst the statuary another one of Beecher's ornately framed (and altogether abysmal) water-colours.

"Anne's doing, no doubt," she sniffed (making a mental note to have it removed and burnt).

As Lord Beecher held little interest in what jewels of wisdom his mother-in-law had to offer, she saw little worth in Beecher. Other than a fourth at cards in those long evenings at home with Anne and Mrs. Jenkinson, she would have seen him as she did most every other man of her acquaintance—a compleat waste of manhood. He was, however, a fast worker. That conclusion came by way of Lady Anne not only sporting a fiancé, but a womb half-gone with child by the time they left Bath. In light of Lady Catherine's attentiveness to all that was decorous, it might have been expected that she would have been most unhappy to learn that her daughter had leapt the nuptial broomstick prior to her wedding day.

However, upon this specific occasion, she was not.

Indeed, she was pleased as punch to confirm that the breeding stock of a lord that she had purchased was not merely fertile, but motile as well. It would have been untidy to have to rid Anne of Beecher after the wedding—not to mention the time that would be lost upon obtaining a pregnancy. But that had not come to pass. She congratulated herself upon the thoroughness of her investigations of Beecher's prolificacy. He had serviced her daughter with unrivalled efficiency. Indeed, from what the servants reported to her, her daughter's solemn demeanour hid a libido of some magnitude. Lady Catherine had been more bemused than offended to learn of it.

"Well, just when one thought there no more surprises to be found in this world," Lady Catherine had reflected in the darkness of her bed-chamber, "one learns that Anne's little love-cranny is just as cock-smitten as any scullery-maid's."

Although Beecher had been secured for Anne by the time Lady Catherine had learnt the extent of his gambling debts, she was not prepared to call foul in the matrimonial sweepstakes. As she saw it, holding that information gave her the whip-hand over her son-in-law. She secretly paid off his creditors, thereby becoming his true obligator. She could sic the dogs of the bailiff upon him at her own will—*that* was a handsome thought, indeed. There would be little meddling from him when she put her plan into play for her grandchild. So long as she held the financial reins, he would back her every move. Moreover, money properly applied would cinch his compleat compliance—perhaps even his assistance.

If there was one thing she had learnt in her life, it was that there were few sorrows in which a good income is of no avail.

Lord Winton Beecher was not about this evening. Everyone in the house knew he was in London—but only Lady Catherine knew he was gambling at Boodle's. She cared little. The proprietor would only allow his losses to reach a level of her determination before his credit was halted. She looked in the direction of the clock once again. Only on the half-hour did she allow herself a glance to reckon the time. It was with dispassion that Yewdell observed the hands of the clock as they slowly circled. And it was with no little irony that he realised that the swinging of the clock's pendulum acquiesced to the mistress's will, keeping time to the beat of Lady Catherine's drumming finger rather than the reverse.

When all thought they would run mad from the interminable wait, the drumming ceased. The lady struck her stick but once, but it landed with a resounding thud upon the floor. At the cracking blow of her stick, all uniformly gave a start, punctuated by a great gasp—and the parrot went into a flapping frenzy, startling everyone out of their stupor. Even Lady Catherine's perversely persistent patience had had enough. (When the silence was finally ruptured, that it was pertinacious Lady Catherine who finally broke it was more startling than the act itself.) Unfortunately, the footman who had the whole of the pocket-square stuffed in his mouth gasped too. He began to turn the colour of a boiled beet, further distraught as to whether to break his stand and extract that which was choking the life from him thus enduring his lady's displeasure or dying on the spot—in Rosings, 'twas no quick decision. Yewdell cut his eyes in the footman's direction daring him to suffocate.

The strangled footmen let out a small, gurgling cough, all others gulped in anticipation, but still the door did not open. This, a unique occurrence for few things did not yield to Lady Catherine de Bourgh's wrath.

Lady Catherine's finger paused atop her stick, her eyes fluttering in exasperation. Just then, as if bidden by the huge Javanese gong sitting quietly in the corner, Dr. Brumfitt threw back both doors, and strode momentously into the corridor. Whilst still wiping his hands, he initiated a small ceremony. Stepping back he hid the bloody rag behind his back and swept his freshly wiped hand in the direction of an equally be-stained nurse who had followed in his wake. Now the centre of all notice, the nurse made an awkward, off-balance curtsy. In her arms lay a squirming, swaddled bundle. She raised the child before her ladyship as if a gift from the Magi.

With a self-conscious flourish, Dr. Brumfitt bowed, saying, "Lady Catherine, your grandchild!"

For one whose arthritic hip had been the subject of a great deal of complaint, Lady Catherine came to her feet most expeditiously. She nodded once, abruptly turned, and with great purpose, carried herself down the corridor. She neither peered at the infant nor took notice of the silence from the room from whence the surgeon had emerged.

Simultaneous to her leave, the enormous beads of perspiration that had formed at his hairline began to seep down his face.

Standing quite still, Dr. Brumfitt closed his eyes and drew a deep, heartfelt breath of stagnant air and mopped his brow. It was not his place to prophesy. He could only praise God above that Lady Catherine believed he had done well seeing that her grandchild survived such a troubled birth. If Lady Catherine spoke no question of it, he was beyond caring the fate of Lady Anne.

64

One Husband— Must Wear Regimentals and Have an Open Mind

For the duration of Wickham's deployment, Lydia and her sons had resided with her parents at Longbourn. As she was, at best, an inattentive mother, this was not a particularly happy arrangement for anyone but her. Yet it had been propitious that she was with them when word of Wickham's valorous death arrived, for when she first learnt of her husband's demise she was very nearly inconsolable. She wailed, wept, and tore at her clothing with such vehemence that her mother feared she might do herself harm. However untenable her marriage had become, at that moment she truly believed that she had loved Wickham more than any living thing (well, save herself—she was grief-stricken, not mad).

Still too bereft to stand, she had herself wheeled directly to church. In that Lydia had not seen the inside of a church since she had lived under her father's roof, her family was quite astonished that her very first inclination had been ecclesiastical, certain that she went thither to beg for her husband's immortal soul. If they were of that opinion, Lydia did not choose to correct their misapprehension, for she had, in fact, had a religious reawakening between the house and the nave. Indeed, as she knelt her thoughts *were* of Wickham. But, she did not offer appeals upon his behalf. Rather, she gave thanks to God above for answering her prayers for Wickham's death. (She gave thanks for that in general and the cannon shot that felled him in particular.) Once that had been done, she guiltlessly hied for home.

Her enjoyment of the blessing of her husband's obliteration was sweet. But quite soon that giddiness was superseded by an even greater delight. For it was customary for the members of the brigade of a fallen comrade to pay their respects to his family. When first she beheld their regimentals in her mother's parlour, she all but swooned. Fortuitously, this discomposure was mistaken for grief and she was rushed her mother's smelling salts. She only allowed herself to be revived by the visage of the handsomest of the officer's kneeling before her waving the salts-bottle beneath her nose.

Having been prest into widow's weeds to mourn for a man of whom she thought very little in life, Lydia saw him much improved in death. She took an officer upon each arm and allowed them to take her upon turns about their park. Whilst she strolled, she touched a pocket-square to the corner of her eye at regular intervals. She thought it quite fitting that at last she found a redeeming virtue in her husband—his fellow officers.

Her good fortune was very nearly met by theirs in not having actually been acquainted with Wickham. They were, therefore, relieved of the necessity of outright lies in finding some good quality of his to praise. These were Whitehall garrisoned officers, many second sons of the aristocracy who gained their rank and their situation through their well-placed connexions. They assumed that because Wickham had been an officer, he was therefore, a gentleman. Thereby they spoke reverently of his courage and respectfully of his honour. For her part, Lydia did remarkably well conveying the correct portion of grief and determined pluck to be believable. Time and opportunity, however, obliged her to become less innocent. There would be only so many days in which and so many officers in whom she could find a replacement for Wickham.

Never the sharpest tool in the shed, even she knew that she had erred mightily in running off with Wickham. (Many a time she groused to herself of un-bought cows and free milk.) The bloom had been off Wickham's rose long before the birth of their first child. Wickham was nothing more than a bounder and a cad. She had grieved for him, in her way, long before she learnt of his death. Regrettably, the lesson that she learnt was only a singular one. She knew that she had erred with Wickham specifically, but did not see that her admiration for the shallower traits of mankind were at fault. Her goal was still regimentals without due consideration to what sort of man's shoulders they adorned. She was, however, astute enough to know if obtaining another officer for a husband was her aim, the time was nigh—such a fertile pool would not be found soon again.

What with people dying right and left, she had been much occupied by mourning and had to hastily practice her rusty flirting skills. Through constant study of her looking-glass though, she perfected a gaze that was half-hidden behind her fan—one which told her comforter that she just might, in spite of her grief, desire him. Her countenance bore a combination of trepidation and fevered despair which rendered the officers *quite* sympathetic. (She exuded just enough fevered despair to put colour in the pallor of her cheeks—she had abandoned actual weeping in that it made her eyes red and her nose run.) She chatted and coquetted quite at her leisure.

Soon, however, most of the other officers tired of observing that Mrs. Wickham's charms did not extend beyond her frontal development and drifted away. They found amusement in the country town of Meryton beyond one semi-grief-stricken hoyden lacking and went on to pay their respects to other deserving widows. Two young gentlemen were more lenient in their diversions and stayed behind. For disparate reasons, they called upon Lydia each day. These young officers were unique in having claimed an actual acquaintance with Wickham. (As there were few amongst his acquaintance whom Wickham did not persuade to loan him money, Lydia was initially a bit wary.) Soon, however, she was convinced that it was her charms alone which Captain Knapper and Major Kneebone admired.

Although they came together, these two officers were as opposite as men could be. Knapper was handsome in his regimentals, but Major Kneebone gave them little distinction. Moreover, Kneebone was not only plain-featured, but, at least in Captain Knapper's company, a bit timid—an attribute that Lydia deplored. The witty and affable Captain Knapper was her particular friend. It was difficult to enjoy his charms properly whilst Major Kneebone skulked about; therefore, Lydia was not above bullying Kitty into entertaining him. But as Kitty was well-employed with her own romance, she was often uncooperative. Hence, in order to be alone with the dashing Captain Knapper, Lydia did not scruple to sneak out of the house to meet with him. The stories he told her and the promises he made were to her wholly credible. It was as if she was once again that desirable, young girl and not a betrayed, and finally bewidowed, wife.

Although Wickham had been the consummate philanderer, revenging herself on him in kind had been only briefly fulfilling.

She had learnt a difficult lesson—for Wickham may have been quick with words of love and alluring touches, but in bed he served only himself. Other than their very first couplings which saw her innocent and easily pleased, her satisfaction thereafter had been accidental. Long disdaining Mr. Darcy's correctness, she was eventually learned enough at love to know that her sister was being pleased in ways that she had been slighted. Lydia was less of a sensual nature than just simply libidinous. Having not had the pleasure of any kind of manly attention in some time, she found herself lifting her skirts with undue haste.

When it looked as if she would have a second chance at finding a husband, it had been her design to do better than Wickham. But, she had vastly underestimated just how hungry she had become for sexual reward. As her vulnerability to the allure of regimentals was well-known, she believed that she could not be wholly at fault for succumbing as she had once again. Lydia told herself this so many times that quite soon she believed that she owned no part of what had come to pass.

She had been seduced.

She had been seduced, but she hoped not abandoned. When Captain Knapper was so urgently called away upon some important regimental duties, he had said he would return forthwith and, after a suitable period of mourning, they would be wed.

Of all this, however, Jane and Elizabeth had been unwitting. By the time these two officers decamped from Meryton, the sisters had breathed a sigh of relief. They had been wholly aghast at Lydia's vulgar flirtatiousness, but Elizabeth's impending birth sent them home. As the trail of officers coming to call had all but stopt, they had believed Lydia would be saved from herself. They soon learnt they were sorely mistaken when Mary apprised them that Lydia "had the morning sickness."

Mary had written of it all to Jane, as she was the oldest sister. (Mrs. Bennet still took to her bed.) It was Jane who endeavoured to make Lydia an honest woman by employing a method of counting that somehow rendered her with child by her dead husband. But facts were facts, and a half-year after she last was in Wickham's company, Lydia was three-months gone. As it is far easier to feign pregnancy than disguise it, Lydia admired Jane's mathematics and continued with the ruse that she was further along than she actually was. All knew, however, that it was imperative that she be rousted out of Hertfordshire and into the obscurity of London until after the baby was born.

Whilst continuing with the fiction of who fathered her child, Lydia had surreptitiously written to the true culprit advising him of her situation. However, she had met with little success. When at last a response was sent, it was not from Knapper at all. Major Hugh Kneebone arrived in Cheapside, full of concern and deep regret on behalf of his friend, whom he had thought was a gentleman. He brought Lydia a letter from Knapper, the contents of which he was clearly witting. It apprised Lydia that Knapper was promised to another and offered her his best wishes.

"So," said Lydia after reading his missive. "So," she repeated wretchedly.

Lydia had dropped the letter and it had wafted to the floor at her feet. Kneebone caught it and attempted to hand it back to her, but she shook her head and drew her hands to her face.

"What shall I do?" she wept piteously. "Where shall I go? My aunt cannot keep us here forever. I shall be forced into the streets with my child!"

If this ploy for sympathy would have been a bit obvious to the casual listener, it was not to poor, bewitched Kneebone. As Lydia prest her tear-streaked face upon his chest (and ran her finger temptingly around the frog-closure of his military jacket), Kneebone found himself quite touched by her wretchedness. Although he professed himself quite ready to leave her to her despair, Lydia insisted he come and sit upon the sofa with her until her heart palpitations had ceased. She allowed him to pat her hand for a spell, but soon picked up the knitting needles from a workbox and commenced to click them as if to add a row to a tiny bonnet (one begun by her aunt and never until then touched by Lydia). This tender sight touched the deepest reaches of Kneebone's tender heart and he was loathe to leave her alone.

This little scene was not unknown to him. He had stood by and watched helplessly as Knapper had left legions of women similarly interfered with in his wake. If they had not been in Lydia's exact predicament, it was not for the want of his trying. When at last the Major took his leave, he had already formed an attachment for this little innocent dove—so in want of a hero to save her from disgrace—precisely as Lydia had planned. She had bid him *adieu* with the recollection of the tear perched upon her dewy cheek (whatever her faults, Lydia took great care of her complexion) to stay with him until next they met. As she put that cheek forward for him to peck her good-bye, Lydia also managed to display a fairly good vantage of her appurtenances. This ploy was but one in her coquetry arsenal (which included wetted petticoats and undersized bodices) and she was quite witting that it had done its office.

Presently, Lydia received a letter from the Major, asking if he might call again upon her. She very nearly whooped aloud. Although it was unapparent to those dearest to her, Lydia was not the simpleton that she once had been. Her humour had entirely left her when she realised that she had once again been left a fool by mistaking a Lothario for a lover. She was pragmatic enough to realise that with four children, finding a man who was willing to take her in wedlock would become increasingly difficult. She was bent on not being left wholly out to dry once again and set her sights upon the only man eligible and naïve enough to want her.

When Lydia wrote to Kneebone in return, she asked him a particular favour. She told him that it was necessary to betake herself to the London lodgings she lately habituated with Wickham to retrieve and catalogue his effects. It was all her poor husband had left her and it was urgent that she turn them into funds for her keep. Ever the gentleman, Kneebone was happy to accompany her thither. These apartments had been far beyond the Wickhams' financial reach and although Lydia did her best to persuade him otherwise, the landlord demanded payment before allowing release of the belongings. That took a considerable portion, but still remaining were a pair of duelling pistols in a rosewood box, a pair of brass spurs, several pair of braces, and a collection of risqué snuffboxes. Lydia professed great regret at having to part with them, but Kneebone saw them put up for auction which brought her near a hundred guineas.

Having him aid her in her endeavours was a stroke of genius upon Lydia's part. By the time it had all been taken care of, Kneebone was quite accustomed to seeing to Lydia and was so compleatly smitten with her (and her adorable little daughter), that he proposed to hold that office from that day forward. Far from believing himself taken advantage of, he could not quite believe his good fortune in finding a ready-made family. That he, Hugh Kneebone, gangly of leg and long of chin, could merit such a match was of unrivalled bliss. Lydia, to him, was the loveliest, most vivacious vixen that ever the world had seen. He cared not who went before him, he was only in want of her upon his arm to make his happiness compleat. As she had not been entirely forthcoming about just how many children she had, her family liked him even more for not breaking the engagement when he was lately apprised.

Lydia, of course, did not return his affection. His only attributes appeared to be his regimentals and a willingness to wed her. She wept buckets the night before the wedding, praying for God to take her lest she have to surrender herself to her new husband's detestable bed.

However abhorrent Lydia may have thought her new husband before their wedding, her opinion had quite altered by the next Sunday. Her bridegroom had been adamant that they attend church, but Lydia fell fast asleep in the middle of the sermon. So satisfactorily did she snore that any wife within earshot thought Kneebone not half so homely as they did before. Indeed, contented at last, Lydia would have whole-heartedly agreed.

The Painting

Sir Robert Morland sat in his coach as it once again rumbled upon the road to Pemberley. Swaying to and fro as the carriage made its way over, under, and through various sized puddles of mud, he impatiently tapped the enormous ruby ring adorning his forefinger against the window whilst imagining what lay ahead. He was not merely anxious, he was all but giddy with anticipation.

It had been both a disastrous and roundly exhilarating experience when last he hied to Derbyshire. The likeness he had taken of Mrs. Darcy had been excellent—his best to date. Therefore, he had been much desirous of putting it on exhibit in London. Mr. Darcy had forbidden the notion out of hand. He paid for the painting and it fell to his discretion where it would and would not be seen. Morland had fairly gone into hysterics. He had ranted and raved, he had wept and pouted, but to no avail. Mr. Darcy was implacable upon the subject. Sir Morland left in a snit, intending to throw himself off the first available cliff.

Mr. Darcy was not so chary of his wife's image that he refused it to be seen—quite the opposite. Every visitor to Pemberley was led first through the portrait gallery, Mrs. Darcy's portrait prominently displayed. Clearly, Mr. Darcy was proud of the likeness, he simply desired dominion over whose eyes were privy to it. Because visitors to Pemberley were many, eventually word of this masterpiece had escaped. To Morland's everlasting delight, its prominence only improved with every retelling. But that had been five years ago and he was much in want of a new commission to enhance his already stunning curriculum vitae.

Hence, when he had seen Miss Georgiana Darcy, now Mrs. Col. Fitzwilliam, in his own hometown of Bath and learnt that the beautiful Mrs. Darcy had given birth, he was immediately intrigued. She was a comely woman, and although her husband could be rather menacing, the man had regular features and was of quite masculine build. Their offspring could not be other than of the most handsome sort. It would not even be necessary for him to walk that purgatorial line between authenticity and flattery to render a painting of them his magnum opus. The recollection of the quarrel that he had partaken in loomed over him like a behemoth. Would Mr. Darcy be forgiving? Sir Morland recalled quite clearly that Mrs. Darcy had said that she intended to have a family portrait done to hang in the portrait gallery one day. His feelings for and about ever returning to Pemberley had unquestionably altered.

Gulping a huge helping of crow, he took pen to paper. He wrote to Mrs. Darcy (not Mr. Darcy—no, never) offering his services once again. Her reply was swift and favourable. They were to be at Brighton for several months and asked him to come immediately to Pemberley upon their return. Once again, he eschewed his policy of having his patron come to his studio in Bath. Indeed, so happy to endure such travail was he that he had very nearly leapt for joy at the prospect. To have his pocket richly rewarded and the privilege of enhancing his own reputation interested all his dearest emotions. The only possible bugbear to disturb him was whether Mrs. Darcy's countenance had maintained its bloom. Betimes motherhood was less than kind to one's charms. To have birthed two infants could not possibly have benefited her complexion. If that was the case, he could always refer to his original portrait of her for direction. If need be, he could employ his unparalleled talents to render her unto canvas in a form befitting his considerable genius.

Indeed, from what he understood, there was to be a precipitous increase within the ranks of the aristocracy. Next to the royal family, those were his very favourite kind of people.

In the months after Napoleon's return to exile, the Darcy family and its immediate circle had proliferated beyond a recognisable number. Pemberley's august halls were now laden with squeals and squalls and all manner of ruckus from a pair of toddlers who were seldom disposed to be shushed. Adding to near anarchy was a gaggle of nieces and nephews who grew so fast and were in and out with such rapidity, Mr. Darcy not only failed to remember their names, he doubted he could identify with any accuracy just which of his relatives were their parents.

Had that not been test enough, Mrs. Bennet was to come to Pemberley. This visit was inevitable, but her lengthy observation of mourning had allowed Elizabeth to avoid that pesky little disagreement over a wet-nurse. Mrs. Bennet would only know that she had employed one, but not that Lizzy was the babies' primary source of nourishment. Elizabeth had been fully prepared to weather her disapproval, but fate intervened by way of the early set of teeth precociously grown by her son. When he began employing those teeth during feeding, Elizabeth concluded with the utmost rapidity that he was old enough to be weaned onto a cup. As he was quite happy to use a cup except when he saw his sister doing otherwise, they concluded that Janie would be weaned at the same time. Thus when she arrived, Mrs. Bennet would be denied the opportunity to engage in a fit of nerves over the matter and Mrs. Littlepage continued on as a second nurse.

Also soon to be on hand was Lydia, who, at last upon the arm of a husband not entirely repugnant to them, was happy for the Darcys to send a coach for her. Darcy had been surprisingly good-humoured about the prospect of having Mrs. Bennet and Lydia under his roof once again. If Elizabeth attributed this new-found magnanimity to a general relaxing of his usual hauteur, she was to be disappointed. Happy he was for Elizabeth's sister to come to Pemberley rather than to have his wife on the road to London. He would endure any inanity if it meant his wife was safe at home. Still, he steeled himself to endure what would certainly be Lydia's continued impetuosity.

"Pray, why does she engage in such rash behaviour?"

Elizabeth shook her head, "One may as well inquire, 'why does the canary sing?' Who knows what is behind any of Lydia's actions? I do believe that we have abused her so often for it that she has quite given up being a flirt for simply yielding on the spot."

Indeed, when they arrived home from Brighton, they had not fully come to an agreement on just how, or even who, would betake themselves to London to see to Lydia. As much as he loathed the entire notion, Darcy had been fully prepared to undertake the office of corralling Lydia himself if it meant Elizabeth would be out of harm's way. But by happy chance before that particular fence was taken, a post arrived announcing Lydia's upcoming nuptials. Although they chose not to attend, the wedding gift they sent with their best wishes was substantial enough to leave Lydia quite happy for them to plead their regrets. In the Gardiners' estimation, Lydia's suitor was a very reliable gentleman of the highest sort. Everyone was astonished that she could be so practical as to marry a man who would actually be a good husband, but they questioned it not (employing the axiom of "not looking a gift horse in the mouth").

Robert Morland entered into this bedlam in quite the same temper he had before. He was accompanied by two assistants, five trunks, and no good word for anyone. When last he came to Derbyshire, he had been in great anticipation of whether Mrs. Darcy's beauty had been exaggerated. Once again he was most anxious to see to see if her beauty had waned and if the aspects of his newest subjects would rival their mother's.

As before, the Darcys had arranged for him to set up his paints in a northern-facing sitting-room. He left his men to see to those arrangements and immediately requested an audience with all the Darcy family members whom he was to paint. He was ushered forthwith into Mr. Darcy's study. Mr. Darcy was standing next to a large, ornately carved, mahogany desk with his hands folded behind his back. His stance suggested that his disposition had not altered after a half-dozen years. As he had before, he did not meet Sir Morland mid-most in the room, but stood with his chin elevated with impervious disdain and one large foot foremost, waiting for Morland to come before him. Although he seldom allowed himself to be humbled in any man's presence, Morland was so eager for this commission that he veritably scurried the length of the room and executed a graceful, low bow.

"Mr. Darcy," said he.

"Sir Morland," Mr. Darcy replied.

That was the extent of their exchange, for then through the door arrived Mrs. Darcy. She was as lovely as he had remembered and was accompanied by two nurses and two babies. Upon spying them, Morland took a great, gasping inhalation. He clasped his hands before him and then looked heavenward, whereupon he closed his eyes and silently mouthed a prayer of thanks. He was altogether delighted at their tiny aspects.

So delighted was Morland that he could not help but gush, "Had your children been paupers, Mr. Darcy, they would still be called exceptionally handsome!"

Mildly offended but uncertain as to why, Mr. Darcy said (with his usual effusiveness), "Yes."

Sir Morland had not waited for Mr. Darcy's reply, for he had headed directly toward the children, arms outstretched before him. To the Darcys' distress, he looked for all the world as if he were going to take one of them into his arms. As neither of the twins took easily to strangers, Elizabeth reached out and grasped one of the painter's hands and began vigorously to shake it. That lured Morland from his quarry long enough for him to regain his composure.

"We are happy that you approve, Sir Morland," Elizabeth said dryly.

But Morland heard her not, his painterly eye was already taking an assessment of his subjects. He immediately saw that both children had eyes the precise shade of ripe hazelnuts as their father's. And like his as well, both of their eyes were encircled by a tangle of dark lashes. Although they were fair-skinned, both had very dark hair—but more brown than black. He then began to circle them, more like a cat and its prey than painter and subject. Their eyes widened as he moved about them, Janie warily putting her two middle fingers in her mouth—the better to take his measure. Suddenly, he gave a great clap of his hands, announcing, "Pray, take me to my paints! I must have my paints!"

Wordlessly, Darcy effected the smallest flick of his head toward the door and a footman moved forward, bowed to Sir Morland, and swung a graceful, gloved hand in the direction of the door. Morland flung his cape over his shoulder, nodded once each to Mr. and Mrs. Darcy, and pranced from the room.

"Well," said Elizabeth, "it begins."

"Yes," replied her husband.

Sally Frances, One Step Closer to the Truth

Fortune is a mighty queer thing. All you know about it for certain is that it's bound to change. Sally Frances Arbuthnot had learnt that lesson well as she had spied on the Darcy house in Mayfair. It had been a tedious business standing outside the wall surrounding that grand house, hoping against hope to strike up a conversation with one of the servants.

Luck had played a better portion than chance that Daisy Mulroney had been familiar with where the Darcy family was domiciled in London. That her long-dead brothers had both been employed by that family had been more than fortuitous, it had been a god-send. Daisy was altogether vague when Sally inquired after her kin, saying only that they were older than she and she did not know them well. But had Sally not been privy to that titbit of information, she would have had either to walk or to beg a ride all the way to Derbyshire to uncover the pertinent facts she sought. Few were unacquainted with the loose-lipped rattling that servitors of great houses were disposed, and she thought it possible that she just might uncover in town what had befallen her brother. Then if she chose to travel all the way to Derbyshire, it would be at her leisure. Although she would have given her life to kneel at his grave, she did not hold out hope that John's last resting place was in England.

New Oxford Street, legend had it, was the "great divide" between the haves and the have-nots. Once Sally passed it and headed toward those nobs of the West End, she automatically smoothed the front of her apron. The street sign was the actual demarcation, but just as certain was an alteration in habitués. On her side of Oxford Street, urchins chased coal waggons, fighting over those pieces that the uneven cobbles had joggled from the sideboards. To the west the streets were not only clean of hoards of scavengers, they were swept clean as a freshly scoured stoop. It was as if the horses that drew the fine coaches waited to relieve themselves until they had left the West End. So certain was she of this notion, Sally pondered how one went about training a horse to befoul on command. She did not doubt there were men employed by these inhabitants of Mayfair for that single purpose. She shook her head at such an extravagance and once again looked at her patched apron in order to detect any tell-tale stains.

Nell had taught her well that a clean apron was a passage to most anywhere she might need to go. But the boots that Daisy had lent her rubbed a blister on one foot and she had begun to limp. As she sat upon a fringe of grass and rubbed her toe, she looked about for a street sign. Once again, she drew the folded piece of paper from her pocket and read, "Park Lane." Not seeing those words at that corner, she closed her eyes, memorizing that name before folding the piece of paper and stuffing it into her boot to cushion her toe. She got to her feet and tried out her patch, found it satisfactory, and then struck out once again.

It was the first time that she had ever ventured into the West End. The streets were bustling with handsome liveries and magnificent carriages and so much richness initially gave her pause. She soon got accustomed to the more wholesome air, and gave herself leave to sniff some geraniums that sprang from a window box in front of one of the shops.

"Looks prettier'n it smells," she opined to herself.

In that she walked with a clean apron and the same air as someone who had every right to be there, no one paid her much mind. That alone gave her a bit of bravura, and she felt herself growing more brazen with every step she took unchallenged. When at last she came upon the street that she sought, she had tired of walking and breathed a sigh of relief that the end of her trek was in sight. But to her great disappointment, finding the proper street was only the half of it. She stood looking in both directions, uncertain of which way to go, for both ways were identically wide and tree-lined. Every house that she saw was grander than the last. So used to the deplorable warrens of her neighbourhood, she felt her lungs constrict at the sight. She had expected to see riches beyond her wildest imaginings, but the opulence she beheld staggered her.

Her awe was arrested by the familiar squeal of an over-laden wheel of a cart behind her. Turning about, she saw a scurvy looking man trundling along pushing a one-wheeled barrow before him. A shovel was slung diagonally over the top of it and its reek was the unmistakable one of manure. She watched him as he wearily crossed the cobbles to go to work on another steaming pile of horse-leavings. It did not look to be his first day of employment. As he finished up scooping and dumping the dung into his cart and betook himself down the lane, Sally stepped up beside him and paced her walk to mimic his slow plodding steps.

"Ye know this street well, sir?" she cautiously inquired.

"Well enough," was his terse reply.

"I am sent by my master," she lied, "to seek the house of Darcy. Do ye know it?"

"Aye," said he, then nothing more.

Sally waited for what she likened a respectable amount of time, then asked a bit witheringly, "Care to prove it?"

Without breaking his slow but steady pace, the man lifted his arm as if it weighed ten stone and raised his equally heavy forefinger in an easterly direction, saying, "Just over there."

Sally looked thither and beheld a home that rivalled the workhouse in subjugating its surroundings. Thanking the man over her shoulder, she betook herself in that direction but stopt upon the sidewalk before it, not actually daring to enter the property. Rather, she stood before it as if to absorb some truth in the sheer prominence of the five-story structure. As she savoured the sight, she noticed that a coach stood beneath the portico. Although she had seen many an impressive carriage upon the street, this one was particularly grand. Four perfectly matched horses were harnessed to the coach. (She knew they were horses, but they bore little resemblance to the nags pulling waggons upon her street.) Two uniformed men sat in the driving-seat, and another stood at attention near the door. Sally realised that if she were patient, soon she would witness a personage of great import emerge from yonder edifice. Having never actually seen any one of eminence, she was much in want of doing so. Therefore, she made herself inconspicuous behind a stone hitching post to await the spectacle to come.

She was not to be disappointed, for in a matter of minutes a small drama unfolded as an elfish, nervous little man exited the door. Sally gave a great intake of breath, assuming that personage to be the owner of the house.

"Aye," she whispered, "the great man 'imself."

Watching with meticulous zeal, she observed every detail of his person—from the buckles upon his slippers to the elaborate arranging of his hair. Expecting someone as rich as Mr. Darcy to own some part of majesty, she did not much like what she saw. His costume may have been as fine as she had ever seen upon man or woman, but his bearing was altogether unremarkable. Indeed, not only was his aspect in total want of majesty, he was pigeon-chested, chicken-legged, and the feathering of his hair did nothing to disguise his balding pate. The only things he appeared to have in any prodigious amount was an aura of gravitas and an overweening smirk. But his demeanour left no doubt to Sally that he was a man of substance.

He proceeded directly to the open door of the coach, but stopt before he entered, turning to vehemently lecture two servants fast on his heels. Although both stood impassively during the gentleman's harangue, Sally was certain that she detected in their countenances a palpable dislike. Before the gentleman quit the two servants, he poked each several times in the chest for emphasis. By the time he took his leave in the coach, it was with such haste that Sally leapt back from the road lest she be overrun. Indeed, she believed she was nearly as happy to see him go as the recipients of his tirade.

Once the carriage was out of sight, she thought it was safe to take herself about the corner to find access to the alley and thereupon, the garden gate. All the houses upon the street were similarly set upon their grounds—house facing the street with courtyard, coach-house, and stable accessed by a separate alley-way. The mews was not hard to locate, for the small garden in the back was as impressive as the rest of the property. She was determined to linger there as long as she could in hopes that she might strike up a conversation with any servant who might pass her way. Her plan was not fully mapped out. She had only come to the Darcy town house for the purpose of reconnoitring—the first leg of what she knew to be a long journey of uncovering what had become of her brother. She knew herself to own no small amount of patience and intended to stand there all day was it necessary. But after hours at attention and with rain beginning to pelt her, she reconsidered whether at fate's mercy was an advantageous position. She pressed herself beneath the boughs of some unfamiliar, flowering bush and tried to avoid the downpour. Her resolve, however, was not put to so severe a test. To her good fortune, a carter soon ambled up the way and halted next to her. He had a piece of canvas over his head for a head-piece, it peeking over his forehead like the bill of a duck. Wordlessly, he peered out at her for a moment and, thereupon, handed her two large packages.

"Thankee, Miss," he said as he toddled off.

Standing momentarily speechless at her luck, she called after him, "No—thank *you*!"

Initiating every bit of daring that she could muster, she then betook herself directly to the stair-steps leading down to the kitchen. Hearing snatches of singing within, she hesitated before rapping soundly upon the door. It was flung back directly by a pot-bellied woman who carried an enormous bowl containing some sort of floured mixture. The corpulent woman said nothing to Sally, but called over her shoulder.

"Adele, delivery! Adele!"

Presently Adele arrived at the door. She had an openness to her face that suggested a happy temper and looked to be not more than twenty. Adele gazed upon the now thoroughly drenched Sally and clucked like someone twice her age.

"Come here gerl—you'll catch yer death!" beckoned Adele, motioning Sally inside.

Sally happily complied. Adele took the packages from her and set them on the table, paying little heed to Sally who was then inching her backside closer to the fire, hoping she would be ignored at least long enough for the rain to cease. In hopes of disguising her curiosity, Sally kept her head down as she sneaked peeks about her. She had heard of just such a room as this one—it was a brushing room where fine folks were relieved of any dirt from the road. One wall housed the bell-board, an apparatus that had also been described to her and she was thoroughly intrigued. Her fascination she tried to keep to herself, lest it become apparent that she had never beheld such device. Her interest, however, was so keen that she was startled when Adele offered her a cup of hot coffee.

"Warm yerself, gerl."

Gratefully, Sally took it and began to drink, alternately sipping and blowing. Adele looked on with satisfaction; clearly she was a woman of a kind disposition. Sally felt compelled to converse and was searching for some point upon which to remark when Adele took the conversational reins with a bit of chatter. It soon fell apparent that Adele's chief talent was that of enthusiastic discourse. So profuse and far-reaching was her conversation, Sally soon saw that if she just kept nodding her head with encouragement, Adele would natter on endlessly. Initially she held out hope that Adele would eventually come around to the subject paramount amongst her interests. Time was fast approaching when she would have to give up pretending she had any coffee left in her cup with Adele still deep in a one-sided discussion about the abysmal weather, hence, Sally cautiously interrupted.

Glancing at the silent bell-board, she asked, "The family aren't 'ere now?"

"Oh, no. No, they stay mostly at Pemberley these days," Adele said, little furrows criss-crossed her forehead declaring her disappointment. "I've not seen them but twice m'self. What with the new babies and all. I s'pose ye heard 'bout the babies—twins, they was! Canna you believe it? Twins! My own Master and Mistress! And they be handsome ones I hear. Not like those Fairburg twins—they were ugly as two babes could be. Not the Darcy twins—no, sir. The girl is handsome like my Mistress and the boy be handsome like my Master! None handsomer…"

At this disclosure, Sally's ingenuousness bade her interrupt again, "Master Darcy? Handsome? Aye saw 'im leave this house today and handsome I cannot call 'im."

Sally immediately regretted such an outburst, certain she had insulted so new and important a friend. Adele looked at her like she had somehow run mad, then she let out a laugh. She laughed so heartily that Sally did not much like being the butt of such mirth.

"Oh, no!" Adele warbled. "Law, ye didn't see Master Darcy—oh, no, no, no! That was my Master's house steward, Mr. Smeads! That under-hung gnome isn't fit to hold Mr. Darcy's walking stick!"

"'Pon my honour," commented Sally.

She was thoroughly mortified to have made such an unpardonable error and whole-heartily pleased to see Adele did not hold it against her. Indeed, Adele was happy to acquaint Sally with all the doings of the Darcy family that Sally had been in want of knowing, as well as several that had never crossed her mind.

Old Dogs, Old Tricks

Wickham was a happy man as the coach neared London. It would be a considerable relief finally to feel the cobbles of London's streets beneath his feet. It had been some time since he had last felt on even keel. Paris was a poor second to London—a *parfait* to the *entrée*. There was but one question to ask: Would London be half so happy to see him?

Even with the distraction of the pretty young woman sitting opposite all the way from Brighton, he rehearsed various renditions of his whereabouts since the end of the hostilities. He had read something once in a periodical about some curious malady that affected one's recollection. Regrettably, it had been in French, a language he had not mastered beyond the usual pillow talk. Still, he had made out that a blow to the head or other trauma was thought to bring it about. He liked the sound of that. A disorder such as this was ideally suited for a veteran who was in want of sympathy but had tired of pretending a limp. Now, if he could just recall what manifestation amnesia took—was it possible to remember one's name but not one's wife? When he was situated, he would do further research.

Although he knew that he would eventually have to seek out Lydia, he thought he might put off that reunion for as long as humanly possible.

Upon his arrival in London, he went to St. Clement's parish in search of Mrs. Younge, Georgiana Darcy's *quondam* governess. He was happy to learn that she still abided in the large house on Gowell Street. It was the same one that she had taken after being dismissed by Darcy on charges of disapprobation, but she had decidedly gone to the bad. After all these years, other than the seediness of her furniture, little had altered in her situation. She still maintained herself by letting lodgings. He hoped that she was still uncommonly susceptible to his charms as well.

In the years since he and Lydia had secreted themselves from her family and his creditors in her apartments, the place had gone to the bad, almost as abominably as had Mrs. Younge. When she answered the rap upon her door, it pleased his ego that upon recognising him she flushed with pleasure and hastily began to smooth the remnants of her coiffure. He was happy to see that she was still the sensible-looking woman of steady age and questionable character with whom he had once allied himself. Although her apron was a bit besmudged and her hair a muss, her utter devotion to him remained true. Indeed, so happy was she to see him, she ousted a paying tenant to have him under her roof once more. Moreover, whilst he went out, she was happy to tend to the child who he intimated was his own.

Mrs. Younge knew him too well to believe that on his forays he was looking for gainful employment—their history told her that was unlikely. Avoiding the most obvious haunts, he stalked the streets with a dual purpose. He was looking for a mark and endeavouring to keep his countenance from being recognised. He knew enough to be well-situated before he attempted to reinstate himself within the boundaries of his old life.

Walking the streets and offering the occasional twirl of his walking stick, he endeavoured to appear what he had also desired to be—a celebrated blood about town—a boxer-funding, rat-hunting, four-in-hand-driving London dandy. His Parisian costume announced him a gentleman. That alone allowed him credit. He marvelled how far faultless boots and confident manner could take him. If laid out judiciously, he might be carried by his creditors for some months. Certainly long enough to find himself a pawn.

Ere long, his buoyancy became forced, for the air in town was not so invigorating as it once was. There was a hint of fear permeating the talk and hurrying the pace of the well-born. Something was afoot. A disquiet had descended upon society as if they knew their lives and circumstances were endangered. Wickham began to scour the newspapers for the root of it. Although since Napoleon's defeat the price of a newspaper had spiralled precipitously, he dug deep into his pockets day after day regardless. Indeed, day after day it became his habit to take his news with his tea. What he read was at once horrifying and exciting. Marauding bands of pillagers were taking to the streets of Mayfair at night. No man of substance was safe. It was an altogether terrifying time to have money. It would have been alarming even to penniless Wickham had he not been so full of guile.

Like most well-rehearsed liars, he had an excellent memory. All the chaos somehow jogged an ancient story of a certain Chinese symbol that meant catastrophe. One side stood for danger.

The other stood for opportunity.

Happiness Is Two Warm Puppies

Beneath the professional surface of the hatching of a commissioned portrait roosted a bird of an altogether different feather. It had been of appetence but incubated in pique.

When upon that prior occasion Robert Morland had been denied leave to take Mrs. Darcy's portrait to be displayed in London, he *had* left in a huff. Although the irritable pronouncer of that dictum was Mr. Darcy, that had not been the only injury he had inflicted upon the painter. There was another, deeper wound to Morland's ego (one he had allowed to fester without constraint). From the very beginning, Mr. Darcy had been a thorn in his side the whole of that enterprise.

Morland was one of the foremost English portrait painters of his day. He was not a founding member, but naturally belonged to the Royal Academy and was considered by many (other than himself) to be the heir apparent to Reynolds. Indeed, he had taken the likeness of kings and courtiers meritoriously enough to have gained a knighthood. But stylistically, his work favoured Lawrence. Both were expert technicians with their palettes and favoured a romantic view that lent distinction to their sitters. Although clearly they both were influenced by the Dutch School, Morland despised being compared to Reynolds. The similarities were undeniable, for both artists' work was distinguished by rich colour and classical allusions. But Reynolds had won acclaim abroad and as he had not, Morland partook a hearty plate of sour grapes and announced himself wholly anglophilic.

Unbeknownst to him, it was this dictum which influenced Mr. Darcy to have Morland undertake another commission. After escaping the Low Countries, Mr. Darcy wanted little to do with anything or anyone with Continental inclinations.

Morland was altogether certain that his knighthood and his enhanced reputation had preceded him unto Pemberley that first excursion. His eminence as a painter was well-chronicled and unquestioned. However, he had held a repute of quite another nature that was not nearly so renowned. Sir Robert Morland, the King's Portraitist, member of the Royal Academy, was also a libertine of epic proportions.

There were whispers, of course. But as members of the fashionable elite more in name than in practice, of the exact extent of his peccadilloes the Darcys had been largely unwitting. That information having been in their hands would not necessarily have precluded his employment with them. They were sophisticated enough to understand that if they excluded every aristocratic philanderer from their London guest lists, it would be difficult to fill three tables of cards. Mr. Darcy's watch and ward over his wife whilst sitting for Morland would not have altered had the man had papers certifying him a eunuch. Upon that first commission with them, Morland had travelled to Pemberley as unwitting of Mr. Darcy's mindset as Mr. Darcy had been of his.

It had been as much an artistic technique for his female subjects to be under his sway as were his feathery brush-strokes. Indeed, infatuation imbued the countenance of a lady with a certain colour to her cheeks and gleam in her eye—and he alone had the key that unlocked her treasures. With his brush as his instrument, he had successfully wooed some of England's most sophisticated women right under their husbands' noses. He did not expect any less from Mrs. Darcy in that she had lived the whole of her existence in some little Hertfordshire township. As Mrs. Darcy had been but a bride when Morland first took her likeness, she was to his mind a plum, moist, delectable, and ripe for the plucking. What country lass, Morland had wondered, could resist a lover such as himself—a man with the charms of Byron and the talent of Lawrence? That combination had been veritable catnip for a slew of aristocratic pusses in the past. But, alas, it was not to be.

Morland had become absolutely enamoured of Mrs. Darcy's considerable charms. But Mr. Darcy looked after his wife's virtue with uncommon diligence. Indeed, no other husband's watch had been half so keen. For that, Morland was truly sorry—he was enormously sorry. For not only would Mrs. Darcy have been a lovely conquest, over the weeks of that sitting her aspect had morphed from an object of his lust to his very heart's desire. That he had been denied not only her body but her painted vision as well was a carbuncle upon his romantic inclinations. He held Mr. Darcy solely to blame for it all. Although Darcy's sentry over his wife was not without its reward to Morland's artistic endeavours (for he had sat with Mrs. Darcy each day and his presence alone did the honours to her complexion), but that her aspect shone upon her husband's behalf and not his was altogether irksome. Although Morland had deluded himself into believing that he had come once again for purely artistic gain, a niggling little pin-prick in his heart told him otherwise. As he neared Pemberley, it became more pronounced.

On this excursion into the wilds of Derbyshire, Morland knew that seduction would be compromised by the nature of the family portrait. Still, he held out hope. Mrs. Darcy had been one of his few romantic disappointments. To at last succeed with her (and thereby salve his tear-stained heart) by circumventing her husband's sentry would be an especially rewarding triumph. It was possible—even probable. With a more aged marriage, betimes a spousal eye might wander. Perhaps Mr. Darcy's guard would be a bit relaxed with the addition of children and a few years of marital tedium.

The image of the lovely Mrs. Darcy wearing a simple yellow frock had stayed with Morland for half a decade. In lieu of having the painting upon display for him to gaze upon at his leisure, he had cosseted that image in the confines of his dearest recollections. When at last she once again stood before him, he saw that, if anything, she had gained in countenance. Her figure was more womanly, her expression more worldly. Her milky-white shoulders were invaded by a few dark curls that cascaded onto the translucent mantle she had casually tied across her rather voluptuous bosom. She sat primly, her hands folded in her lap, but one slippered toe protruded from the hem of her frock, causing Morland's heart to make a small palpitation every time he happened to gaze upon it.

When once again he stood before the towering Mr. Darcy, he bethought the matter.

It soon fell apparent that his romantic designs were once again to be thwarted. With an inward "bloody hell," he resigned himself to temporary celibacy. That Mr. Darcy stood by so sternly was a constant reminder he would have to guard carefully any project in which cupid had any share. Indeed, it appeared that, if anything, Mr. Darcy was even charier of his wife's time than before.

Moreover, this likeness was to be taken as a family—with their dogs.

Forthwith, Morland's attention was wrested from the possibility of seduction to the intricacies of his work. Not only was Mr. Darcy to stand for his likeness with his wife, but she explained that it was to include their children *and* their pets. Morland detested the odd propensity the English had for including their dogs in a family portrait. He soundly disliked it, but he would never have betrayed that abhorrence for he claimed a lucrative second string to his bow by taking those mongrels' likenesses.

It was the usual practice in these circumstances for the dog to be an ancient and devoted piece of fur, curled at his master's feet. Predictably, the Darcys had one quite fitting for that role in a decrepit female wolfhound. That would be no bother; Morland knew that he could re-create that specimen without laying an eye upon the dog. But there was further bother in that for their first birthday, the Darcys had bestowed upon their offspring a pair of speckled spaniels. Between the wolfhound's inertia and the unruliness of the puppies, he saw that he would spend many a day endeavouring to get proper sketches.

Indeed, from the first day the rambunctious puppies ran circles around the hound, causing them all to trip in a heap. Although she howled balefully, she busied herself keeping them contained, behaving as if she was a collie and the puppies sheep rather than majestic scent-hounds. Morland quickly saw that, in fact, the puppies were quite manageable compared to keeping the twins in check. It would come to pass that many days saw him run weeping from the room, ruing the day he had ever inquired after the commission.

Morland's infatuation for Elizabeth, however, ran quite unabated. Indeed, her motherly calm was such that he occasionally wished she would press her cheek to his fevered brow. In lieu of that opportunity, Morland cast his acute eye from their parents and pets to the children themselves. He was as keen an observer of physical traits as of the ethereal. As Janie sat innocently upon her mother's lap, an informal conversation ensued whilst he painted. It was a studied easiness upon Morland's part, knowing full well that engaging in discourse about her children was the surest way to settle both mother and child. Mr. Darcy stood behind mother and daughter with a protective hand across the back of the chair; Geoff scrambled about upon the floor before them. The room that had become Morland's studio was also a makeshift playroom strewn with wooden horses and trumpet for the boy and the requisite china-doll for the daughter.

When the conversation took that intimate turn, Mr. Darcy perceptively stiffened. In time, such a happy subject tempted even his dour countenance into a small smile as his wife danced Janie in her lap causing the child to giggle.

"I must take leave to confess, Mrs. Darcy," Morland peered around the side of the canvas still daubing as he inquired, "that your daughter is not as spirited as her brother. What say you?"

At this liberty, Mr. Darcy was seen to bristle. Sensing his alarm, Elizabeth put a quieting hand upon his, answering Morland amiably, "As you see."

It was an observation that the Darcys had often exchanged. Elizabeth was uncertain if Janie's reticent nature favoured her father or her Aunt Georgiana. If there was one truth alone that Elizabeth had learnt, it was that a placid countenance did not necessarily foretell insignificant feelings. Indeed, recent history did not dispose Elizabeth to hazard a guess what upheaval that propensity might incite. She chambered that troubling thought to the farthest reaches of her mind in ardent hope the occasion to revisit it would never come to pass. Sir Morland's ready acknowledgment of it and exploring the subject so openly did nothing to alleviate Darcy's defensive mien. Soon, however, Darcy's gaze was again cast upon his son as the boy clamoured about the floor in great pursuit of one stubborn puppy which refused to be cornered. Margaret Heff had been sitting to the side, but took that opportunity to go over and hoist the boy into her arms, then caught the puppy and held him for Geoff to pet.

Although Mr. Darcy was content for his daughter to be cosseted like one of her porcelain dolls, the single pampering in which he refused his indulgence was that his son not be carried constantly about.

"Nurse, put the boy down, he must find his legs!"

Margaret did as she was told and she and Elizabeth shared a smile that Mr. Darcy did not see, for he was far too occupied by justifying his outburst. Rightly, he pointed out that had he not put his foot down, it might not have been discovered that young Geoff had an uncanny sense of balance. After that first awkward hoist to his feet by means of his father's coattail, he was rarely content to creep. He waddled about with no undue caution, looking, said Darcy, a bit like a drunken duck. As the baby drew himself awkwardly to his hands and feet before standing, weaving a bit as he did, his father beamed.

"Time will soon be at hand for his first pony," he said.

At that, it was Elizabeth's countenance that darkened and Darcy's hand which gave a reassuring pat.

As the boy went blundering about, Darcy leant near Elizabeth's ear and whispered, "Not one of Jane's children took to their feet in their first year and then not half so well!"

Elizabeth looked incredulously upon her husband's cheerful countenance, wholly taken aback that he had taken such careful notice of the Bingley children's progress. She smiled at the thought, mirth Morland observed and endeavoured to capture.

It was true that Jane's children had inherited their mother's uncommonly handsome features. Her brood was all bounce, blonde curls, and happy dispositions—conditions that could be charged without reservation to Bingley's patrimonial influence. Elizabeth loved them all nearly as dearly as she loved Jane. Indeed, she loved them vehemently and without reservation. It would serve no purpose, however, to point out to Jane that her children were not the fairest of face, had the keenest understanding, or the most promising figures. Those traits belonged to her twins. This observation she shared only with her husband. On this subject, their minds were uncommonly alike.

As a puppy leapt up and nipped at Geoff's ears, he gave out a delighted shriek causing Janie to commence to cry. Ever their protector, Cressida began to howl in concern and

Elizabeth and Darcy shook their heads in admiration of the bedlam. Morland cringed.

Mr. and Mrs. Darcy, exceptional in so many other ways, joined countless generations of parents who took undue notice of their children's most insignificant accomplishment and fancied themselves ridiculously delighted.

And when poor Morland thought that the din had reached its apex, Mrs. Bennet arrived.

Mrs. Bennet Rides Again

Elizabeth's toes tingled luxuriously and they wriggled with spasms. Whilst her feet pedalled against the mattress, her hands flailed over her head until they managed to catch-hold of two spindles adorning the head-board. With fluttering eyelids and arched back, a slow, susurration of a moan began at the back of her throat threatening to turn into unadulterated acclamation—when came a shrill call from outside the door.

"Lizzy!" Make haste!" Then louder, "*Lizzy!* You must come!"

Elizabeth sat bolt-upright in the middle of the bed just as the huge door exploded open, and with it Mrs. Bennet stood, hands on hips, and face florid with anger. Her mother took steps in her direction and Elizabeth drew the bed-clothes to her chin in defence.

"Ma-MA!" Elizabeth exclaimed.

Behind her mother trod Hannah, clearly on the losing end of keeping Mrs. Bennet from Elizabeth's bed-chamber. Hannah was at least as determined as Mrs. Bennet and therefore overtook her mid-most of the room. In a flash she was to Elizabeth's bedside holding a salmon-coloured, tabby dressing-gown by it shoulders out before her. Elizabeth verily ripped it from her grip and drew it about her shoulders, but her still-trembling hands were errant of the sleeves. Hannah retreated whence she came, but Mrs. Bennet was intent upon her own purposes and held her ground in the middle of the room whilst wailing for Elizabeth to follow.

"Pray, are my children well?" Elizabeth gasped, trying to ascertain the extent of the horrendous event that demanded she be rousted from her bed.

"Pray, they cannot be better! It is your own dear Mama who has been trespassed upon!"

With an involuntary roll of her eyes, Elizabeth could not disguise a wince of disgust, "I will be right there Mama."

"Spare me that look, Lizzy, for I am cruelly used!" she then fled the room, clearly of a mind her daughter was to follow.

There were several curses that visited Elizabeth's mind as her mother quit her bed-chamber. She aired a few low utterances when she had thought her gone. But, added to her disturbance through the half-reopened door, her mother added, "I am sorry to have broke your rest, but when you come we will be of the same mind."

When at last the door was soundly closed, Elizabeth said, "Bless me! My mother has compleatly lost her senses!"

"Forgive me, Lizzy," said Darcy from deep beneath the bed-clothes (and half-way down the mattress), "if I take leave to question whether someone can lose that which she never owned."

He then threw back the counterpane with a heave and drew himself to the pillow next to Elizabeth, observing, "Impeccable timing your mother has."

His hair was in a compleat muss and he instinctively ran his fingers through it in a small attempt to tame his curls.

"Actually," Elizabeth smiled, "insofar as I am concerned, it *was* impeccable."

Either from being hidden beneath the bed-clothes or through investing no small amount of time in pleasuring his wife (possibly both), perspiration drenched his hairline into tiny ringlets. Hers had already begun to evaporate, but the expression she bore suggested she was not altogether keen upon sorting out her mother's most recent pother with any haste. Both, however, were duly conscious they might be descended upon again at any moment. Hence, masculine resolve inevitably waned, leaving her to promise herself that she would repay the compliment at their earliest convenience.

Elizabeth drew to the side of the bed, wrapping her cascading dressing-gown about her as she rose. Standing, she rearranged it about her, allowing him a teasing flash of flesh. He rose upon one elbow to better admire the view.

Said he, "You are, indeed, indebted to me for a later engagement."

Turning her head slightly akilter, she eyed him with unadulterated desire, saying, "Handsome thought, indeed. Do not suppose me desirous of being released from such an obligation."

With all due reluctance, she knotted her sash about her waist as if to steel herself for what next bother her mother had found—it was not difficult to surmise that Sir Morland was at the root of it. She headed for her toilette, but as she gained the doorway, a backward glance caught sight of his sinewy leg and it gave her a slight catch in her throat. She dared not to let her thoughts stray, however, and wondered what sort of bolt would be in place to bar their door by nightfall.

As it happened, there was not one bolt but two and both were exceedingly stout. Elizabeth was already reposing upon the bed when Darcy slid them both into place. He was wearing his silk dressing coat, but cast it off before he reached the bed. It pleasured her to see that he was not wearing his night-shirt. His nakedness suggested that a recommencement of their interrupted love-making was imminent.

Because their door was secured, they had absolutely no inhibitions. Because his nakedness exposed a tumescence of some magnitude, they were in absolutely no hurry either.

From the very beginning, the Darcys had bid Mrs. Bennet make their home her own. They made that invitation without reservation and in compleat understanding and undiluted repugnance of its implications. As a woman who had little turn for economy, Mrs. Bennet was quite happy to bask in the opulence of the Darcys' home—and test her daughter's patience and her son-in-law's forbearance. Unhappily for her nerves, Elizabeth had no scheme in place to tolerate her mother's most objectionable habits. Darcy, however, had his own singular method—one well-documented and therefore absolutely feasible. Elizabeth was witting that it was a compleat sham, but she entirely forgave him. She only wished that she had a deafness which could suffer a sudden recurrence as had he. Instead, she had to sit about listening to her mother's endless insipidness and watch as her husband sat happily engrossed in a book, appearing oblivious to every moment of indecorousness his mother-in-law inflicted.

Although Mrs. Bennet had arrived with all the brouhaha only she could employ, she had been unhappy that her visit was not the jewel in the crown of the Darcys' summer. Although she was wholly unacquainted with Morland's work, she was perceptive enough to understand his importance—he, regrettably, did not return the favour. Hence, she behaved toward him as if he was a servant of Pemberley and was not at all discreet in her opinions upon how the painter employed his brush. Because of her general lack of tact, she was relegated to the grand salon, a room exquisite enough to harbour her nerves with excellent furnishings. Yet, unless Elizabeth sat there with her, she would not stay for long and would invariably invade Morland's makeshift studio where she amused herself by being disagreeable to him and absorbing enough insult to furnish conversation for the evening.

Initially, Mrs. Bennet was inspirited by her travel. It had always done her heart good to see how well her daughters married. Having four daughters wed and her tenure at Longbourn assured by Mr. Darcy's generosity, one might suggest that it was to her good fortune that she at least had the office of widowhood upon which to martyr herself. Indeed, after a germinal burst of good-humour, she quickly reverted to her more familiar guise of affected grief. She genuinely mourned her husband, but was incapable of fatigue whilst enumerating her loss. Upon her crape-wrapped throne, it was still hours after her arrival that she felt composed enough to bid the twins be brought before her.

"They are apt now to survive," she explained. "Bring them to their Grandmamma!"

Elizabeth did as she was bid, but reluctantly, for she was not inclined to have her children appraised and poked like fat capons on market day—a compliment her mother would no doubt pay.

Although he was torn between desiring to shelter his children from such a menace and guilt over leaving such an unpleasant chore to his wife to bear alone—ultimately Darcy left it to Elizabeth to sort out her mother. (He had bid Mrs. Bennet good-day, and so far as he was concerned he had had his daily dish of detestable duty.) Curled and powdered, the twins were given an audience before their grandmother. When first she laid eyes upon their tiny countenances, she could but swoon.

"Lizzy! They are verily two peas in a pod! Not a soul saw fit to tell me that they were identical!" She turned and looked upon Elizabeth as if in accusation, "*Identical!*"

"Actually," Elizabeth cautiously pointed out, "they are *not* identical."

"Not identical? Not *identical*?" perturbation gifted her voice a full octave. "I fancy they are identical. Do you suppose that I am blind? Any fool can see they are quite identical."

Here Elizabeth wavered. She knew it was quite useless to impose reason upon her mother when she had come to a determination, but she thought it imperative that her children not be characterized wrongly. Therefore, she attempted to explain how they could not be actually identical.

"Yes, Mama, I should say they favour each other exceedingly. But, as one is a boy and one is a girl, they cannot possibly be absolutely *identical*."

"Oh, what does it matter?" she scoffed.

"Yes," agreed Elizabeth, "what does it matter, indeed?"

As it was a rare day when Mrs. Bennet's tactlessness was over-estimated, she did not disappoint her daughter's anticipation then. (Elizabeth would scarce allow anyone to touch her babies but Nurse and Darcy, it might have been curious to see what unfolded if Mrs. Bennet had held out her arms, but as it happened, she did not.) After a bit of chin-chucking and respective fussing, she stood back, turned her head a bit (the better to assess their features), and tsked several times.

"It is a shame they are not fair like Jane's children nor half so lively as Lydia's," she said, then added, "but with such a fortune to promote them what does that matter? It is enough that they have survived and we must be happy with that."

Elizabeth gritted her teeth and gave a silent prayer that her husband was out of earshot of that particular observation. With all due consideration of the source, her motherly pride still could not allow her to keep her tongue. Cheeks flaming, she found herself sorely wanting in composure.

She said tersely, "They have their father's eyes and their mother's contentment."

"I suppose you should be happy with that, Lizzy," her mother allowed. "Bingley cannot be father to every child. Your boy *is* a good sleeper." As Elizabeth related it later to Darcy, it was as if Mrs. Bennet was capable of sucking the air right out of the room.

"Somewhere, somehow, a village is being deprived of an idiot!" Elizabeth stormed.

His wife's outrage allowed Darcy to be amused. This single fortune was her saving grace. For had he been unamused, Elizabeth felt certain her mother's querulous demands might have begged her felled by some sympathetic atrocity by their servants. As it was, once their bed-chamber door was barred, they managed to avoid her most of the day. And most of the day, she kept close watch over Morland's work. Torn by unrequited desire for the daughter and abhorrence of her mother, Morland spirits suffered grievously. Regrettably, as this portrait would include so many, accordingly lengthy was Morland's stay.

To sustain himself through the day, he kept a chalice filled with spirits next to his chair. But all the champagne he drank brought no courage to him in the face of Mrs. Bennet's illiberal mind and constant observations. By late afternoon, he stared out with tiny, blood-shot slits of eyes and looked upon her as if she bore a particularly vile infectious disease. This disdain did not faze Mrs. Bennet, nor could Elizabeth encourage her to enjoy the calm pursuits and amusements usually pleasing to country ladies.

Mrs. Bennet had not been there a fortnight ere her general dislike of Sir Morland (and his of her) was sharpened into outright loathing. That fractious arrangement soon paled, however, when lately come to Derbyshire was Lydia—sporting a new husband, an infant daughter, and a small, ragamuffin woman-child as a nurse.

Goddess of Discord, Goddess of the Hunt

If Mrs. Bennet was Eris, Goddess of Discord, Lydia was a self-appointed Diana, Goddess of the Hunt. Indeed, in her own eyes Lydia had proven herself to be a husband-huntress of supreme acumen and she wagged her latest conquest to Pemberley to display prouder than a pointer placing a retrieved mallard at the feet of his master.

Lydia had become Mrs. Wickham prior to her Elizabeth's illustrious marriage, but Mr. Darcy's loathing of her spouse had meant that Lydia had been invited to Pemberley but little. Although Pemberley was an exquisite estate, her exclusion from its premises had never much bothered her. Her pleasures had been far more immediate. Bonnets and beaus excited her admiration. But in the few short years of her marriage, those bonnets had become increasingly tatty—along with the men who deigned to press their lips to her knuckles. When first they were wed, Wickham had seemed charmingly knowledgeable in the ways of love, but she had tired of him almost as soon as he had of her. Still, as she was of concupiscent nature she had positively provoked Wickham's husbandly urges and had dropped babies of him with the regularity of the season. So long as he kept her in new frocks and had a nurse to see to their brood, their marriage had gone quite swimmingly. A plethora of shops of which to avail herself had even allowed her to consider Wickham's eternally roving eye as a challenge. To catch him *in flagrante*, kept her amused to no end. In the end it had not been infidelity that had doomed their marriage, but their great propensity for running into debt.

Like many a portion-less young man, Wickham had made living upon credit, a carefully arranged work of art. But that, as all things, knew it limits. Soon the bailiff and his man began to impinge upon their spending. The single merit that Wickham had found in Lydia was her unparalleled ability to talk over a creditor. Their marital roles saw Wickham as the artful spender and Lydia the wily evader. As a team, they had for some years managed to keep one step ahead of their debts. When at last there were no funds for new frocks (nor even trim for her bonnets), Lydia had had enough of Wickham. That compleat disaffection coincided nicely with his deployment to Belgium. Initially, she had been happy to be rid of her husband, their debts, and her motherly responsibilities, and to live once again as a daughter in her father's house. All too soon the shine wore off that penny and her restless nature once again proved her undoing. She had been wholly unrepentant for her wantonness so long as she believed her lover's vows of rescue. When he proved to be a bounder, she was no less contrite, but felt the unkind sting of desperation. In the end, the very trait which disturbed her morals was what rescued her. Her high animal spirits had enthralled and thrilled the very sensible Major Kneebone. Lydia was as exhilarating to him as a glass of champagne to a teetotaller.

Although Lydia would swear unto the death that she had not settled for young Kneebone in lieu of her paramour, when he arrived upon her doorstep with the unhappy news that she had been crossed in love, so eager was she to escape her family's governance that he might as well have had a bull's-eye painted upon his forehead. So far as Lydia knew, he had little to promote himself but a commission and an admirable lack of guile. As he was hopelessly romantic enough to want to rescue a damsel of questionable virtue in distress, her respect for him was marginal—but what she would settle for in a husband had dwindled with her prospects. When it was uncovered that he had an aunt who had an affection for him of the magnitude that rivalled the balance she kept with her banker, that spelled l-o-v-e in Lydia's newly defined dictionary.

Remarkably, this near-debacle of love did the unimaginable—it inspirited her with a new-found sentience. When once her family believed sensibleness would be forever lost to her, she was compleatly humbled to have been saved from the clutches of a fate worse than death—living out her life in her mother's house seeing to her own unruly pack of children. Although her Aunt Gardiner believed her vows of repentance would not last out the year, she dutifully wrote to Elizabeth and Jane of their sister's lately found gentility. (The considerable merit of at long last being shed of George Wickham was enough to give even Elizabeth reason to be hopeful.) Hence, upon wedding her second husband, and having borne four children ere she was two and twenty, Lydia had, if not the actuality, a passable appearance of respectability.

The Gardiners had been put in the awkward position of reviewing Major Kneebone's qualifications as husband for their niece. Their general opinion was that, at that specific juncture, no offer of marriage to Lydia could be looked upon altogether meanly. Elizabeth received a letter from her highly distraught aunt which arrived forthwith of this courtship. Mrs. Gardiner was appalled at Lydia's betraying the strict rules of mourning by entertaining the notion of marriage before the year was out.

"Dear, Lizzy, we have done what we can to check her outrageous behaviour, but she refuses to hear our admonishments," she wrote.

Elizabeth knew that the time had come for her to apprise the Gardiners the exact nature of Lydia's latest pregnancy and that she had begun mourning her husband long before his death. Therefore, Elizabeth replied immediately, delineating Lydia's pregnancy timeline and that propriety be damned (or words to that effect), to save Lydia from herself it would be essential that she be married forthwith. Initiallly, Elizabeth made the same error as Mrs. Gardiner in supposing Major Kneebone the seducer of record. Hence, Major Kneebone received a welcome befitting a cad making an honest woman of Lydia rather than as her rescuer. Unacquainted with the Gardiners and the subtle nuances of their good manners, he remained wholly unwitting of their misconception. Mr. Gardiner went through the motions of interviewing the candidate and found him a living, breathing individual who was neither previously promised nor currently incarcerated—and, insofar as they were concerned, he was altogether admirable husband material. Mrs. Gardiner had written forthwith to Elizabeth and Jane, failing compleatly in disguising her delight at the prospect of marrying Lydia off so promptly. Indeed, there was not a whiff of disapproval at the prospect of Lydia's remarrying without the proper period of mourning. As the Gardiners were people her head turned to quite naturally, her aunt's good opinion caused Elizabeth to exhale a generous sigh of relief. She had no need of hearing that he was moderate in his address and gentlemanlike in his manners—but she was happy to all the same. Indeed, was it not for his choosing to marry Lydia, he would have been judged an altogether agreeable and estimable young man.

Ecstatic over being conveyed to Pemberley in an equipage of unrivalled majesty, Lydia had prattled to her new husband of the prominence of her sister's husband all the way to Derbyshire. Upon their arrival, however, it was Mrs. Bennet who stood in fluttering welcome beneath the portico. (She had stood upon an upstairs balcony for a most immoderate time watching for their coach to clear the lodge-post, then made haste to be the first to greet them.) It was not her mother alone who Lydia had come all this way to see, and it was with some impatience that she allowed kisses and introductions.

Having been apprised of the arrival, Elizabeth stood in the enormous vestibule in order to keep them from charging in upon her husband without due warning. Lydia was most effusive with her praise of all things Darcy. She could not tell Elizabeth enough how happy she was to be at last welcome at Pemberley and, in the same breath, relate the highlights of their journey—up to and including having passed by Princess Caroline's abode and happening to catch sight of that personage and her alleged Italian lover entering a royal coach.

"Imagine, Lizzy! Her livery was not half so handsome as ours! We were so near to her I could all but smell her scent—truly she must issue an intolerable smell—she looked quite podgy and altogether dirty and unkempt. It is no wonder that Prinny keeps his mistresses. He married her bigamously, did he not? Would it not be outrageous to have such an ugly little tart as queen? Although I must say—we have done far worse!"

Indeed, all of that information was delivered not five steps inside the doorstep. From that notorious subject, she flitted to another with such haste that Elizabeth had no opportunity to interject a word. Her next train of discourse was of greater interest to her audience for it pertained to sights that were beheld in the Derbyshire countryside.

"You have never seen a more crowded thoroughfare in London than the road betwixt Nottingham and Matlock," she explained.

Lydia's costume was new, a tribute to her husband's generosity. (Her bonnet was a milliner's wonder, a series of pheasant plumes projecting out at such an angle as to poke him in the eye for his trouble.) In between her various observations, Lydia introduced her new husband who had been nodding both in agreement with Lydia's last bit of information and to avoid her chapeau's weaponry. With Mrs. Bennet trilling and ejaculating her delight behind them, Elizabeth escorted the couple to the large salon where Darcy stood awaiting them with unprecedented formality. Introductions, therefore, were exchanged somewhat awkwardly, Lydia simpering and giggling whilst Elizabeth attempted to take her new brother-in-law's measure. She was full curious as to whether or not the Gardiners' estimation of Kneebone had been inflated by hope. It was readily apparent that he bore not a whisper of Wickham's twinkle-eyed smirk, indeed, whilst she and Darcy gave Kneebone a detailed evaluation, he appeared neither off-put nor put-out, but remained impassively hospitable to their examination. When Lydia spoke to him, he looked upon her with such devotion, it was impossible for Elizabeth not to forgive him his amorous judgement.

His hair was straw-coloured and unruly. He had used more than a dollop of oil, but it had not done the office of keeping a few sprigs of a cowlick plastered to his skull. (In an oft-used manoeuvre, he nervously scratched his fingers across the crown of his head to tame that one wild lock.) His epaulets disguised narrow shoulders, but he had a thick wrist—the ruddiness of which gave him the appearance of a farm boy lately come to town. Thoroughly prepared to despise the fellow, Darcy was happy to find him not at all appalling. Elizabeth did her best to keep Lydia corralled so the gentlemen could converse uninterrupted. Therefore, Darcy learnt that Kneebone's not seeing action in the latest hostility fell not to his disinclination to put himself in harm's way, but that he had seen action in the Peninsular campaign—carrying a fragment of a musket-ball in a portion of his person that remained undisclosed.

Hearing that subject arise of his heroism, Lydia hastened to exclaim, "He was mentioned by name and with honour in the *Gazette*!"

"Ooooh," exclaimed Mrs. Bennet. "A hero, indeed!"

Kneebone's ruddy complexion coloured the approximate shade of a ripe tomato and Lydia rushed to his side and patted his arm with affection. As she had not witnessed that which the other female parishioners had forthwith of their wedding, Elizabeth remained somewhat suspicious of Lydia's apparent alteration into a devoted wife. But Kneebone covered Lydia's hand with his in a comforting little gesture and said that she wanted him to quit the guards and sell out of the army. He, however, was unwilling to live solely upon his aunt's allowance. With that remark, a silence ensued, not of a particularly deadly variety, but awkward enough for Elizabeth to want it filled. Therefore, she told Darcy of the unusual liveliness of their local roads.

"Pray, what do you make of it?" inquired Major Kneebone of Darcy.

A small expression of concern crossed his countenance (one so tiny only Elizabeth detected it), but he replied benignly, "I fear it was not a good crop year. Some cottagers seek a means of employment in the east."

"Many believe that the Corn Laws are to blame," Kneebone said mildly.

Just as mildly, Darcy replied, "I would agree with those who do."

Knowing that many large landowners were avaricious enough to have supported a law that enriched their own pockets at the peril of those who could least weather the high cost of bread, Kneebone looked quite astonished at Mr. Darcy's position, "Indeed, did you stand among those landowners of Derbyshire who opposed them publicly?"

"Yes, I did."

"Would it be far too bold of me to observe that those in favour of such decrees are merchants and bankers who claimed their property through default and not, like yourself, true lovers of the land?"

"Yes, it would be bold," said Mr. Darcy, "but not incorrect."

Both men then exchanged a moment of understanding—one disrupted by the flamboyant interruption of their mother-in-law.

Mrs. Bennet demanded an alteration in the topic of their discourse, announcing, "Politics, gentlemen! Is there any subject more tiresome to ladies? Do desist!"

"Mama, some ladies are in want of information of that sort," insisted Elizabeth, unhappy at the prospect of not furthering the subject of keen national interest. "You are quite unfair to our sex!"

She had not an ally in Lydia, however, for beyond her husband's past heroics, she disliked the discourse. Elizabeth saw immediately that she was over-ruled if not outnumbered. A servant offered the men a glass of claret and Mrs. Bennet took both her daughters by the arms, insisting they leave the men be. Elizabeth gave a longing look over her shoulder, hoping against hope that her husband would rescue her. It was a point of pride that Darcy did not exclude her from what usually came under the banner of men-talk (the pride was for her husband's lack of male-prone insecurities, not for her own acumen). As her mother whisked her away, it was the first time in her recent recollection that he had not rescued her. Upon this occasion, she supposed, it was acceptable. Indeed, it was her duty to rescue him. Lydia's behaviour when in his company was inexcusably forward. Even in the presence of her new husband, she could not keep her hands to herself. If he could escape her, he would—and Elizabeth would not have to peel Lydia's fingers off his coat lapels.

Darcy was by then deep in conversation with Kneebone which left the ladies to betake themselves to the nursery and admire Lydia's newborn. Whilst Elizabeth led the way, Mrs. Bennet was happy for the opportunity to lament the recently departed Wickham for he had been a particular favourite of hers. Amongst her few admirable qualities was that Lydia was the one daughter who did not scruple to confront and correct her mother's many misconceptions.

"Oh, do not speak to me of Wickham," she said with finality; "he was black at heart, hollow and black!"

"But dear, sweet Lydia," said Mrs. Bennet only slightly chastened, "Wickham had such a handsome countenance and an open, pleasing way. I cannot believe all that you say of him is true."

At this, Lydia snorted. For her part, Elizabeth was altogether uneasy having Lydia within Pemberley—sporting a new husband or not. Just the mention of Wickham's name gave her a small shiver down her spine.

She had not said a word to Darcy of the ghostly visage she thought she had observed when taking leave of Brighton. Darcy had made it clear that he had no true evidence whether Wickham had or had not perished upon the battlefield of Waterloo. In light of no other information, they had chosen to believe the official notification of his death. She had successfully kept that worry in the farthest reaches of her thoughts. At least that was where they stayed until his name was spoken in her presence. She listened as Lydia quickly returned to better humour, warbling and preening over her new daughter for Mrs. Bennet's benefit. Elizabeth gave all the appropriate adulations to the baby's aspect and admired her good nature, taking her carefully into her arms, but as she did so, she was overtaken by ever-increasing unease. It was a disconcertion that could not be appeased by the notion of Lydia procuring an adoring and gentlemanly husband. Lydia had overcome widowhood, adultery, and imposture with unseemly effortlessness. Indeed, Lydia had always managed to overcome life's many struggles without sacrificing much of anything save time and conscience. Elizabeth was torn between pity for Kneebone and holding out hope that Lydia would come to merit him.

"'Twas a great sadness for your mama not to attend this wedding, Lydia. Married twice and I had not the pleasure of witnessing either one!"

With unsparing precision, a tear then sprang from the corner of Mrs. Bennet's eye. With a dainty flourish, she withdrew a gauzy, lace-trimmed handkerchief from her bodice and dabbed at it without conviction.

"Oh, what does it matter?" retorted Lydia dismissively. "The flowers were unexceptional and I was forbidden to wear lace. If we had not gone into the vestry to sign the registry, I should not have thought much had come to pass at all."

Suddenly jealous of her possessing her baby, Lydia had taken her gurgling daughter from Elizabeth, jiggling her a bit upon her shoulder. As this manoeuvre was clearly not one that Lydia regularly employed, her movements were clumsy. The baby began to fuss a bit—whereupon Lydia began to jiggle her more zealously.

"'Tis a pity," offered Mrs. Bennet, reaching out and fluffing Lydia's bobbing tendrils, "that swaddling is no longer done."

Mrs. Bennet and Lydia commiserated that sad fact emphatically, nodding and waggling their eyebrows in unison. It was then that Elizabeth's attention was arrested by the young nursemaid. The girl, who was no bigger than a mite, bore the precise expression of one of much longer years—one who had spent a great deal of time witnessing the many follies of her fellow man. Indeed, Elizabeth was quite certain that the girl's countenance mirrored her own contemptuous dislike of the display before them. At that very moment, the girl's gaze caught hers—and she thereupon cast her eyes deferentially to the floor. Her cheeks flushed with embarrassment as if she had been caught in some covert act. Elizabeth had wanted to speak to her, to bid her not to be afraid—for the sight of her countenance had given her stomach an added twinge. The girl, however, stepped back with head still bowed and folded her hands in front of her.

Lydia continued to jiggle the baby who then began to cry with some vehemence. Sighing with equal resolve, Lydia thrust her toward the nursemaid, who then enveloped the child in her small arms and immediately began to hum. Elizabeth looked at the girl once again, but she had turned away with the baby toward a homely wreck of woman who sat in the corner already opening her dress-front in anticipation of the feeding. Quite involuntarily, Elizabeth grimaced. It was a trial not to snatch Lydia's baby from her, but she held her ground.

With a quick whisper, she bid, "Pray Lydia, your wet-nurse, is she…entirely reliable?"

Lydia looked upon her as if she had run mad, impatiently replying, "Of course. Can you not see she is rich with milk?"

"You do not take my meaning…" Elizabeth began to explain, then the little nursemaid turned to her with such an expression of reassurance, she quit the subject entirely.

"Come, Lizzy," said her mother, turning up her nose at the thought of witnessing the very act she had vociferously avoided for herself and her daughters. "We must implore the Major to tell us more of his aunt."

"She keeps a box on Drury Lane," announced Lydia. "She is sickly and Hugh is her only relation! Can there be a happier thought?"

For some reason, Lydia's return to indecorous self-centeredness was a very present relief. It was as if Elizabeth had been waiting for the other, very large shoe to drop. She did not even bother to attempt to admonish her.

As they quit the room, she looked back upon the little nursemaid as she stood stroking the baby's head whilst the other woman nursed. Carefully and quietly she closed the door. Somehow, beyond all reason, she was comforted and had no further concern for the baby's well-being.

Footsteps Retraced

Since that fortuitous day on which she became employed by Lydia, what Sally knew as true had been twirled three-hundred-and-sixty degrees and then back again.

To what her family had just uncovered of the nature of Lydia's husband and marriage, Sally Frances had long been privy. She knew it all because loquacious Lydia had merrily admitted to much of her family's travails, and what she had not put forth she had hinted at broadly enough for Sally to have surmised. Lydia had not shared these private matters with Sally because she felt any kinship with her baby's nurse. Indeed, because her Aunt Gardiner did not offer her a sympathetic ear, she simply had no one else to listen to her prattle. Sally was, and always had been, a very good listener. She came, however, with a bias.

Sally's penurious perspective gifted her little respect for well-born folks who by accident crossed her path prior to her turning up on Gracechurch Street. That point of view had not been challenged during the days she had lain in wait for an excuse to make her way to the Gardiners. In that her first glimpse of that breed up close had been Lydia, her regard did not immediately improve for that specimen. After a very few weeks under her supervision, Sally held out little hope for the English race in general if Mrs. Wickham represented the ruling class. Had the Gardiners not arrived home and proved Lydia was not, as a rule, typical of her society, Sally might have been so dejected as to give up her project to search out her brother's history altogether. Although Sally thought Mrs. Gardiner was a fine woman, she was well aware that she was disapproving of Lydia bringing someone into their home without references (and, truth be known, with a street address that would have struck fear in her heart). Lydia asked nothing of her except was she capable of caring for a baby. Mr. Gardiner was in trade and from what little she saw of him, he was as kind as his wife. Their children were so well-behaved that whilst Lydia complained endlessly about them behind her aunt's back, Sally seldom was aware they were there. If any one indicator of Lydia's being a societal aberrance, it was the Gardiners' barely concealed dislike of her character. (In time Sally would learn that Lydia may not have been the most admired lady of her class, but neither was she a compleat peculiarity.)

It had quickly fallen apparent to her that Lydia was an immodest strumpet who used her wiles far more ruthlessly than any woman of the street. Yet, her aunt, Mrs. Gardiner was the finest lady Sally's eyes had ever beheld. True her home was not one-tenth as fine as the Darcys' house in Mayfair, but it was still grand by any standard Sally had ever had. Even Lydia had been little bother to her as she only paid a visit to her daughter once a day. Mrs. Gardiner had attended to the little girl with far more dedication than Lydia.

Sally's opinion of Major Kneebone was not quite so mean as that of Lydia. Despite his uniform, he was basically a man of books and quiet pursuits which was not the worst sort—although, clearly he was a dunce when it came to women. As Sally had witnessed the whole of their courtship, she was well aware that Lydia had seduced the Major as surely as if she had sat in a cheap dressing-gown in a window in Seven Dials. (Indeed, she thought those tarts a tad more honest.) They made quite an odd pair, which only disposed Sally to believe that there was no accounting for some people's taste. That Lydia's nuptials had attracted an invitation to Pemberley was as serendipitous an event as Sally had ever fathomed. She had been saving her pennies to sit aboard a post-*chaise* and she ended up travelling all the way to Derbyshire accompanied by the finest livery in three counties.

When they prepared to take their leave to Derbyshire, Mrs. Gardiner drew a loosely woven, aubergine shawl from about her own shoulders and gave it to Sally for the trip.

"Here, my dear," she had said, "you must not catch your death."

Sally was taken so unawares that she could hardly croak out proper thanks. But she had taken it from her with such reverence, it was unlikely that Mrs. Gardiner thought it unappreciated. Indeed, Sally felt the sting of tears at her generosity. (Lydia had given her a chintz gown and a used pair of high-low boots, but that had been more to please Lydia's sensibilities over the austerity of Sally's coarse, fustian costume than as an act of generosity.) The shawl played no part in Sally's elevated regard of Mrs. Gardiner as a lady, but it certainly solidified it. Surprisingly the esteem she held for the Gardiners did not translate into the same for the rest of Lydia's relations. As the Gardiners held all of Sally's admiration, she had little in reserve for anyone else. She believed it quite impossible that the whole of Lydia's family could be half as good as they.

Because Sally held the baby, she had ridden all the way from London inside the coach and upon the seat opposite the Major and Mrs. Kneebone. The aging wet-nurse, Malmsy, had ridden upon the top with a footman. Hence despite her apprehension of riding knee-to-knee with her employer halfway across England, Sally had felt fortunate to have been out of the rain. Major Kneebone was clearly a gentleman in having offered his seat inside to Malmsy. Lydia had said, "Pish-tosh—do not be a fool!" and he had wordlessly betaken himself inside the coach.

With every mile that drew her closer to Pemberley, ever-greater was her disconcertion. Despite her brother's high regard, she vowed to herself that she would despise them all. Indeed, she even refused to allow the estimable approach to Pemberley House as it came into view through the winding avenue of tulip trees to excite her anticipation. By the time, however, they drew to a stop beneath the portico, though she still clung dearly to her disapproval, it had begun to waver.

Indeed, forthwith of their arrival, her opinion wavered wildly from disgust to awe. That first was occasioned by encountering Mrs. Bennet. For the first to greet them was a lady of middle years and shrill voice entirely unknown to her. She greeted Lydia Bennet Wickham Kneebone with excessive determination. Sally stood dutifully by whilst both ladies cooed and kissed, professing undying affection. Major Kneebone was then introduced and the older woman declared herself to be excessively happy to make his acquaintance. Although Kneebone seemed pleased enough, Sally found the trilling voices unappealing. She loosened the blanket about the baby for proper inspection of her—one that did not then come about.

Sally meant to follow them through the huge entryway, but a servant caught her attention and directed her to wait. Malmsy was just then climbing from atop the carriage and bags were being unloaded from the boot. Without fanfare, they were herded toward a curved staircase. As she ascended it, she overlooked the huge black and white diamond pattern upon the floor, the statuary, and the gilded mirrors, and checked herself from gasping in awe. Overhead the entire ceiling was a brilliantly painted mural of winged angels, infants, naked women, and beasts. She had never imagined such magnificence, but feared that the scenes depicted might invade her dreams. She also wondered if the shrill woman who had met them outside was the beautiful mistress who had engendered her brother's loyalty and devotion. She shook her head free of such a notion and endeavoured with great concentration to take the stairs without a misstep.

The nursery room that had awaited them at Pemberley was as fine as anything Sally had ever imagined. She walked about eying the place in wonder and explaining it all to the silent newborn. Without instruction or much consideration, Malmsy took her seat in a nursing chair in the corner. Overtaken by sheer glee at the notion of such fine surroundings, Sally giggled and shrugged her shoulders at Malmsy, whose face cracked oddly, exposing two bottom teeth. It was the first smile she had witnessed from the woman, and that it took the form of a leering jack-o-lantern did nothing to ruin the moment of jubilation for Sally. Even in so small a position as a baby-nurse, the opulence of her surroundings persuaded her to pretend she was no less than a princess. She had thought the Gardiners' fine home in Cheapside to have been the apex of all that was grand. She had no words for a castle such as Pemberley. She could not make herself put the baby in a crib, but walked about the room as if in a daze, by turns looking out of the window upon a lawn adorned with white marble statuary. Sally paced the room once again, altogether stunned at this fortunate turn of events.

Her reverie was forestalled by the intrusion of an unknown personage in the room. It was a lady—a most handsome lady who walked directly to her. Sally was so taken by the exquisite visage that she did not immediately notice that fast upon the heels of the fine lady was Lydia and the woman who had greeted them upon their arrival.

The lady spoke to her but looked at the baby's face, saying, "Good day, Miss. Pray, may I take her?"

Sally nodded dumbly and handed her off. The baby stirred and the lady began to shush her and sing. Sally knew she was not to look at the lady—she had already learnt that would be unseemly of a mere nurse. Rather she should cast her eyes upon the floor, but she felt as if her eyes were beguiled from their duty and took another peek. Suddenly, she felt self-conscious and tugged a bit at her cap.

Lydia called the lady "Lizzy."

The lady called Lizzy said, "She is a sweet baby, Lydia. She favours you."

Just who the baby did and did not favour seemed not a subject that was favourable and was awkwardly abandoned. Slowly, perceptively, Sally began to determine the relationship of each of these gentlefolk. They were mother and daughters. Raucous Lydia was sister to the divine lady called Lizzy? Heresy. She squinted her eyes, taking it all in.

Perhaps her eyes betrayed this knowingness, for when the lady called Lizzy returned infant Sue to her open arms, she peered curiously at her. Lydia curled her nose at her. She was tempted to sneer at her, but dared not. Quickly, furtively, Sally cast her eyes away, feeling as if she were of some guilty knowledge. Before she had courage enough to look up again, both the lady and Lydia were gone. In that void, Sally was unsettled.

The single drawback to her entire undertaking was that she would be hard-prest to steal away to talk to the stable-folk about her brother. It would be risky, but she was determined to do it. She could not come in all this stead and learn nothing. 'Twas imperative.

72

What the Gods Have in Store

When Elizabeth reflected upon this time, neither her mother's disputatiousness nor her sister's inanity were brought immediately to mind. All she would recall was her husband's caressing touch and her children's delighted smiles all wrapped in a glorious, golden glow. Even the morning they rode out toward the far hills, the sun upon their shoulders was merely a kiss, promising the day to come to be as grand as the last.

The other shoe that Elizabeth anticipated fell, but it one was of an altogether different style than expected.

They awaited for the third day of Lydia's visit ere they took out upon horseback. It was not an unusual occurrence; it was a habit they took full advantage of when there were disagreeable relations in visit. Enhancing this decision was an uncommonly fine morning. Indeed, they would have been happy for this occasion had they not been running in defence of their very sanity. Despite the vexation of Lydia's trying presence, Elizabeth was in fine enough spirits. She had come to be easy with leaving her children for a few hours at a time. As those occasions were few, she cherished them. This day too held an additional pleasure. It was her first outing upon her beloved mare, Boots, since foaling.

Darcy had honoured Elizabeth's wish to present the colt as a gift to Fitzwilliam. It had been her intention since she learnt that Scimitar was the foal's sire. However, she had the good sense to wait to mention it until her husband's displeasure over the inadvertent breeding had waned. Much to her relief, his pique over the entire affair seemed to have disappeared altogether. Indeed, when at last she had nerve enough to broach the subject, he had behaved as if she had run mad to think he might have been of another mind upon the matter.

That told her that there was absolutely no remaining rancour towards Fitzwilliam—which was a happy thought indeed.

They made a little ceremony of it, gathering Georgiana and Fitzwilliam in the courtyard for the presentation. Elizabeth held Boots's reins and Darcy stood at attention in a manner that suggested the entire idea his. With great formality, he then bade Edward Hardin to lead the handsome colt out onto the cobbles. If any doubt had lingered over just which horse was his sire, all was forgot. So precise were his markings, he looked as if Scimitar's replica.

Perhaps thinking of her own son's likeness to his father, Elizabeth whispered in her mare's ear, "Poor Boots. I know how you must feel. It looks as if you had no part in it at all."

After the adulation of the colt's likeness had faded, Darcy reached out and took the reins from Hardin, and with great gravity, handed them to Fitzwilliam. The Colonel stood momentarily stunned—both by the colt's resemblance to Scimitar and the grandness of the gift. As unlikely as it was, tears seemed to threaten Fitzwilliam's countenance. But he and Darcy both put up such a masquerade of nonchalance that neither Elizabeth nor Georgiana dared remark otherwise.

It would be months, however, before Fitzwilliam would take possession of the colt, for it was not yet fully weaned. In the meantime, Elizabeth was happy to give her mare a little freedom. The frisky colt kicked jubilantly when turned out into paddock, and, like sons everywhere, did not look back when Elizabeth rode off on Boots. Secretly, Elizabeth thought of them as motherly cohorts escaped from their offspring for a truant day of play. Indeed, the wild extravagance of racing beside her husband made her heart hurry (in a way that was surpassed only by the liberties enjoyed of him of an amorous nature). Darcy, however, appeared quite of an opposing mood for he had spoken but little the entire morn. She felt a small pang of conscience that her kin and their abuse to his sensibilities had altered his spirits.

As had become his habit since their very first ride together, Darcy had always legged her up and onto her horse. Whilst she arranged her right leg over the side-saddle pommel, he situated her left foot in the stirrup. (Because upon every occurrence of this favour, his hand slid beneath her skirt and up the calf of her leg, it could be assumed his wandering touch was not a misplacement.) It had always been one of her particular delights to know of that intimate gesture, but unwitting to those surrounding them. It was a test to keep her countenance from exposing her private titillation from any witnesses. This day had been not different, indeed, she believed his hand lingered more than it had in the past, even giving her a gentle pat once she had been situated soundly in her saddle. Any overt affection had always been quite abhorrent to him. The very act of taking his hand upon a private stroll betimes left him somewhat ruffled. His effusive (his wondrous, exuberant, exhaustive) affection in private, however, removed any hint of reproof she may have entertained to offer. She wondered, therefore, if this overt act might foretell unusually pleasurable acts to come.

His reticence once they had taken leave suggested he was more thoughtful than amorous. Lest she accuse herself of unbridled wantonness, she refused to allow herself to be unhappy by such a turn of events. She did not hesitate, however, to reinvigorate her libidinous anticipation with the reminder that when he was disposed to be alone to ponder some vexation, he did not hesitate to take out upon his own. But, she thought it odd that he invited her along only to ignore her. After several attempts to beguile him into conversation met little success, she decided that frankness was necessary.

"Shall we go all this way without you speaking two words together?" she asked.

She did not like the tone of her own voice. It sounded uncommonly like a complaint rather than the tease she meant it to be. He turned about and looked upon her. His eyes were piercingly direct. So piercing were they that she unconsciously shrank in her saddle. Still not uttering a word, he nodded for yonder grove and gave an encouraging heel to Blackjack. The big horse responded splendidly increasing his leisurely walk into a gentle, rocking-horse canter. It was not necessary for her to nudge Boots, for the moment Blackjack cantered on, Boots followed in kind.

The sun was not yet high, but the shade still felt good upon her shoulders as she pulled Boots to a stop beneath a huge oak. Just as Darcy alit, a hare leapt from its burrow, startling them. Both horses reared, but Boots did not immediately settle down as Blackjack had. The mare continued to dance about, even kicking out with one leg severely enough to have called it a buck. Darcy relinquished his reins to catch Boots's bridle. She continued to half-jump, but he a put a soothing hand upon her nose, called to her in a soft lowing voice. Elizabeth believed herself to have done an admirable job of not being thrown, but refused to rule out that possibility whilst the horse continued to skitter about. Boots settled, but Darcy clung to the bridle and put his free hand out to Elizabeth in encouraging her to dismount. She let loose the reins and fairly leapt to him, and the momentum cast them both to the ground.

Lying atop her husband was not her least favourite position, but she feared that the odd elbow or knee might have done him damage, hence she immediately rolled from him and sat up.

"Have I inflicted on you any permanent harm?" she asked worriedly.

"I am always at your service to break any fall that may betake you," he laughed.

Both looked at Boots who was clearly confused by what had come to pass, for she had never reared with Elizabeth before that day. As if to rid herself of all the commotion, she gave a shuddering shake of her head. She then hung it low as if aware she had somehow caused great injury.

"Oh," said Elizabeth, "'twas not your fault, Boots..."

"No, it was not her fault. It was mine and mine alone," Darcy announced. "I should have ridden her first myself to ascertain her readiness to be reacquainted with a rider before allowing you to take her out."

Elizabeth opened her mouth to chide him for such an affront to her equestrian abilities, but did not. The expression he bore when he drew himself to one knee, bid her to be quite of another mind altogether. He reached out, cupping her chin in his hand.

Said he, "It is my duty to inquire of you, Lizzy. Have you injured your...have you been injured?"

She stifled a smile at his delicacy and shook her head almost as emphatically as had Boots. His hand dropped from her face and he knelt before her. His expression of concern, however, remained.

He said, "We must talk."

The gravity of this statement was not lost upon her. Her heart had not yet stopt racing from her small scare ere it was sent skittering again with anxiousness. She took his hands in hers (more of a comfort to herself rather than to him), to gird for what was to come.

"Bingley must retrench," he announced abruptly.

"Retrench?" she repeated dumbly.

"Yes."

"How could that be? Why? Jane has said nothing to me," Elizabeth was stunned.

"I am certain Jane knows nothing of it. Bingley only just disclosed the state of his affairs to me."

She sat in silence, her mind at the same time racing and suspended. It was an odd sensation—one she could not elude long enough to form further question.

In the resultant quiet, he said, "There is more afoot in the country than any of us had reckoned, Lizzy. When your sister related observing many waggons carrying belongings upon the road, she may not have exaggerated."

"If so, it would be a first," Elizabeth interjected sourly.

He emitted a small harrumph of agreement before continuing.

"What we witnessed returning from Brighton was only the beginning of an exodus of working men who have had to uproot their families and move east for work."

"Those men upon the beach…?"

"I cannot imagine what mischief they may have wrought," he admitted.

She shook her head, still unbelieving, "I am well aware high taxes and bad harvests have caused much hardship and unrest—but what has this to do with Bingley? Now that the war is over, Napoleon's embargo has been lifted upon his merchandise. I was of the opinion all was well."

"I fear it may well have come too late."

"Jane knows nothing of it?"

"Bingley has gone to London even now to speak with his bankers. They have impeded the movement of his shipments," he gave an imperceptible shake of his head at the thought. "It is a fruitless cause."

"They will lose their home," she said finally. Then realising the magnitude of that fact, "Jane! Poor Jane!"

"That may well be their fate unless someone comes to their aid."

"You have a plan?"

"I have a plan."

She smiled broadly. Her husband was, and always had been, a rescuer. At that moment she cared little how it came about, she wanted only to bask in the pleasure of his chivalry. He, however, would not allow that.

He said, "It involves a man I despise."

She looked at him quizzically, saying, "Had we not agreed to believe that George Wickham is dead?"

"Contrary to my previous comments," he said, "Wickham is not the only despicable man in England."

With that, he stood and put forth his hand, "Rise, please, and thither I shall take you."

She stood brushing grass from her skirts, mumbling that she was uncertain if she wanted to see any man in league with Wickham. He legged her upon Boots once again in repetition of the same seductive manner that he had employed when first they had taken their leave. She could not, however, give it her undivided attention. She could think of nothing but Jane and how distressed she would be on Bingley's behalf.

"You, sir," she cautioned, "must behave yourself, lest you tempt your wife from the business at hand."

He did not respond, but leapt upon his own saddle with an oft employed manoeuvre—one that she came to believe was employed only for her benefit. If it was, that made her happy twice—once because it displayed his considerable brawn to a propitious degree and second because he wanted her to see it.

Darcy's intended destination was a neighbouring estate. It was the home of a family that had long been a thorn in Darcy's keenly felt sense of righteousness.

Thomas Howgrave was a gentleman only by the most generous definition of that term. He had fathered a son by his housekeeper—a deed not unheard of among the gentry. The insult to his station as Darcy perceived it was not having an illegitimate son, but that he had ignored the indiscretion and the product of it until a particular situation necessitated him producing an heir. It was not the illegitimacy that affronted Darcy, but that he only chose to claim paternity when it fit his purposes—and Mrs. Howgrave was happy to stand arm in arm with her husband and the proof of his betrayal. Indeed, Darcy was known to have publicly snubbed young Henry Howgrave on more than one occasion. As to why Darcy had done the unthinkable in leading them to the Howgraves this day, and just what was their connexion to Bingley left Elizabeth altogether perplexed. She had no doubt there would be method to this madness—but madness it seemed nonetheless.

He led her to an overlook above the house.

"'Tis a very pretty prospect," said Elizabeth. "I did not expect that family to have such a handsome home."

Elizabeth turned her horse, expecting to proceed down to the house. Darcy put up his hand to forestall her.

"No?" she looked at him questioning.

For him to come all of five miles only to overlook the house of a man he did not esteem was quite bewildering. She had supposed that he had business there. The unlikelihood that he would have taken his wife to pay a call to such a man presented itself. Hence, she still desired an explanation.

"I wanted to see if you approve," said he, "of the house and its grounds."

"Why, yes. As I said, I find it quite pleasing."

"It is but five miles from Pemberley."

Cautiously, she agreed that, indeed, it was but five miles—her hindquarters vouched for the distance. She believed if he did not soon explain his cryptic remarks she might lose all patience.

At long last, he did thusly, "I want the place for Jane and Bingley."

She was torn between delight at the prospect of having her beloved sister close at hand and true chagrin in the realisation that Jane might soon be homeless. She looked again upon the property and pictured Jane's brood running and playing upon the broad expanse of lawn. It was a pretty picture indeed.

"Yes," she said, then more emphatically, "yes! It would be ideal! That is, if the interior is half so lovely as its façade."

"The decorations, I am quite sure, would be little problem for the two of you," he smiled.

"I know you will soon reveal to me your design," she raised an eyebrow—one suggesting that not a hope, but a demand.

"I do not yet have it all in place," he said; then cautioned, "do not speak of any of it to Jane."

"Of course not," she replied somewhat piqued that he thought that caution necessary (and somewhat contrite in realising that it probably was).

"Now that the elder Howgrave is dead, his son has inherited the estate of his grandfather. It was this inheritance which prompted my disapproval of the lot of them."

She nodded her head, recollecting the grandfather who wanted a male heir, and the unseemly manner in which the son endeavoured to procure one.

"Young Henry Howgrave is in want of parlaying his heroics in the Low Countries into a seat in Parliament, but he cannot from this district. He is willing to pay Bingley's debt in exchange for Kirkland Hall which carries with it a seat in Parliament, one that Bingley has not chosen to take," he explained.

That only answered a small part of her larger question. It remained unclear to Elizabeth how then Bingley would be able to purchase Howgrave Manor. Her husband's expression was one of unmitigated satisfaction, hence she felt he had everything in place for that to come to pass also.

"Once the bankers are paid, Bingley's merchandise will be released. That represents a considerable fortune—enough to purchase whatever estate he so chooses."

"You are quite pleased with yourself, I see," she teased.

"I must admit that I am—quite," he said. He then looked to the eastern sky and pointed with his crop, "The sky darkens—I am certain." Taking out his watch and looking at it, Darcy commented, "Yes, it is not all that late. We must make haste for home."

"One question, dear husband," said she. "Does Bingley yet know of the arrangements you have made upon his behalf?"

He shook his head, no. Then he drew his reins to the left and gave Blackjack his heel, causing the big animal to wheel about.

"Come," he called.

She took but one look at the sky ere she duplicated his manoeuvre, urging Boots toward home.

Headlong Passions

The sky did not withhold its deluge further than the outskirts of Dronfield. They had prest on in the vain hope that they could at least reach the more familiar area of Lambton before the heavens opened. There Darcy knew all manner of barn or outbuildings in which to take refuge from an impending storm. Those were the glens and downs of his youth. Here he was familiar only with the roads.

As they began to be pelted with the first large drops of a summer storm, Darcy spied a stone edifice down a small incline. They veered to its leeward side perchance to keep the worst of the storm from them. Fortune saw it to be a ramshackle shearing barn built into the side of a hill and open upon one end. They quickly dropped to the ground and led the horses under the shelter behind them.

Although it had lay unused since the spring shearing, it still stunk of dung, urine, and, increasingly, damp wool. But there was hay residue upon the ground and several broken bags of wool at one end. As it did not look like the rain would stop in much haste, Elizabeth removed her bonnet and shook her head a bit in hopeless attempt to dry the tendrils of her hair that were plastered to her cheeks. Seeing the tempting pillows of wool, she made herself comfortable away from what she knew would come to pass from the horses. They immediately obliged her by, first one then the other, employing a convulsive head to tail vibration that did the job of expelling excess moisture from them, but drenching everything around them. Knowing it then safe to tie them, Darcy led them to a post, but a clap of thunder made them stamp restlessly. He talked soothingly to them whilst Elizabeth began unbuttoning her soaked jacket. When she caught Darcy's eyes, she patted her hand invitingly upon the canvas bag next to her.

"I think not," said he taking off his jacket and giving it a fierce shake, "nor should you either."

She frowned at that in wonder just what fastidious quirk made him pronounce a bag of wool an unworthy perch. As it was an expression she had employed before, he recognised it immediately as one which suggested him overly captious.

"Sheep ticks," he announced.

"Sheep ticks?" she repeated. "My father had sheep and I have never heard of such a thing. I think you are making that up."

"*Longbourn* had sheep, it is likely that the only thing your father did was to count them."

Her hair was dripping, and her riding habit clung to her in a clammy, uncomfortable fashion leaving her a bit short-tempered. She was not prepared to capitulate to him just yet.

"I suppose that you, sir, did for your sheep more than my father did for his?" she retorted.

"As a boy, indeed I did," said he. "I have been bitten by many a sheep tick and refuse to submit myself to that injury now. This is a sheep fold and I dare say it is rife with ticks. Sit there amongst them if you will. I choose not."

She was inclined to further the argument by insisting that it was unlikely any sheep had inhabited lately enough to have left any blood-sucking insects behind, but her contentiousness was arrested. As he busied himself with loosing the saddle girths to allow the horses a rest, she allowed her gaze to take in the length of his frame. Soaked to the skin as he was, she could not help but notice that his aspect did not bespeak his usual meticulousness. Indeed, his hair in a muss and his costume soaked lent a rakishness to his attitude that she found altogether fetching. As he removed his jacket, she could not help but tell him so.

"I say, you look quite the brigand, Mr. Darcy."

"I dare say your curls have seen finer days themselves, Mrs. Darcy," he retorted.

She threw back her head and had a good laugh, allowing, indeed, that was no doubt true.

He added, "I also hope that he who owns this barn does not begrudge us this shelter."

"Surely, no one could be so cruel as to deny that in this storm," she said, "despite how disreputable we appear."

"There was a time when that would be true," said he, "but there are many on the road and some are not above pilfering when they can."

The thought of the poverty that drove those poor souls from their home was one she had little time to contemplate. Suddenly, she leapt up. She was sent halfway to Darcy before she realised that what had affrighted her was the bleat of a half-grown lamb—one most likely escaping the rain in the same fashion as themselves. She did not see her husband smile at her alarm for she immediately looked down and around the sack upon which she had sat and saw two small, glittering, coal-black eyes staring back at her.

"Oh, Darcy! What a precious little mound of fluff!"

As she reached out to pet it, he clasped her hand, holding her back, saying, "Do not—the ewe may be about."

No sooner than that was said, that particular danger came scrambling forward. Both Darcys leapt for the surest escape which was a ladder leading to the loft. Darcy stood his ground half-way up, attempting to regain some dignity. Elizabeth thought it all rather hilarious, but as the ewe maintained her mean watch, she thought it best to wait her out in the loft rather than on the creaking ladder. Darcy, however, kicked out with his boot several times in a determined, but ultimately vain, attempt to shoo her away. Elizabeth rose upon her knees and peered down at both him and the infuriated ewe.

Laughing, she called, "Retreat! She may have ticks!"

The look he gifted her was not quite as mirthful as hers, but he did climb up the ladder and onto the loft. They both looked down upon the sheep which, in turn, butted hard at the ladder. Darcy caught it before it fell and they both pulled it up onto the loft beside them lest they be marooned.

"This rain may well let up before the sheep," he said with his usual pessimistic perspective.

As a person of the more optimistic persuasion, Elizabeth began to claw hay into a pile for a more comfortable wait. He granted the ewe with one more dour look, but Mr. Darcy's glare—intimidating to all who fell under it—was useless on this sheep. Hence, even he knew when he was defeated and joined Elizabeth. When at last they were settled, they lay their damp jackets across the hay to dry, then lay back to listen to the rain as it struck the roof. In a moment, a banging noise behind them again brought Darcy to his feet only to see that the door to the hayloft had been left unlatched. He thrust a board against it to temporarily batten it.

When Elizabeth queried, "Pray, will that determined ewe come round here and find us?" it was only partly in jest.

He rose upon one knee and peered over the edge of the loft, "She is still fast to her watch here."

"A pity," said she.

Rising, she came up behind him and put her arms around his neck, placing her cheek next to his. Directly, she began to unbutton the first buttons of his waistcoat. He attacked from the bottom and their hands met mid-most of his chest. He grasped her hand, turned, and prest her back against their pallet of hay. Their long looks were to the accompaniment of the rain as it pounded the thatch of the roof and began to find its way through and then to drip upon the back of Mr. Darcy's head. They picked themselves up and found a dryer spot. The dampness and the chill were excuse enough if she had needed one; she nestled against him. He dutifully rubbed her arms and back and then blew upon her hands to warm them. Knowing there were far better means to encourage circulation, she lovingly stroked his cheek with the backs of her fingers, her forefinger trailing then to the tip of his chin. She whispered the beginnings of an ancient rhyme.

"Dimple in your cheek, a living you will seek; dimple in your chin, you'll have your living brought in."

He smiled.

She asked, "You have both, what does that foretell?"

"You have neither, what does *that* foretell?" was his rejoinder.

"It means that your son has a dimple in his chin and your daughter has none."

"Speak to me not of dimples," he said huskily.

As it was his bidding, she then raised her lips to his—a chaste kiss that did not remain so. As his tongue probed her throat, so did her hand make its own inquiry, sliding down the inside of his leg to find the firm evidence of his desire. (It had not been her intent, but since Brighton, she most particularly noted that was the only weapon he had concealed within his breeches.) With the barest of caress, his manhood presented itself at attention as dutiful as a soldier. Had her lips not been so thoroughly engaged in another employment, she would have smiled at how easily his member was provoked. She caressed it once again for no other reason than the pleasure of how easily she governed his...governor.

With that last caress, the kissing was not abandoned, but their attention to it was compromised by both pulling and tugging the tail of his shirt free with what became almost a frenzied abandon. Whilst he attended to the buttons on his breeches, she ran her hand up and beneath his shirt-front. He was left then to attack her skirts on his own—but he was immediately rewarded when she wrapped one liberated leg over his and began to massage his calf with the heel of her boot.

"Lizzy," he gasped. "Lizzy."

As she had embedded her lips against his neck, he did not hear her call out his name in return. Her mouth formed the first letter, but with the second, it altered into something akin to a moan. The rain pelting down, the smell of the aged hay, and the occasional bleats from below were a far greater aphrodisiac than either would ever have guessed. It was, however, no small operation to engage in the intimate manner they intended without the elements of their pastoral setting being the occasional bother.

Indeed, although when his hand found the back of her knee and thereupon cast her skirts aside, the wild abandon with which he was taken did not altogether preclude a small worry for her bared bottom being pricked by other than himself. It is the nature of such activities, however, that the deeper in the throes of rapture one becomes, the less any troublesome stems are noticed.

And because their rapture transcended the prickly nature of their bed, so did their vigilance. Hence, when there came a call from up the hill, it was a moment ere they realised that they had attracted unwanted attention. As Darcy was withholding himself with admirable restraint and Elizabeth was amidst a primeval swoon, it was he rather than she who first noted an intrusion. When he fell to the side and immediately began stuffing his shirt and his swollen member, she, understandably, was somewhat miffed. She grasped him by the buttons of his waistcoat and very nearly apprised him of the extent of her displeasure when she suddenly came to the realisation that something was amiss.

Before she could inquire the nature of the disturbance, he put his forefinger to his lips to silence her. Once again they heard a voice, this time it was accompanied by the rapping of a staff upon the doors he had just closed.

"You there!" the voice growled. "You will not steal my wool! I'll have the bailiff on you, I will!"

Only then did they see the sack of wool hidden in their loft. There was the merest flick of a moment when both entertained the possibility of identifying themselves to the owner of their shelter. Simultaneously both considered and rejected that plan in that their present occupation would be apparent—and therefore lend the Darcy name little distinction. Therefore, as the man impatiently rattled the door, Elizabeth straightened her costume with the utmost rapidity and claimed their coats, Darcy quietly slid the ladder back in place, stepped over and down a few rungs before offering Elizabeth his hand to follow his lead. Just as the intruder was having his way with the door, Elizabeth was only halfway down and nigh unnerved with panic, hence she veritably leapt into Darcy's arms. (In fortune, he managed to both break her fall and to keep to his feet.) With no thought of the belligerent ewe, both ran for their horses, Darcy hastily legging Elizabeth onto her horse. (It goes without saying that this manoeuvre was employed with such haste that it eschewed the usual accompanying caresses, but it had its own distinction in nearly propelling her over the other side.) He leapt upon Blackjack and they raced like blazes for Pemberley with the scream "Thieves!" ringing in their ears.

Fortunately, the rain had lightened by then to a mere drizzle allowing the remainder of the journey to be uneventful save for the disgrace done to their costumes by the mud-spattering run for home.

They were still giddy with the triumph of their escape when at last they arrived. Happily for them there were few who witnessed the embarrassing state in which they returned. The groom who took their horses made a point of not staring at them, and Darcy, refusing to slink away in humiliation, stood for a full ten minutes and detailed just how their horses should be cooled down. This predilection for maintaining his dignity at all costs was a particular torment to Elizabeth just then. But upon their walk back to the house, Darcy did the unlikely and took her hand. He whispered the promise that they would directly remedy the coitus that was *interruptus*. The hand-holding alone made up for any adversity they had encountered, but she smiled to herself as she thought of the many ways he would repay that debt. Indeed, he would have immediately had not they been stopt upon the staircase by Smeads with an important missive.

When Darcy took it in his hand, they both recognised the significance of its black border.

He tore it open quite hastily, but did not speak. Rather, he simply held the card betwixt fore- and middle finger and handed it to Elizabeth. With equal measures of gravity and impatience, she retrieved it. Her eyes scanned the letter quickly for it was the briefest of announcements. It read that his cousin, Lady Anne de Bourgh Beecher's soul had departed this earth and her mortal remains would be laid to eternal rest as soon as family could be gathered.

As summer's heat was at its peak, they must take their leave with all due haste.

Love's Labours

"Are they all horrid?" asked Mrs. Jenkinson incredulously. "Are you quite certain that they are *all* horrid?

A question, however innocently proffered, was no less an act of insubordination to Lady Catherine de Bourgh than a slap across the face. Her countenance registered that displeasure without any sympathy for her late daughter's companion whatsoever.

"Gothic novels, Mrs. Jenkinson? They are, every one, horrid and base!" she bellowed. "And in my daughter's possession! The stupidity to which you are favoured by nature, Mrs. Jenkinson, knows no bounds!"

Forthwith of Lady Anne's demise, Lady Catherine had ordered her bed-chamber stripped to the walls of every trinket or memento of her daughter's having lived there. Hence, the offensive literature had been uncovered within hours of Anne's death. A chamber-maid had discovered Anne's private store of reading materials and dutifully delivered them to Mrs. Jenkinson who had been charged with overseeing the project. Stricken with grief, such an act of finality as she had been engaged in was not to her liking. The single merit she saw in it was that it kept her from Lady Catherine's attention. Hence, this unearthing was most unwelcome. But she did what duty demanded and scurried to her mistress, the most well-used of the lurid books in hand as evidence.

As Lady Anne had been so undisciplined as to expire without so much as a by your leave to her mother, Lady Catherine had been most decidedly unamused. Initially, her ire had known no direction. To have the quaking Mrs. Jenkinson before her was absolute manna for her most urgent need—an unbridled vent. Given only the merest moment for contemplation, Lady Catherine had concluded that the demise of her charge fell compleatly to a lack of diligence on Mrs. Jenkinson's part. As Lady Catherine saw it, if her treasured daughter had sullied her mind in so unspeakable manner, Mrs. Jenkinson *had* to have been remiss. Her daughter certainly had not the wherewithal to employ such stealth. One would have to be a dolt to have been oblivious to such activity.

"I paid you good money to watch over my daughter, and to what end, I ask you?" She continued her diatribe, "I should have you repay me every penny!"

The novella her ladyship held in her hand (and periodically cast to the floor and stomped upon) was *The Mysteries of Udolpho*. It had been Lady Anne's favourite and therefore the ideal volume to endure Lady Catherine's outrage.

Mrs. Jenkinson was truly unwitting of Anne's bent for lurid prose. Perhaps she was a dolt to have been unmindful of Anne's surreptitious doings. Had she been aware, she certainly would have hied to Lady Catherine with that intelligence with all due haste. She was shocked, mortified, and not a little conscience-stricken to learn that guileless little Anne had duped her so shamelessly.

In that much of Lady Catherine's umbrage stemmed from the fact that the culpable party was long past hearing a vituperative lecture upon the evil and foul writings. Unused as she was to insubordination, being denied the ability to vent her fury upon her newly departed daughter, she looked upon Mrs. Jenkinson as the next best thing. But not only did she choose to accuse her of a lack of vigilance over her daughter, she was disposed to suggest to Anne's companion that reading novels of that ilk had been injurious enough to Anne to have weakened her for childbirth.

One of Lady Catherine's most finely honed skills was to identify personal weaknesses. She could sight the person who was most susceptible to brow-beating with great dispatch. The laying of guilt was her special gift. Mrs. Jenkinson was both heartbroken over Anne's death and aware that her own existence was in jeopardy as well. Her very life depended upon gaining another position. That would depend solely upon a recommendation from her employer. Therefore, so far as vulnerability went, the poor woman may as well have had a sign reading "sitting duck" hanging about her neck. To Mrs. Jenkinson's further misfortune, when Lady Catherine smelled weakness, she did not relent until blood was drawn. She wailed away until her victims were beaten prostrate. Having spent the better part of a decade under her rule, Mrs. Jenkinson had never been a match for her employer. Now, at her weakest, she merely served as a receptacle for Lady Catherine's bereavement-driven wrath.

Her ladyship had always despised weakness—in herself no less than any other. She was a remarkable specimen of stalwartness, both in disposition and constitution.

However, her daughter's death had gifted Lady Catherine something akin to grief. She had not been so indecorous as falling into a weep, but initially tears did threaten her countenance. To a lady who prided her command of every matter great and small, that had been unforgivable. She was notoriously impatient with the short-comings of others, and was no less rigid with herself. Therefore, she refused to admit that she was guilty of undue sentiment and set out to badger, berate, and deride any persons who crossed her path. Regrettably, the first such person had been poor Mrs. Jenkinson, and it was she who bore the brunt of the grieving mother's method of lamentations.

Lady Catherine was then halfway through a stack of black-trimmed mourning announcements, and did not much want to be interrupted. There were any number of details to which she must attend, but making arrangements for the care of her granddaughter was not amongst them. Prior to Anne's lying in, a wet-nurse and baby-nurse had been employed and taken residence in a room within the upper reaches of the house. The baby's care had not altered whatsoever with her mother's death. Lady Catherine had gone so far as to have the baby unwrapped for her to count her fingers and toes. The only sentiment she showed had been to lean forward and mindlessly kiss the baby's forehead before waving her away.

All who witnessed Lady Catherine's actions that sad day were properly appalled at her lack of tender feelings. All of her servants feared her ladyship. A few even harboured a measure of respect. Most, however, despised her as imperious and dictatorial. Yewdell knew Lady Catherine more intimately, by his reckoning, than any other member of staff—and most probably her family as well. He, alone, witnessed what others did not. She was undeniably authoritative, her air was not conciliatory, and her arrogance was unrivalled. But she was not as unfeeling as she wanted others to suppose.

When Mrs. Jenkinson had come shuffling before her bearing testament to her daughter's disobedience, dishonour, and compleat lack of discernment, it was not surprising that she flew into an aggrieved snit, lashing out at the nearest object. As it was unacceptable for a daughter of hers to have been guilty of such offences, it was necessary for her ladyship to lay the blame upon someone else. Unfortunately, Mrs. Jenkinson did not have the forethought to take her leave with any haste and it fell to her spindly shoulders to bear the brunt of Lady Catherine's considerable displeasure. It was a pitiless, one-sided row. Lady Catherine was relentless in her censure, all but convincing poor Mrs. Jenkinson that it was by her hands that Lady Anne had gone to her eternal reward. Lady Catherine's premise was that the tremblings and vibrations that books of a lurid nature wrought upon the innocent hearts of their readers caused injury to her daughter's weakened chest, thus causing her to be unable to withstand childbirth.

"It is a clear case of injury through omission!" Lady Catherine squawked, adding for good measure (lest the poor woman was not compleatly taken amort), "You, woman, could not have driven my daughter to her grave any more certainly than had you prest a pillow across her face and smothered her yourself!"

With that last harangue, Mrs. Jenkinson stopt wringing her pocket-square, prest it to her mouth to stifle a wail, and ran from the room. Yewdell dutifully opened the door for her to make her passage and just as dutifully closed it behind her. Because of Yewdell's vigilance, Lady Catherine's last bit of diatribe failed to follow the hysterical woman up the staircase. Hence, she was spared the denunciation of "Murderer! Heartless murderer!" that rang out upon her fast-retreating footfalls.

There was not a person in the service of Rosings Park who remained uninformed of their employer's attack upon the heart-broken Mrs. Jenkinson. Disgruntlement, which had kept its head prudently low, began to behave more blatantly, yet no one was disposed actually to rebel. Times were far too unsteady for anyone to mutiny. Lady Catherine did not pay her staff well, but she paid them regularly (save for her personal maid who in lieu of pay often had to take her ladyship's cast-off apparel), and few were inclined to risk their positions to take the part of one old woman. After taking stock of their options, most were inclined to think kindly of their own necks and meanly of Mrs. Jenkinson's.

As usual, Yewdell kept his own counsel on the matter. He neither aligned himself with the grumblers nor defended Lady Catherine. Properly, his main concern remained his feet. The slippers that her ladyship had demanded he wear never became more comfortable. He had returned to wearing his old ones, but Lady Catherine had pronounced them unacceptable. They had been at logger-heads on the subject and he had worn a pair of clogs just to inflame her. Now, of course, he had reverted once again to the torturing pair for appearances sake. Lady Catherine would disapprove if his looks were less than exemplary when the family gathered.

Into this testy atmosphere the Darcy branch of the de Bourgh family arrived at Rosings Park. Darcy and Elizabeth had taken leave of their children for the first time and both were uneasy, although they exhibited this disquiet in decidedly opposing methods. Elizabeth talked far too indiscriminately and Darcy would not speak two words together. Their single uniformity was that neither spoke a word of their children. This oddity was not lost upon Georgiana, and she smiled knowingly.

That she rode with them upon their pilgrimage to pay their respects to their cousin was the culmination of a great deal of argument. This, not because her company was undesirable, but because she was great with child.

Indeed, she had insisted upon travelling there against the advice of everyone. Fitzwilliam had threatened to physically restrain her, but that threat was met with little more success than any other dictum Colonel Fitzwillliam issued to his delicate wife. With her uniquely demure demeanour, she flatly overruled him. He shrugged his shoulders in a manner suggesting one who had given it his all but had been defeated by superior forces. Neither Darcy nor Elizabeth had fared better with their arguments. Elizabeth had gone so far as to relate to Georgiana her personally experienced travails of childbirth upon the road. In wanting to persuade Georgiana, Elizabeth had employed all due hyperbole. Regrettably, it had little effect upon anyone save her husband. It soon came to her attention that Darcy had turned an ominous shade of grey. She retracted those descriptions with all due haste, but the damage had been done to his sensibilities.

He appeared to be unable to look squarely upon her countenance.

The discomfiture that observation wrought upon her did not leave her until long after they arrived in Kent.

*T*he Gathering

"What dreadfully hot weather this week," said Lady Catherine, flapping her fan. "I fear it keeps me in a continual state of derangement."

No member of her company dared to contradict that statement, most certainly not Darcy and Elizabeth. Elizabeth had been jumpy as a cat since their arrival, Darcy was merely glum. Her ladyship's deportment upon the occasion of the interment of her daughter's corpse had been curious indeed and did little to improve their humour. They had been altogether uncertain in what temper they would find her. Anger, melancholy, anything seemed a possibility save the one that greeted them. For Lady Catherine sat in her favourite high-backed chair, directing servants upon their rounds of offering refreshments. (It was an unfortunate irony that chair was the very same one she had awaited that which occasioned this sad gathering, but it remained unacknowledged.) At that moment, her most pressing interest was for her guests to know what lengths her hospitality knew.

"Do enjoy your sorbets," she admonished. "It will be the last ice we see this year."

With every exultation to her guests, Henry the parrot squawked. Lady Catherine sat in her usual majesty ignoring the fact that every time he did, her guests cringed. She had dressed in half-mourning lo these many years since Sir Lewis's passing, hence the lustreless black bombazine of her dress was no great departure from her usual attire. Hence, Henry the macaw's garish feathers were at odds with the nature of the gathering. The only clue that there was anything amiss for Lady Catherine herself was that the old-fashioned powdered wig she wore was exceedingly ill-kempt (looking for all the world as if a unsheared ewe had curled upon her head and lately died). Her costume and toilette never quite recovered from the disappointment she had experienced some half-dozen years before when her favourite nephew threw over her daughter and aligned himself with that Miss Bennet. So deeply was she bothered, she had seldom found reason to entertain. Indeed, having fallen into a decided funk, she all but withdrew both herself and her daughter from society. Upon those few occasions when invitations were issued from Rosings, the primary purpose had not been to entertain. It was to offer opportunity to those of her neighbours who desired her condescension the privilege of laying themselves before her prostrate with obsequiousness. Anne, however, was so seldom in good health that she frequented those events but little. Those of less sympathetic leanings standing patiently in the foyer for the viewing noted that this was the first social gathering that Anne had graced in some time—and glanced with a snigger at her flower-draped body laid out for inspection.

"These ices are the last we can look forward to this season," her ladyship repeated, still fanning herself, "so you must partake."

She flicked her fan closed and rapped the wrist of a man sitting to her right. His collar and plain, black suit identified him as of the clergy (had the carefully arranged dolefulness of his countenance not). He had introduced himself to the Darcys immediately upon their arrival. In the few minutes they conversed with him, it was apparent that Lady Catherine had done the remarkable in finding a vicar suitably unctuous to fill Mr. William Collins's shoes. The gentleman did not actually resemble Mr. Collins in any way but by his grave, stately air and formal manners. He walked in a hunched, prissy manner as if suffering a case of the piles. He looked to be no more than thirty but had a small paunch and unsuccessfully covered his balding pate by the artful arrangement of a few sparse strands cultivated from behind his ears. His most prominent feature, however, was his sense of self-importance—rivalled only by his veneration for his patron. He had introduced himself as "Mr. William Henry Pratt, faithful servant of God, dedicated educator of Hunsford Parish, and grateful vicar under the condescension of the illustrious Lady Catherine de Bourgh."

"It is a sad, sad day for Rosings Park, the County of Kent, and His Majesty the King that we have to lay to rest a true flower of England such as Lady Anne de Bourgh," he announced. "I have taken pen to page and written, I flatter myself, a sermon to compliment Lady Anne's memory with the utmost compassion thereby offering her dear mother succour to her wounded breast."

No doubt he had repeated that same speech to each and every ear at Rosings Park. That Lady Catherine kept Mr. Pratt at her elbow suggested he had rendered it unto her more than once as well.

Even before she gifted the vicar with a rap as a reminder to partake of his sorbet, few dared refuse Lady Catherine's demand. Her demeanour, under the circumstances, was so peculiar it had instigated hushed whispers. Although it was her stated office, she did not behave as if bereft. Indeed, had one been unapprised of the circumstances of the gathering, it would have been supposed that she was the hostess of an afternoon tea. She accepted condolences, but did not speak of her daughter's demise directly. That was a difficult thing to do as Lady Anne's mortal remains, cautionary plate of salt sitting upon her thin, dead bosom, was displayed directly opposite her. It sat in the broad doorway, a velvet rope between the coffin and the path designated for tenants and neighbours to pass by to pay their respects. Lady Catherine was happy, however, to expound upon the clamour emanating from the doors that opened onto a grand promenade. As she explained them, her plans were for what could only be described as a shrine.

Indeed, in the distance was the insistent sound of stonemasons' hammers as they chinked gouges from an enormous slab of Italian marble that lay incongruously upon the manicured lawn. That marble was meant for a twelve foot sarcophagus that was to adorn Lady Anne's coffin. Another, even larger, piece of pink marble was then being unloaded, giving Lady Catherine the great pleasure of describing the levers and pulleys necessary to do so. This monstrosity bore the tell-tall traces of delicate grey veining which announced its rarity. This piece, she explained, was to be sculpted into Grecian pillars upon which crouching male figures' upturned hands would support the four corners of the mausoleum. Each of the four edges of the cornice would be adorned with a frieze depicting the seasons. The only decision left was for her to determine which of the scriptures would be engraved beneath Anne's name. That would be transposed upon a replica of a scroll to be held by the figure of a six-winged seraph with bas-relief cherubs tugging at its skirts. Whilst a number amongst her company gave the appropriate sighs of admiration, not all were awestruck. The haste that must have been employed to have the marble and men already hard at work only two days after Anne's death remained unremarked.

"Who does she suppose she is burying, the bloody Earl of Carlisle?" grumbled Fitzwilliam under his breath to Darcy. "She could better have spent her time getting the body underground than arranging all this folderol!"

It was true. Those who were witting of the ravages the heat wrought upon a corpse also knew that the grimace that was beginning to plague Anne's pale face did not stem from a lack of peace made with God.

He immediately was regretful of his remark, for he looked about to discover that he stood directly to the left of Lady Anne's widower, recognising that gentleman by his short stature and elaborate mourning attire. He nudged Darcy and flicked his head in Beecher's direction. Beecher then moved with amazing grace across the room to his mother-in-law's side. A bit of a smirk upon his countenance, he took her hand in his and prest it to his lips. She glanced at him as he did so, but gave him little more notice as she was still enraptured by her architectural creation.

Observing Beecher's mincing walk and fawning ways, Fitzwilliam forgot all regret upon his behalf, whispering to Darcy, "Still the veritable tulip I see."

"I see he suffers his loss well," replied Darcy. "I have never seen a finer waistcoat sported by one bereaved."

Whilst consoling his mother-in-law, Beecher's eyes darted about, appraising the comforters who had gathered in Lady Catherine's large parlour. His eyes stopt abruptly, having caught sight of the handsome tailoring and, if he wasn't mistaken, equally exquisite boots belonging to Mr. Darcy and Colonel Fitzwilliam. Having previously had the pleasure of making their acquaintance, Lord Beecher moved before them, bowing majestically.

Before Beecher could utter a sound, Darcy anticipated him, saying, "I am very sorry for your present sorrow."

Seemingly taken aback, Beecher muttered, "Yes, yes. I thank you for your kind words. We are very much in grief."

Fitzwilliam echoed Darcy's sentiments and Beecher complimented his concern as well, nodding in Georgiana's direction, he added, "I pray your expected event will end more happily than ours."

Fitzwilliam was altogether aghast and thus rendered speechless. To have alluded to Georgiana's condition was unspeakably indecorous. Neither was he particular pleased to have pointed out the obvious danger that they faced. Had he looked in Darcy's direction, he would have seen that his friend's countenance echoed his. As was Darcy's nature, he met indecorousness with extreme formality. He bowed curtly, turned his back, and strode away, leaving Fitzwilliam to contend with Beecher's unseemliness alone. Having been to the wars, Fitzwilliam knew Beecher had spent time in the West Indies. After time in warmer climes, it was sometimes difficult to reacquaint oneself with the niceties of society. He chose to believe this indignity and his previous familiarity in naming

Georgiana fell to his being an unseasoned traveller rather than overt crudeness. Certainly his aunt would not have allowed Lady Anne to have married other than a gentleman. He endeavoured to put those affronts behind him and offer some helpful advice.

"I fear," he said tightly, "your sojourn in the West Indies has made you forget yourself. Society in England is unused to such frankness."

"Of course, can you ever forgive such rudeness?" Beecher said. "This sadness has been very trying. I scarcely know what nonsense finds its way out of my mouth. I meant no disrespect."

His words were humble, but his expression remained somewhat haughty. Still, Fitzwilliam was not the sort to hold mere words against another gentleman. He had witnessed far worse injury inflicted by his fellow man. He was happy to believe Beecher a victim of something recognisable to him rather than a compleat boor—a condition for which he had no explanation. Yet, Fitzwilliam had limits upon what ill-traits he would accept from another. Beecher was obviously a dandy, but Fitzwilliam had felt pity for Anne all her life and had hoped that his poor cousin at least had been honourably settled for a small portion of her life. Darcy, he knew, held no such hope, privately pronouncing Beecher a fortune-hunter.

Believing himself to have won Fitzwilliam's sympathy, Beecher took him by the arm and steered him from the others, immediately launching upon a story to test that kindness. It involved Fitzwilliam's least favourite subject, but one the unsuspecting Beecher thought a soldier of the crown would enjoy.

"Are you, Colonel, one of those soldiers who considered Napoleon's disturbing the peace of the Continent as a personal kindness?" he laughed. "What ever shall you do with yourself now that Wellington has given us tranquility?"

Fitzwilliam was not unused to such abuse, and he answered mildly, "Once one has witnessed war there is nothing quite so dear as peace."

Darcy then approached Fitzwilliam, touching him upon the elbow, "Forgive my interruption, Fitzwilliam, you are needed."

He nodded his head in the direction of Georgiana who was sitting upon a settee at the far end of the room. Elizabeth was fanning her. She did not look entirely well and Fitzwilliam nodded curtly to Beecher and hurried to her. Beecher smiled at his hastening and sauntered up to Darcy.

"The Colonel is a very dutiful husband," Beecher sighed. "What is it they say of courtship and marriage, Darcy?"

Darcy stood mute.

Smiling amiably, he answered his own question, "Courtship to marriage—a very witty prologue to a very dull play."

That was not a theory to which Darcy subscribed. Despite his disinclination to converse with such a man, he could not help but retort, "There are occasions when I have known that to be true. Perhaps it is thus when the match is insincere."

If Beecher believed that observation was directed toward him, he did not display umbrage. He did, however, defend his marriage, not scrupling to employ his dead wife's name.

"I am happy to share with you that your cousin Anne often told me that she had loved me from first we met."

"In cases such as these, I must take leave to observe that there is a road from the eye to the heart that often does not traverse the intellect."

Darcy did not see what sort of response his remark had upon Beecher's countenance, for he immediately betook himself in service of his sister. Elizabeth had warned him that Georgiana felt unwell and was much in want of Fitzwilliam escorting her upstairs. That sounded remarkably like an imminent birth to him. He wished that Georgiana had listened to Elizabeth and not taken the journey to Kent. In her present state, chiding her for not taking that advice would have been unwise. But he could not keep from worrying. Indeed, he felt himself become increasingly anxious as he awaited Elizabeth to return to his side with the news of Georgiana's condition. He stood apart from the other guests, nervously pulling at his cuffs, hoping against hope that Beecher would not again seek him out. Whilst one eye he kept upon his guard for that gentleman, the other he kept trained upon the stairs. After some time, Elizabeth appeared. She had stopt midway down the staircase and beckoned to him. He was to her side in an instant.

Employing no artificial formality, she said, "Her time is come."

The expression she bore suggested just how imminent her time was. That concern was immediately shared by Darcy.

"Has the surgeon been called?"

She nodded that he had, but said, "I fear the baby will arrive ere does he."

She knew enough of his discomfort of the subject not to employ the word "pain" in her description of Georgiana's condition. Still, the furrow between his eyebrows deepened and she patted his arm in a motherly fashion.

"Dare not," said he, "conduct yourself as if I were a child."

He immediately regretted that objection, but his regret was tardy by half. Her countenance registered a hurt of some magnitude. Still, she remained true to the issue at hand.

"We must perforce be calm," she said. "We have no reason not to expect all will be well."

After being petted like an infant, his least favourite thing was being advised to be calm. Hence, his initial pique was reinstated.

"Of course," he said curtly.

The mood of this wait was not to improve, for once Lady Catherine heard her niece had been taken to the straw, she abandoned her watch over her daughter's corpse to sit with Darcy and Fitzwilliam. Elizabeth escaped by reason of frequenting Georgiana's bedside.

Upon the untimely demise of Lady Anne, Dr. Brumfitt had hastily removed himself from Rosings Park. To his horror, Lady Catherine had issued no reproach. Had she rebuked him, had she screamed epitaphs at him (yea, had she threatened to draw and quarter him and throw him to the pigs), he would have been frightened, but not nearly as alarmed as he was in her silence. When he was recalled to Rosings, it was only with the utmost fortitude that he made himself board Lady Catherine's carriage. He knew not what lay before him and he was far too wretched to inquire of the driver for the particulars. When he arrived, Lady Catherine did not receive him, but he was relieved to learn that his services were welcomed once again. Only upon learning that did he once again draw an easy breath.

Regrettably, that news was met by an equal relaxation of his sphincter (that had been in a puckered state since Lady Anne's passing), thereby causing him to spend much of Georgiana's labour perched upon a chamber-pot in the servants' quarters. Chasing up and down the staircase did not leave him much time to monitor Georgiana's progress. Of this turn of events her husband and her brother remained unaware. In fortune, Elizabeth had assisted in Jane's deliveries, therefore she had little trouble performing those duties to which the surgeon was unable to attend. Georgiana was as stout-hearted as any soldier's wife, bearing down with determination. If she was afraid, that remained unapparent. Indeed, she had enough wits about her to direct Elizabeth's hands to help her daughter into the world. When she handed the baby to her mother, between them was exchanged an acceptance of a bond eclipsing any that had gone before.

Once she had washed the baby, swaddled her, and placed her in her mother's arms, Elizabeth betook herself to announce the birth (passing Brumfitt upon the stairs). Both relieved and ecstatic, Fitzwilliam rushed to Georgiana's side to adore his wife and his newborn, leaving Darcy and Elizabeth with the awkward task of sitting with Lady Catherine and keeping her company.

The line of viewers had dwindled with the light, and Lady Catherine gave the orders to have her daughter's coffin sealed. As she had gone to await another child to be brought into the world forthwith of those instructions, Mrs. Jenkinson took that private opportunity to creep next to the coffin and place therein the tattered copy of *The Mysteries of Udolpho* and the cross and chain Anne had received at her confirmation. It lay to her to weep and to keep watch as the coffin was nailed shut.

It was altogether fitting that when Fitzwilliam returned from his introduction to his daughter he announced that it had been their agreement that her name should be Anne.

The Proposition

As the Darcys and Lady Catherine sat about awaiting their turn to see the newborn, no one had much to say. Those unspoken thoughts of Anne's very different parturition imbued the air around them with a sickly, sticky uneasiness. Darcy had been out of sorts since arriving at Rosings. He had a private audience with Lady Catherine soon after their arrival that did nothing to alleviate his mood. Having been privy to what transpired when last Darcy hied to Rosings with a mind to settling a score, Elizabeth knew how torn he must be. He had left to his aunt's discretion the timbre of their continued relationship. She had refused the baptismal and Elizabeth assumed their connexion irreconcilable. When death visits, betimes those rifts are repaired. She hoped that so, for Darcy's sake, not hers. Family meant a great deal to him.

When Darcy was invited to meet his niece, he invited Lady Catherine to join him. She, however, demurred. It was a surprising choice. Elizabeth could not imagine that her ladyship would prefer her company to any other. Lady Catherine had been cordial to her. At least she was cordial in Darcy's presence. In his absence, such as then, she largely ignored her. This tacit agreement between themselves was very much to Elizabeth's satisfaction. She had offered her sincere condolences upon their arrival and was happy not to be called on to engage in those discourses particular to funerals.

"Nothing improves one's reputation like dying," she had observed to Darcy as she listened to boundless remarks alluding to Anne's handsome face, svelte figure, keen intellect, and unrivalled kindness.

Having known Lady Anne, even platitudes seemed useless. Hence, she sat at that moment admiring silence more than any other occupation. So quiet was it, Elizabeth nearly leapt from her seat when Yewdell entered the room and announced Dr. Brumfitt awaited.

Curtly, Lady Catherine bid him enter.

He sidled in, standing but one jump from the door. He did not address Lady Catherine, but Elizabeth. He bowed with a quick little dip of his head and eyed Lady Catherine with wide-eyed apprehension. She busied herself adjusting her skirt, giving him the courage to address Elizabeth. He hemmed and hawed a bit, giving Lady Catherine to snort derisively.

"Get to it, Bumfitt!"

He immediately quit stammering and put forth a piece of paper. Upon it were several notations and a figure. It was his bill. Elizabeth reached out her hand and he inched his way forward until he was near enough for her to snatch it from his fingers. It was a tidy sum he charged for standing by Georgiana's side with his watch in his hand to time her contractions (which came with no less frequency than that of his bowels), and he submitted a bill for full services rendered. Dr. Brumfitt was clearly of a mind that Georgiana's delivery recompensed that of Anne's too, for even he had not the gall to ask Lady Catherine for payment for a dead patient. He was greedy, but not stupid.

"God heals and the surgeon hath the thanks, eh Bumfitt?" Lady Catherine harrumphed.

Elizabeth discretely folded the bill and nodded to Brumfitt, whispering she would see that it would be attended to. He acknowledged that promise and made for the door, Yewdell delicately closing it behind him.

"Will there be anything else, Madam?"

Lady Catherine shook her head and resituated herself in her chair. Yewdell then withdrew from the room. In the silence that followed, Elizabeth felt compelled to make some remark.

All she could think of to offer was, "However timorous Dr. Brumfitt's demeanour, I believe his devotion to his pocketbook commendable."

Lady Catherine neither smiled nor glowered, but simply nodded her head. Elizabeth folded, then unfolded her hands, smoothed her skirt over her knees, and folded them once more. She had just decided to excuse herself and make her way to Georgiana's side when Lady Catherine spoke.

"Have you seen my granddaughter?"

"No, your ladyship, I have not had that honour."

Rather than pulling the bell cord for a servant to bring the infant to her, she rose, issuing the command, "Come."

Elizabeth could do nothing but follow her up the stairs.

They were but half-way up, when she realised that Lord Beecher had joined them. She turned about with a start at this notice and he smiled genially. She nodded in return, but an uncomfortable feeling gripped her spine, causing her to shudder involuntarily. By the time they gained the upper reaches of the house, the stairs had narrowed. The passageway they entered was lit by a series of torches, and she felt as if they had entered the farthest keep in a castle. When at last they reached the door of the nursery, she entered a perfectly well-tended room. It was composed of ancient furnishings, but there were several nurses on hand to see to Lady Catherine's granddaughter.

As would most mothers, Elizabeth went directly to the baby's side to admire her (and compare her to her own children).

"What a beautiful baby," she gushed, employing not a single bit of exaggeration.

She truly was a pretty newborn, having not the misshapen head expected of such an arduous trip down the birth canal. Elizabeth was prepared to offer her admiration and depart, but Lady Catherine astonished her by asking her if she would like to hold the baby. Her first impulse was to beg off, but she feared that the infant would not often feel the comfort of caring arms. The nurses looked to be more efficient than loving.

Tenderly, she took the motherless baby into her arms, who snuffled a bit but did not stir from her sleep, and cooed softly. As she had done with her own, she drew the backs of her fingers across the baby's brow. Before returning her to her cradle, she kissed her upon the forehead. A nurse came forward, but Lady Catherine shooed her away. Once again Elizabeth was very aware of Beecher's presence and wondered their design—for she was certain they did not bring her all this way without one.

At last Lady Catherine spoke, the beginnings of her scheme unfolding.

"It is as if it were that day a generation past, dear Elizabeth."

Dear Elizabeth—*that* was a dead giveaway. Her scheme must be a weighty one indeed, Elizabeth thought to herself. But she would not allow her countenance to register that detection.

Mildly, she inquired, "Whatever do you mean?"

"Why, it was but that long ago that I stood with Darcy's mother just as we are here."

Her voice had taken on an odd softness. Elizabeth was convinced the woman *was* actually recollecting.

"Truly?"

"Yes, indeed," she continued, "we stood over Lady Anne's cradle just as you and I are here. Poor, dead Anne!"

Elizabeth was well aware that if Lady Catherine was prepared to employ pity for her means, she would employ every shot in her locker. Yet, she remained aloof, refusing to give Lady Catherine any assistance. She looked at her keenly, but Elizabeth continued to gaze upon the baby.

"From their cradles, they were meant for each other!" She boomed, then remembered herself and repeated softly, "From their cradles, they had been meant for each other. But that was not to be."

Giving up all semblance of apathy, Elizabeth then looked directly at her.

"No, that was not to be," she said evenly.

"No," Lady Catherine repeated.

That capitulation gifted Elizabeth her very first sense of triumph. She somehow felt, however, it was not a feeling that would last.

Beecher interjected, "That is history, Elizabeth. Today is another day."

She could not disagree with those observations, but she refused to admit it in apprehension of what he thought this day would bring.

"Yes," agreed Lady Catherine, her eyes ploughing silent daggers at Beecher's chest, "today is another day. We have before us another opportunity to unite our families as Darcy's mother had wished unto her dying days."

Lady Catherine's design fell glaringly apparent. Although Elizabeth did not want to despise any future bride for her son out of hand, it was a compleat impossibility that she would force her darling son into a marriage conceived by anyone or anything other than his own wishes. She harboured no doubt whatsoever that she would never agree to such an arrangement. At that moment, however, she could not be certain of Darcy's mind. If Lady Catherine employed his mother's name and his dead cousin's memory, might he be prevailed upon to agree to such a scheme? It had long been her fear that in marrying her, he might have believed that he had betrayed his mother's wishes. She had been so certain of Lady Catherine's hatred, she had never once entertained the notion of employing such a gambit. Perhaps, she worried, she already had gone to Darcy. Why else would Lady Catherine have had the audacity to approach her?

"My son is yet a baby. To speak of such arrangements now is ludicrous."

The curtness of that opinion was not lost upon anyone there. She had hoped merely to evade the issue, but her true feelings could not help but burst forth. Whilst she mentally flailed about for the least objectionable way in which to extricate herself from this exceedingly uncomfortable situation, the ill-humour Darcy had harboured since hearing of Anne's passing visited her thoughts. She did not expect that he would celebrate such an event, but neither did she believe that singular occurrence to cause him undue discomfiture. She had a firm feeling that something else was afoot. This rumination was not distinct, it passed through her mind in a wild jumble. She still scarcely knew what to say to Lady Catherine. Beyond objecting to her ridiculous plan, the only remarks that came to mind involved accusations of insanity. She looked at Beecher, compleatly flummoxed as to what part he had in it all.

In imploring her to agree, Lady Catherine once again employed Darcy's mother's name, "I am certain my sister is looking down upon us as we speak, praying for this promise to come to pass."

"I believe," Elizabeth said, "we should allow our children to have their own mind in such matters. I am certain my husband agrees."

Lady Catherine raised one eyebrow, "Are you? His sister has just named her daughter after mine. I have already spoken to Darcy. It is clear that time has altered his opinion upon the matter. Family has become ever more important to him."

Lady Catherine's tone had returned to a more familiar one. That was actually a relief for Elizabeth. It was easier to remember her as the foe that she had been, rather than the grieved mother that she was this day. She did not for one moment believe that Darcy had agreed to such a plan. That was an outrageous supposition. More likely was that any moment Lady Catherine to begin to call her an insolent, headstrong girl—that she had sullied the hallowed alls of Pemberley. But she did not.

She did worse.

She looked upon her with an odiously knowing countenance. Drawing up into a reasonable facsimile of her husband's hauteur, Elizabeth begged her leave. Lady Catherine gave a curt nod.

"Time has come," she said as Elizabeth made for the door, "for you to recognise the family to which you are wed."

She fled down the stairs, one last, ridiculous ploy of Lady Catherine's ringing in her ears. It was proffered, however, by Lord Beecher.

"We shall call the baby after you, Cousin Elizabeth."

Elizabeth was incredulous. Such indecency! If they would sell that baby's name so cheaply, Elizabeth shuddered at what other designs they might have for a helpless infant. As she betook herself with great haste down the steps, she was plotting wildly as to how she might rescue that baby, hence, she literally bumped into her husband as she rounded the newel-post. She apologised for her distraction, took a calming breath, and inquired as to Georgiana—betaking herself in that direction ere he had the opportunity to gaze upon her troubled countenance. She was not prepared to engage in the touchy discourse necessary to sort out the entire matter. There were far too many buried hurts and apprehensions. It took her a while to come to one conclusion, however. It was a recollection of some comfort.

Lady Anne was called after Darcy's mother. If Georgiana named her child after someone, it would have been her mother, not her cousin, Elizabeth reassured herself.

"That is one thing I know to be true."

Sweet Sorrow

Every room at Rosings was more extravagant than the last. It had not altered since last Elizabeth visited, but she had. When once she was overwhelmed by the sheer magnitude of the edifice, now she saw it quite differently. Now used as she was to Pemberley's exquisite decorations, she saw the difference between the two houses clearly. Rosings was opulent, Pemberley was elegant. With worn upholstery and scratched floors, Rosings replicated the aging dowager who was its mistress. The drapes were kept drawn so neither could be seen in the harsh light of morn.

Having been to crumbling St. James palace, Elizabeth certainly understood Darcy's explanation for Rosings's condition.

"Early in her marriage, my aunt employed the same decorator as King George, believing his decisions to be sacrosanct and did not question any expenditure," Darcy had told her. "She is the most parsimonious woman on earth in small matters but has thrown good money after bad in adorning her home with the most outlandish decorations in England."

They slept in the same room Darcy had inhabited upon his long-past visits to his aunt. It might have been expected that their brief respite from their children would have gifted them with a tantalising sense of freedom. Rather, it did quite the opposite. In the embrace of life's alpha and omega, both Darcy and Elizabeth were out of sorts. In times such as these it was a parent's inclination to draw their children to their breast and remind themselves of the fragility of life. Moreover, Elizabeth sought the comfort of her home in which to ruminate upon those questions that troubled her. It had been a subtle transformation (perhaps influenced by her father's death), but the thought of Longbourn no longer elicited melancholy recollections. It was a revelation for her to realise how compleatly Pemberley embodied her notion of home.

She lay upon her side of the bed without even an errant foot to remind her that her husband was but an arm's-length away. Coupling had not even been considered. Such selfish longings seemed altogether out of place with a coffin one floor below. Had that not been the case, the sheer forbiddingness of the place would have dampened the most fervent desires. It was a wonder any procreative activity had managed to flower in these bed-chambers. That understanding made her curious about Anne's marriage. She was not even privy to where she and Beecher had wed. They had met in Bath, perhaps they held their nuptials there. That thought was to be a comforting notion. Anne had been a sad creature indeed if she never once enjoyed the lists of love. She realised then that she had come to believe that Lady Anne's wedding and pregnancy was through her mother's wishes, rather than her own. Having faced Lady Catherine and Beecher over her granddaughter's cradle, she had little doubt of it. Lady Catherine was perfectly capable of sacrificing her daughter to profit her family name. From what she knew of poor, weak Anne, childbirth must have frightened her to her very bones. How could such a fragile girl be expected to weather such a daunting event? Elizabeth hoped that her pregnancy was due to Anne's own desire for a child and not her mother's for an heir. She wanted to believe it, but the spectre of Lady Catherine made her think that Lady Anne was far more frightened of her mother than of dying in childbirth.

Initially, she had, as any mother would, empathised with Lady Catherine's loss. She even felt a nagging sense of guilt—the same conflicting rush of emotions that betakes one when an enemy meets with misfortune. A rational creature knows that ill-feelings had no part in it, but cannot help but fear (or hope, depending upon one's rectitude) an ownership in that injury. Elizabeth's step had been heavy with that culpability up to the moment Lady Catherine endeavoured to coerce her into sacrificing her first-born's life on the altar of Family Connexions. The notion that Darcy, in any way, shape, or form, agreed to such lunacy troubled her keenly. A week ago, she could have laughed at such a notion. Not a day's time underneath Lady Catherine's roof and she would believe her beloved husband capable of the most heinous of transgression? That was a question she had not yet addressed.

And she would not address any of it with any haste. She had vowed to herself that Lady Catherine's walls would not hear her broach any point of possible contention with her husband. It was not beyond Lady Catherine to have eavesdroppers about. Indeed, added to Elizabeth's unease, she had the odd notion that she was being watched. This and other apprehensions made her quite anxious to return to hearth and home. She had given Hannah instructions to begin preparing her trunks for the trip home when they departed for the burial. She knew it might be premature. Georgiana's ill-timed childbirth meant she would be kept to her bed for weeks. It would be even longer before she would be able to travel.

The Darcys rode in the same carriage with Fitzwilliam when they returned from the burial. It had been an extravagant event, particularly in such a small hamlet as Hunsford. Lady Catherine seemed not to be happy for the out-pouring of sympathy. Indeed, as the cortège grew, she seemed less appreciative of that sentiment than the crushing all those ill-bred feet did to the flowers about the gravesite. Other than Lady Catherine's decided ingratitude, the only other matter of note was that Anne was not laid to rest next to her father. One could only suppose that lay to the fact that her mother's plans for her daughter's monument would have Lord Lewis's pale in comparison. Indeed, after that first anxious flurry of attention to his place of rest, it seemed never to have been tended to once. In that Rosings Park had been his ancestral home, one would have thought his widow would at least have made a point of giving his remains a place of respect rather than a barely discernible stone lying amongst the weeds and rabbit burrows.

Lady Catherine's notion of family and consequence continued to be disagreeable.

Elizabeth shook her head of such thoughts, glad to have such an unhappy event behind them. She also thought it prudent to employ a moment that she knew to be private economically. There were arrangements upon Georgiana's behalf that must be agreed upon.

"I suppose it would be best for me to stay here with Georgiana," Elizabeth offered.

There was not a bit of tentativeness in her voice, given she thought she might run mad if forced to stay any longer under Lady Catherine's roof. Her duty was decisively divided, however, between wanting to stay and care for Georgiana and return to her children. They were in capable hands, but they were not her hands. To her good fortune, the decision was made for her. Neither Darcy nor Fitzwilliam thought her staying was a reasonable proposition.

"Thank you for your kindness, Elizabeth," said Fitzwilliam. "I know Georgiana would not allow you to forgo your own children to care for her. It is not as if she would be helpless, for my aunt has more servants than any three estates put together. She will not want for care."

He turned to Darcy to see if his mind was alike. Darcy nodded his head and gave the briefest of smiles.

"As much as I would like to have her home, that appears to be the only answer," he agreed. "I have to wonder if having Georgiana here might give my aunt something with which to engage her mind rather than her recent loss. She seemed quite pleased to be of service last evening."

Elizabeth felt a bit of giddiness stir in her stomach and turned her head to look out the crack left by the window shade, lest they see the delight her countenance registered at the notion of escape. She was then calculating the months mandatory for mourning a cousin and was happy in knowing that they would be out of their black by Christmas. Their children would be old enough this year to enjoy that celebration. The sudden realisation that poor Anne would never enjoy another Christmas (if, indeed, she had in the past) stole her sudden flash of good humour. She also worried for the tiny baby whose brow she had kissed. She did not relish the notion of her growing up in the wretched gloom of that nursery. From the looks of him, there was little chance that Beecher would rescue his daughter—indeed, if Lady Catherine would even allow it. Again, she searched her mind for a way to save the baby, but for naught.

There was one thing that would either save the tiny girl or be her downfall.

The de Bourgh fortune was not entailed away from the female line. She wondered what arrangement Lady Catherine had with Beecher. There was little doubt that he was a fortune-hunter, as to why she had encouraged the engagement to be formed with him remained an enigma. There was one certainty. Lady Catherine had a plan. Lady Anne certainly would not have gone against her mother's wishes.

"It is all so puzzling," she said aloud, startling herself.

Accordingly, both Darcy and Fitzwilliam inquired, "Pray, what is puzzling?"

"Anne's marriage—I cannot in all good conscience call it a romance. Her health troubled her so that she was seldom out in society, but she married a man who is by no means respectable. Even if Lady Anne fancied him, I cannot believe that Lady Catherine would have allowed such a match."

"In his favour, his admiration for rank and connexions rival my aunt's," said Darcy.

Having not had the pleasure of his company, Elizabeth resorted to respectable hearsay, "Georgiana believes his society to be irksome."

"I would wager that he has not a sixpence of his own," said Fitzwilliam knowingly.

"There you have it," announced Elizabeth sheepishly, "we have proven that no one is happier to point out one's shortcomings than his relations."

"You may claim him if you want, but he is not my relation," Darcy announced with such vehemence, Fitzwilliam and Elizabeth had to laugh.

"I do not think we are allowed that choice, dearest," Elizabeth said, instantly regretting it.

The subject of undesirable kin was one that always had been avoided—and not because of her own vulgar relations. Indeed, since Lady Millhouse's revelation over just who was and was not his kin, Darcy had all but given up despising Elizabeth's mother and sister. Right then, Darcy's thoughts did not mirror hers. If he thought of Wickham, he gave no indication.

"I will simply regard Lord Beecher as someone else's problem until his remarriage makes him so."

That seemed a suitable way of looking at it for all of them, and by the time the horses gained the portico their humour was much improved. So merry were they, they had to reclaim their countenances before being handed out of the carriage. Elizabeth removed her gloves and was heading for the stairs to oversee the arranging of the trunks, when she was stopt by the voice of Yewdell calling her husband's name.

"Mr. Darcy, sir, an urgent letter."

A carelessly folded piece of paper lay atop Yewdell's finger-tips. It was from Pemberley. An icy chill enveloped her spine making her walk clumsily in the direction of the missive. Few urgent missives beheld good news. Had she been inclined, she was unable to take the letter herself, for Darcy had snatched it from Yewdell before she could. With great deliberation, he took the letter and placed it inside his waistcoat, and with a graceful sweep of his hand indicated for Elizabeth to precede him up the stairs—a reminder to keep one's private matters private from the help. She did so, but did not take a breath until they had gained their assigned bed-chamber. The word "urgent" echoed with such reverberation in her mind, she feared that it might be heard by others.

Once the door had closed behind them, he hastily retrieved the missive, tore off the seal, and walked to the window for better light. Elizabeth followed him so closely, when he turned to tell her of its contents, he stepped upon her foot—an injury that remained unnoticed.

"It is from Bingley," said he.

"That cannot be, they planned to spend the season in London."

He handed her the letter and she saw that the letter had been directed to Pemberley from London, and forwarded to Kent. A deep, satisfying exhalation issued from her lungs. That information reduced her apprehension for her children immediately, but not for her family compleatly. She had written to Jane telling of Lady Anne's demise and their travel plans. Undoubtedly, their letters crossed in the post. What could possibly be amiss? The letter had been "urgent."

"I must away to London," Darcy said with finality. "Immediately."

"Is he well? Is Jane well?" her voice became ever more urgent itself. "Are their children well?"

"It is," he said, "a matter of business."

He patted her much in the same manner that had so recently offended him. She was miffed enough to be inclined to point that out to him, but that might disturb the nature of their conversation. Therefore she did not (and congratulated herself upon being the better person).

"I can only assume that this business is the matter we discussed?" She would not be happy with so little information of such important matters.

"Yes, it is the same," he replied. "I would tell you more if I knew more, but I do not. He merely wishes my assistance upon a matter of some urgency."

Hidden beneath the hem of her skirts, she gave a small, indignant stamp of her foot. She disliked not knowing—particularly when her family was involved. She saw that their trunks were well upon their way to be readied to travel. Darcy called for Goodwin and told him that he would leave for London in an hour. Goodwin's countenance registered his approval of their destination—he had been unhappy at Rosings almost as sincerely as had Elizabeth.

Before Goodwin became more animated than usual, Darcy said tersely, "I will be travelling alone."

Goodwin's and Elizabeth's countenances both fell. Neither was aware that they were of such like minds, for Goodwin had immediately begun to retrieve Mr. Darcy's belongings and Elizabeth was still at his elbow.

"I believe I should travel with you," she reasoned. "It will be a treat to see Jane once again—it has been months."

"It is better that she not know of any of this, Lizzy," he explained. "I can meet with Bingley covertly. She need not know that I am there. If you come as well..."

She understood that rationale, but was still not happy. He seemed not to notice, for he had busied himself going through papers in a small satchel, tucking some under his chin, others in separate stacks.

"Furthermore," he said without looking up from his employment, "you must stay here."

"You cannot mean to leave me here, alone with your aunt?"

"You will hardly be alone—Georgiana and Fitzwilliam are here as well. I know you are much in want of seeing your children. No doubt they miss their mother. We will all be home soon."

"They miss their father too," she said dejectedly.

"I beg your pardon," he said absently.

She rose and walked away from him, drawing back the heavy, velvet curtains and looking vacantly out a window, which looked not to have been cleaned for some time. She licked the tip of her forefinger and rubbed it against a spot to determine which side had been neglected. The spot smudged. Mr. Collins extolled the expense of Lady Catherine's glazings. She would be most excessively displeased to see one of them in such a state. Elizabeth mindlessly grasped the hem of her sleeve with her palm and fingers and began patiently to rub all the dirt from that pane. When she had finished, she looked at her cuff. It was grey with ash residue.

"Come winter," she said idly, "they must adjust the flue in that fireplace."

That was what she said, but not, however, what she thought.

"What?" Darcy said impatiently, picking up the chosen pages and stuffing them in the satchel.

"You will, no doubt, presently show me your pistol and tell me how to use it," said she, recollecting the invidious leave-taking in pursuit of his errant sister.

Impatiently, he again repeated, "What?"

She closed her eyes, her back still to him, "I said, I bid you good-bye."

"Yes," said he, "I bid you good-bye."

It appeared quite easy for him to take his leave from her with nothing but a pat upon her head. How dare he patronize her in that manner? How many times had they vowed that they would never again travel alone? Had that been merely hyperbole? She was endeavouring with all her being to be angry, but truth was, she was hurt. And humiliated.

She could hear that he had not walked to the door, but she could not turn about to face him. She simply could not. If she did, he would see the huge tears that had welled in her eyes had begun the trip down her cheeks.

"I refuse to be a weepy wife," she told herself. Then aloud, she said over her shoulder, "A safe journey."

He answered her not. But she did hear his footsteps. She heard them all the way to the doorway, then through it. She did not turn about until she heard the sound clunk of the enormous door close behind him. His leaving her side without kissing her good-bye did not bother her in the least. She loved him no less than she ever had, but she had concluded that until she determined what agreement he had made with his cursed aunt, she could not, in all good conscience, offer her…affection.

There was no doubt of that.

Clandestine *Tête-à-tête*

She refused to stay alone in that room for another moment. She considered taking leave for Pemberley at first light. She would arrive before the children would be put down to their night's sleep. That notion pleased Elizabeth exceedingly and she gave those instructions to Hannah and Goodwin. If he could be happy leaving her, then she could be happy betaking herself home to those whose podgy arms would be extended to her. She did not much relish the long ride alone. She would have Hannah and Goodwin to keep her company. No doubt he had taken their coach to London, the three of them would have a cosy trip in the smaller carriage, but that was of little matter. She chose not to think of his displeasure when learning that she had returned to Pemberley alone. Alone and unarmed upon the road. It was only then that she worried that he may not have taken his pistol with him. He had told her of the danger upon many of London's streets. If he was to meet Bingley other than at his home, what must that street be like? The notion of returning to Pemberley without her husband began to lose its lustre. She would be just that much farther from him if some catastrophe should befall.

It was early afternoon; Darcy would be in London long before nightfall. That was a comfort. She was no more easy with him travelling alone than he would be for her. Yet, she could not elude the suspicion that she had formally been rendered an unwanted accoutrement. She knew that he had much to occupy his mind. In being unforgivably miffed, she felt as if she had fallen into some wifely trap—one where the husband embarks upon some lofty duty, leaving his wife to be an unreasonable shrew. But she was miffed.

She refused, however, to sulk. She believed the proper tonic for her mood was to see her children once again. In the meantime she would busy herself—and avoid Lady Catherine. She quickly determined an ideal solution—she would make her way to Charlotte's home. It was the same cottage that she had occupied as wife to Mr. Collins. Darcy had arranged for her to keep it in lieu of any claims against Longbourn. As those homes were very dissimilar in worth, he had settled a sum upon her to redress the difference. Charlotte was not of effusive nature, but she had appeared pleased. She had exchanged letters with her at Christmas, but Elizabeth had not seen her for some time. She had only glimpsed Charlotte at the gravesite. She had her son with her. He had grown substantially since last she saw him. He had a dull look to his eyes and had grown fat-bottomed like his father. He looked nothing like Charlotte, who seemed to be thinner each time she saw her. She feared one day that her figure might become so insignificant as to be literally blown away with the first strong wind.

Not being in her usual conversational mood, Elizabeth had prepared what subjects she would address. Firstly, she intended to ask her opinion of the new vicar. She would be interested to learn if Charlotte saw the resemblance to her dead husband. She initially entertained the possibility for a match—then quickly determined that it was unlikely that Charlotte would want a suitor. She had never thought highly of men or matrimony. Her first marriage was simply of convenience. For a woman of small fortune, marriage had been her only alternative. Presently, she was a well-provided for woman of steady age and character. She would have little need of a second marriage.

Thinking back upon Charlotte's alliance with Mr. Collins (possibly the silliest man in England), the memory could not help but make her sad. She had hoped her friend might find love at last.

"I am not romantic, Lizzy," Charlotte had once told her.

Perhaps, Elizabeth thought to herself, I am too romantic. Charlotte wants nothing from life but a good fire and no one to trouble her. She looked placid. Was not placidity a more favourable state than her own present distress? She had no answer for that. She gazed upon her reflection in the looking-glass and tied the ribbon to her bonnet so tightly it almost choked her. It was a pleasant sensation. She strode to the door and looked each way down the corridor. She stepped out her door, once again stopping to listen for footfalls. It was a simple matter to pay her respects to her old friend, but she strove to avoid having to explain herself, particularly to Lady Catherine. Hearing nothing, she went directly to the staircase and from thence, made her way through the scullery and for the rear door.

She had but put her hand upon the door-knob when she realised she had not put on her black gloves. In her hesitation over returning for them or defying convention, a hand reached out from the shadows and clutched her wrist. Had she been of her normal composure and not been so skittish, she might not have shrieked as she had. She also might not have caught the handle of a convenient pot and raised it above her assailant's head. In fortune, she did not bring that instrument down with any force, for if she had, she would never have forgiven herself.

"Lizzy!" Darcy whispered.

He had caught her weapon-wielding hand by the wrist and held it suspended. Her eyes grew large at what catastrophe had been barely averted.

"What do you mean lurking about the scullery like this? You nearly frightened me out of my wits."

"I apologise, I did not expect to find you in the same corridor that was my own means for a secretive re-entry into the house. What brings you here?"

"Much the same as yours, but of opposite intention."

"Where do you go in all this stealth? The minute your husband leaves, you take covert leave of the house?"

She was tempted to be coy over her reasons, but could not engage in an activity that was so foreign to her nature.

Hence, she said, "My intention was to steal across the lane and pay my regards to Charlotte. I took this route simply to avoid the house's mistress."

"My intentions were less noble," he replied, "but richly rewarded."

She looked at him. She blinked. The hands that had loosed her wrists found her waist. He drew her hips solidly to his.

"Oh," she replied.

He lowered his head as if to kiss her, but did not. He prest his temple against hers and drew it across her forehead, much as she had employed her fingers across that of Anne's daughter.

Whispering against her ear, he said, "I have yet to take my leave without a kiss to hurry my return."

He then kissed her upon her forehead. Although it might have appeared to be, in no manner did she see it as fatherly.

Still whispering, he said, "No matter how burdened are my thoughts, you are never far."

"You returned to give me a forgotten kiss? I am all astonishment."

"I would travel farther for less."

"Whose favours tempted you thusly?" she teased.

"She is a saucy lady, one not of your acquaintance," was his rejoinder.

Before she could reply, his hands guided her backward, pushing through a partially opened door. She came to rest against a shelf, one of many that spanned from eaves to floorboards. Without removing his hands from her waist, he kicked the door shut with his heel. It shut soundly enough for her to wonder if they were heard. Her throat suppressed a giggle. The thought of granting favours in the pantry under Lady Catherine's roof delighted her in a way that was most audacious. (That she was about to behave in so illicit a fashion was titillation enough—that her lover was the man her ladyship had done everything within her power to keep from her had absolutely no influence over her—or at least very little.) He leaned down to kiss her and she raised her lips to meet his. But theirs was not the pursed-lip peck of farewell often seen of departing spouses. Theirs was the moist, hot, tongue-probing kiss that would not allow containment. Little could curtail their passion, and only one concern elicited any adjustment.

It had always been a small inconvenience that he was so much taller than was she. Not that she begrudged him that height; indeed, his carriage was positively...splendid. When they kissed, however, it was a bit of a stretch (but one well worth the effort). Early on there were more occasions when this difference was an issue, as they were disposed to kiss at odd moments. Although their love-making may have begun toe to toe, it most frequently ended in their bed. When once they had coupled whenever and wherever passion overcame them, they had of late become less adventurous. She had not realised that alteration had come to pass until in the darkness of this unfamiliar closet, she heard the familiar sounds of her lover's desire (at least what she could hear of him over her own laboured breathing). Had she had the wherewithal to study the matter, she might have supposed she had happened upon the root of her increasing interest in their afternoon rides. It was an adventure of possibilities.

At that moment, however, more immediate concerns needed addressing, for although she had wrapped both arms and one leg about him, the matter of elevation was reasserted. Passion (particularly their passion) was not inclined to await for adjustment. Their lips were still locked in a kiss which was more distinguished by enthusiasm than aesthetics, therefore, neither looked about for architectural features suitable for positioning. They did, however, grope. In the past he had prest her against a brace (a door, a window sill, a book-shelf), and would have then, but when her searching hand found the organ evidencing his arousal, he was momentarily distracted. Indeed, when she ran her hand across his tumescence, he momentarily had a weakening of the knees.

Although her appraisal told her there was little room for improvement, she stroked him. The quiver beneath her fingers gifted her an inward smile.

Evidently, that caress signalled an escalation of their ardour from the preparatory to the quintessential. He did not put his hand upon hers in encouragement, for that was quite unnecessary. Rather, he grasped her hair, urging her head back, exposing her neck momentarily ere he began to kiss it. Her neck was but a brief investigation, his hand finding her knee and struggling for her hem. When he had successfully surmounted the obstacle that was her petticoats, his hand glided up her thigh, fingers spread as if to leave as little of her skin unstroked as possible.

"A moment," said she loosing her clasp upon his manhood. Gasping, she repeated, "A moment."

For that moment little was heard but panting, hers mingled with his.

Finally, he croaked, "What? Pray, what?"

"Did you," she began, paused for a moment to regain her breath, then continued, "agree to promise our son to Lady Catherine?"

Again, he said, "What?" but with a tinge of exasperation.

"Did you, or did you not, promise our son to Lady Catherine's granddaughter?"

"What?" He repeated once again, then with irritation, "I did not."

He still had his hand beneath her skirt, but it had quit its progress.

"She told me that you did."

"Can we not speak of this another time?"

"I think not."

With resignation, he removed his hand compleatly, placing it impatiently upon his hip.

"I may have said something to that effect, I cannot recall," he confessed. "When first we arrived, she took me aside and implored that ridiculous notion of me. I, of course, denied her. She began to weep, Lizzy. What was I to do? She had only just lost her daughter. You know that I am not disposed to be swayed by a woman's tears. However, observing a woman of her temper weep was exceedingly discomposing."

In the shadows, he looked to Elizabeth for reassurance that she would agree upon that point. She was silent, but he believed she was not in disagreement.

"I said whatever I could to satisfy her and not compromise our son's future," he related, admitting, "I may have…I told her that I could make no such promise without your agreement."

"I *knew* you would not agree to such a scheme!"

"She approached you?"

"I fear this is so."

"And you said nothing of it to me?"

His words now were in the accusatory. Although they had been whispering, she lowered her voice further.

"I did not want to speak of it whilst we remained under her roof," she explained, and then became irritated at having fallen prey to Lady Catherine's machinations once again. "That woman drives me to distraction!"

"How far might you be distracted?" he teased, his hands once again finding her waist, thumbs undulating upward to her bosom. As she had yet to fully regain her breath from their previous endeavours, it was but a short way to reach the throes she had just begun to enjoy. Their respite did not dispose them to betake themselves up the stairs. It was unspoken, but both were not of a mind to share their inclinations with anyone else in the house. It *was* remarkable how quickly his manhood was reinvigorated.

Indeed, having previously scaled the obstacle of her skirt it was no bother, but that of his height was re-addressed. In fortune, of the many shelves lining the pantry it was easy to find one of convenient height to accommodate them. From thence, they happily resumed their love-making and it was but a few caresses ere rapturous fulfilment was enjoyed.

Regrettably, accompanying this climax was an event that was unplanned. The shelf employed for the aforementioned bracing was not as resilient to repeated prodding as was…Elizabeth. Hence, with the last shuddering throes of passion, it shattered, smashing to the floor. This crescendo was not nearly as quiet as theirs. Indeed, they were fortunate to escape uninjured. And, escape they did with no small haste. They quickly reinstated their costumes and hastily exited.

Standing innocently outside the wreckage, Darcy said, "I suppose I must be on my way."

"And I as well," said she.

He reached for his hat, tapped it upon his head, and said, "A pleasure."

"To be sure," replied she.

Without anyone being the wiser, both took their leave by way of the back passage, he to his patiently waiting carriage and she to the path to Charlotte's.

Upon her way, she hurried her step and looked over shoulder to be certain he had not espied this giddiness. He walked away with his usual purposeful stride. With excessive adoration she watched him stride away—a regard which happened to treble upon espying him returning her gaze. When their eyes caught each other's in identical over-the-shoulder glance, both countenances were over-spread with the same heightened shade of rose. Whilst he strode on with even greater determination, Elizabeth could not keep a small skip from her step.

The Vicar's Widow

Still experiencing the frisson of amorous consummation, Elizabeth's visit to her old friend brought her back to her senses. Returning so hastily to the world of restraint and fastidiousness would have been jolt enough, but as it happened her polite call upon her old friend was strange indeed. That peculiarity had little to do with Charlotte's corporeal self. (Her thinness Elizabeth had first noticed whilst they stood amidst the rabbit runs criss-crossing the graves.) Since she had journeyed to Pemberley after Elizabeth's confinement, Charlotte had altered in other, less identifiable ways. Endeavouring to pinpoint such alterations did not come easily.

Charlotte seemed quite pleased to have Elizabeth's visit (if she was not she put on a decent air of welcome despite it). When last they saw each other, Elizabeth had still been in the throes of those conflicting humours of new mothers which were largely comprised of fatigue and unmitigated joy (with a dollop of self-disgust and a dash of pique). There were so many callers, they had little private conversation. Of her friends, Charlotte had seemed to be least influenced by her elevation in station. (To not have to suffer toadying or snobbery was a considerable relief.) Their discourses had remained those easy chats of their girlhood.

This day had begun no differently. Indeed, their conversation was garnished by a few speculations that could be considered gossipry. Primarily amongst these conjectures were those that often surrounded the death of the well-born. An alteration in a household always meant an alteration in servants. Speculating upon which servants would receive their dismissals and which would obtain a legacy entertained not only those amongst the staff, but the community in general. Upon this occasion, conjecture did not favour Mrs. Jenkinson. This talk of Lady Anne's passing reminded Charlotte of a particular point of unhappiness.

"That churchyard is a compleat disgrace," she exclaimed before Elizabeth had taken a bite of her sweet-cake. "It is inexcusable of Mr. Pratt to ignore it so. It certainly was better cared for when Mr. Collins saw to it."

In that single sentence, Charlotte answered several of Elizabeth's questions. She was certain Mr. Pratt neglected nothing that Lady Catherine did not approve. She also saw that it was folly to entertain the hope that the new vicar might replace the old in ways other than in the pulpit. Charlotte clearly kept notice of his failings. That was more the pity, for Elizabeth had never quite given up hope that she might find happiness. Eventually Elizabeth would learn that certain souls did not seek happiness, but merely to be left to themselves. Regrettably for Charlotte, every step she took in the direction of peaceful seclusion gifted her two toward relentless torment.

"Our vicar does not like his cottage and envies me ours," Charlotte said with satisfaction; "they are identical but for the improvements I have made."

Elizabeth was happy she had not brought up the subject of the vicar. He seemed to be a sore spot with her. She did not want to irritate her unduly. Charlotte was not only thin, she was very nearly emaciated. She had a haggard look about the eyes that Elizabeth had seen the beginnings of at Pemberley. At the time, she had attributed it to her being a notoriously poor traveller. However, the true source of this emaciation was revealed not a quarter-hour into their visit.

As Charlotte had kindly inquired of their health, Elizabeth was happy to relate the latest antics of her toddlers. She had just begun her account of them when Chauncey Charlemagne Collins marched into the parlour, picked up a miniature trumpet and stood before his mother and let loose with a sputtering blatt into his mother's face. Even in the face of what she had witnessed of him previously, this impudence stunned Elizabeth—but only by half of what was to follow.

He threw down his instrument and commenced to stomp his feet and simultaneously scream at such an ear-piercing level; Elizabeth was forced to cover her ears. Charlotte neither attempted to correct nor to chastise Chauncey. Her countenance was claimed by a discernable expression of defeat. Chauncey then betook his considerable bulk upon her lap and began to unbutton the buttons adorning her bodice with his chubby little fingers. Ignoring the intrusion of her person, Charlotte sat with a mortified expression upon her countenance whilst he exposed her breast and began to suckle. She took her shawl and tossed the end of it across her child and exposed breast, but he refused it, swatting it away without interruption of his feeding.

"Perhaps, I shall return at a more convenient time," said Elizabeth, rising to go.

"No," said Charlotte, "please stay.

She spoke mildly, but behind her eyes was a plea. It was heart-wrenching to Elizabeth and she could not deny her.

Charlotte attempted to explain her son's effrontery, "His dinner-time is half-past two. He can be very determined."

"Yes," agreed Elizabeth.

It was unfortunate in avoiding Lady Catherine's table that she had intruded upon Chauncey's. In smaller cottages, she knew well, the inhabitants were more dedicated to the noon-hour for their mid-day meal. She was not pleased to have imposed upon Charlotte. Her imposition was not, however, Charlotte's worst. It had to have been the behemoth of a child perched upon her lap. Elizabeth certainly could have weathered the child's temper and ill-manners for he was but five years old. Many sins could be forgiven in so young a child. She had made a point of not criticising another's child lest her children's misbehaviour be fodder in return (if, indeed, they were *ever* to misbehave). It had been her observation that she and Darcy were like every other parent who sit about watching their children's antics and fancy themselves delighted. Charlotte, however, did not appear delighted whatsoever. She looked to be afraid and drained—literally. Chauncey's enormous bottom covered Charlotte's diminishing lap, his feet nearly reached the floor. It reminded Elizabeth of the cuckoo-bird she had read about in one of her father's wildlife volumes. The mother cuckoo would lay an egg in a sparrow's nest and when the enormous cuckoo baby hatched, it shoved all the other sparrow eggs out of the nest and the poor mother sparrow would drive herself to an early death feeding the huge and demanding cuckoo baby. Elizabeth looked at Chauncey and all she could see was a huge pin-feathered cuckoo baby—bearing Mr. Collins's countenance. She was all but sickened. She simply could not leave without making some effort to save poor Charlotte not from Chauncey but from herself.

"Have you considered weaning?" Elizabeth ventured.

"Oh, no, I could never do that," she exclaimed with no little vehemence. "I could not bear the poor child's disappointment if I were to deny him."

"I see," replied Elizabeth, and surely she did see.

"I must take my leave," she announced, rising. "I must ready myself to return to my own children."

Suddenly, that desire became ever more intense. Her own circumstances, not those of wealth, but of those riches of the heart—a loving (if occasionally maddening) husband and adored children—made her extraordinarily blessed. It was a bittersweet observation in the face of Charlotte's unappetising lot. Charlotte always had been a bit of an odd duck, pragmatic, but kind. It had always been her desire for nothing more than a comfortable home. She had to believe that Charlotte now saw to be needed could be a satisfaction in and of itself.

"Please, Lizzy, do not take your leave before you see my new gander," she begged. "Chauncey, be a good little man for Mama now. We must show Mama's friend our lovely poultry house."

Remarkably, Chauncey immediately released his mother's teat and arched his back and slid to the floor, wriggling like a happy puppy. He took Elizabeth's hand, calling out some unintelligible instructions. Elizabeth allowed herself to be towed outside. It was there in the sunlight, carefully making her way amongst the fowl that Elizabeth was able to lose a little of the uneasiness of her visit. A tour of Charlotte's handsome garden, boasting hollyhocks and daffodils, still did not allow her to forget her mind's-eye picture of mother and son.

"I hope you can forgive my interference, Charlotte, for you have been a mother longer than I have," she said. "But you must know that your son must be weaned sooner or later. If you do not soon, you may be forced to sit on *his* lap to nurse him."

Elizabeth smiled, hoping that her little jest would soften her criticism. Charlotte did not exactly return the smile, but she did not appear offended. Indeed, as Chauncey ran wildly about the garden after a rabbit loose from its hutch, she nodded as if to accept the truth of Elizabeth's observation.

Then, she laughed, "That would be quite the sight would it not?"

"His school-mates, no doubt, would be unforgiving." Elizabeth laughed as well, but she hoped her point was not lost on Charlotte.

"You are right, Lizzy." Charlotte said quietly, "But he is a gift from God. Are we not to take them and love them as god gives them to us?"

Elizabeth said, "Is not teaching them not to need us the greatest gift that we can give them?"

At first Charlotte appeared alarmed at the notion. Presently, her expression softened. Before she could respond, Chauncey ran to her, crying that the rabbit had escaped through the hedge.

Elizabeth bid them good-bye and gave Charlotte an especially generous kiss. She returned to Rosings with renewed hope that Charlotte's spirit would rally.

She had but gained the postern when she was met by Lady Catherine's servant with a letter in his hand, much as been handed to Darcy earlier. She took it more eagerly than she intended, hoping to see it from Bingley. She had already begun to compose in her head the anticipated contents—it was all a mistake, all was well, Darcy need not come, Bingley is not ruined. Once she had it in her hand, she attempted to mimic her husband's nonchalance as she took the stairs, but her excitement made her hurry the last few steps. To have Jane's house saved and her husband returned made her very nearly euphoric. When she gained her room, however, her mood altered decidedly.

This letter too was marked "urgent." It was not, however, directed to Darcy, but to her. It was not from Bingley. It was from Lydia.

When the black-edged missive arriving announcing the death of Mr. Darcy's cousin, Major Hugh Kneebone insisted they impose upon the Darcys' hospitality no longer. Lydia was disappointed, but she allowed her new husband to inveigle her to return to London in the very fine equipage sporting the very fine livery of Pemberley. Under those particular circumstances, she was happy to return to what her new life as Mrs. Kneebone had to offer. A house in Chelsea, courtesy of his aunt, was a very good enticement.

"I shall regret leaving the apartments afforded us there," Lydia recollected upon the road back to London. "The prospect from my window was quite pleasing!"

Major Kneebone ducked his head slightly and reddened, mildly mortified at his wife's ribaldry. Her high spirits had intrigued him from the very beginning—it would be unfair to expect other of her after he had made her his wife. The prospect of which she spoke betokened a particular statue, of a nude male. He was uncertain of the sculptor, but it was an excellent rendering. The artistry, however, was lost upon his dear wife. She could but point and titter. In fortune, such silliness imbued Lydia with an impish voluptuousness that requited his every marital hope.

The Darcys were fine, fine people. Like the Gardiners, he saw that Lydia's kin were of the best sort. Why Lydia did not think she could have found assistance from such a well-placed sister could only have been attributed to sweet Lydia's desire not to be a burden to her kin. Lydia's unselfish devotion to her family was commendable. She *had* been excessively unhappy to leave her mother. There was an impenetrable bond between them that a mere man could never fathom. It was a beautiful thing to see. Mrs. Bennet could occasionally be a tad…high-strung, but her likeness was so very similar to his adorable, new wife, he could but love her in the same measure as did dearest Lydia. One day, perhaps, life would be so kind as to have that lovely woman come live in his home allowing him to enjoy both their lovely smiles each day. He smiled even then as he thought of it.

He rapped lightly up the roof of the coach, "Hurry on, sir! Our new abode awaits!

By the time Major Kneebone introduced his lovely bride and her infant daughter to their new home, they were so weary from their travels, they were ready to take their rest. First, however, Lydia had to admire every room and every accoutrement therein. Whilst she enjoyed them all, Kneebone withdrew to the nearest bell-pull to call for tea. However, sitting in (appropriately) their sitting room was a guest. Major Kneebone had thought to have a housekeeper open the windows and place fresh flowers to welcome them. He had given no instructions as to allowing admittance to any manner of unknown persons. As Lydia went trilling about, Major Kneebone introduced himself to his caller. Major Kneebone was unalarmed, for he could see by the cut of his coat and the leather of his boots that the visitor was clearly a gentleman.

The caller stood, then bowed with exquisite form. Before, however, he had opportunity to introduce himself, Lydia did for him.

She also shrieked, then fell to the floor in her first bona fide swoon—just after she uttered the invective, "Wickham!"

Motherless Child

Lying in an unfamiliar bed under the eye of servants wholly unknown to her, Georgiana was a bit out of sorts. The doctor had given instructions for her to lie flat, and, under no circumstances was she to attempt to rise.

"Simpleton," she accused him silently, her emotions were far too stirred to lie still.

Indeed, she was thoroughly exasperated with the worthy doctor. Dearest Elizabeth had been of far greater service to her during her labour than the intestinally compromised Dr. Brumfitt. They had both been astonished that Lady Catherine had allowed him to return to her premises in that Lady Anne's care had been less than a stellar success. (Indeed, understanding Lady Catherine's temperament, it was an astonishment he had not been hung from a gibbet upon the nearest crossing.) The more Georgiana thought of him, the more indignant she became over his incompetence. Any country midwife would have been preferable. Indeed, he had been as useless as—what was that crude expression farmers use? Oh, yes—more useless than teats on a boar.

She laughed inwardly at the thought of what her gentlemanly husband might say if he were witting that she had even heard such a coarse term, much less employed it. So far as she was concerned, he would never learn of it. She could never affront his sensibilities in that manner. There were strict rules for a lady's comportment. She knew them well. Indeed, at one time, those rules were the guiding force of her life. She clung to them when she had no will of her own. Having thrown off that yoke so thoroughly (she considered herself to have been to the wars as certainly as any soldier), she wondered would she ever be happy again with calm country pursuits and amusements. Although she fully intended to retain her respectability with all due diligence—for both her husband's and her brother's sake—she knew it would be an impossibility for her to compleatly abandon her pursuit of the healing arts.

Because of that interest, Georgiana had been more keenly attentive to the particulars of Lady Anne's demise than the average curiosity seeker. However, her own unexpected accouchement had not allowed her to learn just what led to Lady Anne's passing. It was the general consensus that Anne fell victim to what most frequently took a mother's life during childbirth—that of bleeding out. It grieved her that she had not been by her cousin's side to suggest to the surgeon the application of cobwebs, for they were known to have a coalescing effect.

Indeed, her remedies were many and now that she had been enfolded into the exclusive league of ladies who had experienced childbirth, Georgiana was thrilled to know that she too could attend the labour of others. A surgeon with his dirty hands and brusque manner would be rendered unnecessary. She knew not which blessing she admired most—loving husband, beautiful daughter, or the future good she would do. She could not have been more delighted had she had another book accepted for publication. Even then, she was fast on the subject of her next piece of writing. After her marriage, she had largely abandoned her fledgling writing career. At one time, literary composition had been her most comforting pursuit. Of late, she had found other, more gratifying means of satisfaction. But she thought in due time she might want to explore the possibility of a work of nonfiction, incorporating two of her great loves—writing and the curatives.

"Perhaps, a treatise upon the Therapeutic Advantage of Bloodletting," she mused, "published under a pseudonym, of course."

"My dearest," said Fitzwilliam, "you have awakened."

Georgiana only then realised that her husband sat in a side-chair just beyond her reach. As Fitzwilliam rose and approached the bed, so did a nurse bearing her freshly arranged newborn. Georgiana attempted to raise herself upon her pillows, but two servitors hurried forth and plumped them for her. As soon as she was situated with her daughter tucked in the crook of her arm, Fitzwilliam inched forward so as not to miss a moment of the presentation.

As the baby squirmed and threatened to cry, Fitzwilliam leaned over and kissed the single ginger curl that protruded from her tiny cap.

"I daresay, Darcy, I know not who is more beautiful—my wife or my daughter."

Darcy had entered the room, but remained near the door as if to protect the couple from his intrusion. History had instructed him that this was to be a moment of uncommon intimacy for them. Georgiana, however, spied him there and held out her hand to him. Only then did he walk forward and take it, kissing her knuckles. For a moment, his countenance was threatened. But he quickly reclaimed himself.

Said he, looking upon the tiny bundle she held, "It appears, my dear sister, that search beneath the gooseberry bush was a great success."

As all three had been told at one time or another that beneath the gooseberry bush was where babies came from, both she and Fitzwilliam laughed appreciatively—both at the nature of the jest and that her staid brother attempted to make one.

"If you can possibly spare me," Darcy continued, "I must away briefly to London."

Georgiana was busy fussing with the baby and acquiesced to her brother's departure with a smile. Fitzwilliam, however, rose and accompanied him to the door, curious as to what urgency might have precipitated such an abrupt departure.

"Is there any way I might be of assistance?" inquired Fitzwilliam.

The answer Darcy gave was both heartfelt and unsurprising, "You can be no greater service to me than allowing me to know that you are at my sister's side."

He took Fitzwilliam's hand and shook it firmly. Thereupon he cast his other arm about him, drawing him into the first embrace they had ever shared.

"Elizabeth abides," he assured him, "should you want for anything."

Without actually saying the words, he bid him good-bye.

Fitzwilliam watched as Darcy strode off down the hallway. With a thoughtful furrow between his brows, he returned to Georgiana and the baby.

"Do you happen to be privy to what business your brother might have in London?" he inquired mildly.

Georgiana shook her head. They punctuated their exchange with a gaze that shared a bit of concern as to the nature of Darcy's away. It was unusual for him to take his leave unaccompanied by his wife. When within hours Elizabeth visited Georgiana's bedside to advise them of her own imminent leave-taking, again they exchanged glances. However, they accepted her regrets of company with the same agreeability they had Darcy's. Upon this occasion, however, Fitzwilliam's offer of assistance was ever more fervently proposed. Indeed, he followed her out of the room to insist upon it. Therefore, Elizabeth felt compelled to give some sort of explanation, but knew employing the name of Wickham would not be to Georgiana's benefit.

"My sister Lydia," she said cryptically.

"Ah, yes," replied Fitzwilliam.

As the good colonel had met Lydia and knew of her history, Elizabeth did not need to elucidate further.

When he returned to Georgiana, whose eyebrows had risen in inquiry, the single name was all he employed as well. In doing so, he had to eschew the protocol of the lady's proper title of Mrs. Wickham.

"Lydia," said he.

Georgiana's brows immediately knitted, announcing his circumlocution not a compleat triumph. Immediately thereafter, Georgiana's countenance returned to its former glow. It was as if she had willed herself not to allow past transgressions to haunt her present happiness. It was a decision of which Fitzwilliam whole-heartedly approved.

Having bested that small bugaboo, Georgiana had opportunity to address another, far more serious one.

"Have you had the opportunity to admire my cousin's poor motherless baby?"

"I must confess that I have not." he replied, "I have had another baby much upon my mind."

She smiled and patted his hand, but explained her inquiry, "I held her a bit before poor Anne was laid to rest. I was most distressed…"

"Pray, could that be what brought on your labour?"

She gave him a withering look, making it clear to him that he was to hear her out without placing blame for her daughter's early arrival. Before she continued, however, an odour emanating from her daughter bid Georgiana to unwrap the blanket one revolution. Thus exposed, she observed approvingly of the colour of the stool therein and nodded for the nurse to see to her.

"Oh dear God in heaven!" exclaimed Fitzwilliam when the odour wafted in his direction.

As the nurse moved forward to take the baby, Georgiana reproved the new father, "I would think that a colonel of the cavalry, successful participant in the Peninsular and Waterloo campaigns would not be felled by a mere scent."

With great efficiency, the nurse whisked the baby from Georgiana and out the door. Fitzwilliam recollected himself, and had only begun to defend his sensibilities to his wife when came a knock upon the door-frame then. The door had been left open and Yewdell stood there stiffly at attention, his toes carefully arranged at the threshold.

"Beg pardon, m'lady," he said. "Your servants have inquired if they might have the honour of looking upon the young mistress in the nursery."

"Of course," Georgiana replied. "They are very welcome."

Beyond the door and Yewdell, stood Hannah, Goodwin, and Georgiana's recently acquired lady-maid, Lucy. All wore properly reverent expressions, but Hannah's eyes twinkled. That made Georgiana smile. Before he closed the door behind him, Yewdell extended a gingham-wrapped gift. It was tied with a string and he seemed embarrassed to proffer it. Seeing as Yewdell was shy of coming into the room, Fitzwilliam rose and took the package from his hand. A nervous giggle was heard from behind Yewdell as the gift was tendered and Yewdell frowned at the indiscretion.

"Thank you, Yewdell," said Georgiana. "You are so very kind."

"Oh no," said Yewdell, mortified to be identified as the giver of this paltry gift, "'tis not from me—Mrs. Darcy's woman, it is from her hand."

"Hannah, you say?" Georgiana glowed with delight, insisting, "Do bring her forth!"

Hannah then sidled into the room, wringing a pocket-square anxiously in her hands and still trying to stifle her nervous laugh. Only then did Georgiana nod to Fitzwilliam to untie, then unroll the gift.

"I only just finished it, m'lady," Hannah said proudly. "I've been working on it lo these many months. Wasn't it the luck now that I happened to bring my work-box with me on this trip—what with you taken to the straw like you did."

At that point, a tiny, gossamer shawl of considerable glory was revealed and Hannah got the best of her babbling by pressing her pocket-square firmly to her lips. Although she quieted herself, she veritably beamed with pride. Unaccustomed to handling delicate items, Fitzwilliam struggled for a moment to find two corners with which to display it for Georgiana's approval.

"Oh, Hannah!" Georgiana exclaimed, "I have never seen anything quite so lovely!"

"Mrs. Darcy," said Hannah, "she gave me the yarn but I did the knitting m'self. I suppose it is from both of us."

She fell quiet as Georgiana caressed the shawl, saying, "Please take it to Nurse and wrap my daughter in it now."

Hannah gave a quick curtsy, retrieved the shawl, and headed out the door. Yewdell had stood silently during the exhibition and gave a resigned sigh when at last Hannah betook herself from the room. After he had excused himself, the sweetness of the moment turned melancholy for Georgiana.

"I do wish," she said, "that Mrs. Annesley had lived to see our daughter."

In the silence that followed, the unspoken regret was for Georgiana's mother as well. Mrs. Darcy's death in childbirth was rarely brought into conversation. Indeed, throughout Georgiana's confinement it was a forbidden subject. Now that she had successfully delivered, that ban had been lifted.

"It is sad," she observed, "so very sad."

Fitzwilliam agreed—but warily—that it was sad, indeed.

"To think the poor child will not ever have a mother's arms to hold her."

Again, Fitzwilliam nodded his head in hesitant agreement of the inherent sadness of such a situation, only then realising that Georgiana was referring not to herself, but to her cousin's daughter.

Georgiana continued, "I cannot bear to think of that baby alone, forever, when our child will have us both for all her days."

Indeed, so great was her empathy, she began to weep.

"I cannot bear it," she repeated.

"There, there, my sweet," soothed Fitzwilliam, "Lady Catherine is well and will see that she has her every wish. She will want for nothing."

"She will be in great want of the one thing Lady Catherine cannot give."

Lady Catherine's great love affair with herself was of legend. Hence, it was unnecessary to delineate her aunt's motherly short-comings. Fitzwilliam's logical mind leapt ahead, knowing just which way this wind was blowing.

"She would never give her up," he announced with finality.

With that statement, Fitzwilliam, the tactician, gave up more of his position than he intended. That he had already determined Lady Catherine's answer meant the question was one that he would entertain. Georgiana knew that in having her husband agreeable to taking Anne's baby to their home, half of the sizeable battle that lay ahead had been won. It fell to her then to devise an arrangement that would entice Lady Catherine to let loose of her granddaughter—and have it all seem her ladyship's design.

A piece of cake.

The Talent of the Dead

The missive sent by Lydia had been, for her, succinct. She related that Major George Wickham was back from the dead and she was in a bit of a muddle. She could not quite make out just who had the prevailing claim upon her services as a wife.

"Major Kneebone is threatening Wickham to a duel in my honour, and I know not what to do!!!"

The three exclamation points did not make Elizabeth think for a minute that the craven cad of a deserter who was George Wickham would engage in a duel with a living, breathing gentleman of the blade. But Kneebone seemed the sort who just might think he had to protect his wife's honour.

"Honour! Lydia?" Elizabeth snorted. "Surely that is a jest!"

Elizabeth set out immediately and alone for London. She made her regrets to Lady Catherine by note. That was not the best of manners, but she was not of a mind even to speak to Lady Catherine, much less make her privy to the Bennet family business. She knew that two post riders coming in one day would start tongues to wagging from all corners of the house. Not wanting to worry Fitzwilliam or Georgiana, she explained away their hasty leave-taking in the simplest and least alarming terms. Georgiana was happy to hold her daughter and not worry of what she did not know. Fitzwilliam was less complaisant.

"Are you certain all is well?" he asked, worriment testing his countenance.

"We shall both return before Georgiana misses us," she assured him.

She had her lone footman see to the carriage. As she had suspected, Darcy had taken the larger coach. Her reason to hie for London with all due haste was one of such import that she felt little compunction in doing so. It was her intention to return before Darcy. It would be much easier confronting him with what had gone before, than to vex him with what must be done. It was only on the road to London that she thought to wonder if her driver or her footman was armed. Because Darcy had armed himself, she chose to believe at least one of her men was as well. She did not ask. It would have made little difference in her decision. This matter of Wickham must be straightened immediately. She was happy that she had taken the trouble upon Lydia's new marriage to inquire of her Uncle Phillips what the law said concerning the return of a husband thought dead. In his letter containing that information, with the kindest of words he had told her that she worried too much—that Wickham was for certain dead and buried in some grave in the Low Countries.

"A good riddance it would be," said that wise man.

Armed with what she knew of the law, she was prepared to advise Lydia that there was a choice to be made. When a man was thought to be dead and reappeared after his widow, in all good intentions, re-wed, said wife's second marriage was not necessarily null and void—the wife could choose which marriage to uphold.

"If Lydia does not have the sense God gave her to choose Major Kneebone, I wash my hands of it all!" said Elizabeth aloud to no one but herself.

She had been compleatly satisfied with the gentleman who had taken Lydia's hand in marriage. He seemed the sensible sort, a man under whose influence Lydia (and thus her family) might at last be free from alarm and affliction. She feared, however, that all would not end happily. Major Kneebone seemed to be a kind and loving man, but it perplexed her how a man with those qualities might think he would find happiness with a young woman such as her sister. He could not be a fortune hunter; Lydia had nothing but debts. It could not be a meeting of the minds, for he was a thoughtful sort and Lydia had not picked up a book but to use it as a weight for pressing the ribbons of her bonnet. Kneebone could not be such a simpleton not to know that he was being used. All Lydia ever had to promote herself had been her girlish allure.

"The only thing not in his favour was his taste in wives," thought Elizabeth meanly, before chastising herself for it. She fitfully mused over the appearance of so many vexations coming to light in so short a space of time—Anne's death, Bingley's ruin, Charlotte's lot—and now the spectre of Wickham had re-entered their lives. Somehow filtered through her thoughts came a few appropriate lines.

"When sorrows come, they come not single spies; but in battalions," Elizabeth repeated.

At least, she reminded herself, Georgiana had successfully given birth. She refused to acknowledge that said lady was also, for the foreseeable future, a captive in Rosings Park's ominous machinations. At least Fitzwilliam was there to guard her. Georgiana was safe unless Lady Catherine employed that most effective weapon of hers—the one even Elizabeth's own resolute husband had little defence against. Who would have thought that the formidable Lady Catherine would have stooped to a lady's most offensive ploy? Tears. Who would ever have thought?

All of this rumination relieved her of the most vexatious thought of all.

As the months drew on and Wickham had not reappeared, she and Darcy had become increasingly sure that he was dead. It was not a troubling thought. His death would have been far more bearable to all concerned than his survival. She had very nearly prayed for that, only retreating when she realised such a wish as not only uncharitable, it was a sin. Wickham had committed enough sins for her not to contribute to the further sullying of righteousness. Still, she could see no one who would benefit from his survival. Not Lydia, not his sons, and most certainly not Darcy. She knew her husband had never quite come to terms with the fact that Wickham was a half-brother to him. If he could not manage that notion in light of Wickham's death, she was loath to imagine his struggle upon beholding the living, breathing embodiment of his beloved father's adultery. The single way she could keep her own mind from running wild with the implications of it all was to refuse to think of it. She would address each problem as it arose. For now, she had to reach Lydia before she made a disastrous decision.

Elizabeth notified neither Jane nor the Gardiners of this latest catastrophe, and she prayed that Lydia had not either.

Her coachman knew his way about the streets of London, therefore they arrived in a timely fashion. When she approached the door, she gave an inward exclamation at the stateliness of the Kneebones' new home. She had expected something more modest.

"We are in such an uproar," Lydia burst out when she saw her.

"Have you informed Uncle Gardiner?"

Elizabeth's first interest was to see how contained this incident was. She held the single hope that she might make arrangements for Wickham's withdrawal without Darcy's immediate knowledge. There was a modicum of guilt that accompanied this scheme, but she endeavoured to rationalise her decision of covertness on behalf of her husband's abhorrence of the entire subject.

"Nay, I have not," replied Lydia. "I have only informed you, Lizzy. But," she looked around and behind Elizabeth, "I had hoped that you would have brought Mr. Darcy. He has taken care of everything before. I believed he would be best suited for this as well."

So much history was involved in Lydia's statement that Elizabeth was disinclined to recall just how often her dear Darcy had been called upon to rescue various members of her family. He was on just such a mission then (in the Bennet family's defence, Bingley was his friend as well). She dared not share the particulars of his mission to loquacious Lydia. Bingley's financial woes would be in the newspaper in five counties by daylight. She saw the same girl with the piercing eyes holding Lydia's shawl-draped baby. She stood resolutely rocking the infant in her arms. Elizabeth knew nothing of the girl's background, and doubted Lydia did either.

Elizabeth asked Lydia for reassurance of her discretion, "And to no other?"

"No, Lizzy, I have said nothing. I am much in want of assistance, but I do not know how all can be put to right without Darcy's intervention."

Every time Lydia addressed him as "Darcy" rather than "Mr. Darcy," Elizabeth cringed. That familiarity was exceedingly vexing. (Every time Lydia ran her hands upon his coat-front, she had to choke down the desire to smack her atop her head with a fan, but she would address that failing upon another occasion.) Indeed, Elizabeth was happy that Darcy was not there. If he had to weather Lydia and Wickham—she knew not what means he might employ to be rid of them. Yes, she had been wise to exclude Darcy from this ordeal. And Lydia seemed disinclined to leap into Wickham's outstretched arms. This was very good news, indeed. The plan she had devised to rid them all from him forever might actually succeed. She meant to tell him of the rumours of his desertion. Hearing that, he might find it in his best interest to take his leave.

"Pray, Lydia, what did Major Wickham say? Was he explicit in his expectations?"

"His expectations?!" Lydia exclaimed. "He expects that I am to return to his bed forthwith! My own dear Major Kneebone means to fight him in a duel, Lizzy! What ever are we to do?"

Major Kneebone had said very little throughout this exchange, which had taken place in a commodious parlour, immediately after Elizabeth persuaded Lydia not to keep her standing in the doorway. The good Major appeared discomfited. Whether this discomposure lay in his outrage over another man challenging him to his wife, the prospect of a duel, or his wife's putting him forth in a duel not of his making remained temporarily unexplored. The single fortune in Elizabeth's mind was that she did not find Wickham perched like a cat with a canary on their settee when she arrived. Not only was she unprepared to face Wickham, the murdering deserter, she most certainly did not want to intercede in a duel of honour. As to what next she would she do, Elizabeth was uncertain.

"When does Major Wickham return? Not at dawn, I pray," she asked ruefully.

"Not at dawn, but Hughie is to meet him tomorrow morn," said Lydia, displeased with Elizabeth's attempt at a jest.

Major Kneebone was displeased as well, unhappy for Mrs. Darcy to be involved in matters that should rightfully belong to the men-folk.

"I thank you for coming, Mrs. Darcy. I was unaware that Lydia had alarmed you. These are matters for men to decide. You can rest assured that I will see to Lydia's best interests," he said proudly.

Masculine pride was a characteristic with which Elizabeth was exceedingly familiar.

"I do not question your gentleman's honour for a moment, Major. But as my husband is much taken at the time by matters of business, I come in his stead. My father is dead. I will speak for the Bennet family on Lydia's behalf. I am most familiar with Major Wickham and how he must be worked upon."

It was a bit audacious, but entirely true. She believed she had an ace in the hole when it came to manipulating Wickham.

"It is a sticky situation, indeed, Mrs. Darcy. Although Lydia has been legally married, Wickham claims otherwise. He has told me that the law says he and Lydia are still rightfully wed, he claims that he will have me jailed for bigamy," Kneebone said, worry lines threatening his forehead.

"Well, if that's the law, the law is an ass!" burst out Lydia. "The eye of the law is a blind idiot and I am certainly *not* married to George Wickham—that...that...that..." she sputtered. "He is no kind of a husband to a wife! Oh, black, black and hollow heart has he—the bloody blackguard!"

"There, there," soothed Kneebone to his nearly hysterical wife, clearly unperturbed by her foul mouth. To Elizabeth, he said, "I confess, I do not know the law, but ours cannot be the first instance of a husband returning after his death had been reported."

Suddenly, Lydia pointed directly to her baby-nurse, "You! Yes, you! This is all your fault!" Turning about, she explained her accusation, "She was whistling!"

Disgusted at such idiocy, Elizabeth told her, "That is but an ancient myth. Ill-tidings can still come about when hens do not crow and young girls do not whistle."

The girl fled the room with the baby and Elizabeth gave Lydia a reproachful look. Lydia seemed unchastened however. Elizabeth was happy to have some actual facts upon which to act. Indeed, it was with no small amount of self-satisfaction that Elizabeth gave her legal accounting, "As it happens, my Uncle Phillips is an attorney. We have taken the precaution to inquire of him just what is done in cases such as these. Wickham either does not know the law, or is purposely misleading you—the second I might guess, such a man as he is. Truth of the matter is that if a wife remarries upon reliable word of her husband's death and that husband is found later to be otherwise, the wife has the right to choose which husband to retain."

Kneebone was noticeably relieved, clearly certain that he knew his wife's mind. However, a strange expression overspread Lydia's countenance, and in it Elizabeth saw clearly the girl of sixteen who Wickham had seduced. Was Lydia recalling those moments of infatuation—had Wickham's return rekindled them? In that moment she saw it was imperative to keep Lydia from Wickham's clutches or she might be vulnerable to his easy words. In fortune, Kneebone did not recognise vacillation on his wife's countenance. Elizabeth saw then (had she expected any other) that Lydia's fiercest enemy would be herself. She also experienced a giddy sense of hegemony, having come to the rescue as she had. It was fleeting, but altogether pleasing.

"Pray, is Major Wickham on hand to engage a meeting?"

The sense of command she had just felt began to waffle ever so slightly as she recalled the last time she had endeavoured to influence George Wickham—it had ended badly. (It had ended with Wickham being escorted from Pemberley at the point of a sword wielded by Darcy, but she would not allow that recollection to sway her.) It did begin to fret her just what Wickham would say in his own defence—he most certainly would have a long, involved, logical, and totally false justification for all that had occurred. It was also possible that he might deny it all. It might be imperative that she call his bluff—deny his denial. She was certain that she was a match for a seasoned liar such as Wickham. It was said that the ends justify the means. She had once wondered how a man such as he was to be worked on. She was now fully informed as to that device. What she meant to do could only be called exaction—or extortion, blackmail, or coercion. None of those words were pretty, but then neither was the ilk of Major Wickham. She had right on her side—if indeed saving Lydia from herself was right. Had she not also been her husband's protector (he would never think himself in need of protection, but that was neither here nor there) against Wickham's re-entry into their lives she might well have given Mrs. Kneebone the letter of the law and let her stew in her own juices. But as many times as Darcy had defended her honour, she felt it was a noble calling to come to the defence of his. Righteousness gave her courage.

"Major Wickham gave an address to meet him in Limehouse—it is a public house," said Kneebone.

"It is there where they are to duel!" interjected Lydia.

"I shall meet him instead," announced Elizabeth.

"No, Mrs. Darcy," cried Kneebone. "I could not allow a lady to venture there. It is a very low establishment in the worst sort of neighbourhood."

"I have been in worse, I am sure," she recalled the public house to which her kidnappers had taken her—a place she was apt never to forget. "I have my footman, I shall be well-protected."

Perhaps her countenance displayed more assurance that she felt. Regardless, Kneebone acquiesced.

"But, I must insist that I accompany you. Your husband would never forgive me if I do not," said Kneebone.

Knowing the truth to that particular understanding, she nodded her head once in acceptance. Lydia also invited her to stay in their home to await the meeting. Elizabeth thought that an excellent notion. She did not much want to go to the Darcy town house, where she might encounter her husband. It was imperative that this matter be reconciled beyond his notice. If Darcy learnt of it all, he would meet with Wickham and she could not be certain of that outcome. Darcy, no doubt, was wearing his pistol. She saw the correctness of that precaution—the streets were alive with thuggery and worse. It was ironic that she saw great need for Darcy to be armed but did not hold the same fear for herself. She had but one goal—to relieve her husband of confronting (and possibly doing violence to) Wickham.

She would do what she had to do.

The Cunning and the Taken

Wickham had always been most particular in his dress; his vanity demanded nothing less. The governing principle of his life had been the ceaseless search for pleasure. To be chained to a room with spit upon his waistcoat—even this baby's—was becoming increasingly offensive.

With the fussy baby upon his shoulder, he paced the floor and patted her back, but to no avail. Indeed, her screams increased. She had been fed, he knew not what else to do. Still juggling the infant girl, he walked purposely to the door, threw it back, and bellowed, "Henrietta!"

Recollecting himself, he reduced the volume of his voice by half and allowed her name to roll off his tongue like marzipan, "Henri-etta, my sweet plum-cake!"

There was no immediate response, but in a moment he heard the reassuring steps of his landlady, Mrs. Younge.

"I cannot keep taking these stairs every time that infant cries, Mr. Wickham."

Her mood matched his, and as it was she who was owed money by him, her righteousness was indignant, indeed. Despite that, she took the baby from him, placed the child upon the bed, and began to clean her.

"When did you last see to this child? Oh, never you mind—if something unpleasant needs to be seen to, men are sure to escape it!"

He sat down upon the bedside and watched with a version of tender attention peculiar to those observing another do one's dirty work. The baby quieted immediately. Mrs. Younge owned a singular position in Wickham's heart. One measure a mother, sometime lover, and a large part, dupe—she had fed him when he was hungry, taken him in when he had no home. And when he was penniless (which was often), he could charm her out of a few coins to jingle in his purse. She was a once handsome woman of a certain age, and had maintained a semblance of gentility. She was, however, given to listening at the keyholes of her tenants for entertainment. He had known her when she had, through the auspices of false recommendations, been hired as Georgiana

Darcy's companion. Their long acquaintance had advanced when she aided him in his aborted elopement of Georgiana Darcy. He had promised her two-hundred pounds if he had been successful. When Mr. Darcy thwarted that scheme and ran Mrs. Younge off for having been a conspirator, she had never held that against Wickham.

"We were found out," she laughed, as if losing her position had not been a financial set-back.

The one thing she liked above all else was putting something over on the gentry. That it was a bust mattered not, she still enjoyed the thrill of it all. She liked it most especially when young Wickham came up behind her and gobbled kisses upon the side of her neck. She maintained as respectable a house as could be found in that neighbourhood and considered herself a lady in all ways except situation. And when Wickham happened by, she always had a room. She gave him allowance on his rent, and when it had accumulated to an unusual degree, he talked her into a bum-tickle in exchange for his arrears. Although she was at least twenty years his senior, he thought it a fair trade—she was firm of thigh and very enthusiastic. Her other tenants were well aware of their arrangement and when encountering Wickham in the passage-way occasionally mocked him.

"That old wreck of a woman? A young buck like you?" they would tsk.

Wickham remained unchastened, and always had the same response, "There is something to be said for bedding a woman of her age."

"And what would that be?"

Wriggling his eyebrows lasciviously, "They are always *so* grateful."

That was not even a compleat falsehood, for Mrs. Younge had been more constant to him than any other of his lovers. But, he had to acknowledge even she had her limits.

"Wickham, dear," she announced an inveiglement by raising her voice into falsetto, "I am afraid I must ask you for your rent. I have expenses, y'know."

He heaved a great sigh of exasperation, "Henrietta dear, *you* know that I have too many irons in the fire at present to bother with such mundane matters. All my planning will come to fruition forthwith, and when that comes to pass, I will pay you twice what I owe—no, thrice!"

Mrs. Younge let loose with what could only be described as a giggling snort. Inwardly, Wickham winced for it was a sound quite familiar to their love-making.

"Oh, dear me! I quite forgot," she said, picking up the baby and handing her directly to Wickham.

He stood up with the baby and walked her about whilst Mrs. Younge dug about her apron pocket for a letter. When Wickham spied it, he hastily thrust the baby to her in exchange for the post. He quickly broke the seal and read. Whilst he pored over it, Mrs. Younge looked upon the sight, her eyes bright with greed.

"Pray, what is it?

"Patience, woman, patience," he said irritably. His French was unremarkable when it came to grammar, thus his progress was slow. When he reached the end, he smiled with satisfaction, refolded it, and stowed it in his waistcoat, smiling mischievously.

"At last! A meeting is to take place! I must have my frock-coat pressed!"

With an expression that portrayed both resignation and anticipation, Mrs. Younge said, "I suppose you want me to look after the baby?"

"No, my good woman, you must say good-bye to this darling baby girl," he looked upon her gurgling countenance with something akin to regret.

Indeed, it would be with considerable regret he would give up the child. He had done all he could to keep from forming an attachment, but had been largely unsuccessful. That, he supposed, was because of her resemblance to his beloved Césarine. She had dark hair rather than the copper of her mother's, but otherwise she was her spitting-image. Early on he had fancied that he would have liked to keep her as his own, but ultimately, pragmatism willed out. He simply had not the funds. It would have been delightful to have had the wherewithal to send the precious girl to the best schools, engage the best governesses and see her grow up into the spitting image of Césarine—and dare any man to come near her.

He would mourn her as if a daughter.

Marie-Therese Lambert had proposed to meet with him at the north gate to Kensington Gardens. He was not altogether happy with such a public meeting place, but he was too anxious to make the exchange to haggle over minor details. He must keep his eye on the prize and not let small vexations get in the way. Once the meeting was set, he became increasingly anxious for it to take place. Every time he looked upon the baby's angelic face, his little-used heart felt a rent. Whilst he called her his *chanton*, he tenderly gathered a few strands of her fine hair and tied it with a tiny pink bow, readying her for the transferral.

"Lydia should have given me daughters," Wickham concluded. "I would have been a different father had I been gifted with daughters."

Altogether oblivious to the dubiety of such a notion, he chucked her under her chin and pursed his lips in a kissing noise. The little girl smiled and cooed. He cocked his head to the side, smiling with approval.

It would, he admitted, be difficult to give up the baby—she had given him such unexpected joy. But he had known all along this day would come—perhaps not so soon as it had. Still, Wickham had to congratulate himself upon his cunning. For although Du Mautort had complained of his poverty with great dedication, his mother was far too determined to have him return home for it to have been only to solace a mother's heart. The only surprise was that it was the young viscount's death rather than his father, the Count's that brought his plan to fruition. Wickham supposed that Du Mautort caught his disease from the low prostitutes to whom he resorted after Césarine's death. Still, had not Césarine confided in him the baby's true father, he would never have thought of it all.

"Is not fate peculiar?" mused Wickham. "So seldom could he afford Césarine's time but yet it was his seed that stormed the citadel of Césarine's womb. Alas, to be a young blood once again!"

The baby carriage was one that Mrs. Younge had found for him; it was old, but serviceable. The driver of his hired coach did not want to take it, and when Wickham insisted, he tossed it aboard with little concern for its fragility. Regrettably, this callous deportment bent one wheel and the carriage squeaked and wobbled as Wickham pushed it along. It was not necessary for him to endure this indignity for long, for he espied Marie-Therese directly. She had not appeared to have altered since last he saw her upon the sorrowful day of Césarine's demise—except for a small little crease between her eyebrows that aged her from the young girl he recalled.

Her expression, however, was not what caught his eye. For around Mlle. Lambert's pretty throat was a necklace worth a king's ransom. It was the ruby and diamond creation he had last seen about his true love's neck. He despised seeing it thusly, for it not only reminded him of poor Césarine, dead in her grave, but that Marie-Therese had bested him in its confiscation after Césarine went to meet her maker. She was also using exceedingly bad judgement to have such a treasure upon her person, even in the lovely grounds of Kensington Park. It was broad daylight, but the increasing number of marauders traversing London's byways would leap at such a valuable accoutrement. They would not give a second thought to shoving her to the ground, ripping it from her neck, and running like blazes. She had no one accompanying her. They would be gone ere she could call for assistance. What could Marie-Therese be thinking? He had once thought her uncommonly clever. He supposed what passed for cunning in Paris meant little upon English soil. Suffering to an audacious degree the illusion of his own cleverness, that thought made him bolder still. Poor Mlle. Lambert, she was but a lamb to the slaughter.

"*Bonjour*," he said, touching his fingers to the brim of his hat. "You have never looked more handsome. London air does your complexion compliment."

At that remark, she restrained herself from looking about at the yellowish grey haze that passed for air in London. Even in lovely Kensington Gardens it was discernible. Wickham did not note her scepticism and believed his advantage over her was substantial. Therefore, he was happy to be generous in his compliments. It was not, after all, mere flattery. She was ravishingly beautiful. He simply had never noticed her beauty as she had always been over-shadowed by Césarine.

She returned his greeting, "*Bonjour, Général* Wickham."

At this, Wickham had to smile—the girl still believed that he was a general—how droll! He would just have to humour her.

"As unhappy as I am to lose this precious bundle here," he sighed heavily, the carriage wheel squeaking almost loudly enough to drown him out, "duty calls. I must return to my command. It would not be in the baby's best interest to travel behind us in a laundry waggon. I must have, however, assurances that she will be taken care of properly. I could not bear to allow her leave without that. As it is, my heart will break each day that I do not awake to hear her lovely laughter."

He fancied that the exact mixture of resignation and sadness, and looked at Marie-Therese to gauge its impact. Her countenance remained altogether inscrutable. But then, courtesans were not known for their exhibition of pathos. He was then troubled by a pang of anxiety.

"Are you certain that you can care for the baby upon the return trip? She did not take to the sea on our journey here…"

"Care not, *Général*, I travel with a nurse."

"I should have known that you would come prepared," he said.

Then suddenly, he felt the need to get their exchange done as quickly as possible. He owned an abrupt need to begone. He wanted his money and cared not to look back.

"Shall we sit?" he suggested, pointing to a bench. "We must hurry our agreement lest we be observed."

It was an excuse, of course. No one should have cared at all what came to pass between them.

"As you wish," she agreed mildly.

They did then sit, Wickham stationing the baby carriage between them. He was thankful the baby was asleep, oblivious to the racket the decrepit carriage made. Marie-Therese sat unmoving, her reticule bulging temptingly in her lap. She made no move to proffer what was in it. He had heard the clink when she sat—the sound of one-thousand sovereigns.

"Do you have the funds?"

"In gold, as you asked."

"I was saddened to hear of Du Mautort's passing. He was a good and great friend."

"He was an impetuous boy. He took no greater care of himself than did Césarine," she observed. "Losing both her son and her husband left his mother inconsolable—or, should I say, almost inconsolable?"

There, they both almost laughed, but regained their countenances. Wickham went so far as to reinstate a business-like mien. Marie-Therese remained placid. Wickham looked at the necklace about her neck. A number of things crossed his mind at that time. The first amongst them was that in the aftermath of war, France's economy was even worse than England's. A piece of that carat weight would be worth much more in England than in France. He did not for a moment think Mlle. Lambert was aware of that. Courtesans were not known for their grasp of economics either.

"I see," he ventured, "that you rescued at least one piece of Césarine's jewellry from her creditors. It must have been at great cost."

"*Un peu*."

He did not for a moment think she retrieved it legitimately; he knew that she had pilfered it from about Césarine's dead neck. That only instilled within him greater determination.

"To see it once again…I can think of nothing but my own, darling Césarine."

Was it? Yes. He believed it was. A tear—a tiny one, but still a tear—had begun at the corner of his eye. By sheer will (and an odd bit of blinking), he managed to encourage it out of his eye and onto his cheek. Was it possible to be missed? No, was not. Marie-Therese reached in her reticule for a piece of linen and dabbed at the corner of her own eye as well.

"She loved you so, *Général*!"

"And I, her!" agreed Wickham.

It was true, he had loved her. If he was to give up her child, could he not have a memento? He put it to Marie-Therese just like that. He worried that he had been too blunt—nuance is all in some negotiations.

"But, *Général*, it is not worth but a pittance compared to these funds Countess Du Mautort will pay for the return of her granddaughter. It would be too unfair."

"I cannot think of that now," cried Wickham. "I only asked to be repaid for my expenses in saving this baby—which, as you know, have been substantial. The heart, however, knows only of love. I would be forever in your debt if you would do me this favour!"

Sitting pensively, Marie-Therese mulled over his request. Then, with the greatest of reluctance, she unclasped the necklace. Suddenly apprehensive, she looked carefully about, to be certain no eyes of the wrong sort might espy them, Wickham noted her sudden caution, but allowed the treasure to be placed in his out-stretched palm. He then scooted the handle of the carriage over to her. She shook her head, however, and picked the baby up in her arms. The baby had awakened and looked winsomely in Wickham's direction.

"I prefer this," she said.

She held the baby close to her bosom. It was clear to Wickham by such a posture that she had little experience with babies. He was happy to have been assured of the awaiting baby-nurse. They both stood. Awkwardly, he offered her his hand. She loosed one hand and extended it. He kissed her fingers, slipping his treasure for safe-keeping into his waistcoat. They walked a little ways together, then Wickham asked if he might kiss the baby good-bye. He was feeling true remorse when he drew back her bonnet and bent to peck her upon forehead. Thereupon, Marie-Therese said she must return to her hired carriage lest it not wait for her.

Wickham doffed his hat, "*Adieu*."

"*Adieu*," repeated Marie-Therese.

"Her name," he had almost forgotten to tell her name, "is Eliza."

She nodded, unimpressed. It was likely that bit of sentiment on his part would not survive the crossing. No doubt Marie-Therese or Du Mautort's mother would christen her something French. As he watched her walk away, his eyes were mesmerised by the fetching swing to her undercarriage. He thought it peculiar that in all the decadence amidst which he found himself in Paris, he had never once tasted the delights Mlle. Lambert had to offer.

"A pity," he said as he sauntered away.

83

While the Cat's Away

"I cannot believe that even *you* would do such a thing!" exclaimed Goodwin, an expression of mortified incredulity upon his face. Hannah, however, refused to be cowed.

"Miss Darcy—er, rather, Mrs. Fitzwilliam—said it was lovely," Hannah sniffed. "She wanted it wrapped about her little babe immediately! You heard her yerself!"

"What more could the poor thing say, delirious with fatigue as she was?" Goodwin insisted.

This conversation occurred upon their return trip to Pemberley, the two servants bickering as if an old married couple. As usual, Goodwin was unhappy with Hannah's lack of circumspection in the presence of their betters. And just as routinely, Hannah was unapologetic. Goodwin had always held it against Hannah that she had not come up through the Pemberley ranks to obtain her position. He saw her as a plebian upstart—devoid of those nuances necessary to be worthy of such an exalted position as hers. As for Hannah, every time Goodwin got in a snit over some distraction, his Adam's apple bobbed quite vigourously. Endeavour as she might against it, that sight titillated her beyond all reason.

"Law, Goodwin, you were just as anxious as me to see that baby," Hannah said, expertly altering the subject from her forwardness to a turn they shared. "If t'were left up to you she'd be repeatin' the responses afore we had chance to admire her. I ask you, what good would my shawl do her then?"

Goodwin had known Georgiana the entirety of her life and was even more anxious than Hannah to have a look at the latest Darcy progeny. Therefore, he gazed with great dedication out the coach window and harrumphed—this being his standard response when he had no rejoinder. His temper had always been a bit compromised when it came to Hannah—a predisposition that had not moderated even after her protection of him during his period of indisposition. It had not been exactly spelled out, but the meaningful looks she gifted him told him that she had shielded him in his hour of need. He despised her for it. He used every shot in his arsenal of acerbity and she still remained blissfully unaware how exquisitely grieved he was to find himself beholden to her.

Their relationship might have remained skewered upon the horns of obligation had not a mutual enemy made it necessary for them to join forces.

Yewdell had told her that Mrs. Darcy had bid them return to Pemberley shortly after she had taken leave for London. Hannah was not altogether certain why she had requested them to do so, but it was not her place to question any instruction by her lady. There was certainly no reason for them to stay on at Rosings Park. Indeed, Hannah was happy to depart from the fine house regardless.

"I never saw a handsomer house with an uglier air about it," mused Hannah as she watched Goodwin impatiently adjusting his black arm-band. "It gives me the shivers—and not just because of the wearin' of the black. I don't know how that Yewdell can bear it."

For once Goodwin did not argue her observation. He had had a similar foreboding. Still, he was most unhappy to be sent back to Pemberley. Whatever business Mr. Darcy had in London, Goodwin was exceedingly unhappy not to accompany him. He felt that most firmly. To watch as Mr. Darcy hied for London without him gifted him an alarm remarkably similar to that which had troubled him the summer past. He did not think that he would again take to the flask, but with each mile put between him and Mr. Darcy, it was an increasingly vexatious temptation.

By the time they arrived at the gravel drive leading up to Pemberley House itself, Goodwin all but flung himself from the coach in a fit of agitation. He did not even direct the unloading of the trunks before he made his way through the portico and headed up the stairs. Hannah saw the makings of a bender when she saw one and was fast upon his heels, fully intending to move heaven and earth to keep him sober. A slip such as that and that loathsome Smeads would use it against poor Goodwin. She was not so certain of Mr. Darcy's mind on the matter that she believed Goodwin's position safe from dismissal. She could not have that.

When they reached the second set of stairs, Hannah was losing her breath, but wiry Goodwin had barely broken a sweat. He headed directly toward Mr. Darcy's study—a location known to contain not only a cellaret holding several fine bottles of brandy, but also Mr. Darcy's infamous silver flask—the very one that Goodwin had employed for his past imbibing. As both Hannah and Goodwin were intent upon their own objectives, they came to a near collision with a small group of tourists just then departing the nursery.

From behind their group came the voice of Smeads, saying, "Hurry along if you will. Time is of the essence."

In the summer months, when touring the countryside is a happy past-time, it was not unusual to have compleat strangers ask permission not only to walk in their gardens, but to view the rooms within as well. They were always graciously admitted and had been chaperoned either by Mrs. Reynolds herself or one of her trusted minions. After his mother's death, Smeads accommodated these requests meanly, making certain any visitors understood such hospitality was a transgression against his time. Never, however, in all Hannah's days at Pemberley had she seen other than invited guests upon the floor of the family apartments.

Because of the oddity of it, Hannah dared to take a peek beyond the milling bodies and into the room they had just taken leave of. She was much in want of learning the excuse for such audacity—certain above all else that the children would not be within. She was truly appalled to see Margaret Heff standing mid-most of the nursery. In her arms sat Janie, sucking furiously upon her middle two fingers whilst little Geoffrey clung with great determination to her skirt. Although Janie was clearly uneasy, the children looked more curious than afraid. But Margaret's eyes were wide—large enough to reveal an exceptional array of emotions. Foremost amongst them was fear, seconded by confusion, and topped off with a significant degree of distaste. She looked as if she would like to question what had come about, but Hannah knew her cousin to be far too new in her position to question Smeads's authority.

Whilst Hannah uncovered the extent of the breach to family's privacy, the little band of excursionists remained clustered at the doorway, nattering with great satisfaction amongst themselves over the sight they had just beheld.

"Lovely children," said one stranger to another who nodded in agreement. "They look to be a healthy pair. Not often the case with twins I understand. Oftentimes they are simpletons."

It was readily apparent to Hannah and Goodwin what sort of malfeasance was afoot. But, such was the bustling nature of the group that Smeads led, he only espied Hannah and Goodwin as they elbowed their way through the visitors. No fool he, Smeads quickly squelched the expression of horror that had invaded his countenance and composed his aspect into one of righteous indignation. (The best defence always a good offence, he intended to head off any accusations thusly.) Hannah had no ready censure as her mouth was quite agape. Had she looked at Goodwin, she would have recognised that their minds were quite alike in this matter.

There was no other trespass Smeads could have incurred that would have infuriated Hannah quite as much as one against the children. Her hands curled into fists and she hit the sides of her thighs with them in a fury she had never before quite entertained,

"Out!" she screamed at the nondescript troop of sightseers, "Out! Out! *Out*!"

As they made haste for the grand front door, Smeads made as if to slide in behind them, saying, "Very good. Very good," as if their expulsion was entirely his doing.

Goodwin would not have it, however, and went so far as to put his hand upon Smeads's shoulder to keep him from trailing out with the others.

Smeads whirled about at that affront, hissing, "Unhand me you churlish oaf! How dare you? I shall have your position, I will!"

He then turned about with a bumptious flounce, but had the misfortune to collide into Hannah Moorhouse's considerable bosom. She folded her arms across herself with such vehemence that she nearly took off a bit of his nose. Goodwin betook himself to Hannah's side and together they presented a united defence against any further intrusion into the Darcys' nursery. As they had not seen money exchange hands, they had no proof that Smeads was selling admission to ogle the twins, but they were altogether certain of it. Hannah intended to confer with Goodwin as to how to address the subject with the Darcys. If they were to engage in a pitched battle with the house steward, they knew their line of attack must be perfected. For her part, Hannah was quite certain just knowing that Smeads allowed persons unknown to them to reach the nursery level of the house would mean retribution of some sort against him.

Her musings of just how and where Smeads would be meted out his comeuppance was curtailed. Hannah and Goodwin were buttressed together so solidly that Smeads had no where to go but whence he came. Regrettably, hearing the commotion, the corridor's self-proclaimed sentinel, Cressida had come to investigate the rumpus. As the air of disdain which affixed itself to Smeads's countenance included in the bargain an upraised chin and heavy-lidded glower, he did not see the dog as she slunk behind him. Not surprisingly, Smeads tripped over Cressida. Goodwin instinctively reached out for him, but Smeads's momentum threw him beyond reach. The initial impact did Smeads no great harm. However, the reverberation of his cranium as it bobbed down each step was such that few who heard it were soon to forget.

As his body took several revolutions as he made his way down, the only loss he suffered worse than his dignity was of several of his teeth. However, the percussion of his body as it jounced down the stairs shook the silver coins he had taken in payment from the tour loose from the purse he had pinned to his small clothes. As he was knocked out of his senses for the better part of an hour, there was ample opportunity for it to be gathered in evidence against him.

Cressida appeared altogether unwitting of her heroics. Still, as Smeads remained a bit unwell for some time, the dog was happy to find his portion of shepherd's pie in her dinner dish that night—almost as much as cook and her kitchen maids were to serve it to her.

How Far the Fall

As outraged as they were at Smeads's audacity, Hannah and Goodwin were disconcerted as they anticipated Mr. Darcy's return. The thought of being chief witnesses against their nemesis was a privilege, but still a bit daunting.

Although those who had paid their admittance fee to see the twins had been hustled away, the footmen doing the hustling had seen Smeads take his horrifying tumble. By the time his body came to rest at the bottom of the staircase, he looked like a bloodied rag doll. Although Hannah stood petrified, Goodwin had taken the stairs with such haste that he reached Smeads before his body came to a rest. He did not, however, go to him. One brave footman cautiously stepped forward and delicately prodded him with the toe of his shoe. Smeads stirred, causing the footman to leap away as if having roused a snake. Goodwin only shook his head.

With surprising aplomb, Goodwin took charge of the situation, snapping his fingers for two footmen, one each to grasp his arms and legs to drag Smeads below stairs. (Having the house steward in such an indecorous attitude and in full view of anyone who might come upon the scene would have been unseemly.) As they lifted him, Smeads began to groan—loudly.

Hannah worried that Smeads might have broken a limb, but Goodwin seemed unconcerned. He led the way as the footmen hauled Smeads, bemoaning and bewailing, off to repair in his bed in the servants' quarters. Hannah, however, remained behind. There she waited in barely contained tremulousness for Goodwin to return with an assessment of the seriousness of Smeads's injuries. It had been a nasty fall and all the blood spewing from his mouth made it difficult to determine what part of him bore the worst of it. Directly, Goodwin returned, acerbically offering an apology that Smeads's injuries did not appear fatal.

Hannah needed more specifics, worried whether Smeads was awake and looking for retribution. Goodwin merely smirked, allowing that the steward, indeed, had ceased gibbering. After that initially unforthcoming assessment, Hannah managed to elicit from Goodwin that Smeads's injuries included a severe head-ache, the loss of several front teeth, and a swollen upper lip, but no broken bones. Contusions to his nether-end were a probability, but no one was inclined to take a look to determine absolutely.

Hannah wrung her hands at the extent of Smeads's injuries, uncertain whether to be happy or not that his injuries were not grave. She was glad for him to be incapacitated whilst they waited for the Darcys' return, but the worry that somehow she and Goodwin would be found in fault continued to nag her. After ascertaining that the steward was much to his bed, Hannah managed to gather up the courage to look in on him herself. Even in his compromised state, he remained an intimidating figure. Hence, she dared go no nearer to him than the doorway. From that distance, she could see that he was returning to his former self.

A young scullery maid had the misfortune of being the handiest servant when Smeads was brought to his bed, and it was she who inherited the office of his caretaker. By that time, his lips had begun to swell and his demands were garbled. She stood over him and dithered, having not a clue as to how to aid him. After several repetitions of his barely intelligible instructions, she assisted him to a sitting position. Smeads repaid her, however, with a sputtering scold upon her ineffectual performance of that simple duty. His swollen lips made him sound a bit like a duck, therefore she had to cover her mouth lest she laugh out loud. Hannah gasped on her behalf, knowing what might befall her if Smeads caught sight of her amusement.

But before he was finished with his jabbering tongue-lashing, he began to gag. The maid then had the pleasure of thwacking him between his shoulder blades to dislodge an incisor that had wedged in his throat. Whilst engaged in this activity, the maid espied Hannah at the door and rolled her eyes heavenward. She then held out a hand as he spit the persistent tooth into her palm. Hannah had nodded to her in sympathy, but was too jumpy to stay longer lest Smeads espy her.

Having seen for herself that indeed Smeads would likely survive, Hannah returned to discuss the matter more thoroughly with Goodwin. Two aspects of the troubling events Hannah saw as propitious. Not only had they had the opportunity of ridding Pemberley of its cursed steward, but she and Goodwin had been thrown together as partners in that enterprise. It would be necessary for her to consult with Goodwin upon many occasions before the Darcys returned lest Smeads not be given his rightful comeuppance. There were also several aspects of the events which remained unclear to her.

Goodwin and Hannah both understood that whilst Smeads's abuse of his position was extreme, it was not uncommon for servants to be guilty of employing lucrative schemes which treaded the fringes of embezzlement. Smeads's infraction, however, was so flagrant an abuse that it would eventually have had to come to light—far too many people were witting of it. If one were to engage in such antics, most knew enough to keep witnesses to a minimum. Smeads's audacity, however, knew no bounds. Indeed, the extent of his gall was as astonishing as it was foolish.

Hannah and Goodwin concluded that it was propitious that Smeads was exposed so compleatly. For if he had not been, the house would have had to suffer whispered accusations amongst the under-servants, everyone awaiting until someone garnered enough pluck to reveal all to the Darcys. Hannah and Goodwin's education may have been shy on the side of philosophers, but they saw first-hand the corrupting nature of power in Smeads. It took true strength of character not to exploit power—as Mr. Darcy so aptly demonstrated.

The other issue which plagued Hannah and Goodwin (besides their steward nursing a badly bruised cranium) was why Yewdell had insisted upon their hasty return to Pemberley. Both had independently concluded that he meant to expose

Smeads's malfeasance. What injury Smeads had committed against Yewdell to inspire such retribution, they had not a clue. So far as they were aware, those two men had no connexion.

They knew not why Yewdell did it, they were simply glad that he felled the tyrant.

Fortune Favours the Fools

The exceedingly rich drama involving Smeads was not the only entertainment for those who remained behind whilst the Darcys were away. One rife with those emotions singular to romance played out in plain view of all who cared to notice. The players, however, were altogether astonishing.

Just because the Darcys were away, work did not cease upon their family portrait. Sir Morland's work had progressed to the point that the sitters' likenesses were imprinted upon his mind with uncommon authenticity. Hence, when the Darcys took their unscheduled leave, he was able to sit happily upon his upholstered stool and dabble away, humming with satisfaction.

Once her daughter's duty to Mr. Darcy's relation took her from Pemberley, Mrs. Bennet saw it as her duty to watch over her daughter's house, her daughter's servants, her daughter's children, and, most intently, her daughter's painter. (She would have appointed herself watch and ward over her daughter's pigs and fowl as well, but there were only so many hours in a day.) As she believed that one could not be doing justice to one's employment in a happy state of mind, Morland's contentment outraged Mrs. Bennet.

For his part, in the Darcys' absence, Morland expected Mrs. Bennet's renewed scrutiny. With Mrs. Darcy no longer there to mediate their squabbles, he looked forward to those testy exchanges to rage quite without restraint. To remind himself that he despised Mrs. Bennet, he took measures to make certain that she was banned altogether from the salon were he painted. Indeed, his assistant was stationed outside the door to bar her admittance. Insofar as Mrs. Bennet had not intruded upon him for some time, he had congratulated himself that he had thought to do it.

Yet, after several days of self-prescribed solitude, his passion for his art idled. He began to miss Mrs. Bennet's persistent intrusion into his work place. Her outrageous interjections and opinions had heightened his colour. Indeed, after such episodes, the blood coursed through his veins with unbridled fervour. He began to consider in what other ways he might renew his passion in that same manner. Whatever it was, he thought it most certainly would not include that tempestuous Mrs. Bennet.

As it happened, Mrs. Bennet had not trespassed upon him simply because she had not chosen to do so—not because of his silly little sentry. If she truly wanted to enter a particular room in her daughter's house, a mere mortal would not have stopt her (although the bolts securing the door to her daughter's bed-chamber had done their office with great efficiency). As it happened, her youngest daughter, Mrs. Kneebone, and her new husband had been visiting and Mrs. Bennet's attention had been much occupied by entertaining them in the largest, and most elegant of Pemberley's parlours. The Major was not particularly witty, but she never tired of dear Lydia's gossip.

Because of the bereavement suffered by the Darcy family, the Kneebones felt it only proper that they took their leave as well (in truth, it was Major Kneebone who insisted). Once both her daughters and their husbands had taken their leave from Pemberley, Mrs. Bennet had little to amuse herself. Indeed, it took but a single evening of nothing but her own company ere she thought of an offence of Morland's that had remained unaddressed. Mrs. Bennet believed that her daughter Lizzy was far too tolerant of that man's daily inebriation. Now that the house was in her able hands, time had come that the painter's sins against God and his fellow men be addressed. She was in want of confronting him immediately, but was thwarted. He was not an early riser.

"Nursing his head due to an over-indulgence in spirits, no doubt," she sniffed.

Knowing to do otherwise would be fruitless, she waited until she heard the bell toll eleven and then made her way to the room Morland had commandeered as his studio. Although his master's instructions were explicit when it came to Mrs. Bennet, Morland's minion was still unable to stop her from bursting through the door. He did manage to put up enough of an obstruction to slow her down and the resultant fuss was great enough to give warning of her imminent intrusion. Moreland had removed the protective canvas from the painting, and was just then putting out his paints. When he heard the commotion, he ceased and turned towards the door expectantly.

Mid-day was not near as complimentary to a lady's complexion as candlelight, but the northern light (Morland demanded it for his sittings) was still favourable to a woman of Mrs. Bennet's years. Indeed, she was still a lady of some handsomeness. With flattering light and the particular care she had shown her toilette that morning, she was at her best. Moreover, her pique had heightened the colour in her cheeks. As she wafted across the room, she stopt a half-dozen steps away from the painter (making certain she kept the light streaming in from the windows at her back). The fragrance with which she had drenched herself caught up with her, engulfing them both.

Morland caught the scent and he raised his nose as it involuntarily took a whiff. It did not escape him that her cheeks bore a rosy hue that could not be entirely attributed to her state of agitation. Sometimes, he mused, loveliness is found where one least expects it. (Had her eyes always been that striking shade of green?) The proposal Mr. Darcy had put to him on her behalf did not look quite so repugnant from this vantage. It was surprising how much more fetching a countenance was when it was accompanied by a healthy-sized commission.

"Sir Morland!" she exclaimed. "I am come to insist that you no longer indulge your taste for spirits in my presence."

That, of course, was an ill-considered demand. She immediately realised her error, but before she could qualify it more rationally, he bowed.

"If Madame would refrain from my company, would that not solve the dilemma?"

"I think not," she blustered. "You should refrain from my company!"

"I must point out, Madame," he said civilly, "that you have come to my studio, I have not come to you."

He gave her a gracefully indulgent bow despite himself, adding, "And if you did, I would not have the pleasure of beginning my day with the vision of your very lovely frock before me. The lace is lovely. Is it new?"

Mrs. Bennet was quite taken aback by both his civility and his compliment. It was not new. Upon the sixth month anniversary of her husband's death, she had dared to add a small bit of lace to freshen one of her black bombazine gowns. Therefore, she stuttered a bit in reply.

"Why, yes," said she, "it is new. No, I mean—not altogether. It has been refashioned."

Whilst Mrs. Bennet's interest in the painter was born primarily of boredom, they both had a substantial mercenary streak. (She might not have been happy to know that his attention to her was inspirited by monetary gain, but she would have understood it.) However, by the time Morland saw Mrs. Bennet, literally, in a new light, the enforced celibacy he had endured during his long sojourn in the country bade his masculine appetite take notice. Hence, he liberated all the charm that had lain dormant for months.

"What ever you have done, I must say it is quite fetching."

She peered at him suspiciously—absolutely refusing to admit that she had sought out his admiration. It took her a moment before she recollected herself and returned the courtesy with a dip of her knees. Instinctively, she caught hold of the fan that dangled from a cord about her wrist (it too was black, but the tassel was silk) and had it unfurled by the time she arose from her curtsy. From behind its flutter, she batted her eyelashes several times. A titter escaped her lips before she managed to collect herself.

He swept his arm in the direction of his work-in-progress, inviting her to view it. She closed her fan and made her way in that direction. Her walk was prim, but her figure was arranged to suggest that she might, despite her widowhood, be cajoled from her bereavement.

"What say you, Madame?" Morland said as he stood proudly next to what he saw as a masterpiece.

It was the first time that she had been allowed to see it. Even she had admitted that the earlier portrait that he had done of Elizabeth had been exquisite ("If only it had been of Jane," she had said, "now there is true beauty.") This one even Mrs. Bennet could see was extraordinarily fine. Upon this occasion she had the good sense not to wish it had been of Jane's handsome family instead. Indeed, she did know how to admire it enough.

"Your work is most excellent, Sir Morland," she gushed. "You give my daughter's family a great compliment. It is, indeed, the most handsome rendering I have ever beheld." Then she added, "'Tis such a pity that it will not be displayed in London for the enjoyment of all. That would be such a triumph!"

Upon this matter, they exchanged commiserating looks on behalf of Mr. Darcy's implacability. That gentleman had remained unmoved upon the subject of public display of his family's portraits. On the subject of Mr. Darcy's pride, they were of like minds.

"I thank you," Morland bowed. "I am happy to know that you approve and understand the loss to my reputation."

Morland gazed upon Mrs. Bennet with renewed interest. He had never noticed how dazzling white was her skin—for a lady of her years. Indeed, her hair had not a hint of grey and her complexion was well-tended. Few women could wear the black of mourning with her success.

"I find it impossible to believe that you have married daughters, Mrs. Bennet," he exclaimed. "You cannot be more than a girl yourself!"

As a woman who never quarrelled with a compliment, she gave another flutter of her fan and dropped her gaze demurely to the floor. It had been far too long since she had been looked upon with an admiring eye. She had cared for Mr. Bennet, but no one thought their marriage to be one of abiding love. He had found much greater diversion in mocking her than professing his esteem. She was not truly tempted to succumb to Morland's charms—she was far too cognizant his reputation extended beyond that of his skills of an artistic nature. Still, a woman of her ego was not one to rebuff chivalrous attention when it was presented.

"Pray, has Mr. Darcy approached you, my dear Mrs. Bennet," he queried, "upon a further commission he has proposed?"

"No, indeed, he has not."

"If Mr. Darcy has not yet spoken to you of it, I dare not anticipate him," he said, feigning humility.

As he expected, Mrs. Bennet commenced to wheedle him into his own bidding. In doing so, she once again began flapping her fan—behind which she simpered to an alarming degree. Although he begged her to desist, his surrender was swift.

"Mr. Darcy has requested that I take your likeness when I have compleated my present work."

Upon hearing this, Mrs. Bennet was dumbfounded. (The rarity of such a happening was such that it was a shame only Morland was there to witness it.) She was absolutely astonished to learn that Mr. Darcy held her in such special regard. Initially, she stood mouth agape, but momentarily her jaw began to move with such rapidity, it was remarkable that she uttered not a sound. Had he known that she was so easily silenced, Morland might have brought Mr. Darcy's request to her attention long before. (His new-found admiration did not forget her loquaciousness.) He stood nodding patiently until at last she regained her voice.

She managed to croak out a response, "You honour me, sir!"

Although he was becoming increasingly happy to do so, Morland had dragged his heels a bit when Mr. Darcy had initially asked him to take another commission. Although there were few men who dared deny Mr. Darcy anything, Morland's ego sometimes took him down the lane of impetuosity. He knew it unwise to reject Mr. Darcy, but the thought of spending the time he must to do Mrs. Bennet justice whilst listening to her carp was objectionable. Of course, he did not say this to Mr. Darcy. Rather, he patiently explained that in some instances, the chosen subject did not suit his artistic sensibilities. When Mr. Darcy increased his offer by half, Morland reconsidered his position. Even with that additional incentive, Morland had remained sullen over the prospect of such a portrait; ruing his plight as one no man should have to suffer.

It had been a curiosity to him as to why Mr. Darcy was so keen upon a portrait of his mother-in-law—she had neither title nor position beyond her connexion to the Darcys. Initially, Morland believed Mr. Darcy was willing to spare no expense in having his irritating mother-in-law busy for much of the day. However, when informed that the likeness was to be taken at the Bennet family home of Longbourn, the Darcys' design fell unerringly apparent. Plainly, it suited them not only to have Mrs. Bennet's afternoons occupied, but to have her spend them in fair Hertfordshire. The additional stipulation that this sitting was to be taken beneath the spreading arms of an exceptionally fine oak to the east of the house itself, Morland saw as being Mrs. Darcy's particular wish, not her husband's.

Morland was entirely sympathetic to their plight, he was just not entirely certain about being sequestered with the quarrelsome Mrs. Bennet for such a portion of time that a sitting would demand. He had toyed with the notion of declining. In the end, the call of his pocketbook over-ruled his reservations. He steeled his resolve by reminding himself of just how charming he could be when he put his mind to it. The new side of herself that she had displayed was a relief. He would not have to employ all of his wiles to beguile her and that made his decision all the happier. True, his history suggested that he liked his romantic conquests not so long in the tooth, but he had courted less handsome women to ensure the success of his work. If he had not quailed at the prospect of wooing that portly duchess with the wrinkled décolleté and foul-smelling breath, a mere country lady would be but child's play.

The one thing he never thought it would be was a pleasure.

86

Irony's Sting

Upon the succeeding afternoon, Mrs. Bennet seated herself in a wing chair and admired Sir Morland as he put the finishing touches upon the Darcys' portrait. Afterward, he escorted her about the promenade. They uncovered a common interest in gossip and he introduced her to the health benefits of champagne. Theirs was not quite a romance, but he suspected that he would have little trouble obtaining Mrs. Bennet's agreement to have her likeness displayed in London. Theirs was enough of an attachment, however, to catch the attention of the servants. Most were astounded, but all who worked above stairs were happy that Mrs. Bennet had found a diversion that did not include cavilling to them.

Hannah and Goodwin were gladdened too for her distraction. Had she been witting of Smeads's plummet down the staircase, Mrs. Bennet's eager interest would not have been trifling. No doubt she would precede them in the telling of the incident to Mr. Darcy. The longer they had to think of it, the more certain they were that it was imperative to present their version of events before Smeads did.

That worry, however, directly became quite irrelevant. It was not above a day and a half later that when the same scullery maid who had inherited Smeads's care went to bring him his morning broth, she found the bed empty. He had taken his leave with only a few belongings and under the cover of darkness.

The little maid came running to report this distressing turn of events to Hannah—who then immediately notified Goodwin. Hannah had been happy to learn that Goodwin was up and tending to his chores (an indication that stress had not tempted his sobriety). He was as compleatly astonished as Hannah. They could not make out for the life of them why he had taken off like that. It would take several weeks for them to learn the whole truth of it. But the whole truth would certainly not be a comfort.

Within the first week, word returned to Derbyshire that Cyril Smeads had made his way to London. Few were caught unawares by that news. Still, his reason for taking leave remained a mystery. They could only surmise that he recognised the untenableness of his actions. Given a little objectivity, Hannah and Goodwin understood it as well. Mr. Darcy would never forgive a breach of his own privacy much less that of his children's. The more thought was given to the matter, the realisation came about that once Smeads regained his senses, he had, no doubt, fled for his very life.

However, they were quite amazed when they learnt that upon stealing away from Pemberley, he had first made haste for Rosings Park.

It was learnt that his reason for making for Kent fell to his misapprehension that his services as Lady Catherine's spy within the Darcy household would be rewarded. He had even expected to have been elevated to a similar position in her household.

Although their paths rarely crossed, Smeads's reputation of boundless arrogance and unrivalled disputatiousness was well known to Yewdell. Had he not been witting, it was doubtful that they would have been friends—stewards and housekeepers of large manor houses were a bit chary of each other. Hence, to his mind, Yewdell had good reason to want Smeads sent packing even had he not been privy to the spying. Moreover, Smeads also had a reputation of avariciousness, but had not taken a pence from Lady Catherine for his services. Yewdell was no dolt. If Smeads did not take money, he expected some other reward. It was probable that his own situation was threatened. Because of this, Yewdell took action.

Although she monitored every expenditure within her household with an exceedingly keen eye, in matters of servants, Lady Catherine valued Yewdell's judgement. Therefore, Yewdell had only to remind her of Smeads's easily compromised loyalty for her to see there was no place for him at Rosings. Indeed, with the Darcy kin visiting, she refused to see Smeads at all. He stood, hat in hand, at the rear door whilst Yewdell had the pleasure of delivering her ladyship's refusal. If Yewdell bore a smirk as he did, Smeads was far too crest-fallen to notice.

The last was seen of Smeads, he was serving drinks at Boodle's. He had a second string to his bow there as well—one of procuring female companionship for the customers. Word had it that it was a line of work for which he was richly equipped.

Angels Avenge

To soothe himself of the loss of his tiny companion, Wickham took himself to the nearest bijoutier. Even he dared not keep such a treasure on his person long. He had to make himself not pat it in reassurance—that was a dead giveaway to the light-fingered where one stowed his money. It was fortunate that he was near Mayfair. There were more jewellers within a half-mile of where he walked than in any spot in England.

He did not, however, stop in the first one he came across. He knew he must choose carefully. It must be the most exclusive of shops to handle such a singular item. In fortune, he found a suitable one quite promptly. It had a tasteful sign. It read: "Fine Gems, William R. Smythe, Proprietor." He drew a breath, tugged his cuffs straight, and entered.

The walls and cabinetry were of mahogany, but little merchandise was evident other than a case of watches.

"Good-day to you, sir," said the natty gentleman behind the counter.

Wickham was not fooled by the man's dapper appearance, "Your employer, please."

The man bowed curtly and betook himself behind a curtain. After a moment of inaudible mumblings, a second man appeared. He was not half-so fashionable as his clerk, but his flawless tailoring announced him not your average shopkeeper. He was a small man, however. He stepped upon a stool hidden behind the counter to raise his stature high enough to do business.

"My name is Smythe, I am the proprietor. May I be of assistance?"

Wickham was not the least bit fooled by the name Smythe. The man had an indistinct accent—perhaps German. Moreover, Wickham disposed not to tell, but to show what he had to offer. Slipping his hand into the breast-pocket of his waistcoat, he withdrew the necklace by one clasp. It revealed itself with a slither—as if he had charmed it like a snake. Mr. Smythe could not help but gasp. He reached for it.

"Tsk, tsk," Wickham shook his head.

Immediately, the man withdrew his hand and unfolded a piece of felt. Wickham carefully arranged his treasure upon it. Smythe gasped again.

"I am jeweller to the Prince Regent himself and rarely do I see something of this distinction!"

Wickham was leaning against the counter upon his elbow, his fingers nudging the necklace with seeming idleness, but pushing it imperceptibly in the jeweller's direction.

"I am told this once adorned the neck of Queen Marie Antoinette," he lied.

"I do not doubt it for a moment," said the little man, shaking his head with true astonishment.

His tone thereupon altered, his voice conspiratorial.

"There are," Smythe whispered, "those who would pay handsomely for a piece such as you have."

"Do you indeed think so?" Wickham said, endeavouring to conceal a smirk.

"Yes, yes. I believe so," the man hurried on. "If you would be so kind as to allow me to have a look with my glass?"

With the merest flick of his head, Wickham allowed it. Even more quickly the man produced a glass, caught it in the squint of his right eye, and bent forward. Drawing his gaze carefully from one end to the other, he observed each and every stone.

"Ah," said Smythe. "Ah," he repeated, Wickham beaming ever-more greatly with every movement of his quizzing glass.

Then he said, "Oh."

Wickham stood up, placing both hands upon the edge of the counter, but remained quiet.

"Oh," the man said again, then, "uh, oh."

By that last comment, Wickham's head had inched ever-more closely to the jeweller's until they were almost touching foreheads. When the jeweller at last rose from his investigation, he almost bumped noses with his client.

"I fear I have bad news for us both," he apologized. "This necklace is not as it first appeared."

"No?" Wickham said tightly.

"No," Smythe repeated. "The setting…one can see the error. It is exquisite workmanship."

Without thinking twice, Wickham wrested the glass from Smythe's eye and held it to his own, taking the same care as did Smythe. He saw nothing (not even that the chain attached to the glass was about Smythe's neck and choking him). He released it and extended an upturned palm. It was a plea.

"What then can ever be the matter?"

Smyte replied simply, "Why, it is the stones."

"The stones?" Wickham repeated dumbly.

"Yes, the stones. The rubies, the diamonds…"

Tightly, Wickham stopt him, saying, "I know of which stones you speak. I do not know what is amiss with the stones?"

As he asked the question, he knew in his heart the answer. Hence by the time the man uttered what he truly did not want to hear, he was already acclimating himself to the realisation that he had been duped. He really did not have to listen to the rest of what the man had to say, it meant nothing to him.

"They are paste, sir," Smythe said with finality. "True, they are the best I have ever seen, but still paste. So many exquisite pieces are arriving from France, I was so taken with the notion of what it could be that I did not immediately see what I should have."

Clearly, Wickham was devastated. Indeed, so wretched did he look, the man feared he might burst into tears. Indeed, Wickham thought that a distinct possibility. He placed both hands upon the edge of the counter, his legs suddenly having no strength.

He stood resting his weight there so he could catch the breath that seemed to have been knocked out of him. Smythe reached out and patted one hand with true compassion. Suddenly, the true impact of what had occurred hit Wickham. His reaction was not one of benign acceptance. Because he desperately wanted it to be true, he leapt to attack.

"You lie, sir! *J'accuse*!"

He knew that word in French. What was suddenly crystal clear to him was that he was crossed, but not by little Marie-Therese, but this man, Smythe.

"I have heard of such as you! Your assessment is a sham—then you pretend sympathy and offer to take the gems for a pittance! You little Hun…little…bloody Hun dwarf!"

"Sir! I am offended by such accusations! Begone from my establishment!"

"Happily!" sniffed Wickham.

Angrily, he picked up the necklace and stalked out.

Once outside, he bethought the matter. Perhaps it was true. With slightly less bravado, he entered another shop. Then another. Each had exactly the same answer as before. The only additional intelligence he uncovered was that the French forgeries were the very best.

"You were fooled by nothing but the finest imitation."

"How reassuring," Wickham had replied without enthusiasm.

Knowing that anyone in a position to acquire such a necklace would be disinclined to purchase it without authentication, he finally accepted fifty pounds for the setting. He was happy to get it.

When at last he trudged back to Mrs. Younge's establishment, he was in low spirits, indeed. He avoided her, for he knew she would inquire first if his intrigue was successful and if told the truth, she would secondly demand his outstanding rent. In his frame of mind, he thought it unlikely he had the wherewithal to employ his alternate means of payment.

In fortune, Mrs. Younge was busy elsewhere and Wickham managed to take the stairs without her intrusion. He made for the door of his room, opened it, stepped in, and then carefully closed it behind him. It was then that he saw a tri-folded letter that had been shoved underneath the door. He automatically stooped and picked it up. He immediately recognised the hand, but he would have known the author without looking at it. What gall—no doubt she wrote only to rub salt in his wounds. He could not bring himself to read it just then and he dropped it upon the table next to his bed. Thereupon, he wrested himself out of his coat and sat heavily upon the mattress. When he began to tug off his boots, his eyes lit upon the empty cradle sitting vacant in the corner. From there, his eyes spanned the length of the room, taking note of every item of baby paraphernalia that remained. Fitfully, he picked up a basket and went from item to item until all had been secured within. Thereupon, he crushed the basket into the opening of the cradle, picked up both and set them outside his door.

"Mr. Wickham? Is that you?" sang out Mrs. Younge.

His answer was to soundly shut the door. In a moment he heard her scratching at the door, but he refused to answer. He simply could not respond and sat once again upon the side of the bed and put his head in his hands until she left. Only when she quit his door did he pick up the letter and open it. He thought he knew all that it would say.

But he was wrong.

Dear Major Wickham,

If you have not yet learnt, you will soon know that the necklace that I gave you in exchange for the bébé is—I believe this is what it is called—fake.

"Yes," he agreed, "that would be an accurate term. Your English, Marie-Therese, is much better than my French."

Thinking he knew all the letter would say, he was not reading it carefully, thus he did not immediately recognise that she had used his proper rank.

She went on:

I would say that I was sorry for the deceit, but I am not.

When dear Césarine told you that the bébé was by Monsieur Du Mautort, it was a lie. The baby is yours—or should I say was begat by you? She did not want you to know that. Her reason for that deceit may be unclear to you. This letter is to explain to you why.

You are unaware that Césarine knew you long ago—when you were said to be a student. Her father was your tutor. She knew it was unlikely that you would recall her, for your women were many. Perhaps you do not even now.

Stunned, Wickham quit reading for a moment to see if he could, indeed, recall. There was a bit of a recollection, but it was indistinct. His brow furrowed. This was absurd—he knew Césarine in England when they were but children? It was possible, he supposed. He read on.

She became with child from you. You abandoned her and the child. You lied to her even your name. She was sent away and forced to give up her child. Thereafter she became the Césarine you met in Paris. Why Césarine took you to her bed again remains to me a mystery. She said she did not love you and never did she believe you loved her. Such is the nature of desire. It has no reason.

Césarine was a good mother. She went to great expense and much time to find the bébé that she had given away. When she fell with child by you again, she could not bear to kill it. The bébé was to be taken to a convent of her choosing. She did not want you ever to know that you were Babette's father. That is her name, Babette.

You seemed to have been fond of Babette, but I do not truly believe it. You love no one but Major Wickham. If there is some bit of love for Babette inside your heart, you need not worry for her. She is with her sister who will see to her always.

I am,
Your Daughter,
Marie-Therese

Carefully, he reread the letter, this time noting every detail. Just as carefully, he refolded it and placed it upon the table next to him. From beneath his mattress he withdrew a half-bottle of gin. It was not his favourite drink, but it would do in a pinch. He did not bother to look for a glass, but upended the bottle. He then lay back upon his bed, one arm behind his head.

He lay in that exact attitude until the next morn.

The Divine Duel

It was easy in the aftermath of this misadventure for Wickham to locate Lydia. She had decamped from their previous dwelling, but she had few alternatives. He knew she would go to her family. Her Aunt and Uncle Gardiner had come to her rescue once before. As they were her only relations he knew to be dwelling in London, in seeking her, he sallied forth first unto Cheapside. Still, he was disinclined to show his hold card. Catching sight of an appropriately impoverished boy, he called to him.

"Here, lad," said he, offering him a coin. "Ring the bell and deliver this package at yonder door. If the lady to whom it is addressed is not within, find out where she can be found."

He knew not to give the boy the half-penny beforehand—he had had little snipes take off with his money. This one was delighted to have such a lucrative assignment, grabbed the box, and betook himself across the street directly. He did not inquire (nor did he care) why the gentleman did not take it himself.

The box had only a folded newspaper inside. If it was opened, it might seem a tad odd but nothing more. He had read that paper and was current as to the unrest and mischief about in England in general and London in particular. That news did better office as senseless delivery than use to him—politics had never been his forte. Other than having himself delivered as cannon fodder unto Napoleon's elite guard, he gave not a fig what happened in the world beyond his own. He watched as the boy went to the door, pulled the bell, and a servant answered. The maid held up the box, rattled it, peered at the name upon it, scowled (aha! Lydia had been there), retrieved a pencil from behind her ear, and wrote something upon the box. Perfect. As the boy hied back to his side, he congratulated himself upon his stealth. He certainly did not intend to travel all the way to the ridiculously bucolic county of Hertfordshire only to learn she was not abiding with her father if he could avoid it.

Quick as that, he had an address for her new lodgings. Indeed, he was quite pleased with himself. He sent the boy happily upon his way, joyously flipping the coin.

"O to be a carefree youngster with no worries to bother me!" thought Wickham as he watched the lad dance away. Sometimes he refused to pay the child after it had compleated his bidding, claiming malfeasance of some sort against them. This day, upon the cusp of a bright new scheme, he felt generous.

"Look here," he said to himself upon seeing the Chelsea address. "What has my darling wife been up to since her loving husband has been to the wars? Perhaps those sisters who are so pecuniarily blessed have at last taken pity upon their poor relation and settled some funds on her. Oooh, welcome home, Major Wickham."

It was then he saw something else upon her address, "What is this?"

He looked more closely, "Mrs. Kneebone? Mrs. *Kneebone*?"

He was outraged.

The more he thought of it, the more umbrage he took. Could his dear wife not have waited the proper mourning period before she remarried? After all, he was a war hero! Moreover, if that was the same drudge of a Major Kneebone that he recalled from his regiment in Brighton, he found further insult.

Not that he needed it. He had a plan and it had nothing to do with reinstating himself in Lydia's household. Actually, her remarriage was a tremendous boon. He had been torn as to what would be his next move. Although there was a great deal of chaos within the country (he had witnessed roving thugs and random mayhem had spilt out of the East End and into the West), one thing was certain. Anyone who could claim to have any part of Napoleon's downfall was given carte blanche in his homeland. So far, he had avoided the inevitable moment when he would be recognised. He had only toyed with the notion of claiming amnesia and done nothing to research as he had planned. Marie-Therese's letter offering money for the baby had led him to believe that unnecessary.

In learning of Lydia's remarriage, he was privy to helpful intelligence. That told him the single thing he had been unable to ascertain—Major George Wickham was thought dead, not a deserter. She would not have remarried had he been thought still alive. He knew that. It was probable that he now had a choice. He could claim to have been lost and returned to the bosom of his family which would entail a great deal of invention (of which he was ably capable), or he could eat an enormous helping of humble pie (of which he was not). In light of Lydia's hasty remarriage, there loomed a more palpable alternative. If his inconstant wife was well settled, her prosperous sisters might be willing to purchase both his leave-taking and his silence.

Little Marie-Therese's ruse had ruined his original brilliant (or so he thought) scheme. The thousand pounds was to have given him a stake to establish himself wherever he might have wanted. That recollection brought him a disagreeable train of reflections. Chief amongst them was the notion of him desiring a new start—a renaissance. It was all he desired. Was not everyone deserving of another chance—to amend those failings they had encountered? If he had a purse, he could return to the Continent—his handsomeness had not waned—this time he would find an heiress in need of a husband. A thousand pounds would be quite adequate.

One possibility that he had considered was to cadge enough money from Lydia to fund a return to Paris. If that girl did indeed believe herself his daughter, their connexion was not severed. If she still had the original gems from the necklace (which he was sure had been genuine in Césarine's day), she was in possession of a considerable fortune—one of which he would be happy to relieve her. He could either convince her that he could exchange them to her advantage in England, or he would simply steal them. What he would not do was allow himself to take any drubbing lying down. This new turn of events, however, may not have altered everything, but it certainly painted it another colour.

What he had not done was truly address Marie-Therese's outlandish accusations. He had avoided them. He intended to continue avoiding them until he could use them to his advantage. That he had not one daughter, but two, was wholly pleasing to him. If what they said was true and that he had even *another* chance bairn still at Pemberley, that would be admirable indeed. He enjoyed the prolificacy of his loins—if they did no damage to his pocket. One small discombobulation asserted itself, however. If Marie-Therese was correct, he was most grateful not to have acted upon his initial impulse to seduce her. There were few things that were beneath him, but even he drew the line at incest. That and folk-dancing.

He was anxious to confront Lydia and hired a coach to hurry his way to Chelsea.

When he had confronted Lydia, her reaction was even more rewarding than her jingle-brained husband's. Both were superb in their astonishment of his return. They had not even asked where he had been. Lydia had threatened to swoon and run about rending her garment like some crazed Turk. Her opposite in every way, Kneebone stood in a stupor, his mouth agape exposing an abominable inattention to the condition of his teeth.

Wickham *had* to congratulate himself. He had handled his role of aggrieved husband superbly. His poor, wounded heart lay upon his sleeve. Kneebone had actually called him out! Actually duelling for Lydia's honour? That was rich. Of course he agreed to it—what else was one to do? Lydia had thrown herself between them, begging poor Kneebone to reconsider. Under no circumstances did Wickham intend to entertain such a notion, but one must always display a willingness to defend one's name as a gentleman.

All of that, and the clear evidence of the presence of an infant whose age made its paternity another bartering point for the dissolution of their marriage, made for it a most profitable call.

He knew that it would be but a matter of time before Lydia would call upon her family for remedy. It was unlikely that her father would be who she would contact. Wickham had learnt at the time of their marriage how little that gentleman was good for. He even believed he had detected a speck of indecision upon his wife's countenance. That might be a problem. Under no circumstances now did he want her back. The more he thought about it, the more he thought his withdrawal worth. He became increasingly eager to see who would come forth as arbiter over the situation. His anticipation was keen.

Wickham had chosen to meet with Lydia's arbiter in the tavern below his lodgings. It was suitably disreputable, the better to display his financial…amiability, suggesting him a destitute, struggling veteran of the wars. No doubt he had also chosen it to keep his well-born callers uneasy.

Upon learning of their destination, Elizabeth suggested to Kneebone that they hire a hack rather than take her carriage. She thought it best to be as inconspicuous as possible in considering the unfortunate neighbourhood they would be visiting. Therefore, she wore her simplest dress and went so far as to pull the lace from her plainest bonnet. Major Kneebone insisted upon wearing his uniform, however, which in and of itself drew attention. He also wore his sword which made Elizabeth excessively uneasy. Lydia, whose costume was gaudy on her severest days, was dressed in her finest frock. This day she was in want of displaying to Wickham just what he would be forgoing was he to give her up. Hence, she wore a bizarre hat and her most revealing dress. Although the days were still warm, she wore—at eleven in the morning—an ermine muff. Elizabeth recognised it as once belonging to Jane who had thought it and its glass beads tasteless.

At mid-morning the streets near the Thames still stunk from the previous night's revelry. As Kneebone handed the ladies out of their hired coach, he gave a coin to the driver, telling him to wait. Then, once again he attempted to dissuade the ladies from taking such a meeting.

"This is not a safe area, Lydia dear. And you Mrs. Darcy, can I not make other arrangements?" asked Kneebone with increasing apprehension.

The ladies were far more resolute than he, Lydia charging forward as if on a regimental excursion herself. Elizabeth was just as determined, but history told her to be wary. She rethought, however, her initial inclination to meet with Wickham alone. They had to step around two bodies to get to the appointed address, and she was not altogether certain one was merely unconscious.

"Do the authorities not take the dead from the street?" whined Lydia. "This is abominable business."

Kneebone toed first one recumbent form and then the other. In fortune both responded and he and Elizabeth exchanged a look of relief. Regrettably, one disturbed figure sat up and retched in his lap, inviting Lydia to shriek and both she and Elizabeth lifted their skirts to their ankles and hurried their step.

"Oh, Lizzy! Where are clogs when we need them?"

(That was an astonishment. Lydia had always had to be threatened to wear clogs in bad weather. However fervently Elizabeth hoped to see an improvement in Lydia's prudence, she was not certain an alteration in what footwear she was disposed to wear was a true gauge of it.)

The further they betook themselves along the foetid streets, the more anxious the three of them became. By the time they located the public house Wickham had chosen for their meeting, Elizabeth had serious misgivings about the entire venture. Those reservations did not lessen upon seeing Wickham's countenance again. He, however, looked surprised upon seeing her. She was uncertain whether that was in her favour or not.

Wickham bowed with the same unctuous manner he had always employed. It was still difficult to believe she ever thought him charming.

"Sister Elizabeth!" he exclaimed. "How well you look. It is a great honour to see you."

The question as to why she was there was unasked, but implied. However, she did not offer to explain. Lydia believed that no silence should go unoccupied and began to talk enough for everyone. She complained about Wickham's choice of meeting place, that he wanted to meet, that Kneebone would not duel him no matter how badly he wanted to and, most of all, how much must she lay down for him to leave her be?

Elizabeth was uncertain whether Major Kneebone groaned inwardly as did she or not, for she dared not look in his direction. He had been as coiled as a spring since they had left Chelsea. She was less certain than Lydia of his intentions toward Wickham.

Wickham behaved as if he was taking afternoon tea, motioning them to a trestle table in the far corner.

"Had I known you were to be here I would have arranged to accept you in the Green Room at the Argyle, Mrs. Darcy," he smiled.

Elizabeth was self-conscious and wanted to be done with the meeting as quickly as possible. There was a moment when she was uncertain how to step over the bench to sit down and Kneebone tugged the huge wooden seat far enough away from the table so that she and Lydia could inch their way down and be seated. Kneebone remained standing, his hat in the crook of his arm. Wickham looked at him and smirked. She was curious where Wickham had been, he looked well-tailored and she assumed she had not been wrong in supposing his choice of public house a manipulation. Contrary to her want of hasty dispatch of their business, Wickham was bent on small talk which, under the circumstances, seemed ludicrous. Indeed, as a trio of men, cup of ale in hand, joined them at their table and no one bid them leave, she became exasperated.

"I beg you, sirs," she addressed them, "may we have privacy for our discourse?"

The men turned to each other, hooted, and pretended high manners, mocking hers, "Woohoo! She begs us she do! What else will she beg us, I ask you!"

Kneebone turned to the men menacingly demanding, "Leave us!" And they did directly.

Relieved, Elizabeth quieted Lydia who was still enumerating Wickham's shortcomings as a husband and had only arrived to count three of a possible hundred, saying to her, "Lydia dear, you may post a letter upon your own time."

Wickham grinned. Elizabeth wanted more than any other thing she could think of at that time to rid the smile from his face.

"May we be frank, Mr. Wickham?"

"I most humbly desire that, Elizabeth."

She ignored his familiarity, "We have been advised by our attorney…"

"Mr. Phillips, I presume—lovely man. He still owes me five pounds from cards," Wickham interrupted.

"Let her speak, Wickham," Kneebone raised his voice.

It was incendiary.

Wickham retorted, "I do not recall one Major is to command another Major in what he may or may not do. I am an officer of the Waterloo battle and a gentleman. I have a history with this lady, we are friends! I beg you leave this conversation to us!"

"Since when was your name ever described in the annals of glory, Wickham?" Lydia cried.

"I do not care to be spoken to in that manner by a woman who arranges her hair with a pitchfork and dresses like a Covent Garden tart!"

Wickham had half risen. Elisabeth rose as well as she could from behind the table and put her hand between them, but to no avail.

"You, sir, are no gentleman," boomed Kneebone. "Of that I am certain. You are an adulterer and a card-cheat."

"You Kneebone, who claimed you are friend to all things demure in a woman, have taken Lydia to your bed! What hypocrisy!"

Although she had never heard them before, Elizabeth knew fighting words when uttered—and there had been more than a few just exchanged. She grabbed Lydia by

the hand to make away, but both were tangled in their skirts whilst attempting to escape the bench.

"Draw your weapon, Kneebone," snorted Wickham, pulling a knife from his boot.

In a flash, Kneebone unsheathed his sword.

Suddenly, to the shock of all in the room, the cocking of a pistol was heard. To her horror, Elizabeth saw that Lydia had withdrawn a tiny single-shot pistol from her reticule.

When Kneebone turned to look aghast at his wife, Wickham slid the point of his blade to his fingers and drew back to throw it at Kneebone. With that came the report of Lydia's gun. The bullet hit the knife with a ping and ricocheted into Wickham's foot. He did not immediately react, but looked at his foot in wonder.

Lydia looked at the still-smoking end of her gun, saying, "I thought I would be a better shot than that."

"What ever do you mean?" cried Kneebone. "That was magnificent! You shot the knife from his hand!"

"I was," Lydia groused, "aiming at the curl in the middle of his bloody forehead!"

Only then did Wickham begin to hop about, endeavouring unsuccessfully to kee from howling in pain, "Are you compleatly mad, woman?! Discharging a weapon me! This is a first even for you, Lydia!"

Instantly, Lydia was by Wickham's side, "Oh dear! Poor Wickham! What h done? What have I done?"

Lydia was still keening whilst endeavouring to put her arms about Wickham bone was even more aghast than that she had discharged a gun, "Lydia, dear

Elizabeth had had enough. She grasped Lydia by her bonnet strings and f from Wickham, dragging her through the crowd that was just then beginni in the hopes of seeing a person lying dead from malfeasance.

"Come, Major Kneebone!" she demanded.

He had been standing as if a statue, arms out-stretched, still murm dearest."

At last Kneebone regained his composure and clutched Lydia abo ing her up and over what various personages lay in their way to the h bled into the coach and neither of the ladies waited to be hand Indeed, Kneebone climbed onto the top with the driver, wresting once atop. He flapped the reins wildly but could only urge them

It was good enough for them to make their escape.

When they arrived home from the encounter with Wi quite happy to have escaped—not only with their lives, bu well. Disturbed by that possibility, they sat with the drap day, with Kneebone taking periodic trips to the window ders. In time, Lydia realised she would not be dragged unrepentant. Still, in light of attempted murder beir bourhood in London, Lydia begged Elizabeth to kee Elizabeth agreed readily. She truly did not care for I light of her similar exertion in his aunt's direction

the conclusion that her entire family was a threat to tranquillity. Hence, she was not inclined to be called forth to the magistrate as an accessory to such a crime. Had anything more than Wickham's dignity (and only a tiny bit of his big toe) been injured, the outcome might have been quite dissimilar.

After the initial fright was over, Elizabeth was so angry with Lydia, she was all but rendered speechless, "Really, Lydia!"

She did not inquire as to where Lydia had acquired a pistol. It seemed pointless. After all, Lydia was not entirely to blame. Hers was not the first weapon drawn. The entire fracas recalled to Elizabeth an episode in her own life that was not so benign. In want of not recalling that horrifying event, she suffered from a headache that evening. In light of such a fiasco of a negotiation, as Elizabeth saw it, their largest challenge was not that nothing was decided. What most worried her was the revelation that Lydia was not immune to Wickham. Kneebone was not inconsolable, but clearly was miffed—uncertain which held the greatest weight, that Lydia endeavoured to kill Wickham in his defence or that she threw herself at Wickham's feet after the fact.

As for Lydia, she vowed to Kneebone that she had not meant to go to Wickham as she had, but, "When I saw what I had done, I could not bear to be his murderer."

Kneebone allowed that grounds for remorse, but did not appear altogether convinced of her loyalty. It was then that Lydia came to Elizabeth to implore her to be rid of Wickham on her behalf.

"If you do not," she said, "I cannot answer for what might come to pass."

It was the first time in Elizabeth's recollection that she saw tears in Lydia's eyes that ere truly meant and not a ploy. Even as a child, Lydia had taken advantage of her other's partiality and her position of youngest sister, wailing like a banshee at the allest injury and weeping buckets with any cross words. Elizabeth knew that neither eebone nor Lydia could be trusted to meet with Wickham again. Such a violent oute had made her more resolute against Darcy engaging him as well. Her initial inct to see Wickham alone had been correct. Having seen him for as brief a time as ad, she did not enjoy the idea at all. As to how to make contact with him, she was ely at a loss. It did not take intuition to tell her that she had not seen the last of him. er a sleepless night, the next morning she bade a messenger to deliver a note to am that she had scribbled late the night before. When she gave the boy the s, Lydia tried to read what was written in the letter over her shoulder but she folded it and shooed her away.

ad written:

ad not the time to tell you, we have been advised that the law reads that in cases ours, a wife may choose between her first husband and her second. Moreover, if is proven, the husband has morally dissolved the marriage as well. I only ask you dia in peace.

hoose not to desist, I must advise you that information to your detriment will inst you.

course, was a compleat bluff. They had no real evidence, only hear-say. as officially a hero, killed in hostilities for the crown. At that moment she e not to meet with him again—most certainly not alone in a vile tavern. e longer she stayed in London without advising Darcy, she knew she was

at risk of injuring his trust. She was even more convinced after that altercation the previous morning that she wanted Darcy nowhere near Wickham.

She sealed the folded letter with red wax only and handed it to the boy with a half-crown for his trouble. The boy looked at her in wonder, gave the coin a bite just to make certain it was real, and took off on a hard run. Elizabeth marvelled at his sense of purpose. When she closed the door and turned, Lydia stood before her.

"We will have to wait," Elizabeth said.

Lydia turned and walked away. The little nurse was standing by the doorway holding the baby. To the girl's astonishment, Lydia took her daughter from her, prest her to her breast, and carried her into the sitting room. The girl looked directly at Elizabeth. Neither quit the gaze.

At last, Elizabeth asked, "Pray, do I *know* you?"

"No m'am," Sally answered, then seeing her opening, said, "not exactly."

A Turn or Two

The little servant girl with the searching eyes had quite a tale to tell.

It seemed that the Darcys had sorely underestimated the extent of behindhand prattle that came in the aftermath of war. It not only traversed Derbyshire, it made its way to London and beyond. Hence, Sally had been very much upon his trail, when her path crossed Wickham's.

When the Darcys supposed that only they were privy to the heinous crimes of George Wickham, they were greatly mistaken. As much as those within the inner circle of their servitors dedicated themselves to maintaining their privacy and abhorred its betrayal, those in more distant positions were not so circumspect. Indeed, the greater the distance, the more injudicious the talk. There may have been only whispers, but they were pervasive. The member of Wickham's command with whom Mr. Darcy spoke in the field hospital in Belgium recognised not only that Mr. Darcy was a man of some means, he knew in what county those means largely existed. Whilst initially it was only a matter of curiosity who the tall, aristocratic man was, once one was privy to it, soon was every other soldier (at least those whose wounds bade him sensible enough to be told). To have a man such as Mr. Darcy labouring as a stretcher-bearer had been a fine sight indeed.

The grenadier who was important enough for Mr. Darcy to comfort became equally memorable. Both names were murmured from one end of the hospital to the other. Upon the return of those surviving soldiers to their home counties, those names were repeated. The means by which the young grenadier John Christie received his wound were recounted and the name of the officer responsible were hissed from one person to the next. These soldiers who surrounded the young grenadier—those near enough and alert enough to be privy to the tale—were not officers. The few men of rank injured were sequestered upon the far wall, away from the riff-raff which comprised the enlisted men. Hence, the disgrace Major Wickham employed in service to his King remained unknown to those who might take legal interest in such an occurrence. There was but one man who knew both who Mr. Darcy was and heard what John Christie said of his commanding officer. That man was not inclined to speak publicly—far too many men who reported such misdeeds came under undue inspection by the authorities. He spoke his mind in more than one ale-house, but no more.

That man had been but one of many who despised the act but thought little of that over-sight, for it was the way of the world. It was only one of the more conspicuous injuries done to the working man by those who comprised their betters in the established order. Indeed, word of such a crime as Major Wickham's only served to inflame the perturbable masses. What Sally learnt from stealing away to the Darcys' stables was only a slight variation of the truth. (Even the high-born believed any story worth retelling had to take a bend or two.) It had enough authenticity to redirect Sally's quest from finding her brother to finding his killer and seeing that, if the law did not exact vengeance upon her brother's behalf, she would. The only thing that stood in her way was the question of whether that officer was kilt in the battle or had deserted as some had said.

Sally had always been quick to make friends and that remained true at the Pemberley stables. In that she had only brief periods of time to escape Lydia's watch, it was remarkable that she found Edward Hardin's wife with such ease. It had been even more astonishing to Sally that when she told Mrs. Hardin that her brother's name was John Christie, that lady scooped her into her arms and hugged her to her generous bosom.

"I loved that boy as if 'e were my own," she said.

Hearing that such a kind woman had looked after her brother made Sally all but cry with pleasure.

"Law, now, gerl," Mrs. Hardin said, "he was a fine lad. You can be proud."

That her pride could be extended to her brother's induction into the grenadiers was added pleasure. That he had given all he had to give to the King upon the field of battle was not. She was not altogether surprised. Not receiving another letter after his deployment supposed to her that was his fate. The particulars Mrs. Hardin whispered were of grave importance to her. But these came not in buckets, but in a trickle. With each creep down to Mrs. Hardin's kitchen, more of her brother's situation fell apparent.

That her mother had once worked as a maid at Pemberley was one of the first surprises—she had always thought it was one of her mother's tales. Sally had to explain that John was but her half-brother, but of this Mrs. Hardin seemed already aware.

Mrs. Hardin was shelling a bowl of peas with precision as she talked, expertly inserting her thumbnail into the pods, evicting the peas from their snug home and into her dish.

"Here gerl," she said, "make yerself useful."

Thereupon, she grasped a handful of peas and dropped them into Sally's lap. Sally had never shelled peas, but she was observant and caught on in a hurry.

"Your mama worked at Pemberley, did ye know that?"

"Nay," replied Sally, "I would think that if I worked in such a fine house I would never want to leave it."

Mr. Hardin looked at her carefully, gauging her words.

"Do you know your brother's pa?" she asked cautiously.

"I only know that my mama weren't married to him," she answered straightforwardly.

Mrs. Hardin barely recalled the events that she related, but filled the holes in her memory as best she could. She was far too loyal to her husband's employer to pass on those allegations of a youthful dalliance with Abigail that had taken on a life of their own after her death. Word filtered back from the Continent that Mr. Darcy had sat bedside of John Christie's dying body, enough for some of those in Pemberley's service to surmise that their connexion was of a particular kind. But the Hardins knew better. The last houskeepr Mrs. Reynolds had put that fallacy to rest for good. Had Sally arrived a twelve-month before, she might have heard a far different story than she did. Because whilst Mrs. Reynolds had squelched that earlier rumour, she had confirmed another upon her deathbed. For those who nursed Mrs. Reynolds in her last hours were privy to that woman's revelation to Darcy regarding George Wickham's paternity. That was one bit of information that Mrs. Hardin thought twice about sharing. At last, her loyalty to the boy whom she had thought of as a son bade her tell his thoughtful sister what was thought to be the truth of his death. She related it in detail, not omitting Mr. Darcy's overseeing his final hours.

Hence, before Sally left the Hardins' kitchen, she had obtained a great deal of intelligence. That it all dawned upon her slowly did not make the absorbing of it any less painful. But once she accepted that her brother was dead—kilt by Major George Wickham in the act of that devil's desertion, the rest was only a means to what ends she sought. She knew her brother's murderer was George Wickham and that he was Mrs. Darcy's brother-in-law. Mr. Darcy comforted her brother on his deathbed. Mrs. Darcy's sister, Mrs. Wickham, abided with her uncle, Mr. Gardiner in Cheapside until her marriage to Major Kneebone. Major Wickham was both said to be dead, and said to be a deserter.

"Anybody who knows that scoundrel don't think for a minute he didn't run when the fightin' heated up," observed Mrs. Hardin.

Sally had but caught a glimpse of Mr. Darcy at Pemberley. She could only tell that he was a proud man, given to prideful ways, but she would have liked to shake his hand.

Then, quite without warning, Sally found herself under the same roof as her brother's murderer. She did not know if it was a boon or not that she had been unaware of it until after the fact. Everyone was in an uproar, she fancied that she could have leapt upon him and garrotted him before anyone could stop her. It was her intention to take the retribution against Wickham that the army had not. She was still uncertain whether his family actually knew of this Wickham's deeds. Clearly, Mrs. Kneebone was not witting of the talk. (It was clear she was not because everything she knew and then some came out of that lady's mouth.)

When her eyes had met with Mrs. Darcy's that day due to Mrs. Kneebone's unprecedented claiming of her daughter, Sally truly did not know what to do.

Mrs. Darcy took her aside, asking, "Pray, what is our connexion?"

"My brother's name is—was John Christie."

With that correction, an expression of sympathy overspread the lady's face. She first put her hand upon Sally's shoulder, squeezing it in gentle comfort. But as the first tears that she had shed for her brother since learning of his fate began to pool in her eyes, Mrs. Darcy drew her into her embrace.

"There, there," was all she said.

In a moment, Sally made herself hush. Mrs. Darcy let go her and she stood back. A hint of her exquisite fragrance, however, remained

"He was very brave," said Mrs. Darcy.

"I don't know 'bout that," said Sally. "I do know that he was murdered by Major Wickham."

It seemed like the right time to tell all she knew and discover, in return, what his kin knew as well. Mrs. Darcy's countenance only registered enough surprise to suggest that what had taken her aback was not what she knew, but that she knew it.

"I don't think Mrs. Kneebone knows that. What say you?" Sally asked with a plain-spokenness unaccustomed by gentlefolk.

"No," Mrs. Darcy answered, "I know that she does not."

"I aim to kill 'im," Sally said, "bein' as no one else seems inclined to."

Mrs. Darcy was mildly taken aback, but regained her composure quickly, "Not that I disapprove of that man being held accountable for his misdeeds, but I think it best that we leave retribution to the courts."

"Don't treat me like I don't know nothin', m'am," Sally told her bitterly, then thought to add, "beggin' yer pardon."

"I did not mean to speak to you with condescension, but I do not withdraw my advice," said Elizabeth.

"I shouldn't be meddlin' in rich men's affairs, eh?"

Sally knew that she had stepped over a line that few crossed without reproval. She would have jutted her chin in pure stubbornness, but Mrs. Darcy was too nice for her to insult her in that manner. She had to remind herself that she was not in Seven Dials and there were manners to be observed. She knew it was possible that she would be dismissed, but as she had located Major Wickham, Mrs. Kneebone's temper was not a particular inducement to stay.

"Can you remain at the ready?" asked Mrs. Darcy. "The limb of the law may need your assistance."

Suddenly, acting as Mrs. Darcy's accomplice seemed the most important task imaginable. Sally set her vengeance aside—for the moment.

The Piper's Wages

"I am aghast!" exclaimed Jane. "I am aghast, distressed, and vexed."

Such a pronouncement from his gentle wife was of a sort Bingley had hoped never to hear. But, in truth, he supposed keeping their imminent ruin a confidence from her was not altogether wise. In his defence, he had kept his financial failings from her not to protect himself, but her. Jane, however, was incensed (or the closest expression of pique of which she was capable).

"Charles, how could you?"

"I did not want to worry you," he explained.

It was a dicey business, protecting his wife's sensibilities. She despised few things, but being denied the opportunity to assist another in any of life's hardships was amongst them. Bingley looked pleadingly at Darcy, who in return raised his eyebrows in an expression that was both commiserative and an indication of a reluctance to be drawn into what some might describe as marital discord. He had been called urgently from his cousin's funeral to Bingley's side for two reasons—both of equal distress to Bingley. The first was to help him salvage some part of his fortune and the other was to stand by him whilst he apprised his wife of their situation.

"Does Lizzy know, Mr. Darcy?" asked Jane.

Darcy did not for a moment believe that that question was indicative of Jane's being embarrassed by her sister knowing of their ruin. Jane could but be inquiring because she would not want her dear sister to worry upon her behalf.

"Only the smallest share," he answered.

Jane appeared comforted—as was Bingley. Having finally relieved himself of the catastrophic news that he had been keeping for some time, Bingley felt light-headed and found a winged-back chair in which to collapse. Jane rushed to his side, drawing a linen pocket-square from her sleeve and commencing to flap it before his face.

"Nicholls! Come! Mr. Bingley is unwell!" she called to Bingley's man.

"I am not so unhinged as that," Bingley replied, holding up the flat of his hand to dismiss Nicholls, who had come hastily into the room.

Bingley then stood and motioned Jane to be seated in the chair. They exchanged places and then Bingley and Darcy began to talk about methods of retrenchment.

"I will sell my jewellry," said Jane, not a hint of reluctance in her words. "And my father's legacy—of course—I will assign to our creditors."

Caroline, Louisa, and Mr. Hurst sat in a row upon a divan, but none could think of a single thing to give up to defend their finances. Darcy turned and looked pointedly at Mr. Hurst.

"I suppose," that man said, "I could give up my one set of duelling pistols."

"Not those," interjected Louisa, "I suggest one of your long guns."

Finally, disgusted at what little progress was made, Darcy concluded, "I think it is imperative that you give up Kirkland Hall."

A chorus of dismay erupted from everyone save Bingley. He had resigned himself to that probability.

"You cannot, Charles," erupted Caroline. "Where will I go? How shall I entertain? I could not possibly stay in town out of season!"

Jane rose and walked to Caroline, putting her hand upon her shoulder. "There, there, Caroline, Charles will think of something. You must not despair."

With this sympathy, Caroline attempted to relieve herself of Jane's comforting hand and leapt to her feet, "Father should have employed a banker to oversee our money, Charles! You have run us to ruin! You are not fit to be a night-soil man!"

She then stomped to the fireplace and began angrily stabbing the ashes with a poker. As far as Darcy was concerned, he hoped she would betake herself from the room altogether. From the mortified expression upon Bingley's countenance, he did as well. Even sweet-tempered Jane was, in the first time of his recollection, gifting Caroline's back something akin to a glower.

"I am happy to know your true feelings, Caroline," Bingley replied.

"I believe," said Darcy, "accusations are unhelpful."

Caroline turned and gifted him a spiteful glare, but he cared not. Therefore, neither did he notice the alteration in her countenance as she bethought herself. Darcy had but one goal, to save Bingley from compleat and utter ruin.

"You must free up some capital, Bingley," Darcy told him. "Time is of the essence."

He knew if Bingley did not, he would not be able to pay the taxes on the fortune of crates of fabric that were waiting idly aboard to be unloaded into his warehouse. Nor would he be able to pay lading costs to the shippers for the cotton waiting equally idly dockside to be loaded. Did he not forthwith, all would either be confiscated or fall prey to land pirates who were even then stealing cargos from other ships unable to unload due to taxes owed. As Darcy saw it, there was little choice. Bingley needed cash—a lot of it. But if he could free up some equity, he could salvage his business. He would not be quite so rich as he had been, but he would not be ruined. Several times Darcy had offered a personal loan (for which he would never demand repayment), but Bingley had refused.

"I must stew in my own juices," he had said.

Bingley did see then that Darcy's plan was his only course. As did Jane. Mr. and Mrs. Hurst sat seemingly stunned, of no use to any discussion. Caroline still fumed from the abhorrence of the notion that she should have to curtail any of her wants.

At last, Bingley agreed, "I will send my card to Sir Howgrave."

Sir Henry Howgrave received his knighthood for recognition of his heroics during the Waterloo engagement and, as he was much involved in politics, had offices in his home near Whitehall. He had agreed to see Mr. Darcy with no small amount of glee. (He did not, of course, dare exhibit any trace of that unseemly pleasure.) Mr. Darcy asking to see him meant that Mr. Darcy wanted something of him. To be in the position to oblige or deny Mr. Darcy as he saw fit was the cherry on the considerable cake of his year.

He had never forgiven that man's cut some half-dozen years ago. Mr. Darcy had refused him, not only to court his sister, but to dance with her as well. Supposedly, Mr. Darcy disapproved of his familial…indecorousness. From the rumours he had heard, he hardly thought Mr. Darcy in a position to point fingers at paternal wandering eyes. Ah, was not life sweet? Society's leper in one life, society's darling in another. He withdrew a looking-glass from the drawer of his desk and exposed his teeth, checking for any errant fragments of his dinner. Satisfied, he went to the door and bid Mr. Darcy and his friend Bingley to enter.

Mr. Darcy did so with unparalleled dignity. Howgrave marvelled at it. He had never seen another gentleman to rival Mr. Darcy's bearing. At one time he had tried to effect it himself—but to little avail. He had not the leg to pull it off. Indeed, since his return from the wars, he had grown stouter. Self-consciously, he ran his hand across his waistcoat, then caught the tips of it and pulled, pretending to straighten it.

"I thank you for seeing us, Sir Howgrave," said Mr. Darcy.

"It is nothing," replied Howgrave. "Do call me Howgrave."

"As you wish," Mr. Darcy replied. "May I have the honour of introducing my friend, Mr. Bingley?"

After these formal introductions, Howgrave asked his guests to be seated and they both moved to do so, Mr. Darcy expertly sitting without having to flick the tails of his coat from beneath him like the average man. Was there any limit to this man's finesse? Howgrave attempted a bit of small talk, but Mr. Darcy was disinclined to engage thusly.

"Mr. Bingley wishes to sell his estate," said Darcy.

Howgrave nodded in recognition of the statement. Mr. Darcy did not much like to fuss about—got right to the point, the man did. But did he think Howgrave was a bloody estate agent? He was determined to be a member of Parliament, although up to that moment he had not yet determined by what means. He would not suffer such foolishness. The man, Bingley, seemed altogether content to have Mr. Darcy talk for him throughout their meeting. He sat there like a puppy-dog waiting to have his stomach rubbed.

Perhaps Howgrave's countenance exposed his lack of esteem for Bingley's wants. Regardless, Mr. Darcy continued, clarifying his opening statement.

"He would like to sell it to you in exchange for your estate and a settlement of cash."

"What makes you believe," countered Howgrave, "that a lowly public servant such as myself would be in a position to accept such an offer? And, if indeed I was, what would tempt me to entertain doing so?"

"I believe, Howgrave, that the privateers that you own under an alias would make you wealthier than many in Parliament, should you make that run. I also understand you are but little at home in Derbyshire. You business keeps you much at town."

No idle rich man he, sighed Howgrave. Darcy had done his homework. Howgrave knew Mr. Bingley but by reputation—which was excellent. He was also quite cognizant that one of the accoutrements of Bingley's estate was a political seat, now vacant. This was interesting, indeed.

It was quite expeditiously then that an agreement was made. Howgrave and Bingley shook hands. The one hindrance to the expeditious completion of their transaction was the unavailability of the funds for several days.

"For reasons which I do not care to explain, it would behoove Mr. Bingley to receive this money as soon as possible."

By that time, Howgrave had lost interest in the specifics of Bingley's finances. He was a man of action. Once his agreement was reached, little did he care what others needed to do so long as they upheld their end of the bargain. He walked the gentlemen as far as the door of his office and closed it abruptly behind them.

Bingley and Darcy looked at each other, both relieved that their meeting was met with such success and mildly perplexed to have been turned out so rudely. For his part, Darcy expected nothing else from Henry Howgrave, but Bingley decided to find offence. He was a good-natured man, but the preceding months had used up a good portion of his patience. As Howgrave's maid brought them their hats and gloves, Bingley was anxious to go and went out the door and headed to the coach. Hence, Bingley was climbing into the carriage when Darcy was still only halfway down the steps and still donning his gloves. When he looked up, Darcy's attention was arrested by a lady ascending those same steps directly in his path.

It was Juliette Clisson.

Bonjour, Juliette

Darcy had heard that Howgrave had engaged an exceptionally beautiful mistress of French descent. He had not allowed himself to conjecture just who she might be. He believed he cared little for such information. Indeed, even then he would have done nothing but tip his hat to her had she not stopt before him and spoken his name.

"Mr. Darcy," said Juliette.

"Mlle. Clisson," he touched the brim of his hat.

"You have had business within?"

"Yes. Mr. Bingley and I have compleated our business with Sir Howgrave," he nodded in Bingley's direction.

"This meeting is nothing but chance, I know, but it must also be fate," she told him.

He noticed that there was only a trace remaining of her accent. He was disinclined to see their meeting as fateful and was disposed to go upon his way. Seeing her then recalled the last time they had spoken. It was upon a London wharf under circumstances he would have liked to forget. However, she stopt him by quickly saying a name that she knew would do just that.

"I intended to send you a note. A lady within has word of George Wickham, a man whose whereabouts I understand interest you."

The name did its office. He stopt and turned directly to her, waiting intently for what further she had to say. After listening a moment, he motioned to Bingley, then sitting in the coach, that he would return directly. He then took Juliette's elbow, steered her up the steps, and re-entered Howgrave's house.

Inside, she took his hat, gloves, and stick and handed them with her gloves and reticule to a servant. There was no sound from the room he had just left with Bingley and she led him to a large sitting room upon the opposite side of the house. Sitting upon a settee in the centre of the room was a lovely girl. Her gown and accoutrements (to say nothing of the knowing look upon her face) supposed to Darcy that she was not a young lady of the gentry. He could not be certain, but she looked vaguely familiar. By then, he had begun to question whether his decision to return with Juliette had been altogether good judgement.

As if she detected his instinct for flight, Juliette took his elbow and introduced the girl.

"May I present Mlle. Marie-Therese Lambert." Thereupon she gave a nervous titter (one quite unusual for her), saying, "But I have forgotten. You have met my dear Marie-Therese above a year ago."

The titter as much as the date reclaimed his memory, "Yes. At my cousin's home."

He could feel himself flushing and was immediately piqued at his own disorder. To find himself standing in Howgrave's house in the company of two ladies of exceedingly expansive sensibilities was most disconcerting. He was beginning to question Juliette's motives. She put that apprehension to rest directly.

To Marie-Therese she said, "I met Mr. Darcy upon the steps just now. He has very little time, but I assured him that he would want to hear your intelligence of his friend, Mr. Wickham."

"He is not my friend," Darcy corrected, his voice tight.

"That does you credit, Mr. Darcy," said Marie-Therese.

She had lost the hardness that he had found so offensive when last they met. Then, she had been not only forward, but almost lewd. Her demeanour had not improved beyond criticism though, for he noticed that she had not lost her coquetry. Perhaps, Darcy mused, that became ingrained in one who depended upon such mannerisms for her livelihood.

Juliette regained his attention when she asked him to sit down. He refused with a quick shake of his head so cursory as to be nearly impolite.

Despite this, Juliette proceeded, mildly inquiring, "I believe that you wish to know of this Wickham's situation?"

"Official word to his wife said he was a casualty of the Waterloo action."

"I believe you suspected otherwise," Marie-Therese said. "As of three days ago, he had rooms with a Mrs. Younge near Gowell St. For the price of his arrears she was happy to tell me all she knew."

Darcy's expression barely flickered upon receiving this shocking intelligence. If Marie-Therese had expected the reticent Mr. Darcy to expose his private thoughts to her, she was mistaken. It was a moment before he spoke—a moment during which he turned his back and walked to the fireplace. He placed one hand against the mantle and the barest closure of his eyes betrayed the significance of his feelings. This small concession to his disconcertion was exposed to his company through the mirror hanging above the mantle and they exchanged glances. Directly, he returned. His hands behind his back, he stood remarkably straight, resting his weight majestically upon one foot.

"May I inquire as to your connexion with Major Wickham?"

Marie-Therese had not deviated from her placidly coy demeanour, but she did then. Momentarily, her eyes flashed. She knew that he supposed her connexion with Wickham was through the nature of her avocation.

"May I ask you, Mr. Darcy, as to *your* connexion with Major Wickham?"

He gave her a slight bow as if to say, "*Touché*."

Her request for him to divulge his business before she divulged hers was entirely correct and he recognised that.

"Major Wickham is the first husband of my wife's sister."

Marie-Therese nodded at both the information and his acquiescence to her request. The only thing that remained to be seen was if she would be equally *un*forthcoming as had Darcy.

"Mr. Wickham seduced a good friend of mine when she was but a child. She had an infant by him that was taken from her."

That was hardly a shock to Darcy. Wickham had made seduction and betrayal his life's work.

"I am sorry for your friend. Her injury is not the only one Mr. Wickham has inflicted."

"In my friend's case," Marie-Therese said, "his seduction was carried out under your name."

"What?" Darcy said, before reclaiming himself. "I do not take your meaning."

"I believe, Mr. Darcy, that you do. I suspect it is not the only time he acted thusly. I would hope he might be meted out the justice he so richly deserves. I fear only those injuries he has inflicted against the crown are punishable."

Darcy did not say, but his countenance agreed with the probability of that statement.

"I believe my company is witting that Mr. Wickham is presumed dead. That he is not and has spent these months other than with his regiment will demand a military tribunal."

Marie-Therese thereupon handed Darcy a folded piece of paper bearing Mrs. Younge's address. He did not look at it, but tucked it into his waistcoat.

"I thank you for this inteligence," he said stiffly. "I must now bid you good-day."

With a curt bow, he turned. Juliette put an unforgivably intimate hand upon his forearm.

"Must you?" she asked.

With that question, Marie-Therese stood and betook herself from the room. A piece of handwork that she had been working on remained upon one seat of the settee—the only evidence of her having been there.

"Yes," he replied, "I must."

"If you *must*, then you *must*."

The implication was unappreciated.

"I do as I *choose*."

Juliette's eyes flicked away then returned. She realised that she had over-stepped that invisible boundary that he kept about himself. His eyes remained trained upon her to a vexatious degree.

"I intend to marry Howgrave," she announced.

"My best wishes."

"He has a home in the country—one not far, I understand, from Pemberley," she smiled, "we will be neighbours."

"Indeed?" he said mildly. "I bid you good-day."

When he took his leave, she crossed her arms, smiled satisfactorily to herself, and, with uncommon grace, claimed the middle of the settee. As he took his leave, a smile of similar expression tempted the corner of Darcy's mouth. Juliette's, however, was abruptly lost upon sitting on Marie-Therese's abandoned knitting needles.

It was an expression of mischance that would be replicated upon learning that her soon-to-be husband had given up his country home in favour of the larger but more distant residence of Kirkland Hall.

Wherefore, Mr. Darcy

It was but a few hours before Elizabeth learnt that Wickham would call her bluff.

> *Dearest Elizabeth,*
>
> *My price for stepping aside in favour of Major Kneebone is ten-thousand pounds by seven o'clock tonight. I will await above the public house of our previous meeting.*
>
> *If you are unable to raise this sum, I would be happy to make alternate arrangements.*
>
> *Yours,*
> *George Wickham Esq.*

With the utmost reluctance she had concluded that she could not keep Darcy from the negotiations with Wickham. Indeed, as much as she had wanted to spare her husband,

Wickham's demands were far beyond her means. The jewellry that she owned, she did not count as truly hers, as most were Darcy family heirlooms. Moreover, those which were not were of such sentimental value because her husband selected them especially for her she would never contemplate exchanging them in such a disreputable manner.

And an exaction was what it was. *Wickham* was exacting money from them in exchange for Lydia's freedom.

That he had not taken umbrage when faced with the barely veiled accusation of her note, she knew he was fully guilty. That realisation sent such a cold shudder through her body, her fingers began to shake. They were still shaking when she entered a coach and hied to Jane's in search of her husband. Although Lydia had taken to her bed by the time Wickham answered her note, she knew Major Kneebone was most anxious to know of it. She took extra means to escape, but did feel a certain compunction at doing so. Until she spoke to Darcy, she thought it best no one else be privy to it and even left it behind for safe keeping. The one thing she would not do was show her husband the note itself. His implication in offering her "alternative" means of paying him was unambiguous—the cad. Was there no depth to which the man would not sink?

By the time she reached the street and hailed a carriage, her knees had weakened. The driver of a hack coach had been lounging next to his horse, feeding it bits of the apple he was peeling when Elizabeth appeared. With all due haste, he opened the door and flipped down the steps, but did not offer his hand to help her take them. When that small discourtesy materialised, she straightened her shoulders and pulled herself aboard.

She was happy that had been necessary. She was far too used to being pampered. She could certainly fend for herself if need be.

After that fit of self-delusion, she realised there had actually been a time when she would have thought nothing of entering a coach without assistance. Pemberley saw to her every whim even before she had one. At that moment, that had not been altogether disagreeable. The thought of her husband's cosseting was even sweeter. In the face of a blackguard called Wickham, she was no match. It was time to seek assistance. She would go to her husband and see how Jane and Bingley fared. She would put the matter before them. Indeed, the thought of her husband's rescue cheered her considerably.

Once the decision had been made, so anxious was she to be there that she did not take the time to return for her own carriage. The man who drove her was kind to his horse and thus deserving of the crown she paid him to take her to Belgrave Square. When she handed him the coin and begged him to please make haste, they left in such a hurry she was thrown back against the seat. She clasped the hand-hold and held on for dear life.

"Jane!" Elizabeth called.

Holding out her arms and extending her fingers, she rushed to her sister's own outstretched arms.

"Lizzy! It is so *good* to see you!"

Jane was in a small sitting room upon the second storey of her home. Two of her children played at her feet, the remnants of some unidentifiable project strewn about them. Jane had been perched upon the edge of her chair admiring their handiwork, but leapt to her feet when she saw her sister.

It was uncommonly refreshing for her to see Jane once again, but she was uncertain how she might broach the subject of Bingley's urgent letter to Darcy. She was certain that it had pertained to their financial straits, but was not disposed to reveal that she was witting of their predicament. Moreover, she still did not know if Jane was aware of any of it at all. Once Elizabeth was before her, Jane could not withhold what had just come to pass that very day within her own walls. Hence, before Elizabeth had done more than begin to untie her bonnet, Jane took her hands and burst out with all.

"Oh Lizzy, my poor Charles!"

That told Elizabeth that Jane had been made aware of their impending ruin.

"Do not fret, Jane. I know that Darcy has a plan!"

She knew part of that plan, but not all.

"Yes, they have gone there now. I cannot tell you when they shall return."

"To Sir Howgrave's?"

"How ever did you know?"

Elizabeth told her she only knew that an agreement was to be reached with that man. She did not want to tell Jane of the necessity of moving from Kirkland Hall, even though she was delighted to have her so near. Therefore, their conversation became stilted—Elizabeth not wanting to betray all she knew and Jane knowing so little to tell. In that quiet, Elizabeth had no choice but to tell Jane why she had come to London. But, before she could, Jane inquired.

"Why are you come to London by yourself, Lizzy? I know Mr. Darcy would not approve. He assured me that you were at his aunt's."

The doings of Rosings Park were enough to entertain their conversation for some time—poor Anne's untimely passing, Georgiana's childbirth, and Charlotte Collins's discomfiting situation—all were subjects they would have been able to engage in discourse for hours had not Elizabeth had other tidings as well.

"Directly after Darcy's leave-taking for London, I received a very urgent letter from Lydia," she reported. "I have been at Lydia's these last two days."

Jane placed the flat of her hand against her chest, fingers extended in alarm.

"Dear me! Whatever can be the matter now?"

The tiniest shred of exasperation in Jane's voice was understandable. Elizabeth was sorry that she could not prepare her for the news that she was about deliver.

"Major Wickham has returned."

Jane did not speak, but she blanched. She sat, alternately blinking and opening her mouth, but nothing came out until at last she exclaimed, "Sweet Mother of God!"

With Jane still flabbergasted, Elizabeth endeavoured to answer those questions that she knew Jane would most have liked to ask. She would not, however, relate to her the extent of Wickham's crimes. Darcy had told her that in confidence. It would be up to him to confide that at a time of his own choosing.

"I do not know where he has been or by what means he has returned," she explained. "I have been far too busy trying to keep Major Kneebone and Major Wickham from duelling for Lydia's hand."

She took a breath, uncertain if that was what it was called when two men fought over the same wife, and looked at Jane for further instructions. She nodded and Elizabeth took that to mean she should continue her monologue.

"My Uncle Phillips advises us that, in cases such as these, when a husband has been thought dead and his wife remarries, that wife may choose which husband she would like to keep."

Having at last regained her voice, Jane exclaimed, "Certainly she will choose Major Kneebone!"

"Would that I could be certain that she will," replied Elizabeth.

She then related the meeting with Wickham, including the near duel, but omitting the gunfire, "Although she professes she loves Major Kneebone, Lydia was far too sympathetic to Wickham to be certain of her heart. Indeed, I fear he may yet sway her."

She was happy to have information of the sort to share with Jane proving Wickham's wickedness without resorting to revealing he was thought a murderer. She was quite fearful Jane might be swayed by the notion of Lydia following her heart in the matter. Thereupon, Elizabeth took a deep breath and confided in her the true reason for coming.

"Wickham has vowed that he will leave Lydia be for a payment of money. That he will proves that his designs on Lydia are not in her best interest."

"For shame! What kind of a man is this?" exclaimed Jane.

In answer to that question, Elizabeth resorted to the imprecise, "When the truth of Wickham's flight from his family and his regiment comes out, it cannot be a happy business. Lydia is well done with him."

Jane nodded in concurrence and did not question her further on Wickham's misdeeds. Surprisingly, Jane was not opposed to doing what had to be done to be rid of him.

"It is a distasteful business," Jane observed, "but do you know how much would have to be laid out to secure his riddance?"

"Ten-thousand pounds."

Putting her hand across her gaping mouth, Jane gasped. She quickly looked to see if her children noticed anything amiss. They kept on with their playing, occasionally arguing over ownership of certain toys. Looking upon them gave Elizabeth a tug at her own heart. Only lying alone in bed at Lydia's had she allowed herself to think of her children home alone without her. Even with everything working itself out perfectly, she could not look forward to seeing them for several days. That thought tugged at her heart mercilessly. She knew alleviation of that pain would best be remedied in her husband's arms. Suddenly, that need was paramount to any other.

"I must go to Darcy," she said abruptly, "he and Bingley will know what to do. Wickham has demanded I return with his inducement forthwith."

Jane wrote the address of Howgrave's house upon a piece of paper.

"I do not know the way…" Jane apologised for having no directions.

"I have a good driver."

Elizabeth smiled to herself that Jane was unwitting of her manner of travel through the bustling (and occasionally dangerous) streets of London. It was still early and the days were long. If she hurried, she could locate Darcy and be done with Wickham before nightfall.

She was quite satisfied with her driver. He knew the streets well and was happy to do what ever she bid so long as she kept feeding his hand coins. The address she had given him was not so far away from Bingley's house, but an over-turned dray carrying several barrels of ale had caused a near riot on one of the thorough-fares. By the time she reached the address, she was afraid she might have missed her timing. When the driver pointed out the house, she was greatly relieved to see Darcy's coach had not gone.

"Here," she told the driver and he came to a halt. As she reached for the door handle, she caught sight of the handsome figure of her husband upon the steps and was overcome with relief. A few minutes more and they would have missed Darcy entirely. Things appeared to be working out perfectly. Would he not be surprised to see her?

With the unerring bad luck of certain happenings, the moment she caught sight of her husband was one and the same moment in which he took Miss Juliette Clisson's elbow and began escorting her up the stairs. She watched as they walked through the door and into the house. Elizabeth watched as the door closed behind them. She even sat there a moment to ascertain that her eyes had not deceived her.

"Can I 'elp you out?" inquired the driver, aware of the niceties expected by certain clientele.

"No."

That had been spoken in a voice entirely too soft for him to have heard. Therefore, she repeated herself, making certain there was no mistake.

"I said *no*!" And without hesitation she bade him, "Drive on!"

Second Verse, Not as the First

It was a desperate ride through the streets to return to Chelsea, but she had not a moment to spare. Such was their haste, they had taken more than one corner upon two wheels (and nearly brained a poor horse that had the misfortune to get in their path). Hence, by the time she reached the Kneebones she was in a similar frantic state ere she had left. But she knew time was of the essence if she was to return and take her own coach and horses to the nearest public stable and see what price they might fetch. She arrived accompanied by her footman and driver both sporting the elegant Darcy livery, and the stable's proprietor looked at her as if she had run mad when she did not haggle and took several hundred sovereigns less than the coach and animals were clearly worth. When she stuffed the gold into her tiny reticule, she had to jiggle it for the coins to settle enough to pull the draw-string. From the expression he bore, she thought the man suspected her of some malfeasance, but she had little time to care. She hired a coach to take the footman, her driver, and herself back to Lydia's.

Both of her men were too appalled to ask her what they were to do, but she gave them money and told them to take a post to the Darcy town house—she had no idea what else to do with them, they were of no good to anyone lurking about Lydia's. They walked off mumbling to each other, but Elizabeth was far too busy to worry about their opinions either. She counted the money that she had left and shook her head. It did not seem enough to tempt Wickham and she gave a small stamp of disappointment. There were acquaintances in town that she could importune, but she had neither the time nor the inclination to draw outsiders into such a wild scheme.

Kneebone happened upon her at that moment, and as he had happened upon Wickham's note, he was ready truly to do him harm. Elizabeth argued against it.

"I know this man, Major. I believe he could not possibly hold to that large of a demand. If we offer him a substantial enough amount, I believe he can be worked on," she said, adding, "I have obtained five-hundred pounds. Perhaps that will do."

"Perhaps twice that will do," he countered, putting his boot upon the arm of a chair.

From there he withdrew a wad of bank notes. Astonished, she watched as he counted.

"Five-hundred thirty-five and," he counted from his jacket pocket, "four half-crowns and a tuppence."

"Keep your thirty-five and change, Major. One thousand is a good round number!"

She had been delighted at her luck. Putting a finger to her lips, she bid his silence and stole away.

By the time she arrived at Wickham's her giddiness had waned. The pace of the hired coach was not leisurely, but neither was it the hooves-flailing ride to Chelsea. Therefore, she had nothing to do but rethink what she had seen upon the steps of that house. Indeed, the vision of her husband escorting Juliette Clisson would not leave her thoughts in peace. She had employed every device imaginable to make it not what it looked for all the world to be. She was alternately incredulous and furious. The realisation that he took his sweet leave and left her in the clutches of his scheming aunt whilst he gad about London with a former lover made her angry. Exceedingly angry. The angrier she became the more willing she became to shove the thousand pounds down George Wickham's sorry throat.

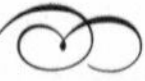

The entrance to Wickham's rooms above the tavern was through a separate doorway and up two sets of stairs. The stench was much as she had encountered in the ale-room, but added to that distinct odour was that which came by way of the stair-well's oft alternate office as handy latrine. She endeavoured to take as little air as possible into her nostrils as she made her way up the steps, but had to exhale when she was accosted by an elderly man who peered at her with rheumy eyes.

"Lookin' fer Wickham?" he squawked.

Clearly she was not the first lady come in to pay that man a call. She nodded.

"If you please," she replied daintily—and much unhappy to be noticed by anyone of any social strata entering lodgings harbouring George Wickham.

He pointed up the next flight of stairs. Upon the landing, she was taken by surprise at how much less foul it was than the establishment below. When she rapped upon his door, Wickham immediately opened it. He wore neither his coat nor a neck-cloth. Nor had he bothered to button his shirt. Believing it not an oversight, the display of his chest hair made her stomach roil more violently than had the odour in the hallway. Certainly he had not the gall to employ seduction against her. A quick image invaded her thought—one of Wickham making little kisses up her arm. She gave an involuntary shiver.

He bowed and bid her enter (exhibiting only the smallest limp due to his encounter with his wife). His room was much in keeping with what she suspected of the other apartments—comfortable with splashes of gentility. Clearly the landlord of the rooms had once been above their present situation. She saw two sitting chairs, an escritoire, and a barren fireplace with a low bed hidden behind a half-drawn curtain. Because the stink of the entrance had not wafted this far, her nostrils had cleared enough to detect an odour of another kind—one of which she was distinctly familiar. She was certain she smelled the after-scent of a baby. That, however, she attributed to a previous tenant. Whatever would Wickham be doing with a baby? Outrageous notion.

"So," Wickham said to her, "I suppose Darcy has enough attorneys in his pocket to have what he wants."

"Darcy knows not of this," she said, then was instantly sorry for she saw Wickham's eyes flicker with triumph. The first point went to Wickham. This transaction had begun badly. Indeed, he moved boldly forward.

"I know Lydia, and she will have me back," he threatened.

"Wounds tingle most when they are about to heal," Elizabeth countered.

"What is Kneebone? A nothing. Was he mentioned with honours? No," he said petulantly.

"As a non-combatant, his name was not mentioned in newspapers. He obtained his wound in the Peninsular campaign."

"And you believed him when he happened to drop that into a conversation?"

"Some men are not disposed to lies," she retorted. "You would not be aware of them."

"Harrumph. *Cowards in scarlet pass for men of war*," he quoted.

"Yes. Spoken like one who would have first-hand knowledge."

Wickham looked at her keenly—more keenly than she liked, but she did not shrink back.

"I do not take your meaning, Mrs. Darcy."

Time had come for her to show her hand. They both knew it.

"I know that you are a deserter. I know that you killed one of your own soldiers to make your away. You are a coward and a murderer. That you are a liar, thief, and adulterer is beside the point. Major Kneebone accuses you of cheating at cards—I should not be at all surprised of that either," she said angrily.

Wickham was not altogether stunned. He knew that something was afoot. However, the extent of what she knew was remarkable. As they both listened to a clock ticking loudly upon the barren mantle, a few beads of perspiration broke out upon

Wickham's upper lip. It was only with a concerted effort that he did not blot it with the back of his hand. As she was not as astute as her husband in the study of the nuances of prevarication, Elizabeth did not know to look for such a sign. By her own particular detection, she knew she had him all the same.

He said, "You cannot possibly prove such an outrageous accusation."

That statement was not delivered with the same outrage he professed. Still, she knew she must put something forward to suggest that she could.

"The boy you killed was in our employ. My husband talked to him upon his deathbed. He was explicit as to your guilt," she said evenly.

To her utter astonishment, he guffawed, "Ha! For a moment, I thought..." Thereupon, he caught himself, "I did no such thing."

Indeed, for a moment he had thought that there was evidence against him. He was shrewd enough to know that Darcy's allegation he claimed to have heard from a now-dead boy was flimsy indeed.

"There is nothing—no proof. There is nothing but unsubstantiated hear-say!"

Elizabeth was disinclined to enter into a "Yes you did/No I did not" argument with him. She also did not know what the next step should be. That had been the last shot in her locker. He had murder thrown in his face and he had laughed. What next was she to do?

Wickham saw then a truth. It was best for him to make his away from England. General opinion could turn against him did Darcy go public with what he had heard. Wickham quickly assessed the possibilities. Elizabeth wanted to protect her sister from him. Because she stood before him without her husband's knowledge, he believed that there was little she would not do in her sister's protection.

"My demand is ten-thousand pounds," he said, then voice lowered, "or something of similar value."

Elizabeth eyes flickered but little, holding out her reticule, she said, "I have one-thousand. You will have to make do with that for there is no more now."

"There is always more, Elizabeth," said Wickham. "Darcy pays more for a horse."

The mention of horses gifted Elizabeth with a twinge, knowing as she did that she had all but given away Darcy's horses. It also occurred to her that she left the document that she had written out for Wickham to sign in the hack coach. If he took the money, she had nothing in return.

"My husband has no part in this," she told him. "This is all you will be offered."

Impulsively, she threw out what she hoped was further incentive, "I can send you more later—when you are settled."

"Ha!" he laughed again. "And allow you to know of my whereabouts? Do you think me a fool?"

"No, I do not," she answered honestly, "but when I say there is no more money to be had at this hour, I speak the truth."

He looked keenly at her. Thereupon he casually drew a small armchair between himself and the door, dropped nonchalantly into it, swung one leg over the arm, and let it slowly begin to swing.

"Perhaps, there is another recourse."

Had Wickham's expression not, the noise from the ale house below gifted Elizabeth an anxiousness she did not like at all. If she had to scream, it was unlikely she would be heard. Even if she was, it was even less likely any of that establishment's habitués would be moved to come to her rescue. (That she saw it necessary to contemplate screaming was no comfort either.) A bit tardily it occurred to her that a man who would do murder would be unlikely to have any qualms over committing a lesser crime. Indeed, she had just offered him enough money to escape to the ends of the earth.

Although her ruminations were silent, it was as if he heard every word.

Near Miss

Upon returning with Bingley to his house in Belgrave Square, Darcy had come to a course of action. He knew he must confront Wickham himself. It was a temptation to inform the constabulary and wash his hands of it all, but he had felt some primeval need to confront him with what he knew. Only then would he see if a man dwelled therein, or was Wickham the blackguard he looked to have become. Darcy's single equivocation was whether to tell him of their true connexion.

It was not as if he had not studied upon the matter with all due vigour, for there had been many hours in many days when there was little else of which he could think. At one time, he believed that was Wickham still alive that it would be his unhappy duty to apprise him of the fact that they were half-brothers. Of late his thinking had begun to alter. That direction of full disclosure seemed less and less to harbour a worthy end. While initially he had believed that revealing such intelligence was only just, he had begun to be of the opinion that he was being wrong-headed—that his argument for doing so was born of contrition for his father's short-comings rather than the result of rational thinking.

Because the boy, John Christie, had no living relation and Wickham had been thought dead, Darcy had seen no point in pursuing charges against him. Any lingering doubt he might have had to as Wickham's guilt was there no longer. Having learnt that Wickham was still alive proved to his mind that John Christie's death-bed accusation was true. A murdering scoundrel dead was one thing, one walking the streets was an entirely different matter. The only thing that he was curious about was where Wickham had been all this time. Whatever it was, he believed that Marie-Therese Lambert knew the truth of it. Clearly, Wickham had not been devoting himself to some benevolent society—unless it was one dedicated to the betterment of ladies of the night.

Darcy had never told anyone but Elizabeth of Wickham's crimes, but the unseemliness of meeting a lady of Juliette Clisson's renown upon a public street and escorting her into a house demanded an explanation to Bingley. Bingley had waited patiently for him, and upon his re-entry into the coach, he thought it best that he not only understand who Juliette was but what intelligence she might have that would bid him behave in such a manner. That Wickham was not dead would be an astonishment to poor Bingley, he knew—it had been a shock to him.

Darcy told Bingley that Wickham lived and the story behind his disappearance. It was an excellent tale, one Bingley listened to with rapt attention. Still, Darcy did not explain his past connexion with Juliette, only that she was a consort of Howgrave's who told him she had word of Wickham. Bingley was not so easily put off.

"I say, Darcy, seldom have I seen a more handsome woman. She certainly looked to know you intimately."

It was as always between them. Bingley knew not to ask his friend so personal a question, but would make a statement and wait for Darcy's response. If the answer was a negative, Darcy would reply thusly, and if yes, he would not remark upon it. He would only refute, never verify. That Darcy said not a word then might have raised Bingley's eyebrows, but he asked nothing more. Noticing Bingley's expression, Darcy was moved to do the unthinkable. He elucidated.

"We were once acquaintances," was all he would say. (Well, it was fairly elucidative for Darcy.)

What Darcy did tell Bingley was of his intention to confront Wickham, withdrawing the paper with the address on it and showing it to him.

"Are you familiar with this address?"

"Indeed I am, Darcy. And it is not a fit place. It is near my warehouses at the docklands, but I do not go there alone—nor should you. It is the home of every vice—thieves, whore masters, even killers. There are women who will approach you and men who would be happy to do you harm. Again, I say that if you must go, do not go alone," said he.

Indeed, after having heard what he had of Wickham's deeds, Bingley was convinced that Wickham was not merely untrustworthy, he was a danger, "I must repeat, my advice is not to go at all—leave it to the magistrate."

Darcy was not imprudent, but his personal scruples did not include allowing another to give him leave upon which street in London he walked. He had resolved what he would do and he refused to deviate from his decision. Bingley soon let the matter drop. He was most anxious for his own business and, in hope of inducing Darcy to leave Wickham to the law, inveigled him to accompany him to the docks.

"These men have been more than patient," said he. "I must apprise them immediately that all is well and payment will be forthwith."

Darcy was of the opinion that Bingley's business could wait until morning. "If what you say of that neighbourhood it is true, you would do better to wait until morning."

Reluctantly, Bingley agreed, not noticing that he acquiesced to the same argument that Darcy refused. When they arrived at his house, Bingley hurried to tell Jane of their success, leaving Darcy to make ready for his own evening. Although the dinner bell soon sounded, Darcy was neither in the mood for food nor the company of Bingley's self-indulgent kin. If he had to sit across from Caroline Bingley after her behaviour to her brother, he knew it likely he would be uncivil. In that Bingley's situation was largely repaired, he cared little for suffering the praise for bringing it about. He told the servants he was not to be disturbed.

Jane would have thanked him profusely had he come to dinner, but did want not infringe upon his privacy under any circumstances. Still, she had learnt from Bingley that they had not seen Elizabeth and she knew that Darcy would want to be told that his wife was in town. Indeed, Jane was also curious as to why they had not seen her when she went to Howgrave's house. So concerned was she that she slipped a note under his door to that effect, also surmising that perhaps Lizzy missed them there and returned to Lydia's. Regrettably, Darcy recognised Jane's hand and thought it was simply a thank you, picked it up and tossed it unopened upon the bureau. He had more important matters upon his mind.

He had another reason for seeing Wickham that evening. If he did, he could make for Rosings at first light, stopping at the magistrate on his way out of town. It sounded to him as a perfect solution, for he was much in want of telling Elizabeth of Wickham being alive. Moreover, he had much arrears of affection to pay her for leaving her at his aunt's house. But he solaced himself with the understanding that his Lizzy would want to keep Georgiana company—there was much two mothers could find to discuss. The image of his beloved wife looking after his beloved sister and her newborn was one that gave him great pleasure.

Thinking of Georgiana so happy at last lent him greater resolve in bringing Wickham to justice. That cad had brought misery to every life he touched.

Once Wickham was located and held, all would be well with them all.

Darcy had not rehearsed a speech in which to accuse Wickham, presuming the words would come to him when he saw that dastard's face. How he would go about siccing the authorities on him remained uncertain other than reporting all that he knew. He supposed that there would be a trial and he would have to testify all that he heard. All would depend upon what defence Wickham offered—whether he had someone to lie for him. Darcy had resigned himself to the possibility that he might be acquitted. Death-bed accusations held a great deal of weight, but his testimony might be cast out as hearsay. Moreover, as his enmity against Wickham was of legend, he might be accused of having made the story up out of whole cloth. Nothing was cast in stone. Wickham might walk away a free man. The single certainty was that Darcy himself would not walk away from his duty to report both the murder and desertion.

He handed the paper containing Wickham's address to his driver. It was not a location with which he was familiar. Indeed, his driver looked at him a bit curiously as to what sort of business he could have there. Darcy chose to ignore that man's questioning aspect. Clearly, the section of London they would be travelling was of dangerous by-ways and menacing denizens. He was unarmed, but he knew his man was. As if reading his mind, the man patted his waistband. Darcy nodded and bade him drive on.

When he had first heard Mrs. Younge's name mentioned by Mlle. Lambert, he had not been altogether surprised that after all these years, she was still in cahoots with Wickham. He wondered of *their* connexion. Other than co-conspirators, he had always thought there was something odd about the duo. He surmised Wickham had simply beguiled her into being his dupe. Wickham could be quite charming when he found reason to be. From the address of her lodging house, she had dropped several notches down society's ladder. He had no sympathy for her as she had proven herself to be Wickham's match when it came to scruples.

Impatient, he rapped upon the roof of the carriage and asked his driver how much farther they must go. He could see that with every street they passed, the buildings became more dilapidated, the citizens less reputable. The man replied that they were nearing his destination. He saw that to their fortune, for the streets had also become narrower and soon looked to become impassable.

The driver pulled the horses to a stop, hopped down, and opened the door.

"It is just over the street, sir," he said, pointing.

Mr. Darcy did not inquire of his driver how it happened that he knew such an area so well. The man was loyal and hard-working. He asked nothing more of his servants. If he had risen above his circumstances, Darcy had nothing but admiration for him.

The sign said Gowell Street and it appeared to be the keeper of more offensive businesses than Darcy had ever seen together on one stretch of cobbles.

"There?" Darcy pointed with his stick.

Between a horse boiler and an ale house was a sign that said "To Let," with a faded yellow arrow pointing up.

"I believe so, yes sir," the driver said.

It was dusk. The lights inside the establishments were visible but not yet of service. The lodgings were upon the far side of the street and Darcy picked his way along the walkboards until he was even with it, cautious of ascertaining his surroundings before he made his way there. He found a fair-sized column and stood behind it, observing the doorway across the street. He had been standing under a half minute when a hack coach drew up to the door. There were far more waggons than coaches upon the street and he wondered if its occupant could be Wickham. When the door opened, it was to the other side and he could not see who was within, but he saw a woman's feet and skirts drop to the ground. She tarried momentarily and Darcy assumed that she was paying her fare. He continued to watch, curious to take measure of who she was, for from what little he could see, her footwear supposed her to be a lady. Oddly, she looked to be wearing a pair of slippers not unlike a pair of Elizabeth's. The sight of them unsettled him, but he reassured himself in the knowledge that his wife was safe in Kent. If the owner of those slippers was a lady, he had no doubt that she was to call upon Wickham—he was certain. It occurred to him that he was observing a tryst in progress. Wickham was notorious for his affairs with women of all levels of society. He was nothing if not democratic in his assignations.

He was watching intently, hoping for the coach to draw away from the walk so he might identify the lady before she entered the building. Although a small part of him was simply curious as to the identity of Wickham's caller, Darcy saw the lady's arrival as a detriment to his mission. He was contemplating whether to wait for her to leave before knocking upon Wickham's door when he was called by name.

He turned angrily, not wanting his name to be used in so loud a fashion, lest Wickham be warned. When he saw who had called to him he was alarmed.

Nicholls, Bingley's man, had alit his mount next to Darcy's coach and was scurrying up the walk in his direction. He called out again before Darcy could hush him.

"Mr. Darcy! Mrs. Bingley says that you must come immediately!"

"Be quiet, Nicholls, you shall announce to all that I am here!" he whispered harshly.

"Sorry, sir!"

Nicholls was more breathless than his horse, which looked to have run a great distance. At Darcy's insistence, Nicholls bent over, putting his hands upon his knees and endeavoured to regain his breath. After a half minute, he croaked out his message.

"Mrs. Bingley says that you must come! Mr. Bingley received word that scallywags were intent on burning his cotton if he did not come pay them all he owes! He has gone alone to Ratcliff Highway wharves!"

Darcy's insides heaved at the the name, but he remained outwardly calm, asking, "Do you know the way?"

Nicholls nodded.

All thought of Wickham had evaporated whilst Darcy determined the best course of action.

"Did he go on horseback?"

Nicholls nodded again.

"Then I shall as well."

Again Nicholls nodded, uncertain as to what he had agreed. Whilst watching Darcy obtain his footman's weapon, gain directions, and mount his horse, however, he gathered a fair approximation.

As for Darcy, he knew Wickham would just have to keep.

95

Two Times Crossed, Once Found

By the time Darcy reached the quay next to Bingley's warehouses, it was fully dark. From what he could see, he thought he was too late. A torch-bearing mob of men were leading a saddled horse up the sloping road and away toward the row of taverns lining the wharves. Some men were in front pulling the reins, others were at the rear—crowing and slapping the beast for encouragement. As the raucous hoard headed up the street and disappeared into the fog, Darcy eased up beside a building so dilapidated that it looked as though a strong wind would blow it over. He alit, but held tight to the lead having just been shown clear evidence that horses' ownership only went so far as who held the reins.

After the mob had disappeared, it was quiet as death except for the lapping of water and creaking of ships that were sitting idle by their mooring. If it had been daylight he would have been arrested by the sight of a forest of masts beyond the decaying warehouses with blind windows. As it was, he saw little and heard only an occasional voice, so he knew the ships to be inhabited. He did not have the smallest notion where he might find Bingley, and in the quiet, he became increasingly alarmed as to in what condition he might find him. Therefore his search was both high and low, not knowing whether he was looking for a man or a body. His initial search was fruitless and as the fog thickened, he began to chastise himself for leaving his men and Bingley's behind.

"Where are you Fitzwilliam when I need you?" he asked himself silently. He would have given anything to have his reliable friend with him just then. He had thought he was only to intercede upon a negotiation, perhaps to thwart violence. Clearly he was tardy, but to what, he still was uncertain. From the raucousness of the mob, they had to have been requited in some manner other than the theft of a horse. The longer he searched to no avail, the more he believed he might be visiting the magistrate upon Bingley's behalf rather than Wickham's.

He decided that he must give up stealth. He had a weapon; if the mob returned, so be it. He had to find Bingley and was having no success through quiet search.

"Bingley!" he called. "Bingley!"

It was then that he heard a whispering sound. He stopt and listened closely, his heart racing, then called again.

"*Bingley*!"

"Here, damn it! Here!" Bingley whispered. "Keep your voice down or they will return."

It was too dark and foggy to see anything much farther than a few feet, hence, when Bingley popped up right next to him out of a wooden barrel, he nearly leapt out of his skin.

"Bingley. Thank God you are all right! You gave me a fright."

"Gave you a fright? *Gave you a fright*?" his voice grew shrill. "I say, I'll tell you about a fright!"

Darcy only noticed then the nature of Bingley's habitation in the barrel—it appeared to be of the nude variety. Darcy peered into the barrel to be certain. Indeed, it was true. He was naked.

"Bingley, where are your clothes?"

"I left them for the laundress," he retorted sarcastically, "Where do you think they are? They are being paraded about this despicable purlieu upon the persons of the most ill-mannered louts I have ever had the pleasure of meeting!"

Darcy was both amused and relieved. Whilst helping Bingley climb from the barrel, he took leave to observe, "You seem most fortunate to have lost nothing more than your costume and your horse…"

"And twenty-thousand pounds!" he veritably shouted.

"Twenty-thousand pounds?" he repeated, incredulous. "How could you have been so foolish as to come alone with such a sum?"

"It was *their* money," Bingley reasoned. "I came to pay them. I did not expect them to rob me of their money! They would not even allow the courtesy of an explanation!"

Bingley was still so affronted by the ordeal and explaining it with such excitement that he seemingly forgot that he was naked as the day he was born. Darcy kept saying "Yes,

yes," whilst taking off his frock coat for Bingley to cover himself. Regrettably, as fine as it was, the specific cut of that coat did not lend Bingley's private parts any privacy.

Darcy looked at the situation and suggested, "Here, Bingley, take it off and use the sleeves to wrap about your waist lest you be arrested before I can get you home."

Bingley was far too upset to employ the proper manoeuvres for that, hence, Darcy tied him as best he could.

"There. Perhaps that will hold until I get you home."

Further apprising the situation, he added, "I suppose we can ride double."

Bingley finally gave up his ranting, and Darcy, unused as he was to legging anyone onto a horse other than Elizabeth, was having difficulty with Bingley. At last he said, "Here, I'll mount and then pull you up."

That seemed like the proper solution. Indeed, it appeared to work perfectly, but when almost in place, Bingley spied something in road.

"Belay this!' he said, leaping down. "Look! There! My boot!"

"We have not the time, Bingley."

"You do not understand!" Bingley whispered loudly over his shoulder. "It is not that it is a boot! It is that it is *the* boot!"

Bingley had dropped and run toward what he had seen lying on the ground. Darcy could hear his bare feet as they pattered along the cobbles. He endeavoured not to laugh, but Bingley was a hilarious sight.

"Look here!" Bingley stood up triumphantly holding a boot. "Look here what they dropped!"

"I do not see why you are so happy for one boot, it will do you little good," groused Darcy. "Now if we see the other one—that would be happiness, indeed."

In that moment, however, Darcy understood. Indeed, he saw bundles of notes falling from the boot onto the road. Whilst bidding Bingley hurry, Darcy leapt down to help retrieve the notes, resorting to tucking half of them in his waistcoat whilst Bingley hopped around, giddy with joy.

Darcy could not help but ask, "How did you manage to walk with all this tucked in your boot?"

Bingley did not reply, but scurried back to the horse. Darcy remounted and put his hand out for another tug up.

Bingley was behind him then and Darcy urged the horse forward. From some indistinguishable location the sound of laughter erupted. Both turned and looked, then Darcy gave the laden horse his heel again hurrying him on their way. Once they cleared the wharves, he drew the horse to a kinder pace. And upon their way, much became apparent. Chief amongst it was that the mob of men only wanted to be paid. They had taken Bingley's horse and clothes only against his debt. In their revelry of seizing those items and the gentleman's horse, they did not notice that they had dropped a boot. It would have made a great deal of difference to them to have realised that in that boot was Bingley's twenty-thousand pounds.

"You can be sure that they will return my property or I will certainly deduct its value from what I owe them," said Bingley indignantly.

As their horse made for Belgrave Square, Bingley repeated, "You can be sure of that."

What the Cobbles Know

Belgrave Square was not half so foggy as those neighbourhoods near the wharves. Hence, by the time Darcy arrived at Bingley's house, Mr. Bingley was most anxious to dismount and betake his nakedness inside.

Darcy had made for the back of the house. Their descent from the saddle was hindered by reason of the agglutinate nature of Bingley's skin against the leather of the saddle in warm weather. Indeed, it took him a moment to disengage his nether-end. Darcy drew his leg across the horse's neck and leapt down, allowing Bingley room to wriggle himself loose. Jane had been beside herself with worry since Bingley's leave-taking, hence she was out the door and by his side almost before Darcy had dismounted.

"Charles! Charles!" she called. "Whatever is the matter?"

Upon seeing the lack of costume upon her husband, she thought the worst (in truth, she was not fully aware of what was worse than being cast naked into the street). Bingley was so very relieved to have gotten away not only with his life, but his twenty-thousand pounds, he was all but delirious with happiness.

To Jane's appeal of explanation of all that came to pass, Bingley replied, "I am not disposed to stand here in this indecorous manner and tell you the details of our evening. Suffice it to say, I am safe and all is well."

Darcy was quite relieved himself. Intending to disguise that as he did all emotions, he set to issuing orders for seeing to the weary horse, and had regained himself enough to then inquire as to the coach and men they left in a neighbourhood that did not look altogether safe.

Jane assured him, "They have been here for some time. Nicholls is drawing Charles's bath as we speak."

Bingley made haste for the house, hugging his boot to his chest.

"I must return Darcy's coat," Bingley called over his shoulder as he made for the house.

Jane laughed, quite happy to have her husband home and not lying murdered and robbed in the street, then said solemnly to Darcy, "I would ask you to come in and sit down, but I know you must be in a great hurry to go to Lizzy."

"Yes, I am. But, I will wait until morn. I have another matter to which I must attend before returning to Kent."

"Pray, you do not know?"

"I beg you, it appears I do not," he said tentatively.

"Lizzy is here in London."

"Here?" he repeated. "Where? Why?"

Jane's countenance announced many things that her voice did not. Foremost was that trouble was afoot and Elizabeth was deeply involved with it. Jane quickly explained all she knew of it. She told him things that he already knew such as that Wickham had returned from the dead. But she also told him what he did not know. He had not been informed that Wickham had demanded money from them to leave Lydia to Kneebone. He also did not know that Elizabeth had come to Bingley's that day and set out to intercept him at Howgrave's house in order to gain his help.

The possibility that Elizabeth might have witnessed what occurred upon the steps of that house troubled him but briefly. He knew his Lizzy far too well to believe her capable of wilfully misinterpreting an altogether innocent meeting. Clearly, she had arrived behindhand of his departure. If she was not with Jane, he concluded that she had returned to Lydia's.

He dearly hoped that she had not endeavoured to go to Wickham's on her own.

"Surely, she would not be so foolish as to think she could bargain with such a man," he said under his breath.

Jane supplied him with Kneebone's address. He did not wait for his coach. Censuring himself, he leapt upon the flagging horse, and bade Jane goodbye. He cantered off down the street toward Chelsea, issuing apologies to his mount as he did.

Darcy knew Chelsea a sight better than the wharves, hence he made excellent time. Regrettably, that speed was to the detriment of his mount. When he stopt in front of Kneebone's house, he tied Bingley's horse to the hitching post and patted the heaving horse's neck in thanks. The horse immediately began to drink from the trough. Darcy plunged his hand in the water to be certain of its temperature. It was still relatively warm from the afternoon sun. He let the horse drink a bit then walked him to another post and tied him once again. He would have preferred to have turned the animal over to a groom for a good rubdown. Indeed, he was beginning to feel as if he could use some caring for himself. It had been an exceedingly long and discomfiting day. He prayed that Elizabeth was sitting in Lydia's parlour awaiting him. He prayed that all the way to the door and through the vestibule.

Regrettably, Elizabeth was not to be found. What was found was Lydia in an unusually constrained attitude and Kneebone, fraught with worry.

"Mrs. Darcy left several hours ago to meet Mr. Wickham. I have vehemently chastised myself for allowing her to keep me from accompanying her," he said wretchedly.

Darcy was unimpressed with what he conceived as belated remorse. To learn that his Lizzy had taken it upon herself to go bargain with George Wickham herself in the worst of neighbourhoods…

"My God," Darcy declared.

The realisation just hit him that the woman he had seen exiting a coach in front of Wickham's lodging had been Elizabeth. It sent a shock through him so strongly that he had to take a step back. Quickly, he thought to ascertain that certainty.

"Did she take her carriage?"

"No," replied Kneebone dolefully, "she hired a coach."

Darcy caught himself before he let out a curse. If he stifled it outwardly, he did not inwardly. He cursed again and again in his mind.

"What did she hope to accomplish?" he asked fretfully.

Kneebone withdrew Wickham's note from his waistband and handed it to Darcy.

"Ten thousand pounds," he read, then said, "He does not think his silence cheap."

Suddenly, Lydia entered the conversation, "No he does not. And what does Lizzy take to him I ask you? A pittance of what he asks. I cannot imagine what she is thinking."

Disinclined to believe Lydia the best purveyor of information, Darcy turned to Kneebone for an explanation.

In offering it, Kneebone said, "Mrs. Darcy took her leave earlier in the day. It was my information that she intended to seek her family's aide in paying Wickham his vile demand. When she returned, I assumed she was unsuccessful, for she took her coach, sold it with the horses, and sent her coachmen away. The five-hundred pounds she received, I matched. She intended to offer that to Wickham in exchange for his giving up his right of husband to Lydia."

"Would this all not have been necessary had Lydia simply denied Wickham as a husband?"

Pointedly, he looked at Lydia. He knew what Mr. Phillips had written Elizabeth. She had showed him the letter. In the silent intensity of his gaze, Lydia turned away. Darcy was thoroughly disgusted with Lydia. He was not altogether happy with Kneebone either, but he knew that man had his hands full with the wife he had chosen and lent him a small bit of allowance for it. He also gave him allowance because he felt a certain amount of guilt himself. He felt certain that part of Elizabeth's reason for going to Wickham herself was in his defence. He had made no effort to conceal how the very thought of Wickham unstrung him.

"My horse is spent. Do you have one?"

Kneebone shook his head, "A coach for hire can usually be found upon the corner."

Darcy said nothing, but took another look at Wickham's note before wadding it up, tossing it upon the table, and taking his leave.

Kneebone stopt him, offering a long great-coat, "Here sir, you will find the air has a chill this time of night."

He realised then that he had not retrieved his other coat, "I thank you."

Kneebone was almost as tall as Darcy. He was thinner, but the coat was generously cut. Had Darcy bothered to notice the tailoring, he would have approved.

Upon the steps, he stood a moment endeavouring to allow his eyes to adjust to the dark. In the distance, he saw the glow of a pipe and the outline of a horse and coach. He knew the hour was late, but was uncertain of the time. He should have checked his watch in the light before he left.

He was also glad that Kneebone had loaned him the great-coat—the wind was picking up.

"Mr. Darcy?" a voice said out of the dark.

Designs Most Fowl

Recuperation from childbirth required of Georgiana a lengthy sojourn at Rosings Park. During that stay, a drama quite of another sort was unfolding. That Sir Winton Beecher was at its centre was no great astonishment. That the consort in this affair was a long-standing (if not altogether inventive) husband-hunter, Miss Caroline Bingley, was a tad unexpected.

This alliance all came about through the agency of a detestable fowl.

Once the hoards of consolers, comforters, and those who inevitably came only to gawk, left the family to mourn on their own, the air of reflection and familial solidarity dissipated with great rapidity. Had Lady Catherine's proposal to Elizabeth gone better, perhaps her ladyship would have been in better humour. As it did not, she was not. In her sullenness, she occasionally cast a disputatious look at her son-in-law. He, in turn, refused to rise to the bait. To Beecher's way of thinking, he did his part and felt he should be duly compensated. If that Mrs. Darcy would not fall for her ladyship's schemes, that was very unfortunate, but no skin off his aristocratic nose.

Not surprisingly, Lady Catherine saw it quite differently. The monetary arrangement they had arrived at for Beecher to join forces with her to induce the Darcys to commit to a future union betwixt their families was based purely upon results. As the results of their combined efforts were not a success, she believed their arrangement null and void. Words and looks were exchanged with enough regularity to keep the animosity at a peak.

Eventually, Beecher was content to sulk in silence. Lady Catherine's temper, however, was not so easily quieted. Although their joint venture of persuasion had been thoroughly quashed, Lady Catherine did not give it up with any part of good grace. Rather than understand her proposition was ill-advised, she blamed their lack of success wholly upon Beecher. (In lieu of an introspection that might suggest her unhappy with him for higher crimes.) Her esteem of her daughter's twit of a husband had never gone beyond gratitude for the motility of his seed. She had thought, however, that the effortlessness with which he had charmed her daughter would translate into similar success with others of her sex. She then saw an error in her judgement—not a feeling that she enjoyed. It brought to her recollections of past miscalculations of a humiliating nature. If she was once again to be foiled by her nephew's wife, she preferred to have a scapegoat upon which to heap the blame.

"It was, after all, my opinion early on that Anne's passing alone would not soften that lady's heart. Anne was nothing to her," Beecher said inadvisably. "Moreover, it has been my experience that one must not reveal one's hand prematurely."

Reminding her of his gaming ways and suggesting that he had been right and she in error in the same breath did not endear Beecher to her ladyship. Indeed, she was most displeased. The only part of her scheme that went right was having obtained Darcy's qualified agreement. Because of that small triumph, Lady Catherine chose to leave it alone for then and pursue it upon another occasion. In the meantime, she had sweet Georgiana and her lovely nephew, Fitzwilliam, to keep her thoughts occupied. Although her design for her own daughter's future with Darcy had been thwarted, Georgiana's was still a match of which she was most pleased. In truth, Fitzwilliam's conviviality endeared him to her in a way that Darcy's reticent nature never could. But then, marriage had nothing to do with companionability and everything to do with condition.

She had been surprised by Georgiana's marriage to Fitzwilliam, but only a little disappointed. A titled husband would have suited a lady of her station better, but a husband from their own family ranks was still suitable. It was still possible that Fitzwilliam would yet earn a title for his heroics—if he would only accept. That was one of his few failings—he eschewed acclaim. Nevertheless, that Georgiana was taken to the straw within her walls she saw as providential. Lady Catherine was well-aware of the affection Darcy held for his sister. Georgiana giving birth within the august halls of Rosings Park and naming her daughter Anne was another link in her chain of renewed family unity. She intended to keep the dear girl with her as long as possible. In doing so, she was not above invoking her dead daughter's memory and a mother's broken heart. Lady Catherine had been almost stunned at how well that ploy had worked on Darcy. At one time she had believed him to be a man unmoved by such pathos. She supposed that decline in what had been his finely honed sense of perspicaciousness was inevitable. It was an observation not unfamiliar to her. Once a man fell under the throes of womanly wiles, all good sense went missing.

Although Lady Catherine despised womanly wiles when she perceived them to have been employed by another, she was not so resistant to such ploys as to scruple to use them herself. Regrettably, she was compleatly unaware that she had never quite mastered the art. Hence, when attempting to engage in such tomfoolery, the effect was betimes lacking. (The expression upon Darcy's countenance when she had endeavoured to weep was one less of compassion than appalled incredulity.) She had bruised her dignity in resorting to such a device, but was disinclined to argue with success—Darcy had capitulated. Two can play that game Miss Bennet!

As she mused over that marginally successful ruse, Lady Catherine looked again upon Beecher. Summoning the thought of her illustrious nephew, the comparison did not do Beecher's aspect any kindness. As he sat slumped in his chair nursing his wineglass, powdered and curled to perfection, she had to repress the desire to whap him atop his head with her fan.

As if divining her thoughts, Beecher set down his drink and looked upon her.

"What?" he said impatiently. "What?"

"You sir, ask no questions better than you answer them."

At that nonsensical response, Beecher stood and walked the length of the room. There, he reached out and imperceptively corrected the hang of the frame for one of his water-colours. Upon his return, he passed by Henry's perch, and as if doing a bit of divining of his mistress's thoughts himself, Henry let out a screech and took flight in Beecher's direction. The tether kept Henry from doing any damage beyond a loss of dignity—at the feather-flapping squawk, Beecher leapt two-foot into the air and did not regain his composure gracefully.

"That bloody bird!" Beecher squawked (doing a passable, if unintentional, imitation of Henry). "He does that again and I'll have him for supper!"

With all her considerable hauteur, Lady Catherine rose to her feet.

"You sir," she announced, "have said quite enough! Be gone from my sight!"

It had not been Beecher's design, but being banished from her ladyship's presence was no great punishment. Indeed, he thought it not altogether unseemly to betake himself from her presence and all the way to London—an atmosphere far more to his liking. There, people of condition were happy for his company.

It had long been Caroline Bingley's habit to troll the matrimonial waters employing the time-tested method of winnowing out eligible husbands by perusing the newspaper's weekly obituary column. Had she not been apprised beforehand that the death of Darcy's young cousin left a grieving widower, she would have honed in on him regardless. Other than his relative youth, she was attracted to Lord Beecher for the same virtues as had been Lady Catherine—he was titled and kept a carriage. Of the more questionable of his attributes, she remained blissfully unaware. Had she been witting, they would not have served her purposes as they had Lady Catherine's. Gambling was a vice that would have troubled her, but a mistress simply meant that was one obligation she would not have to fulfill. (Fertility not only served no purpose for her, it was undesirable.) Caroline wanted only the title (and the yellow livery was quite nice). Indeed, his turn for foppish wardrobe and London society was all she desired in a husband.

When espying Beecher sporting a black band and salving his poor, wounded bosom in the card rooms at Almack's (Boodle's still held markers for him that Lady Catherine had not yet settled), Caroline made a beeline for him, the recuperation of his heart much upon her mind. Long past her bloom, had Miss Bingley not employed the name of Darcy as one of her connexions, Beecher would not have been half so ready to have her be his chief consoler. Quite expeditiously (and with the help of copious amounts of wine), Miss Bingley's hand was stroking his waistcoat and his arm snaked about her waist. Although it was certainly observed, no one within their milieu actually raised an eyebrow at their familiarity. Although mourning demanded any new alliance be kept in confidence for a full year, society over-looked a husband's lack of dedication to a spouse's memory with far greater tolerance than a wife's.

All might have gone without mishap had Beecher's vice of gambling not been so intimately intertwined with that of drink. But as a man who clearly did not own the intuitive mind required to be successful in games of chance, luck absolutely fled from his side as well when he was in his cups. Caroline remained constant to him during his trial, for she had been so dedicated to her search for a match, when at last one was at hand, she was not inclined to let him slip through her fingers. Indeed, she allowed herself to be escorted to the tables each night, but did not play herself. She draped herself across the back of his chair, but she could do nothing to avert the catastrophe she saw unfold as hand after hand went greatly to the bad.

Although it was a precipitous decline, one particular hand incurred deficit so substantial that Beecher could not leave the table without writing out an acknowledgment of debt promising several of his prize racing ponies as collateral.

The key to the misunderstanding that came about was whether the horses in question actually resolved the debt or were held in abeyance until Beecher could cover his wager. Beecher had believed them security. Therefore, first he cajoled, and when rebuffed, Beecher begged his creditor to relent. As he held the horses in far greater esteem than he ever felt for a mere wife, the prospect of losing them sent him into a plaintive keen sufficiently pitiable to have unmanned Herod. However the gentleman was not Herod, but Alphonse Parr. He was not a man of sport, but of business. Parr had, without compunction, evicted widows and orphans from his properties. Beecher, however, was unknowing of Parr's disposition and when the man insisted upon taking possession of the precious mounts, Beecher slapped him across the face with his glove. Unfortunately, he did this in a public hall and all about the room gasped, knowing well what that meant.

Even Miss Bingley exclaimed, "Dear God in heaven!"

At Beecher's attack, Parr demanded, "Name your weapon, sir!"

From the wavering expression of effrontery upon Beecher's countenance, it appeared that he may have reconsidered the depth of his injury. As a gentleman, Beecher knew that if he did not appear to defend his honour, his societal death would precede his actual one. Parr's nose curled just a bit, as if he had detected the odour of fear that was then emanating from the area of Beecher's spine.

Gathering himself just a bit, Beecher boomed, "Pistols," with a far greater degree of certainty than he felt.

His choice of gun rather than blade was precautionary—his shooting experience was limited to toting a long gun on his shoulder during the odd grouse hunt. (He had taken out a pistol once or twice, but had never actually shot anyone—he was, after all, a gentleman.) However, he had never wielded a blade of any kind. He thought no better of taking exercise with a foil than he did of those bloody grouse hunts into which he was occasionally coerced. With a gun, he had reasonably presumed that he had at least one chance to hit his opponent. Feint and parry were compleatly foreign to him.

There was the issue of a second. Beecher had not the happy manners that made for fast friendship of other gentlemen. If he had incurred this engagement in the county of Kent, Lady Catherine's connexions would have made it far easier to marshal someone to stand with him. As it was, Miss Bingley had been prest into service of supplying him one. Caroline had the audacity to think her brother a candidate. She pleaded with Jane to speak to him, but surprisingly, Jane refused, citing Bingley's keeping to his room due to some business he had endured upon the wharves. Beyond those monetary, Caroline had little time for the particulars of her brother's affairs and scurried for the more sympathetic ear of sister Louisa. (Caroline's memory of her recent denunciation of her brother had conveniently failed her, but Jane's would not be so forgiving.) Mrs. Hurst was happy to dragoon Mr. Hurst to do the job—as being the keeper of the Flask of Courage was an employment that merged quite nicely with his own proclivities.

Mr. Hurst had served his office by plying Beecher with liquid courage until the appointed hour. But, when Beecher arrived at the appropriately secluded spot, his trembling knees remained unsettled. The bravado he had enjoyed the night before had fled, leaving him with bleary eyes and a fierce headache. Moreover, it was such an outrageously early hour. Indeed, he regretted that he had attempted the few hours of sleep that he had.

"Get on with it, I say!" he demanded.

Parr nodded benignly, threw his cape over his shoulder and took his position. Impatient and irritable, Beecher shot first and missed. Protocol then gave Parr the freedom to take his own shot. To his credit, Beecher stood his ground to receive his punishment like the gentleman he believed himself to be—temporarily. By the time Parr had taken aim, Beecher peeked through squinted eyes and was most affrighted by looking down the barrel of Parr's pistol. In the following moment, Parr drew a bead upon the largest target exposed to him which, unfortunately, was the broad expanse of Beecher's buttocks as he was making his away. In fortune, that area of the human form is the one most cushioned for such an assault, hence, Beecher was taken down, but not killed.

The return trip to Rosings Park was, however, a tad uncomfortable. This, not only for Beecher who had to endure the trip to Kent lying on his stomach and swilling laudanum, but for Caroline's lap upon which he reposed. As he was merely incapacitated, not dead, Miss Bingley did not desert him. (Indeed, she was so dedicated, one would have thought she had burnt her bridges everywhere else.) As his closest relative, her son-in-law's care was remanded ultimately unto Lady Catherine. In that Caroline advised her ladyship of the deep and abiding friendship she shared with Georgiana, she was asked to stay on for so long as she liked. Georgiana, of course, was quite astonished to see Caroline once again—almost as astonished as she was to learn that Miss Bingley still regarded their friendship as a dear one. Although Lady Catherine and Miss Bingley were of similar minds upon many things (not least amongst them as admiration of rank), Caroline's design upon Beecher became apparent.

Lady Catherine was very attentive to those tenets governing societal behaviour. Unlike her peers in London, she did not turn a blind eye to a widower transgressing the conventions of mourning. Even in Beecher's compromised health, she saw a romance in progress.

She was most displeased.

The Convalescence

Lady Catherine had all but washed her hands of Beecher, giving Georgiana the opportunity to undertake the somewhat thankless office of over-seer of his repair. Caroline Bingley was keenly interested in Beecher's recuperation, but was queasy of illness of any kind and thereby delighted to have her friend's intervention on his behalf. Fitzwilliam, however, protested, insisting such activity was far too taxing for so new a mother. It was a bit cumbersome to direct Beecher's care from her own bed, but Georgiana was delighted for the opportunity to employ her store of remedies. Hence, she sweetly, but firmly, over-ruled her husband's objection.

At one time, Miss Bingley had pursued a close friendship with Georgiana (but her devotion to Darcy's sister had waned once he had married Elizabeth). Of late, they had little in common—for Caroline could no more satisfy Georgiana's thirst for thoughtful discourse than Georgiana could hers for what colours would be fashionable next season. Having stumbled upon her long-lost friend at Rosings Park, Caroline was quite happy to renew their acquaintance—a connexion that she hoped would influence Lady Catherine in her favour.

Recalling the difficult young girl she once knew, Caroline was rightly impressed with both Georgiana's expertise and her self-possession. Indeed, she listened closely to Georgiana's instructions and followed the servants as they shuttled back and forth fulfilling them. As her ladyship had made it clear that she was still quite irked over the blossoming of her son-in-law's unseemly romance, Caroline's scampering between Georgiana's bed and Beecher's accomplished dual purposes. It gave the appearance of dutifulness to her lover and kept her from under Lady Catherine's disapproving glare.

Although not happy to have his husbandly concern rebuffed, Fitzwilliam's recollections of Georgiana were similar to Caroline's. Hence, he smiled indulgently upon her as she issued orders. Despite her neice's choice of patients, even Lady Catherine (whose parsimony with compliments was of legend) could not be at variance with the conclusion of her niece's cleverness. Indeed, she insisted that the Fitzwilliams sojourn at Rosings for as long as they liked.

The death of a mother in childbirth was a common-place event even in Kent. Whilst Georgiana believed that beneath her aunt's seeming indifference to Anne's death lurked a wounded heart, she doubted that the usual remedies for such a tragedy would benefit one of Lady Catherine's dispostion. Although that lady had come to admire the Fitzwilliams' newborn each day, she had not paid the same attention to her granddaughter. Granted, she issued a number of edicts upon that baby's care, but she had not once visited her since her ill-advised crib-side confrontation with Elizabeth. It was clear that an attachment between grandmother and granddaughter had not been formed. The recognition of that lack of affection gave Georgiana the impetus to pursue her aunt's approval for bringing Anne's baby home with their own.

In truth, it was not one, but several seemingly unrelated sentiments that combined propitiously in supporting Georgiana's suit. The sheer economy of raising two girls together and the possibility that Beecher might employ his parental right to the child held no small sway over Lady Catherine's opinion. But in the end, it was that the Fitzwilliams would be spending a great deal of time at Pemberley which decided the matter in their favour. Having her granddaughter situated in close proximity to the Darcy heir-apparent pleased Lady Catherine no end. (Indeed, she was quite happy to have thought of it.)

Knowing that the baby would be brought up with love gladdened Georgiana even more.

The Wicked and the Just

Wickham did not visibly start at the spectre before him, but his pupils contracted noticeably. He stood, picked up a glove, and flicked it nervously against his other palm.

With a remarkably level voice, he said, "I did not expect to see you here, Darcy."

"No," said Darcy, "I do not expect that you would."

Once Darcy's eyes had swept the room, he stood gravely still—eyes levelled upon Wickham.

To Wickham's mind the early evening chill was not significant enough to merit the long coat Darcy wore—that made him even more nervous than Darcy's sudden appearance. He was troubled that it obscured his figure, thus whether he was armed. He could ascertain only that he did not wear his sword. Darcy was also unaccompanied by a second—that was of comfort. But Wickham's toe throbbed and he cursed Lydia under his breath. He was happy that he had managed to pull on his boots. He would not have liked to be confronted in his stockings.

"No second?" Wickham smirked, then quickly sobered.

Initially, Wickham had never quite believed that tale that had travelled the length and breadth of England of Darcy slaying three men. But that unhappy occurrence of being invited to take his leave from Pemberley at the point of Darcy's blade bade him rethink the matter. This night he thought it best to keep his distance from Darcy—particularly in light of engaging in clandestine meetings with his wife.

Elizabeth, however, was gone, and he was sporting a lump the size of a potato upon the side of his head thanks to the heavy swing she took at him with her gold-filled reticule. Wickham was uncertain what prompted Darcy's visit—was he there because he knew of what had come to pass upon her visit or because he did not? Elizabeth had inadvertently admitted that Darcy knew nothing of her coming, hence, it was possible that he learnt of their meeting and this confrontation was prompted by jealousy. Wickham knew not whether to admire that possibility or despise it.

All these considerations crossed, flitted about, and then abandoned Wickham's thoughts in the seconds he recognised Darcy stood before him. But then, his fast-thinking was one of his keenest attributes—that secnd only to the quickness of his tongue.

As Darcy still stood in silence, Wickham knew that he was being called out in some manner. If not a duel, what? He felt compelled to break the stalemate.

He laughed nervously, then spread his hands, and said, "May we talk man to man, Darcy?"

"Any other manner would be curious," replied Darcy.

It was clear no quarter was to be granted. It was also clear to Wickham that if he was to wriggle out of the tight spot into which he had situated himself, he would have to draw upon all his powers of persuasion. Failing that, he would break and run. He was, even then, calculating his exit strategy.

"It has been a long time," he ventured, attempting to stall.

"Not long enough," Darcy retorted. "Your commanding officers will be surprised to know you are alive."

Darcy stood between Wickham and the door and it did not appear that he intended to move from his position—one that blocked exit from the room. Wickham was both irked and frightened. Soon, however, fright overcame his pique and his brow began to perspire. He had always despised his propensity to that weakness. As any good card-player knows, one must never reveal the lack of hold cards. Impassivity was all if one was to have the upper hand. A sudden twitch began to trouble his left eyelid.

They had stood before each other for a full five minutes and why Darcy was there remained unexplained. Whatever it was, Wickham knew that it could not be good. The lack of promise of situation bade Wickham assess alternate routes of escape. A window was behind him. He believed the shutters were open, but the sash was closed. Damn.

When at last Darcy made a move, Wickham jerked like a startled cat.

"I have here," said Darcy reaching into his coat, "a document."

Wickham exhaled mightily and immediately set about to reclaim his composure.

"A document?"

"Yes."

Darcy then walked purposely to a game-table that stood mid-most of the room. He placed his gloves upon the edge and then placed the tri-folded piece of paper in the middle of the chessboard that decorated the lacquered top. Wickham, however, dropped his gloves to that same table, then strode to the cellaret standing against the wall. He opened the cabinet door and withdrew a bottle of claret and two glasses. He kicked the door closed with the heel of his boot and thereupon, returned to the game-table. He placed the glasses and decanter upon it next to the still-folded document.

Once he had seen that Darcy held not a weapon, but a legal document, he allowed the exultation of triumph to wash over him. It was a heady feeling to have the whip-hand over the proud Darcy. Had he been wise, he would have enjoyed his win and left it at that. But Wickham had never been particularly wise. Granted, he had an innate talent for chicanery. But he was sly, not wise. That lack of wisdom then allowed him to entertain the notion of gloating over his victory.

"A drink, my old friend?" he said amiably.

"I am not your friend," was the reply.

Wickham shrugged, "Suit yourself."

He poured half a glass and upended it immediately. Wiping his mouth with the back of his hand, he thought to apprise Darcy of the wine's fine quality.

"A mistake, my friend," he said, picking up the decanter and holding it to the light. "This is a particularly nice bottle of…"

Suddenly, Darcy reached out and grasped the decanter by its neck and cast it to the floor.

"I am not," he said evenly, "your friend."

"Testy, testy, Darcy," said Wickham with a smirk. Then, most unadvisedly, "'Tis a pity your wife could not come with you. I have enjoyed our meetings most decidedly."

With that, Wickham stepped back, his hand at the ready by his waistband. There lurked a small pistol. It was but a single-shot—a pea-shooter, they were called—a lady's gun—Lydia's gun—but one that could fell a man—even a man of Darcy's size. Darcy, however, did not advance even at that provocation.

Wickham raised one eyebrow, as if to dare him to advance.

To his astonishment, Darcy smiled, "I believe from the size of the contusion on your head that you would do well to stay away from my wife."

So, Wickham realised, he had talked to his wife. That irked him no end.

Darcy picked up the document, opened it, and set it before Wickham. That reminded Wickham that he was to win this confrontation. Still, he could not help but touch the goose-egg near his hair-line.

"Have you no pen?" Wickham asked.

Darcy flicked his head toward the escritoire.

"Yes," Wickham simpered, "of course."

Employing every device of relish, he sauntered there and back, holding the pen aloft in one hand, the inkwell in the other. He set the inkwell down, dabbed the pen in it three times, then held the pen to the light.

"Does it need mending?"

"Get on with it," demanded Darcy.

"I suppose I should read it first."

Wickham picked up the paper and held it close to the candle, reading it in the quasi-silence of lip-accompaniment. Satisfied, he laid it down, but still did not sign.

"You understand, it is not that I do not trust you. But, under these particular circumstances, might I bear witness that you have sufficient funds in exchange for this signature. Bloody war. It has made paupers of so many gentlemen."

It was Darcy's turn to sigh, and he gave a generous one of disgust. He reached within his waistcoat, retrieved Bingley's bank notes, and tossed them into the middle of the table.

Still holding the pen aloft, Wickham picked up a bundle and appraised it. With the money before him in a tantalizing mound, he quickly scratched a signature upon the paper.

Darcy reached out and yanked it from beneath his pen before he had time to blot.

That impatience had little effect upon Wickham's mood—which was by then bordering upon the giddy. "I am most excessively grateful," he said scooping up the notes.

He gave Darcy a swooping bow.

"Good day," Wickham said amiably.

Darcy did not respond. He picked up the document and refolded it, stashing it again in his waistcoat. Darcy took up his gloves and strode toward the door. At the door, however, he paused.

Looking directly at Wickham, he said with no small gravity, "I *do* have a second, Wickham."

Wickham smiled and then lost it, uncertain of Darcy's meaning.

Darcy was disinclined to explain. With one parting look, he took his leave.

"What sort of enigmatic rubbish is that?" Wickham said aloud, mimicking Darcy. "*I do have a second.*"

He picked up his gloves and stopt, brow furrowing. He bethought the matter further. It was troubling. Then he shook that thought from his mind, certain that Darcy was only playing with him. But then, Darcy was not much of a gamester. What could be his design?

Shrugging his shoulders, he pondered more important matters. It was imperative that he make his money safe. But first, he must count. Carefully, he arranged each stack, counting the notes in each. It was indeed, ten-thousand there. He put his hands over his face and rubbed his eyes—thinking he might just weep with joy. Mrs. Younge, of course, had no safe. But there was a strongbox in a room behind the tavern. He would borrow it until he could find permanent means of stowing his booty. A canvas bag lay upon the escritoire. He took it and began to stuff the notes into it. It had been the one that had held the ruby necklace for his brief ownership. To refill it with such a fortune gifted him no small delight.

"What is it they say about luck?" he asked himself. "Oh, yes. 'Luck is what happens when preparation meets opportunity.'"

Wickham made for the door and began to don his gloves. He stopt once again, perplexed. There was something wrong with the fit of his gloves. The appearance of his costume was one of his many conceits. He refused to leave his room unless dressed as a gentleman. He pushed between each of the fingers endeavouring to press them into place, but to no avail. He looked at his hand. The fingers of the gloves were a knuckle-length too long on each finger. Furiously, he withdrew them both and cast them to the ground. Realising that Darcy had mistakenly taken his gloves and left his own, Wickham settled himself.

"Let Darcy have my gloves," he thought. "I now have the funds to buy all the kid gloves I should want."

The thought of gloves he could buy was rewarding. Still, he could not help himself from looking once again at Darcy's gloves lying in a heap upon the floor. It was not the fineness of those gloves that so bothered him. The many gloves that he would buy would be just as fine.

What truly vexed him was the thought that even then Darcy would be endeavouring to don the gloves he took by mistake. It was not that Darcy's gloves were too long for him that riled Wickham so, but that Darcy would realise that his were far too small.

But, then size really did not matter. Did it?

What Went Before

When Mr. Darcy left Major Kneebone's house, he stood momentarily upon the stoop determining the location of the nearest coach for hire. From the shadows, Sally Frances called his name.

That he wore Major Kneebone's coat was no impediment to her recognition of that man. Mr. Darcy's presence was of a singular kind. Sally had seen him upon several occasions at Pemberley. Such was the observation of those who knew the couple that after Mrs. Darcy's arrival, Sally knew it would be only a short time ere Mr. Darcy came after her. It was nice to know of a married couple who loved each other as they seemed to do. Had it not been for the Darcys and Gardiners, Sally might have believed love and respect between a married couple was only that of fairy-tales.

Sally was as much Mrs. Darcy's ally as she was hers against Mr. Wickham. She had wanted most especially to go with Mrs. Darcy when she saw Mr. Wickham, but Mrs. Darcy had asked her to stay in case Mr. Darcy came looking for her. Sally had no doubt that he would. Mr. Darcy, she had heard, was given to rescuing folks.

It worried her that Mrs. Darcy might need rescuing. She intended to have Mr. Wickham sign a paper giving up his right to Mrs. Kneebone and pay him for his time. (It came to light she had a second document—one Sally understood equally well.) But the coachman had returned to his stand only to find that document in the seat of his coach. In fortune, he observed Mrs. Darcy's doings and knew Sally was of her acquaintance so he returned the document forthwith to her. Sally had it with her then, tucked beneath her shawl. Mr. Darcy had been right to borrow Mr. Kneebone's coat. Had he left in the same shirtsleeves he arrived, he might catch his death. Mrs. Darcy would be heart-broken was that to happen.

When she called Mr. Darcy's name, it was clear he had no recollection of her. Still, he peered at her, not with suspicion, but curiosity. He answered only yes, that he was Mr. Darcy and waited for her to speak again.

"Are ye in want of yer wife?"

"Yes."

She liked Mr. Darcy—he was a man of few words. Garrulous men were to be suspected she had learnt long ago.

"My name is Sally Frances Arbuthnot and I know where she went."

"Thank you, Miss Arbuthnot, but I know as well," Mr. Darcy said. Then he eyed her again, "I was just in that neighbourhood—but it was daylight still. I fear I may not find the way in the dark. Do you know Gowell Street?"

"Like the back of my hand," she assured him.

"Come," he commanded, "I will pay you well."

"I had no doubt ye wouldn't," she assured him, "but I got my reasons fer helpin' ye."

As they were crossing the street to the single remaining coach, Sally brought forth Elizabeth's lost document.

"Mrs. Darcy forgot this in her coach. The driver brought it to me."

Darcy took the instrument from her and squinted in the dim gaslight to discover its contents. Ever in want of being of assistance, Sally said, "It's a paper sayin' that Wickham is dead, and one that says there ain't no Wickham no more."

Mr. Darcy looked at her in a singular manner and she added defensively, "I can read."

"Is the coachman here who took Mrs. Darcy to Mr. Wickham's?"

Sally was not about to allow Mr. Darcy to leave her behind, but she did not have to fib to obtain that objective, "Naw, sir. He went 'ome."

Mr. Darcy opened the door to the coach as Sally told the coachman their destination. She began to scramble in, but Mr. Darcy took her hand and helped her in like a proper lady. Sally was altogether pleased to be treated as such. So pleased was she, she thought it only fair to apprise Mr. Darcy of all she knew of the despicable doings of wicked Mr. Wickham. In doing so, she also thought it prudent to advise him of her connexion.

"That soldier he kilt? He was me brother," she told him.

That information gifted Mr. Darcy the strangest look.

"Your brother?" he repeated, then queried, "Your family name is Arbuthnot?"

"He's me half-brother—same Ma, different Pa."

"I see," said he.

"I mean to kill 'im," Sally announced.

"Who?" Mr. Darcy inquired.

"Why, Mr. Wickham, of course," she said impatiently.

"I believe it best to let the authorities see to Mr. Wickham."

"That's just what Mrs. Darcy said," Sally marvelled.

"Mrs. Darcy knows of your connexion?"

"Indeed," Sally replied, "I'm her associate in this business."

He looked at her a bit dubiously, and she retorted, "She *told* me I was."

His smile was not of the condescending variety. Apparently, asking for help from the likes of her was a turn of his wife's that he admired.

"I gotta tell ye, sir, that this time a night things can get a might rowdy down around Gowell Street."

"No doubt."

He seemed unfazed by such a notion, and Sally wondered would he remain unfazed when faced with the likes of Seven Dials night life? Moreover, she wondered when faced with the likes of Mr. Darcy, would Gowell Street be fazed by him? It might be necessary for her to call upon past associates to make their way unassaulted. She had not been to that neighbourhood for many months, but she doubted much had changed.

Indeed, the coachman arrived at an approximation of where Darcy last had been taken. They had approached it from the other end, so Darcy's sense of direction was a bit askew. The street had been fairly bustling at dusk. The girl's description of what he would find when he arrived had him expecting a veritable circus of drunkenness and debauchery. A circus he did not see. The street was dark and almost deserted. He did not leave the coach until he caught sight of a landmark he recognised. The one he saw was the upturned arrow barely visible in the low-cast lights from the windows.

He opened the coach door and alit, placing but one page of the document in his breast pocket, the other he folded again and tucked into his waistband and instructed the coachman to wait.

He told Sally Frances Arbuthnot, "I thank you for your aid. I shall go alone."

"Ye ain't leavin' me," said Sally, leaping to the ground—having given up hope that her impetuosity would be rewarded by him taking her hand and escorting her from the coach.

"I think it best if I proceed alone. The streets are altogether vacant. I see the lodgings but a few steps from here."

"Vacant, huh?" Sally snorted.

Darcy put his hands upon his hips, dissatisfied at his charge's impudence.

"See here, Miss," he began.

Sally grabbed his hand and tugged him into a shadowed niche. He had the good judgement to follow her lead and to be quiet. Two men crept by them, one carrying what could ably pass as a bludgeon, in the other's hand, a knife glinted. Their whispering discourse involved the gentleman they had just seen and interest of where he might have gone.

"Rowdiness?" he mouthed to Sally.

She shrugged, but Darcy was affrighted to his toes. His own head was not his concern. His fear was for Elizabeth who had trod upon these very steps not hours before. Silently, he looked skyward, begging God to look after her. Rather than cautioning him, the appearance of the men merely spurred his determination to locate her. His compleat recollection of her abduction and its aftermath had not yet descended upon him, but it was on the cusp of his thoughts. His heart told him to draw his pistol and walk down the middle of the street until Wickham's door, march up those stairs, and kick open the door. His head insisted otherwise lest his rashness incite her murder.

"I must enter those lodgings," he whispered to Sally. "There by the arrow—upstairs."

He all but took a step onto the walkway, when Sally again tugged his arm.

"This way!"

Into an alley and up several buildings, Sally found an unlocked door. Weaving through barrels containing reeking substances the contents of which he chose not to ponder, they made their way through what appeared to be a kitchen and into some sort of parlour. The remains of a silk scarf strewn over the top of a lamp cast a reddish hue through the room. It occurred to Darcy that such an arrangement was a fire-hazard, but by the time his eyes adjusted to its particular glow, he was non-plussed enough to have forgotten that trail of thought.

Seated about the room were several ladies, none of whom were fully attired. One nearest him immediately rose and went to him, putting her arm around his waist, announcing through a grin that evidenced a single tooth, "This 'ere's mine!"

To the murmurs of the others' disgruntlement of having been forestalled, Mr. Darcy unwrapped her arm from about his waist, observing, "I do beg your pardon, this is a misunderstanding."

Not so easily rebuffed, the heavily rouged, scantily clad sexual vendor investigated the goods beneath his great-coat, saying, "See here, pretty feller, doncha worry, I'll be gentle."

To that, screeches of laughter erupted.

Mr. Darcy announced (far too primly), "Unhand me, Madam."

"'Unhand me' sez 'e," the woman mimicked. "'Unhand me'—like 'e's some little virgin! Take off that hat and them gloves and I'll shew you what ye been missin'!"

Gratefully, his guide through this particularly lewd bawdy house then spoke in his defence, "Leave 'im be! 'E's after a murderin' scum, 'e is." To the general lack of sympathy upon their faces, she added, "This murderin' scum 'e's after is a gentleman!"

"Ahs" of appreciation were heard all round. One plump tart, wearing curl-papers and an orange kimono knew the description well.

"Ye must mean that feller who lodges across up the street, in Mrs. Younge's house. He keeps more than one chit in pink stockings," she said knowingly.

Just then came an interruption.

"Oh hush-up, Mellie!" said a voice from the stairs. "And take those curl-papers out yer hair. How'd ye think a man's gonna want to tail ye lookin' like that?"

Once again, Darcy's new admirer clamped on to his waist with one arm and sent her hand scurrying for the inside of his leg, "Whoa Papa Bear! What family jewels ye got."

Whilst endeavouring to unpeel her fingers and disengage the personage attempting to caress his vitals, Darcy caught sight of possibly the oddest looking apparition of his recollection. Before him stood a female, no more than four foot tall, her yellow hair and ermine tippit much in evidence.

"Daisy!" Sally cried, "I been lookin' fer ye."

"I been right 'ere," said Daisy, unsuccessfully endeavouring to hide her delight at seeing her young friend. "Brought us a customer, did ye?"

To the woman with whom Darcy was still wrangling with over ownership of his genitals, Daisy demanded, "Let 'im be!" Then to Darcy apologetically, she offered, "I can do better for ye, she's got a face to inspire chastity if ever I saw one."

"I thank you, no," replied Darcy, giving Sally a flick of his head of indication that she was to explain that, which by nature of his lack of intelligence of it, he could not—for he had no idea what they were doing there.

Sally stepped between them, "We need to get over two houses without 'im gettin' thumped."

Daisy did not ask unnecessary questions, but beckoned them to follow her. They trooped up the stairs through several bedrooms that were unoccupied and one that was (both tenants far too engaged to be aware that they were transgressed) to a window facing another across a small divide.

"Are ye lookin' fer a woman?" Daisy asked suddenly.

Taken aback, Darcy answered, "Why, yes. Indeed I am. At least," he corrected, "a particular lady."

He thought it important to make that distinction.

"That why yer after this gemmen?"

Sally interrupted, "Nothin' like that, Daisy. Remember the feller that I told ye kilt my brother? 'E's after 'im. 'Is wife is too. She come 'ere to get rid of 'im not to...ye know," she ended with a fit of decorum. "This 'ere's Mr. Darcy."

With only the moonlight shining upon them, the unmistakable grunts and groans of humping in the background, Daisy looked Mr. Darcy up and down.

Mr. Darcy allowed this measure taken without complaint. Although he knew not of their connexion, he believed if he was to accept her assistance, he must acquiesce to her inspection.

This inspection was longer than Darcy anticipated. Even Sally wondered what Daisy's perusal of Mr. Darcy's person meant.

At last, Daisy turned and pointed to the window across the way, "Go through there to another stairs. Up 'em and across the other hall. That'll put ye in Mrs. Younge's landing. Mr. Wickham's at the far end of the hallway."

It was then that Darcy again pondered obtaining the help of the authorities. He also once again wished for Fitzwilliam's accompaniment. Darcy thanked Daisy, but put the flat of his hand out at Sally, "If my wife is being held, there may be trouble. You must stay here. I'll not have anyone else endangered."

Laconically, Daisy interjected, "Yer wife ain't there."

"What?" said Darcy, one foot out the window.

"She left hours ago."

"Are you certain?"

"Am I certain?! Course I'm certain," she said indignantly. "Nothin' 'appens on this street that I don't know. She left 'im cold-cocked, she did."

"There was an altercation?" Darcy asked worriedly.

"I wouldn't call it that 'specially," she said. "I wuz downstairs when he called for some ice. They said she 'it 'im with her bag up-side 'is 'ead. 'Ad it comin', so's I hear."

"Then she is alright?"

"Perfectly, so's I heard. Left in the cab that brung 'er."

Darcy whispered, "Thank God," under his breath.

Daisy asked, "So—ye still after this feller?"

With renewed determination upon his countenance, Darcy nodded once firmly.

"Yer wife," Daisy asked, "she yer only wife?"

With an expression that suggested the ludicrous nature of such an inquiry, he replied in the positive.

"Jes' askin'," was Daisy's explanation.

Darcy still intended to confront Wickham. He had not come all this way to return without that pleasure. But he wanted not only justice done to Wickham, but right done as well for John Christie's sister.

To her, he said, "I intend to lay out to Wickham money in payment for…" Here he bethought explaining himself, "It matters not my reason, but he is owed. Anyone here who sees fit to confront Mr. Wickham over past grievances will be free to do so. I only advise you that I intend to report Mr. Wickham to the authorities. I shall tell them that he's done murder to a soldier under his command and then deserted his post. Mr. Wickham knows this will be my intention. After I leave, what becomes of him will be of no interest to me."

"Ye can be certain, Mr. Darcy, that I will be waiting for you to take yer leave," said Sally.

"Here," Darcy said, reaching in his waistband and removing his pistol, "Wickham will be desperate. He is not to be trusted."

"Thankee," said Sally, "but yer gonna need it."

"I think not," he replied. "And I bid you good-luck."

"And you as well."

Taking off his hat, he started out the window once again, this time, Daisy stopt him, "Careful someone don't cut ye another smile."

She put her finger beneath her ear and drew it swiftly under her chin and across to the other one.

"I will keep that in mind," said he.

Drawing his other long leg through the window, he paused, then leapt across the divide and pulled himself through. Then he disappeared into the darkness therein.

A Rescue of Sorts

When Darcy took his leave of Wickham, he was in a furiously satisfied temper. By the time his boots hit the cobbles, he was still seething with rage, gratification, and a sense of finality.

He took leave so embroiled in those emotions, he took to the street with hard steps and chin tucked. He had been exceedingly disinclined to return by the way whence he had arrived. He did not think his dignity would survive one more trip through that Gates of Hell of a brothel. He had not seen the girl, Sally, as he left, but he sensed her presence. What satisfaction he had not received from Wickham, he was certain she would exact.

The streets looked as vacant as they had before, but then he knew better what menaces lay there and could see rustlings just beyond the fringes of window-light. He kept walking, shoulders back. Still, he slowed a bit as he put on his hat. He dug into his pockets for the gloves he had stashed within. He sought them in defence of his fastidious nature rather than the chilly air. He drew them on whilst keeping careful watch about him, and when he could not fit his fingers into those of the gloves, he stuffed them back in his pockets without another thought. Only his own custom-made gloves fit him properly. These, he knew immediately, must have been someone else's.

Looking about for his hired coach, he wished he had his walking stick. (It was small defence, but some.) His coach was not to be found. He had been so single-minded in his confrontation with Wickham that he had not let small details derail him. Only then did he recall the haste with which that coach had departed. Having never had occasion to sit in a hired vehicle, it had not occurred to him that his demand for the driver to wait would not be heeded without a coin in payment. He cursed himself for his cosseted life—not knowing what any street urchin would know.

The late hour was of even more particular notice to him now that he was without a coach. Few people were on the streets and not a horse was in sight. Dogs were certainly about, he could hear their howls as they scavenged for scraps. One animal began to follow him, for he had determined it was better to not to stand as if waiting for someone lest he be beset upon. His pace was certainly no guarantee of safety, but it improved his mood to be on the move. His intention was to move away from the wharves, but the yellowed fog that shrouded his feet made it difficult to get his bearings.

He was very aware of his fine attire. Kneebone's coat, he noticed only then, was a finely tailored one and very conspicuous. That coat alone would be deemed worth cutting his throat for by the denizens of this district. He endeavoured to walk quietly, still his footfalls echoed in the dampness. He rethought his distaste of returning through the brothel. Might that miniature brothel owner have advised him?

A crash of glass, a woman's screams, and a man's laughter bade him pick up his pace—to where he was altogether uncertain. He then rethought his decision to have given the girl his pistol—chivalry would not allow that, insisting he believe it better that she be armed than he. In truth, he had not altogether trusted himself to face Wickham with a weapon at the ready—it would have been too great a temptation to employ it. He had done murder once in his life—that was quite enough.

He then sensed shadows behind him and turned to face his attackers rather be taken from behind.

To his great relief, he saw only that a second dog had joined the first following behind him. Both stopt and returned his gaze, unafraid. He clapped his hands and said, "Scat," dispersing them—for how long, he knew not.

Ahead of him, he espied a cross-street and made for it in hope of finding a street sign. It was then that he heard an odd sound. It was maddeningly familiar, but he could not place it. It was either a squeal or a whistle—perhaps an animal in distress. Whichever it was he cared not, but he walked briskly in that direction to determine its origin.

There it was—he heard it once again. It *was* a whistle—one of a singular nature, known only unto himself. He strode with even greater determination in its direction. When he came closer, he saw a carriage, but one that he did not recognise. It was once a fine carriage, but it had seen better days. As he drew nearer, the mist thinned and through it he saw the coach more clearly. He recognised it—but not only because of the livery. He recognised the pale face protruding from the window, peering at him almost as dearly he did at it. The feeble whistle then ceased. By the time he reached the carriage door, the driver had released the brake and started upon his way. The door opened and the steps were tossed down, he leapt upon them on the run, drew himself into the carriage and slammed the door behind him. He quickly rapped the roof with his knuckles, thereupon doffed his hat to stick his head out of the door to call to the driver to make all due haste. When the driver obliged, the coach leapt forward causing the occupants to be tossed against the seat backs. Only then did the breath that he had been holding release into a huge sigh of relief.

"I was astonished you heard me," Elizabeth said.

"*I* was astonished I heard you."

"You do not think I have improved?"

"No, I do not—nor do I think you should."

"One never knows when it might be useful," Elizabeth said.

"With any luck, it will never be necessary for you to employ it again," he answered.

With that, he wrapped his arms about her, crushing her to his chest. Thereupon, with similar enthusiasm he planted a kiss upon her lips—one that she returned with particular warmth. Still holding her, he pushed her back at arms length, unable to stop himself from gazing upon her.

Before he could chastise her, she said, "I am sorry I was no nearer than I was. Only luck found you. It does not look at all as it did in the daylight."

He could not have agreed more, but did not say so.

Happy that she did come, still he admonished, "You should not have come down here alone. It is unsafe."

"Unsafe you say—and for you as well. I have a driver and a footman, and what do you have?" She chastened him in return, reminding him, "I have been sick with worry for you. I would never sit back to await your injury."

"I hired a carriage," he answered mildly, reminding her, "as did you the first time here."

She ignored that, "Where is your hackney? Why did you not pay him to have him await you?"

He was disinclined to address that particular error upon his part, hence he altered the subject.

"What coach is this? Kneebone said you had sold your coach and horses."

She knew this would be a sore point. As much as she would have hoped the subject would not arise, she new it imperative to reclaim them forthwith lest the purchaser resell them. Therefore, she identified the location. To her relief, he seemed remarkably unvexed.

"I'll have my man go there directly," he replied mildly.

"This one I obtained from our Mayfair house," Elizabeth explained. "The coach was dusty, but two good horses were stabled there."

Both knew that there were many other things of which they must speak.

"How did you know where to find me?" he asked, wondering at her intuition.

"After I left Wickham…"

"I saw a large contusion upon Mr. Wickham's head. I understand that it was through your doing? My compliments for your aim," he interrupted her.

"Did he tell you that?"

He shook his head, but did not explain further. The tale of the brothel would wait.

She continued her story, "I returned to Lydia's to repay Major Kneebone the money with which I struck Wickham and he advised me you had sought Wickham—and," she held out her hands, "*vôilà*, I am here. But, you should not have worried me so, I have spent all day endeavouring to keep you from facing Wickham—but to no avail," she stopt, suddenly alarmed. "Pray, you did not do him harm did you?"

"No, I did not," said he, withdrawing a document from his waistcoat "I paid him to sign this."

She took it from him. Recognising her own hand, she looked perplexed.

"Lydia is free of him! Wherever did you find this?"

Rather than answering, he employed a gesture that meant—do not ask.

"Did he refuse the other?" she inquired.

"He did not see it." He felt in his waistband and breast pocket, did not find it and said, "I discarded it."

The expression upon her countenance was a blend of disappointment, contrition, and disapproval.

"Perhaps I should not have endeavoured to rid us of Wickham employing only my own volition. But I truly believed—I still believe—that to have him sign a disavowal of his name would the best course. That paper would mean that George Wickham was dead, forever from our lives."

"Lizzy, I understand, I truly do. You wanted to spare me contending with Wickham. If he signed that disavowal, he would take his leave under an assumed name, never to bother us again. Despite the name, in his breast Wickham's cold heart would beat. It would be unfair to turn him onto an unknowing populace free to do murder again if he so chooses."

She sighed, "Then nothing is done. Wickham is free to haunt us all."

"No, not necessarily. I gave him a stack of bank notes and a running start ere the dogs were set upon him—so to speak. I left him and a pistol in the able hands of your associate," he explained.

"Beg pardon?"

"Little Miss Arbuthnot."

She raised an eyebrow, then smiled.

Quite formally, Darcy said, "We shall report Major Wickham's reappearance to his regiment. I will give testimony to what I know of his crimes. We shall leave it all to fate."

"Fate may not find much left of Major Wickham," she observed. "I do not suppose you told him of his connexion to you."

"No, I did not. If Wickham survives, I will leave that to fate as well."

She was curious, "How much did you have to lay out to Wickham for him to sign away his husbandly rights?"

The understanding that in any other situation Wickham would have been happy to pay Kneebone to take Lydia off his hands remained unremarked upon.

"I honestly have no idea," said he. "It was Bingley's. I must determine that and repay him."

Without fanfare, she asked, "Pray, sir, may I inquire as to how it came about that upon Regent Street this very afternoon your arm was adorned by your former lover?"

Now that he was safe, it was clear that the events of the day had not worn out the resentment she had formed upon beholding that abhorrent sight. At her inquiry, however, Darcy gave a slight shake of his head. Indeed, for Elizabeth to have happened upon him at that very moment proved the unerring misfortune such circumstances invariably attract. He knew her too well to suppose her pique was merely because of the unseemliness of being seen upon a public street with a woman of Juliette's reputation.

He hurried to assure her, "Our meeting was coincidental to my visit to Sir Howgrave..."

The arching of her brow reminded him mid-sentence that he had employed the term "coincidence" when characterising his last encounter with Juliette. When he had used that term to describe their meeting once again, he had believed that it was nothing but happenstance. In looking at it through Elizabeth's skeptical eyes, he began to rethink the matter. Still, that she believed it was possible for him to be beguiled by another woman insulted both his honour and his reason. His indignation lasted only long enough for him to recall what his own resentment would have been had their positions been reversed—had he seen her upon the arm of a former suitor. At the thought of it his breath grew heavy. He closed his eyes to rid himself of that image.

When their eyes at last engaged, all his resentment was lost. Hers, however, still festered.

Regrettably, the depth of his empathy temporarily stole his powers of speech. As he struggled to conquer the catch in his throat, Elizabeth grew uneasy. His discomposure to her looked uncommonly like contrition. As to what act might have caused him remorse, she awaited to hear with more than a little impatience. This rising anxiety too was betrayed by her countance. Noting the subtle arrangement of her features into what could best be described as dubious, he hastened to reassure her—but met with little immediate success.

"I happened upon Mlle. Clisson as I—or I should say as Bingley and I—had just taken our leave of Sir Howgrave's apartments," he explained.

"I did not see Mr. Bingley."

"Of course not." He reminded himself to be explicit. "Bingley awaited in the carriage, for my business with Mlle. Clisson was of a private nature."

"Indeed?" she said, a raised eyebrow intimating a sardonicism her inquiry did not.

Unappreciative of the cynicism of her eyebrow, he replied a bit defensively, but this time had the good sense not to employ his former lover's name. "She advised me that a visiting acquaintance had news of Mr. Wickham. I returned with her to Howgrave's to hear what the lady knew of Wickham's situation. I asked Bingley to wait in the carriage due to the delicacy of the information."

"What business did Mlle. Clisson have with Sir Howgrave?"

"They are affianced."

That was a curious bit of information, but of the particulars of their connexion she would inquire upon another occasion. Instead she asked, "It was through her agency that you learnt that Wickham was in London?"

"Yes. You can imagine my surprise and dismay."

Indeed, she could.

"I fear that I will always be an ungenerous wife. I am unhappy to admit to such a failing, but there it is."

It would have been easy to accept the lightness of her tone and speak no more of Juliette Clisson, but Darcy believed that the time had come for him to put her mind at ease on the matter once and for all.

"I must have you understand, Lizzy, that my ineloquence cannot allow me to tell you the depth of my feelings for you. I am left only to say that my heart is, and always will be, yours alone."

He took her hand in his and pressed her palm to his lips.

From the back of her throat came a small sigh. Had she been granted at that moment the gift of speech, she would have assured him that his articulacy was in no way lacking. As it happened, she could not. Indeed, it was her own feelings that were so entirely inexpressible. She sat in that confounded attitude, with only the backs of her fingers stroking his cheek to tell him how very dear he was to her. In return, his hand trailed up her arm and took her earlobe, gently rubbing it between his forefinger and thumb. Within the wordless relm of a shared gaze, they exchanged vows of everlasting love.

Quietly, he asked, "Have we at last put all to rest?"

Chastened, she nodded.

In time, he said, "You will be happy to know Bingley is saved."

"The business to which you were attending with Sir Howgrave—it went well?"

"Indeed, the Bingleys will take possession of Howgrave's manor directly," he was delighted to tell her.

It was a comfort for Elizabeth to know that Bingley had been, indeed, with Darcy, and he had not been entirely alone when he encountered Juliette. She fully realised that it had never been her husband's intentions she doubted, but Mlle. Clisson's. Still, the manner in which he reassured her of his constancy she knew not how to admire adequately.

They were interrupted at that point by their driver.

"Begging your pardon, sir, but what is our destination? A cross-roads awaits us."

Darcy asked Elizabeth, "What shall it be? To Bingley's for corroboration? Or shall we hie for home?"

"Home," she said. "It has been but a few days, but feels as if a year—I long to see my children!"

"Our children," he corrected. "I admit to that longing as well. I have seen far too much of these streets for one day—yea, for a lifetime."

He rapped upon the roof, calling, "To Pemberley."

The Sweetest Thing

When Wickham threw back the door, his already jangled nerves were once again abused. For before him stood a girl. She was almost grown, but was not of his acquaintance.

"Hello, Wickham," she said as if she knew him.

"Do I know you?" he asked.

"No."

"Do I know your mother?" he said wanly.

"Actually," she said, "you do."

She brushed past him and walked in.

He had had just about enough of this. Indeed, one must draw the line at some point in accepting the paternity of every base-born infant in the country. Certainly there were other men capable of reproducing. The satisfying thought crossed his mind that his nemesis (despite the size of his hands) was barren in that department. Darcy may have a wife to covet, but he had not given her a child. Ha.

He looked at the girl before him wondering what she might want. Her figure was trim, complexion altogether lovely, and she looked to be more than sixteen. As her age gifted her the single requisite that he had endeavoured to abide in his many seductions, he instinctively smiled.

"Don't bother shewing me yer teeth, I ain't buyin'," she announced.

Immediately, he adjusted his countenance to profess indulgent indignation, "Whatever do you mean?"

"I come 'ere on business."

"Now why is a pretty girl like you wanting to talk business? It will put a furrow in your lovely brow," he simpered.

Withdrawing her pistol did the office of removing any part of humour from his countenance.

"What is this?" he demanded. "A robbery?"

"Maybe just murder."

Immediately, Wickham lost all umbrage and began to inquire just what animus did she hold against him. Sally was disinclined to pussyfoot about it.

"The soldier you murdered…"

"I did no such thing," he denied. "No such thing ever occurred, no one saw it, there was no such soldier."

Employing the "my dog did not bite you, my dog does not bite, I do not have a dog" defence, Wickham believed himself thoroughly covered insofar as responding to the charge laid at his door. Where *had* all these people learnt of this, he worried. He had truly seen no witnesses.

Not put off whatsoever, Sally continued, "It did occur, it was witnessed, and there most certainly were a soldier. He was my brother and I aim to have you die for it."

"Now, now, let us think this matter through," Wickham began to try to talk his way out of it. "If I did harm to your brother, it was a most grievous error upon my part. I would *never*…"

Although the weapon made him uneasy, he had not feared Sally's accusation. If Darcy was not disposed to put charges against him himself, he must be of a mind he had not enough proof to put in him gaol. If Darcy had none, what proof could this girl have?

At that moment, another person walked into his room. It was the pint-sized lady of the night he had seen strutting up and down the walkway. Odd creature, her. Had he the time, he might have had a taste, but as it was, he did not. Upon this occasion, she did not appear ready to contract business of her usual calling. She flounced across the room and stood next to Sally.

"Ye told 'im yet?"

"Not yet."

"Then git on with it!"

Sally nodded, "I was jest remindin' 'im of 'is crimes."

Thereupon, Sally put before him the piece of vellum that had dropped from Mr. Darcy's waistband. Sally was truly very sorry for taking as she had done, but she had not been altogether forthcoming with Mrs. Darcy. She knew more than she let on. For behind the hands and in the kitchens of those who were employed by Mr. Darcy, more than her brother's killer had been revealed. The servants are never quite so benighted as their employers would like to think. It should not have been surprising that the talk that had swept across Derbyshire of young Mr. Darcy having fathered a child by the servant girl, Abigail Christie, had at last righted itself. Before going to her great reward, Mrs. Reynolds arrested the runaway talk by naming the true culprit. Those who knew Mr. Darcy were quite easily persuaded that it was not he, but George Wickham who defiled the girl and was father to John Christie.

Indeed, Mrs. Hardin knew the tale and was willing to share the particular irony that Major Wickham had unknowingly killed his own son. It made for a much better story too. No one bothered to do anything about it since Major Wickham was thought dead. In light of the improbability of Wickham ever returning, any number of folk announced they would have been happy to do justice by that boy had not it already been done by Nappy.

"The soldier you killed was my brother—my half-brother," Sally told him. "My mother's name was Abigail Christie."

"For that you have my sympathy," Wickham said testily, not at all happy to be held at bay by a pair of females sporting a pistol with a barrel the size of a blunderbuss.

But then, an alteration overspread Wickham's countenance. One could see the wheels of his brain turning with precision as if he had a hole in his cranium. As Daisy was unwitting of all that Sally knew, only she saw them as the little cerebral pistons performed, assessing, cogitating, and then, at last, eureka.

"That soldier was Abigail Christie's son? My son you say? No, it cannot be!"

Slowly, to make the realisation as painful as possible, Sally nodded her head.

"Bloody hell!" Wickham stamped his foot. "I have the worst luck!"

Immediately, Wickham appreciated the full extent of his jeopardy. He had largely thought of the young ladies with the pistol as all in good fun. A trick—a game of wits. The expression the younger girl wore was exceedingly solemn. Nothing at all seemed amusing.

Wickham recalled that he had a bargaining tool. He made his play for his own pistol, but Daisy raised the gun menacingly. Sally found the tiny pistol and held it on him too.

Hastily, he began babbling, "I have money. I can pay. I have more money than you ever imagined. Here, here…"

Grasping the canvas bag by its bottom, he gave a yank, sending neatly tied packets of notes spilling across the table top, one skittering onto the floor. He made a move to retrieve it, but Sally raised the end of her weapon menacingly at him when he did. Hence, he stood—arms raised, palms out—certain they would make for the money. The only question would be whether they would kill him or not. He had seen men killed for a groat in these parts of London. The only hope he had was that the sight of this money would make them drunk enough with delight to leave him alone.

Whilst Daisy eyed the money, Sally ignored it. She handed the pea-shooter off to Daisy and strode to the table. With one swoop of her arm, she swept the money aside and slapped down a document before him. Having two documents to sign in one evening was altogether a singular occurrence. He knew not what to make of it. This time, he did read it. He read it carefully. He did not understand.

"This document states that the signee swears that he is not Major George Wickham. That George Wickham died in battle on June 16 in the year '15. Why would I sign such a thing?" He looked at Sally, "Moreover, why would *you* want me to sign it?"

Daisy juggled the pistol whilst merrily picking up the notes and stuffing half of them in Wickham's canvas bag, the other half in her bodice. She had pulled the rags out that had held office of her undeveloped bosom and thought this a divine replacement.

Showing Sally, she laughed, "What ye think, Sal? Better'n the real thing?"

Sally only allowed herself to smile a moment. She returned her attention to Wickham's question.

"I figure there are worse things for some men than killin'," she answered. "Get to it!"

Reasonably, Wickham inquired, "What am I to sign? If am swearing that I am not George Wickham I must have a name."

He was genuinely perplexed—as was Sally. She had not given that much thought, but Daisy thought anointing Wickham a name great fun.

"I know," she said, "I know! How 'bout Harry Butts? Or, or," she thought more, "Dick Flaccid?"

"Could not we just use Dusty Rhoades?" Wickham said dejectedly.

Laughing to herself into near hysteria, Daisy suddenly stopt.

"You thought of something, Daisy?" Sally asked.

"Yea," she said solemnly, "I did."

Sally raised her eyebrows, waiting.

"Sign your name *Thomas Reed*," she said.

When Wickham hesitated, she put the barrel of the pistol against his head, demanding, "Write."

Wickham shrugged his shoulders and did as he was told. His position was firmly on the side of doing whatever it took to remain alive. His signature was exacted with none of the foolish antics that he had employed with Darcy. When he compleated writing, Sally whisked the paper from beneath him, handed it to Daisy to witness, and when this office was compleat, rolled it like a scroll.

"Am I to be told why I signed such a document?"

"Ye shouldn't be bothered with signing away that name," Sally told him. "It ain't what it ought to be anyhow."

"Oh, no?" said Wickham flippantly, certain Sally was barking mad. "What should it be? Harry Butts?"

"No," she said, "it could've been Darcy."

So incredulous of such a statement, Wickham did not even bother to appear so. He simply awaited her to attempt to explain such a ludicrous notion.

"Folks that know say that yer a bastard to Mr. Darcy's father."

Wickham's attitude did not alter. Not for a moment, at least.

"Mr. Darcy knows it too. I don't blame 'im fer not wantin' to claim yer."

In an aside to Daisy, Sally said, "Ye should see that Mr. Darcy's little babies—two of 'em, like two peas in a pod!"

"Twins? Son-of-a-bitch! I bet they keep 'em busy!" Daisy exclaimed, both temporarily forgetting themselves.

Wickham, however, had not.

"What…? How…?" Wickham attempted to form a question.

Recollecting herself, Daisy explained, "There's so much talk, ye were bound to find out anyhow. That old housekeeper, Mrs. Reynolds, said it's so."

"What does that have to do with you? Why would you tell me this and have me sign that document? What is it to you?"

"Well," she explained, "I was gonna kill ye, but I got to thinkin' sorry as ye are, that was too good for ye. I thought that would hurt ye worse—that and this."

With that, Sally took Lydia's pea-shooter, drew her bead, and shot. Her aim was quite good. Wickham fell to the floor writhing—both hands over his crotch, screaming, "You bloody bitch, you bloody bitch, you bloody bitch!"

Daisy stood looking at Sally in wonder. She did not ask a question, but Sally chose to answer it all the same.

"I figured that getting' shot in the nuts was the other thing that would be for him worse that dyin'. That'n, 'e'll never sire another bastard."

She stepped over Wickham, who in one last desperate move, tried to grab her ankle. She shook him off like a playful pup and she and Daisy betook themselves out the door without looking back.

As the door shut soundly behind them, they could hear Wickham's screams in the background—even over the sounds of the ale house below.

Sally raised her voice over the din of it all, "Tell me, Daisy, why'd ye pick that particular name?"

"It was my brother's name," she said. "Tom escaped from Newgate. If 'e uses it, they might nail 'im fer it."

Sally pursed her lips and nodded as if she understood, "I see."

Shaking her head, Daisy said, "Ye don't see, really. Tom Reed was my brother what Mr. Darcy kilt. Fer that matter, Tom got my brother Frank kilt by Mr. Darcy too."

Sally's countenance was then quite astounded, "Mr. Darcy kilt yer brothers—don't ye hate him fer it?"

To hear such a thing of proud Mr. Darcy was altogether astonishing for Sally. She could not imagine such an occurrence—nor could she imagine that Daisy had a pistol in her hand and did not exact retribution when she had the chance. Indeed, she had even aided Mr. Darcy.

Daisy shrugged her shoulders which caused a slight shuffling of her note-filled bosom. As she retucked her stuffing, she had only one further comment upon her long-dead kin.

"Seems there was bad blood. Knowing Tom," she observed, "he had it comin'."

Peeling off one note from her many packets, Sally stuffed it under Wickham's door. He had stopt bellowing and had begun to whimper.

They passed Mrs. Younge heading up the stairs as they strolled down. Sally looked upwards momentarily before she offered an agreement to Daisy's conclusion.

"Don't they all 'ave it comin', Daisy? Don't they all?"

Homeward

Once they were at last upon their way to Pemberley, Darcy closed the window-shade but was stopt before he could don his hat again.

"Do not," said she.

Without looking in her direction, he set it upon the opposing seat.

"If we must travel, I like this carriage especially," she said settling herself against him.

He looked upon her with both tenderness and puzzlement, saying, "This one? It looks to have seen its day. I am astonished to know we still own it."

She nodded her head, reminding him that it had been stored at their London house.

"We have newer, and if I do say so myself, finer carriages."

"I like this one," she explained. "I selected it particularly for our return home. It has a history."

Several of their carriages had history, for much had come to pass upon their travel home to Pemberley. Of those most notable, he could think of none that he would recollect with any fondness. The kidnapping was one journey that was most abhorrent of all. He recalled that coach most particularly because of the cotter pin that had been disturbed causing him to leave her and seek repair. This was not that coach. Another coach came to mind which was accompanied by a considerably less abhorrent recollection, but still inflicted an injurious memory. That had been the coach in which she had laboured and given birth. When he had arrived home that day past, he had seen it sitting near the portico. The interior had been stained with blood—he was beside himself with fear. The picture of the condition of those seats was imprinted in his brain as if branded. The first one he could never again bear to gaze upon and had it sold. The other had been reupholstered. The coach in which they rode had no history to him.

Seeing that he did not understand her meaning, she aided his memory.

"There was another journey," she said, "of which I see you have no recollection. I am very much offended, for it has never quite left my thoughts lo these many years."

His expression did a very good job of wanting to know of what she spoke, but ultimately he did not. As words had not prompted him, she thought to illustrate. Meticulously, she lowered each shade. It was dark, but that did not matter, it was only an approximation, not an actual re-creation. He sat very still as she went about her demonstration, if he knew yet what she meant for him to recollect, he did not remark upon it.

"Upon the past occasion, it was you, sir, who lowered these shades."

"Is that so?" he inquired mildly. "What then came to pass?"

It remained unclear if he had guessed that she was referring to her second journey to Pemberley—the first as his wife. That occasioned upon a bright winter day and this was an early autumn night, but she was not deterred—the weather had been unimportant. What was pertinent occurred inside and the coach was as it had been then. There was one exception.

The early part of their journey had been unhappy for two reasons. Firstly, the road had been unduly rough due to heavy rains, straining the springs of the coach. This bouncing would have played havoc upon her nether-end even had she not been so sore due to her introduction to marital duties. He had offered her a pillow, it was the most indiscrete cushion she had ever seen—of puce satin, tasselled all around—one she refused from mortification. The second reason for her displeasure had been his general demeanour, for he had been exceedingly distant—to the point of rudeness. Their wedding night had been for her one of rapturous bliss—an enjoyment that she had not kept to herself. In the bright light of the morn, she feared that he had been off-put by her enthusiasm for physical congress the night before. But, he was not. It was not her libido that had frightened him, but his own. He had not been the tender lover that he had intended.

Indeed, it had all been a misunderstanding.

The pillow was not for her mortification, but his.

It was not upon taking their vows that they had truly become as one. That had been man's unification—not even the throes of passion they had enjoyed that night were sufficient. They had become truly joined together in the coach the next day. It was there that he had truly communed. He had lain open his heart and she had as well. They had become one heart of two parts. They had, of course, also enjoyed repeated unifications of an erotic nature which had made the memory all the sweeter. What was intimately passionate within the hush of darkness of their bed-chamber had become unabashedly erotic in the rocking carriage—face to face, compleatly clothed—but beneath, their sexes united—a secret shared. She could never think of it without a frisson deep within her feminine reaches.

That had not been a singular journey in that they had been intimate upon other occasions in the carriage, but never with quite such wild abandon. He could not have forgotten, whether he would want to recall it was another matter entirely.

To his inquiry, she said nothing more, content just then to bask in the recollection by herself. Neither wanted to speak of Wickham, Lydia, the girl Sally, or anything that had come lately to pass. It was a silent agreement. She laid her head against his shoulder and crossed her ankles upon the seat next to his hat.

Although she thought herself content to let the matter rest, her act of nonchalance was an announcement of another subject and she wriggled her feet as if to tempt him. She thought it an impotent attempt, certain his spirit had been sapped by what he had endured by meeting with Wickham. Still, she slipped off her slippers and wriggled her toes in her stocking feet. When no sound came from him, she looked to see if he had fallen asleep. When she did, he caught her face in his hand and raised her lips to kiss. That kiss began chastely but did not remain so. Indeed, hands were employed, limbs stroked, until at last escalation was inevitable.

It was a large coach, but for a man of long leg such as he, manoeuvrability was limited. (It had been some time since they had engaged themselves thusly inside their coach—their love was not old, their need just less often so immediate.) Hence, when strokings no longer fed their hunger, it took a moment for knees and elbows to relocate. Once he had drawn her upon his lap, her skirt billowed over them both, obscuring their union even from their own eyes—and made it difficult for his hand to find its way to the buttons on his breeches.

"Your gowns please me better when otherwise engaged," he complained.

He became increasingly impatient to release himself, but she was wise enough in love-making by then to know that hindered eagerness would be rewarded to them both. Indeed, when at last he freed himself, his tumescence was one of particular glory. As it was hidden beneath the volume of her skirt, however, she was unable to admire it. But when he grasped her by the buttocks and drew her forcefully down upon him, she was made fully cognizant of the magnitude of his instrument. Indeed, such was his ardour that she could not stop herself from crying out. That was but a momentary pain, and as she was the one who was the initiator, she believed it unfair of her to complain (involuntarily or not) and stuffed one fist in her mouth lest she cry out again.

He was gentler then, but was in such heat the last, powerful thrusts of love were engaged upon the seat opposite. With the last convulsions of passion passed, he sat back, pulling her back upon him in their original position—their bodies still engaged, but the mechanism fast waning. Her arms were still tightly about his neck, for the flutters had not entirely ceased within her. (It would be a while before she examined the ridges her teeth made in her knuckles.)

"Pray, Lizzy," he inquired, whispering in her ear, "did I…? Were you injured by my efforts?"

"No," she said, "never."

It was a point of pride to her never to admit that the generosity of his member had been injurious to her person. Had she given it thought, she might have understood that resolve to have been birthed upon their first night together. He *had* hurt her and he had been all but overcome with remorse. She did not want him ever to restrain himself on her behalf. Her pride demanded she gave as good as she got—so to speak.

At her denial of any injury, he wrapped his arms about her, massaging her back in solace.

"I think you are too brave, my love," he whispered. "You must tell me if I am not gentle enough."

From the sound of the carriage wheels, they could tell that the cobbles of London were no longer beneath them. The rocking of the coach announced their speed had increased and they were fast on for Pemberley.

She drew back and looked at him with a half-smile and ran the back of her fingers across his chin, "You are gentle upon those occasions I want you so."

"You mean then, that you do not need this?"

He had in his hand a pillow. It was not the exact shade of the one she recalled, but it was red. Where it had been hidden, she had not a clue. For it was undeniably tasselled.

And not at all discreet.

Acknowledgments

It is Sourcebooks editor, Deb Werksman, who bears the distinction of single-handedly rescuing my first book, *The Bar Sinister*, from the bowels of self-publishing purgatory. Still, throwing one's work open for critique can be a harrowing experience. But Deb managed to hold my hand through it all, insuring that I weathered the ordeal relatively unscathed. Not only did she polish my manuscript, but she astutely retrieved its original title. When *Mr. Darcy Takes a Wife* was published, it was to general applause (and only a few wails of outrage). To those who were delighted by it, I grant Deb a large portion of the credit. To the indignant few—well, I am happy to have her share the blame.

I was fortunate once again to have Deb's guidance for *Darcy and Elizabeth*. For her wise counsel, she has earned my undying gratitude. I would also like to thank her associates, Susie Benton, Elizabeth Meagher, and Stephanie Frerich for their invaluable editorial contributions and Megan Dempster and Anne Locascio for their exquisite work on the cover art.

Additional thanks to Lynne Robson, who graciously acted as our Derbyshire tour guide.

About the Author

Linda Berdoll is the author of the number one bestselling Jane Austen sequel—her first novel, *Mr. Darcy Takes a Wife.* Linda Berdoll is a self-described "Texas farm wife" whose interest in all things Austen was piqued by the BBC/A&E mini-series of *Pride and Prejudice.* Four years and much research later, *Mr. Darcy Takes a Wife* (originally titled *The Bar Sinister*) appeared, to the acclaim of readers and the horror of Jane Austen purists. She and her husband live on a pecan farm in Del Valle, Texas. Although she admits that she eloped in a manner similar to Lydia Bennet's, to her great fortune it was with Darcy, not Wickham.